The Adventures of Elizabeth Stanton
Series

Volume 3:
Of Kings and Queens and
Troubadours

Vic Broquard

Published by:
Broquard eBooks
http://Broquard-eBooks.com
author@Broquard-eBooks.com
103 Timberlane
East Peoria, IL 61611

Artwork by Crooked Willow Studios

For Morgan and L. Ron Hubbard

Table of Contents

Chapter 1 An Unfortunate Beginning

"It's another boy!" Godwin pronounced excitedly, as he wrapped my new baby body in a blanket and handed me to his wife, Naessa. These people have a very thick accent so I will translate instead of boggling you with it.

Though exhausted from the exertion of childbirth, sweat lining her face, she managed that smile that only a new mother can wear. She cradled me against her warm body, letting Godwin finish cleaning her up. Her lovely voice spoke softly to me, "Welcome, Ket of Cuch Glyn. Glad to have you join our growing family. You are named after my grandfather. Long may you live, my son." To her husband, she said, "As soon as you have me looking presentable, go fetch our children, and let them see our new addition to the family. Then, I must rest. I'm getting too old for this childbearing," she teased. Indeed, this fifth child, coming rather late in her life, had been the most difficult of all to bear. Later this year, she would mark her fortieth birthday.

"Aye, you rest. I'll bring them, Fianna is dying to see her new baby brother," he answered her, while he finished wiping away the mess of childbirth. A few minutes later, their four other children crept into their parent's room, sheepishly at first, unsure of themselves.

Godwin explained, "Don't be shy; mother and son are doing just fine. Come. Let us introduce your new brother. This is Ket." Naessa spread my blanket a little more open so that her other children could get a good look at me. He continued, "Ket, this is your oldest brother, Garth; he is fifteen. Next is your older brother Rath; he's twelve this summer. Next, is your youngest brother, Fian, who is only four. Finally, this is your older sister, Fianna, who turns three next month. Ket, I'm Godwin, your fisherman father, and that is your mother, Naessa, our Priestess. You have a fine mother in Naessa."

Fianna asked, "Mommy, why does Ket look so crinkly and reddish? Is he sick?"

Both my new parents chuckled. "No," Naessa explained to her only daughter, "this is just the way new born babies look. He will look just fine in a day or two. You all looked just like this when you were born." Fianna rubbed her nose, accepting her mother's pronouncement for the time being anyway. "Now, you all go to sleep. Mommy's quite tired. Ket and I both need to get some sleep too. Tomorrow, you older boys get to do all my chores, at least for the next few days." Garth and Rath smiled; both had been through this drill twice before. While their father went fishing, they had to do all her chores as well as theirs, including cooking the family's lunch and supper. Their father handled breakfast duties. While they didn't like all the extra work, since they were in charge of the cooking, they helped themselves to two extra hot cocoas each day, which more than made up for their extra workload in their minds. Hence, both smiled when they heard the news. Cocoa was an expensive, imported, rare commodity in this small fishing village.

Vaguely I watched them all leave. I was still in shock over "It's a boy!" All my plans were dashed in that instant! The lights dimmed in the room; Godwin left only a single oil lantern going. It must be nighttime. I sensed him giving Naessa a loving kiss, and she, he. Then, I felt him kiss me. I'm not sure where he slept that first night, though. I was too wrapped up trying to get a grip on what had just happened to me. My new body fell into a deep sleep, snuggled up against the warm body of my mother.

My name is-was Elizabeth Stanton, originally, and my dearest friends used to call me Bethany — at least it was Bethany, that is Bethany Madelyn Adid, until some time ago. I've had two lifetimes of female bodies and now have just gotten that role down pat. I'd spent several months before the birth tonight working out ways and means of getting Naessa to name me Bethany once more. However, now I find that my new body is male, and I'm to be called Ket! If you are getting confused, can you imagine the confusion I'm experiencing these past few minutes!

You see, I, like you, am a being — an immortal spirit. I've lived in many bodies and will have as many more as I desire, assuming the world, our playground, is not destroyed. It began some fifty years ago. I was part of a group of like-minded people, the druwids. In my group, I was revered as the Wid Bethany — the title, which I took nearly nine hundred years ago now, as I sit here and look back on my past. I am Truth and Knowledge. Yes, you may call me a witch, a demon, or a heretic, but, in doing so, you mark yourself as just another Blind One. I chose this road — this path I follow — knowingly and willingly. I do it for all mankind, even you.

I guess I ought to back up and explain my life up to this point in time — to try to undo the confusion. For me, it all began in 550 AH (After Hodhekansis, the legendary twins and founders of Megalos) in a small village called Uru in the northern part of the rolling green hills of the Greenway here on Tarra. Who I was and where I've been before coming to Tarra are blocked in my memories. Believe me, I've tried to crack that black veil which hides more of my past from me. The earliest memories I can see are running and playing tag with other children in Uru one spring morning.

Uru at that period in history was one of the first farming settlements on Tarra as far as anyone knows. No written records date from before 558 AH. We know that writing was invented by the great artist and philosopher Niccolo Helios in the land called Megalos. Geography plays a vital role in understanding what has happened to me and to so many others. Let me begin properly with a description of the planet we all call home, Tarra.

Tarra is a blue-green world about eight thousand miles in diameter consisting of vast oceans and one enormous continent shaped much like a dog bone — that is, the two huge continents we call Eastern Tarra and

Western Tarra are physically joined by one long, narrow, nearly impassable desert region that is some two hundred miles wide and three hundred miles long. Where this narrows joins the roughly circular lobes of the two continents, two towering mountain ranges block any passage into this desert region that goes by the name of the Desert of Desolation. On our side, Western Tarra, the blocking eighteen thousand foot range is called Kathas, while on the Eastern side, the similar range is named Helios Grande after the great Sun God himself. None of us really knows what lies in Eastern Tarra because no one has been there and returned, though through the centuries, I have heard tales of some who have tried.

Straddling the southern side of the Desert of Desolation is a huge, rocky island, Megalos, which is four hundred miles long but only one hundred miles at its greatest width. Here on the Western Tarra side, Megalos nearly touches the continent. The Sallow Firth, as it is called, is two miles wide yet only three feet deep at low tide! Yes, horses and people often walk across the Firth, but there are ferries for those with money and passes from the Emperor of Megalos. The eastern side of Megalos is some twenty miles from the rocky coast of Eastern Tarra, but here treacherous tides thunder against many hidden rocks in that wide channel. From the dawn of time, Megalos and Western Tarra share the annals of history, both good and bad.

Now Western Tarra is roughly divided into halves by the great Med Sea, which opens onto the ocean at the western most part of the continent. This pale blue sea is nearly eight hundred miles long; its width varies between fifty and a hundred miles. Along the northern shores of Med Sea lie the principalities of the Seven Sea Princes. On the eastern shore of the Med Sea, abutting the Sea Princes, is the arid land called Juda Arad which stretches all the way to the Kathas mountain range. My early years last lifetime were spent living in various towns in Juda Arad, but more on that in a moment. All across the southern shore of Med Sea lies the giant Red Desert uninhabited and proven unpassable. South of the Red Desert lay the Southlands with rich, rolling green savannahs and forests, rich in animal life but with few, dark-skinned inhabitants. The Southlands and Megalos share a close relationship as far back as anyone can remember, though not necessarily a good one.

North of the principalities of the Seven Sea Princes is a mountain range known as the Appian Way. These spectacular eight thousand foot tall, granite peaks stretch nearly across all of Western Tarra dividing the continent in half. The lands above the Appian Way are divided by nature into three roughly equal sized areas. At the far north lies the cold but timbered lands called Volksholm, whose people are called the Axemen. To the east is the Northern Steppes, an arid land home to nomadic horsemen called the Galts, while to the west lies the Greenway, a land of contrasts. Greenway consists of heavily forested, rugged hills interspersed with lush green valleys. My original village of Uru lies in the north central portion of the Greenway.

Many islands both large and small dot the lengthy coastline. However, of note is the large island called West Reach, or Cymry as we locals call it; it lies some ten miles off the coast of the Greenway and is a large island kingdom unto itself. Though largely unpopulated, it plays a role in this story, obviously.

The world at this time is roughly divisible into three political camps. Megalos, rumored to be the cradle of civilization, has great marble-stone cities, is very hot during summers, and has produced the first great thinkers, including the great artist and inventor Niccolo Helios, who I met years ago. The principalities of the Seven Sea Princes are the feudal city-states of wealthy men, who sail the Med Sea trading there, as well as up and down the coastline of Western Tarra. Finally, all of the lands above the Appian Way, are inhabited warring hunter-gatherer groups or primitive farming communities. However, everywhere, rule is by the strongest sword and the mightiest forces, of which the Megalos Centurions are reputed to be the best at this time in history.

Megalos is an old civilization dating back well over five hundred years and currently has the highest level of civilization of any land, though of technology might be a better statement. They are ruled by Emperor Titus, a young man recently placed into power by the Church of Sol. Originally, these people worshiped the Sun God. Their Senate made the laws of the land, while the Emperor carried them out. However, over the centuries, the Senate became an ineffective ruling institution and the Emperor became all-powerful. Their previous Emperor Hiro turned the entire empire into a promiscuous brothel, at least from my point of view. When the Emperor drugged me and tried to rape me, I killed him, forcing a change of power. The Church of Sol took on more power and placed Titus on the throne.

However, for many years, Megalos attempted to bring their version of civilization to the barbarian lands. Definition of barbarian lands: any land not theirs. Long ago in the depths of history, they conquered the Southland, at least the eastern sections. Their soldiers are called Centurions and are bronzed-skinned, carry enormous shields, and fight often with spears and short swords. Some even ride war chariots into battle. They fight in tight formations and have been unstoppable in their forward march across all the lands. Now in the Southlands, they operate wealthy gold and gem mines and have taken many dark skinned natives back to Megalos as slaves. Today, there are many second generation slaves on Megalos, who know only of life as a slave and nothing of their original homeland or people.

Perhaps some thirty years ago, the Centurions conquered the land adjoining the Southlands, Juda Arad, taking its vital port on the eastern edge of the Med Sea, Al Barq. Next, they proceeded to attack each of the Seven Sea Prince cities or sectors or principalities, one by one, beginning with Zargarb and ending with Velona. Their style of assault was interesting because they built a straight, level, paved stone roadway from where they currently were located right up to the next city to be attacked. Once that city fell, they resumed their road construction toward the next target. Thus, they were assured of rapid supply and movement of soldiers.

My original land was the Greenway, north of the Appian Way, a land of farmers and hunter-trappers, and sparsely populated. In contrast to the cities of a hundred thousand or more in the Lands of the Sea Princes, our largest city, the port of Calgary, only boasts some thirty thousand people. Only one other town in the middle of the Greenway, Brownsville has a population over ten thousand. Most of the towns and villages have only a few thousand, while we do have numerous hamlets of fifty to a hundred inhabitants.

Yes, all this does tie together. In the Greenway, several hundred years ago, one man, Alabaster Benjamin Crowley, founded a special group of people, called the druwids. We are usually trained from about the age of six to become a part of this group, because it took ten full years of study to learn what was required. The druwids are organized into Circles of seven members, each with their own specialties. The Protector is a highly skilled fighter whose task is to defend the others. The Loremaster is wise about Nature, plants and animals. The Planner is skilled at design and construction of buildings and such. The Judger is both a conjurer and an arbitrator of justice. The Communicator is skilled with telepathy and acts as the communicator between members of the group and other Communicators in other groups. Thus, distance plays no part in holding us together. The Healer is highly skilled in all aspects of healing the sick and injured. Finally, the Wid is the wisest and the leader of the Circle because the Wid is always seeking to know all about everything in the world. Wids are the rarest of all the druwids and hardest to become. I was a Wid in my Circle, the Lightning Circle, before my untimely death.

Now every druwid is skilled in healing; it's just that the Healer has far more skill than the rest of us. The entire purpose of Alabaster's druwids is to protect and serve all the people of the Greenway. To that end, most of the druwids live out among the small towns and villages, protecting, healing, arbitrating disputes, and helping with new constructions. We live to help our people and our lives are dedicated to helping them. As an aside, every druwid is a being, just like all the others on Tarra, but a druwid is not located in their body's head, but rather some distance from it. Most of the people on Tarra are stuck solidly in their heads. Druwids derogatorily call them the Headers, a disgusting word rarely spoken.

Further, because of our intense study and total love and devotion to Nature, yes, you may say that we worship Nature, we have developed powers that many find remarkable. We can bring into existence fire, ice, and lightning. My specialty is lightning. Given a cloud in the sky, I can cause a bolt to strike where I desire. However, the druwids only use these intense powers to protect our people from the raiders. In the past, the raiders came from the Galts of the Northern Steppes or from Axemen of Volksholm.

My first lifetime, I was called Elizabeth Stanton, and I was the Wid of my Lightning Circle. Back then, Centurions from Megalos were attempting to conquer the known universe, bringing their version of civilization to the "barbarians" of the world. Already, they had conquered Juda Arad, and were moving across the Sea Princes, when my Circle got involved. Alabaster figured that the Greenway would be next on their conquest list, and he sent my Circle off to obtain more knowledge about them, an attempt to find out their strategies, tactics, and some way we might defeat them. After traveling across the Sea Princes, my Circle headed to Megalos, passing through Juda Arad and then the Southlands, before visiting Megalos proper. Alabaster died before we returned from our long journey, but using what we learned, I was able to avoid a Centurion war with the Greenway.

For several years, I relaxed and enjoyed a normal life. Roy, our Protector, and I were happily married and we had three lovely children. I could not have been happier. Unfortunately, that came to an abrupt end for me. Far to the east in the Greenway, King Randolf, who was building his own empire, made a treaty of some kind with our enemy, the Galts. Some thousand of those raiders joined his cavalry and foot soldiers near his wooden fortress at Redun. Just north of his lands were those of Erline Herbiscus, a renegade druwid, that is, she knew how to control the weather and bring down fire and lightning, but refused to be a part of our group, preferring to be her own master. Her forces were arrayed opposite the King's army and the Galts. Worse still, the Centurions, thousands of them, were building the new road system nearby and would likely get caught between the warring factions. I met with Erline and got her agreement not to start the conflict. I then tried to speak with King Randolf under the universal white parley flag. He was insane, ignored the flag, and killed me with an arrow in my forehead.   Into that confusion on that dark and stormy day, Alabaster appeared. Yes, he was there, a being alone, for he still had not chosen to acquire a new infant body. Together with Erline, he and I let lose a tremendous volley of over a thousand lightning strikes, eliminating the King and most all of his forces, including the Galts. To all outsiders, especially the nearby Centurions, it appeared as if another one of the freaky storms of Nature had occurred.

Alabaster helped me obtain a new purpose. The prophets of Juda Arad long predicted the coming of their Great Messiah, the Son of God, Jehosa, who would set them free of the Infidels or Centurions. Alabaster send me down there to learn what I could of this Great Messiah's methods, in hopes that I could emulate them in our Greenway later on. Hence, I headed off to find this Great Messiah, who was just a young boy at this time.

Luck was with me. I picked up a new body, that of a young girl who had just been bitten by a viper. The being who occupied that body decided it was dying and departed. I took it over and the body survived. I became a very close friend of the Great Messiah, Jes Amir, and I learned most all their religious history as it was taught to Jes. Later, we were married and I bore him three children. During our time there, Jes, after picking ten disciples to follow him, roamed the land, preaching the word of Jehosa.

Yes, I would have to say that Jes was the Son of God, for I saw him perform many miracles. True, he would heal the sick and infirm, but also he had the ability to help a person move out of his body and discover their true state, that of an immortal spiritual being. To free his people, his plan was to educate them so that they could become free, powerful beings as they once were, and thus, the Infidels or Centurions would have no impact over them any longer. His goal of freedom was misinterpreted by the prophets of Juda Arad to mean that he was going to lead a rebellion, a war against the Centurions.

When the Arads realized that he was not going to war, they took it upon themselves to attack their overlords. After three days, the entire rebellion was completely squashed with a large loss of life among those who rebelled. Meanwhile, Jes pretended to be crucified upon the cross and then be resurrected from the dead as the most powerful way he could imagine in a last attempt to communicate and reach his people. He left it to his disciples to spread the word far and wide. Then, in secret, Jes, our family, and his brother's family left Juda Arad and ended up in West Reach, or Cymry. Here there was no Centurion presence.

Above all, Jes wanted to nurture his bloodline, who, he claimed, were the rightful heirs to be Kings of Tarra. Hence, we needed a safe place to raise our three children, and West Reach was the only place on Tarra where we could be completely safe.

Now the religion known as Jehosanity took on three versions. Obviously here in Cymry, Jes, and after he left, I, preached the message that we were all spiritual beings. I added in harmony with Nature, which also happened to align with the local religion practiced by the original inhabitants of the island. One group of his disciples founded the Church of Jehosanity in the Sea Princes, calling it the Bandar-Hamah version or simply the Northern Orthodoxy. Finally, another disciple traveled all the way to Megalos and there he founded his Church of Jehosanity. All three sprang from Jes's teachings.

At this time, a pair of orphaned Galt twins, Mikhailovich and Zdlenka Strokova, accomplished a feat that had never been done before. After having a "magical sword" built to their specifications, they managed to unite all the clans of the Northern Steppes into a single fighting unit. Their cavalry, or wild barbarians as they were known by their victims, swooped down from the steppes and conquered all the Arad, driving the Centurions out of that land. Then, they conquered all of the Sea Princes, looting and pillaging the major cities. Finally, they headed into the Southlands to get to Megalos itself, until they were within a hundred miles of Sud and Megalos.

In stepped the disciple of Jes, Yazi Rigan, who now calls himself Pope Yazi I. A master of sweet words, he manipulated the Centurion beliefs, preaching his version of Jehosanity. He made a bargain with the emperor, who gave him some land for his master church, and proclaimed that Jehosanity was now the official religion of all Megalos. In return, Pope Yazi I promised a miracle: the Hand of Jehosa would intervene and destroy these barbarians from the north. Shortly after this, the Galt barbarian horde was crushed and Mikhailovich beheaded, ending the Galt invasion.

All right, that is the history as it is known at this time by the parties involved. However, and this is a big however, I discovered a vastly more sinister and evil undercurrent at play here on Tarra, one that may even account for why the vast majority of spiritual beings are so thoroughly convinced that they are a fleshly body and not a spiritual being. During my travels, I encountered two secret groups of strange creatures, one located in the inaccessible, high peaks of the Appian Way. The other is located in the impassable Red Desert near three tall pyramids.

The ones in the Appian Way are giants with grey skin and with three toes on their feet. They have some machine in the shape of a pole. When a being's fleshly body dies, they have been ordered to report in to this machine. Personally, I have watched numerous spiritual beings, whose bodies have just perished, slavishly follow this implanted order. Once they arrive, the pole is activated and the beings are literally sucked into the pole, where all their memories, their mental pictures, are completely scrambled! Once they are completely dazed and totally confused, they are given the order to go get a new baby body and, when it dies, to report back here once more. They then take off like a bolt of lightning to carry out that order.

The group in the Red Desert operates similarly, though their bodies are even stranger. I liken them to that of a fifty foot tall praying mantis! The mantises seem to collect spiritual beings from the southern portions of Tarra, while the Grey Creatures collect those from the northern half. At first, only my Lightning Circle and Alabaster knew about these creatures. When Alabaster's body finally died of very old age, he took on the task of spying on the Grey Creatures to gain more information. Jes, my late husband and the Son of Jehosa, also found out about these creatures.

For years, Jes brooded over the impact that they were having on his people. We both speculated that these two sets of creatures were somehow interfering with the humans on Tarra, though we couldn't prove it. Our hypothesis was that they could be acting as a hidden influence, perhaps causing all the wars and conflicts between the different peoples on Tarra. At the very least, they could be responsible for convincing immortal spiritual beings that they were a fleshly body. In the end, Jes had to do something about these Grey Creatures. He left us safely on West Reach and traveled to their location, high in the Appian Way. After spending some time spying on them, he found one of these creatures alone and attempted to kill its body.

Alabaster was also in the vicinity and he did a Mind Join with me, so I could watch what happened. I pleaded with Alabaster to help save Jes, because I knew these creatures had immense powers, far beyond anything that I could muster. In the end, the creature, though wounded in both legs by Jes, smashed his fist into Jes's face, killing him instantly. I watched in horror as Jes was then sucked into the machine and his memories scrambled. In vain, Alabaster tried to free him from the diabolical trap, but he too became trapped. Alabaster's last message to me was that if he did not contact me within the next thirty years, I was to find him, for he would need my help.

Unfortunately, these Grey Creatures detected my presence and attempted to suck me into their contraption. However, the secret to their machine is simply not resist its effect and then it cannot pull a being into it. I escaped. Back in my house in West Reach, I continued preaching the truth of our spiritual nature. Additionally, I began a special ceremony. Whenever anyone in our town died, that is their fleshly body died, I would Mind Join them with their relatives and friends. In this way, they could say a final farewell. However, I also effectively blocked their implanted command to return to the Grey Creatures in the Appian Way.

In hindsight, I think this is what finally brought me to the attention of these diabolical creatures. One night while I and Sarah, my daughter, were riding back after delivering Sunday sermons, the Grey Creatures attacked me. They had some kind of flying machine that hovered over our position. While I escaped, they were relentless in coming after me. Not wanting to bring harm to my fellow townsfolk or daughter, I left in secret, intending to hide out in the foggy portion of the island known as Tewdwr. Footnote: my two grown boys had already donned their mantles of Kings and ruled over a pair of towns each. I also did not want to bring this down upon their heads either.

I was found almost at once and attacked by one of these Grey Creatures. While it instantly killed my body with a massive fist blow to my face, I again escaped. Even though they had a portable sucking device and tried to capture me, I eluded them. In frustration, they reversed their tactics, which took me by surprise. A massive energy bolt smashed into me, blacking me out, as I dove deep under the ocean just off the coast.

I waited for a time until I thought it was safe to emerge from underwater. When I did, to my shock, several years had passed! I don't know yet how many. I had intended to join with the baby that Naessa was soon to have, which would have been my sister, Fianna. Can you imagine my double shock? Years had passed, not days, and I now had a male body, which I've never had.

In the near darkness of that first night, I was too dazed to compute, to think logically. *Whatever am I going to do now? I don't know how to be a man. I don't want to be a man; they'll probably want me to be a fighter and I hate fighting. Wait, that means I'll have to become interested in women! How can I ever do that anyway? I will continuously have to keep my real nature, a woman, a secret from them. This is going to be so awkward. Besides, I don't want to use brawn. I use my brains. They'll surely want me to work fields or forge steel or fish or hunt. But I want to organize things, to nurture things. Woe is me. I've really screwed it all up this time!*

Time! I forgot Alabaster. I'm supposed to rescue him! I'm absolutely certain he really got messed up in the Grey Creature's trap! Let's see, thirty years would make it about 618 AH. How long have I been unconscious anyway? What year is it? Think. Think. Probably at least three, more like four years. Okay, let's be optimistic and say four years have passed instead of a couple months. That would make the year now about 607 AH. Oh no! This body will only be eleven years old when I'm supposed to go find Alabaster and help him recover! I'm doomed! I have already failed to help the one person in the whole universe that I most want to help!

In the dim background, I heard a small voice saying, "Mommy, why is Ket crying so much? Is he hurt?"

Naessa answered, "No, Fianna. I'm not sure what his problem is. Let's see. He's just nursed, so he can't be hungry. He hasn't yet slept so maybe he is just overly tired." I felt her fiddling with my arms and legs, testing them. "He doesn't seem to have any broken bones or anything. Maybe he is upset, Fianna. Come. Let's talk to him and sing to him. Maybe that will calm him down."

"Maybe he is having a nightmare, do you suppose?" my sister suggested.

"Ah, that could be it too. You are probably right," mother replied, as she began to speak soothing words to me. "There, there, little Ket. Remember, Ket, we are the Annwn, the Children of God. It is our lot in life to be allowed to experience life to its fullest. We must endeavor to triumph over evil, hardship, and travail. By experiencing life in its completeness, we continue to strive for our spiritual purity of being. So Ket, you must rise above it all." Then, she began to sing a soothing lullaby, and Fianna joined in too.

Get it together, Bethany! You now got everyone upset! I relaxed my tense grip upon the baby body, and it stopped crying. Finally, it dozed off and I floated over to a chair by the fireplace and the dim lantern that burned throughout the night. As my awareness finally rose, I sensed the house was now quiet. Fianna was sleeping beside her mother on the opposite side from Ket. Seeing them, I realized once more just how much I enjoy motherhood and all that goes with it. This lifetime, I would be denied these pleasures; that thought brought me down in to grief once more. Time passed; I dropped off into a deep sleep.

It's all my fault that things got so messed up this time. Maybe I should just try to forget all my past, everything, all of it — pretend to just start over this lifetime. It would be so easy to just forget everything about my past. I could begin with a new, clean slate! Suddenly, I realized just what it was that I was thinking!

Good grief, Bethany! Wallowing in self-pity again! Knock it off. You would never be able to live with yourself if you forgot the druwids and Alabaster! Wait just a darn minute here! I'm getting everything so confused, so mixed up. I **am**. *I am a spiritual being, not a body. Look, my last Arad female body just got killed. I didn't! Here, I am now going to make use of this nice new Cymry body — Ket, it's called. But no matter what happens, I am not this body. I am not male or female. I am me. Okay, so I have thus far not played the role of a male since I came to Tarra. I guess I can learn. Besides, this mess up is likely to happen every time I have to acquire a new baby body — it's 50-50, boy or girl. I can see that for the others on our world, who have been here quite some time, this constant fluctuating between male and female bodies has to be terribly confusing indeed, from lifetime to lifetime! It's no wonder people want to forget their last lifetime.*

Besides, I did choose Naessa and this location for safety. The main thing is, Bethany, to keep your ownerships straight. Naessa's body gave birth to this Ket body. We are both spiritual beings playing the game of mother and daughter, er, I mean son. I just need to keep the games straight. I do feel much more relaxed now. Truth sets us free, that's for sure. Maybe Alabaster will be okay on his own and will try to contact me; maybe he'll not need my help after all. I'd not be surprised if he didn't; he's so powerful. I guess the thing to do now is just sit back, relax, and let this Ket body grow up.

Finally, I was at peace with myself. Going to war with oneself can be quite nasty. You suffer all the damage.

Chapter 2 Childhood Problems

"Mommy, why is Ket crying?" asked my sister, Fianna, her young voice full of concern. I was about two years old; it was the middle of the night. Images of that grey creature smashing in my head seemed more real than the room. Yes, I was shrieking and crying, trying to fend off the hideous creature.

The soothing voice of my mother cooed, "There, there, Ket, it's all right. You're just having a nightmare. None of it is real; you're just having some bad imaginings." She was rocking me gently back and forth, as my hands got tangled in her curly, long red hair. Turning to Fianna, she added, "Yes, Ket is having another one of his nightmares."

"He seems to have a lot of them mommy. How come none of us have nightmares?" she asked.

In her priestess manner, she replied, still calming me down, "We all are here to triumph over hardship and travail. Ket has his own things to overcome. Each of us face different things, Fianna. But you know, Fianna, you are right about Ket. He seems to be having these nightmares once a month, when the moon is at the first quarter. I wonder if the moon has anything to do with his nightmares? Let's watch and see how he does next month, shall we?"

She was right! I had no more nightmares until the next quarter moon. A month later, there I was shrieking and crying near midnight once more. Fianna thought that their having figured out this pattern was interesting, and she plied our mother for reasons for why this was so. Of course, Naessa had no real idea of what was going on with me — about all my small body could say was "Mamma and Pappa."

However, I can't tell you how much I owe to my little sister's suggestion. "Mommy, maybe Ket is scared of the dark. Maybe we could leave a lantern going in the room when the moon is nearly first quarter; then he might not be scared." Such a simple idea, and yet so powerful. Sure enough, after two years of having to deal with my nightmares, Naessa was willing to try almost anything. It worked perfectly. You see, when the images came back into my mind, because of the dim lantern light, I could see my room, the bed, covers, walls, and such. The world about me was more real now than those frightful images in my mind. Result: true, I still woke up on that particular night each month, but now I could keep my orientation to this world, dimming the mental images down. No more crying, shrieking, and waking everyone up.

The next calamity occurred when I was three. My hair was long and red, and it was time for my first haircut. Okay, they probably cut it before this time, but I was too young to realize what was happening. In this village, the usual haircut for the young boys was simply done. Their parents placed a bowl over the child's head and cut off all hair that was visible. Understand though, that once the boys grew into their teens, they tended to let their hair grow to their shoulders.

As I realized what Naessa was trying to do to my hair this fine spring morning, I began to wail and protest. "No, I don't want it cut. Don't cut my hair. I want it long." I pleaded, I protested, I cried, I bawled and pleaded for her not to cut it off.

"But Ket, all boys have their hair cut short so it won't get in your way," Naessa countered.

"I want it long," I countered, "just like Fianna's."

"But Fianna is a girl, Ket," she countered.

"Girls have long hair," added Fianna, who always seemed to be around me when anything was happening. I was her little brother, and she was looking after me. "Boys have short hair," she stated quite flatly, as if she were making an astute pronouncement of some magnitude that was irrefutable.

"But I want it long," was all I said.

"People will think you are a girl, Ket," Naessa added. My face flushed as red as my hair. How could I tell her I thought of myself as a girl, not a boy? This was getting so confusing. I dearly love long hair, but that was when I had female bodies. Nevertheless, I continued protesting so adamantly, that she finally gave up, saying, "Okay, Ket. I will not cut it today. However, if you get teased that you are a sissy, don't come crying to me, you understand?" Of course, I agreed.

For the next two years, periodically, I had this same discussion, more or less, and not only with Naessa, but also with my father and three older brothers, none of whom could understand my adamant insistence on having long hair. The name-calling didn't occur until I was around five years old, but by then, there were other considerations that lay behind other village children teasing me about being a sissy.

One of these considerations Naessa and Fianna really appreciated, and that was my dogged insistence to help around the house and grounds with daily chores. By now, my three older brothers were off at dawn, helping dad with his fishing or else tending our fields just outside of the village. That left Naessa and Fianna to do all the other chores that a large family generates. I pitched in and washed dishes, helped mend clothes, and helped with the cooking. Fianna was very impressed with how well I did the outside chores, milking the goat, gathering the eggs, and feeding our few domestic animals. Normally, she would have to do all these herself, but just as soon as I could manage them, I always beat her to them, doing them all before she had the chance. I think that my sister really appreciated my help, because it gave her more free time later in the morning to go out and play with her friends.

Often, I would overhear mom and Fianna chatting about how

wonderful it was that I was helping with all the household chores. It seems that when my older brothers were growing up, they had never wanted to do them and only did the outside chores when directly ordered to do so. Fianna observed, "Mommy, Ket is more like a little sister than a brother, isn't he?" I blushed as I overheard her comment to mom.

The next consideration became clearly visible when I was around six. By then, the other boys my age or older were playing with wooden swords. Daily, they would divide into two groups. Using wooden swords, they would have a mock battle, pretending to be heroic fighters and invading Axemen. Of course, I hated this game and refused to play, making up some excuse that I had some chore to do first.

When they boys began their mock battle, I would always be found tinkering with the chickens or brushing the goat, always around our house. One day Fianna asked me, "Ket, how come you aren't over there fighting the great battles? Boys do that you know," she explained patiently, using her "I know what I'm talking about" voice. Then, she had another thought, "Won't anyone let you be on their side? I'll ask mommy to make them let you join in their game."

I had a horrified look on my face, as I replied, "No! Don't do that! I don't want to play at fighting. I hate fighting."

"But Ket, men are supposed to defend us all. Women don't fight; men do. You're supposed to be able to help defend us."

"Fianna, fighting doesn't solve anything. People only get hurt or killed. Fighting should be a very last resort when all else fails. I hate fighting with swords and such."

"But how will you be able to defend me if some bad guys come, Ket, if you don't learn to fight?" she tried her pleading voice, hoping to melt my determination.

I looked her squarely in her blue eyes and said, "If it comes to that, Fianna, I'll use a pole to fend them off. But I'll not be a party to swordplay, ever." That settled that or so I thought and hoped. It didn't — it only raised the name calling of "sissy" to a higher notch.

When I was seven, it all came to a head one day, and Fianna witnessed it. About a dozen boys, mostly older than me, began to break into their teams to play out their new battle scenario. Someone pushed me into the group, saying, "Hey, you guys get Ket."

"No way! We don't want that sissy! You take him," the self-appointed leader of one side retorted. He was about ten years old and weighed about half again as much as I did. I'm still not sure exactly how it all happened, but soon, I was surrounded by the boys, who were insisting that Ged, the ten year old leader, fight me. I tried to break out of the circle, but the others kept shoving me back inside the circle.

Egged on by the others, Ged said, "Okay Ket, now I'm going to teach you sissy a lesson. You yellow coward. I'm going to smash every bone in your body with my trusty sword!" He waved his wooden sword through the air menacingly. From a corner of my eye, I spied Fianna looking terrified. I realized that she was almost ready to run to find mother to have her put a stop to all this bullying. Too late, Ged began rushing at me.

Instantly, all my former druwid training came rushing back to me. I effectively dodged out of the way, and the game was on. He lunged. I darted out of the way. Fianna pushed her way into the crowd of children who had gathered to watch this "for real" fight. "That's no fair," she cried out, "Ket doesn't have a sword to defend himself!" I saw Ged grimace in reaction; she spoke the truth.

He realized that beating up an unarmed younger boy would likely get him in trouble, so he momentarily halted. "Okay, someone give sissy Ket a sword." Reluctantly, several offered me their swords, all of which I refused.

I grabbed a small fence pole-type stick and faced Ged and the crowd, saying calmly, "Fighting is not a good answer to any problem; people just get hurt or killed. All I need to stop you is this fence pole. I warn you, if you continue to force me to fight you, you will get hurt."

"Bring it on, sissy Ket," Ged taunted, confident that he would now be able to beat me to a pulp and not get in trouble for doing it, since now that I had a weapon. Many in the crowd laughed loudly at me; everyone knows a pole is no match for a sword. They catcalled and egged Ged on. Little did they know. While the crowd began shouting and cheering Ged to teach me a lesson, the fight began in earnest. I spied Fianna clenching her face with her hands, praying that I wouldn't get badly beaten up.

Again, Ged lunged at me swinging wildly. I dodged and carefully began to observe his rather clumsy, boyish fighting style. Three swings later, I stopped dodging and began the offensive. My first swing landed on his shins, knocking him to the ground. Now he grew angry, which only made my task easier. After knocking him to the ground two more times, I said, "Had enough?" I hoped he was finished and would let me go. No, I had injured his manly pride! I had forgotten about this aspect of males. He jumped up more determined than ever to put me into my place.

His anger took over, displacing the little skill that he had with the wooden sword. My next strike connected with his wooden sword, sending it flying out of his hands, effectively disarming him. "Now, had enough?" I asked, certain that he would choose to end it here. However, I had only really pushed his buttons.

Men were supposed to be able to fight. His male self-pride simply would not let him quit, even when logic dictated otherwise. Suddenly I realized the impact of this cultural detail between the sexes. I could disarm him a hundred times, and he would still attempt to retaliate and get me back. I thought it was just sheer boyish stupidity. Nevertheless, he continued to try to attack me.

At last, I said, "I've had enough of this. If you don't stop, Ged, then I will have to end it." He continued to charge at me, waving his sword menacingly at my head. I whirled as his blow swiped through thin air; my pole came down sharply on his head, whack! He crumpled to the ground, out cold. The crowd of children was stunned. Not a word was said as I dropped the pole, pushed through them, and walked out of the circle toward my sister, who had a huge grin on her face.

She put her arm around me and said, "You showed him! I knew you weren't a coward or a sissy! Good going, Ket." Smiling, I found I enjoyed her praise. Just then, I saw mom standing far to the back and realized that she must have seen the whole fight. For a fleeting instant, I figured that I would be in trouble for having knocked Ged out like I did — I mean, doing real fighting and not play fighting. However, she had a smile on her face, which drove such thoughts out of my mind.

When we drew close to her, she commented, "Well, Ket, I think that Ged will think twice before he challenges you to another fight. You did well. Your father will be pleased. Come on inside; it's nearly lunch time." Fianna walked inside holding her head tall, immensely proud of her little brother. Yes, thinking back on it now, all the sissy talk had been really bothering her for quite some time.

The next problem I had centered on learning how to do things. Here, parents generally began by teaching young children how to count, progressing from there into doing simple arithmetic. Certainly, children had to learn the spoken language, including a vocabulary and sentence structure. Simultaneously, they would systematically teach their children life skills, such as how to care for the domestic animals, how to fish, how to grow crops, and so on. Of course, girls soon end up being taught a very different set of skills than the boys. I guess you could sum this all up by saying a child must be educated.

Can you see my problem? I used to be a Wid, a highly knowledgeable druwid! I already knew math. Last lifetime, I used to be able to speak a number of different languages. I knew basic life skills, at least those at which women must be proficient. As they began to instruct me, why, I figured I already knew all about it. Couple that attitude with the fact that I had a new small body, which had not yet become fully coordinated, and you get a recipe for troubles.

I'd get so frustrated doing some simple tasks. For example, one day, mom began to instruct me in how to milk the goats. "But I already know how to do it," I protested in my usual gruff, whining voice that often got me my way with her.

"Okay, then go ahead and show me," she said in her exasperated voice. "Five children and you are the most obstinate," she muttered to herself.

Intending to show her, I proceeded to make a mess of things; my small hands had not yet been trained, or perhaps it was coordination that was lacking. Funny, now I was being just as obstinate and stubborn as Ged had been. *Could I be sliding into a male personality?* I wondered, as red faced, I let her show me some skills and tricks that worked with my small, not so coordinated hands, and so my basic education went, full of frustration.

Over supper that night, dad brought up the topic I dreaded most. "Ket, we should start you in on learning skills for your future. What do you want to be? A fisherman like myself and your older brother perhaps? A boat maker, a blacksmith, a fighter, a merchant, a keg maker. . ." He rattled off a lengthy list of trades. My oldest brother, Garth, was soon to have his own fishing boat. However, both my other brothers wanted to be fighters, here called guardians of the peace. We all knew just how much this was costing our father. Paying for a new fishing boat wasn't cheap nor were the quality steel swords that he had purchased from the Highland Clans for my brothers.

I felt quite trapped. Last two lives, I had been a decent cook, could sew, and perform all the normal domestic duties, ignoring all my real skills, which I had learned as a druwid. "You would make a fine fisherman, Ket," my older brother Garth encouraged me. "It is really fun and very peaceful out there fishing in the bay. No hassles either. You'll like it."

"Nah, you should join up with us, Ket," broke in Rath. "We heard how you bested that bully Ged. You would make a great keeper of the peace. Come and learn how to fight with Fian and me."

I blurted out, "I don't want to fight. I don't want to sit around in a boat in the bay all day. I don't want to be a blacksmith, a baker, a merchant, a bar keeper, or a farmer." I rattled off a rather extensive list of local trades, hoping to put an end to their suggestions. If I ruled them all out, maybe they would just leave me alone in my misery.

Finally, mom commented, "Well then, Ket, you've ruled out most everything. What is it, pray tell, that you *do* want to do?" I detected some sarcasm in her voice; she was losing patience with me.

"I want to travel and see the world, but that isn't a trade," I answered very truthfully. After a pause, I added, "I would like to learn how to sail a fishing boat, to navigate, and all that. How hard is it to learn how to make a fishing boat?" In the back of my mind, I imagined myself making a small sailing boat and sailing from West Reach over to the mainland so I could go searching for Alabaster.

The relief on both my parents' faces told me I had scored a small victory. Thereafter, twice a week dad took me out fishing with him, teaching me how to sail and navigate our treacherous bay. Another two days each week I spent with Gar, the shipwright, learning basic woodworking and ship building skills. Further, twice a week, I got to accompany Fianna and her group who roamed the nearby countryside, foraging for honey, berries, and nuts for the long winter; that is, I got to travel around the nearby country.

Fianna was very happy that I could go on these trips with her.

However, all wasn't doom and gloom here in Cuch Glyn. Our small village contained thirty-two homes and business buildings. Mostly made from grey stone with thatched roofs, the village sprawled roughly semi-circular around the cozy bay. Grey sandy beaches stretched about a mile north and south of the village. We went swimming nearly every day in the warmer weather, usually in the middle of the afternoon.

Normally the coastline around here consists of beach fronts that ranged from perhaps fifty feet wide to a mile, where our village was located. Beyond the beaches, towering cliffs rose, often some hundred vertical feet. Giant stones dotted the water in random patterns, except where the stones created small natural harbors. Nearly all these harbors sported a small fishing village here along the western coastline of Tewdwr.

Streams, brooks, and occasional rivers cut and dropped their way down the cliffs to drain into the ocean. These natural cuts in the cliffs provided easy access to the vast hilly grasslands that formed most of Tewdwr. Here, flocks of sheep grazed. Often, each village had a communal flock tended by several shepherds. These coastal villages traded wool, mutton, and volumes of dried fish at inland towns and villages scattered across the green grasslands and woodlands of Tewdwr.

Rain. It rained nearly every day. Rare indeed was a day of sunshine without any clouds! Okay, you might call it gloomy. Grey days predominated. Yet it was the fog that always intrigued me! Just after supper, fog banks would come rolling in from the ocean. I loved to sit on shore and watch the swirling fog clouds move toward me, engulfing my small form, turning the village into a ghost town.

When I was eight, I was allowed to accompany the family on its biannual trip inland. In the spring and late fall, my dad packed up our horse with bags of dried fish and bags of wool. Leading the overloaded horse, we walked the ten miles to the inland town called Baegar, home to perhaps a thousand folks. Here in the open-air markets, dad would trade his supply of fish and wool for the other essentials that we needed and couldn't make or find in our village. One of these was, of course, cocoa leaves, which we children dearly loved. This trip, dad got us children a new pair of shoes, and he even had mom get a new dress.

However, what really caught my eye was the carnival! Fianna said, "Come on Ket! You've just got to see the circus." She led me to a large open area just at the edge of the town. Here five wagons, all gaily painted in reds, greens, yellows, and blues, formed a circle. Clowns in funny looking clothes worked the growing crowd of children, performing crazy antics that never failed to generate laughs and clapping hands. What got my interest almost at once was music! Three adults were playing music on a flute, guitar, and drum. Many older children, especially girls, were dancing to the music.

Fianna pulled me into the dancing area and began to show me how to dance. "I look forward to this all year long," she explained, and then began to show me how to make the moves. Soon, I was dancing along with her, but my mind was enthralled with the music. I had forgotten how much I loved making music. Although I didn't recognize any of the songs, I still loved them. One man played several songs on a whistle or flute held in one hand while beating a drum with his other hand. He even moved around the area, slow dancing to his own music.

Time flew by. Next thing I knew, Naessa had come to fetch us, "I knew I'd find you two here," she commented. "Fianna spends all her time dancing, Ket. Now come on, Fianna; dad wants to get you some shoes before we head home." Reluctantly and still dancing, we two followed her, dancing until the music finally died away.

We found dad at the cobbler's shop, waiting for us. "Ah there you two are. Come on; we need to measure your feet and get you some new boots." Fianna went first, gaily trying on several, looking for the prettiest pair she could get. An idea formed in my mind. I looked at her old shoes. They seemed to be still in good repair; her feet had just grown too large for them.

While Naessa and Fianna picked among the boots, I asked dad, "Dad, are flutes expensive? Could I get a flute so I can make music? If I can get a flute, I'll wear Fianna's old boots. They're still okay, and my feet are still smaller than hers."

"Well, I don't know," came his undecided reply. "Are you sure you would wear them? They are girl's boots after all."

"Sure, look, they will fit me," I hastily answered, taking mine off and putting hers on so that he could see that they really did fit me. "Please, dad," I begged in my most pleasing manner.

Finally, he said, "Let's see what your mother has to say about this." Shortly, Fianna, with a contented, satisfied look on her face, reappeared, showing off her new boots. Naessa was right behind her.

"What are you doing wearing my old boots?" she asked, as she spied me wearing her old ones. Mom's eyebrows rose, though she said nothing.

Dad answered, "Ket wants to get a flute instead of shoes. He says he'll be satisfied and wear her old ones. What do you think dear?"

Mom looked at me sternly, "Those are girl's boots, Ket. You'll be stuck with them until next year if you do this. Are you sure you want to do this?"

"Oh yes! I really want a flute so I can learn to play music!" I enthusiastically replied, putting on my most begging facial expression.

"Well, it's his first time coming to town. I suppose it is okay. Can we afford it?" she replied. My heart sank; perhaps the cost of a flute would be far too great. I watched as dad traded my old boots and some wool to pay for Fianna's new boots. I held my breath as we walked across town to a shop where dad thought we could find a flute.

A half hour later, we were heading back home, our horse now loaded down with the newly acquired supplies we needed. Fianna kept looking down at her new pretty boots, while I held onto my wooden flute for dear life. It had suddenly become my most prized possession. However, I waited until I was back home and alone before I tried to play it.

All this led to a dramatic shift in my life. Each evening after the prayer meeting and then supper, I would usually sit on the docks watching the fog bank roll in. The others usually went to the inn. Since my parents now thought I was old enough to accompany them, I got to go with them. Inside the inn, local musicians played traditional tunes and sang songs while the villagers drank pints of mead and chatted. Fianna and many other young girls also took this as an excellent opportunity to dance, and I saw at once why she knew how to dance so well.

This communal meeting was an aspect of our village that I had forgotten about. Yes, last lifetime when I had come to this town attempting to elude the Grey Creature following me, I had enjoyed a night of music and song here in this very inn. Memories came back to me as I listened. How could I have forgotten this detail, I wondered? Music, I could learn much from these three musicians!

Suddenly, I realized my way out of this mess. Musicians. I remembered many years ago back in the Greenway, musicians often traveled throughout the lands playing for local villages along the way. If I could become a troubadour, why, I could indeed travel the world so that I could search for Alabaster! Finally, I had the answer that I desperately wanted. For the first time, I settled down to learn all that I could from our local musicians.

I think my parents were finally happy with me. At age eight, from their viewpoint, I stopped being the obstinate, stubborn child. I began to learn from them all that I could in earnest, quite a change for me. I went out to sea on Mondays and Fridays with dad; I studied with Gar, the shipwright, on Tuesdays and Wednesdays; on Thursdays and Saturdays, I roamed the countryside far and wide with Fianna and her friends, foraging for the village. But every night, I was at the inn practicing with our musicians, until I became good enough to join them entertaining our village.

Our bay was about two miles wide at the shoreline, gradually extending to ten miles where it met the ocean proper. On all outward sides giant, jagged boulders of lichen covered granite protruded, like enormous teeth of some gargantuan monster. Close to these boulders, passage was incredibly treacherous; the current and tide surges could reach out to an unwary craft and suck it into the boulders, crushing it at once on the sharp stone. However, inside our bay, the fishing was generally good, though dad often ventured out to the open sea. On those days, he always brought home significantly larger catches.

His craft had a single lateen sail and a small rudder. It could seat six adults, but normally dad went out alone or with one of us kids with him so he had sufficient room for his catch. When I went with him, he carefully taught me how to handle the boat in all kinds of weather and how to navigate, especially when the fog bank rolled in earlier than expected. He respected my wishes and didn't attempt to turn me into a fisherman. By the time I was twelve, I was skilled in handling these small boats. He also promised me that one day he would take me on a trip to some nearby bays and coves along our rocky coastline.

After working under Gar's guidance for years, I successfully built my own small sailing boat. I had the callouses to prove it, but I was very proud the day we launched the Lucky Lady. Thereafter, at least once a day I took her out for a spin around the bay. I truly enjoyed the private time while sailing, no cares in the world. Yes, I frequently took Fianna with me; we were almost inseparable growing up.

Yet, now I had a new skill, working with wood, and I began in secret to build my own guitar and lute. If I were to be a troubadour, I would need to be able to make my own instruments. I had already carved two new flutes, but they had been failures. I discovered getting the finger holes correctly placed was extremely critical, if one wanted the correct notes to sound. Before I began my third attempt at flute construction, I began to work out the mathematics of the hole position versus the intended notes. This time I was confident the flute would be more playable than its two predecessors were. I was in better shape, though, with the two stringed instruments, because I was merely copying a pair that our local musicians played each night.

The foraging trips I took with Fianna and her friends were some of the happiest times of my childhood. Usually she went with six of her girlfriends, all nearly her age, accompanied by Rob and myself. Parents insisted that at least one young man accompany the girls in case of trouble. Rob was two years older than I was, and he was training to be a fighter or guardian of the peace. Hence, he carried proudly his shiny metal sword and often bragged to the girls about how he was here to protect them. Secretly, I saw that he was really trying to impress the girls, something which I was not. I had to carry a stout pole with me so that I could play the role of protector if some trouble came our way. The girls sometimes teased me playfully calling me their "pole man." Rob did his best to ignore me completely.

Each trip generally took most of the day, as we traveled probably a good ten miles out into the surrounding rolling green hills and forests. Each trip covered slightly different ground, so I got to see a large part of the immediate surrounding countryside. Tewdwr is like no other land I had seen on Tarra. Emerald rolling hills, sometimes dotted with small glens of timber, displayed more shades of green than I imagined could exist. True, it rained nearly every day, which probably accounted for the abundant growth.

Sometimes when we didn't find much to bring back, Fianna and I would lay down in the plush grasses and gaze over the landscape and the distant sea, at least when the weather cooperated and we could see that far. On one of those days, she said lazily to me, "Are you really going to one day take your flute and travel all around the world?"

"Yes, I plan to do it, once I'm old enough to be on my own," I replied.

"But won't you get lonely? I mean you'd be so far from home and from us," she replied with a sigh. "I know I'll miss you very much, Ket."

"Oh sure, I'll miss mom and dad and you, Fianna, most of all, but I have something I have to do."

"Won't you tell me what it is that you have to do? Why you have to travel everywhere?" she pleaded with those big blue eyes of hers. Seeing that I was still reluctant to open up, she added, "If it is a secret, I can keep a secret."

We were close, Fianna and I; she was always looking out for me. My brothers were so much older than I and were totally engrossed in their own lives that they seldom spent much time with me. Yet, Fianna was always there. I sighed. I longed to confide in someone. "Okay, sis, but you must promise me that you'll not tell anyone." Of course she enthusiastically promised.

I had not gotten much farther than explaining that we were all immortal spiritual beings when she interrupted, wondering if a spirit was a ghost or something. "Look, can you get a mental image of our house?" I decided to try to reach her as best I could. She closed her eyes, and I could tell from her smile that she did. "Now that is a picture in your mind. And this is your physical body," I pinched her slightly. "See, body and mind." She nodded. "Now, who is looking at that picture?" This was the moment of truth. I held my breath.

"Why I am, of course," she flatly declared, as if I had asked a stupid question. "Who else could be looking at my picture?"

"That's you, Fianna, the looker at the picture. That's you, the immortal spiritual being."

"Oh! Me? I never thought of it that way," she said, her eyes opened wide.

"When our bodies die, we just go and find a new baby body. That's what happened to me. I got killed nearby our village, and I took this body when it was born," I tried to keep it simple, omitting the former identities that I had just before my body had been slain by the Grey Creature.

"How can you remember who you were? I mean before you got killed?" she asked, her eyes full of curiosity and disbelief.

"I can. How about you? Can you remember anything from before you moved into this body?" I asked, suspecting that I would get the predictable "No." She surprised me.

"Well, when I was little I had these awful pictures of an old man drowning in the ocean. I was afraid of the water for a long time, until dad taught me to swim — that was when you were only three," she said determinedly.

"See, you can remember too, but sometimes it is sad things that we remember," I replied.

"Well, mommy said it was just nightmares and not to give them any mind. Say, were your nightmares coming from remembering how you died, I mean your body died?" she asked.

Fianna's question caused me to re-evaluate my sister. Such an astute observation or conclusion! "Yes, yes, that was what gave me nightmares. I woke up, couldn't see where I was at, and got confused between being in our house and being killed that night. Your idea of keeping a lantern going saved the day for me! I've never said how thankful I am for your help with that, Fianna." She fairly beamed as she recalled those early days.

"Were you a great fighter — I mean before you got killed? Did you die in a great battle?" she asked, extremely curious.

"I was a priestess, rather like our mother, not a fighter. And no, I died all alone just up the coast from our village. No glorious combat — just got my face completely smashed in by this bad man. Don't worry. That man is no longer anywhere around here," I answered truthfully and tried not to get her worried.

She gave me the queerest look before she spoke again. I could see her mind whirling. "So you were a girl before. Now you are a boy. Isn't that confusing?"

"Yes, I have been very confused and frustrated. This is the first boy body I've had."

"Well, then Ket, now everything makes so much more sense. No wonder you didn't want to fight with swords and roughhouse like the other boys. You are really a girl. This is so confusing. I know I would be confused, but it makes so much sense. I've always thought of you more like my little sister than my little brother. Well, I shall just have to help you get things straight, about boys, I mean. I do know a lot about boys," she said with determination in her young voice, as if she was somehow going to solve all my problems for me.

"Thanks. Anyhow, I had this very, very good friend, a really, really great man. He got into some very bad trouble helping me out, and he asked me to promise to come and rescue him, if I did not hear from him. Well, I still haven't heard so much as a peep from him. I don't even know where on Tarra is now is. Yet, I made him a solid promise that I would find him and help him. I aim to keep that promise. He is the most important person on all Tarra, as far as I'm concerned. I'm not going to let him down."

She sat in silence for a minute before she replied, "Yes, if I made such a promise, I would do everything I could to keep it. After all, what else is there but our word, our pledge? You should go, find him, and help him, Ket, really you should. But why not tell mom and dad about it? Maybe they can help you go and find him?"

"They won't understand, really they won't, Fianna. Please don't go telling them any of this, you promised," I reminded her.

"Oh, I won't tell; it's a secret between you and me. Here come the others. I guess we ought to be heading home," she said as we got up and went to join the others for the long walk home.

The final problem that I faced occurred when I was nearly thirteen. I reached puberty and experienced the body's male-hood for the first time! Yes, I was shocked, surprised, and then very curious. Remember, I was more than familiar with being a woman and her sensations, but this was totally new and different. I found myself being aroused by many of the young women in our village and found the bulge rather embarrassing to say the least. Yet what shocked me the most was how quickly the passion came and went, totally unlike that I experienced as a woman. Suddenly, I had a great insight into men that I wished I had when I had my two earlier female bodies.

However, now I was torn into halves. My physical body was drawn to the young women, especially those who were in my sister's group of friends, but me, I wasn't; rather I was used to looking at handsome men. Now I realized I was in for a great deal of difficulty and had no idea how to deal with these emotions and sensations.

Of course, when Fianna found out about all this, she offered her advice and help. "Go with your body's urges," she suggested. However, she soon found that I was a keen judge of men, particularly the young men she had begun to take seriously. For the next couple years, she was always asking me what I thought about this boy and that; she trusted my female experience implicitly.

In return, she gave me clues about which young women were interested in me, though their attempts at flirting gave them away. Yes, for the next two years, Fianna and I grew even closer. Then, two disasters struck within a week.

By this time, I was fourteen and she was seventeen. Both Garth and Rath had married and moved to different villages, beginning their own families. Fian, now eighteen, still lived at home, even though he was now officially a guardian of the peace. As usual, I spent this fateful Tuesday working on shipbuilding with Gar. Late afternoon, I packed up my tools and headed home to meet dad when he sailed up to the dock. One of my chores was to help him unload his catch, gut, and clean the fish. Now that I was fourteen, he was even letting me help him stake them out to dry in our back shed. However, when I got home, a dense fog had already rolled in across our bay. I saw no sign of dad's small boat.

Prayer time came and still dad had not returned. Naessa wasn't particularly concerned, though, because occasionally he would come in late, usually with an above average catch. Hastily, we went to the church and mom held the brief service. When we got home and ready to eat our dinner, still dad failed to appear. "No sense in letting everything get cold; let's eat. Dad should be home anytime, and there will probably be more work than normal," mom commented. I glanced at Fianna; she, me. We were both getting a bit worried; I couldn't remember dad ever being this late getting back. Fianna fidgeted and ate little, and I knew she was worried.

Once we had eaten, she and I quickly did the dishes. She whispered, "Do you think dad's all right? He's terribly late. I'm getting really worried. I think mom is too, though she is doing her best not to show it."

"Yes, this isn't like dad. Let's get these dishes done really fast, just in case," I replied, washing all the faster.

A few minutes later, we joined mom, who still sat at the table, toying with a cup of half-drunk tea. Her eyes appeared distant, as if she were trying to see her husband. She couldn't hide the worry on her face. Fianna sat beside her and said, "Mommy, I'm awfully worried about dad. This fog is so dense. How will he find his way here?"

This brought a little life to mom's face. She looked up and commented, "We lit the four dock lanterns. He should be able to make them out when he gets close enough."

"I'll go and check on them, mom, make sure they are still shining brightly," I volunteered, wanting to do something useful. Besides, I began to have a bad feeling in my stomach. This was not like dad at all. Every year, at least one fisherman would have a string of bad luck, a miscalculation, which sometimes ended with their boats smashed upon the rocks, even their own deaths sometimes.

Outside, the fog was very dense; I could only see about ten feet in front of me as I approached the four lanterns, which still shone brightly. I walked to the very end of the dock and stood looking out to sea, straining to see his little ship and sail heading my way. I saw only rolling black fog. Until now, I hadn't used my special druwid powers much at all, keeping a low profile for several reasons, the biggest was that I didn't want to draw the attention of the Grey Creatures to me or our village. *Besides, sensing in this direction will not likely draw the attention of them — it's out to sea, opposite of their location in the Appian Way. I have to find out about dad.* I was just relaxing and letting my mind expand outward when I heard and felt Fianna timidly approaching me.

When she neared, I could see that she was crying, tears trickled down her face. I put my arm around her and had her sit on the edge of the dock beside me. "Don't worry, sis. I'm going to find out what's happening with dad right now. Don't let anything disturb my concentration. I need complete quiet. I haven't done this in a long time."

"Done what?" she sniffled. "How can you find out?"

"I'm going to mentally contact dad and locate where he is at. So keep everything very still and quiet." She gave me a strange look, and I could tell I would have a lot of explaining to do later. She complied and I continued to expand my awareness out towards the ocean in an ever-widening arc. When I am doing this, I lose all sense of time. After what seemed to me to be an eternity, I made contact and had located him. He was nearly unconscious, clinging to some rocks far out at the very edge of the bay. Hence, I decided not to plant any thoughts into his mind, calculating that he might be so startled that he would lose his grip and maybe drown.

"Come on, Fianna. I found him. He is still alive. I think he ran into the rocks at the edge of the bay on the south side. I have to go rescue him. Give me a hand getting my boat ready," I told her, taking charge of the situation. Again, she gave me a very queer look, but helped me put some rope and two lanterns on my small boat. I was now very glad that I had learned to build small sailing crafts.

As I was about to shove off, she finally could contain her questions no longer. "How can you do that? You should not go to sea in this fog. How will you ever find him? If he got smashed up on the rocks, won't that happen to you? How will you ever find our dock coming back? How. . ."

I cut her off, "No time to explain. Tell mom to get warm blankets ready and a lot of hot broth. I think he will be really cold by the time I get him back." Using an oar, I pushed off from the dock and hoisted my little sail. "See you in a little while, Fianna. Please don't worry about me." Then I could see her face no longer, only a grey shape in the fog, surrounded by the pale glow of the lanterns. I adjusted the sail and began tacking my way out into our bay. I kept my mental connection with dad and his location firmly in mind and made my way in that general direction.

I knew that I could navigate to his general location, but once there, if I drew close, I too would get smashed upon the rocks. As I slowly sailed the couple of miles as the crow flies, I pondered what I ought to do when I got close. The winds were definitely not cooperating, blowing inland. Time passed pitifully slowly as did my outward progress. Finally, I could hear the crashing thunder of waves pounding upon the hidden rocks ahead. When I calculated I was as close as I dared, I dropped the sail and stowed it. I tied an oar to the rope, laid it carefully in the water at my side, and watched it move and bounce with the waves and current. This way, I could tell which way the water was moving my boat. Luck was with me, the currents were slowly taking the boat back toward shore.

Stripping down to my shorts, I prepared to swim to him. I tied a short length of rope around my waist. The long rope I tied securely to my waist and to the bow of my boat. Then I carefully slipped into the chilly waters, holding on to the side of the boat. I unfastened one lantern and began swimming using a breaststroke while trying to hold the lantern up out of the water so I could see where I was going. I swam slowly, still maintaining my contact with dad. I sensed he was now very weak and prayed that he could hold on a little longer, but as precarious the situation was, I refused to quicken my pace. Soon, I felt the surges of the underwater currents as they ebbed and flowed from the barrier rocks ahead. The noise of the crashing waves drowned out all other sounds.

Twice, I ran into hidden underwater rock outcrops, nearly cramping my legs in the process. Then I saw him just as a wave hurled me upwards towards the suddenly appearing black boulder masses. Wham, I hit the rocks, nearly knocking my breath out. My lantern was smashed in the process. I felt his cold, shivering body. "I'm here, dad. I'll have you rescued in no time," I called out reassuring him. He did not reply.

Despite the challenge of surging waves over this bit of nearly submerged rock, I finally managed to get the short length of rope around his waist. Gently, I pulled him off the rock; his grip was so weak by this time that it was not beyond my strength. I began swimming back toward my boat, keeping him on his back and his head up as best I could. I still could see virtually nothing but a dim glow where my boat's single lantern glowed in the dense fog. However, his weight I couldn't carry much further, so I began pulling on the rope, gently moving my boat toward me. After an eternity, the boat banged into my head. Now I had to figure out how to get dad up and into the boat.

Limp and unconscious now, dad was no help. Oh for the strong arm of an adult at this point! My teeth were chattering. I knew that I couldn't take much more of this cold water myself. *Think, Bethany, think!* I plopped both his arms over the side of the boat and then dove under water and swam up as hard and fast as I could, catching his legs and pushing him up at the same time. Dead weight fought me back, but I managed to get him half onboard. Then, I had another idea. I untied the rope around my waist and tied it to his waist, throwing the other end over the boat into the water on the other side. Then, I swam around, grabbed the rope, tugged, and pulled. It must have looked hilarious: a great big unconscious man slowly sliding into a small boat, while a teenager nearly walked up the other side of the boat, nearly parallel to the water! I fell backwards in a giant slash when his body suddenly lurched fully into the boat. Quickly, I scrambled back in, turned the boat around, hoisted my sail, and headed back toward shore.

The fog was so thick, of course, that I couldn't see where I was going. I was sailing rapidly, what with the slight wind at my rear, but I was sailing blind. If I kept my head, if all else failed, I could just run the boat aground somewhere on our lengthy beach. However, then I would have the problem of getting help for dad quickly. "Use your brain, Bethany," I said to myself. I reached out ahead and sensed Fianna and mom, using them as a bearing. Sometime later on, again, how long I had no way of telling, I faintly spied a vague light ahead and made for it. Slowly the light grew, but I almost rammed headlong into the dock, so suddenly did it appear out of the fog. I had navigated perfectly back to our own dock!

A crowd of people was standing there, talking. Cheers went up when they suddenly spied my small boat. "Look out, you are going to smash into the dock," someone yelled, somewhat too late. I hit it with a dull thud.

"Dad's alive, freezing cold, and unconscious. Help him please," I called out, my own teeth chattering so badly that my words barely were audible. I felt strong arms lifting me out and a warm blanket quickly wrapping me up. Someone carried me inside our house, while behind me, I heard much commotion as several men brought dad.

Hot cocoa and a warm fire soon brought me back to my senses. Everyone congratulated me on the dangerous rescue of my dad. His prognosis was good. He'd bunged up his right leg rather badly and had nearly died from the long exposure to the cold, but he would live.

By the next day, I was the talk of everyone in the village. Everyone said that Annwn must have been guiding me, for there was no other acceptable answer for this rescue. None could ever recall a rescue like this in the dense fog. It had to have been the divine intervention of Annwn. I let them devise their own acceptable explanations for what I had done. Naturally, Fianna would have none of their divine intervention explanations and late in the afternoon, we walked out into the grasslands so I could explain to her in private. Yes, I had to tell her every detail. Surprisingly, she accepted it readily, though she had no idea how I could have done it.

Thankfully, by the next day, things were back to normal, and I was no longer the center of the entire village's attention. I hate being the center of attention! Of course, dad wouldn't be able to go fishing for some time until his leg recovered. Then, there was the problem of no boat; his had been destroyed on the rocks. I volunteered to let him have my boat until another could be found. He hugged me and thanked me generously. In fact, Gar and I promised to begin building him another boat the next day, though it would take us several weeks to make one as big as he needed; mine was only a small two-man boat. Unfortunately, this project was never completed, due to the second disaster, which struck on Friday afternoon, when three heavily armed cavalrymen rode into our village, demanding our attention.

One acted as spokesman, he was perhaps twenty-five, sporting long blonde hair with a nearly-there beard that was still rather thin. Overall, he had a covert look about himself; I didn't trust him from the moment I first saw him. "Your attention please," he said in a domineering voice. "I'm the official representative of King Albert I." Most of the villagers had a hard time understanding him because he spoke with an accent associated with the southern region known as the Layamon. However, I instantly recognized his accent and realized that it was we who had the thick and nearly undecipherable accent, not him. I guess it is just a matter of viewpoint.

From the blank looks on the small crowd who had gathered to hear him, I presumed that no one had ever heard of this king from the southern portion of the island. I certainly had not. He continued, "King Albert hereby annexes your village into his kingdom, this twenty-first day of June. In return for his protection from enemies, you are hereby ordered to send two wagonloads of grain and one of wool to his keep in Bregia each fall at harvest time. In return, you are granted the right to work this land that he now claims as his rightful property."

Fian spoke up for Cuch Glyn, "As the officially appointed Guardian of the Peace, we will do no such thing. We do not need any protection. This is Tewdwr, not Layamon. We don't recognize this foreign king. So ride away and never come back," he said as his ire grew.

My mind raced trying to make sense of this ultimatum. There used to be a duke who led Bregia, at least when I was last there so many years ago. Now they had a king. Could my children last lifetime who became kings and queen, could our children have started this push toward dividing the land into kingdoms? I was so caught up in trying to grasp the situation, that I didn't pay close attention to their ensuing conversation. Perhaps I should have.

Angry words soon came to blows. In Fian's defense, I will say that they fired their crossbows first, wounding two young men. Enraged, Fian and several others attacked the three with great violence, pulling two off their horses, and killing them outright with their swords. The third, the spokesman, though wounded in the scuffle, managed to gallop safely away.

By nightfall, the confrontation was the talk of the entire village! Naessa ordered the two slain men be buried, but she had to insist strongly before anyone actually carried out her order. That night, we musicians didn't play at the inn. Rather everyone was there discussing this new problem. By bedtime, the consensus of agreement was that Fian and the others had taught them a lesson, and they would not be back, leaving us alone.

None of the adults would listen to me, only Fianna did. When we were snugly in our respective beds later that night, she asked me why I disagreed with all the adults. I replied simply, "Power hungry men will not take no for an answer. I've seen something like this before, many years ago. Mark my words, sis; they will return in force and try to enforce their will on our village." She didn't reply and fell asleep pondering my prediction, weighing it against the predictions of the adults earlier this evening.

Nothing happened the next day, and by nightfall, everyone pretty much forgot about it. On Sunday, as usual, I accompanied Fianna and six of her close girl friends on our usual foraging hike across the emerald green countryside. The other boy, who carried a sword, didn't come with us; instead, he stayed in the village in case further trouble might come. After delivering supplies to two young men who shepherded the village's flock of sheep, we went berry hunting. By mid-afternoon, we headed home, several sacks filled with early season berries.

The girls' spirits were high, and as usual, they chatted about their prospects for getting some new clothes and their boyfriends, of course. Fianna finally convinced Gylee to let her red hair down so its richness showed instead of having it wrapped in an old maid's bun as she normally did. "I'm sure more boys will notice you this way," she declared, and her four friends heartily agreed. Gylee, just fourteen, let Fianna undo her bun and arrange her hair, while we paused for a short break. "See, I think it looks good. What do you think, Ket?"

I blushed at the unexpected thrust into this dangerous arena. I swallowed and looked at Gylee. "Yes, you look much more attractive this way." I kept it short and to the point. "You look youthful now and more desirable — I mean, not that you weren't before. It's just with your hair up in a bun you look much older and like you aren't inviting the attention of boys." The girls giggled and looked away from me. However, Gylee's broad smile told me that she liked my comment, but I hoped she wouldn't think that I was now interested in dating her. Before anyone could get to thinking along that line, I suggested we continue our walk back to our village.

"Looks like rain is coming again," Fianna announced shortly after we had begun walking once more. Quickly, we halted, put on our rain cloaks, and continued walking. As soon as the sprinkles began falling, we pulled the hoods up over our heads. However, we all enjoyed walking along in the warm spring rain. The air smelled so fresh and invigorating that our spirits rose even further. In Tewdwr, rain was a daily occurrence, welcomed in fact.

We were on the last tall hill before Cuch Glyn when we saw the catastrophe drawing close to our village. At least fifty cavalrymen were charging full speed toward our village, coming up the sandy beach from the south. I surmised they must have come down the river slice about five miles further south. Around here, the cliffs were a hundred feet tall and impassable, save where the brooks and rivers cut a gash in their sides. Obviously, these men wanted the attack to be a total surprise. Fianna started to scream, but I quickly put my hand over her mouth and ordered all of us to drop down on the ground and seek cover as best we could. I was responsible for their safety.

We crawled to a spot about a mile northwest of Cuch Glyn, hiding behind an outcrop of boulders, three feet tall, covered with lichens and moss. From here, we could see what was happening below us. The riders entered the village and began killing everyone who came outside their homes to see what was going on! Some were cut down by sword swings; others took quarrels to their chests and heads. It was a frightening slaughter. We only had three young guardians of the peace who could actually do some fighting.

I watched as old Gar tried to defend himself with a pitchfork before he was cut down. I felt sick to my stomach. Dad hobbled out on his sore leg to stand alongside my brother Fian, who was vainly swinging his sword in all directions to little avail. Dad was trying to protect him by swinging an oar from a boat. "Not this again!" I cried, as images from my earlier lives came flooding into my mind. Yet again, my family was being killed right before my eyes.

When dad and Fian both fell, Fianna cried out, "Ket, *do* something!"

"Look, you girls stay here and be quiet. Whatever you do, do not get their attention. If you do, they are likely to ride up here and rape you or take you away as their sex slaves! I'm going to try to help dad and Fian."

"Be careful," Fianna whispered, suddenly terrified that she might lose me too. I suspect she regretted her outburst.

A stroke of lightning flashed, struck the hills far off, and the thunder rolled ominously across the green land. I began running toward our village and trying hard to also concentrate on bringing down lightning on my command. Yes, in my previous two lifetimes, I had been exceedingly good at commanding lightning; it was my specialty. However, for the last fourteen years, I had not done it even once; I was a bit rusty. Yet, a skill once well learned never leaves you. By the time I reached the edge of the village, I had it under my control, but I was forced to make crude motions with my hands to help me concentrate on just the exact spot I desired lightning to strike.

Actually, if one can observe, it is a simple thing to do, really. First, there is a tiny, nearly invisible arc that goes up from the target to the energy cloud; nearly instantaneously, the power surge flows back down that line, striking the target. Hence, all you need to do is move, alter, adjust, or create that tiny, thin energy line, and Nature does the rest. I put one end of my beam on the nearest cavalryman and pushed the line up into the black clouds. Wham! Blazing lightning came back down, killing the man and horse, knocking him some ten feet off his horse in the process. One down, forty-nine to go, I thought to myself. Worse still, some cavalrymen began throwing flaming torches up onto our thatched roofs. Here and there, roofs were burning.

I lost count quickly as I approached our house. Damn, mom had come out to tend to my wounded dad and brother. Before I could get to her, several crossbows twanged, and I watched in horror as she collapsed on top of dad, several quarrels sticking out of her back. Wham! Wham! I let lose bolt after bolt, killing those who had shot mom. Now my rage increased, as it often did when I encounter such wickedness. I grabbed dad's oar to use to help fend off the cavalrymen who charged at me. Wham! I took out another. Now a new idea formed, I intentionally pointed out to each man, indicating with my arms, that I was causing the lightning to strike them, which it did momentarily afterwards. My intention was to strike fear and terror into these men, who were doing the same to our village, give them a taste of their own medicine.

Soon it was obvious to the attackers that I, and I alone, stood in their way of conquering the village. They weren't stupid and stopped attacking the defenseless villagers, concentrating on me. They dared not get too close, so they tried firing quarrels at me. However, my druwid training kicked in full steam. Some I merely dodged; others, I deflected with a swift motion of my arms; a few others, I simply caught and let drop onto the cobblestones. My retribution was swift. Wham! Wham! More and more bolts rained down on the attackers, bodies and horses flying in all directions.

Then suddenly, it was over, nearly as quick as it had begun. The remaining half dozen cavalrymen, including the same one that had come days earlier with the ultimatum, stared at me, turned their horses around, and galloped off as fast as they dared on the wet, slippery cobblestones. I watched as they vanished south along the beach. I stood frozen for several minutes, trying desperately to overcome my rage and violent anger. That had always been my Achilles heel. I get so enraged that I go nearly insane and cannot stop myself. I had Willow help me regain control that first time, but here, I was alone and on my own. If I couldn't recover, there was no one to help me.

By the time that I had calmed down, the girls had raced down into our village, seeking out their families. Fianna came rushing up to us, crying, "Mom! Dad! Fian!" Her words helped pull me out of my rage. I turned to her and together we knelt beside their bodies. Carefully, I rolled mom over; she was still alive, barely. She looked into the tear-filled eyes of Fianna and whispered, "I love you." She moved her head ever so slightly to me and said, "Take care of Fianna." Those were her last words; her breath left, and she slumped lifeless before us. Tears and rain drenched both our faces.

I moved mom off dad to see how he was. He had died from a severe wound to his neck and chest. I crawled over to Fian, but didn't need to look carefully; the heavy rain was moving a huge pool of blood down toward the bay. He was also quite dead. However, the roar of flames caught my ears. Our roof was blazing. I closed my eyes, pulled in more rain, and then more rain. It was all I could think of to help put out the fires. Soon, a heavy deluge flooded down upon us all. The sounds of sputtering and steam foretold the extinguishing of the flames. It worked. While a dozen homes would need new roofs, the rest of the house had been spared. True, all our homes were built of grey stone, but inside, timbers supported the floors and roof. Had I not been able to get the fires out, we would have had just grey stone shells for homes.

For what seemed like an eternity, Fianna and I knelt there beside our fallen family, our arms around each other, neither saying a word while the heavy rains pounded down on us. Around us, women were wailing; girls and boys crying. All were in shock. Fianna's voice finally reached my ears, her voice high and shrill, as if coming from some distance away, "You said this would happen. They should have listened to you, Ket."

I bawled back, "It wouldn't have made any difference. They would have still come. The outcome would still have been the same."

The voice of an old man sounded behind us, "It is our lot in life to suffer the travails of life. Today, we have all suffered a great tragedy, a tragedy beyond words. Yet, greatness comes to those of us who can overcome the challenges of life. Naessa would want us to believe this and say this, I'm sure." Conna, our blacksmith, began to take charge; he had occasionally conducted our prayer services when Naessa was unable to do so. "Come, children. Let the living gather in the church to pray for our loved ones and to take an official counting of those that still live."

He began moving around the village, ushering all grieving folks toward the church. Drenched from rain and tears, slowly everyone filed into our church. We feebly looked around, noticing how many were missing, particularly when Conna himself finally entered, walking up to the front with the weight of the entire village on his shoulders. Shocked, I reckoned only half our village survived! Children and teenagers made up the largest percentage. Only ten adults were present. Slowly, grief halting his words at times, Conna led our prayer service, but I heard none of his words. I was still in shock, still trying to keep my rage and anger at bay.

As he neared the end, I finally actually began to hear what he was saying. "What do we do now? Well, with so many lost, we can't stay here. As soon as the rain lets up, we must properly bury our loved ones. All must lend a hand in digging the graves. Then, tomorrow let us gather up all that is of value and pack our horses. We will walk to Baegar and seek help there. I am sure the folks there will help usl. Perhaps in time, we can return to Cuch Glyn and rebuild our village, but right now, we must stay alive and survive."

"I hear that the rain is letting up. First, I want you children to go home, grab a shovel or anything you can dig with, and go to our cemetery. Dig one giant grave. We few adults will gather up our fallen and bring them to the cemetery. Anyone with healing skills, please report to me when we adjourn; we have ten that are still alive and need help. Let us overcome this travail; let us all work together."

One teenager yelled out, "I'll not dig a hole for those bastards who did this! Let them rot!" Cheers arose in response.

Conna commented, "We will salvage what horses and equipment we can. We'll place the beasts that did this on the beach and leave their bodies for the buzzards to eat. Those men were not human and deserve nothing civilized." Everyone cheered loudly and began to leave to carry out his orders. I was certainly glad that someone had stepped up to lead us survivors. For an instant, I fretted that I might be once again thrust into that role.

As it is, I used to be a healer in my last two lives. Though I had not really practiced any thus far, I knew I had a responsibility to help heal our wounded as I could. "I've got to stay, Fianna, and help with those that need healing. You go on ahead and help the others dig a proper grave for them.

I'll join you as soon as I can."

"Okay," she muttered feebly. Then, she looked at me with a funny expression on her grief-stricken face, "I didn't know you knew anything about healing."

"Never had any need to use it," I replied truthfully. I gave her a loving hug and she left, joining up with several of her girlfriends. I waited for Conna.

Slowly everyone left the church, all except Conna, me, and one older woman, Dana. I know that Conna was quite surprised to see me volunteering. He said, "Ket, are you sure that you know something about healing? I've never known anything about it." Dana also gave me a curious look of disbelief.

"Yes, I know a lot about healing," I replied meekly, adding, "Please just don't ask how it is that I know. I'm very out of practice." Both nodded. I followed them out of the church. Miraculously, the adults had carried the wounded into the inn and done what little they could for them before coming to the church service. I was gratified that they were all together in one, dry, warm place.

Dana took charge, "Ket, let us examine each together and compare what we think must be done to each." I was sure that she didn't believe I knew the first thing about healing. I simply agreed, anxious to know what we actually were facing here.

In a half hour, we finished making our survey. We had six with quarrel wounds; none were life threatening, but all had to be removed and the wounds bled, cleansed, and bandaged. Four others had severe sword cuts, mostly to the arms and legs. All had hastily been bound to slow the bleeding. When we had finished comparing notes, Dana was greatly impressed with me. "I didn't believe you Ket. I made you make each diagnosis first before I gave mine. Forgive me for doubting that you know something about healing."

"I'd feel better handling those with the sword wounds, Dana. I don't think I have the physical strength to pry out some of those quarrel bolts. Some are stuck in bone. I'm only fourteen," I suggested, knowing that I really would have an awful time on at least three of them.

"Boys aren't known for their sewing abilities, but I concur. Have at it then. I'll inspect each one before you bandage them up, if you don't mind," she insisted.

"That would be great!" I replied, "That way, if I make a mistake, it can be corrected." I think she liked my attitude. We set to work. By now, many kettles were boiling away; the adults had the foresight to get a lot of water going before they had gone to the church, so everything was ready for us. I marveled how they had such a presence of mind to get the wounded here into the inn, temporarily bind the wounds, and get water going. All I could do at that time was kneel in shock over my dead parents and brother.

An hour later, covered in blood, I finally stepped back from the last patient. Dana once again came over and carefully looked over my work. "Good, Ket. I don't know where you ever learned how to sew this well! I do declare I've never seen a male sew this well, Ket. You've done a terrific job. Go ahead and bandage her arm." I blushed, but she did not see it, and hastily I bandaged her arm. My clothes and body were so bloody, that I went outside and headed for the bay. The sun had just gone down; fog was rolling in; the rain had ceased altogether. I dove into the chilly waters. In five minutes, I climbed out, refreshed, all traces of blood gone from my clothes. I ran home and quickly changed into some dry clothes and headed back outside to find Fianna.

Our cemetery was just outside the village on the northern side. There, I found the children and teens had been very busy. Conna had shown great wisdom in putting all of them to work at once. Instead of standing around doing nothing and feeling the degradations of being utterly useless, all of them, including Fianna, felt like they had accomplished something important. They had, in fact. A huge grave awaited the arrival of our loved ones. Gone was the total shock and massive grief. Instead, grave, determined faces greeted me when I arrived. Shortly, the adults began bringing our dead, laying them carefully in the pit.

Finally, Conna presided over the mass funeral. Everyone, including the smallest child, pitched in to cover up the bodies of our fallen. No one spoke, but the looks of stoic determination graced each face. It took us about an hour to finish up. Conna then spoke, "Now each of you will return to the inn. There we will have some supper. I think it best if we all sleep together tonight at the inn." One by one, everyone wandered off toward the inn. "Ket, Fianna, stay a moment. I must have a word with you."

I wondered what he wanted now. As far as I could tell, everything that needed to be done immediately had already been accomplished. What could he need done now?

"Ket, I will be honest and frank with you. Sincerely, I thank you for what you did to save our village. I know you did something godlike. Lightning does not strike the way it did here today. In my youth, I heard tales from travelers about magical people who, they say, could bring down lightning from the sky. I never believed those tales until today. I don't know how you did it or who you really are. Annwn god is perhaps testing us, but it doesn't matter. Six attackers got away. I know they got a very good look at you, Ket. I know they now know that you are their main foe here. From now on, Ket, you are a marked man. I didn't believe your suggestions a few days ago, but after today, I doubt your wisdom not. However, I feel it in my bones that our enemies will now try to hunt you down like an animal. If I was their king or leader, that is what I would do. That is why I say, Ket, you are a marked man."

I hadn't thought this far ahead; he was right. I had openly defied all of them and they had a good look at me. From my experiences, I knew in my heart he was quite right. If I were this Albert king, I'd spare no effort to hunt this Ket fellow down. He went on, "My advice to you, Ket, is you must leave the village and this area entirely, perhaps taking on some kind of disguise so that you will not be recognized. Tomorrow when we all pack up and leave for Baegar, you head somewhere else. That way, no one will know where you have gone. There may be spies in Tewdwr; trust no one."

"Fianna, I'm afraid you must go with Ket as well. You are his sister. If you come with us to Baegar, eventually, someone is going to catch up with you and attempt to learn where Ket is at through you. Even if you have no idea where he is at, you would very likely be tortured, raped, or worse. For your own safety, you need to disappear along with Ket. Maybe later on, you could come back and stay with your older brothers. I will get word to them that they, as well, could be in danger."

While I fully agreed with Conna's observations regarding myself, I had forgotten about Fianna's safety. I looked at her and was surprised at her reaction. Stoic determination lined her face as she said quietly, "I think you're right, Conna. I'll go with Ket. Besides, after today, I'll only feel safe when I'm around Ket." I squeezed her hand tightly in mine.

"Come; let us go get some dinner and sleep. We all desperately need both," he said, leading the way back to the inn. The mood in the inn was somber and, though I felt ravishingly hungry, I ate minimally. Soon everyone curled up on blankets wherever they could find some space. Fianna and I wrapped ourselves in a pair of blankets and holding each other tightly, we both soon fell asleep, exhausted beyond words.

The morning came too soon. The adults had awakened early and prepared breakfast for us. I was grateful for this small kindness. Once we had eaten, everyone dispersed to their respective homes to gather up their belongings to take with them on the journey to Baegar. I must say Fianna and I both felt horrible entering our silent home all alone. Both of us cried for a time. Finally, I broke the silence, "I'm going to get my instruments first. I always intended to travel around as a traveling musician, a troubadour. So I guess now is as good as any to get started."

"We'll need lots of clothes, blankets, cooking gear, and food," Fianna began rattling off useful items. "I'm the oldest, and I ought to take charge of the things that I do know about, Ket."

"Great, Fianna. That would be perfect."

"Have you thought about a disguise, Ket?" she asked.

"Not really," I replied honestly. "I have no experience with disguises. Any suggestions?"

She gave me a secret grin, a teasing one at that, "Well," and she let her voice dwindle for a moment. "Yes, I think I have the perfect disguise, one that might suit you even better than you think."

"Okay, sis, out with it," I playfully teased her back. I had no idea what she had in mind.

"Well," she continued to keep me in suspense, "they are going to be looking for a young man and his sister, right?"

"Yes," I said feigning impatience.

"Well, we could disguise you as a young woman. We'd then be just two young women traveling around as musicians! What do you think? Besides, unlike the other boys around here, you would be more comfortable in such a disguise. I can't easily disguise myself as a boy; my breasts are too full. You are only fourteen, so yours would still be small, if you follow me."

"Fianna, you never cease to amaze me! It is positively brilliant! I can play the music and you can dance. Together, we ought to be able to entertain others and get our lodging and food in exchange. Brilliant. This Albert king certainly will not be looking for a pair of women. Brilliant!" I gave her a loving hug as a reward. "Okay, then from now on, I am called Bethany."

She giggled, "Okay, Bethany. I like that name, by the way. Now we need to get you looking like a young girl. It shouldn't be too hard. Come on. Let's see what we can do." Together, we rummaged through her and mom's clothing. Three years older, Fianna was slightly taller than I was. After some experimentation, we settled on three outfits for me and three for her. It felt slightly strange to be leaving all my familiar male clothing behind, though. One outfit for traveling consisted of a light dress over pants so that riding or walking would be comfortable. In fact, dressed this way, one could hardly tell the difference between Fianna, me, and her girlfriends with whom we had hiked the countryside. We packed a spare set as well as a dressy collection, just in case we needed to look more formal. Several cloaks were also stowed, I confiscated several of mom's; we would need protection from the rains and possibly against colder weather.

I gathered my musical instruments, all three of them, packing them securely in leather carrying cases. I added a bag containing all my wood working tools, which turned out to be the heaviest of our sacks. I stowed dad's large fishing knife in the side of my boot and joined Fianna in the kitchen. I found that she had already amassed a large pile of camping essentials and was pleased that she had taken command of this aspect of our trip and was both willing to do so and was competent at it. I told her so and she smiled, "I'm almost ready to be married so I should know how to run a household and family, K — I mean Bethany." She blushed. However, we were both startled to hear a knock on the front door.

"You'd better get it," I hastily said. "I look like a young girl now. We'd best not give away my disguise so soon." She smiled and raced for the door while I rather hid in a corner of the kitchen. Presently, Fianna returned beaming.

"That was Conna saying goodbye; he left us four of the newly acquired horses. He figured we would need them to pack all our things. He also said that the others were leaving and would be telling the others that we were running late and would catch up with them. So now, we are alone here in Cuch Glyn. Do you suppose this will become a ghost town?"

"That's good to hear. We are taking quite a lot of stuff with us. Don't worry. I suspect that after the adults recover, they will come back here, re-roof the houses, and perhaps fortify it from attacks maybe. Come on; we ought to hurry up. How much food have you packed?"

"Enough for two weeks," she promptly replied. "Got all the cooking stuff, lanterns, and oil. Oh, I forgot the tinder boxes. Can't leave without those."

"Say, did mom and dad have any coins or gems, anything we could use to pay for anything, like room and board?" I asked. Always before when setting out, I had taken a rather large amount of readily traded valuables, coins, and gems usually.

"I hadn't thought of that. Let's see," and Fianna began rummaging through all the likely spots where she thought our parents might have kept any such funds. I certainly had no idea of what, if any, real funds our parents might have had. I felt awfully stupid for not having paid any attention to this detail about my parents, but then I also hadn't anticipated their untimely slaying. From Fianna's smile when she returned, I figured she had found something. "Look, Bethany, I found us ten coppers and one silver. I know it is not much, but that's all I can find."

"Great, it is better than nothing," I complimented. "Let's see how we can pack all this on the horses. Then, if there is any room left, let's take along all that we can manage to use in trade. Folks always will trade for dried fish, especially the more inland we go." We began carting packs and sacks outside to the four horses.

Neither Fianna nor I had any training in the use, care, and handling of horses. However, we both had ridden a few times. "Oh dear, how do we do this?" she said downhearted, realizing she had no idea what to put where on the horses.

"Don't worry, sis, in my last two lives I've had plenty of experience with horses, though admittedly, I often let the men deal with them. The main thing is the weight must be balanced on their backs; one side can't be heavier than the other is. With any luck, all my experience with horses will come back to me. If not, we'll really look the part of two young girls going off on a trip," I jested. She chuckled, but looked relieved. In the end, we were able to stow an additional two weeks' worth of supplies that I intended to use in trade.

It was nearly noon before we were finally ready to set out. Fianna suggested we eat lunch before getting underway so as not to use up any of our supplies. I agreed, "While you are fixing it, I'm going out to the dock. There are several things I want to practice before we go and when there is no one around to see me doing these things." She gave me a curious look, but headed back into the kitchen to rustle us up something for lunch. I walked out to the end of dad's dock and stood looking out over the bay. A dark bank of clouds was slowly moving our way; it would rain again in the afternoon.

Until the attack on our village, I hadn't used any of my druwid powers or spells as you might call them. Now that I was on my own once again and responsible for my sister's safety, I wanted these very rusty skills to be at the ready. I concentrated and worked on bringing down fire from the sky, placing it out over the bay so it was extinguished soon after it came into being. I was rusty, that's for sure. A skill long unused takes some practice. Fianna came out with a plate of sandwiches and drink; she sat down and watched the show, as she called it. "Oh, that was a good one," she occasionally commented softly, trying not to interrupt me.

I stopped and joined her, "Okay, I have fire back under my control, lightning too. I still have one more to practice, and then we can go. Oops, I ought to do the blue light one too." After gulping down my food, I went back to my conjuring, bringing sheets of ice into existence and letting them fall into the bay. I found that I was very rusty indeed with the ice sheets. At first, they appeared as a sheet of water, which fell like rain into the bay. Fianna laughed while I said "Oops!"

I found the conjuring of the blue light in my hand easy to remember. A druwid is never without a light source. Finally, satisfied that I could call upon these old skills of mine should I need them, I was finally ready to depart. We stood hand in hand and looked silently at our old home for several minutes. Fianna did have tears welling up in her eyes, though she tried to stifle them. "Hey, it is okay to feel sad, sis. We're leaving our home; our parents are gone; we have lost a lot that means something to us. It's only natural we feel saddened. Come on; we best be on our way."

I helped her onto her horse and gave her the reins of another. Then, I mounted mine and took hold of the fourth set of reins. We each could ride and lead another behind us, making better time. We rode up the small river valley just north of Cuch Glyn, where the river had cut a passage through the tall white cliffs. Once up on the rolling green hills, Fianna said, "Now which way do we go?"

"We can't go north after the others, because this Albert king fellow would assume that is the direction we would have gone. I need answers to what is going on politically around here that would drive a Layamon king to invade and brutally attack a Tewdwr village. It makes no sense to me, but then I was never big on politics. I think the thing to do is head back into northern Layamon to where I used to live. When I left, some druwids were on their way there to continue my work. If they are still there, maybe we can get some answers and find out what is going on around here. Besides, when I left, my sons were kings and in charge of four towns, while my nephews and niece were kings and queen over a couple nearby towns. So even if the druwids are not there, my children might have answers."

"That's okay with me. Lead on, Bethany. But you know it is *so* utterly strange to hear you talking about *your* children. You're only fourteen. Weird indeed! Oh, yes one other thing. Mom always brushed out my hair at night. I know that I ought to do it myself, but it would look more like we're sisters if you would brush it; I'll brush out yours for you."

"Sure thing, sis. I really like long hair flowing behind me. Always have."

"Yes, well, yours is nearly a foot longer than mine. I had mom keep mine shoulder length, less fuss, she always said, but you look really good with it that long. Do guys like it that long too?"

I turned toward her and winked, "Mine always did."

"I think then that I shall let mine grow longer like yours," Fianna declared. "Do you suppose that we will meet many boys our age?"

"You betcha," I replied.

Chapter 3 On the Trail

Our first afternoon on the trail, June 16, 621 AH, brought a mid-afternoon shower down upon us as Fianna and I casually rode southeastward from the village of Glyn Lach. Although we donned our capes, we still got soaked to our skins. We therefore stopped well before sundown to camp in a sheltered glen of ash trees, primarily so we could dry out.

All the deadwood around us was wet, frustrating Fianna's attempt to light a fire, while I tended to the horses and the unloading of our gear. "Allow me," I teased. A small blaze of fire appeared just above her nicely stacked firewood, slowly settling on it, crackling and spitting, as the wetness turned to gas, and the wood finally ignited.

"Now that *is* handy," she exclaimed. She fixed our supper and together we cleaned everything up. Silently we watched the rosy red sun set behind a bank of clouds.

She stoked the fire once more, and we lay down beside each other on our blankets, gazing up at the stars, which peeked out from behind cumulus clouds. She said, "Okay, Bethany, I think that I have been patient long enough. These past few days, I have seen things that can only be called magic or the work of a god. I think you owe me a full and complete explanation. After all, whether I want to or not, I'm now just as involved in all this mess as you are. I should at least know what is going on, especially with you, my brother. Here, you can brush out my hair while you explain absolutely everything." She teased me and poked me in my ribs with her hairbrush.

I was surprised how easily brushing a woman's hair came back to me. Memories of brushing out Sarah's hair came back to me. As I performed this loving task for her, I began, knowing that my sister had to know the truth. Truth sets one free, not lies and deception. "My first recollection is playing in the soft, powdery dirt in a tiny village called Uru in the Greenway. Bethany Stanton, okay, Elizabeth, was my name, and I was six years old." I explained a bit of the geography of Tarra to put my original home into some kind of perspective for her.

"In the Greenway, there are some very special people whom the locals call their Guardians. We call ourselves druwids. Our purpose is to aid, protect, and assist the people in the Greenway." I went on to explain how Ellen had stopped the Galt raiders and had become my mentor, teaching me the druwid ways. After describing how my family had nearly been killed in an ambush on our way to Karka, I rapidly summed up our ten years of extensive training. I told her about the other members of my Lightning Circle and our special abilities that we had trained so long and hard to be able to perform.

"Now the entire druwid movement was founded by Alabaster Benjamin Crowley; he was the ultimate Wid and lived to be something like two hundred and fifty years old."

"But that's not possible!" Fianna protested. "No one lives that long!"

"I agree with you, sis. I don't know how he did it, but I assure you he was really old when we first met him. Powerful beyond belief! He taught us something very special: how to avoid being harmed by another bringing down fire and lightning upon us. I think that was the hardest thing I have ever had to learn how to do!"

"You, you're saying you can't be harmed by a lightning bolt?" she asked incredulously.

"If I am being attacked with them and I am alert to it, nope. I did just that later on to save my daughter, but this is getting way ahead of my story." I explained the political situation of that time, the Centurions of Megalos out to conquer all of Tarra so she would grasp why my Circle was given the mission to travel to the Sea Princes, which were at that time under attack. I did carefully avoid telling her details that probably should still be kept a secret, however.

She was appalled at how women were being treated in the Land of the Seven Sea Princes during that time. When I explained how Simon, who was pretending to be Simone, managed to affect a major change in the treatment of women there, Fianna cheered to the sky. I knew she would really appreciate hearing that detail. Then, it was on to the land of Juda Arad, where the deeply religious people had been living under the domination of the Centurions for many years. When I told her about their belief in the coming of their Great Messiah who would free them from the infidels, she asked if this was prophesy or reality. When I told her about the signs in the sky, the new bright star, which faded away in a week's time, she was impressed. However, she reacted badly when I told her about the Centurion governor who promptly had all the newborn babies in Al Barq slain, hoping one of them was this Great Messiah.

All this led to our traveling all the way south to Megalos proper. She was expecting an island full of barbarous people, but my description of Niccolo and his art and inventions got across the view that one cannot judge a country solely by the actions of some of its citizens. She cheered when I described how I had to kill their evil emperor who had drugged me and tried to rape me. "Can you teach me to do that? I think it would be super if I could do that if someone tried to rape me."

"Sure, if you have ten years to spend every waking hour learning," I replied.

"You are teasing me?" she asked, not quite sure.

"No, remember that I said that we seven in my Circle trained for ten years to learn how to do all these things. Yes, you probably could learn them, but Fianna, it would take tremendous dedication to learn it all." She was satisfied, if only somewhat. I continued the tale of our adventure. She was saddened to learn of Alabaster's death just before we returned home, but was cheered by the fact that my Circle became the leaders of the druwid movement, the All Greenway Circle. However, I had to spend much more time telling her about our marriages and our children. She asked many questions, particularly about childbirth; I could tell she was perhaps a bit frightened about the prospect. "As long as I'm around, Fianna, you have nothing to worry about, I promise you that!" Her sigh told me that she accepted my promise and relaxed.

Next, I briefly described how we handled the Centurion problem by making a mutually beneficial treaty, avoiding a war. Finally, I had to explain how I had gotten my young body killed by an arrow to the forehead. She laughed, "Everyone knows that you can't reason with an insane man." It was my turn to laugh at myself.

At last she understood why Alabaster had given me my next mission, to find out all about this Great Messiah, in hopes we could use the data to help our people. "But before I get into that mess, I have to tell you something that only a handful of people in the entire world know about. It is something so utterly fantastic you may not believe it. I hope to god you never have to see them with your own eyes." Now she rolled over and paid careful attention. I described both the giant Mantis creatures in the Red Desert and the giant Grey Creatures high in the desolation of the Appian Way. When I described what they did to spiritual beings, she grimaced. Yet, it was such an wild and unbelievable thing that I don't think that she truly believed they existed.

I went on with my story, telling her how I had acquired my Arad body of a young girl who had been bitten by a poisonous viper. I rapidly sketched out my life there including marrying the Great Messiah, Jes Amir. Again, she had me tell her all about my three children. I knew that having a loving husband and raising a family were her real goals in life. Inwardly, I promised myself to do everything in my power to help her achieve just that, though just now, I had no idea how to do any of that.

Next, I carefully explained about the teachings of Jes, the miracles he performed, and about his disciples. It was crucial that she fully grasped that Jes was the Son of God, at least some god, that Jes was not a normal person, that his skills and abilities made those of us druwids pale in comparison. It took some doing, but I felt that I finally managed to convince her of that detail. I told her about the rebellion and how so many of the young men of the Arad perished at the hands of the Centurions. I told her about our flight to West Reach and of our finally settling down, carving out a new town near the border of Layamon and Tewdwr.

"Remember those evil Grey Creatures? Well, here's where they come back into the story." I described how Jes had attempted to attack and kill one of them, how he had been killed instead, how he had been sucked into their mind-scrambling machine, and how Alabaster had helped me see everything that happened, including Alabaster being sucked into the infernal machine as well. I told her of his last words to me, that if he did not contact me within thirty years, he was in big trouble, and that I was to come and find him and help him out. Finally, Fianna fully understood my promise to him, why I had been so insistent on leaving Cuch Glyn and traveling the world.

"There's a bit more," I added. Though the hour was late, I explained what my life had been like after Jes had died, how I had tried to help people, and how I had incurred the ire of these Grey Creatures. She was more than a bit spooked when I related how one had come after me in some kind of flying machine, attempting to kill my daughter, Sarah, and me. She fully agreed with my idea to flee to Tewdwr, in hopes of hiding from them. Although I had already told her a bit about how I had gotten killed, this time, she could put it all into perspective.

She gushed, "Now I really see how my suggestion of keeping a lantern going at night helped you out, Ket, er, I mean Bethany. Golly, if that had happened to me, I would still be having nightmares about it! I just had nightmare about drowning in the ocean. Say, that would mean that I was an old man before, wouldn't it?"

"Yes, it would certainly seem that way to me, sis. Very few people can recall who and what they have been in their lives before this one. I'm not sure why they want to forget about that life, but I have some ideas why. First, they just had a painful experience, more than likely, dying, I mean. That would be a good thing to want to forget. Also, after one gets a new baby body, one no longer has the things that one used to have. It's like starting over; only the new body can't do much of anything for so many years. But it is very late; we ought to get some sleep."

"I only have one more question, Bethany. I've seen you heal, bring down lightning, start fires, and even make a blue light appear, but there is one thing that I have not seen that I really must, if I'm to wholeheartedly go on this mission of yours. Can you really communicate between minds? I figure you must have done that when you rescued dad. But can you do it to me?"

I am proud of the way you have responded to all the disasters we've just experienced, Fianna. I placed my thought into her mind.

She blushed. Her eyes opened wide. She sat bolt upright staring at me. Finally, she found words, "God Ket, that is so, so, so utterly *intimate*! That is the one thing I really wish I could do! Would it really take me ten years to learn how to do that?"

"Probably, not everyone has the talent to do it or so I have observed. I'll try to teach you how to do it, sis," I broke down and agreed. How could I not?

"I love you, little brother!" she declared and hugged me tightly. We

44

snuggled together to keep warm and soon fell asleep.

Glyn Lach appeared before us around mid-afternoon the next day. Earlier, I had picked up the signs of a trail and we had followed it. Gradually, the track became well worn, and I was sure we were heading for a town or village. I hoped it was Glyn Lach. Cradled in a small green valley surrounded by numerous trees, lay this quiet village of some fifty stone buildings. Picture the grey stone walls, the multitudinous shades of green, the brown thatched roofs, and the deep blue sky with billowing white-grey cumulus clouds and you have what we saw as we rode slowly into the village. Wisps of grey smoke twisted their way into the sky from several chimneys, along with the telltale clanking of blacksmiths. There was at least a pair of them, sounds echoing each other. Children were running and playing about the cobblestone streets, and they waved hello as we rode slowly past them.

Finding the inn was easy; it was the largest building other than the church. We dismounted and tied up our horses outside. We looked at each other, took a deep breath, and walked inside. I decided to do the talking. The proprietor of the Boar's Head Inn was obviously the man in the white apron, known as Gamling. "Good sir, we are a pair of traveling musicians, troubadours, if you please. We would like to trade some evenings of music and dance here in your inn in return for food and lodging for ourselves and our four horses." I thought for a second, trying to decide if I had left anything out.

"Well, I don't know," came his drawl, while pulling on his short beard. "We have local musicians who play every night in here. How do I know you are any good?"

"Well," Fianna interjected coyly using that tone of voice that often got her way with mom and dad, "let us play in here tonight. If everyone likes us, then you give us a room and board. If they don't, why, we'll leave tonight, and you've lost nothing. How's that?" She knew he would agree for he had nothing to lose and everything to gain. However, she didn't consider that he might not be of good faith, that is, we would be liked, and he would still refuse the deal, claiming something was wrong with our playing. Then again, what seventeen year old girl would entertain such thoughts?

"You girls have yourself a deal," he said without hesitation, and we shook hands on it. Here in Tewdwr, a handshake consummated a bargain. In this land, men valued their words. "I'll tell you what — seeing how's you probably want to clean up, change clothes, and such, why don't I give you a room where you can store your stuff? If it works out tonight, you can sleep there. If not, you can pack up and leave."

Suddenly a voice interrupted him, "Gamling, where are your manners?" A matronly woman, also wearing an apron, walked up to us. "If it doesn't work out, I'll not have you sending these young girls out in the night! That isn't civil. If it doesn't work out, girls, you can still spend the night, but

I'll make you help me wash up all the dishes in the morning to pay for the room. Isn't that a whole lot better?"

We grinned and so promised, Gamling grumbled, but had no intention of going against his wife's pronouncement, knowing she was right. A half hour later, we had stowed our many sacks in a small room. Next, we changed clothes into our fancier performance dresses. I assembled my instruments in the musician's corner of the inn. Then, we went for a stroll around the village. Fianna got the great idea to find some wild flowers. She nimbly made us each a headband of flowers; now we really looked like entertainers. We chatted with many townsfolk during the afternoon, explaining that we were going to be entertaining them at the inn this evening. Finally, we went with everyone when they filed into the church just before supper to pray. Joining them in prayer services I believe made us much more acceptable to the folks of Glyn Lach.

Around six, the usual musicians filed into the inn, but they already knew we were going to be playing as well. There were four of them, all middle aged, and we got along very nicely with them. Soon the inn filled up with a larger crowd than normal, and it was time for us to play. I began playing a lively dance tune on the lute so Fianna could do her dance. Soon the other musicians joined in with me, and a large number of people began to dance with and alongside of Fianna. Yes, we were quite acceptable to the folks of Glyn Lach. We musicians had a lot of fun, playing song after song. As usual, the festivities were over long before I would have desired. I love making music, though Fianna was quite pooped and flushed, having done far more dancing than she was used to doing. Gamling complimented us, "The room is yours. Leftovers are in the kitchen out back, help yourselves." He was more than pleased with our performance; he'd had more customers in here than normal.

The other musicians had packed up and were heading for the door, while only a handful of people remained; some were staying overnight at the inn, I guessed. One young lad asked us, "Say, do you know Lyneth's Lament? Here's a copper if you can play it for me?"

I looked at the young boy who had yellow hair cut in the traditional bowl over the head pattern. He sported no beard yet, which told of his youthfulness. His blue eyes seemed be begging for the song. "It is such a sad song," I replied. "Are you sure you want to hear my rendition of it?"

His smile and twinkle in his eye answered me. "Okay, then." I got my flute and sat on the edge of a table, paused momentarily, mocking up the sad mood of the song. Soft and low, the notes began, hinting at the great loss of her husband. Soon the notes doubled and the pitch rose overall, reflecting her inner turmoil and anger over her untimely loss. After a crescendo, the notes once more sank downward and slowly, as she accepted her fate, her loss. Okay this was the traditional rendition, and I should've stopped. There are times when a musician is moved by the emotion of the moment. While playing it, memories of the recent loss of my parents and brother came to me, I saw tears swell in Fianna's eyes, and I knew that she too felt as I did. I didn't need telepathy to tell me that. I continued the song, improvising as I went along, ebbing and flowing with my mood, as the images of the past few days came and went in my mind. I don't know how long I played before concluding. I lost total track of time. Stop, I finally did.

When I looked up at our benefactor, I saw he was as moved by the piece as we were. Strange to see tears of great sadness in a youthful boy's face, rather out of place. He slowly placed a copper coin on the table for me, bowed to me, and said simply, "Thank you." He turned and headed off to his room. I was correct in assuming that some who were still here were staying at the inn as well. Fianna collected the coin and scurried off to bring us some long overdue supper from the kitchen. I gathered up my instruments, put them back into their cases, and carried them to our room.

Gamling commented to Fianna as she was carrying a plate of food to our room, "Mighty fine playing. You two can stay for a few days, if you like. I think I have the better part of this bargain, if you know what I mean," he teased her. She smiled back and thanked him.

I'd already used the chamber pot, so I began eating while Fianna used it. Although we were brother and sister, I still felt she needed her own privacy, as much as we could get, considering the circumstances. She smiled and joined me; we were quite hungry. "I think it went quite well, Bethany. We even made a copper from that young man. Strange song request, though, don't you think? Not what I would have thought he would request. Ah well, you played wonderfully tonight. Gamling says that we can stay on for a couple more days."

"Yes, you danced really well, yourself, sis. Okay, I'm going to try to sense if Alabaster is anywhere around here tonight. I'm really rusty at it, so I'll wait until everything totally quiets down."

"I'm pooped," she declared, and hastily got ready for bed. Actually, she was asleep almost as soon as her head hit the pillow. We had not even had time to brush out our hair. Time enough for that on the morrow, I thought. I had been putting off searching for Alabaster long enough. I relaxed and began concentrating, remembering just how he appeared as a spiritual being. Every being is distinctive in some way, Alabaster more so than others. Even if his mind was still scrambled, I should be able to sense his presence.

Now if there was not the consideration of the Grey Creatures or the Mantises to interfere, I could easily search the whole of Tarra from this room, with a high certainty of locating him precisely and most likely establishing a Mind Link with him. However, if I accidentally included one of these evil creatures in my awareness, they would instantly become aware of me and come after me once again. I just could not risk bringing down the wrath of these nasty beings. Hence, I would do as I had long planned, search small areas at one time only. I planned to travel the land and search mentally only in that neighborhood. With luck, these evil creatures would never detect my presence. Unless — there is always an unless — unless I accidentally encountered one of the Grey Creatures here in this area in disguise. I knew from my last life that they could disguise themselves as humans and walk undetected among us. Undetected by most, that is. Even my daughter, Sarah, was able to detect them, once she knew what that cold chill indicated.

Quietly and determinedly, I began expanding my awareness outward over the village and beyond. I searched what I thought would be about a five mile radius or so, but then remember, I'm a poor judge of distances when doing these mental gymnastics. I sensed many beings, but not Alabaster. Then, I partially undressed and crawled in beside my sister. I had not expected to find Alabaster here. Actually, I had no idea whatsoever where he might be. I prayed that he was not in the Northern Steppes with the barbarian Galts or up north with the burly Axemen; traveling there would be very challenging indeed, if not life threatening.

We actually stayed here for a full week. In the mornings, we washed the prior night's dishes and helped clean the place. In return, Gamling gave us a copper each day. Further, I spent as much time with the local musicians as I could, learning a dozen new songs that our own musicians in Cuch Glyn hadn't known. Fianna was all for this, since the more songs we knew the better we could perform our troubadour duties. Besides, she was enjoying collecting the copper coins; right away, she appointed herself in charge of our finances.

A kind farmer graciously allowed our horses to graze in his pasture, so we didn't need to worry about their care either. Afternoons we had free. Together, we took long walks around the countryside just outside town. Yes, we felt free and light, ready to face another evening's performance. Finally, it was time to move on to the next village, further to the south and east. We parted with the innkeeper and his wife, who invited us to come back anytime, and we thanked them profusely for having welcomed us to their inn.

All our gear packed, we finally mounted up and rode slowly out of the village. Children enthusiastically waved goodbye and many an adult did likewise. We felt elated that our first attempt at being traveling musicians had gone so well. Our spirits soared as we headed out, following the directions we were given for Glyn Lowri, a slightly larger village closer to the border with Layamon.

Suddenly, I was brought back into the reality of what we were doing: two young women traveling about the land all by themselves. "We are being followed," I whispered to Fianna. The gay smile vanished instantly from her face. "Don't look back. Single rider, I think."

"Someone is following us from the village, perhaps?" she asked.

"Probably. Let's ignore them and see if it is just a coincidence. I'll be on my guard, though, so don't worry," I added, knowing that she would be anyway.

"I wish I could bring down fire from the sky to protect myself," she declared. "Always before, I just assumed that someone would always be around to protect me. You know, he was always waving his sword around us girls when we were out gathering in the countryside. Can't you teach me how to do something to protect myself? I feel so defenseless."

"First, you have to be able to observe the obvious. From there, you can learn how to defend yourself. I think I can help you learn that, sis." I knew that I was definitely going to have to train her in defensive fighting somehow. I resolved to begin tonight when we camped out. We had already decided to spend the night under the stars so that we could arrive in this next town mid-morning. It wouldn't do to arrive at sunset.

After another mile had passed, our follower picked up speed, intending on closing the distance between us. Fianna was slightly nervous, but I said calmly, "Let's halt, dismount, and wait until the person comes to us. It doesn't necessarily spell trouble, sis, because it is only one person. If it was a number of riders, then I would be somewhat alarmed." She seemed reassured and dismounted, trying the horses to the loiwer branches of a nearby tree.

We waited only a few minutes before the rider came cantering up to our position. Spying us, he reined in, with his horse pawing the ground letting off some energy of the fast ride. It was the young man who had paid us a copper to play Lyneth's Lament! I remembered seeing him several other evenings, mostly hidden in the background of the crowded inn. He dismounted. "Hello, musicians. Please excuse me, but I was trying to catch up with you. I want to have a word with you — a private word, if you take my meaning. The village back there has many spying eyes."

"Well, you caught up with us," I commented, indicating that it was acceptable for him to say what he wanted. In the clear light of day, I could see his features far better than in the dim light of the inn. He was indeed a young boy, scarcely older than I was, I guessed, maybe fifteen. Since he had stayed at the inn, it was obvious that he was also traveling. His horse, though, was clearly not the usual farm horse you'd find around Tewdwr. I'm not a fine judge of horses, mind you, but this mare had superior conformation and held her head proudly. Like us, he had numerous bulging sacks and packs tied to his saddle.

"We've not been introduced," he began in his boyish voice. I guessed his voice had not yet undergone that major change; mine had not yet, at least. "I'm called Cal, Cal of Leebrook," he hastily added. Somehow, I wasn't convinced. There was that slight hesitation before he added the village portion. A seed of distrust entered my mind and I stayed alert. "I too am a musician, just getting started as you two are doing. I've been meaning to ask, are you two sisters?"

Fianna replied for us, "Yes, sisters. I'm Fianna and this is Bethany of Cuch Glyn. We are just getting started, too. We did well in the last town. I'm glad you enjoyed our music and dance."

"Very pleased to meet you, Fianna of Cuch Glyn," Cal said in a rather grandiose style, taking her hand, and bowing slightly toward her. She flushed with the attention of this rather handsome young boy.

"And more than pleased to meet you, Bethany of Cuch Glyn. You are already a great master of music," he said, taking my hand, which I offered following Fianna's lead, as he bowed slightly toward me. I didn't blush, and I still did not trust him. "Your name is a bit unusual for Tewdwr, is it not?" he added, looking me straight in the eye.

"I didn't name myself," I half-lied. From the corner of my eye, I caught Fianna cracking a smile. "What instrument do you play?" I changed the topic swiftly.

"A dulcimer. Having listened to you several nights, I thought that a dulcimer might be a great addition to your sound." Suddenly, I detected that he was now uncertain of himself, that is, gone was his social tone and banter. He added, as if he were unsure how to say this, "I would like you to listen to me play a bit. If you like it, then I would like you to consider letting me join up with your group." He added hastily, "Of course, I would follow any orders you two might make, since this is your group."

Realistically, I had no choice by to give the boy a chance to play. If he played poorly, then he would grasp why we couldn't accept his offer to join us. I wasn't intending to add more people to our music group. But then, he was a man, and I began to think that traveling around the countryside accompanied by a man might prove valuable. While I was pondering the significance of this, he quickly got his instrument from his saddle, unpacked it, and looked for a place to play. He found a boulder and sat down, placing the stringed instrument in his lap. He had two little sticks or hammers, which he used to strike the strings.

He stuck up a familiar tune, a lively one. I'd never heard a dulcimer before and was instantly enthralled with its sound. Cal was right. It would blend superbly with any of my three instruments, the flute in particular. When he finished the tune, Fianna said excitedly, "Wow, Cal, that is really good. You play very well." He blushed at her compliment, but he knew that I knew that he had to impress me, not Fianna.

"Yes, you are right. Its sound is amazing and would blend with me."

Encouraged, Cal said, "Here, listen to this one. It's my version of that lament I had you play." He was off playing Lyneth's Lament. Played on the dulcimer, the moving piece was incredibly more impressive than with solo flute. There was no doubt about it, Cal could play, but also here was a man who had great sensitivity. It took a tremendous sensitivity to play this lament and make it communicate the intensity of emotion Lyneth felt over the loss of her husband. Cal was obviously not your normal fighter-type male; he had sensitivity akin to mine.

While he was playing, I quickly got out my flute and joined in. It is one thing to play solo and quite another to play ensemble with others. If he were to join us, given the limited amount of rehearsal time we likely would have, he and I would have to be able to play together. In this piece, the flute part would naturally take the lead, so I listened to see if Cal would insist on leading or if he would adjust to my playing. To my amazement, he adjusted, which is what I think impressed me more than anything about his playing. Cal instinctively followed my lead, knowing his part had to back up mine in this piece.

I glanced at Cal and saw that he was watching me as well as he could while playing. There was a knowing twinkle in his eye that told me that he knew that I was testing him on this very issue. He gave a slight nod, and then he changed his pattern, beginning a slight improvisation on his part. Suddenly, I was on the spot! He was testing me! For the music to make sense, I would have to pick up on his subtle change, follow him, and then add to it in a solo fashion. I began to concentrate more on what I was doing. Cal was no dummy, that's for sure.

When we finally finished, I looked at him, and he, me. I said, "You certainly pass, Cal. That was great playing."

He smiled, or perhaps even blushed, and said, "And you passed too, Bethany. Yes, we have established that we can readily play very well together. That is the primary requisite to making great music, wouldn't you agree?"

I had to agree with him, though I saw where this would lead. Fianna gave me a slight nudge in my rump. I knew she thought Cal was perfect. "Okay, Cal, so you want to join us, is that it?"

He carefully put his instrument back in its leather carrying case before speaking. "Yes, I have been traveling for some time now looking for just such an opportunity."

As much as I was beginning to like Cal, I felt that it was my immediate obligation to let him know our true intentions. "Cal, we are really traveling. I mean, first we intend to travel the length and breadth of Cymry. Once we've done that, we intend to head for the mainland and travel widely around Tarra, visiting nearly every land, of course, probably not that of the Galts and the Axemen. We mean to travel, do you follow me?" Now that I said it, I figured any normal person would be very downcast about leaving the island, let alone traveling so widely.

Cal's eyes opened wider than I could imagine they could. "Eureka! Holy cow! Why I never expected this." Fianna's growing smile suddenly faded. She felt certain that Cal was so shocked that he would quickly beg our pardon and leave. Cal was excited.

"This is even better than I could have ever hoped for," he exclaimed, exuding enthusiasm. "This is absolutely perfect! Fabulous!" After a slight pause, he added, "Just as long as you don't go into the steppes or up north where the Axemen live. This is precisely what I want to do as well!" He was so excited that he could scarcely contain his emotions. Fianna's gigantic grin echoed her viewpoint on all this. How could I do otherwise?

"Okay, Cal. Would you like to join with us? Mind you, you have already said that you will follow our orders. I must stress right here at the onset, that what I say goes, no matter how strange or difficult or crazy it may seem at the time. You must also give me your word that you will never try to take improper advantage of my sister or me?" I added that last, because I didn't want Cal to try to start making advances to Fianna, though I know at this point in time, she would welcome them.

"Yes, to both! You have my sworn word. I would never, ever, even remotely take any unseemly or improper advantage of you two beautiful women. Never. I give you my solemn vow on that. If I should ever do any unseemly thing to either of you, you may kick me out of the group at once! Thank you, Bethany of Cuch Glyn! I don't know how to thank you for giving me this opportunity!" What made matters worse for me was that I knew instinctively he was genuinely and completely sincere. There wasn't the slightest trace of deception in him about any of this. I was beginning to doubt my original observation of Cal.

Cal added, "Further, since I'm the only man in the group, I pledge myself to protecting both of you as I can. Realize though that I'm not a fighter, have no such training, and am not very strong, but I will die trying to protect you both from harm. You have my solemn vow on this!"

Just like a young man, I thought, in the presence of two beautiful young women. However, under the circumstances, I would have thought far less of Cal had he not made such a vow. Fianna blushed. No man had ever made such a pledge to her, and she did not quite know how to respond. I quickly spoke up, "Gratefully and gladly accepted, Cal. You are right. It is perhaps a bit unwise for two young women to go traveling about the land unprotected in any way. We both know that you are a musician and not a fighter, so don't worry, we'll not expect such heroics from you. Just do what you're able, if it is needed, and we'll be more than satisfied."

Fianna added, "Are we going to camp here tonight or go further?" I detected that she would be more than willing to stay put and get to know Cal better.

"Let's stick to our plan. We need to travel another five miles before camping, if we are to enter Glyn Lowri in mid-morning so we have time to arrange things." That settled, we mounted up once more, riding three abreast.

Cal looked at me, getting up the courage to tell me something. I can always tell when a man is about to tell me something personal. Oops, that is my prior lives speaking. I'm a man now; I keep forgetting. "Please don't take this the wrong way, Bethany, but I have wanted to tell you this since I first laid eyes upon you." I held my breath, hoping this was not some lovesick boy. "You have the prettiest, long red hair that I have ever seen anywhere. It is just incredibly beautiful, and I wanted to tell you that." Cal blushed and my cheeks reddened for the wrong reasons. Fianna also blushed. He added, "You don't often see such really long locks and yours is, well, impressive."

"Bethany has convinced me to let mine grow. I want mine to get as long as hers," Fianna came to my rescue and hers as well. "I always had mom keep mine shoulder length so it was out of the way, but hers is just incredible so I'm letting mine grow too."

I recovered my voice and replied, "Thanks. I really do love long hair. It sure is red isn't it? Say, Cal, you definitely speak with a Layamon accent not Tewdwr. Where is Leebrook anyway?" I hastily changed the subject without making Cal wrong for having complimented my hair.

"Is that why his speech sounds slightly funny to me?" Fianna interjected.

Cal's face definitely flushed this time. "Well, yes, I thought that I had picked up your accent fairly well, but I guess I haven't. Leebrook is down south in Layamon, as you have noted." Again, I had that eerie feeling that Cal was not being totally truthful with us on this. Yes, he did have a Layamon accent. I remembered my own difficulty when I first arrived in Cuch Glyn while running away from the Grey Creatures. I thought that the Tewdwr folks had the thickest accents imaginable.

On a whim, I said in as close to proper Layamon dialect as I could remember, "There are quite a few towns in Layamon, Bregia, Nuadilan, Amathon, Bedwyn, and Brea, as I recall." Both Fianna and Cal turned to look at me, eyes wide open.

Cal spoke first, "Say, you do a pretty good job with the Layamon accent. I could still tell that you did not come from Layamon natively, as I guess you could tell with me. If we travel around the world, isn't language going to be a big barrier?" I could tell from his body language that he was trying to change the subject.

"From what I've gathered, if you can speak reasonable Layamon dialect, why, you should do well most everywhere on Cymry, except in Tewdwr and perhaps the highlands of Ruadan. However, once we get to the mainland, we will have to learn the Sea Prince dialect and that of the Greenway and Juda Arad, and perhaps even that of Megalos, if we ever get that far south. I ought to be able to manage all of those fairly easily. You might say I have a knack for languages. Fianna though, you are going to have to work on them, I'm afraid." Cal, on the other hand, said little, only staring closely at me for a minute as we rode along. I began to wonder if I had blurted out too much, but then I needed to have a way to cover my knowing so many languages and only being fourteen.

Again, Cal changed the subject, "I know it is not altogether proper to ask a lady her age, but I am curious just how old you two are. I am fifteen myself."

"Oh, that's an easy one," Fianna gaily replied, thankful for a chance to add to the conversation. "I'm seventeen and Bethany's fourteen." Then, she became quiet, realizing that Cal might think it a bit odd for us to be taking orders from the youngest person in the group. She had no fast explanation for it and hoped that Cal would not inquire further.

"Great, we are all about the same age. Say, what do you call your band? Have we got a name?" Cal replied.

I hadn't thought of this detail yet. "Er, no, Cal, we don't have a name figured out yet. With just the two of us, it didn't seem as important as it does now that the group is larger. Okay, gang, any suggestions?" I replied, thankful for the turn in conversation topics.

Fianna began suggesting names, "How about Cloudy Days or the Red Heads? No that won't do now that Cal has joined us. Glyn Minstrels, the Vagabonds, the Happy Vagabonds?" Cal chuckled and added some more ideas. I suggested that since we expected to play across the mainland that our name should be indicative of West Reach. "Cymry Rockers, Cymry Minstrels," Fianna kept on inventing names.

Cal began laughing, "Say you can stop anytime now, Fianna. I like the sound of Cymry Minstrels. How about you, Bethany?"

"Yes, Cymry Minstrels has a nice ring to it, though I wonder if anyone off our island knows that Cymry is our name for West Reach?" I added thoughtfully.

Undaunted, Fianna suggested, "Well, then, when we are on the mainland, we can be the West Reach Minstrels. That is fine with me. How about you two?" We agreed, now we had a name for our group.

The dark clouds formed again in the early afternoon; we just had time to don our cloaks before the rains came as usual. We were not in any hurry, so we let our horses amble onward. Cal broke in on my thoughts, "Say, where are we going and does anyone know how to get there? We don't seem to be on any actual road or anything."

I took a deep breath inhaling the freshness of the rain before replying. "Glyn Lowri, a slightly larger village closer to the border with Layamon — that's where we are headed. As far as I can tell, we are still on the track that leads there. Have you been there, Cal? We haven't."

"I don't see any track. Besides, how can you see where you are going in this rain?" Cal replied somewhat chagrined. "Yes, I was there about three weeks ago. Nice little village, friendly people." Cal watched me look down at the ground out in front of our horses.

"Yes, still on the track," I replied. "We planned to stop about three or four miles from the village so we could arrive in Glyn Lowri in the morning. That way, we have time to work out a deal with an inn, get settled, and ready to play. Do they have a nice inn there that we could use, Cal?"

"Sure, there are two. Both would serve our purposes," Cal answered above a clap of thunder. We rode on until the rain stopped. "Hey, look at that! A rainbow." We looked back over our shoulders to where Cal was pointing.

"I just love rainbows, don't you Cal?" Fianna commented. "Say I count five rainbows there. See, three join together on the main one and two more join together just below it. You know I once saw seven rainbows at the same time. I'll never forget that sight."

"Yes, they are really enchanting. I always look for them after a rain, ever since I was a little. . ." Cal stumbled over his words and quickly added, "lad. You have me beat, Fianna. I've only see five, like today. Some say that seeing rainbows brings you good luck. I like to think so. Leastwise, it's never brought me bad luck. I always look for them. How about you, Bethany? Do you like rainbows? Are they considered lucky in your village?"

"Rainbows are a natural phenomenon — sunlight reflecting off water particles high in the air," I replied absentmindedly. "Rainbows are another marvel of Nature, and I'm in love and harmony with Nature. I don't think luck has anything to do with them."

Cal gave me a strange look, studying my face. He finally repeated back, "Sunlight reflecting off of water bits? Well, that would seem to make sense. You only see a rainbow after a rain and the sun comes out a bit. Bethany, you sure do seem to know a lot about nature, especially for such a young girl."

His compliment was sincerely meant, and Fianna came to my rescue by explaining, "Our late mother, she was the village Priestess. She taught us a lot of things."

"Oh, I'm terribly sorry! I didn't know your mother had died. That's terrible. Are you holding up okay?" genuine concern was in Cal's voice. However, thinking about our mother's death just a few days ago brought water into both our eyes. Neither of us said anything, but Cal was really sensitive to us, and added, "It's okay. I'm so sorry about it. She must have been a terrific mother. Say, how close are we getting to the village, Bethany?" Cal respectfully changed the subject, for which I was grateful.

I sniffed a bit, dislodging my watering eyes and nose and glanced about me. "Yes, my guess is this is about where we want to stop for today. Let's see — over there in that grove of ash trees — that would make a good spot to camp. I see a little brook, and there ought to be plenty of firewood. Let's make for that grove and setup camp."

Next, I had to confront setting up a community camp, which I hadn't had to consider before now, when it was just Fianna and me. I desperately needed to go to the bathroom and suspected the others did too. We would have to be careful about personal hygiene with Cal nearby. I whispered to Fianna my urgent needs. She whispered, "You go back in the trees there, and I'll keep Cal occupied."

"Cal, I guess we ought to share camp duties. I assume we'll all eat together, unless you want to cook your own food," she got his attention. She noticed that Cal seemed a little ill at ease, now that he had dismounted. Perhaps he was unsure of what to do next, she thought to herself, and took it upon herself to help him over his awkwardness. "I usually do all the cooking, though Bethany helps me wash up afterwards. I'm a much better cook than she is, you see. I suppose you have had to eat your own cooking. I've never known a boy to be much of a cook, no offense intended. We've got a lot of dried fish and lentils we can share."

"That would be great," Cal replied. "Of course, I have my own food stash. I didn't expect to find fellow traveling musicians. Yet it is only fair if I pool mine with yours. I'm sure that you are a better cook than I am. Should I unload all the horses?" Fianna got the impression that Cal was trying to think of what chores the boy in our group ought to do. Just then, I came waking back from the trees.

Fianna explained, "My turn. Cal has volunteered to pool his stash of food with ours. I'll do all the cooking as usual, but we ought to figure out who is doing what. Back in a minute." She rushed for the trees from which I had come. Cal quickly excused himself and rushed to another stand of trees very distant from Fianna. I smiled. We all needed to use the restroom, but were too shy to come right out and say so. While they were gone, I unloaded our four horses, piling the gear carefully on the ground. The two came back about the same time, looking more relaxed. I smiled.

Fianna again took charge; camping was similar to housekeeping, and in this, at seventeen, she was nearly an expert. "Cal, you are in charge of fetching a lot of firewood. Bethany is in charge of getting the fire going and washing up the dishes later on." She tried to think of chores that would be fitting for a boy. "Cal, perhaps you can unsaddle the horses and take care of them. Maybe Bethany can help you with that. Usually, she takes care of our horses while I cook."

Dutifully, Cal wandered off in search of dry wood for our fire. First, I helped Fianna unpack the cooking gear and then went to take care of our horses. Cal returned with an armload of branches and said, "Darn, everything is soaked. I'm sorry, Bethany. I don't know how you'll ever get this wet wood lit. I'll try harder on the next load." I detected a note of sympathy in his voice and knew he was sincere.

"Don't worry, Cal. This will do fine. We need about four times this amount for the night," I added. I arranged the wood and waited until Cal was out of sight before I did my short chant. A small square of crackling fire appeared above the stacked wet wood and slowly settled down upon it. I'm always impressed with all the crackling and sputtering wet wood makes as it dries out enough to burn. You can imagine the surprise on Cal's face when he returned later on with another large pile of wet wood.

"How did you ever manage to get the fire going so well in so short a time, Bethany? Very well done. I doubt that I would ever have gotten it going." Cal was impressed.

"Magic!" I teased, but then realized that I shouldn't have said that and wished I could take back my jest. He grinned and went for more wood.

Later on, Cal began to unsaddle his horse. I had three of ours handled already. "Pretty impressive fire lighting," Cal teased me.

"Thanks," I kept it brief and sought to change the subject. "You've a really fine looking mare there, Cal," I complimented him.

"Yes, she is indeed, a very fine horse. I've been wondering about your horses, Bethany. All four aren't workhorses. They almost look like they originally come from the Layamon district to the south, but your saddles are definitely Tewdwr make."

"Gosh, how can you tell?" I asked, though I knew these were some of the confiscated horses from the dead cavalrymen of King Albert. I was glad that Conna had thought to use our local tack instead of what the horses originally wore. Also, I was curious. I had not studied horses much, either last lifetime or this one. "Our village got them in a trade, I believe." Hardly a fair "trade," but it was sufficiently truthful, in that I had not seen precisely from where Conna had gotten them, I justified to myself.

While dealing with his horse, Cal explained about their conformation, body shapes, and markings. It would have been easier to grasp had we also had a workhorse at hand for comparison. Cal certainly did seem to know his horses though and came dangerously close to the mark, "The way these four act, one might think that they had once served in the cavalry. They are particularly well suited for your traveling needs, I might add." He struggled with his heavy saddle, lugging it over to the campsite. Somehow, I got the notion that perhaps I was a bit stronger than he was, physically, though still a year younger. Perhaps it was because I had been working hard at shipbuilding, which took a lot of effort. I noticed that my hands still bore woodworking callouses and suddenly realized that I would have to be a bit more careful. Fianna's hands had none. I hoped that Cal wouldn't notice my hands, and I kept them clasped behind my back as he returned.

Together, we made a horse line so that all five were secure and couldn't get away, yet all could graze to their heart's content on the lush green, tall grasses. "Supper's ready," called Fianna, and we went to join her. "Cal's better at getting provisions that we are, Bethany. Look, greens! He's got lots of greens." True, we had forgotten to bring any real vegetables or lettuce along with us. He smiled over his small victory.

Once dinner was finished and the dishes washed, Cal setup his sleeping arrangements and brought out his sword to show us. "Like I said, I promise to try to protect you ladies. I do have this very small sword, but I'm not very good with it. However, I do keep it by my side at night, just in case." Fianna did the obligatory oh's and ah's bringing a smile to his face. However, I noticed that his small sword was more likely a large dagger used with the short sword and dagger fighting style, but I didn't say anything about it. No sense in embarrassing him over a dagger. What caught my eye further was the rather large ruby set in its pummel. This was no ordinary, cheap dagger. I really didn't know how much weaponry cost around here, but my guess was one could buy perhaps ten normal daggers for the same amount as this dagger probably cost him.

For a while, we sat in idle chat around the campfire. Then, Cal brought up the topic I dreaded most. "Say, where are we headed after this village? I was heading north, hoping to travel the length of Tewdwr. I've never been way up north on Cymry." I got the distinct impression that Cal would very much like us to go that way, and not just because he was already intending to go that way. I didn't know what to make of that bit of intuition, so I ignored it. Coming up with my own reply would be sufficiently challenging.

"Well, we had intended to make for Bedwyn, Brea, or Nuudilan next," I began, trying to figure out some way to make our destination seem plausible. That I needed information was the real reason we were heading there, and I had some vague idea that I might make contact with that druwid circle, which was supposed to come and take over my work just before I was killed some fourteen years ago. However, nothing prepared me for Cal's reaction.

He face grew very pale, but his voice rose in pitch, "Oh no! You don't want to go there, not there of all places! Not now, please no!" Both Fianna and I stared at him and suddenly his ghastly pale face flushed crimson.

"Why not?" I asked, unable to grasp why he was embarrassed after being shocked; I couldn't think of a proper counter.

"They are at war. All Layamon is at war. Kings are fighting kings. It is wholly unsafe to go riding around Layamon right now. You'd be stopped and maybe even arrested as a spy or worse. It's absolute folly to enter Layamon right now. That's why I left there a while back, to escape all the fighting. Why would you want to go there?" His composure was back to normal.

"Well, troubadours are supposed to be knowledgeable on all the current events of the land so that when we visit a village, we can bring them the latest news along with our music. Frankly, at this point, I don't know what is going on anywhere. Fianna and I can't tell anyone any kind of current news. So I thought we ought to visit Nuadilan or Brea first and learn what is current there before we head to the highlands. Besides, it will give us a chance to learn how they speak, and perhaps get rid of our heavy Tewdwr accent. We've never seen towns as large as these are supposed to be. We wanted to see what life was like in a big town." I was pleased with all my "right reasons."

From Cal's down-turned face, I could tell that he thought all my reasons for visiting Nuadilan were quite correct. He finally said, fighting hard to hold back tears, "What you say makes a great deal of sense, really it does, honestly. But, but if you insist on going into Layamon, I'll have to stay behind." Using a disguised arm motion, he wiped the growing wetness from his eyes. He added, "There is no way I'll enter that section, not at this time anyway, maybe in a few years when things calm down. Not now. If you are really going to go there, I'll, I'll just leave you tomorrow and go my own way."

Fianna was crestfallen; she looked at me pleadingly, "Bethany, he can't leave us. He's only just joined us."

"Well, Fianna and I both need to know much about what is going on in Layamon. How well versed are you on recent events and such in Layamon? I have heard many things over the years and have vowed to find out the truthfulness of them. I know a bit of history of the area around Nuadilan especially, but not the rest of Layamon. You know, curiosity killed the cat. I want to know more. Do you know much about the goings on there? If so, maybe I can find out as much as I need to know without going there?" I tried to allow him a chance to get out of this mess, but it was dependent on his actual knowledge, which I really doubted that he would have.

My words brought a gleam of hope to Cal's eyes. I could tell that leaving us was about the last thing that he wanted to do. He was sincere in his pronouncement and grasped at this straw as his salvation. "I know quite a lot, really I do. What do you want to know?" Before I could begin, he added in a very serious, solemn voice while looking at us both, "But you must promise me that you will *never* ask me how it is that I might know these things, promise me!"

We both did.

Chapter 4 The News, According to Cal

Now I was on the spot. I had to know what had happened there during the last fourteen years since my death. What had happened to my daughter, Sarah, and the druwid circle? I had to know the current situation, especially as it related to this war. "Cal, I need some answers. However, just as we have promised not to inquire how it is that you may know these things, similarly we must ask you not to inquire how it is I know what I know and ask what I do. Do you so promise?"

He looked at me in complete disbelief and then broke out laughing. "A double entente it is!"

"A what?" asked Fianna.

"A formal, friendly understanding between factions," Cal replied. However, the man definitely had a command of the language. He was definitely not a country bumpkin. My guess was that he had been well educated in Layamon. "I promise I will not ask, though I may well be surprised by your questions, Bethany. Please don't confuse my surprise with an inquiry, okay?"

I smiled, "Okay, same with us." Now I was on the spot. I had to figure out a way of asking what I wanted to know without raising undo suspicion. However, I realized just then that I had been putting off this entire line of thinking until I had actually reached one of these towns. I had no idea of what I would ask when I got there. Hence, I might as well practice with Cal.

"I know that over a dozen years ago, some people who immigrated from Juda Arad built the four towns of Bedwyn, Brea, Nuadilan, and Amathon. At that time, the villages were thriving, and many native Cymry folks moved into those cities as well. As I recall, there was some kind of religion that they practiced, Jehosanity or something like that. I've been told that they had a woman High Priestess who everyone loved. Do you know anything about this?" I thought that this would make a good starting point. I wondered if he knew any history.

Cal's eyebrows rose markedly as I spoke, and his eyes never left mine. He waited until he was sure I had finished. Perhaps he was also trying to figure out how best to answer. I realized we must be playing some kind of cat and mouse game, with neither of us knowing the rules. "Yes, I believe you are essentially correct. As I recall, the name of that Holy Blessed Mother was Bethany Madelyn Amir. She was responsible for the construction, growth, and popularity of those towns. When she disappeared, her daughter, Sarah, I think was her name, tried to carry on in her footsteps. But no one could replace the Holy Blessed Mother."

My gods, he does know what I am talking about! I think Cal saw the shock on my face, and I was glad we had our bargain in full force. "Did some others arrive to help this Sarah out after the Holy Blessed Mother disappeared?" I could not resist finding out what had happened to my daughter and if the druwids actually arrived.

"Now that you mentioned it, yes, seven strangers came. They were always around Sarah. As stories go, she fell in love with one of the young men. She married Percival Penton." I could not conceal my smile. So she'd found her man, a druwid, just as I had dearly hoped she would. That meant in all likelihood, she would have been well cared for and may still be alive and well. He had finished and an awkward silence fell. A Penton? Could he perhaps be related to my dear friends Sarah Jane and Raphael Penton? I dare not ask that question, though.

"Is she still around and preaching? Are these strangers still with her?" Oops, Cal had not stated that she had been filling my shoes, preaching to our four churches.

"No, she left for the mainland with the strangers in 605 AH I'm told. The Holy Blessed Mother had three children. The older two brothers, King Ahmad and King Emil, had a violent argument with Sarah over her leaving the island. One night, all eight of them just disappeared and have never been heard from since. The two brothers were very upset and angry with their sister, and never have forgiven her for deserting the island." How could Cal know all this? These were key and relatively private facts that he was relating matter-of-factly. I began to wonder who Cal really was.

I needed time to absorb what he had said and to draw some tentative conclusions. When I did not respond with another question right away, Cal added, "All this is rather common knowledge in those towns. Just about everyone knows about the violent arguments they had. Many overheard them."

That this Percival Penton had decided to leave the island could only mean one thing: the Grey Creatures were on to them as well. He would want to get his Circle and Sarah out of harm's way. Hence, the nighttime disappearance act — at least that is what I would have done. Thus, this meant that for the last dozen years, my sons and the children of Josh Amir would have been on their own; they had to lead. "Okay, for the last dozen or so years, how has been the rule of King Ahmad, King Emil and their cousins, King Hadid and Queen Ros, wife of the King of Aine?"

Once more, Cal gave me the queerest of looks. He hadn't said anything about Hadid and Ros, yet I apparently knew of them. "Ah, this could be a very long tale. How much detail do you want to hear? How about Fianna making us a cup of tea? All this talking is making me thirsty, and we have no mead." She jumped at the opportunity to be of use; however, she kept her ears totally focused on our conversation. All this was new to her, and she found it intriguing.

Cal explained, "I do have possibly some bias in discussing such. Be forewarned. Anyhow, you want to know how things have gone. My honest and frank opinion is that everything just went very much downhill after the Blessed Holy Mother disappeared. King Ahmad became obsessed with gaining ever more lands and building more towns. He could not expand westward, because his brother controlled Bedwyn and Brea. King Ahmad thrust his expansion southward. With each new town he founded or took over, he built wooden fortifications similar to those that the Blessed Holy Mother had made for Nuadilan . Eventually, all the other dukes and earls began to take note of this expansionism. They too began to fortify their major towns and proclaimed themselves kings too. Five years ago, King Albert I came to power in Bregia. He is a ruthless, pigheaded, vile man. He raised an army to put a halt to King Ahmad's territorial expansion into southern Layamon. To give you an idea of just how low King Ahmad had sunk, he even tried to force his own daughter to marry this pig of a king, Albert, solely and only to avoid a war. Everyone knows this, though. It didn't work. For years, the two forces have been skirmishing on border towns and villages. It is unsafe for anyone to even pass through southern Layamon, these days. I've even heard rumors that King Albert I is planning to expand his domain into southern Tewdwr, but I don't know if that is true or not." My face crimsoned, but the darkness of the evening hid my red face from Cal — Fianna's too, as she approached with a pot of steaming tea.

"What of the other brother, this King Emil?" I asked, hoping to avoid any further discussion about Albert's expansion plans.

"No two brothers could be so totally different! Unc — King Emil is content with the size of his kingdom. He has carried on the religion of his mother, the Blessed Holy Mother, building great churches in her honor. Many of the faithful around Layamon make a journey to her shrine in Bedwyn. I myself have seen it. I doubt there is a larger church anywhere in Cymry. Her shrine is splendid, a wonder to behold. One day when it is safe to journey into Layamon, you really should visit the Shrine of the Blessed Holy Mother and see for yourselves. Right now, it is too dangerous to go there, especially you being from Tewdwr and all. Before I left, I heard rumors that a great battle is coming between King Ahmad and King Albert I. We don't want to be anywhere around that area, believe me!"

"Hum, if there is supposed to be this big battle, won't King Emil come to the aid of his older brother?" I asked and then grimaced. Cal had not said which brother was the elder. My blunder did not go unnoticed; Cal picked up that detail immediately.

He said only, "As I said, no two brothers could be so different. We have it on good authority that King Emil will under no circumstances ever come to the aid of his brother's petty wars. King Emil has stated that his *older* brother is totally in the wrong for waging this war. Everyone knows King Emil's position; it's common knowledge." (Cal emphasized the word "older" while looking me straight in my eyes.)

"What about the cousins then?" I asked changing the topic slightly.

"King Hadid has expanded eastward, uniting outlying villages. It is said his lands extend all the way to the ocean, but I suspect its width is perhaps only five miles. Other nearby dukes and earls have likewise proclaimed themselves kings over their lands. In King Hadid's favor is that he has never waged war on any of his neighbors. He claims that he wanted to get to the ocean so he would have a chance at fighting the Axemen raiders. He says the raiders have never ever gotten inland enough to his primary fort. The King of Aine is allied with King Hadid and likewise has built up strong fortifications in his southern highlands portion of Ruadan. Trust me on this one again. It would not be wise of us at all to enter the towns occupied directly by King Hadid or King Aine themselves. Word has it that they are paranoid about spies infiltrating their strongholds. I heard a rumor two weeks ago that some traveling merchant was beheaded for spying. No one was certain for whom the man was spying though, so I took that one with a grain of salt. However, we really ought to avoid those two towns. I would like to keep my head for a long time yet."

"You are probably right. I don't want to lose my head either," I jested. A period of silence ensued, as I digested all this information. Thus far, I hadn't detected any sign that Cal was lying to me. However, rumors are rumors and not fact. Still, even if I had managed to get into these towns, I would only be hearing rumors there, unless I somehow could get an audience with my children. Just now, I had no desire to meddle in their affairs. I had to find Alabaster. That was the single most important action I could take. We had to put a stop to the Grey Creatures and the Mantises. All else was totally secondary. Thus, I decided not to ask about my grandchildren, a blunder I would later regret. I changed the topic, "So how is this religion they founded going?"

For an instant, I thought I saw a great relief come over Cal's face, but it was fleeting. He jested, "Somehow, I don't picture you two as deeply religious. Troubadours are not known for deeply held religion doctrine."

Fianna took offense at his insinuation, protesting, "We have always prayed every evening before supper at the church."

"I'm sorry, Fianna. I meant no disrespect. There is a huge difference between praying to your gods and being fanatical about your religion. Believe me, I pray as well to the Blessed Holy Mother when I can. No, I'm talking about religious fever. As far as I'm concerned, it borders on fanaticism. Let me explain. In particular in Bedwyn, everyone worships the Blessed Holy Mother and her Holy Teachings. They believe that each of us is an immortal spiritual being inhabiting these fleshly bodies. It is our task to become one with Nature in order to regain our spiritual freedom. Many in these four towns are absolutely fanatical about preaching the ways of the Blessed Holy Mother."

"However, just north of these four towns in the realms of King Hadid and to a lesser extent, King of Aine, they worship the original ways of some

Great Messiah, who they call Jes Amir, the husband of the Blessed Holy Mother. Honestly, you can expect a Holy War to break out between supporters of these two religious beliefs any day now! I could never ever figure out how this Great Messiah and the Blessed Holy Mother could have ever lived together as man and wife. Why, they must have had knockdown drag our fights everyday over nearly everything! Well, at least the two do agree on one thing: that we are all immortal spiritual beings inhabiting a fleshly body, but that's about all they can ever agree upon. If you ever want to see a wild argument between two ordinary, quiet men, just mention this topic and watch the sparks fly! I made that mistake once! I'll never do that again! It was wild!" Cal was really caught up in his tale and missed entirely my flushed face and rising anger over what had been done to the teachings of Jes and me. I had an urge to march into both churches and set them straight! My anger subsided as my basic purpose to rescue Alabaster came back to mind, thankfully.

Again, I finally duplicated the silence in our conversation. I quickly thought up another question, but was too hasty. "What of their other son, Mac Dez, I believe he was called or something like that," I added the last to make it seem more plausible that I had heard rumors.

Again, I came under Cal's intense scrutiny. "You ask the strangest questions, Bethany of Cuch Glyn. By the way, you see now why I was surprised at your name. It was also the name of the Blessed Holy Mother, who I worship. But never mind that, Mac Dez, I was told, died in a hunting accident shortly after the disappearance of the Blessed Holy Mother. I can't imagine what you want to know next," Cal insinuated in a teasing manner. I returned his smile.

"I know it is late, but I have got one more thing to ask. Now this one might seem awfully queer and strange. Take your time before you answer; search all your rumors and firsthand information if you have any. About King Ahmad, does he or did he have some kind of advisor or person around him, who seems unusual in anyway? An advisor, perhaps, who is supporting or suggesting this continual warring mess? Someone who makes your skin feel creepy or sends chills down your spine when you are around him?" I was trying desperately to remember Sarah's description of the Grey Creature, who was masquerading as a man so many years ago. I'd forgotten the words that she had used to describe it.

I honestly didn't expect the reply that I got. Cal became instantly vehement, "Snake Tongue!" I detected intense hatred behind those words. Cal paused for a moment and got control over his emotions. "Yes, Ahmad has this nasty man I call Snake Tongue. Rodriguez is his name. Ahmad believes everything he says, and what he says is all bad, if you take my meaning. I don't know of a nastier person on Tarra, excepting maybe King Albert I. Why do you ask? Is it important? Whatever you may do, never, ever get near Snake Tongue!"

Neither Cal not Fianna was prepared for my reaction. Instant anger flared within me, "Damn!" I cursed and stood up, making fists in the air. The evil Grey Creatures were actively leading my own son to ruin, undoing all our good work in Layamon. Suddenly, I realized I had an audience; my face once more flushed scarlet. I sat back down and picked up my empty teacup.

I knew that I had to give both of them some kind of explanation for my reaction. I couldn't tell them my suspicion that Snake Tongue was really a Grey Creature in disguise. "On this world of Tarra, there are some very, very, very evil and nasty beings who are working for our destruction. It seems that Ahmad, who ought to have known better, has come under the influence of one of these to his own detriment. It can only result in his untimely death. 'Nuff said."

Fianna correctly concluded that I was referring to the Grey Creatures that I had previously told her about. On the other hand, Cal's reaction was quite interesting. "Wow, Bethany. You are an incredibly insightful young woman! Only a few of us in Layamon can see what has actually happened to King Ahmad. You don't even know him, and yet you correctly diagnosed what has happened to him. I tip my hat to you, only I don't have one," he jested. Yet, I knew he was sincere in his praise. From Cal, I received an unexpected outpouring of genuine admiration and respect. From this point on, the aloof wall that had separated us evaporated. Cal now very much respected me; I found this heartening.

I changed the topic once more, after refilling my teacup. "Okay, Cal, that's all the things I need to know. Thanks. I think it is now more than clear that we ought to follow your advice on which towns to visit. Only we don't want to go back into Tewdwr just now, save that section for later. We need to visit as much of our island as we can — that's safe to visit, mind you. You are hereby in charge of our itinerary, at least until we can get to the mainland."

"Thanks, I promise I won't let you down!" Cal answered enthusiastically. After a few minutes he said, "There is one thing that I was wondering about, can I ask a question?"

"Sure thing, ask away," I said, without thinking.

"What about adding more musicians to our group? You know when we are finally able to get to the mainland and are putting on shows, we ought to have more musicians with a greater variety of sounds and songs — you know, in order to keep our audience's interest up. We want to be really good so that everyone wants to hear us no matter where we go, right?"

"Yes, you have a good point, Cal. Besides, there is more safety in numbers. We should keep an eye out for any others who might want to join up. However, they must pass an audition, as you did Cal. They have to be able to fit in with the rest of us. Also, they're going to have to be willing to accept my decisions as final. Some men might not, you know."

"Great! Yes, I know *that* only too well," Cal added. I wondered what he meant by that.

In the spirit of honesty, I decided to give Cal just a bit more information on my true goals. "Cal, I just want to let you know that one of the main reasons that I'm traveling all over Tarra is that I'm looking for someone. When I find him, I'll know it and I'm pledged to help him."

"That is a noble purpose, Bethany, and honorable too. Does he have a name? Do you know what he looks like? Where he is at? Maybe I can spot him one day," Cal offered. I was afraid he would so respond.

"Again, don't ask further. I don't know where he is, his name, or his appearance. I will know it when I find him, on that you can be certain. Consider this is my personal quest and leave it at that. No questions asked." He nodded his agreement, though I knew his mind must have been racing, speculating upon the hidden meaning of my words, my quest, and my goal. I was sorry that I had to leave him in mystery, however.

By now, the hour was very late. We turned in; as usual, Fianna and I snuggled together. Cal slept on the opposite side of the fire from us, his dagger, I mean short sword, at his side in case of trouble. Dawn came altogether too soon.

After Fianna fixed breakfast, Cal and I got the horses ready. He was good with horses, I discovered. What he might lack in physical strength, which would come naturally as he grew into full manhood, he made up in cunning. He used his mind, in other words. We had five horses to saddle. He got three done during the time I got two ready, and he teased me about being a tad slow. I was beginning to like this fellow, whatever his past might be. I knew he was hiding much from me, but then I was hiding much from him. Still, our friendship grew.

Again, I amazed him by picking up the faint track that led to the village long before he spotted the signs before us. As planned, we made Glyn Lowri around mid-morning. The village was just as he described. Further, Cal took charge and made the arrangements to play at an inn in return for our keep. "I presume that we want two separate rooms," he added after he had already made the arrangement. We nodded and accepted his tease. It felt good to have another person I could rely upon.

Next, we went to our rooms, cleaned up, and then held a practice session. Cal had a further surprise, he presented Fianna with a pair of gourd rattles he had. "Now you can shake them in time to the music and add a bit of a percussive flavor to the dances." She was elated and just had to try them out. We played for about an hour and broke for lunch.

The long afternoon loomed before us, until I made a valuable suggestion. "Cal, both Fianna and I need to learn to speak without the thick Tewdwr accent. Perhaps during the afternoon, you can work with us." It only took me about an hour, after which I could lose the accent at will. Fianna, on the other hand, felt that she was learning a new language entirely. Cal had superior patience for such a young lad to nurse and coax her along, always being encouraging. Remarkable, I thought. Thus, for the next couple of weeks, learning to speak without the thick Tewdwr accent was the task. We Tewdwr folk insist on adding 'th' to the endings of most words, making words hard to understand. I often wondered how this variation ever came into being, but then I had never made a study of linguistics yet.

Okay, if you want to know about this Tewdwr accent, here are a few little sentences:

Aye, that be'th ol' Demna. I be'th Goewin. Sure got'h a spare'th room. Don'na get'h man'ie stranger'ths 'round here. Be'th welcome 'ere at Ram's Head. 'Ere on business'th?

And here is the same sentence as would be spoken in the Layamon region:

Aye, that'd be old Demma. I am Goewin. Sure, I got a spare room. Don't get many strangers around here. Be welcome at Ram's Head. Here on business?

Once more, our concerts were well received, and we stayed here for an entire week, accumulating nearly fifty coppers for our efforts. Cal insisted that all the funds we made go into a group fund, designed to help all the members out. I thought that was an incredibly wise idea, and Fianna appointed herself "Keeper of the Funds."

At night when we had retired to our rooms and after brushing Fianna's hair, I would lay down, concentrate and expand my awareness, spiritually searching for the presence of Alabaster. Thanks to the forewarning from Cal, I knew that at least one Grey Creature was on the island, but perhaps there were more. I had a dilemma. The one thing that I didn't want to do was to have my presence discovered by a Grey Creature. That would certainly become fatal once again. Yet, I had to search systematically the southern portion of the island for him from here, because we dare not physically travel there. I had to risk detection if I were to rule out Alabaster being down there.

Thus, it was that I developed a different searching technique. Always before when I tried to locate someone mentally, I'd first expand my awareness wide, encompassing all the desired space and all the spiritual beings located there. Then, I would narrow my focus down onto the specific person I wanted to find. If I did that here, I would become aware of all the Grey Creatures that were here as well. Worse, I knew that they would instantly notice me as a result, and the game would be over before it really got started.

Thus, my bright idea was: would it work in reverse? That is, first, narrow my focus to the specific nature and beingness of the person I wanted, Alabaster in this case, and then expand my awareness outward, sensing the presence of this single spiritual being. If it would work, I wouldn't sense the presence of any Grey Creatures and thus they wouldn't sense me. I tried it out on the sleeping Fianna and it seemed to work.

However, she lay but a foot from me. Next, I decided to see if it would work to locate my older brother, Garth. Ten minutes later, I proved it would work.

Over the next few nights, I satisfied myself that Alabaster was not located anywhere in the south of our island, particularly the Layamon region. Further, I was sure he wasn't around southern Tewdwr either, for that matter. However, this procedure still carried some risk of exposing my presence to these Grey Creatures. I had no idea about the Mantises. Perhaps they were just as acute to my presence as well. I dared not do this searching wholesale across Tarra. Besides, even if I could locate Alabaster from here, by the time I could physically get to him, the creatures could easily have already found him and disposed of him. I decided to stick to my original plan, travel the land, and search small sections at a time, avoiding at all costs being discovered by the true enemies of man.

Near the end of our stay, after the crowd thinned, Cal took us over to a table and spread out a piece of parchment. Using a quill pen and small bottle of ink, he began to sketch us a map, his long thin fingers nimbly drawing the outline of the lands about us. "Here is the bottom half of Cymry. Here is the Ath mountains that divides the central highlands of Ruadan from your green hills of Tewdwr. Now down here is the river Daneas, which divides Tewdwr from the southern section, Layamon. Right here at the very bottom of the highlands is the area controlled by the King of Aine and Queen Ros. Just south of there right next to them and stretching all the way to the ocean on the eastern side is the lands controlled by King Hadid. Now here, these four dots just south of Hadid's area are where the Kings Ahmad and Emil rule. Emil has these two, Bedwyn and Brea. Here are Nuadilan and Amathon. I'm pretty sure that King Ahmad has taken control of all this area." He drew an oval shaped outline around much of the central portion of Layamon. "Way down here is the major port of Bregia controlled by King Albert I. The last information I have is that Albert has stretched his dominion up the southwestern coast toward Tewdwr here." Cal was dangerously close to our home of Cuch Glyn. Okay, now back over here by the Daneas river about halfway from the western coast to the Ath mountains is where we are right now, according to my best guess, anyway. Now I've been asking around, and I believe that there are three more villages before we get to the Ath mountains. No one knows whether we could cross them on horseback or not. However, I believe that we should be able to travel along here, just north of the Daneas river, and when we get to the Ath range, we cut north for a while. This way, we should be able to completely bypass any troubles with the King of Aine."

"Mind you, I have no idea what we will find up there in the highlands of Ruadan. I've never been there. But music is music everywhere, so we should be all right," Cal added.

"Good thinking, Cal," I complimented him, then added, "If all goes well, we travel up the central portion of the highlands until we hit the rocky barrens of Ruthcroghan, then veer eastward once more coming down through the Dark Forest, across the Lir River into Moyrath. I think we will face the most danger when coming down the eastern side of the island. As I recall, this is where the Axemen primarily raid."

"Interestingly enough, Bethany, for the last few years now, there hasn't been hardly any Axemen raids. No one knows why, though many have speculated that our kings have become too strong for them. I think that is just wishful thinking. Anyway, I assume that we are going to try to cross the ocean from somewhere along the eastern coast, is that right? Or are we planning to come full circle and go back through Tewdwr?"

"Ports, Cal, everything hinges on where we can get passage on a Sea Prince ship — that and the cost factor. I wish I knew how much it is going to cost us to buy passage to the mainland. You don't happen to have that information handy, do you?" I jested.

"Sorry, I don't have a clue," Cal replied somewhat downcast.

"Well, we can always sell our horses; probably that would be enough," Fianna speculated. "Besides, I don't think we can take horses across the ocean. We can always get new ones on the mainland, can't we?"

Chapter 5 The Highlands of Ruadan

During the first week of July, we drew close to the Ath range. Each day these rugged, grey granite teeth steadily grew in size. At last we halted our due east passage; we could go no further. Jagged and sharp giant's teeth rose before us. Cal explained that the Ath was more rounded and even on the highland's side, but dropped off sharply on the Tewdwr side. I spent an hour examining the sight before me. Spectacular and forbidding, the Ath formed a natural barrier, dividing the island into sections. I estimated they weren't that tall here, perhaps rising up two thousand feet. However, the rise was so steep, sheer, and jagged that one couldn't even climb over them without special gear and ropes. Still, Fianna and I enjoyed the beauty of the Ath before we headed southeastward following the edge of the Ath.

Within five miles, this natural barrier began to lower and two miles further along, Cal led us slowly eastward again. I spied a little used track that led southeast. Although Cal couldn't see this faint trail, he told us that the King of Aine's lands lay in that direction, perhaps ten miles further along. By late that afternoon, I spied a river off to our right, and I recognized it. "Daneas, right?" I pronounced. Cal confirmed it. Just to the east lay Queen Ros, I suspected, while just to the south, where the shoreline sported a dense patch of trees, lay the four towns that I had helped build some twenty years ago. Beyond that lay two armies fighting over land rights — a fight probably instigated by the Grey Creatures. I shuttered involuntarily at that thought. I had done my best to properly train and raise Ahmad, but I couldn't live his life. I couldn't make all his decisions for him. I was just thankful that Emil had better sense and wisdom than his older brother.

I got to thinking about children. When their bodies are small, we do everything we can to protect them from getting hurt. I had called it baby proofing the house. As they grow older, we teach them the values we believe will carry them through life on a successful path, particularly toward spiritual freedom. Yet, in the end, our children are spiritual beings themselves and must make their own choices, for good or ill. I wondered if some day far down the line Ahmad might once again inhabit a new baby body of mine; if so, we might hold a discussion about the actions he had taken this time — assuming, of course, he could still remember them. I smiled; if that happened, I promised myself that I would help him remember them.

Fianna brought me out of my reflections, "Bethany, can we camp along the river for the night? I would dearly love to take a swim and wash everything in sight. I feel so grubby, even my hair, but is it safe to camp here?"

"Cal, I defer to you? Would we be safe on this side? Are we too close to Aine's lands?" I asked. My own hair and clothes stank as well. I could definitely use a bath.

"Well, we are awfully close, but I need one too. Perhaps we can risk it, but can we do it without lighting a fire tonight? I think a campfire might be a bad idea — this close and all," Cal replied hesitatingly.

We veered right and paralleled the river for a time. I saw no signs of any tracks, save those made by deer. A small partially concealed glen by the river made an excellent campsite. Boulders from the Ath rose on three sides of the glen, so we could only really be seen from across the river, which was several hundred feet across, though I had no idea how deep it might be. Into the glen we rode, dismounted, and made our camp in the middle of the afternoon.

As Cal and I were removing the saddles, I noticed a bit of blood on his saddle and pants. "Did you hurt yourself?" I asked innocently.

Cal's face turned beet red, and he seemed very flustered. "Ah, yes, I, ah, foolishly cut myself on my sword a while back. Nothing serious, just silly. Nothing to worry about," he hastily added. "Come on; we had better hurry up. Fianna will want to go for a swim soon, and it isn't safe for her to swim alone." I detected his rapid change of subject and went along with it. Cutting yourself on your own sword has to be very embarrassing. Funny, though, the blood was more in the center of his saddle.

It didn't take us long to get our towels and our spare traveling clothes. As predicted, Fianna wanted to get into the water as fast as possible. "Just keep the noise down, Fianna. Be as quiet as you can," Cal worried. Then he added, "You girls swim here closest to our camp. I'll go down river a ways to give you your privacy." Fianna thanked him, made for the water, and began undressing rapidly. I followed slightly behind her.

I knew this would be tricky, pretending to be a woman and taking a bath naked in the river was risky. Most of the time, I kept my shirt on to hide everything. Yet, I relished the bath as well as Fianna. Both of us were used to going for a plunge in our bay nearly anytime we felt dirty, which was usually every day. We loved swimming in the warm waters of the bay in the summertime. We each helped the other wash our hair and then scrubbed our traveling clothes. At last, we waded out, dried off, and donned our spare set of clothes.

Then, of course, came the lengthy ritual of drying and combing the tangles out of our hair. I told Fianna I thought hers was definitely getting noticeably longer, whereon she cooed in pleasure. Two hours after we began, she and I walked back to our camp to figure out what we could fix for dinner without using a fire. We still had plenty of dried fish with us, since we had not yet needed to trade it for lodging. Died fish, apples, and the last of Cal's greens would suffice, though I longed for my cup of hot tea. Fianna came to my rescue with a clever idea; she put tea leaves in a pot, filled it with water, and set it out in the sun to catch the last rays of the afternoon.

"By supper, we should have some sun tea, not as strong, mind you, but tea nevertheless," she pronounced.

"You amaze me, Fianna. Where did you learn that trick?"

"Mom, silly," she replied. "Oh, here comes Cal. He looks all cleaned up, doesn't he?"

Over dinner, Cal suggested that by this time tomorrow, we ought to reach another village, one in which it would be safe enough for us to play once more. Hence, we spent the rest of the day practicing our music. I definitely enjoyed our lazy lifestyle.

The next day, we traveled north and east. Cal was very relieved when I announced that I spied a track and even more relieved when it became so plain that he could see it as well. He felt certain that we were on the right path, even more so when it joined what had to be a well-traveled road that led mostly northward. We were back in the civilized portion of the island once more.

Cal's estimate was not far off. Later that afternoon, we rounded a bend and before us lay the sprawling town of Aberdeen. The land was different from any I had seen on Cymry before. The valleys were filled with large stones with grasses growing between. Every so often, a stand of trees grew tall. That this was civilized land was plainly evident. The farmers had removed the stones from their fields, placing them in rows, marking the boundaries of their fields. All across the land to the west and east, fields of grain grew, outlined by the two to three foot tall walls of stones. It was quite picturesque indeed.

Aberdeen was by far the largest town we had encountered to date. I estimated that there were perhaps several hundred quaint stone buildings and a population of several thousand. In the distance, I could see numerous flocks of sheep grazing on the rising hillsides. Yet it was the people themselves that really caught my eye or rather their dress styles. Plaids — all their clothes were woolen plaids, and all with nearly the same style and color. Fianna's comment spoke for me as well, "Look! They all wear dresses!" Indeed, the men and boys wore a plaid skirt that came only down to their knees; plaid socks stretched up, ending somewhere under their skirts. The women's dresses, however, came down to their ankles. Yet men and women all wore the same type of white cloth shirts.

Yes, they stared at us as we stared back at them, when we rode into their town. We looked as unusual to them as they did to us. Quickly, we asked for directions to their largest inn. Once we found it, the Lamb's Head, Cal and I dismounted and went in search of the innkeeper, while Fianna took charge of watching over our five horses. Cal, now comfortable in his role, opened discussions with the innkeeper, "We are the Cymry Minstrels out on a tour, visiting towns and villages, bringing news and music for one and all."

Really, it ought to have been me making the deals, but rightly, Cal had said that the innkeepers would be more comfortable bargaining with a man than a young girl. Booking a gig was more of a man's role, and I couldn't deny him that. Yet, I had to maintain my disguise, so I let Cal do it. The first few times he had been overly self-conscious, I thought, but now he seemed to have the knack of it. Soon, he had made our usual arrangements; we could play all evening in return for two rooms and our meals. Here, mead was extra, but none of us drank, so that wasn't a problem.

An hour later, the horses were stabled, our gear stowed in our rooms, our performance dress clothes on, and we were setting up to play. This time, the inn was prepared for musicians. Indeed, there was a raised platform in the back, a stage from which to perform! Fianna's comment spoke for us all, "Now this *is* more like it!" Slowly, the inn began to fill and around six pm, the innkeeper joined us on stage. We were actually getting an introduction this time!

He raised his hands to get people's attention, then said loudly, "Tonieght, wie heve tee Cymry Minstrels weeth us to sharee neuws and plai fer us. Tee yung lassie will e'en dance fer yeu! But ferst tee neuws!" While the crowd clapped and hollered for news, the innkeeper motioned for one of us to come center stage and relay the news. I gave Cal a nudge, hoping he would do it for us. His face was white, but he realized that this was a man's obligation. I felt a bit like a heel for thrusting this shy lad into the limelight, but it would be unseemly for a young woman to relay the news.

Cal cleared his throat, and spoke in an squeaky voice at first, until he got the hang of it. He relayed the rumors of the war between King Ahmad and King Albert I, of Albert's push into Tewdwr, of the intense refusal of King Emil, King Hadid, and King of Aine to become involved. Cal assured them that this war would never reach Aberdeen. This they seem pleased to hear. Finally, one man yelled out, "Eenuff of neuws! Pleey, pleey!" Cal quickly returned to us, more than a little relieved. We began to play our liveliest dance tunes. Fianna, shaking the gourds in time, danced and whirled on the stage. The crowd appeared to enjoy the festivities, and we all settled down to a long evening's merrymaking.

The hour was getting late, when our worst playing nightmare arose. Suddenly, someone called out, half drunken, "Pleey Aberdeen Rose!" Quickly, the crowd began chanting for that song. Unfortunately, it had to be a local song we did not know. Embarrassed, Cal tried to explain, but the crowd wouldn't accept his apology and kept on insisting for that one. For the first time, I was truly at a loss for what to do. We all must have looked rather silly and embarrassed, standing dumbfounded upon the stage.

Suddenly, out of nowhere, a young lad yelled, "Ie'll sheew 'em!" A young lad wearing the usual plaid skirt with long socks and carrying some kind of plaid bags with wooden sticks sticking out of it climbed up on the stage with us. "Fello mee," he said. He stuck a stick in his mouth and began to huff and puff like mad. The bags inflated. Bagpipes! I finally recognized what this funny looking instrument was. Then, the nasal sounds of the reeds and drones began to fill the room, as the crowd cheered. This must have been their favorite tune, I surmised.

It was a slow dance with an easy melody. Quickly, Fianna picked up on its rhythms, began to dance, and shake the rattles, while the crowd clapped along with her. Soon, Cal and I, playing my guitar, joined our bagpipe savior. In fact, we had to play the song twice before the crowd was satisfied. At last, the innkeeper announced the music was finished for the night; it was getting late. Slowly most of the crowd wandered home.

I quickly and profusely thanked our benefactor and introduced ourselves, "I am Bethany, our leader; this is my sister Fianna; and this is Cal. We are eternally grateful for your rescue. You play very well indeed. It is the first time I have actually heard a bagpipe. It sounds wonderful indeed!"

"Aye, lassies, tis does. Needs e druem, thew to soond beatr. Naem's Fergus O'rylee, aet yer serviece," and he bowed low to we girls, nodding politely to Cal. "E tep fer yea ahl, they's aelways be awantin Aberdeen Rose 'round 'ere."

Ah accents. Fianna was listening intently to Fergus, trying hard to understand him. He said to Fianna, "Yea pleyed goud. Bein loong tieme sience e 'eard some o tweuns. Leat me buy u all a ale." From the look on poor Fianna's face, he could tell that she was struggling to understand him. Surprisingly, he then said, "Can you understand me better if I talk like Layamon folks?"

Her eyes popped wide open, "Yes, yes, I can."

"Ah, Tewdwr folk, you be. I can still understand you. Okay. I said, lassie, you played good. It's been a long time since I have heard some of those tunes. Let me buy you all an ale. Please?"

"Sure!" Fianna replied, without even looking at me. Off we four went to find a table that was still reasonably clean. Only a handful of people were still in the inn, finishing their drinks. Again, I figured these were probably staying in the inn as we were.

"Thanks, Fergus, for the ale. I really like the sound of your bagpipes. Have you played them long?"

"Yes, since I was a wee lad. I know most of the songs you'll find up here in the highlands. I'm nineteen, by the way. Fianna, you have the prettiest hair and eyes that I have ever seen."

She blushed and said, "You probably just have not seen many redheads up here in the highlands."

"Aye, you are right there, lassie. Not many Tewdwr folks up here. Still, you and your sister have really brightened up the evening 'round here. Thanks for coming to Aberdeen. Are you staying long?"

"Oh, we usually stay in one town for about a week," Fianna gaily replied. "We are not in any rush."

"Say, Fergus, could you perhaps teach us some of the more popular songs of the highlands?" I interjected. "After tonight, I can tell that we need to learn lots of local songs. By the way, you do speak good Layamon. The local accent here in the highlands is a bit hard to grasp, as is Tewdwr to you all, I expect. Where did you learn it?"

"Thanks. From my mother. She taught me a number of Layamon songs too, but I haven't heard them for quite some time, before tonight, that is. You all are very good musicians, and Fianna, you dance so well!"

"Thanks," she blushed and fiddled with her hair absentmindedly.

"Tell you what," Fergus continued, "I'll be glad to teach you the songs I know. If Fianna will allow me to take her for a walk and show her the sights of Aberdeen in the morning, I'll spend all afternoon teaching you as many songs as you care to learn. Will you?" he looked longingly at Fianna.

"That would be great!" Fianna replied, but then quickly looked at me for reassurance.

"Super, Fergus. Thanks. But don't you have to work or something?" I replied, slightly annoyed that he was really making a play for my sister.

"Nah, I'm on an extended holiday. I'm staying with my uncle here in Aberdeen. I have nothing better to do than to walk this pretty lassie around the town and play music with you. Thanks again. I reckon I'd better go now. Innkeeper wants to close. It's getting late and you are probably tired after that concert. I'll come by mid-morning, if that is all right with you, Fianna?"

"You bet!" she bubbled, and Fergus picked up his pipes, bowed to we lassies, and left. Hastily, we finished our ales, picked up our instruments, and headed for our rooms.

Cal's comment spoke for all of us, "What an incredible stroke of good luck we had tonight, you know, with Fergus. Golly, we might have been kicked out of our gig if he hadn't come to our rescue!" I didn't have the heart to tell him I was a little worried about his flirting with my sister, though.

Safe inside our room, Fianna asked, "Well, what do you think of Fergus? Isn't he just really cute? So polite, so like a fine gentleman, isn't he? And he likes our music, too."

"Just watch yourself, Fianna. Be a bit careful around him. We don't know anything about him. He does speak Layamon though."

"Ah, don't worry, Bethany. I know how to take care of myself. I intend to have a good time with him, that's all." Still, I grumbled.

The next day, around mid-morning, Fergus arrived at the inn. He wore a clean dress and sported a large broadsword around his waist. Spying me eyeing it, he explained, "My father taught me how to fight rather well. I can handle myself in a fight, so your sister will be perfectly safe with me. No need to worry. And my mother taught me not to fight, by the way, so I prefer not to fight, if you take my meaning." I did feel slightly reassured.

Shortly after lunch, the two returned to the inn, both their arms were loaded. "Look, Bethany, Fergus has bought us some flowers; it'll spice up our show tonight." I took the flowers out of her hands so she could better manage the other bags she was carrying.

"I brought everything," Fergus explained, "all my instruments. Variety of sound, you know."

"Double thanks," I said, still a bit abashed that he was giving me flowers. Soon, I forgot about everything else but music. First, using his bagpipes, he would play a song, and then we would join in, going over and over it until we had it learned. Each time, when he was sure that we had picked up the song, he'd put down the pipes and accompany us on one or more of his four different types of drums. I particularly like the wide variety of sounds he could get from the one he called a dumbek. Depending upon where it was struck, one got a shrill beat or a deep throb.

When we took our first break, he brought out another instrument. "Lassies and lad, this is called a shawm, a tenor shawm to be precise, double reed inside the cap here." He played it a bit. Oh, there was nothing like that incredibly mellow, slightly nasal sound! I fell in love with it immediately.

"Can I try it out, Fergus? I just love its sound!" I exclaimed enthusiastically.

"Aye, but normally men play the tenor shawm, for it takes a lot of strength to play it. Lassies probably can't play it, but you are welcome to try." He handed it gently to me.

Its finger holes were similar to my flute and my fingers had to stretch a bit to cover all the holes. Yes, it did take a rather strong breath pressure to sound, but quickly I adapted. I struggled until I could get a scale of notes out of it that sounded good. Fergus commented, "Well done, lassie! You are the first woman I've known that could blow the thing."

"Are these expensive?" I asked.

"Aye, lassie. I could buy two or three bagpipes for one of these. Lucky was the day when I found this one for sale. Here, I have two other instruments to try out. This one looks like a hollow cylinder with holes. I call it my buzzy, but around here, it is a racket, makes only a soft noise, though." He played a bit on it. Indeed, it was a bass, buzzy sound, which I thought would blend in nicely with our dulcimer and lute or flute.

Next, Fergus produced what he called an alto capped horn. It was not a horn; rather it had a double set of reeds inside a hollow cap. A good deal of breath pressure was required to make it sound, but its alto pitch, though not loud, also blended with our dulcimer and lute. I had to try his capped horn, but found it much harder to play than the tenor shawm. Fergus chuckled at my attempts, "Aye, lassie, I had a good deal of trouble getting that one to sound well."

Thus went our afternoon. Soon it was getting close to performance time, just after sunset. Fianna suggested, "Say, why don't we let Fergus play along with us tonight. I'm sure he would love to, and besides, I think our audience would like the sound variety." As kind and generous as Fergus had been to us, I could not refuse. Besides, he said that he would love to join us.

Yes, the audience loved the addition of Fergus to our troupe. The rest of the week went by altogether too swiftly. Every day, Fergus would take Fianna for a stroll about the town in the mornings, and together we would all practice during the afternoons. Without fail, each evening, he joined us on stage, claiming he was having more fun than he had for years.

Finally, we had to depart and continue our northerly journey to the next town or village. We said our farewells to Fergus and thanked him immensely. Fianna even gave him a kiss; I settled for giving him a hug instead. Cal seemed a bit embarrassed about the show of emotion and shook his hand warmly. Then, we rode off, leaving Aberdeen behind us.

"Well, financially, we did well there," Fianna reported, as we leisurely rode down the well-traveled path. "We took in thirty coppers all total. Not bad. It's triple what we got any place else, but then this was the largest place we've played so far."

After a while, Fianna said, "By the way, Bethany, Fergus warned me that under no circumstances are we to ride out into the countryside — where all the moors and ponds are located — no matter how pretty they might seem to us. He says that there are hidden bogs there that will suck you right in and drown you. He says it is treacherous to walk on the moors without a guide who is familiar with that moor."

"Thanks for the warning. Say, did Fergus ever tell you what he does for a living? He seems to be on vacation. But from what, I wonder?" I asked.

"No, is that important? He says he travels a lot and learns songs, but that is about all he said. I think he said that he has a younger brother and two younger sisters, but he never said where they live. Is that important?"

"Probably not, just curious," I replied.

"I think he really liked me, don't you?" she asked me.

I knew I was on thin ice, so I replied carefully, "Yes, sis, he definitely liked you. No doubt about that." She beamed and we rode onward.

Cal added, "Oh absolutely, Fianna! I would say that he was smitten by you. Too bad we could not just settle down there. I'm sure he would have offered to court you immediately. Yes, I think he was rather cute too. I can't get over the men's dresses, though, so quaint. I wonder what they have on under them?" Cal then flushed and became silent. Yet, I too, wondered what the men wore under their very short skirts. In the rush to learn music, I had forgotten to ask him about them. I guess Fianna had other things occupying her mind than details of their dress code.

The next day, we arrived at a smaller village about a quarter the size of Aberdeen. It was called Rylie, home to perhaps five hundred people. Once more, we made our bargain with a local innkeeper. In advance, we decided to stay only one night because it was so small. Our evening gig went without any surprises this time, thanks to all our preparations under the guidance of Fergus. I found that playing this evening was wee bit lonesome. I too missed the sounds that Fergus had added to our group. Fianna was quite moody, I noticed.

After our successful one night stand here in Rylie, we pushed on northward. The directions we were given suggested that a large town lay fifteen miles further on up the road. Dunedun, it was called and boasted over five thousand inhabitants, by far the largest town we had yet encountered. More importantly, it was the home and fortification of King Rory Ross. For the first time, we might get an invitation to play for local rulers, something that made us all a little nervous. Fianna did suggest that our coffers might fare better playing for a king, however.

We camped what I judged would be five miles from Dunedun. Off to the side of the road lay vast rolling hills and bogs. Wild flowers were everywhere, but Fianna again cautioned us about treacherous bogs and drowning. Hence, I chose to camp close to the road, gambling no one would come by during the evening or night. I was, of course, wrong. Several wagons passed by in both directions as well as two riders. It was the first time we all felt slightly vulnerable camping out in the open, easy prey as it were. Yet, nothing amiss happened.

Mid-morning, the splendor of Dunedun greeted our eyes, stone buildings sprawling across a wide valley. Perhaps two miles in diameter, the town was entirely surrounded by a low stone barrier wall, four feet tall. The road led straight to a gatehouse with two armed guards milling around. Yes, this was a fortified town, safe haven for King Rory Ross. We had to spend three coppers just to enter the town! However, thanks to Cal's quick thinking, we also got directions to a large inn from one of the guards in return for our coppers.

Rossmead Inn was huge and boasted a musician's stage. Cal didn't have the slightest trouble making our usual deal to play in return for lodging and food. The red-faced innkeeper's bargain was simple: he would try us one night. If we worked out, he wanted us to agree to a week's stay, playing every evening, of course. Cal readily agreed. After stowing our gear and seeing that the horses were properly stabled behind the inn, we took a short stroll around the immediate area of the inn. Shops lined the street, if only we had sufficient funds actually to purchase anything. We satisfied ourselves by window shopping. I was surprised to see that even Cal enjoyed looking in all the shop's windows, gazing at this and that. Men usually don't like to just look — I had observed when my parents took us to the larger town to go shopping twice a year.

Soon it was show time once more. Cal really lucked out this time; no one asked for news at all. They only wanted entertainment, so we gladly struck up a lively tune. When we had finished our third song, a quiet voice to our right said, "Mind if I join you? Did you miss me?"

It was Fergus! He'd obviously followed us. With his arms full of his instruments, he walked quickly to join us. Fianna instantly helped him unload his instruments. "Sorry I am a bit late. Okay, what song is next?" We really didn't have time to say much else, as the crowd grew impatient for the next song. Fergus joined in playing his tenor shawm, which I admit added a great deal of sonority to our sound.

The hours passed quickly for us. Finally, the innkeeper interrupted us, "If I doen't stoep teem, thee'l pleuy til daen! Coem bek en tee morro fer mor." As quickly as we had begun, our gig was over. He shook Cal's hand, promising to promote us during the day tomorrow. I didn't know what he meant by that, but we soon found out. The next day, he sent cryers about town, saying loudly, "Come to Rosemean Inn! Hear the Cymry Minstrels, limited engagement!" Yes, the next night we played to a full house.

Again, Fergus bought us a round of the finest ale before we could say much of anything. "You're back," I said as soon as we sat down at a vacant table, waiting the ale.

"Ah, I could say that I was in the area, heard you playing, and stopped by," Fergus said coyly, adding, "but I expect you wouldn't believe that one." We all laughed; he was right. "Would you believe I had to make a business trip to Dunedun?"

"Fergus," I drawled, expressing a teasing disbelief.

"Didn't think so," he jested. "After you left, I realized just how much fun I had playing with you. Since I'm on vacation, more or less, my time is my own. So here I am. Can I play with you while you are in Dunedun, please?" He was literally begging us to let him play, looking at each of us in turn, and saying, "Please."

How could we resist? "Sure, Fergus. We do have a much larger audience to please, and you do add depth to our sound," I consented.

"Oh thank you, thank you!" he exclaimed expressing genuine relief and appreciation.

"I'm rather glad to see you here," Fianna said, her eyes never leaving him. "Do you know your way around this large town?"

"Oh yes, my fair lassie, yes indeed. Been here many times," he explained to her. "Would you care to accompany me for a walk around the town mid-morning?"

"You bet!" Fianna gushed, hardly concealing her excitement. He beamed and grinned from ear to ear. I glanced at Cal. He was smiling broadly as well, so I surmised that Cal also liked Fergus. Maybe I was just being too cautious with my sister's welfare.

Fergus sipped some ale and stated, "You know, if we get a good crowd in here tomorrow night and it goes well, I'm sure that King Rory Ross will very likely send for you to come play for his court one night this week. He often does, you see, bring the most popular entertainment into his court. Have you ever played for royalty?"

"No! What an honor that would be," gushed Fianna, still staring constantly at Fergus.

"Yes and no, it goes both ways. I've played for King Rory a couple times now. True, the acoustics are good in the small dining hall, up in the minstrel's gallery, but the audience is often small, and not as attentive as are the folks here in the inn. Personally, I play for people to enjoy, not for the status. Anyhow, if you are asked, really it will be an order, so I'll go with you. I know the ropes and can help you with the details, though there aren't that many. It can be a bit daunting playing for the king and his court, mind you, that is, if you want me to, I will," he added, realizing that he was perhaps just a little too assuming.

I answered for us, "Fergus, if we are asked to play for the King, why, I insist you play with us and handle the details on our behalf. Honestly, we are just starting out our careers as troubadours. Any help would be most appreciated, thanks." He relaxed and seemed more at ease with us. He and Fianna then chatted idly for a while; Cal and I packed up our instruments and headed to our rooms. She joined us a bit later, cheeks flushed.

"He kissed me!" she bubbled and danced around the room. "I do hope we get to play for the King. I've never seen a king and would like to meet one, how about you?"

I laughed, "You know, King Ross could turn out to be an old man, bald, and wrinkled, you know." She laughed and we prepared for bed.

The next day, Fergus met us, and this time we all went for a walk with him. Cal and I were also curious about this large town. He led us to the main shopping section of the town, which wasn't too far from the inn. "You can get almost anything you want in one of these shops," Fergus explained. "Only be careful you're not overcharged. Merchants tend to do that to outsiders, such as yourselves."

We walked and window shopped mostly. Actually, about the only things we really needed to trade to get or to buy with our meager funds were food supplies. Ours was running low. However, Fianna just had to stop by the dressmaker's shop and examine all the beautiful gowns and clothes displayed in the front of the store. Fergus and I stayed near the front door, content to watch Fianna as she ogled over this dress and that. I was surprised that Cal also seemed rather interested in the dress construction.

While we were standing around waiting on Fianna and Cal, I asked Fergus discretely, "Say, there is one question I have been dying to ask one of you fellows, but I'm not sure that it is entirely polite to ask it."

He gave a chuckle, saying, "Whisper it then."

I did. "What do you guys wear under that short skirt?"

He roared. "I knew it! I knew it!" My face reddened a bit. "All outsiders are curious about our kilts. They are called kilts. We wear shorts under them. If we didn't, we'd freeze our you know what's. We stay cool in the heat of the summers. Kilts are a great invention, don't you think?"

"I couldn't say," I teased back. "And while you stay cool, your women's long dresses keep them hot?"

"Modesty, my young lassie, modesty. Our women are too modest to show much leg, otherwise they might be mistaken for a Lady of the Night, if you grasp my meaning," he replied. I dropped the subject; fortunately, Fianna and Cal were finally ready to move on to the next shop.

"Excellent workmanship," Cal commented to me as he passed. "Very fine seamstress here." I wondered how he could tell that detail. Were boys educated differently in Layamon these days?

Fergus stopped beside a weapons shop, "In here you will find the finest blades to be found anywhere in the highlands or on Cymry for that matter. Steel by Clayton, that's the brand name. My broadsword was made in this very shop."

Cal asked, "Was it very expensive? I mean how much would a blade about the size of mine run?"

"Oh around fifteen gold pieces, I would guess. The maker would match your body size and speed with the blade, so that you would have a perfectly balanced blade, suited to you. It's well worth the money."

We laughed and I added, "None of us has ever seen a single gold piece, let alone have fifteen to spend on a blade." He seemed to understand our position, however.

The day passed peacefully, and we even got in an hour's practice before we donned our performance clothes and walked on stage. This second night, the large inn room was absolutely packed. It was standing room only. Men and women stood behind the others lucky enough to have found a seat at the tables. The barmaids could barely move about filling the orders. Again, we were formally introduced as the Cymry Minstrels, and the gig was on.

This night, the audience was very responsive and lively. I noticed they preferred both fast dance tunes and slow laments about equally. It was hard to tell who had more fun, the crowd or us. The evening ended in no time, with the crowd begging for more. The innkeeper refused, saying to come back tomorrow night for more. Once again, Fergus bought us a round of ale as we unwound. We needed to relax. I never realized how caught up in the excitement I had become until now.

Taking a big slurp of ale, Fergus stated, "Now that is what I treasure about making music. They loved you! Did you hear their reactions and responses? You are really good."

Fianna gave him a hug and said, "You were playing too, so they liked you too, and you are really good too." I smiled, knowing she was right. I wondered if I ought to ask Fergus if he might like to join our troupe, but then thought better of it.

The next day, an immaculately dressed man wearing the finest made kilts came to the inn asking for us. When we came to him, he stated formally, "Are you the Cymry Minstrels?" When we said we were, he continued, "King Rory Ross hereby requests that the Cymry Minstrels play for his dinner this Saturday night." Fianna squealed with glee; her wish had come true. Cal had the presence of mind to ask where we were to go and when and how long we were to play. I realized that it might be a bit unseemly if the youngest woman in the troupe asked these sorts of questions. I thanked Cal for doing that once the man had left.

When Fergus appeared later on, Fianna rushed to him to relay the news. He did not seem surprised that we had been asked. Cal relayed the critical information to him, and Fergus knew exactly where we needed to go. It wouldn't do to get lost in the town while trying to get there to play for the King. Fergus also said that probably we would need to play only about half the time that we did at the inn. "Just remember, that the King and his court will be dining while we play, chatting among themselves. They will not be as attentive as the folks are here at the inn."

We played four more nights to an equally packed house. I figured that the innkeeper was making a bundle by having us play; it looked like he was doing a terrific business. After our gig on Friday night, which was to be the last night before playing for the king, the innkeeper came by and settled his account with us. While we would still spend another night here once we finished playing for the king, we wouldn't be expected to play. He gave us four gold pieces and thanked us, telling us we were welcome to come by and play again anytime we were in town.

Needless to say, Fianna was exuberant. In our room, she lovingly touched and caressed her gold coin. I, of course, had seen plenty of gold coins in my previous lives, and was more impressed with his generosity. "Heavy coin," was my comment. Cal didn't seem all that impressed either, now that I think of it. Perhaps he too had seen many gold coins. For Fianna, this was truly impressive, and I let her bask in her enjoyment. She'd earned her reward with all that dancing.

Saturday morning when Fergus joined us, Fianna tried to give him his coin, but he told her she should keep it, that he didn't need any money. We both then asked if our performance clothes would be acceptable at the king's court. Having seen the immaculately dressed courtier, I was worried our rather crude dresses would be an affront or worse. Fergus put us at ease, "Nay, lassies. You are fine. Remember, they are not going to be looking at you; rather they are going to be mostly listening to the music while they eat and chat. Oh yes, once the meal is done, there is some likelihood that the King will request a formal dance. If so, we should play slow, stately dance tunes for a while, as they dance before us. Sometimes they do and sometimes they don't want to dance after eating."

Late afternoon, Fergus led us through town to the King's residence. Actually, once we found the place, I realized it would be impossible to miss. His residence was huge and entirely surrounded by a ten-foot tall stone wall. To gain entry, one had to pass through the guardhouse, which was heavily garrisoned. Inside the grey walled compound, I counted a dozen stone buildings, and at least one was the stables. The manor house was a large, stately stone building, single story. Two doormen stood at attention before the oaken doors. As we approached, they opened them wide for us. Fergus took the lead; he had been here before and knew where to go. Hence, it wouldn't look so awkward for us.

We walked down a long hall and entered a small, inconspicuous door. I wondered where we were going. However, as we stepped inside the room, I found that we were actually on the stage; this was the musician's entrance! I looked out on a Great Hall, boasting the largest table that I had ever seen in all my lives, at least thirty feet in length and could seat several dozen people. Currently, only several servant maids were present, busily bringing things to the table. At the far end and facing us was a giant chair, whose back must have risen six feet above the seat, obviously the King's chair, I surmised. Quickly, we went about getting our instruments out and warmed up. We even had time to play a tune to test out the acoustics. I was amazed. Fergus was right, the sounds carried marvelously in this spacious hall.

Just then, a middle aged man, dressed in a fine plaid kilt, but whose protruding belly indicated his hearty appetite, entered with a lovely middle aged woman on his arm. She was dressed in a very fancy plaid dress. Both wore small golden crowns. King Rory Ross no doubt.

With perfect speech, the King introduced himself and his wife, Kathleen, and thanked us for coming to play for him. "Ah, I see Fergus is joining you tonight. Very well, he does play a mean horn." Fergus bowed, but said nothing. They turned to walk to their places at the table, but the King turned for an instant and said, "We'll dance tonight, Fergus." I presumed that Fergus knew what that meant and guessed we would need to play some slow dances.

I was right. Fergus quickly explained which dances we should play when they wanted their dance music. I hoped that I could remember them. "Don't worry lassies. I'll tell you which ones to play as we go along." I calmed down, realizing that I was getting jittery. Fianna was outright nervous, and even Cal seemed a little ill at ease, not nervous, but worried. I wondered why but had no time to ask. At this moment, a fanfare of trumpets announced the arrival of the king's guests for the evening meal, and some twenty others, dressed in their finery, paraded into the room, taking their assigned places at the King's table. Once they were seated, the King spoke loudly, "Tonight, we are entertained by the Cymry Minstrels. Let the music begin!"

That was obviously our cue and we began to play. Unfortunately, there was not much for Fianna to do but shake her gourds. No one was watching us or her dancing. She contented herself with adding percussion. Between songs, Fergus loaned her one of his drums, and she added a strong rhythm section, though occasionally dancing about the stage as well. As time passed, I began to empathize with Fergus. Playing for the inn crowd had been exhilarating; this was more like a practice session with no one listening. I was very glad when the king finally announced it was time for the dance.

This was more like it. The couples spread out around the room and danced slowly to our tunes. Fianna was even honored by the King, who asked her to step down and dance one round with him personally. She was a bit giddy when she climbed back on stage. I think she will be telling her grandchildren one day about how the king personally danced with her! Finally, the guests began leaving, and the evening's festivities were over, our part finished. One of the king's servants handed Fianna a small pouch, expressing the King's gratitude for having played this evening. Quickly, we packed up everything and exited the side door. A guard was there to make sure we found the exit, or so he said. I knew better; he was just being polite.

As we walked back to the inn, I commented, "I see what you mean, Fergus. That was very boring. I was high when we finished playing at the inn, but this is such a letdown, you know. I much prefer playing for the common people."

"Aye, lassie, I knew you would see it my way. After all, you are musicians. However, there is a side benefit to playing for the king. Did you look in that pouch, Fianna dear?" She hadn't.

We stopped while she opened the heavy pouch. Her eyes nearly popped out of her head as she spread out twenty-five gold coins into the palm of her hand! For once, she could say nothing. She had no words. Fergus said it all, "The King pays well for services rendered." Once again, Fergus would take no money, but said, "Tonight, I'll let you buy the round of ale." We did.

After taking a slurp of ale, Fergus asked, "So tomorrow you are off once more, I take it? Heading north still? Lots more towns up there and two more kings, if you are lucky."

"Yes, yes, we are, Fergus," Fianna replied with a sigh. I knew she was already pining over the eminent departure of Fergus.

Over my ale mug, I looked Fergus straight in his eyes. "Fergus, what are the odds that when we get to the next larger town that we'll look up and there you'll be instruments at hand?"

He roared, before saying, "Probably an absolute certainty, lassie." Fianna grinned unable to conceal how that pronouncement pleased her. "I've never had so much fun making music ever before. I don't want it to end, if the truth be said."

"Well then, since we can't keep you from us, I shall have to ask you to join us, at least for a while. Will you?" I asked. Fianna thought that I would never get around to asking him.

"I thought you'd never ask. Yes, yes gladly. I'll not be a bother, honestly I won't. I don't need any funds, so you may keep all that is earned."

Cal was smiling broadly as well, so I knew I had everyone's agreement to add Fergus to our troupe, at least temporarily. "Fergus, I should be straight and up front with you right from the start. Our plans are to visit the towns on up to Ruthcroghan before angling down the east coast, past the Lir River and into Moyrath. Once there, we intend to find a way to cross over to the mainland. We all are going to travel all over the mainland, learning local songs and playing our way, real troubadours, if you please. We hope to be on the mainland before winter comes. So you can leave us anytime you want. If you don't want to go any further than the end of the highlands, we understand. This is your home. We can't ask you to become vagabonds as we are." There, I had said it all. He could leave when he felt like it.

Once again, I had totally underestimated a man. He slapped himself in the face as if he could not believe this was real. "Eureka! Pay dirt! Such unbelievable luck! I have to be the luckiest man in all Cymry! This is fantastic. Unreal. No one will believe it. Hurray! Hurray for me! Whoopee!" He was standing and jumping wildly around, causing everyone in the inn to look our way, embarrassing me to no end.

"What on Tarra is the matter with you?" Fianna finally asked in her stern, older sister voice.

Fergus sat down and drank the entire mug of ale in one continuous gulp before signaling for a refill and speaking. "Five years! Would you believe five years!"

"What *are* you talking about, Fergus?" pleaded Fianna. None of us could make any sense of his pronouncement.

He belched, excused himself, and began once more, "For the last five years, I have been trying to find other musicians who would join me in traveling around the mainland, learning their songs, and entertaining the local people, not royalty mind you. I don't like playing for the king. After tonight, you have seen what that is like. In five years of searching, I have never found one musician who wanted to join me and do this. And tonight, I am asked to join your troupe and do precisely what I have been attempting to do for five years! It must be a miracle. All praise to Jehosa and the Blessed Holy Mother! I'm the happiest man in the world. Besides, I have really enjoyed being with you, Fianna. You are very special. Not that you aren't too, Bethany," he quickly added, thinking he might have offended me and then further added, "Nor you, Cal." Now he looked rather embarrassed himself.

Cal came to my rescue, "We know, Fergus. A man cannot hide his passion for a woman from observant eyes, right Bethany?" Cal winked knowingly at me. Suddenly, my face flushed. Did I detect a hint of flirting from Cal towards me? I was only pretending to be a young woman, oops, a woman. Cal would be thinking of me as a woman! My face grew very hot indeed. I slurped away at my ale. I had to say something to change the topic fast!

"Fianna does like you too, Fergus. However, we're all set to continue our trek. Do you need some time to get your affairs in order so you may accompany us to the mainland?" There, I had cleverly shifted the topic away from romance.

"Aye, lassie, a few days at most, though. If you ride north and play in each village, I'll catch up with you just as fast as I can, couple of days at most. I don't know how to thank you all properly."

"You already have," I acknowledged. "You have taken your time to teach us the songs of the highlands, accompany us, and even lead us through our first gig for a king. That is more than enough thanks, Fergus."

"Right then, I should be off. Say, is there anything that you need that I might be able to bring with me?" he asked.

I could think of nothing, but Cal answered. "Are you a big eater? Food, I mean. Bethany eats about twice what Fianna and I do." My face flushed. I was a growing boy, I justified; no one noticed me, thankfully. "We need to resupply our food stores a bit, so it would be helpful if we knew how much to get for you and what you like to eat?" I wondered why I hadn't thought of this detail and that Cal had? Did I really eat that much? Well, I'm still growing, I continued to rationalize.

"I've not thought about it. I just eat. Guess you can say moderate. Love ham when you can get it. Honestly, I'll make due with whatever you have. Not a problem. I've never given much thought to acquiring food supplies for a trip. I guess you can tell I've never gotten to the planning stage in my attempts to get to the mainland and travel."

With that, he gave Fianna a solid hug and was off. He was so excited that he wouldn't even wait for daylight to get started on his errands. For a moment, I wondered where he would have to go, what his parents would say, and what he might have to arrange. Cal brought me back into reality with his exuberant, heartfelt words, "Well, we certainly struck a chord with Fergus. The Holy Blessed Mother must be looking over us! He makes a terrific addition to the group, don't you think, Bethany?" Cal smiled my way.

Was he flirting with me again? I couldn't really tell. I knew my face was slightly warm, but I replied, "Yes, we have. He adds so much depth to our overall sound! We are indeed very lucky."

"True," Cal commented. "I'll wager anything that he is sort of a 'man about the world' — you know, a man of experience, who knows things that we don't. I bet he is a much better fighter than I am and can protect us all far better than I can."

"Well, he's already proven that several times over, I mean helping us out of tight situations. I can't tell about the fighting, though. His sword certainly is twice the size of yours, and he is more stoutly built than you are, Cal. No offence, Cal; you are just younger, and your body is still growing into manhood." I tried to be polite about it.

"Hey, you'll get no protest on that account from me, Bethany," Cal chuckled and changed the topic. "But we ought to head to our rooms. Tomorrow we must spend some of our funds on food supplies before we get going." He got no argument from us, and we headed off to our rooms.

In our room, while brushing out Fianna's hair, she felt like talking. "Golly, I'm sure that Fergus really likes me, don't you? He seems like such a nice fellow. I wonder what his family will say when they hear that he is going off to the mainland with troubadours? Do you suppose that his family will approve of troubadours?" I agreed with her mostly and we chatted some more.

"Say, you know tonight, I got the impression that Cal really likes you, Bethany!" Suddenly, she clasped her hand to her mouth, realizing what she was saying and its implications. "Oh my, I forgot, Cal thinks you are a young woman! Oh, dear, Bethany! Whatever will you do? I feel so badly for Cal. Maybe I can tell him that you are still too young to be taking romance seriously," she declared.

I finished brushing out her hair, so she began to do mine. "I felt really awful tonight, sis. I thought he might just be flirting with me; at least he was paying close attention to me, more so than normal. Just between you and me, I sometimes get so confused. Until now, I would always be looking at young men, like you, and Cal is rather handsome, in a youthful sort of way, but I've got a male body for the first time. I just get so utterly confused at times that I don't know what to say or do, like tonight. All I could do was change the topic and hope for the best. Once we get safely to the mainland, I can drop my disguise and be honest with everyone. But until then, it's not safe to do so. I have to maintain the guise of being a young woman. I feel so awful leading Cal on like this. I'm trying hard to ignore him. Mostly, I think I'm not giving him any reason to flirt with me, you think so?"

"You sure do have one huge problem, I will say that. I don't know that I could cope with it all. Maybe we should just hurry it up a bit, try to get to the mainland soon. That would help a lot, right?"

"You have a good idea, sis. When we all get together, I'll see what they think of hastening it a bit, but you didn't answer me. Am I somehow giving Cal the wrong kind of signs?"

She bit down on her lip for a moment, "No, not really. I think that it is more the circumstances. You know, what with Fergus taking a liking to me, it rather puts Cal on the spot, so to speak, to at least make some attempt with you, so that you do not feel left out."

"Thanks, it is so hard for me. I always before had close girl friends with whom to discuss these things. Originally, when I was in the Greenway, I knew absolutely nothing about boys and love and all that. It took one of my girlfriends to point out to me that I was suffering from love and that Roy was in love with me and I, he. I was that ignorant. Even last lifetime, I had close friends with whom I could rely on to help me. Now this time, I've only got you, sis. I hate to be putting such heavy problems on you, though. You probably think I'm nuts or something."

She giggled and replied in her no nonsense, learned manner, "No silly. I'm your big sister. I've always been looking out for you ever since you were a little baby. I think I changed your diapers more times than mom did." I flushed. She ignored that and continued. "Cal seems still very young and shy, a bit nervous around women. He's only just now growing into manhood, I expect, so he probably doesn't quite know how to handle women either. He's probably just as confused as you are with him. I mean, only in a different way that is. I promise I will let you know if you are doing something that might tend to suggest to Cal that you are interested in him, okay?"

I thanked her and we turned in for the night. However, I slept poorly, having nightmares about men kissing me, thinking me a woman, only to suddenly discover I was male. Frightfully embarrassing nightmares! I'd see the shocked, startled, humiliated face of Cal as he discovered that I didn't have a female body, that I wasn't the woman of his dreams. Three times I woke up in a startled sweat; three times I cooled off and tried to go back to sleep.

Finally, just as my body finally relaxed into sleep without a nightmare, something that Fergus had innocently said flashed in my mind. "All praise to Jehosa and the Blessed Holy Mother! I'm the happiest man in the world." I sat bolt upright, all sleep gone from my eyes, all fog from my mind. *This is weird, strange indeed! He looks like he is a native of the highlands. He speaks like one, dresses like one, knows about the highlands, knows their music and their kings, so he must be from the highlands, but, a really big but — why didn't I see this at once! Bethany, you are failing to use your most fundamental druwid skill: observe the obvious!* The natives of this island worship what they call the One God. They call themselves Annwn, the spiritual children of the One God now inhabiting a fleshly body. Their goal is to seek spiritual purity to gain their lost kingdom called Gwynfyd. In Layamon, their very clothes encompass their spirituality with embroidered ornate and colorful knots, circles intertwining, and such. Each person has a design that is unique to their spiritual self. In Tewdwr, the designs were more subdued, perhaps because of the continuous cloudy days and fog. Here in the highlands, plaids ruled, but still, their shirts carried the telltale, but small, embroidered designs of swirls, intertwined ropes, and knots.

No, it was we, Jes, Josh, and I, who brought the religion of Jehosa to Cymry. After Jes departed, I carried on his and my spiritual teachings, while Josh preached his views, which, I admit, were closer to their basic religious beliefs from Juda Arad. Somehow, after my departure from the scene, I had become known as the Blessed Holy Mother, whatever connotations that may have. "What Fergus said does not make sense!"

Fianna rolled over, half awake, and mumbled, "What doesn't make sense? Are you still awake?"

"Fergus. Remember how excited he was when he found out that we intended to go to the mainland. He said, 'All praise to Jehosa and the Blessed Holy Mother!' Not all praise to the One God or the Annwn or Gwynfyd. He specifically referred to the religion we brought here, Jehosanity and the wife of the Great Messiah."

"So, what of it? I don't see anything sinister about it," she commented, rubbing the sleep from her eyes, preparing to defend Fergus.

"Oh, nothing sinister, not like that at all. It's just not quite what I would have expected. Perhaps Jehosanity has spread further north in the last decade. Yet, we haven't seen any of their churches in the towns and villages, only those of the One God. Why would Fergus be a follower of Jehosa? That's what troubles me. I think there is more to Fergus than he is letting on to us."

"Is that all? Go back to sleep!" She laid back down and pulled the covers over her head.

I tried to lie back down, but my mind kept racing down avenues of speculation. Once more, some insignificant detail popped into view. Cal! After Fergus had left, he was very excited about Fergus joining us. He'd said, "The Holy Blessed Mother must be looking over us!" What a strange thing for a man to say. It probably was a slip of the tongue, but he must place great weight on this alternate view of Jehosanity that I had begun last lifetime. Once again, this detail didn't match at all. Certainly, Cal must be from the Layamon region, though I had never heard of the village that he said he came from. Then again, I didn't know all the villages in the regions, far from it. Either the religion I preached had somehow reached his village during these years or he was not from where he said he was from. Now I had two mysteries on my hands! I fell asleep in total frustration.

The next day, I was in an irritable mood from lack of sleep and fretting all night. Cleverly, Fianna passed off to Cal, "It's the wrong time of the month for her." Cal flushed and accepted that as a reasonable explanation. Well, it at least added to my disguise, and I was more than glad to let those two do the shopping for our supplies. I merely watched over our horses and gear. Finally, we mounted up and rode out of Dunedun. I rode out in front, leaving Cal and Fianna following behind, still chatting about all the shops.

A fair number of wagons and people, both on foot and horseback, passed us during the day. By nightfall, we had arrived at another small village, which only had one small inn. Already, the villagers were in the inn being entertained by their own local musicians. Hence, this time, we paid for a night's lodging and arranged to play for them the next night. Surprisingly, the innkeeper had already heard about the Cymry Minstrels. Evidently, word spreads fast in the highlands. He even knew that we had played for the King and was more than willing to meet our price of lodging.

The next day seemed to drag on, not only for me, but also for Fianna — however, for different reasons. Yes, she missed the smiling, cheery face of

Fergus. When the time for us to play came, after the first song, all my melancholia faded away. We were making music once more, playing to folks who really enjoyed our performance. Afterwards, I slept like a rock and was back to normal the next day as we rode on northward toward the next village.

Late that afternoon, I heard galloping horses coming up towards us from our rear. Naturally, everyone was slightly worried, so I moved us off the road to a more defensible position. Brave Cal, drew his short sword and stood in front of we girls. I held onto the five horses, not trusting that to Fianna. Shortly, Fergus came galloping into view, leading a packhorse brimming with bags and sacks of various sizes, all bulging. "Fergus!" We cheered. Okay, I cheered as well. Can I say from relief it was nothing threatening? (You don't have to believe that if you don't want to.)

"You came loaded down!" Fianna commented as she gave him a welcoming hug, once he had dismounted.

"Aye, lassie, I brought all my instruments. Didn't realize I had accumulated so many of them. I figure you, Fianna dear, might be able to make use of some of these. I'll show you when we next practice."

"Wonderful! Thanks, Fergus," she bubbled.

"Well, what now?" I asked. "You know the highlands. Should we press on to the next village or is there somewhere up ahead where we might camp?"

"Well, lassie, it all depends upon what you think we should do first. I was thinking perhaps it might be a good idea for us to hole up somewhere for a few days, and I can show you the instruments, and we can see how to work them into our music, without having an audience listening in to all our goofs. On the other hand, if you think we need to keep moving north, we can do all this perhaps at the next inn we play."

Cal added, "Well, I know some more Layamon tunes that we could learn, you know, expand our repertoire further. I'm for spending a few days without any pressure so we can learn new things before we get back to entertaining."

"I've been thinking too," I took charge. "I think that I would like to speed up our journey in order to get to the mainland sooner. Are any of you opposed to heading to the mainland sooner?"

Cal grinned broadly, "Absolutely not! The sooner, the better as far as I'm concerned."

"Same here!" Fergus added.

Somehow, I wasn't too surprised that there was no resistance to leaving Cymry sooner than planned. "Okay, then in that case, I think Fergus is right. We need to take a few days off, somewhere quiet where we can experiment, learn new songs and such. Once we're comfortable with everything, and then let's get going northward, playing only here and there. Perhaps, Fergus can give us some good ideas which towns and villages we should play."

"Great, lassie, perfect. I know just the place where we can spend a few days. Not too far from here lie some ancient ruins. No one lives anywhere around there, great place to camp." That decided, I let Fergus lead the way.

We rode on up the road for a few miles before turning off onto a barely visible side track. For a few miles, it twisted and turned circumscribing its way around the more treacherous bogs that lay in the dips of the stony hills. At last, all trace of normal travel along the track vanished from my sight. I surmised that there probably were isolated homes out here in the highlands, but where we were going was really off the beaten track, so to speak. Still, I could tell that we were following a track that had been well used, but a long, long time ago.

The sun hung red as it began sinking below the rim of the Ath range to our west. "Here we are," called out Fergus, as we entered a secluded valley. I wasn't prepared for what my eyes took in! In the center of a small, rocky valley stood seven standing stones, just like our druwid standing stone circles! In fact, I could see no difference between this one and all those I had visited in the Greenway. We druwids come to the standing circles to celebrate the coming of spring and fall, holding our ceremonies at sunset. What was a druwid circle doing here in the highlands of West Reach? It had been abandoned ages ago, I could see no signs of recent celebrations on the grounds around the circle. Just what I needed right now, another mystery!

Fergus called out, "Follow me, there is something of a shelter where we can stay up here at the edge of the hollow." We rode a short distance and the shell of a home stood, dark and still. Roughly thirty feet square, the grey stone walls still stood tall and proud. The thatched roof had long ago disintegrated. However, part of the flooring of the second floor still stood. Underneath that, we made camp. I spied the remains of a campsite. Fergus noticed me observing it, and said, "Mine, I'm guilty. I used to camp up here when I was a wee lad. Haven't been here for several years, though. You like the place? Gets kind of spooky at night, what with those weird stones standing there, like dead trees or specters."

"I think it is perfect, Fergus. Well done," I complimented him. As we began unpacking everything, I asked him, "Say, do you know anything about this place? Who put the stones there?"

"Down in Kael, that's the nearest village about seven miles from here, they tell ghost stories about seeing strange people up here dancing in the moonlight. Near as I could tell, that story has been handed down for generations. No one really knows for sure, I'll wager. No one ever comes here; locals claim it is haunted, but I've camped here a number of times and have never seen anything at all out of the ordinary. It's perfectly safe, I'm sure."

We made camp; the men went for wood, while Fianna and I prepared dinner and got the place ordered. I was very glad that we had brought several lanterns with us. After eating and chatting, we all turned in early; no sense in wasting our lantern oil.

The next day, Fergus brought out all of his instruments. We'd already seen several of them. "These are for you, Fianna. They're called castanets. They were imported all the way from somewhere called Vito. I think that is part of the Sea Princes. They are like two hollow blocks. You put them in your hands like this. Now using your fingers, click the haves together." She did and we heard the most intriguing clapping sound we'd ever heard. "As you dance and twirl, why clap your fingers to the rhythm and you'll add a unique flavor to the music. You'll be a part of the total sound!" The castanets became an instant hit with Fianna!

He also had several more wind-capped reed instruments that took a good deal of breath pressure to play. He had a small sized guitar, which played notes in a higher register than my guitar did. Ten different types of drums he laid out in an array. Thus, different ones could be used by any of us to add a different accent to the music. "I even got one that I just cannot play. I brought it along just in case you might be able to manage it, Bethany. Here give it a try." Gently he assembled the longest, largest flute I had ever seen. "It's called a bass flute. Makes the mellowest sounds, only my fingers are too short to reach the holes properly. Give it a try."

I fell in love with it after blowing only one note! Haunting, mellow, you just have to hear the thing play. I noticed that my fingers were somewhat longer than Fergus's. Still, I had to stretch them to their limit, but I could finally manage covering them all and played the most sonorous, low mellow note that I had ever heard come from a flute!

"Wow, all praise to the Blessed Holy Mother!" exclaimed Cal, unable to contain his excitement and awe at this most enthralling new sound. "Now that sound will really add something fantastic to our laments! Way to go, Bethany!" He leaned over as if he were going to give me a spontaneous hug, but his face flushed, and he quickly cleared his throat instead.

"Wow, this is really a find, Fergus! I'll definitely practice like mad on this one; it has so many possibilities! Thanks!"

We camped here for a week, spending long days teaching each other new songs and learning the new instruments. Fergus also knew several new dances that we had never seen. One he called the Crossed Swords Dance. He put two thin swords on the ground, blades crossed. The dancer then did various steps into and out of the four quadrants. Fianna spent three days mastering this new dance. Fergus claimed it was one of the most sacred and traditional dances of the highlands.

The only real difficulty we had camping here was that the only source of water lay a quarter mile away, close to a bog. Hence, it became the men's daily chore to hike there and bring back several buckets for our use. Since they did this chore, I handled the scouring for and fetching of the firewood. We were all glad that we had just gone shopping for more food supplies when we had.

Finally, once we were all satisfied with our practicing, we discussed our next moves, relying upon Fergus to provide the needed insight. There were three more large towns like Dunedun directly between us and the rocky barrens of Ruthcroghan, where we intended to veer to the east and then back southward. Hopefully, somewhere below the Lir River in Moyrath we could book passage to the mainland. "A king or duke controls each of these towns, so you have the option of trying to play for them as you did for King Ross and make a bit of money. Or we could just play for the entertainment of the larger inns there, passing through the smaller villages along the way."

"I guess the critical thing to ask is this," I offered. "Does anyone know what it will cost for us to book passage to the mainland? Certainly, we cannot take the horses, so we will have to sell them in the port town and can use those funds to help pay for our passage. Does anyone have any idea how much we can get for our horses and their saddles?"

Cal looked downcast and poked aimlessly at the campfire. He had no idea at all. Silence fell for a moment, before Fergus spoke up. "Don't know about the passage, but I can make an estimate of our horses. Let's see, my two will probably fetch at least fifty each; Cal's, forty; your four, maybe thirty each. That's around two hundred seventy all told."

"Wow, two hundred seventy copper pieces is quite a lot," Fianna exclaimed rather excited about the financial aspects.

"Er, no, my fair lassie, gold pieces," Fergus corrected her. Fianna's mouth gaped; no words came out. Such a sum was unbelievable for her. I knew we had never seen that kind of money. "Surely, it shouldn't cost more than fifty gold pieces for a ship to take us the short distance to the mainland," he added.

Cal added, "If it does cost more than our coffers have, I do have some money of my own I'm willing to donate to the cause. It's my emergency fund."

Not to be left out, Fergus added, "Me too. I've got a tidy sum tucked away, like he says, for emergencies. So my fair lassies, we shouldn't have a problem paying for passage. The real problem will be finding a boat. Finding one would be easy if we went down south to Bregia. That's the main port of call, I'm told, of the mariners who trade with Cymry."

"Oh no! We can't go down there! Not now, anyway," Cal interrupted, his voice rather shrill and full of genuine fear. "There is a big war going on in southern Layamon. I refuse to set foot there. There must be another way, please."

"Not to worry, laddie. I've no hankering to enter a war zone myself. Besides, we don't want to endanger our lassies here, now do we?" he slapped Cal on his back and winked at him. Cal relaxed a bit.

"That's why I chose this route in the first place," I explained. Of course, there are no ports of any kind where an ocean going ship could dock anywhere in Tewdwr; Layamon is totally out. That leaves the western shores as our best hope. However, I know next to nothing about Moyrath, save the Axemen are fond of raiding there."

"Aye, lassie, they raid for the virgin tall trees there. I'm told they use them for their ships. Funny thing, we're supplying them with the timber to make their boats with which they then use to raid us." We all laughed at the irony of it all. He added, "I've heard that the Axemen haven't been raiding here as much as they used to."

"We have to pass through the Dark Forest first. I've been to its edge once," Fergus explained. "Dense woods, tall trees, very little light reaches the ground. Lots of moss grows on the ground, though. Few live there, mostly loggers. Across the Lir, there are many farmers and some loggers as well, lots more people and towns as well. I've heard that they do ship logs and grain down south to Bregia. Perhaps there is hope that we can find a ship there to take us to the mainland. Good plan, Bethany."

I reached a decision, "Okay then. We all want to get to the mainland soonest. None of us really wants to play for kings, and we don't likely need the funds we might get for doing so. Let's travel more quickly, stop, and play only at the larger towns, where we can also replenish our supplies. Once we reach Ruthcroghan, we veer east and then south to the Lir. Once in Moyrath, we head for the coast and travel down it, looking for a port and a ship to the mainland. Sound okay?"

"Aye lassie, but why go all that extra distance up north? We are about even with the headwaters of the Lir in the highlands right now. We could just head east to the coast and then head on down Moyrath. It would save us days," Fergus wondered.

Curses! Once more, I was on the spot with my friends. I sighed and began, "We have a motto in our group. Don't ask how or why of each other. I'm afraid I have to ask you not to ask me how or why. In reality, I'm making this whole trip for another reason. I'm looking for a very dear, old friend, who I'm sworn to find and render all possible assistance to him, once I find him. All that I know is he is in dire trouble and is located somewhere on Tarra, and not at any place I have thus far been around. Not in Tewdwr, nor Layamon, nor thus far in the highlands of Ruadan. He could be absolutely anywhere, so I have to travel everywhere in search of him."

"Wow. You are only fourteen. I don't understand, Bethany, but I'll respect your admonition. Does he have a name? Could we help you?" Fergus asked.

"Honestly, I don't know what his name is now or even whether he now has a male or female body. But I swear to you all, I'll know him instantly when I find him. Helping him is perhaps the most important thing any of us can do."

Fergus let out a nervous laugh, "I'm afraid I understand you less the more you say, Bethany. I consider that I'm your friend, dedicated to protecting you and your sister from harm in our travels. Could you not find it in your heart to explain all this a little better that I may not be so confused about it all, please dear lassie?"

"Oh, all right, but not without a cup of tea at hand," I relented. My friends deserved a better explanation, even if it seemed wild and crazy to them. Fianna jumped at the chance to make the tea, thankfully. A while later, hot teacup in hand, I launched into an explanation.

"What I am about to say you may not believe. I would have spared you all this, if I could have." Cal and Fergus were more than eager to hear my tale, looking intently at me, occasionally sipping their tea. "We are all immortal spiritual beings which for a time inhabit these fleshly bodies. The cycle of life here on Tarra is birth, growth, decay, and then death, but that is the cycle of the fleshly bodies, not us. We are immortal. For a time, then, we inhabit these bodies and when they die, we move on to another baby body and begin the cycle over once more."

Cal interjected, "Gosh, you sound just like the priests back home speak of the Holy Blessed Mother."

"Or Jehosanity, for that matter," Fergus added.

Fianna declared in her take-charge voice, hoping to bolster my argument with the tiny bit with which she could relate, "Well, I had an old fisherman's body last life and it drowned in the ocean. That's why I was afraid of the water when I was a little girl, that is, until my dad taught me to swim. Now it doesn't bother me anymore." Her tale gave me a breather so I could work out what to say next, without giving too much away.

"Since I came to Tarra, I can recall who I have been and all that I have learned. This is my third fleshly body. That is why I know so many languages, since I've not forgotten those that I used to know. This will become a great asset to us once we hit the mainland. I can speak in most of the local languages we are likely to encounter, and I can teach you too." Everyone chatted about this most fortunate turn of events. Indeed, Fergus had given some thought to the language barrier and was very much impressed that language would not be the huge problem he had anticipated.

I went on, "I have learned a great deal during these different lifetimes. You look at me and see a very young girl. But I say to you, I am me and I still know and can do all the things that I have ever been able to do. I have not forgotten them. Looks can be deceiving," I added that bit for Cal's benefit, hoping to soften the blow whenever it came, when he would find out that I was not a young girl but a young man.

Now I had to be very careful in what I relayed. "On Tarra, there are a few very rare people who are powerful and extremely vital. No, I don't mean kings, people far more important and powerful than that. One of these is my dear mentor and friend who I hold in the highest respect. He died trying to do something I begged him to do to help me out, even when I and he both knew it was hopeless even to try. He was, shall I say, killed in the attempt, and I promised him that if he didn't contact me, I would come looking for him, because he would be in dire peril with his new body. Already, we are long overdue to make contact with each other as promised. Hence, I know in my heart and mind, he is in grave danger, and I must find him and help him. It is the most important thing that I ever do."

Fergus was no dummy; he thought for a moment, and asked, "You mentioned contact. You and he were supposed to make contact a long time ago. Considering all you have said, you must not mean contact, such as we are doing right here around the campfire. If so, I don't understand you. How is such possible? If you can answer this, I will be satisfied with your explanation, though I detect that there is much that you are not telling us."

"You are absolutely right; much I am not telling you, for your own safety, in part. You are my dearest friends. I don't want harm to befall you because of me. Remember, the motto of our group is don't ask, don't pry." Both Cal and Fergus flushed slightly, so I know that my pronouncement affected them. "You both deserve that answer. Promise me that you will tell no one about what happens next here tonight."

Both eagerly did so. "You want to know how we can make contact with each other, how I can find him, here is how." I closed my eyes, and expanded my awareness slightly, encompassing all three of them, and made contact with their minds. I resisted the temptation to pry, sticking to our motto of don't ask. Instead, I placed a thought into all thee minds simultaneously: *Thank you for coming along. You are a great musician and dancer. You are my dearest friends.* I opened my eyes to observe their reactions.

Cal's eyes nearly popped out of his head; he muttered, "Holy Blessed Mother!"

Fergus reacted similarly with shock and surprise illuminating his face in the flickering firelight. "Are you a goddess?" he finally managed to mutter.

"Most definitely not! God, there have been times that I wished I was! No, I spent ten long hard years studying all day and far into the night to learn how to do this skill. It is a learnable skill. Given enough time and training, probably all of you could master it, but it would take years and years of practice under the tutelage of someone who knew how to do this."

Cal's face reddened slightly, "Can, can you read other people's minds, their thoughts too?"

I looked straight at Cal, "Yes, Cal, I can, but please don't worry. I too am bound by our agreement in this group: don't ask. I swear to you that your secrets, your innermost thoughts, are yours alone. I will never ever pry, just as I count on your never pressing me beyond what I feel is safe to say." I looked over at Fergus, "Same with you, Fergus."

"Look, if you believe what I have said tonight, then you are wiser than most priests and priestesses. I believe in my heart that truth always sets men free. Okay," I added to give them a bit more reassurance, "when we are safely on the mainland, I will reveal much more to you — things which might prove deadly to you should you know them while we are still here on Cymry."

Fergus grinned finally and relaxed, hopeful of that prospect, "I'll hold you to that one, lassie. Never have I been more curious about a person than I am of you! Til then, I am behind you one hundred percent. You have my word."

"Mine too," Cal offered meekly, still awed by the experience.

Good old Fianna livened up the seriousness, "Now isn't that *the* most intimate thing — her talking directly into your mind? Golly, I would sure love to be able to do that!"

Fergus roared, "You have a way with words, dear lassie!" He laughed even harder.

"So seriously fellows, I must search the rest of Cymry before I head for the mainland. It doesn't take me long to do my search. I usually do it at night just before I go to bed."

Fergus then suggested, "Okay, lassie. Here's my suggestion. Keefe is the last large town before the rocky barrens. We should head for there at a good clip, and pick up a good deal of supplies while we are there. I've no idea what we will find in the way of towns in the Dark Forest. We don't want to starve en route. Shall we get started on the morrow?"

Chapter 6 The Dark Forest Disaster

During the first week of August, we halted and stared out onto the start of the northernmost portion of Cymry, the rocky barrens known as Ruthcroghan. We had made good time traveling through the northern half of the highlands. I frequently wished that we had not decided to be in such a hurry! The northern half of Ruadan was indeed spectacular! It was a land of innumerable lakes and streams cradled amid the rolling, rocky hills. Under different circumstances, I would have loved to spend months here sightseeing the wonders. True, I suspected life was a bit on the harsh side here, especially in the wintertime. The gorgeous scenery more than made up for it, I concluded.

However, the rocky barrens were just that, an uninhabitable, windswept land that stretched some thirty miles to the ocean. Here no dirt covered the land, no trees grew, no sign of animals or living creatures, save field mice. Grey, barren, virgin rock carved by the hands of Nature stretched out before us, undulating slowly toward the distant ocean. A strong easterly breeze blew nearly continuously, according to Fergus, who had once been here. Yes, it was definitely a sight worth seeing and perhaps spending a few days in exploration, but that was all. Fergus explained that in winter, the entire land would be heavily covered with a blanket of snow, inhospitable, for sure. Also, I detected no sign of Alabaster either in the highlands or here. With three quarters of the island checked thoroughly, only the most unknown portions remained.

We now veered nearly due eastward and entered the Dark Forest. The first day, our easterly path dropped steadily downward from the highlands. Rocky boulder fields slowly gave way to stands of deciduous trees and conifers. At first, the trees were somewhat stunted, broad but not tall. From the directional pattern of their branches, I suspected that they were windswept, particularly in the winter. However, by the second day everything changed as we entered the Dark Forest proper.

Here the trees grew tall and dense. Almost at once, we had to dismount and lead the horses. There were just too many branches to duck and dodge while riding, besides, one could not travel in a straight line — dense trees and surprise giant boulders made any direct progress impossible unless perhaps one was a bird. Birds — the forest echoed with birdcalls. Jays, buntings, cardinals, robins, and a multitude of songbirds chirped their carefree songs.

However, the Dark Forest was also a bit forbidding. Little sunlight reached the forest floor, densely matted with decades of fallen leaves and pine needles. Green moss predominated, growing nearly everywhere, even up the sides of some trees. The air carried a faint odor of decay. Often we would stumble into a log only to have the rotted log crumble from our touch. Yet it was the quiet that I found most intriguing, save for the birds, no sounds could be heard. Even our footfalls and those of our horses were totally muffled in this land. Eerie was Fianna's description of the Dark Forest; she kept expecting something bad to happen to us at any minute. Perhaps, I ought to have listened to her. All this time, we barely talked to one another and then only in whispered voices. Such was the impression the Dark Forest had on us.

The third day we attempted to veer to the southeast, hoping to hit the Lir and follow it down to the coast. Both Fergus and I agreed on our current position and where we approximately desired to go. Around noon, we heard the distant noise of people chopping on trees, an unexpected sound out here in the middle of nowhere. "I wonder who that is?" whispered Fergus. "Perhaps, we should sneak up towards it and see; it's probably just some loggers from Moyrath. But then again, it could mean trouble for us; if so, I would like to avoid it." I concurred and we stealthily moved toward the makers of the noise. In hindsight, whether we took this action would have made no difference in what happened a short while later.

We had to walk about a mile to get near enough to the supposed loggers. Steadily the noise grew louder until I whispered, "It can't be just one logger, gotta be a whole herd of them. I heard hammer on wood too, perhaps metal. What can be going on ahead?" A few minutes later, we caught a glimpse of people moving about, so we halted. I had Fianna and Cal hold the horses, while Fergus and I snuck forward for a better look. We were certain these people did not spotted us.

Axemen! Not just a few, either. There was an entire town of Axemen right here on our own island! Burly men, the smallest weighing in at least one hundred eighty pounds with bulging arms and legs, these were the Axemen from the far north of Volksholm. Images of the Axemen raiders that I had helped fight a decade or so ago back in Bregia when we first arrived on this island came back to mind. These men hadn't changed their appearance in all this time, rugged individuals, strong and hardy. However, I also saw a fair number of their women folk, equally big women, every bit as hardy as their men.

Fergus looked positively stunned. He just stared in total disbelief at this unsuspected enemy town right here in the heart of our own Dark Forest! I signaled that we should retreat; even more carefully, we backed up and joined the others, whispering, "An entire Axeman town is just ahead. We have to get out of here as fast and quietly as possible!" Both Fianna and Cal looked stunned by the unexpected news. Hastily, with Fergus in the lead, we pushed on through the woods, still keeping approximately to our original course.

Fergus drew out his shiny broadsword, just in case. Seeing him make this move, Cal hesitatingly drew his short sword dagger and moved up in just behind Fergus. Obviously, the men were making a show of protecting us women, so I fell back in front of Fianna, who brought up the rear. We had not gone but a quarter mile or so, weaving in and out of the dense trees, when suddenly without warning we spied a small group of Axemen scouts. I cursed myself for not having had the sense to expect just this; scouts out along the perimeter of their town would be a highly logical move.

The six Axemen spied us just as we spied them, about three hundred feet away, off to our left. The Axemen didn't hesitate for a split second. These must have been very skilled, highly trained scouts. From their instantaneous reaction, I knew what their orders must be: allow no one to discover their presence. I knew they intended to slay us so their secret town went undiscovered. Before we could really react, a flight of arrows came at us.

From the corner of my eye, I saw one hit Cal in his chest. We all heard the sickening thud as it struck his body. Another arrow narrowly missed Fergus, who had taken another step in the direction we had been going. Four arrows came at Fianna and me. My training, long unused, came back to me in an instant. I dodged one arrow, deflected another that was heading toward my sister, and caught another arrow that would have pierced Fianna's chest, casually dropping the shaft on the ground. I was a bit too slow to deflect the fourth; it grazed my left shoulder slightly.

I took command during that brief instant while our attackers were preparing another set of arrows. "Fergus, you and Fianna take off that way running as fast as you can. I'll bring up the rear and help Cal. Take my horses and Cal's too."

Clumsily Fianna grabbed a hold of my two horses; though combined with her own, she struggled mightily. "But lassie," Fergus tried to protest, even as he involuntarily picked up Cal's blade and reins.

In that instant, I duplicated all that he wanted to say. *I'm supposed to be protecting you. Cal's badly hurt. They'll be shooting at you in a second. Let me bring up the rear.* "Help Fianna," I called out and turned to face the six archers, chanting as quickly as I could. There wasn't the slightest cloud in the sky, what tiny bit of it I could see. Lightning strikes were thus out. I couldn't risk using fire for fear of starting an enormous forest fire. That left only one action available, which was particularly well suited to the present situation. I conjured up a wall of ice, anchoring it sturdily between several trees. Wham! The next volley of arrows flew, and all struck and stuck in the nearly invisible wall of ice.

"What?" yelled Fergus in total disbelief.

"Run, you fool, run," I yelled and leaned over Cal's fallen body. Fergus, encouraged by Fianna's total fright, finally did as I asked. Cal was conscious and had seen the wall of ice stop the arrows; his eyes were filled with both intense pain and wonderment. The arrow protruded from the left side of his chest, just below the breast. I snapped the shaft, leaving enough for me to grab hold of later on when I had time to pull it out. "Can you walk?" I asked. Cal attempted to get to his feet, but faltered, nearly pulling me to the ground with him.

Shock was starting to set in, and I knew that even if I could get him to his feet, he would barely be able to stumble along. Only one option remained. I helped him back onto his feet and bent down. "I'll carry you. You keep watch behind us and let me know when they get too close or are about to shoot more arrows. That's your job. Watch my back." I hoisted him over my shoulder. Cal looked even more stunned and his hands pulled on my hair. "Ouch!" Quickly, he managed to slide his arms under my long hair, supporting himself on my back so that he could see. Carrying Cal, like a sack of potatoes, I followed Fergus and Fianna.

To my surprise, Cal seemed very light for a fifteen year old boy, either that or my male body was stronger than I had suspected. "They've chopped through the ice," Cal managed to utter, moaning in pain all the while. "They are stopping to shoot again."

I whirled around, chanting calmly. Presto, another wall of ice appeared, again anchored firmly between several trees. I turned around and followed Fergus, who was now only barely visible ahead. Carrying Cal, I just couldn't keep up with them, but that was fine with me, because Fianna was slowly escaping the danger.

A few minutes later, I was panting for breath. Cal had slowly become quite heavy or else I was tiring. Again, I had to throw up a wall of ice to slow our pursers down. "If only there was a cloud! There's never a cloud around when you need one," I muttered to myself. I felt Cal twisting around a bit, shifting the weight of my load, making my job even harder. I was about to ask him to hold still, when he said very weakly, "I saw a cloud overhead between the trees just now."

"Thank you Cal!" I exclaimed, halting and turning to face our attackers. I calmed my mind, reached for the clouds that I couldn't see, and found them. They were small cumulus clouds, probably the remnants of the storms, which must have drenched Tewdwr earlier today. However, I was huffing and puffing so badly, I couldn't concentrate sufficiently. "Gotta set you down for a moment." As gently as I could, I sat Cal back onto the ground. He could see the Axemen running our way, perhaps a hundred feet off at most, waving their axes as they closed for the kill. I took a deep breath and concentrated once more.

I pointed to the lead man, placing that nearly invisible line from him upwards to the cloud. Wham! A bolt of lightning arced down striking him and a nearby tree, sending him flying like a leaf in the wind. Wham! Wham! Two more met the same fate; two others had taken secondary wounds from flying pieces of bark from the trees that were also hit. The remaining Axeman halted and began to tend to his fallen comrades. I picked up Cal once more, but he now passed out completely. Fergus left an unmistakable trail for my keen eyes to follow. I had no idea how far ahead they were, but I just kept stumbling along as fast as I could.

In five minutes, I caught up to the pair. They had stopped, terribly worried that something had happened to me. Fianna had almost convinced Fergus that they had to go back for Cal and me, when I stumbled up to them, exhausted from carrying Cal. "Here, let me carry him. You look done in. How on Tarra you could carry him this far is beyond me! Well done, Bethany!" Graciously, I let Fergus take Cal from me.

"Five of the six are down. Lightning got them. Think we'll not be followed for a while. Gotta find some safe place to hold up. Follow me," I gasped between gulps of air. I took hold of four horses and led the way. If only I could find some defensible location and soon.

Fergus muttered, "Aye, I heard the thunder and wondered where the storm was at." He then became awfully silent.

Here was an ideal situation for a Circle's Loremaster. Had my old Loremaster, Thomas, been with me, he could have found us just such a place quickly, such is the knowledge and skill of Loremasters. I spied be beginnings of a valley on my left, on a hunch I headed on down it. Presently, the sides became steeper and I spotted some small caves, probably natural caves used by foxes to hibernate. This looked promising, so I continued down the valley. Defensively, if they returned in force, we would be sitting ducks downhill from them. Still I followed my hunch and female intuition, only I was not female, I reminded myself.

Five minutes later on, my hunch panned out. I spied a dark opening in the side of the valley. I halted, tied the horses, and went to inspect. Perfect, it was a natural cave sufficiently large to hide us all. "What now?" asked Fianna, when she caught up to me. She had been going slower, watching out for Fergus, who brought up the rear. I noticed that he too was now huffing and puffing under the load of Cal.

"In here, get some lanterns going. Look out for snakes and critters, sis." She and I hastily got two lanterns started, and we crept inside, followed shortly by Fergus, who had laid Cal gently down just outside. We flushed several mice, and there were hundreds of bats clinging to the ceiling, but we could all fit in here. "Okay, bring in the horses and Cal. I have to go back and hide our trail. If they try to follow us, I don't want them to find our obvious trail. See if you can get some water boiling by the time I get back, so I can work on Cal."

"But, lassie," Fergus again tried to protest.

"No but's, just do it. Leave Cal to me, back shortly," I ordered and left. Fianna knew better than not follow my orders, and she set Fergus to work, scrambling around just outside the cavern for wood.

I backtracked a mile and laid down another trail that appeared to lead around the entrance to the valley. Then, I retraced our well-worn path to the cavern, obscuring all traces of our passage as best I could. Again, this would have been a perfect task for a Loremaster, but I had no Circle.

About a half hour passed before I ducked inside the cavern and joined the others. Fianna had a campfire going and our kettle boiling away. I fetched my admittedly minuscule pouch of healing items and knelt down beside Cal, who had regained consciousness. I didn't know whether Fergus was squeamish or not, so I ordered, "Fergus, you and Fianna go to the entrance and keep watch. Give me some room to tend to Cal here, please."

Both hastily followed my request. I heard Fianna say to Fergus, "I think she could be a great healer someday." I smiled, *Could be? No, that was Sarah Jane.* "Cal, I have to pull the arrow out. This is going to hurt a lot. Are you up for it?" He gave me a look of panic. Actually, I don't think I've ever come across someone who "was up to it." "On three. One. Two. Three." I gave a solid pull and out came the remains of the shaft and tip. Cal gave a high-pitched cry of pain and completely passed out. Fianna and Fergus both looked back at me rather sheepishly. Fergus is squeamish — I noted for future reference.

I let the wound bleed, cleansing itself for the moment. I examined the wound carefully, pulling back the skin. I couldn't tell whether it had punctured his lung or not. That was what most concerned me. I examined the shaft I'd just removed and tried to estimate the depth it had penetrated. Not too deep was my analysis, hopefully his lung wouldn't be badly affected. However, he would need several stitches to close the gaping hole made by the metal arrowhead. In order to do that as well as properly bandage it afterwards, I would have to remove his tunic and undershirt. I struggled a bit getting his soft leather tunic off — ever try removing the clothes of an unconscious person? If you have, you know what I am talking about.

Next, came his shirt, which I could pull over his head. *What's this?* Around his chest over his breasts was wrapped a white cloth bandage! Curiosity got the better of me, I carefully unwrapped it. There before me lay two small, perfectly white, well-shaped breasts! Cal was a woman! Stunned beyond words, I sat there staring at him, er, her, for several minutes, as my mind absorbed this startling news. Suddenly, in a flash so many little things about Cal began to make total sense! *How could I have missed all these subtle clues? Boy, am I ever slipping in my ability to observe the obvious!* Then, I remembered my own words, "Our motto is don't ask."

Calmly, I set to work, sewing him, er her, up using the tiniest stitches I could, in an attempt to leave as little a scar to mar her perfect chest as possible. It was the very least I could do for her, er him. Finally, I fashioned as good a bandage as possible, lacking all the proper healing items. I regretted not even having a single healing herb! I promised myself that from now on, as we traveled, I would keep my eyes peeled for healing herbs. Once I had his wound properly dressed, I then re-wrapped her breasts as best I could and put his shirt back on him. I had quite a struggle getting his leather tunic on back over him, however. Finally, I positioned his body in a comfortable position, near the fire and covered him with a blanket.

After rinsing off my needle and hands, I cleaned up everything else, and then announced, "Okay, that's done. How about some dinner?" I was ravishingly hungry now all the excitement was over.

Fianna cooked us up some food, but neither she nor Fergus were very hungry. I ate for both of them! While I ate, she asked me, "Will they find us, do you suppose?" Fianna was still very worried about our plight.

"We'll know for sure by morning, sis. If they haven't come to this cave by then, then we've likely eluded them." She seemed somewhat relieved by my answer. Suddenly, I felt so tired! I was drained. "I'm going to get some sleep. Why don't you two take turns watching the entrance? Wake me at the first sign of trouble." Both were glad to have something to do and walked back together to the entrance. I grabbed a blanket and laid down beside Cal and was asleep almost at once.

Sometime later, Cal wakened; his stirring woke me partially up. The fire had turned to glowing red embers. He struggled to sit up and felt his chest. He looked at me, and his face became redder than the fire's embers! I put my finger to my lips and said, "Shh. Don't ask. Your secret is safe with me. They don't know."

"Thank you," she whispered meekly.

"Lie back down and get some sleep. Your body needs to heal." She did as I asked, though she did begin to cry silently to herself, but soon relaxed and went back to sleep. This was going to be awkward for her, I thought to myself, but then I too fell back into a deep sleep.

I awoke the next morning to the smells of cooking fish chowder and tea. Fianna was already up and at it. "Wake up you two sleepyheads. Sun's been up ever so long. Breakfast is waiting." I sat up and rubbed the sleep from my eyes. What a day we had had yesterday. I glanced at Cal on my right, she, er he, was also trying to sit up, but having an awkward time of it because of the stiffness and pain in her left chest. When she saw me, her face again flushed, but I made nothing of it.

"How is my patient feeling today?" I asked. "Can you move your left arm, Cal?"

He did so, reluctantly. "Why, is that important?"

"Could be. Now have you been coughing up blood during the night?"

"Not that I know of," and immediately he did cough, and spat out red phlegm. "Oh no!" he sounded very worried.

"Some is to be expected, Cal. Don't worry. If the arrow had really entered your lung, you would have been coughing up lots of blood during the night. A little is to be expected. You had a lucky call there. Had it gone in a little deeper, you might not be with us this morning. Unless an infection sets in, I think you'll make a full recovery. I used the tiniest stitches I could to close the wound, so you should not have much scaring there." I figured a young woman would be quite concerned about an ugly scar below her perfect breasts, and I wanted to relieve her from such worries.

"Now had Sarah Jane been here, why she can make the tiniest stitches that I have ever seen! I once helped her sew up an artery in a woman's arm. She had taken a very nasty sword cut and ordinarily would have lost her arm. But Sarah Jane, she sewed the artery back together with the tiniest stitches I have ever seen. Saved her arm too." I babbled on, trying to put Cal more at ease, before I realized what all I was babbling about!

Cal looked at me and said softly, "I don't know how to thank you, Bethany. You saved me from certain death back there yesterday."

"It's okay. I'm not about to lose my super dulcimer player! You, *sir*, are irreplaceable." I emphasized the word as a subtle hint that her secret was safe with me. "Later on, I'll have to take a look at how the wound's healing and all. The others are a bit squeamish, and when I look at it, I'll send them away, as I did last night when I sewed you up." Clever am I, I thought to myself. I've just let her, er him, know that the others do not know about her and will not in the future. Clever indeed.

"Thanks," he said again.

Fergus burst out, "Well, I don't know about the rest of you, but, Bethany, I have got so many questions about yesterday to ask you that I don't know where to start. You are only fourteen, and yet you know how to heal wounds. Yesterday, I swear I saw you actually *catch* one of those arrows in your hand! Then, there were those magical barriers, ice sheets perhaps. You, young lassie, carried Cal all by yourself halfway here, as if he was nothing more than another sack; I was pooped after carrying him the rest of the way. Then, there was all that thunder and lightning, and somehow our pursuers perished. Out here in the middle of nowhere, you, my fine lassie, suddenly find this perfect hiding place right here. Cal, did I miss any?"

Cal's embarrassment had melted while listening to Fergus's dissertation. He said, "I saw several ice wall barriers appear to protect us and slow them down. I did find a cloud in the sky for her like she asked me to — after that, she stopped, and the lightning came, hitting some of them. Don't recall much after that, though. I think I passed out."

I chuckled, knowing that at this moment, I honestly must not answer their questions out of fear for their own safety, should I be discovered, either by the Grey Creatures or by King Albert. "Remember, gang, we operate under 'Don't ask.' I'm afraid I must still invoke our agreement." Both of them stared straight at me, looking like I had just wounded them mortally, pleading for me to level with them. I melted somewhat, "All right, you two. Once we get safely to the mainland, I'll explain myself much more fully. Until then, you just have to trust me, as I trust you."

Fergus laughed, "I guess the 'Don't ask' thing works both ways." I smiled, glad that it did.

"I'm going out to check on things and see if it is safe for us to flee toward Moyrath. You all stay put. Fergus, I'm putting you in charge. You must protect my sister and Cal." he heartily agreed. I gave Fianna a little reassuring hug and headed to the entrance.

Behind me, I heard Fergus comment, "Verily, I may have already found what my mother insisted I find. All praise to Jehosa!"

I heard Cal's soft voice add, "Perhaps some of what my father used to tell me is true; all praise to the Blessed Holy Mother." Fianna said nothing. As I left the cavern, I heard Cal add, "She doesn't even have a weapon! I should have offered her my sword."

The last thing I heard was Fianna answering, "She doesn't like swords, only poles." I smiled; my sister had it right.

Another warm late summer day had dawned. I stood still and listened to the forest carefully. I needed all my druwid training this morning. I absolutely had to determine if it was safe to continue our journey or if we ought to hole up longer. Were the Axemen coming after us in force? If they sent out a large force to find us, eventually they would stumble across our cavern. However, after a half hour's careful scrutiny, I could not detect the presence of our enemy. Still not completely satisfied, I closed my eyes and expanded my awareness, this time sensing for the presence of other minds in our vicinity. To my relief, I sensed none at all. I returned to the others.

"All clear. I think we can safely continue anytime."

"Ah, Bethany, there is one slight problem," broke in Fergus in a serious tone. "The Axemen have setup a secret town in our very forest. It is my obligation and duty to let someone back home know about this evil. Cal and I agree on this; others must be warned — only we aren't certain who to warn. Probably some Kings who may launch a strike to force these Axemen from Cymry. We don't know how to do this, only that we both feel honor bound to do so."

From the stalwart expressions on both of their faces, I knew this was serious. We did not have a servant that we could send back with the message. We did not have any carrier pigeons to send the message. "I don't suppose it would be satisfactory to let someone in Moyrath know and have them send forth the messages, would it?" I replied, thinking rapidly. I could use telepathy, but only if I was familiar with the person. The only king I had met was King Ross. "Look, it is just too dangerous for you to head back to the highlands from here. You saw yesterday that they have patrols in the woods. It took all four of us working together to survive them. One person alone wouldn't have much of a chance at all." I saw that my guess that Fergus was about to volunteer to go off on his own and warn everyone had been correct. He looked downcast.

"Aye, I guess you are right again, lassie. I guess it must be Moyrath. Is that all right with you Cal?" He readily agreed.

"Okay, then let's hit the trail. Today, Cal must ride. He'll be weak from the wound for several days, and I don't want him over exerting himself and opening his wound back up." We packed up and saddled the horses,

Fergus handling Cal's for him. After glancing around for a final time to make sure we hadn't forgotten anything, we cautiously left our cavern to the bats.

Of necessity, we went single file. I let Fergus take the lead mostly because he would think it totally unseemly and unmanly to allow a young woman take point, even though I was more than qualified. I follow immediately behind him. Cal followed me sitting astride his mare, while Fianna brought up the rear. We followed the valley a fair number of miles until the southern slopes lessened considerably in steepness, whereon we veered southeastward toward the distant sea. By late afternoon of the next day, we reached the Lir and paused for a time. Interestingly, I spied another half dozen underground openings along the way.

The Lir was a wide river and deep, I guessed. We could see the forest was much less dense on the opposite shore. How to cross was our hurdle. Lir's current was swift, and there were numerous boulders here and there, churning up the waters even further. In the end, we followed Cal's suggestion, "Maybe if we follow along the river for a while, we'll find a good place to cross."

We had gone perhaps a couple miles further downstream, now on the lookout for a suitable place to camp, when I noticed the absolute stillness of the forest about us. Only the rushing waters provided the background noise. I gave everyone a dire warning. No sooner had I done so than two men stepped out from behind some trees and accosted us, crossbows pointing at us.

"Halt! Who goes there? Speak in the name of King Macayle of Westonheath." I believe we all looked very much relieved. Fergus implicitly acted as out spokesman, much to Cal's relief, only now I knew why, of course.

"We are the Cymry Minstrels on our way to play the towns and villages of Moyrath," he pronounced in a regal fashion. The sentry looked at the bulging instrument bags slung on our horses and satisfied himself that we were musicians.

"You'll come with me; the King has given us our orders. Perhaps you'll get to play for the King tonight." It was not a request; we had to follow him, but I began to have some suspicions. What was a King doing out here just across the Lir? As we walked on down river, we spied their encampment. Hundreds of small tents dotted the forest here by the river. He was here with an army! Could he already know about the Axemen I wondered?

We were led to the King's tent, which was obvious. Gaily striped canvas of immense proportions stood roughly in the middle of the encampment, surrounded on all sides, save the river, with those of his troops. "Wait here," the sentry ordered just outside the tent, while he went inside. Shortly, he emerged along with the King and two of his aides. King Macayle was a tall, thin man, probably thirty, with medium long black hair and neatly trimmed beard. He wore a golden circlet on his head and carried a huge sword slung across his back. His clothes were immaculate with the typical Cymry embroidery across the front of his tunic.

He spoke clearly, "My sentry says that you are the Cymry Minstrels. It would appear so from your instruments. However, he also said that you wandered in from upstream. That has raised my curiosity. Tell me, where have you come from? What route did you take?"

Again, Fergus spoke for us, "Well met, King Macayle, well met indeed! We recently finished playing in the highlands and angled our way down here from the rocky barrens. However, we bring you dire news and at great peril to ourselves! It is the Axemen, sire. We came across an actual town of Axemen, hundreds of them, men and women as well! It seems our foes have adopted a new strategy. Instead of raiding, they have taken up residence. We saw them felling numerous of the great trees. When we tried to leave that area, we were attacked by a band of scouts. Cal, here, was wounded by an arrow. At great peril, we managed to elude them by hiding for a time in a cave." He got down on one knee, "Sire, I beg you to send word of this to the highland kings and to those kings nearby in Layamon. If we don't drive these evil Axemen from Cymry, we may wake up on the morrow to find them our landlords!"

I expected to see King Macayle shocked by what Fergus had said. Rather, the king smashed one fist into his other hand, "I knew it! Treacherous pigs! A town! Come, brave minstrel, you must tell me all that you saw. Just where is this town of theirs? Bring out the royal maps! Oh yes, get these minstrels properly settled; see to it that they have all the ale they desire." The king led Fergus into his tent. Fergus stood as tall as he could, looking as important as he could. "Men!" I muttered to myself.

Cal overheard me, smiled, and said, "Yes." We both grinned; I was really beginning to like Cal a whole lot.

We later learned that for months now, rumors had been coming in to Westonheath of Axemen raiders somewhere north of the Lir. A few weeks ago, the King had set forth to see for himself and to drive any that were found from Cymry. Hence, our news was precisely what he was after. Unfortunately, given our estimates on the size of the town, he had not nearly enough men with him to launch an attack. Thus, he did indeed send forth dispatch riders to the highlands and to eastern Layamon, which more than satisfied both Fergus and Cal.

Since he couldn't go charging after them the next day, King Macayle asked us to play for him this evening. This time, we gave an outdoors concert, and at least half of his troops gathered as close to us as they dared to listen. After the two-hour concert, Fianna was discretely handed another coin pouch by one of the king's aides. She cheerily counted out another thirty gold pieces.

After we had finished, Fergus went off to have a chat with one of the

King's aides. He returned much later, all smiles. "I've got good news for you," he began. "There is a good crossing point about a half day's ride further south. This army crossed there. I have the directions for finding Westonheath as well. You are right, Bethany, a few times a year, Sea Prince ships do dock in Westonheath. We are in luck!"

That night we slept in complete safety; the king even let us use two pup tents. I think we were all very happy with this wonderful news. It meant that soon we could get to the mainland; I could then drop most of my disguise. I was having one awful time withholding so much from my sister and friends. As I fell asleep, I realized that the only reason I was able to get away with holding so much back from them was the simple fact that we all had agreed to the motto: "Don't ask."

The next day, I went in search of their physician or healer. A half hour later, I returned to our tents with some salve and a proper bandage for Cal. I ushered Fergus out of the men's tent and in privacy, examined Cal's wound. Luck was with us, no sign of infection was present. Nevertheless, I put the salve on it and re-bound it using the proper bandages for a change. "Don't worry. When we get to Westonheath, I'm going to get us some proper healing supplies!" She again thanked me.

Surprisingly, she felt she could now give me a sisterly hug. "I've wanted to show you how much I admire and respect you for so long now, but I just couldn't do it, you know, you thinking I was a boy. It would be horrible for you to get the wrong idea," she confided in me. I felt like such a heel still letting her think that I was a young girl. I steeled myself from self-recriminations; it had to be done for her own safety.

"That's all right, Cal. Now we can pretend a little longer and no one will be the wiser," I replied, noting that for some unknown reason I really enjoyed her hug. She had a twinkle in her eyes when I left her, er him.

Mid-morning, we mounted up and headed off down the Lir looking for the wide, shallow fording place. When we found it, Fergus commented, "If we had just kept on following the Lir, we would have eventually found this crossing place. How could you have known? Oh, I get it, another 'Don't ask' is it?"

I chuckled, "No, it is common sense. The patterns of all rivers change as they flow along. It was a near certainty that we would eventually find a good, shallow place to cross. Common sense." From the look on his face, I suspected he doubted this simple explanation, which was the truth. One more day on the trail found us at the outskirts of Westonheath. All afternoon, we passed by well-tended fields, interspersed with groves of trees. Evidently, Moyrath could boast significant grain production as well. However, the farmsteads were all quite small by Greenway standards, anyway. We felt cheerful riding along through civilized lands, quite unlike our experiences in the Dark Forest.

Chapter 7 Westonheath

The large port town of Westonheath and immediately surrounding lands was home to probably five thousand people. Here in northern Moyrath, a curved outcropping of land pushed three miles out into the ocean, forming a natural bay and harbor. Yet, the docks were small; only one ocean going ship could dock at a time. However, I counted a dozen smaller fishing boats plying the waters of the bay.

Most of the homes were block shaped, made from the abundant supply of timber. What got our attention immediately were the streets: they were absolutely crazy, laid out in no apparent pattern or order, zigging this way and that. Finding our way around Westonheath would be similar to navigating a maze. At my suggestion, we paused for a time here on the hill overlooking the town, memorizing some key locations and buildings. We spied what had to be the king's residence, the largest complex in the town. The docks were obvious, only the getting there would be the problem. Finding our way around Westonheath would be a challenge.

"I think our best move would be to find an inn close to the docks. Next, chat with the innkeeper or other likely prospects to find out when the next ship that could take us to the mainland might be here. How long must we wait — once we know that, we can better make plans. I don't think it wise to sell our horses until we have booked passage. We may need to make a hasty get away or continue down the coast. However, I do want to do some shopping for healing supplies. I never want to be in such dire straits as I was with Cal. If he had gotten an infection or if the arrow had been poisoned, well, I just need to find the ingredients for a healing pouch. Enough said."

"How long are we willing to wait around Westonheath for a boat? As long as a month?" asked Cal. I detected a note of concern in his voice, but I had no idea why he was worried, unless he found it more difficult to maintain his disguise while in a large town.

"Let's tentatively say a week. Perhaps longer if a ship really is really coming," I suggested. That seemed to satisfy him and we rode on down the hill and into the town itself. Unlike many of the highland towns, Westonheath had no stone wall or wooden fortifications around it. We simply rode down the hill, picked a street, and entered. Of course, if the town came under attack, so could any enemy. However, I liked the idea of a wide-open town; I'd only designed the fortress walls last lifetime to protect our new towns from the raiding Axemen. Thinking back on it, that was a silly idea, Axemen virtually never raided that far inland. Perhaps, I was thinking about the ultimate safety of my family and that of my brother-in-law.

An hour passed before we finally arrived at the Barrel Keg, the last inn before the docks and warehouse district close to the water's edge. Okay, we got lost or turned around five times, and stopped for directions another four. Fergus claimed folks gave differing directions, but I chalked it up to our total unfamiliarity with the maze of intertwining and dead-end streets. The outer areas contained mostly residential homes, for the most part. The central portion contained the shops and market blocks, where I intended to do some shopping. However, in this part of town was where we got lost five times. Throngs of people only added to our confusion.

The Barrel Keg was a seedier inn than those we had visited before, smoky and greasy. Apparently, the innkeeper saw no reason ever to wash the windows or scrub the floor. Tables were cursorily wiped once a day, however. Fifteen coppers bought lodging and meals for us and stabling for our horses, though after the first night, to the person, we agreed to purchase our meals elsewhere!

Once our gear was stowed in our rooms, we decided to split up. Cal and I went shopping for supplies, while Fergus and Fianna investigated ways and means to book our passage. Soon, Cal and I wandered into the throng of folks wandering about in the market district. "Look for any kind of shop where we might find healing supplies or an herbal shop," I suggested.

After a few minutes, Cal said, "There are so many shops! Why don't we just ask around?" I chuckled, what a wise suggestion, and wondered why I hadn't thought of that. Was I slowly adopting a man's attitude? A half hour later, we finally located one of the three shops that folks tried their best to direct us to — Wainscott's Supplies. "Sorry, Bethany, but I don't know much about healing or what we actually might need," Cal admitted shyly.

"Not a problem, Cal, 'cause most of the so called healers don't either. Do you realize that if a person is ill and sees a healer, no matter what the healer might say or do for the person, one in five will get well anyway? I mean you could rattle Fergus' gourd over their heads chanting 'juu juu,' and one in five would get well from it! Here, you hold things I pick out."

I spent an hour poking through everything in the shop. Actually, I fared fairly well, finding all that I thought I might need, save herbs. Amazingly, Wainscott had not a single healing herb! I spent twenty coppers on bandages and the like, including a nice leather bag in which to carry them. As we stepped outside, I said, "Now comes the hard part. We need to find herbs."

Another hour passed as we visited three herbal shops. No single shop carried all that I really wanted. We were walking along looking for Mabyn's Herbs, when Cal suddenly grabbed my arm and froze. His voice squeaked, bordering on terror; certainly fear filled his words, "Oh no! He must not see me! I have to hide. Bethany, quick, I have to hide! Oh no, he's moving this way! Don't let him see me!"

I was startled, taken completely off guard by Cal's reaction. I glanced quickly in the direction Cal had been looking. About thirty feet from us, I saw a tall, thin man, wearing expensive leather armor; a broadsword hung at his side. He had blonde hair, quite different from the wide range of browns of the local people here in Moyrath. Clearly, he was a stranger in the town as well. Further, the embroidered designs on his overtunic, suggested to me that he was from the Layamon district. I noticed he had a parchment in his hand and was showing it to each person he met as he walked along.

Poor Cal, he tried to hide his face, turned completely around, his back to this stranger. Okay, we needed to hide. I looked around; we were in the middle of the street, surrounded by shops and many people. There simply was nowhere to hide, no alleyways, and no time to flee or duck into a shop. "Oh gods! I'm doomed!" Cal whispered nearly in terror. "Please, don't let him see me."

Think, Bethany! What would Simon do? Simon Donegal had been my Judger and conjurer extra-ordinaire. I began a quick chant, hoping I had not lost my touch. I never was very good with conjuring chants, though. I finished as the man walked up to us. "Excuse me," he said formally, "I'm looking for this woman. Have you seen her? There is a hundred gold piece reward for finding her."

I looked at the parchment. Some artist had made a life-like drawing of a young woman with long blonde hair. No doubt about it, the image was Cal! I replied, "No sir. I have never seen this woman. Sorry."

"How about you, sir?" he asked, shoving the paper before Cal's face. Cal was petrified; his legs were shaking. Any second I thought he might collapse.

Mentally, I continued my illusion. Although Cal was too scared to mutter any words, it appeared that he said, "No sir. I've never seen her." I caught the sideways glance of Cal at me. Then, I muttered softly, "I should be moving on to ask these people."

The man then said, "Thank you. I must be moving on to ask these folks." He nodded politely and moved on down the street to a pair of older women, who were chatting about vegetables.

I grabbed Cal's arm and pulled him along in the opposite direction. Poor Cal could barely walk; he stumbled twice and nearly fell. By the time that we had put six blocks between us and that man, Cal recovered from her shock. "What happened back there? I didn't say anything. My voice isn't that low. I've tried so hard to make it sound low. Why didn't he recognize me? I thought I was done for. Why did he say what you said?"

"People see and hear what they expect to see and hear," I replied. "I'm way out of practice doing that sort of thing. Honestly, Cal, I never was much good at it. You look like a man, so I just added a bit to that illusion. He saw you with long red hair and beard, talking with a deep bass voice with words that I conjured. I then planted the thought to move on in his mind and he repeated it nicely for me. It might not have worked, except that particular man is very easily influence by others, so I got away with my illusion. I doubt that Fergus would have bought my illusion."

"I — I really don't understand, Bethany. Now I *have* put you all in dire peril. That was Captain Wynn, he's trying to find me and take me back. If he finds me with you, he will kill all of you to get to me! Bethany, we must flee here at once!"

"Calm down, Cal. He's just one tall man. I'm sure we can deal with him if need be. However, you don't look like that picture very much, so I don't think you will be recognized. Well, except for the facial features and your pretty eyes. I know; let's dye your hair red and that will help throw people off. Come on. Let's continue to hunt for herbs, and I think I know just what we can do."

A half hour later, I had found what I needed in another herb shop. We ducked into a deserted alleyway. Quickly, I crushed the leaves in a tiny metal pot and then rubbed the mixture through Cal's short hair. Satisfied with my handiwork, I used the last water in our canteens to wash off my hands. "There, you now have brown hair. Just don't get it wet or it will wash out. You now look more like a local man."

"Oh thank you! How can I ever repay you? Do you think it will work?" She gave me a big hug. A strange sensation came over my male body, but I put it out of my mind.

"Yes, he's showing pictures of a very pretty blonde woman with long hair. With brown short hair, no one is very likely to spot the facial similarities. People only see what they expect to see or want to see. We have that going for you. I think you are safe for now. Come on; we ought to be finding our way back. I think I'm totally lost. No," I corrected myself, "we are right here. I smell the ocean. It's strongest that way, so we just make our way that way," I said confidently. Okay so it took us another hour to enter our rooms.

When we got back, Fergus and Fianna were waiting for us; both were quite anxious because we had been gone so long. "We thought something dreadful had happened to you," blurted Fianna. "What happened to Cal's hair?" she suddenly spied his brown hair.

"We ran into some trouble. It seems that someone has placed a bounty on Cal — turn him in for a hundred gold pieces." I related our encounter, adding for Cal's benefit, "Remember our motto: Don't ask."

"But you don't seem like you are a criminal, Cal," Fianna commented.

"I'm not!" Cal said defiantly, and then added, "I'm a runaway. Let's leave it at that." I explained that the picture showed a person with blonde hair, which was why I changed his hair's color temporarily. That seemed to satisfy their immediate curiosity and concerns. I added that I had been mostly successful in putting together a healing pouch.

Now it was Fergus's turn to relay what they had uncovered. "Lad and lassie, we are in luck. Sea Princes ships do dock here and take on grain and the occasional passenger."

"That's great. How soon is the next one?" I asked, interrupting him.

"Well, lassie, that is the slight problem. It seems they normally dock in the fall to purchase harvested grain and produce. The regular ship is not due for two months." Cal collapsed into a chair, doomed, and resigned to his fate.

"However, according to the fellow I chatted with, there is a way to signal passing ships that we need to have one dock here. Fianna and I checked out his story. Sure enough, they have a large signal lantern, which they can light. Any passing ship that has available cargo room may choose to put into the dock, answering the call. We took the liberty of getting the signal lighted for us," he smiled, knowing that we would approve of this stroke of good fortune. "It cost me a gold piece to pay for the signal. The only thing is, there is no telling how soon a ship, which has cargo room, will decide to answer it. However, the harbor master assured me that the lantern will stay lit until one does dock however long that may be. We only need to wait and be patient." He finished with a self-confident look on his face that said "how about that!" We thanked him, especially Cal.

Another thought suddenly struck me, "Gang, I don't think the Cymry Minstrels should perform at all while we are in Moyrath. Cal, wouldn't that person who is looking for you know that you play a dulcimer? That might give him away to his enemy."

"Oh gods! You are so right, Bethany! I hadn't thought of that! No, let's not play here at all. I don't think I'm leaving my room until it's time to go!" he declared.

"Well, I guess we can bring you back some food," Fianna offered. Surprisingly, Cal accepted. Evidently, he was terrified of being discovered. I wondered why someone would place a hundred gold piece bounty on her, but I knew I would just have to wait a little longer to find out.

I love the out of doors, and I simply could not fathom how Cal could stay totally locked up in her room these days. It did make his disguise work more readily, as I realized that he was having a hard time with her personal hygiene activities here in town. It didn't help matters that she was rooming with Fergus and had continually to maintain her disguise. For a moment I thought about making up some excuse to have Cal moved into our room, the girl's room. As soon as I thought of this solution, I realized if I did that, then I too would have a huge problem. I left the arrangements alone.

That night, Fergus, who tended to hang out at the bar every evening listening for news, reported that the only topic of conversation was that King Macayle had discovered that the Axemen had actually settled in the Dark Forest and built a town there. Speculation was rampant on what would happen next covering both extremes. Some insisted that their King would besiege the town and drive them from the shores of Cymry. Others insisted that the Axemen would attack the defenseless town any day now, raping and pillaging everything in sight. Opinions ran the gamut. However, just as I expected, no one took any real action over the news.

Finally, around noon on the fifth day of waiting, a messenger from the harbor master came to say that our boat was just now docking. Hastily, we three, Cal still refused to budge from her room, followed the young lad back to the docks. Fianna gave him a copper for having brought us the word, and the boy was exuberant in his thanks. We stood among a small crowd of folks; many were dockhands, I surmised from their work clothes and gloves, watching the magnificent sailing ship slowly maneuver towards us in the small bay. A half hour later, four ropes flew through the air towards the docks; men with gloves grabbed them. Others joined in and slowly the large vessel was pulled up tight with the dock. I noticed the ship's name painted on the bow: Far Seas.

Once the ship was secured, lads on board lowered a wooden gangplank from the deck down to the dock. A tall thin blonde man, wearing a blue shirt and pants, appeared and walked down to us. The old harbor master was there to greet him. Quickly, we were summoned to join them. The sea captain said, "Harbor master says you seek passage to the mainland." He spoke the Sea Prince dialect, which I understood, but neither Fianna nor Fergus did; both stood there looking rather stupid. I suspected the harbor master would have translated, but I quickly spoke up, hoping my accent would not be too difficult for the captain to understand. It had been over a decade since I last spoke it.

"Yes, captain. We desire passage to the mainland. There are four of us, we rode in here a few days ago and are looking to cross over to the mainland."

"Say, this is an unexpected surprise, young woman. You speak fairly good Sea Prince. I do like your magnificent red hair. Is she your sister? You look so similar," he replied.

I sensed he wanted to find out a bit more about us or was just being courteous. "Thanks. I am called Bethany. Yes, we are sisters. Have you got room for us?"

"You mentioned horses? How many would you be bringing?" he replied.

"I didn't think a ship could carry such large animals, sir. We have six. Is that too many?"

He was non-committal, "Well, it all depends, fair Bethany of the red locks, on just where on the mainland you wish to go. Did you have a specific destination in mind?" Ah, the carefree attitude of the Sea Prince mariners came back to mind. I suspected that this captain was one of those lucky men who owned his own ship and could trade as he chose.

"Just across the ocean. Anywhere in the Greenway or the nearest Sea Prince town would be fine. Not far, I hope. I don't want you to have to go out of your way on our account," I added that last hoping to keep the cost of this venture down.

"Well, then Bethany, I've just come from Calgary and am due to dock at Bregia for some cargo. It would be but a small zig in my path to drop you off at say Fortress d'Grange. How does that sound. I assume you know the city?" he replied. From his tone, I suspected that he thought that I might not.

His eyebrows rose with my reply, "Yes, I know the city. That would be excellent. How much do we owe you and how soon can we leave?"

"It is but a small zig; let's see, four plus six. How does twenty gold pieces sound?" I figured I could bargain with him to get it lowered. However, under our present circumstances, I thought better of it. It might be wise to have him thinking he was making a good profit on our passage.

"Great. Do you want payment now or when we board?" I replied.

Since I appeared to be such a young woman, the harbor master interrupted, saying on my behalf, "It is customary to pay at the time of boarding. You see if you paid in full before you boarded, why, there would be nothing to keep the ship from sailing away without you. Need to keep these wily mariners honest." Both he and the captain laughed at the inside joke.

"Agreed, fair Bethany. We can sail as soon as you are all aboard, that is unless the harbor master has other cargo for me."

"A small amount, if you don't mind. We always take advantage of the opportunities that are presented us," the astute harbor master said. "Probably take only an hour to load, captain."

"Okay, then, we sail in an hour, if you can be ready in that time," the youthful captain answered. We shook hands and left to get Cal, our horses, and gear. You can imagine Cal's relief when we returned saying, "Pack up; we're leaving within the hour." That was music to his ears. A half hour later, all our gear was packed onto our horses; we walked them the short distance to the dock.

However, as we neared, I suddenly halted. Cal let out a stifled shriek. There standing talking to the harbor master and the ship's captain was that same man, Captain Wynn, parchment with the sketch of Cal in hand, questioning the two men! "Damn, that man is relentless," I muttered. "He's the one searching for Cal. Careful, everyone. I know. Fergus, you pay our fee. Cal you bring all the horses, surrounding yourself with all six of them so he can't get a good look at you. With Fergus out in front, my sister and I following somewhat behind, and Cal in the rear in a tangle of horses, we walked slowly toward them.

Luck was on our side. Captain Wynn finished talking to the two. I caught the parting words of the harbor master, "Don't get many blonde women in Moyrath, shouldn't be hard to find." The Captain walked past the confusion of Cal and horses without even noticing Cal. I breathed a sigh of relief.

"Fool has lost a pretty blonde; serves him right," the mariner commented to the harbor master. "Ah, my passengers arrive."

"I'll check on the rest of the goods," the harbor master excused himself.

"Ah, right this way," the mariner captain motioned for us to join him. "First, let's get your gear aboard. Leave the horses; my crew will bring them aboard once we load the rest of their cargo. "Pietto, show these folks to their quarters." A young boy barely in his teens scrambled to the gangplank, waving for us to follow him. Quickly, we unloaded all of our sacks, packs, and gear, hoisting them over our shoulders, and walked up the gangplank onto the ship. Memories of the times I spent over forty years ago on board the Lucky Lady came back into my mind. This ship, the Far Seas, was very similar in design. Evidently, ship construction had changed very little over the years. *You know, one day I ought to be a mariner and see what their life is like*, I thought.

Soon, we found ourselves down in the hold. I recalled how my Circle had moved boxes around to make four separate living areas when we sailed from the Greenway to Velona on the Lucky Lady. This time, the hold was nearly empty. Pietto told us to stow everything forward, saying that the horses would go in the middle. I noticed several crates stowed in the stern of this hold. We did as instructed. By the time that we had everything in a safe place, especially the instruments, two other crew members appeared and began erecting a number of wooden fence walls. After they had two in place, I realized they were making a makeshift set of stalls.

Fergus and I caught on and lent them a hand, which brought smiles to their faces. Further, when I demonstrated I could speak their language, however crudely, they were very pleased and even flirted with me. I could tell that they had never seen women with fiery red hair, especially as long as mine had grown. We all watched fascinated as one by one our horses were brought into the cargo hold. Interestingly, each horse had been blindfolded. One hand explained that this way, they were not spooked. I didn't have the heart to suggest that walking blindly might be even spookier for the horses. Fortunately, all six were loaded safely without incident, and I breathed another sigh of relief.

Once they were secured to the heavy timbers that supported the deck above us, the hands returned to loading what remained of the harbor master's cargo. Since the others had never been on a large ship before, Pietto offered to show us all around below deck. "You can sleep there," he pointed to where our gear was stowed. "Only one night. By morning, we'll be docking." Pietto certainly felt important as he took us on the grand tour. At last, the captain stuck his head down and said, "We're setting sail, if you want to come topside and watch."

After I translated, we all headed back on deck. The mooring lines had already been cast off, and four crewmen were coiling them up on the port side. The captain barked orders, while other crew carried them out, as the

Far Seas drifted away from the dock and began to pivot her bow back out toward the ocean. This time, I knew how to sail my small two-man boat that I had built with my own hands. Now I grasped just what they were doing, a clever combination of rudder and sail. Once we were facing the right direction, the mainsail was hoisted, and we began to move more quickly. The winds were blowing from the northwest now, which was perfect for a rapid departure. For a time, we looked in all directions, as the dock and Moyrath began to grow smaller and the bay entrance, larger. Soon we rounded the bend of the last bit of land and hit the open sea.

It was now late afternoon, I pointed out the readily visible mainland, which stretched as far as the eye could see along the eastern horizon. "Over that way is the Greenway, ahead is our destination, the newest Sea Prince sector, Fortress d'Grange, down that way lies the Velona sector," I explained.

"Aye, my lady, you know your land masses," commented our captain, who had overheard my explanation, catching the names of the places, but not my sentences. "I am Captain Irmino Ponterro, at your service." Politeness dictated that I introduce my companions. I added that we were called the Cymry Minstrels, on our way to play our way across the mainland. "Excellent, excellent. Tonight, you shall all dine with me. Perhaps you will grace my crew and me with a little music, eh?" He winked at me. I smiled back, to keep up appearances.

"We've never played on a moving ship before, Captain, we might not sound so great," I hedged. He insisted that any music would be appreciated, so I consented. Actually, the others were excited, none more so than Cal, who I suspected was free at last from her threat of capture. Oh the smell of the sea. I guess that is what struck me the most on this trip, that and the fact that I now knew a bit about sailing.

Dinner with the Captain turned out to be a very crowded affair. His table comfortably would seat three, including himself. We had to scrunch in tightly in order to fit. The meal, though simple, was delicious, and we thanked him many times for his generosity. A little while later, once darkness had fallen, we went below and got out our instruments. The crew turned on a number of lanterns so we could see fairly well, and the gig was on. Well, mostly on. Just try playing an instrument on a moving, bobbing ship at sea. In the end, Cal gave up completely trying to play the dulcimer. Unused to the rocking, he kept hitting the wrong strings. Instead, he joined in with some drums. When we finished, it was the Captain who thanked us repeatedly; even his six crew members added their thanks. Onboard music must have been a real rarity on their long ocean voyages.

Finally, we turned in for the night, sleeping on blankets beside our gear. Sometime during the night, the ship hove to, just off the Fortress d'Grange. At dawn, the Captain asked us if we wanted to watch the ship dock. We all rushed on deck to catch our first glimpse of this city.

Chapter 8 Fortress d'Grange, the Eighth Sea Prince Sector

Nothing could have prepared us for the sight before us! Imagine an orange and grey granite mountainside, whose peaks stretch from the shore on up to the towering peaks of the Appian Way. Rugged, yet barely passable, on this stretch of the mainland, the mountains of the Appian Way finally settled into the ocean. Yes, this formidable range formed a natural barrier from the land of the Sea Princes and Greenway along with part of the Northern Steppes. Here where the craggy peaks finally lowered was the only passageway between the Velona Sector and the Greenway. Yet it was only barely passable on a thin, meandering track that wandered through the treacherous foothills. Calgary, Greenway, lay perhaps some fifty miles further north from here, while the huge city of Velona was hundreds of miles to the south.

True, the mountainous region before us was indeed spectacular, but that was not all that we could see. Rising like two man-made orange and grey checkered mountains were the twin fortress towers, Fortress d'Grange and Fortress Bellini. Yes, here the first stone castles on Tarra had been designed and built, primarily by Count Basilica d'Grange. These fortresses had withstood two invasions already, the Centurion invasion some fifty years ago and the more recent invasion of the Galts from the Northern Steppes; neither army had been able even slightly to penetrate these massive defenses. In fact, Fortress d'Grange now had the distinction of being the sole land on Tarra that had not yet been invaded or conquered, save the far north land of the Axemen. Historical footnote: It was the design of this castle that Raphael Penton, the Planner of my druwid Lightning Circle, had used to build his fortress complex at Mont Blanc, some hundred miles to the northeast of here. Very soon now, many others would begin to adopt this very same design, as the construction of fortified castles spread to many lands.

The two main castle towers rose over a hundred feet, forming a pair of checkerboard peaks, standing in sharp contrast to the surrounding orange and grey granite, rocky foothills. However, massive defensive walls snaked their way around the hills for miles, enclosing the town, the port, and farmers' fields. Each field, though small, had similar small walls of stone forming its boundaries. The sheer number of small single family stone dwellings was impossible to count, but all lay within the twisting, turning defensive walls that were six feet tall.

As we moved slowly into their small bay toward the docks ahead, which I estimated could handle four of these ocean-going ships at the same time, the sheer size of this complex overwhelmed us all. It was breathtakingly beautiful and yet incredibly practical at the same time. It was still growing! I spied tiny workmen constructing additional walls at both the northern and southern edges. This led me to conclude that the city was still growing, that people were still immigrating here. The sight before us was unlike anything that any of us had ever seen before; we stood in silence, gaping at the wonder before us, not even noticing the crew throwing out the four ropes to the dockhands or the lowering of the gangplank.

"Journey's end," our captain brought us out of our musings, "go below and get your things topside. My crew will lead your horses out to you in a few minutes."

I managed to thank him for a perfect journey before scampering below with the others. A few minutes later, we four stood dwarfed on the dock, piles of gear at our feet awaiting our horses. Admittedly, we were still staring all around at this incredible city. Only when the reins of the last of our horses had been handed to us and the captain shook my hand in farewell did we finally get a feeble grip on our new reality.

All around us, dockhands were chatting among themselves, though only I could understand what they were saying. I realized how awkward and ill at ease my companions were; the speech sounded like gibberish to them. I commented, "Stick close to me or you'll be lost in the ocean without a boat." They needed no further encouragement and walked nearly on my heels as we headed up the long dock toward the large open area between the dockside warehouses.

As we reached the end of the dock, three women carrying broadswords and wearing yellow headbands appeared to be waiting for us to reach them. As I drew close, one began speaking, trying several languages, in rapid-fire succession. She said, "Welcome to Fortress d'Grange" in the Sea Prince Velona dialect, Greenway, and even Juda Arad.

"Whoa! Hang on a second," I replied using the Velona dialect, hoping my accent wouldn't be too severe for her to follow. "I can speak all of those. Which are you most comfortable using?" She and her two companions grinned; my accent must have been
bad, I concluded.

Using Velona, she said, "I'll speak slowly. Welcome to Fortress d'Grange. I am Sister Capriotti, Captain of the Guards. This is not an open city. You'll have to come with me for interrogation. If I deem it acceptable, then you may enter the city proper. If not, we will be forced to escort you out of the city. This is not a request but an order. Save your introductions for later. Do you and your friends understand me?"

"Thanks, I do. They don't speak any of those languages. Give me a minute to explain your orders to them, please. I must agree with your precautions, a very wise move." Hastily, I explained what she had said to my companions, who didn't object at all. I nodded and she led the way into the city proper with the four of us following her closely. Her two guards brought up the rear.

As we walked along, I couldn't help noticing that the streets were immaculate, totally unlike any city I had ever seen. These people took immense pride in the beauty of their city, of that I was certain. Sister Capriotti noticed us looking about in all directions and commented, "First time in d'Grange?"

I grinned and teased, "How could you ever tell that?" She laughed and led us to a stone building just at the edge of the open area by the docks. Large warehouses stood on either side with many people and wagons coming and going. I spied several men moving large wooden crates into one building. We tied up our horses at a hitching rail and followed her inside. One of her guards remained outside watching over our horses and piles of gear.

Inside, the room was about twenty feet square with several stone support columns in the middle. There were two large tables and twenty chairs. She took a position opposite us at one table and bade us sit opposite her. The other guard remained at attention in front of the door we had entered. Presently, another young woman with short blonde hair entered from a side door, carrying a parchment, quill and ink. She too wore a yellow headband, but not the leather dress of the fighters, rather she wore a white dress covered with embroidered flowers on it. She sat down beside Sister Capriotti and muttered something, presumably what language we spoke. Then, she looked at me and smiled.

"This should not take long. Glad you can speak our language. I am Sister Abrienda. It is my task to ascertain if you are to be allowed into the city, so please answer my questions honestly. I can tell if you are lying, mind you." I grinned, a soothsayer. I wondered if she did have some native ability or if she were just an astute observer of the obvious. People who lie often display telltale mannerisms.

"First, for the record, by what names do you go by?"

"We are all from Cymry or West Reach. This is Fergus from the highlands of Ruadan, Cal from the Layamon section, and my sister Fianna and I are from Tewdwr. I am called Ket Bethany, Bethany for short. Together, we are called the Cymry Minstrels, though here on the mainland we will probably say the West Reach Minstrels." She smiled as she wrote this all down on paper.

"Well, that answers my next question, what are your occupations? All musicians, I take it?"

"Yes. Our instruments are outside on our horses, if you need to verify it," I replied, trying to be helpful.

"No need. I have already done so before I came in," she commented dryly, continuing to write. "Are you or any of your party thieves? Have any of you stolen that which does not belong to you?" She watched my eyes and face keenly.

"I can vouch completely for my sister and myself, of course. My friends I have known for some time now, and, honestly, I can say that to my knowledge, none of us is a thief or would even consider stealing from another."

"Very good. Do you or any member of your party have any intentions of harming or betraying any member of this city or the city proper?"

"Certainly not!" I protested slightly.

"Very good. And what brings you to our city? What is your purpose here? How long do you plan to stay?" She was certainly methodical; I will say that.

"It was the closest place where the ship could take us so that the captain wouldn't have to go way out of his way. We didn't want to inconvenience the mariner; he might have charged us more for our passage. We just wanted to get to the mainland. Our goal is to travel all around Tarra — well certainly not the steppes or Volksholm and places where evil lurks mind you — and learn the local music, play, and share our music with the common folk. We have played for some kings back home, but we much prefer playing for ordinary people. They definitely enjoy our music. However, I honestly cannot say how long we want to stay here. We are ignorant of current events, of where it may not be safe to travel. So first, we need to learn all that we can. If you have any musicians here, we want to meet them and share songs. Also, it is quite apparent that I need to learn to speak the language much better, and my three companions have to learn it from scratch before we dare to travel around the countryside."

Sister Abrienda's stern, business-like expression melted away, replaced by a friendly, cheerful smile. "Very good. I will allow you and your party full access to our city. Let me be the first to welcome you to our city. We are all very proud of d'Grange. During your stay, please do not do anything to make us retract your welcome. Since you have two young women in your party, I'm pleased to announce that you don't need to be careful walking the streets of our city. There is no crime here whatsoever, something what we are very proud of as well."

"That is indeed terrific to hear! Amazing. It must be because there are so many of the Sisterhood here. I've seen the yellow headbands everywhere. Impressive."

She looked at me with a surprised look on her face, "You know of our Sisterhood?"

"Yes, a little, mostly historically now, I am afraid. I don't know anything more recent than a score of years ago. West Reach is rather isolated," I explained, still being completely truthful.

"Well, you have much to learn then. However, that also makes my next question easier to ask. While you are here, please note that there are two sections of our city. One section, Fortress Botini holds predominately those of the Sisterhood, while Fortress d'Grange holds the general population. However, the lines are not that hard and fast; these days, everyone mingles pretty much at will. So my question is: in which section of the city do you wish to stay? It is our obligation to see that you get safely to an inn of your choice. These days, however, it really doesn't matter anymore as it used to. Have you a preference?"

I thought for a moment. True, she just said that there was no crime. Still, I respected the Sisterhood highly, perhaps second only to the druwids. "You know, I think that we would prefer to stay in the Sisterhood section. Is it allowed for us to change later on, I mean it might later on be more convenient if we stayed at the inn where we wanted to perform."

"Certainly. I've already said that you have access to the city. You are free to go where you will. Personally, I like your choice. I love music and I hope I get the chance to hear you sometime."

"You bet. When we have our first gig setup, I'll send word to you. Say, do you mind if I ask what must be a silly question?"

"Sure, but I'll be the judge whether it is silly," she grinned.

"Fortress Botini, Botini, I once knew or rather heard of a Sister Lucretia Botini of Velona. Is there any connection? Just curious," I added.

She laughed, though I caught the fleeting notice that my slight slip had not gone unnoticed. "You do have some history to catch up on, Bethany. More than twenty years ago, the fortress was built, and she, Sister Lucretia Botini, was in complete charge of the entire fortress. When you know the full history of our Sisterhood, you may appreciate that incredible honor she gained. Once you are settled, I'll send someone around who can brief you on history and answer your questions, how's that? Now about accommodations."

"Thanks, that would be great. We aren't wealthy, so we need a relatively inexpensive inn, nothing fancy. It should be one where we could play of an evening. Back home, everyone in a village goes to the inn at night for song and dance. We've played at many, many inns. Say, I know my accent must be atrocious. Can you also send someone to help us learn your language? We can pay her."

"Okay, I know just the inn for you. However, around here customs may be quite different from West Reach. Here, we Sisters particularly love dances. Not too far from this inn is our community dance hall where you would be most welcome to come and play. Yes, I'll send someone to help you with language. Actually, your accent is not that awful, really. I have heard far worse in my day."

"Splendid indeed! Yes, I know that we have much to learn. Thanks!"

She rose and asked us to follow her. Sister Capriotti and her two guards headed back to their positions on the dock. While Sister Abrienda led us through the winding, stone covered, yet clean city streets, I quickly explained everything she had said to my companions. "Boy you are not kidding, Bethany. The very first thing we have to do is learn their language!" Fergus declared.

"And learn our way around," added Fianna, who now was hopelessly lost. Cal agreed with her, quietly, fearing to say anything around this soothsayer woman that might jeopardize us. Okay, I will admit it; by the time we reached the inn, I would also have had a very hard time retracing our path from the docks.

The inn was called simply Allegra's — a large painted sign above the main entrance held that single word. Here, Sister Abrienda left us to make our own arrangements. We tied the horses at the hitching rail and entered a small, but carpeted antechamber type room. Presently, a woman in her fifties, wearing a cotton dress with a yellow headband, bustled into the room. "Ah, strangers to our city, I presume. I am Sister Allegra. Welcome to my establishment. I presume one of you speaks my language or Sister Abrienda would still be here." She had a reddish complexion and the traditional short, curly yellow hair.

"Yes, I do," I stepped forward wondering how best to proceed. I had usually let the men in my life handle the arrangements at the inns. Now I was the man, though still in disguise, but had not the experience.

Fortunately, Allegra did, "First, are you planning to stay a day, a week, or weeks? Approximate length is all I need to know first. My, but I do love your magnificent and long red hair dear. I cannot ever recall ever having seen such red hair and so long too."

I blushed, and replied, "Thanks. Probably weeks. We need to learn much before we can travel on our way. We are the West Reach Minstrels; we have come to play music for everyone. However, we need to learn much before we can travel around. Is that all right?"

"Certainly, the longer you stay, the cheaper the rates. Next, for those who wish to stay longer, as you have indicated, we had two choices. One is 'Room and Board' — that is, you get a room and three meals. The other is 'Economy Room' — that is, you get much larger rooms equipped with a small kitchen so that you may cook your own meals, which makes your stay here much cheaper and more like the feeling of home, or so say my guests."

"Wow! I do like the Economy Room deal. We would need two, though. We aren't married, just traveling together. It would be best if the rooms were close together, since we are a team, if you grasp what I'm trying to explain about musicians. Also, we have six horses with us. I didn't see anything but that small hitching rail outside."

She smiled, "My stables are around back, close to the Economy Rooms. All right, then, five gold pieces a week will get your horses well-tended and you a pair of adjoining Economy Rooms. Also, feel welcome to come to the dining room for a meal anytime you don't feel like cooking. Our meals are nourishing yet inexpensive. The menu and costs are posted on a sign just inside the dining room. I assume that you can read?"

"Yes, I think I can. Guess, time will tell, though." I asked Fianna for ten gold pieces, so that we could pay up front for two weeks. Once that had been handled, she produced two very large keys, and we followed her as she gave us a guided tour. The entire second floor consisted of ten small rooms. Just behind this building was an enclosed courtyard, filled with tall plants and many tables and chairs. She explained that often guests preferred to eat out here in the courtyard. There was also a cistern for water. On the opposite side of the courtyard was a long building with a line of doors. We had the two quarters that were closest to the ornate iron gate, which allowed us easy access to the courtyard and our rooms. She inserted the keys and then said, "Now follow me and I'll show you where to bring your horses." She went out of the gate and around behind this building. There was yet another long and narrow stone building, the stables. It would easily accommodate thirty horses, I estimated. Entirely satisfied, we thanked her and went to fetch our horses.

A half hour later, the horses were stabled, and we had deposited our gear inside our rooms. From the outside, I presumed these would be relatively small, but on the contrary, they were rather large indeed. On one end, was the kitchen, small but quite serviceable. The other end held a desk with two chairs and floor to ceiling shelving on which to store everything. A large wooden bed divided the room into the three sections. It was more than enough for two people, and we could meet together as a group in one of these without feeling cramped, probably even hold practice sessions as well. The only glitch was we had not yet gone to the market for supplies. However, our packs were still filled with trail supplies, so we could eat for a couple weeks on that, if need be.

In the courtyard, we found the water cistern, and soon we had water in our rooms and tea brewing on the charcoal stove. Over a relaxing tea, I declared, "Well, so far this is so utterly much better than I ever could imagine! Isn't this just incredible, I mean everything, even the city."

"I feel like a total country bumpkin," Fergus said humbly. "Bethany, I don't know how to thank you for all you've done. Here you are the youngest of us and a lassie to boot, and you end up doing what Cal or I should have done. Thank you. I sure hope she sends someone to teach us the language soon. I feel like a complete idiot and useless. I've never felt this way before. But yes, this whole city and its people are incredible. So clean. I never imagined anything like this. I wonder if all the cities are like this?"

"No they are not. Trust me. I've never seen any city remotely like this one. Oops. Don't ask," I chuckled over my slight blunder. "Say, what say we clean up first. I'd like to wash off a bit. It's been a long time since I could go for a swim."

"I'll second that," declared Cal with purpose.

"I wonder where that door leads?" Fianna added, she had been examining every nook and cranny of our new room. On the wall facing the

125

guy's room was a door, just before the floor to ceiling cabinets began. "Look, it has a key hole." At once, my curious sister took our key and tried it out. Sure enough, she unlocked the door. It opened to reveal another door only a few inches away. It also has a key hole. "What a strange door this is!" she declared.

On a whim, Cal took their key and tried it. Sure enough, it unlocked this second door, which opened into the men's room! "Clever!" Cal exclaimed. "Now we have easy access to each other."

Fianna shook Cal's hand, saying, "We make a good discovery team." We all laughed. Leaving the doors ajar, we split up to clean up. An hour later, the guys knocked on our side door to see if we were ready for company. We were. Fianna had already begun to rustle up some lunch for us. The guys brought their two chairs into our room and we ate.

Once we sat back and began to sip our tea, Cal said quietly, "Okay, we're safely on the mainland. It would be dishonest of me to continue to deceive you all. You have become very dear friends to me, even saved my life, more than once. It is time I stop lying to you all and tell you the truth about me. I just can't go on like this anymore. I hope you'll not think evil of me for my deception, though." Quickly, I closed the doors so that we'd not be overheard.

Chapter 9 Cal's Story

"I am so sorry that I had to deceive you all," Cal began, nearly in tears.

I knew part of her deception, that she was a young woman masquerading as a young man. That was about all. I knew just how hard this was for her. I felt a great sympathy for her. "It is fine, Cal. We know it must be something terrible that drove you to do it. How about just starting in at the beginning? We'll understand." I put one hand comfortingly on her shoulder.

She sighed, took a deep breath and plunged in, "I'm really Caitlyn, not Cal. I'm really that woman the captain was searching for back there in Moyrath." Having said this much, she relaxed completely, the most terrible burden lifted from her shoulders. "Now that I'm on the mainland, I don't have to keep up with this deception any longer. I am the youngest daughter of King Ahmad Amir of Nuadilan . I really have just turned fifteen, that part is true."

Fergus coughed, taken totally by surprise, as was Fianna. However, Fianna, the oldest of us, immediately assumed her sisterly role. "I'm sure you must have had a really good reason, Caitlyn. Actually, I'm glad you turned out to be a woman. I have more company now." She very nearly spilled the beans on my disguise!

Caitlyn felt better now and continued. "My father is Ahmad Amir, the oldest son of the Great Messiah, Jes Amir, the Son of Jehosa, and Bethany Madelyn Amir, the Blessed Holy Mother." I coughed, totally startled by this simple statement. This meant that she was my granddaughter, or rather the grandchild of my last fleshly body. I didn't interrupt her. "When I was a young girl, my father took me to the secret place and showed me that priceless document in which he could trace our bloodline all the way back to the original King of the Arad people. He said that only our bloodline lies directly on the line. We are all destined to be kings and queens of men. It is our heritage. All throughout my childhood, he kept drumming that into our heads. My older brother, Ashley, who is now nineteen, has trained to be a fighter all his life. He is always at dad's side, claiming one day to have his own kingdom, if he doesn't inherit dad's first."

"Last year, dad forced my older sister, Jenny, who was just sixteen, to marry a pig of a king, in a small eastern town of Layamon, Leebrook. She protested and begged him not to do this, but he wouldn't listen to reason. He kept insisting that we become queens and take our rightful place in history, that it was our birthright. I still remember her wailing and crying when that older man who called himself king came and took her away. That was the last time I saw her alive, that is. Six months later, we learned that Jenny was dead. She had thrown herself down a well and drowned. It was

the only way she had to escape her awful fate. After that, I hoped dad would come to his senses. He wasn't always so insane on this bloodline thing."

"However, he then arranged a marriage between me and King Albert I of Bregia, a man three times my age and an even worse pig than poor Jenny's man was! I hated him the instant I laid eyes on him! Like my sister, I begged and pleaded for him not to do this thing, but still he would not listen. I think that was too much for mom to bear. Mira, my mother, she just jumped off the balcony. I watched in horror as she purposely swan dove three stories onto her head. Dad only said, 'Stupid woman!' He didn't even cry at her passing!"

I felt like the lowest of ants. My son — my son had done all this. How had I failed him? How had Jes failed him? We'd tried to give him the best training, knowledge, and wisdom we could. Yet, he turned into an insensitive beast. I felt incredibly awful.

"My uncle is King Emil Amir and his wife is Carmine. No two brothers could be so completely different! They have two sons, Justice who is eighteen and Jamal who is sixteen, and a daughter, Cathleen who is my age. Honestly, I spent most of the last ten years at Uncle Emil's place; Cathleen is or was my best friend. Uncle Emil even tried to reason with Ahmad about me, but insane dad almost fought with Uncle Emil. Only Carmine's intervention prevented an outright sword fight! I knew I was doomed that night to the same fate as my sister!"

"I must also say that I learned an awful lot about my grandmother, the Blessed Holy Mother, from Uncle Emil. He would tell me tales all night long about her. At first, I thought he was making it all up. Once, on my grandparent's and his grandparent's journey out of Juda Arad, — he said he was about five years old at the time, they were attacked by ten Galt fighters, who shot arrows at them. He told how my grandmother had actually caught arrows in her hand mid-flight, and how when the men were wounded and the Galts about to win, she brought a magical fire down from the sky, burning up the attackers and their horses. He said that she had also created a magical giant wall of ice to protect the four children and his grandmother from the arrows. I know this all sounds unbelievable; I thought so too, until recently." She looked directly at me and I flushed.

"Over the years, as you may well imagine, I began trying to find out all that I could about my grandmother. She used to hold the Last Holy Communion Ceremony. This part is true; I know. I have interviewed twenty different families who had her conduct it. Grandmother believed that we are all immortal spiritual beings and that we just inhabit these fleshly bodies. When the flesh dies, the being departs and acquires a new baby body. I'm not sure how this works, though. What her ceremony actually did was a miracle. During the ceremony, the actual person, the immortal spirit whose body had just died, was somehow mentally joined with their loved ones and could say their farewells to each other. Every last one of them claimed that

128

this was the most important thing that had ever happened to them. Unfortunately, the priests who now conduct the ceremony have made a mockery of her ceremony; no one talks to the dead anymore, not really. It's all just faked. Well, maybe the grieving families feel a little better, but a proper wake would do the same."

"I hope you don't mind my going on like this, because it plays a part in my story. You see, Uncle Emil also told me that when the Blessed Holy Mother disappeared back in 603, seven strangers came to Nuadilan and joined with her daughter Sarah. Together, the eight of them continued that very miraculous ceremony for a couple of years. Then, the eight of them also just up and disappeared too. Uncle Emil also swore that those seven strangers had similar powers that my grandmother had wielded. He said that those seven could work magical healing on anyone. He saw them bring fire down from the sky one time and even lightning once during a storm."

"Now maybe you think I'm crazy or something, but I decided that my goal in life is to find more of these strange, powerful people and see if they can teach me. If I really am part of this powerful bloodline of ancient kings, then I want to know all that I can and be able to be strong and wise, not like my pitiful excuse for a father! So yes, as we travel around, I'll constantly be on the lookout for these special powerful people. I just have to find at least one of them. I've no idea how I can possible persuade them to teach me, though. However, first I have to find one."

"Anyway, back to my story. After Uncle Emil and my dad almost came to blows, I cried long and hard in Cathleen's bedroom. I said that I ought to just run away and find these special people. I think that gave her the idea. Cathleen invented my disguise; she cut my hair as a boy's and helped me make up the disguise, even to pilfering these clothes from her brothers. She claimed that they had outgrown them and wouldn't miss them. Uncle Emil found out about our deception, however. To my surprise, he approved. He gave me the sword, a lot of traveling money, and my horse. He said that after I left, he would wait until dad asked where I was and then pretend that I had left for dad's house days ago; he would act terribly worried and call out his guards, sending them far and wide in a search for me. Uncle Emil suggested that I ride north and then either into the highlands or to Tewdwr. I chose Tewdwr because my other uncles live very close or just inside the start of the highlands. I didn't want to risk them discovering me. It all very nearly worked, until we got to Moyrath, where dad's captain of the guards was searching for me."

"There you have it. I would really like to stop pretending to be a man, though, only now I don't know how. I don't even have any women's things with me."

"Oh Caitlyn, don't worry! We can go shopping! I'll let you wear some of mine until we can get you properly attired. Your hair will grow back in no time at all. Mine sure has gotten longer these past few months. Of course, now you'll have to sleep in here, the girl's room. It won't do to have you sleeping in Fergus' room any more. Honestly, I don't know how you managed to carry on that disguise. It must have been just awful, you pretending to be a man." She carried on for some time, while Fergus's face flushed. He had no idea whatsoever that his traveling companion had been female. Meanwhile, I was having a mother's worst nightmare over her son's conduct. Worse, I too was in the opposite disguise, a double confusion.

During the lull, I went to our kitchen to make a fresh pot of tea. I also sent Fergus to the dining room to see if there were any biscuits to be had. I had a sudden craving for biscuits and tea, anything to calm the tempest in my mind.

Chapter 10 Fergus' Story

Fergus, grateful for the time away from us, collected his wits and self-respect. He knew that he ought to tell his story as well. After what all he had just heard, his was tame, if not lame. He returned with an armful of breads, but no biscuits. "I hope one of these will do. No biscuits to be had at the moment." He plopped six different kinds of breads on the table. After thanking him, I took what looked to be a promising loaf and began stuffing it in my mouth.

"My, you do look very pretty, even if your hair is a bit short," he complimented Caitlyn. While he was gone and I kept myself fully occupied in the kitchen, Fianna had undressed Cal and put her into her performance dress. I thought it was an amazing transformation, when Fianna told me to peek. She looked very beautiful! And I told her so, although I was slightly embarrassed at the growing bulge in my pants. I still was not used to this male body. Thankfully, Fergus showed up at that point.

"Well, gang, if Caitlyn can tell her story, it is the very least that I should tell mine. Mind you, mine is pale and tame next to her sad, horrible situation. Caitlyn, I do humbly apologized for any offenses I may have committed upon you; I just didn't know. I should not have put so many burdens on you."

She had regained much of her own self-respect. Getting off what one is intentionally withholding from dear friends does just that: a return of one's self-respect. She said, "You weren't supposed to know, silly. I guess I pulled it off pretty well, for the most part. Going to the bathroom and bathing were the worst parts, though." We all chuckled somewhat self-consciously. I thought that was the understatement of the day, though I dare not say so.

Fergus cleared his throat, Caitlyn and Fianna sat on the edge of our bed and stared expectantly at him, curious to what he would reveal. I think Fianna loved all this intrigue. "First, my last name is not O'rylee. I have used that traveling name since I was thirteen and began traveling around the highlands. My true last name is Aine. Yes, my dad is the King of Aine and my mom is Queen Ros, whose maiden name is Amir. She is the daughter of Josh and Milla Amir; he was the older brother of the Great Messiah, Jes. Josh was the founder of our great churches of Jehosanity. My parents still carry forward his teachings."

Caitlyn blurted out, "You're my cousin!" Fergus flushed.

"Aye, lassie. Only I haven't seen you since I was a wee lad. I must say you grew up mighty pretty." She blushed at his compliment.

Good grief! Ros, I wondered how she had fared. As a young girl, she had been so strong-willed and determined.

He continued, "I really am nineteen and am the oldest of my siblings. My older sister is Rhoslyn who is seventeen; next comes my brother Rhett who is fifteen, last comes my sister Rhiannon who is just eleven. So yes, I'm the oldest and heir to my father's crown."

"Caitlyn, like you, my mother constantly filled my head with similar stories about my grandparents and Jes and Bethany, his brother and sister-in-law, my great uncle and aunt. Can you imagine my reaction a while ago when you were describing the very same stories that Ros used to tell me? My god, they are nearly identical! Sometime you and I ought to sit down and compare stories, see if one of us knows something the other doesn't about our grandparents!" Caitlyn's eyes glowed.

"Anyway, Ros kept telling me that to be a proper king, I needed to learn much. She went on to say I needed to learn wisdom if I were to rule wisely. I would need to know how to fight my enemies. She went on at great length about all this. Dad, he kept chuckling and saying that I ought to be my own man and that would serve me just fine. He loves mom a whole lot, though. Dad says that I ought to travel and learn, says that is all that I need. Ever since I was twelve, I have gone off for weeks at times, traveling around the highlands. I go by the name of O'rylee — that was dad's suggestion. He pointed out that his enemies might capture me in order to get back at him. So O'rylee it's been for years now. No one was ever the wiser."

"Mom was ever telling me about these secret, special, really powerful people. She called them the Guardians and suggested they might be found in the Greenway. She thinks she once overheard the Blessed Holy Mother saying something about that. Anyway, Ros kept telling me about the incredible amount of wisdom the Blessed Holy Mother had. It seems that this woman knew just about everything. No matter what crisis occurred, Bethany Madelyn Amir always knew the most optimum path to follow that led always to success." I blushed and stared at the floor.

"When I was fifteen, Ros took me to the secret place, probably the same one you was at, Caitlyn. I watched as she added all four of our names to the list, right below her name. I looked at that long list of those of my line, and right there, I decided that if I truly am part of this very special bloodline, then I ought to find out all that I can about my heritage. Mom says that I suddenly 'found religion.' Really, I studied, trying to find out all that I could about Josh, Jes, and Bethany. I did learn a great deal about Josh and Jes, quite a lot in fact. However, the Blessed Holy Mother defied all my attempts to find out much of anything. It seems she was always in the background, that Jes depended heavily on her judgment in all things, even in his own religious matters. I think that his relying upon her really upset his ten disciples, but perhaps that is just speculation."

"I swore that I would seek out these Guardians and learn what I could from them so that I might one day be suited to be a ruler of men. Now I'm certain I would fail utterly, should I try to step into dad's shoes. Further, I made a solemn promise to myself that one day, I would know far more about my Blessed Holy Mother. You know, who she really was. How she came by her special godlike powers. How it was that she could have such great wisdom. Honestly, from all that I have heard, it is the Blessed Holy Mother, Bethany Madelyn Amir, that ought to be the queen. Her line should be the kings and queens of Tarra. I mean no disrespect to Josh and Jes Amir, mind you, but she was the true power back of Josh, I'm certain. Maybe Caitlyn can say if such is true for Jes."

"Finally, last year, I began traveling around Cymry far more than usual, in search of ways and means to find out. I knew that somehow I needed to come over here to the mainland. Yet, I'm ashamed to say that I was too insecure to be able to come over here on my own. I'm somewhat of a coward, it would seem. You can't imagine how I felt when I found out that you wanted to travel Tarra and come to the mainland! You gave me the courage to face what I really need to do; you helped me overcome my cowardice. For that, I can't thank you enough."

I made a needed observation. "Fergus, under no circumstances should you describe yourself as a coward. On the contrary, you have always displayed intelligent bravery. As you have witnessed today, we have lots to learn. What would have happened, Fergus, if you had made the journey we just made today all by yourself. Can you imagine standing there before the Captain who spoke the welcome in three languages, none of which you know? Let alone the interrogation of the Sister. No this is reality. You showed not cowardice but intelligent bravery to hold out until the proper circumstances arose, which will allow you to carry out your mission."

Fergus stared at me long before he answered, "Verily, you speak the truth of the matter. I'll not call myself cowardly anymore. What strikes me funny, though, Bethany, is that what you just said sounds, in my mind anyway, like something the Blessed Holy Mother might have said, according to all that my mother, Queen Ros, has told me. Strange indeed. Oh yes, there is one other small detail."

His face flushed and he stopped mid-sentence. "When I left, my mother also told me that I may well find the love of my life on my long journey of discovery. I thought that was a silly thing to say, though. However," and his face turned rather red, "she may have been right." He looked lovingly at Fianna. He stood formally before me, and I wondered what he was doing. "Since I have no way of asking your parents for permission, I will ask you, her sister. Bethany, may I have the most honorable privilege of courting your sister, the incredibly beautiful, Fianna of Cuch Glyn?"

I choked. He was dead serious. If I were being truthful with myself, I had seen this coming for weeks now. I glanced at Fianna, her face told me all that I needed to know. "Fergus of Aine, you have my permission to court my sister Fianna, as long as she so desires your attention."

"Whoopee!" exclaimed Fianna, and she rushed over to Fergus, and the two hugged each other. Now the two could be open about their feelings toward one and other. If love came, so be it. I could think of nothing better for my sister, who had already suffered greatly. She deserved all the happiness she could get. I glanced at Caitlyn; her eyes were wet. I knew that she had seen this coming as well. It also met with her total approval. Hence, there would be no rivalry between these women. I relaxed slightly — one less problem to fret about. Yet, I knew that the time had come for me to divulge my own secrets.

Chapter 11 Ket's Story

I ate another loaf of bread and made more hot tea, before I had the nerve to discard my own deceptions. Primarily, I was undecided about how much to reveal to my companions about my former lifetime. Look at it this way. Suppose a friend of yours began talking very sincerely about former lives that he had lived. How would you handle that? I suspect that if you were somewhat in touch with the former identities that you had been, you might listen and accept what your friend was saying about theirs, right? On the other hand, suppose that you couldn't recall much of anything before your body was, say, five years old and your friend began discussing his former lifetimes. What do you suppose your reaction might be? To top it off, supposing that your friend claimed to have been some important historical person. Can you grasp my dilemma? I knew that my sister had a glimpse of the identity she had before this life — the old fisherman who drowned. However, about Fergus and Caitlyn, I knew nothing. The result, one loaf of bread later, I still couldn't reach any real decision, save to decide as I went along. "Okay, everyone, now it's my turn. I hope you are all prepared."

Fergus and Fianna sat on the bed holding hands. That was a good sign. Caitlyn sat meekly in a chair, though her eyes never left me as she sipped her tea. "Like Caitlyn, I have been forced into using a disguise. I am really Ket of Cuch Glyn. I'm not Fianna's sister but her youngest brother." There I dropped my own bombshell and waited for their reactions.

"You can't be!" declared Fergus. "You, you, you are so womanly, I mean — well I don't know what I mean. You sure fooled me!"

I glanced at Caitlyn. Her eyes were open as wide as they could go; she had a look of tremendous relief on her face, though I knew not from what. "I really am fourteen and a half now. It happened this way. Our dad was a fisherman and mom, a village priestess, Godwin and Naessa. My older brothers are Garth and Rath. Fian died along with our parents that horrid day. I was escorting Fianna and some of her girlfriends on a countryside excursion to gather early spring berries. Oops, I guess I ought to begin slightly earlier. A couple days before this one, three riders came into our village, one of the southernmost coastal villages of Tewdwr. Their spokesman claimed to be speaking for this King Albert I of Bregia. He announced that this king had just confiscated all our land to be a part of his kingdom. Well, our villagers protested and tried to run them off. However, these men shot quarrels at our unarmed men. Well, that started the fight. In the end, the villagers managed to kill the two who had shot the crossbows. The spokesman fled."

"Everyone thought that this would be the end of it. However, I explained that this king would likely return with a huge force to conquer what he viewed as a rebellious village. No one, save Fianna, believed me. Nothing happened for a couple days and everyone forgot about it. That was the day that I was escorting Fianna and her girlfriends berry hunting. When we were returning and were about a mile from our village, we saw perhaps fifty cavalrymen charging up the seacoast. I presume they entered the coastal zone several miles to the south to take us by surprise."

"In horror, we watched the nearly defenseless villagers get butchered. Three men in the whole village actually had a sword, though none was skilled in its use. Pitchforks and boat oars fought against mounted cavalry. All but ten adults in the village were killed, though we managed to save the lives of another six. We watched as they killed my father and brother. When mom came out of our house to aid dad, they killed her too. It was an awful sight to behold."

"Well, that did it. I got very angry and charged into the village. It had already begun to rain. It rains nearly every day in coastal Tewdwr, by the way. I coalesced the storm clouds a bit and began pulling down lightning upon the cavalrymen, one by one. They rushed at me, so I picked up the oar that dad had used to fend off these men. I caught their quarrels in flight or deflected them and continued to bring down lightning strikes upon them. I tried to be as overt and spooky about it as I could. I would point and make gestures at the next victim before the bolt came down to slay him. At long last when only a few of the cavalry remained alive, they routed and rapidly rode back down the coast, fleeing for their lives."

"Fianna then joined me as we examined our fallen family. Dad and Fian were already dead, but I don't think Fianna or I will ever forget our mother's dying last words to us."

Fianna, tears rolling down her cheeks, blurted out, "I love you. That's what she said to me."

"Take care of Fianna, she told me. You see why I am always going to be looking out for my sister?"

"I had no idea," Fergus consoled her. She laid her head on his shoulder. "I'm so sorry for your loss, dear Fianna!" His arms held her tight. Caitlyn looked very pale and shocked.

"We had to keep it a secret. I was never so glad for an adult to come in and take charge as I was that day. Old Conna rose to the challenge, taking care of us all. Oh, yes, I forgot to mention that the cavalry had thrown torches onto many roofs, and half of the village was burning. I simply pulled the storm closer and compacted it somewhat so that we got a veritable downpour, which put out the fires. Mostly the thatched roofs were destroyed, but the rest of the buildings I managed to save. Anyway, after the children had dug a mass grave — over half our village perished that day, the few remaining adults and we children buried our family members. The next day, the survivors packed up everything that was of value and headed inland seeking safety and aid from a larger town."

"However, wise Conna took us aside and pointed out that the king's men had seen all that I had done. He reminded me that the king would very likely now set a bounty on my head and send out all his forces to try to find me and slay me, since I was his only real opponent in conquering southern Tewdwr. We both knew that I had to flee. He also said that I should take Fianna with me. Otherwise, eventually those men would find her and torture her at best to get information on my whereabouts. He suggested that I travel under some kind of disguise so that I wouldn't be recognized. Fianna came up with my brilliant disguise, traveling as a young woman. She helped me into some of her and mom's clothes. Since that day this past June, I have been traveling around disguised as I am, Bethany. We dare not go back to Tewdwr unless I'm prepared to seek out this King Albert I and slaughter him and all his men, singlehandedly. This is, of course, silly. I've no such intention and probably couldn't do that much damage before someone killed this body."

The mood was dense and heavy, so I attempted to lighten their mood. I teased, "I really have a male body. Haven't any of you wondered why I have such a slim chest?" That did it. Suddenly, everyone laughed heartily. In fact, though they had not said anything, they had wondered.

Caitlyn exclaimed, "So that is how you could carry me when I was shot! I felt so awful thinking that a young girl had to carry me all that distance. I know that I couldn't have carried you at all. I felt so badly, but now I don't. What a relief!" She added consolingly, "Honestly, Ket, you really did the wisest thing. This King Albert is a really vile, mean, evil man. He probably has his men still scouring the countryside looking for you. We were lucky we didn't go down into Layamon. I bet he has men watching every town and village there! Two red heads would be spotted at once!"

"You are right, Caitlyn, and, boy was I sure glad that you provided us all an alternative reason not to go down into Layamon! Also, like you, Caitlyn, I don't have any men's clothing with me. I'm afraid I won't fit into yours. I'm a bit taller." She grinned and gave me a loving, knowing smile. I felt warm inside and that bulge in my pant grew once more. I was very glad to be wearing women's clothing so that it didn't show. I had to change the subject. "I couldn't have pulled it off if I hadn't had the help of Fianna." Now, of course, everyone look at her. She just grinned, proud of her minor accomplishments.

"Verily, Fianna, you and your idea probably saved your brother's life," Fergus complimented her. She enjoyed his attention and didn't refute it.

Embolden by the astounding news that I was not a woman, Caitlyn became a bit braver. She came over to me and gave me a big loving hug. "It seems we two have a lot more in common. We both narrowly avoided the clutches of King Albert. I'm *so* glad you are really a young *man*, Ket. You've *no* idea how happy that makes me." I flushed and caught Fianna winking an eye my way. My arms surrounded her soft body, as I returned the hug. I liked her a lot, I thought to myself.

Idle chatting ensued discussing various points, whereon Fianna suggested she make us some supper. I was hungry and time had passed rapidly. As she and Caitlyn headed for the kitchen, I called out, "After dinner, there is a whole lot more to my story." There, I had said it. Now there was no turning back. I had to be even more honest with my dear friends. I gambled on the fact that they had seen me casting some of my druwid spells, which they may assign to a god or goddess. I hoped that they would accept my former identities and explanations of this.

Caitlyn merely said coyly, "I certainly *hope* there is a *whole* lot more." She and Fergus chuckled over her pronouncement. I suspect that both wanted to know just why and how I could create walls of ice and bring down lightning bolts.

An hour later, full of dried fish — I really was getting awfully tired of a steady diet of dried fish — we four resumed our places. Fianna and Fergus sat on the bed, Caitlyn, on a chair opposite me. I could tell she wanted to watch my face closely. Once more, I took up my tale.

"How much I dare tell you about myself will depend in some measure on how well you grasp and accept what I have to tell you next. Indeed, some of what I tell you may place you in grave danger. We'll see how it goes." I sighed; I had to tell them some of this; I just had to.

"We are all immortal spiritual beings; we cannot die. For brief time spans, we occupy one of these fleshly bodies. I am me and have always been me and will always be me. You have to understand that or else none of what I am about to say to you will make any sense to you." For an instant, I wished I knew how Jes was able to move a being out of his head so that he could see for himself what he really was, an immortal being. Unfortunately, Jes had never revealed how he did that to me. Whether I could have gotten that information or skill from him had he lived, I do not know. Thus, I did the next best thing. I had them create a mental picture of our horses and then asked them who was looking at that picture and introduced themselves to themselves, the spiritual being which was them doing the looking. I know, meager at best, but it was all that I knew how to do just then.

Now that they had some vague idea of their spiritual selves, I continued, "Here on Tarra, this is the third fleshly body I have inhabited. Both of the two I had before this one were female. I have the skills and knowledge of being a woman, wife, and mother mostly down pat! Unfortunately, this is my first male body, and I am at a loss with how to deal with it. Many times now, I have felt like a fish out of water. I know it is just a role in the game to play, but I have not yet figured out how to play the man's role! It seems so foreign, so opposite of me. My very nature is that of a warm, loving, nurturing mother. I loathe fighting and detest mortal combat, especially with swords and projectiles! If I am forced to fight, I prefer a simple pole. Fianna can tell you about just that."

She jumped at the chance to describe how the bully Ged had challenged me and how I had knocked him out with a pole. Unfortunately, she did describe all the teasing I had endured, "sissy Ket." Thus, I had to elaborate.

"You see, as a small boy, I wanted to help around the house, doing those things that I knew how to do — things, I discovered, that are normally assigned to the womanly role." They seemed to grasp this, nodding their heads affirmatively, so I continued. "However, as a woman, I have one vice." I paused until they were about to insist on knowing. "I dearly love really long hair. I have always had this passion for it."

Fergus roared, "Now how on Tarra could we *ever* have guessed that one? I don't think I have ever met someone who has longer hair." They all roared once more. I did too; this seemed very petty a vice, considering all else that was at stake here on Tarra.

Caitlyn finally stopped laughing and added, "Please don't cut it now! Actually, I too love long hair, only I had no choice but to cut mine. I know you are a man, but Ket, I know many men who let their hair grow long, well maybe not as long as yours is. It is just that you are wearing it in the wrong style for a man. I can see Fianna's hand in the way you wear it, rather like hers. If you would simply tie it into a ponytail, it wouldn't look anywhere near so feminine." I really began to like Caitlyn even more! I realized now that it would take an act of god to get me voluntarily to cut it short! Why was I so excited about the fact that she did not want me to cut it?

"Verily, Ket, Caitlyn speaks truthfully. Don't cut it man. Do you realize that your flaming red hair has become the trademark of the Cymry Minstrels? At least two dozen men have personally commented to me about your hair. Honestly, wherever we have played, your hair has been duly noted! Now that we are about to go on tour on the mainland, if you go and cut it, I'll bop you on the head!" Again, we all laughed. I had no intention of cutting it.

Still chuckling, I added, "Don't worry, I don't think that even Jehosa could make me cut it. Now then, are you ready for the next revelation?"

They quieted down so I dropped it on them. "Okay then, the identity I used last lifetime, the name that I was called was Bethany Madelyn Amir." I said nothing more, letting this startling fact sink home. Unfortunately, their reaction was what I had feared the most.

Caitlyn cried out, "The Blessed Holy Mother!" She dove to her knees, as only a devout worshiper would. Fergus followed suit a split second behind Caitlyn. The absolute last thing I wanted now was a pair of devout, religiously blind worshipers!

I put on my most grandmotherly attitude, "If you two grandchildren do not get back up there and stop all this silliness at once, why, I shall just have to send you two back home!"

"But," Caitlyn began to protest, so I helped her back to her chair;

Fianna pulled Fergus back onto the bed.

"No but's allowed at this time," I interjected. "Look, I did the best that I was able to do for everyone at that point in time. You can't imagine how badly I feel for what my first-born son, Ahmad, has become! I do not want to be worshiped. I never ever intended that to happen. I do not have any idea how this worship of who I was has come about. Mark my words closely grandchildren, what I *wanted* others to do was to emulate my ways, to be honest with each other, to work together to build a new town and lives, and to learn about their spiritual natures. None of this has anything to do with worshiping a fleshly body that I used to have."

"You both claimed to have come on this venture to learn. It's time that you *did* just that. Now the first thing you must grasp is that it was my fleshly body that was involved in your bloodlines, not me or *thee*! You are a being, just as I am. You have had other bodies as have I and Fianna. So no more worship of a fleshly body."

"Please accept my humblest apologies," Fergus was the first to come to his senses. "It was just the shock of it all. To be fully truthful, Bethany, er Ket, I had my own suspicions all along — not that you are the Holy Blessed Mother — rather that you may be one of the Guardians that I have been seeking. You know, the ice walls, catching arrows — you must admit one doesn't very often see someone doing either, if ever."

I chuckled, "No, you most certainly do not! I only did it in your presence because I could see no other way out of the jam we were in at the time." I sensed that I would have no further problems with Fergus. Caitlyn was another matter entirely, compounded by the fact that she was a pretty woman and I, now a man.

I took her hand in mine. "Look, you wanted to find me and you have. Now you have a chance to learn as much as you can. It is all in your hands now, Caitlyn. Will you rise to the challenge?"

"Yes, ma'am, er I mean Ket, er Bethany," she replied, growing more confused by the moment.

I grinned, "Caitlyn, you have put your tongue on the very first problem that we four have to solve. What the heck am I going to be called?" My grin became contagious. A moment before, we were talking about an incredibly significant topic, yet now, something as simple as a name.

"The problem I have is that I am also in love with my former name, Bethany. Actually, I have managed to be called Bethany in both lives, though admittedly it took some doing on my part to get my parents last lifetime to change my name to Bethany. They had originally named me Madelyn, which I loathed. We finally compromised with Bethany Madelyn. However, what to do now is the real question. Honestly, you two, I have my own problems. I feel like I'm a woman; yet I have this male body. I love to be called Bethany, but that can't be twisted into a male name anyway that I can see. Ket, well I could have found something better. Any ideas?" This was serving a two-fold purpose. While lightning up the mood, it gave them an opportunity actually to contribute to helping me out of a problem. Likewise, they might actually help me out of my problem!

"Boy you are right. How could you twist Bethany into a male's name?" Caitlyn commented, her mind racing to figure something out. Fergus kept muttering variations on Bethany, but nothing worked, such as Thany and Eth. I'd long ago explored all those avenues.

"Hey I know," Caitlyn said with that look of confidence that one has when one has worked out a complex puzzle. "Correct me if I'm wrong, but it seems that folks in Tewdwr only have one name, using the name of their village as a surname, right."

Fianna agreed, "Yes, I'm Fianna of Cuch Glyn. Ket of Cuch Glyn, Naessa of Cuch Glyn."

"Here on the mainland, no one is at all likely to know the towns and villages of Tewdwr; they probably have never heard of it. So how about this: Ket of Bethany, or just Ket Bethany for short? That way you can be called Ket among strangers and Bethany among your close friends?" I suddenly realized that I had done just that earlier, when questioned by the Sister. I had not wanted to lie to her and said I was Ket Bethany!

"Brilliant! Well done, Caitlyn!" I gave her a loving hug. "So simple. I wonder why I never thought of that before! Honestly, me making such a fuss over something as my name. I prefer being called Bethany, especially among you. The outside world can call me Ket. I think that will work perfectly. Thanks. Do you realize I have been worrying about that for nearly fifteen years? What a relief." I meant it.

However, as I hugged her, I felt some resistance, some reluctance on her part, as if she felt a little more distant from me. I knew instinctively something was still troubling her. I'm not known for beating around the tree with matters. "You aren't totally happy with this name thing?" She didn't have that instant body language reaction that I expected to see. No, it was something else. "I see that it isn't what is bothering you. I give up, please tell me, Caitlyn?" Her face flushed; I gathered whatever it was, she found it embarrassing, but I had no idea.

She sighed and resigned herself to speaking. "Suppose that I got married and had a son, and then he got married and had a son." The three of us said in unison, "Ah huh." She continued, "Then suppose I then died, I mean the female body I had died, and then I found a new female body that was not related to them in anyway. Would it be all right for my grandson and me, in the new body, to," she faltered and her face grew even redder. "To, um, have a relationship, I mean as man and wife?"

Now it was my turn to be somewhat embarrassed; I began to sense what she really wanted to ask. Yet the druwid in me recognized the total validity of the question. Nearly everywhere, societies frowned on marriage between siblings or those too closely related: offspring of such a union generally had physical deformities of some kind, though no one knew why, just the empirical knowledge that such resulted from sibling offspring. I filed this away to research more fully someday; I still had this unquenchable thirst for knowledge.

"Spiritual beings are not the same as fleshly bodies, Caitlyn. It would be perfectly fine for you and I, for example, to wed. However, only trouble would likely follow if you and Fergus were to wed. I mean the children of such a union might well have deformities of some kind." The grin on her face told me that whatever was troubling her had vanished; she returned my loving hug. Strangely, I enjoyed it and began to wonder.

"Now then, you two, I have a whole lot more to discuss. With the excitement out of the way, let me begin at the *very* beginning. That way, everything will make more sense to you. Realize that I'm under some obligations not to reveal certain secrets. Yet, I will tell you all that I can so you may learn and understand me better. Yes, you have found one of those that you are seeking. I began my lives here on Tarra as one of the Guardians, only we call ourselves the druwids. The earliest memory I have is when I was girl six years old playing in the powered dirt of the main street in a tiny Greenway village called Uru, back around 550 AH. Golly, has it been that long? Nearly three-quarters of a century ago, jeesh!"

I described how it was that I became an apprentice druwid, how my family had moved to Karka, had nearly been ambushed along the way, and how I had nearly gone insane bringing down lightning to slay our attackers. I described at some length the amount of time we had spent learning our skills. I knew that eventually, probably soon, one of these three would be asking me to teach them how to bring down lightning. After all, that was the very same question I asked Ellen, my first teacher, when I began my studies. Little did I know that learning how to do that action was not normally learned until the tenth year of study!

Next, I covered the era of the Centurion invasion and how my Lightning Circle had traveled all the way to Megalos in seek of some information that we could use to defend the Greenway from the expected invasion of the Centurions. They cheered when I described how, though drugged, I still managed to slay the lecherous Emperor who was attempting to rape me.

"Now realize that the most important person, spiritual being, on Tarra is Alabaster Benjamin Crowley, the founder of the druwids." I made sure that they saw his critical role. When I discussed how my Circle became the leaders after his body died of old age, they seemed very pleased indeed. "Yet, I make mistakes," I continued. How I met my death with an arrow in the forehead was a good lesson for them to learn. "I'm not all-mighty, like some god. I have my weaknesses, frailties, and lack of good judgments, just like everyone else." I think they were humbled by this. I sensed that they began to see me as a person; all three already had the wisdom to know not to try to reason with an insane person. Hearing that I made just such a fatal mistake helped them feel more at ease around me, that I wasn't this all-knowing, godlike person.

I then began the lengthy discussion of the Juda Arad mission and of the Great Messiah. After relating to them much of the story, particularly because of their grandparents, I added, "Yes, Caitlyn, your grandfather really was the Son of Jehosa. He really did perform honest miracles. Of that you can be totally certain." For their benefit, I related about a dozen such occurrences. I stopped when they both were crying tears of joy and happiness. "So yes, your direct bloodline is that of Jes Amir, the Son of Jehosa on Tarra. Incidentally, I find that *that* is more important than Jes's insistency on the additional bloodline running back into the depths of Arad history. But then, that is just my opinion. I let you draw your own conclusions." I continued with the apparent death and resurrection of the Great Messiah, swearing them never to reveal the full truth, for it could well upset all of Jes's preachings.

Next, I related all about our two families moving to West Reach. I couldn't resist flushing out the full details of some of the encounters we had. This way, they knew firsthand the full details of the stories that they were told as children. Finally, I carefully explained what I had done to help get the four towns established and thriving, out in the wilderness of the Layamon region.

"Okay, most of this is just history, really. If I go further, I run the risk of placing your lives in danger. I must ask you: do you want me to continue? It is your choice to make. I will honor your request, either way." I had to let them make their own decisions; after all, it was their lives that would be at risk. Even Fianna wanted to know fully, though I knew that she already knew most of it. Thus, I then began the tale of the giant praying mantises of the Red Desert and the Grey Creatures of the Appian Way.

I finished up by saying, "So that is how your grandfather actually died, Caitlyn. Many of us believe these evil creatures are manipulating human events, just like that one that followed me to Cuch Glyn and killed my body outside the village. I strongly suspect, based on how you described him, that the advisor of King Ahmad is really one of these Grey Creatures, disguised as a human, walking among us. My current theory is that these Grey Creatures are attempting to undo the work I had done here, namely showing people their true spiritual nature and avoiding going back to them to get their minds scrambled before acquiring a new baby body. My daughter Sarah also thought this was what was really happening. I sure wish I could find her; I've so many questions I would like to ask. Maybe one day we will run into her in our travels. Who knows?"

"So now you know the true mission I'm on — I must locate Alabaster in his new body, wherever he is, and help him recover. I'm quite confident that he isn't on Cymry. In the meantime, let us learn all the music we can and share our joy of music with others. What say you?"

"I'm with you one hundred percent!" declared Fergus. Fianna echoed him with a "Me too." Caitlyn added her, "Count me in."

"Thanks. Now then, one other detail. During our time together, I will teach you as much as I can. I doubt that any of you can really dedicate every waking hour for the next ten years in constant study, so don't expect to be throwing lightning bolts around. One more thing, only nine people that I know about can totally neutralize such an attack on themselves and those around them. I mean only nine of us can be attacked with flames falling from the sky and have that attack completely fail. That skill was the last thing my Circle of seven learned from Alabaster, and the hardest! Besides us, only he and his long dead wife could do it. I'm telling you this so that if we should by chance encounter one of these Grey Creatures and it attacks us by using fire, lightning, or ice, I should be able to neutralize such an attack. However, one blow from their massive fist will crush our skulls. They did just that to both Jes and me."

Suddenly I began laughing. When they finally got me to stop, I said, "Oh the irony of it all. You three came on this trip thinking you were going to learn the songs and dances of other lands while hunting for a Guardian. Instead, you have been with a Guardian all along, and now you'll be learning a vast amount of completely different things. Well, okay, we still have to learn the songs and dances." They chuckled too.

Caitlyn said, "So when do we start?" She bubbled a youthful enthusiasm.

"You already have," I smiled. "Tonight was history night. Tomorrow, we begin with observing the obvious, along with everything else that is thrown our way. We have to pick up their language rapidly, get new clothes — the list goes on."

I figured this ought to finish the night and that we would all turn in. However, Fianna was whispering something to Fergus. Occasionally she would look at me with a girlish twinkle in her eye. Fergus did likewise. What were these two up to, I wondered. I stared at him even harder when he went over to Caitlyn and whispered something into her ear. Whatever it was, she definitely blushed and glanced at me. "Okay, what is going on between you three?" I asked, all three were smiling rather sheepishly.

Fergus sat up straight and tall on the bed beside Fianna, who held his hand. "You said earlier that you are having a difficult time knowing what and how to play the male role, right?"

"Obviously," I replied, not knowing where this was heading.

"Will you allow me to give you some advice in this area of life?" Fergus continued.

"Sure," I replied. I still couldn't guess where this was leading.

"Some things are plain to others. On Cymry, it is customary for a young lad to ask permission of a lady's parents for permission to date or court their daughter. That's why I asked you earlier for permission to court Fianna, here. You are being a substitute father for her, you see."

"Yes, I understood that when you did it," I answered, still not seeing at what they all were driving.

"Considering that Caitlyn's mother is dead and that her father has become an enemy, Caitlyn is allowing me to act as her father in such matters. In that capacity, is there anything you would like to ask me?"

Wham! I suddenly got his message! My face turned beet red. I looked over at Caitlyn, who also was blushing, but she stared at the floor, not daring to look at me. Fianna had the largest imaginable grin on her face, she kept nodding her head, as if saying to me: yes, yes, yes. The bulge in my pant grew larger as I looked at Caitlyn. I had earlier seen just how important this social ritual had been for Fianna. Presumably, it was so for Caitlyn. Almost involuntarily, I found myself saying, "Fergus I would like to ask you for permission to court the lovely Caitlyn, if she will allow me to do so."

I saw that Caitlyn had both her fingers crossed. "Oh yes, yes I do," she gushed.

"Then you have my consent!" declared Fergus formally.

"Yippee! Hurray!" exclaimed Fianna. "For weeks now, I've seen how you two have been looking at each other when you think the other isn't noticing. It's as plain as the noses on your two faces; you really like each other. Well done, little brother! By the way, it's customary for you two to hug each other now," she declared using that 'I know what I am talking about' tone of voice. We needed no further encouragement.

"Let's all go for a stroll in the courtyard!" declared Fianna. She took Fergus's arm and out they went, disappearing into the darkness of the large courtyard. Cleverly, Fianna had just given me some private time alone with Caitlyn. I took her arm and we strolled outside as well.

Caitlyn explained, "I've had eyes for you almost since we first met. At first, I was really embarrassed about it — what with me thinking you were a woman and me really being a woman," she confessed. "Then when I saw Fergus falling for your sister and those two flirting with each other, I really felt just awful! You know, because I was supposed to be a man and wasn't. Several times, Fergus suggested that I ought to flirt with you, but I only got more embarrassed. I tried to stay a bit aloof. Can you imagine how awful I felt when you discovered that I was a woman? But actually after that I could at least hug you, you know like sisters."

I confessed, "Well, it was just as awful for me when I found out. I wanted to tell you right then, but I dared not, until we got out of harm's way. I'm sorry I really don't know all the proper things that a man ought to know and say. I suspect that my dad would have explained things to me, had he lived a little longer. Are you sure you like a man with really long hair?" I asked.

"Silly question. Of course! It's just that I'm having such a hard time reconciling you and the Blessed Holy Mother. Part of me sees an amazing man, Ket. Another part of me sees the Blessed Holy Mother, who is so utterly more powerful and knowledgeable and stronger than I am or likely will ever be, that I wonder what you can possibly see in me?"

"I see a beautify young woman with a head on her shoulders — a woman who cannot be stopped by or forced by men into doing actions she knows is wrong — a woman who will take whatever action she can to avoid it — a loving and caring woman — a woman who loves music as much as I do — a woman who is interested in a man who does not know fully yet how to play that role, if ever. Okay, a woman who likes a man with long hair. One of those is totally sufficient," I teased.

She gave me a squeeze and whispered, "No beards, please."

"God, you are right! This body is due to grow a beard! Oh no!" I moaned and meant it. I had forgotten about this minor detail. I was really beginning to dislike male bodies.

"Good," she said as she gave me another squeeze.

That night, we made some adjustments. I moved my things into Fergus's room, while Caitlyn moved her stuff to join Fianna. It was the first night that my sister and I had spent apart from each other since witnessing our parent's death. We both were finally emotionally ready for such a separation.

Chapter 12 Of the Events in d'Grange

I listened to the faint snoring of Fergus, this first night of sleeping as a man in the men's room away from the comfort of my sister. So much had been shared that I just couldn't fall asleep. I marveled at just how well these two grandchildren accepted what had to be startling, almost unbelievable news. I'd held back only what must be shared only among druwids. Already I saw the rewards of getting off those things that I had been knowingly withholding from my friends. Yes, I felt a sense of relief and freedom. Tonight, we four had become intensely close, once the artificial barriers imposed by withholding so much from each other had been eliminated. The future looked bright, as bright as the blue eyes of Caitlyn.

Caitlyn, I felt such a physical attraction to her! I wish Sarah Jane were here so I could ask her opinions about love; she had always been so knowledgeable in matters of the heart. I wondered where she was now. Naturally, this immediately led to wondering what had become of all those in my old Lightning Circle. Were their bodies still alive? If so, they would be very old indeed. More than likely, their bodies had died, long ago. Sandy had told me of Roy's passing. Had they been successful in finding new bodies? Did they, as I, still remember our druwid skills? Thus, the night slipped into day.

When Fergus roused me, I realized that my body had indeed been asleep all night, while I, on the other hand, had not! Strange. "Been thinking, let's see if we can make some of my spare clothes sort of work for you, until we can get some proper men's clothing," he suggested. For a few minutes, I tried on various shirts and pants. All were too big for me, naturally. However, we managed to find a combination that didn't look too awful, at least temporarily. Then, we answered the women's call to breakfast.

Caitlyn looked gorgeous to my eyes this morning and I told her so. She blushed, naturally, and promised to help fix my hair in a men's style. Her idea was simple. She drew it back and tied a bit of rawhide around, ponytail style. Next, periodically down its length, she position additional ties. "There, that's much better." I peeked in her metal mirror and was amazed that it didn't look so feminine anymore. I gave her a hug in thanks.

We had just finished the dishes and were discussing our next step, when someone knocked on our door. I answered because the others couldn't speak any of the languages that our visitor was likely to use. A young woman, around twenty-five with medium long blonde hair and deep blue eyes, greeted me. The yellow headband suggested to me that she might be the promised Sisterhood tutor. "Good morning," she said slowly to make sure that I could understand her, "I am Sister Angelina Arcora. I was told that you need the services of a linguist and a historian."

"Hi, I'm Ket Bethany. We sure do, come on inside," I welcomed her and motioned for her to enter. After introducing the others, I added, "Even more urgently, we also need a guide for shopping. We need some clothes and food supplies."

She looked at both Caitlyn and me, and commented, "Yes, you most certainly do. I know just the place to shop for reasonable clothing that is well made, but not too expensive. As far as the tutoring goes, how frequently do you want to meet and study?"

"Well, considering three of us can't speak a word in any dialect known around here, I'd say as often and as long as feasible. We are traveling musicians and need to get up to speed on recent history, as well as getting the basics of at least the Sea Prince and Greenway dialects learned quickly."

She grinned. I suspected she found this often to be the case. "I can be here six days a week, mornings and afternoons. However, I have a family to care for and will have to go home to fix them lunch and supper. I can be here for three hours in the morning and five in the afternoon. Usually, we accept some kind of monetary donation for this service. If these times are satisfactory with you, then the donation is whatever you are able to afford up to but not exceeding a gold piece a week. How does that sound?"

"Great, just perfect!" I replied, and we shook hands, sealing the bargain. Fianna gave her the gold coin for her first week.

"Very good, thanks," she replied with a smile. "You may all call me Sister Angelina." She then made each of us say her name until we got it properly pronounced in the Velona dialect. Next, she took us on our first shopping trip.

The seamstress shop was only six blocks distant; Sister Augati's Clothing read the large sign over the doorway. Sister Angelina was right; the dresses and clothing were very well made indeed. I have an eye for this detail, compliments of my previous two lifetimes. Naturally, the women had a ball picking out just the right dress for Caitlyn. I needed considerable help finding the proper articles that would best fit my new persona. Fergus and Sister Angelina constantly gave me pointers. I was totally used to wearing whatever hand-me-downs mom had given me to wear that I had absolutely no male clothing-sense. I walked out wearing a loose fitting white cotton pull on shirt, brown pants with a blue sash and a matching blue headband and hair ties. The legs of my new pants were stuffed neatly inside the tops of a pair of brown leather boots, to which a pair of matching blue ribbons had been added at the last minute. Caitlyn declared that I now look like a find dandy; everyone was pleased with my new look.

Caitlyn now wore a white cotton dress that flared out at the knees. She too wore a blue sash around her waist that matched mine. She also wore a matching small bonnet that helped hide her altogether too short hair, which she was now overly concerned about its appearance. Arm in arm, we two couples walked back to the inn. During the course of our stay in d'Grange, we would visit this shop at least a dozen times, eventually special ordering several sets of clothes, including matching ones for our gigs.

Back at the inn, the language lessons began in earnest. While I had mostly to work on getting the proper accent back, the others had to learn from scratch. It was a frustrating, enjoyable, tedious, repetitious, yet pleasurable time for the three of them. On their behalf, I must say that they were all three fast learners and worked very hard. Part of each evening, I taught them to read and write what they had learned to speak that day. However, the end of each day was spent in practicing our music.

Yes, Caitlyn taught us another dozen tunes from the Layamon region; Fergus, a comparable amount from the highlands. Not to be left out, I attempted to recall how the songs went that I had known so many years ago as a young girl in the Greenway, learned during the time my Lightning Circle had spent with the traveling musicians. After some trial and error, I finally figured out how to play that marvelous lament the wife of the leader had taught me. Inspired by that success, I fiddled around on my flute until I could actually play that melody that Willow Windsong had sung to me while I had been temporarily insane, after bringing down hundreds of lightning bolts to kill the cavalry who had, I thought, just killed my family in the wagon. Her song had brought me back from the black abyss into life.

Once I had it worked out, together, we created a full band version. I had completely forgotten the words, but Fianna declared it a lullaby. To all of our amazement, she joined in by using her voice as an instrument, not singing words, but singing sounds. We all got chills hearing her sing like that and we encouraged her to sing along this way whenever she felt like doing so. None of us realized it at the time, but this lullaby would have a very far-reaching impact on our goals here on the mainland!

After three weeks, we felt comfortable chatting with the people we met and finally decided it was time to begin sharing our music with the folks of this incredible city. Just as promised, the Sisterhood dance hall was mere blocks from our inn. We had no problems at all setting up a gig to play for their Friday night dance. Wearing our best outfits, we arrived just after supper, carrying our many instruments. Fianna commented that she felt like a pack animal and we laughed.

The dance hall took our breaths away! We entered the door that we had been instructed to use. It opened up backstage. Yes, the hall boasted a well-thought out musician's gallery, raised about three feet from the main dance floor, but the room was enormous, at least fifty feet square, with many supporting stone columns scattered uniformly around the central sections. Across the back, tables lined the wall, and Sisters were beginning to bring in food and drink, arranging them nicely on the table. Fresh flowers provided an outdoor atmosphere. Lanterns hung from the columns and ceiling, however, fully a dozen illuminated our gallery so that the musicians could see their instruments. Along the two other walls, tapestries hung, depicting the nearby mountains. Rows of chairs sat in front of these tapestries providing a chance for the dancers to relax or for the non-dancers to watch. By the time we were to play, the place was absolutely packed! At least three hundred attended to hear us play.

We tested the acoustics as we setup our instruments. We had no play list, as such. Rather as usual, one of us would call out the next song, as we judged the crowd's needs and desires. I had only a single misgiving: what if someone insisted on a local song that we didn't know? The embarrassment that night when the inn crowd demanded we play Aberdeen Rose still haunted me, putting me slightly on edge.

Now the folks began arriving, so we stopped warming up, watched the people, and waited for some signal to begin. I noticed Sister Capriotti and her two guards arriving, and we nodded towards each other. She did a double take though, as she saw me as a male instead of a young girl. What I found fascinating were the men. At least one third of the attendees were male. True, the preponderance were younger folks; still, some looked like they might be in their sixties and sat on the chairs, intending to have a good time as well. I spied Sister Abrienda arriving, a man on one arm, leading her, while she held onto another woman, who probably was in her thirties. Something was strange about this other woman though, but I could not tell what. She walked and moved with unusual motions, appearing to depend utterly upon the guidance of Sister Abrienda. She help the woman to a seat in the rear, the woman used her hands to feel about the chair before sitting down. Next, the man escorted her towards us, while she was smiling broadly, greeting folks as she passed them, which was a chore since the place was becoming quite packed.

She walked up the short stairs onto the stage, with the man escorting her all the way. She, too, had on a very nice gown, puffed out below the waist. "We meet again," she greeted us. "I just wanted my husband to meet you. This is Fabiano Arcola. Dear, these are the Cymry Minstrels. You will forgive me but I didn't bring my list with your names." I quickly introduced each of us, "I'm the leader, Ket Bethany, this is my sister Fianna, the lady Caitlyn on the dulcimer, and Fergus O'rylee." He seemed very pleased to meet us in person.

Next, she turned to face the huge crowd. She raised her hands high and instantly a hush fell over the room. "Welcome to the Friday Night Dance. Tonight we are very pleased to offer you something you'll find very different from the usual band. Please welcome all the way from West Reach, the Cymry Minstrels!" A loud round of applause followed. I blushed from all this unexpected attention; Fianna and Caitlyn reveled in it. Fergus, evidently, was used to such formal introductions. Quickly, she repeated our names, motioning for each of us to rise, so that everyone would associate the name with the person. Then, with a gracious wave of her hand, she said, "Let the dance begin."

If I had any fears that they would find our dance tunes foreign and not even dance, they were gone after the first dance we played. Dance songs are appreciated everywhere, a fact that I was quickly learning. They were enthralled with Fianna's use of the castanets, entirely different from the normal sounds from the Sea Princes. However, when Fianna did the Crossed Swords Dance, everyone stopped dancing to watch her, a fact that did not escape her, and she improvised even more than normal for her admirers. She got such a huge round of applause that we had to play that one again! As soon as we finished it, Sister Abrienda signaled that it was a break time for us, motioning for us to come down and get some drink at the back tables.

While Fergus escorted Fianna, I did the same with Caitlyn. We all felt much better being firmly attached to each other, while walking through this huge crowd. Everyone offered us compliments as we passed by them on the way to the table. It actually took us nearly five minutes to navigate to the table! It seemed that everyone here wanted at least to say hello to us. Indeed, more than one woman commented about our long red hair, a real rarity in this city. Hence, I was glad that I had taken Fergus's advice and just tied it into a ponytail, leaving it flair out behind me. It did add to our image, no doubt.

It took us even longer to get back on stage. This set, we interspersed some slower laments in with the faster dances and found that they did enjoy them as well. Next, we tried Lyneth's Lament. I began low on the bass flute, a sound rarely heard anywhere; quietly, Caitlyn joined in on the dulcimer. After a bit, the soft tapping of Fergus on the dumbeck added more rhythm; at last, Fianna, clicking her castanets almost seemingly at random, added just the finishing touches. After the climax, one by one the others dropped out in reverse order, until only the low, mellow bass flute trailed off to the last haunting note.

When I stopped, you could hear a pin drop. It was that quiet! In a delayed reaction came the loudest applause of the evening. Quickly, we drowned them out with another loud fast dance, led by Fergus on the bagpipes and with me blowing away on the tenor shawm. Yes, our first gig went far better than we predicted. We lost complete track of time, and Sister Abrienda finally had to interrupt us to call a halt, because the hour was very late indeed. How time flew that night!

We received a thunderous round of applause and then someone began yelling, "Come back next Friday night!" Quickly, many picked it up, chanting the words repeatedly, until I stood up, looked at Sister Abrienda for her approval, raised my hands, and yelled, "Okay, see you next Friday!"

As the people began filing out, still talking about us, Sister Abrienda climbed back on stage and handed me four gold pieces. "I know it isn't much, but it is what our musicians normally get for playing here."

"Thanks, it is more than enough, Sister Abrienda," I replied. "We're not doing this for money; we are doing it for fun and the sharing of music. The crowd's reaction tonight is all the payment we really need, but this will help pay for our lodging and tutoring. Thanks."

She grinned. "Say, are you in a rush to leave?"

"Er, no. We are just packing up our instruments, why?"

"After you get them all packed, why don't the four of you come back to where I am at? I have someone I would like you to meet. I hope it doesn't embarrass you. She is blind."

"Sure thing, give us a couple minutes." We carefully packed away all the instruments and then went to join her. Most everyone had left; she and her husband were standing beside the woman, who they had led in when they arrived. Blind. Now I grasped the awkwardness I had observed when she had sat down. It made sense. I wondered who this woman was.

"Here they come," she said to the woman as we came close, standing before her rather awkwardly. I've never been this close to a blind person before, ever. Neither had my friends. "Minstrels, I would like you to meet Sister Jolina Alwana, the greatest musician in the entire Velona sector, that is, before she was blinded. Sister Jolina, I'll introduce you to them one by one. Is it okay if she feels your face and such?" she asked us. We shook our heads yes. "This is their unusual looking leader, Jolina, Ket Bethany. He is the one I told you who has the longest flaming red hair I've ever seen." She offered her hand randomly into space roughly where I stood.

I reached out and took it in mine, gently shaking it, "Very pleased to meet you, Sister Jolina." With her hands, she followed up my arms to my face, all around it, and of course, onto my hair. A look of amazement formed on her face as she attempted to find where it ended, somewhere around my butt.

"Is it really cardinal red like she says?" she asked.

"You bet," I replied. "My sister's is just a wee bit shorter at the moment."

One by one, she met the others, feeling them as well. Of course, her comment when she felt Caitlyn was to be expected, "My, but your hair is so short! What amazing contrasts." Caitlyn flushed.

Jolina, ignorant of the blush, said, "Yes, I truly enjoyed hearing you play tonight. You are far better than Abrienda promised. Pray, what is the name of that piece you played on the bass flute, the slow, sad, but intensely moving one? When it was done, there was total silence in here. That one."

Caitlyn spoke up, "Lyneth's Lament. It is the sad lament of Lyneth over the untimely loss of her husband. It is an old traditional Layamon song that goes way back in time. It must be hundreds of years old by now."

"It moved me as no other song has touched me all these years. Will you play it for me next week?" Jolina asked.

"Absolutely!" insisted Fianna.

Inspiration struck, or maybe it was the subtleness with which the Sisterhood operated. I asked, "Say, do you still play music, Jolina?"

A harsh, sad look crumpled her face, "No, never since I was blinded."

Undaunted, I asked, "What all did you used to play? You recognized the bass flute without having seen it," I complimented her.

A smile erased the downcast look, "Silly boy. I would know that sound anywhere. I used to play one years ago. I used to play so many instruments. Let's see, I had three different flutes, a lute, guitar, mandolin — so many, I've rather forgotten now. No, I never played the bladder pipes, though."

Memories of how Isabel had been when my Lightning Circle found her came back into my mind. She'd lost both hands and was trying to die, claiming to be useless. Of course, she was not. For a year, she had been delivering basic druwid training to the two young sisters who were looking after her. We had helped her get her self-respect back, and she recovered so well that, later on, she actually became a Wid for the All Greenway Circle. Somehow, I saw a bit of Isabel in Jolina here.

I asked quietly, "Jolina, do your fingers still work?"

"Yes, why? There is nothing wrong with them; it is my eyes," she said slightly annoyed.

"Well, that's good to hear. How about your ears and mouth? Do they still work?"

"Of course!" she definitely sounded very annoyed with me, like it was I who could not see.

"That settles it then!" I declared. "There is absolutely no reason whatsoever to keep you from playing all the music you want to play, now is there?" I knew what her response was going to be; she did not disappoint me.

"Can't you see that I am blind? I cannot play. I cannot see!"

"Jolina, honestly, we both know that that is a pile of bologna! Haven't you sometimes sat outside at night and played for yourself to the heavens above? Haven't you had to play some places where there was almost no lantern light by which to see?"

"How did you know that? Why, yes, I used to love to play by myself late at night. How could you know that? Oh yes, I do remember once we played this inn where the innkeeper probably had never cleaned the lampblack from the lanterns in years. We all fumbled around so, trying to get set up."

"See, and weren't you all still able to play somewhat decently, despite the limited lighting?"

"Well, yes, we made mistakes, but it went as well as could be expected," she replied.

"Great! Well, then I will be expecting to have you come round to our inn early tomorrow afternoon. Bring whatever instruments you wish. You can teach us all the songs you know, and we will teach you all the songs we know. How's that for a fair trade?"

"But I can't see," she protested.

"I don't care whether you can see. I care whether you can make music, and I see no reason why you can't make all the music you want, with proper allowances for booboos, of course. That goes with learning any new song. Practice makes perfect, we musicians are fond of saying back home. Are they fond of saying that here too?"

"Well, yes, but. . ."

"Sorry, I will not accept any buts. You must come!"

The soft, kind voice of Sister Abrienda added, "I'll go with you myself, Jolina."

Begrudgingly and timidly, Jolina said, "Okay."

We said our farewells and went to get our things. Meanwhile, Fabiano Arcola took Jolina's arm, leading her out of the dance hall. Sister Abrienda, tears swelling in her eyes, and emotionally overcome, came up to me, "I don't know how to ever thank you enough. I have been trying to get her to resume her playing for the last four years. Never once would she. Thank you from the bottom of my heart for giving her another chance."

"Don't worry. We'll have her playing up a storm in short order. Besides, think of all the songs she can teach us," I replied. We hugged each other.

That was the topic we four chatted about all the way home and then some. At first, all three of them couldn't figure out why I was asking this blind woman to come play with us. Then each one of them realized who and what this woman represented: the greatest musician in Velona. All three of them continued to compliment me over and over for my brilliant, quick thinking.

True to her word, Sister Abrienda brought Sister Jolina to our inn the next day, just after lunch. She brought a flute and a guitar, slung over her back. Yes, it was very awkward at first, getting her into an unfamiliar room and comfortable in a chair where she could play. Yes, Jolina complained that she was totally out of practice and probably couldn't see well enough to play right anyway. I teased her saying that she couldn't see at all, unless she had been pulling my leg. Of course, she and everyone else had a good laugh over that one.

I thought it wise to begin with some slower pieces so that she could get used to playing without sight once more. It was a very wise decision on my part. True, her first attempts were riddled with missed notes and such. By the third pass at it, you couldn't tell that the maker of the music was blind. The fourth pass through, we began joining in, making our own booboos as we tried to learn the sad ballad. When the afternoon ended, she had taught us four slow tunes, and we had taught her Lyneth's Lament.

However, before she left, she ask me if she could try out my bass flute. "Actually, it is Fergus's instrument, but his fingers are too short for the holes," I commented as I handed it to her, wondering how this would go. As I had, she found it difficult to reach the holes; they were so far apart. Nevertheless, she rapidly caught on to its dimensions. After her fourth pass through the melody, she had it down pat on this new instrument. Delight shone on her face as she began playing for herself. We musicians do that from time to time — play solely and only for our own gratification. This was her time for herself. We listened enthralled at the complexity of variations she invented right before our ears, so to speak! In that instant, I realized just how far above me her playing and skill actually was!

When she finally finished, she handed the instrument into the air for someone to get. I took it and said, "I have so much that I can learn from you. I feel like a total amateur!" Between sniffles, Caitlyn and Fianna echoed my words. Even Fergus recognized that he was in the presence of a real master musician. I looked at Sister Abrienda, who was sitting on the bed, tears of unbridled joy streaming down her face.

Jolina answered me, "You aren't really that bad; you just lack polish and more of a feel for the music. All that will come in time, if as you say, you continue to practice."

"Will you try to come here every afternoon, please, Jolina? We have so much to learn and share with each other?" I begged, unwilling to lose this incredible opportunity that had landed in our lap.

"Yes, I will, that is, if I can get someone to bring me," she replied with an air of confidence and certainty in her voice that we hadn't heard before.

"I'll bring you or one of my aides will if I can't get away, Jolina, you can count on that! Thank you all so very much. It is getting late and I need to get her home. See you tomorrow, same time?"

"Yes, that would be terrific," I said, as we watched them awkwardly navigate the room and courtyard.

"Well, that handles that problem," declared Fianna, in her older sister's tone. "With enough time, we'll know all the songs of the Sea Princes. Way to go, Bethany!"

Caitlyn, though, surprised me, "Actually, if you ask me, I think that Bethany just performed a miracle right before our eyes, if only we opened them to see it." Fergus and Fianna both gave her looks that showed her they had no idea what she was saying. She elaborated, "Look you two. Here is this incredible musician who somehow lost her sight. Ever since then, she hasn't ever played a note. Bethany somehow has just gotten Jolina to play again, and she is so much better than we all are that it's not funny! I say that is a miracle!" she heftily declared.

"You are right, Caitlyn," Fianna agreed, "how totally unobservant of me. Of course, it's pretty amazing." Fergus agreed likewise.

The druwid in me stepped in, "Caitlyn gets the prize for today with her keen observation of the obvious. Yes, today, we have given Jolina back her self-respect. She may be blind, but she still can make all the music she ever could. Well done, Caitlyn!" The other two gave her a round of applause.

Later that night, Caitlyn and I went for a late night walk around the block. We discovered just why the streets of this city were so clean. Late at night, the cleaning crews go around. They have a cylindrical wagon full of water to wash filth away, and they pick up any litter and wash away any debris. We chatted briefly with several of the crew, both men and women; we found that they took great pride in keeping the streets so clean. I was indeed impressed; no other town or city I had seen did this.

Every afternoon for the next three weeks, Jolina came to play and teach. We all worked harder on our music than ever before. On the next two Friday nights, we again played for the Sister's dance. However, on the third Friday night, we gave them something that they would never forget. We placed a fifth chair on stage, empty, as we were introduced by Sister Abrienda. However, instead of playing when she gave me the cue, I stood and walked over to the side of the stage, raised my hands, and said loudly, "Tonight, we have asked someone very dear and special to us to join us in playing for you. I hope you enjoy her playing as much as we do."

I moved behind the wall, gently took Jolina's arm, and escorted her to her chair. At first, we heard gasps of shock from here and there in the throng, then absolute silence. Fergus counted out, "One, two, three, four," and we began to play a lively dance tune, one known here in the Sea Princes. Yes, we had worked out ways for Jolina to get the proper cues to begin. However, it was much easier for her just to jump in, once the song began. The noise from the applause after that first song was positively deafening!

Just before we took our first break, we played Lyneth's Lament, with Jolina taking the solo bass flute part. Honestly, her rendition of it made our attempts look completely amateurish; she was that much more in tune with the music than we were, though honestly I must say that after these past three weeks, we had improved vastly. When her solo drifted off into silence at the end, again there was total silence before the crowd exploded with applause. During the overly long break, absolutely everyone wanted to shake her hand and talk with her. I spied only a few dry eyes in the whole place. We felt like this was Jolina's Welcome Back Concert for all of d'Grange!

The weeks following Jolina's return to performance, we received offers to play at many other dances. In fact, we ended up playing every Friday through Monday nights, which began to add much needed finances to our pockets. Our morning language sessions now focused upon learning a bit of the Greenway dialect and that of the Arad. We were told that there were a significant number of immigrants from Juda Arad now residing in the Sea Princes.

Additionally, now that we could speak their language fairly well, the history lessons began in earnest. These, of course, were just what I wanted; many of my lingering questions would be answered. I'll share the important highlights with you.

After the Galt invasion some twenty years ago, when the barbarians had left the conquered towns, the nobles rebelled against both the ruling Princes and their Priests of Tur. In their place, they installed Ruling High Councils, made up of the key wealthiest nobles, the prince, the church priest, and a Sisterhood representative. Yes, because of the Sisterhood's key assistance in the chaotic aftermath of the invasion, the tradesmen all wisely chose the Sisterhood to represent their interests. (Naturally, the nobles, princes, and priests had evacuated the cities just before they fell, returning many months later, when they assumed that it would be safe for them to return. The Sisterhood, on the other hand, came in almost the very day that the Galts left each city, bringing in much needed supplies as well as some semblance of law and order.)

The only city, which did not follow the lead of Zargarb and Solamina, was Velona. Abandoned by the Sisterhood during the time of the Great Plague during the Centurion invasion, a plague set upon them by their very own prince, and once more abandoned by the prince and priests during the Galt invasion, coupled with a population nearly halved by the plague, Velona today is a land of lawless bandits, preying upon any and all travelers. Only those accompanied by a strong Sisterhood fighter group can hope to pass safely across this sector. Even today, d'Grange continues to accept immigrants from the Velona sector, seeking a better life, free from the lawlessness found there.

Additionally, the High Councils have uniformly begun building what they claim will be an impenetrable barrier wall completely around the six key cities. They swear that never again will these cities be sacked by an invading army. I have my doubts about that, though.

More interestingly, the Sisterhood has now risen in popularity, seen as the true saviors by the common working folk. In many ways, its members have become far more integrated into daily life in the Sea Princes, nowhere more abundantly, though, than in d'Grange, where they share equal power and responsibility with the d'Grange family rulers.

What I found very intriguing was the abrupt change in religion in the Sea Princes. With the exception of the Priests of Tur and the actual mariners, the god Tur has been abandoned in favor of Jehosa. The Northern Orthodoxy of Jehosanity has spread like wildfire throughout the Sea Princes, again primarily because these people, many originally immigrated from Juda Arad bringing the religion with them, came unselfishly to the aid of the common man in the chaos left when the Galts finished sacking the cities. They came bearing food, supplies, and manpower to help rebuild homes and businesses destroyed by the barbarians. True, many months later the princes and nobles returned and began dumping vast amounts of their own wealth into the economy, but had it not been for the tireless efforts of the Sisterhood and these Missionaries of Jehosanity, few of the cities' population would have been alive when the nobles finally returned.

To my surprise, I learned that the priest most responsible for all of this had been Bandar Dero, one of Jes's ten disciples! I felt very relieved and happy that at least one of the chosen men had indeed followed through with Jes's request to spread the word of Jehosanity far and wide. Little did I know, however, just how altered Jes's teachings had become.

What of the land of Juda Arad? Invaded and conquered first by the Centurions, then later completely sacked by the Galts, then passed through repeatedly by the Galts for four years as they launched their attacks on other lands, Juda Arad has become a ghost land. Its once thriving cities reduced to mere ghosts of their former splendor. By all accounts, the vast majority of the native Arad people had immigrated to other lands. Only those who had not the means to make the long journey to at least Zargarb or those who had lost the will to do so remained, eking out the barest survival.

What of the Galts? Once their leader had been beheaded and his sister long lost as well, the army disintegrated into warring clans once more, fleeing north from close to Sud, the city in the Southlands just opposite Megalos, the island home of the Centurions. Some ravaged Juda Arad once more on their way back to the steppes. A few chose to stay in the Arad. As far as the Sea Prince cities were concerned, nary a Galt raider has appeared in the Sea Princes since 589, some thirty-two years now. For most, the four-year reign of terror was a distant memory or merely a history lesson for the younger folks.

Closer to home, here in d'Grange, we learned much about its history. Originally, Count Basilica d'Grange had begun construction of the primary Fortress that still bears his name. During the Centurion invasion, he became allies with the druwids of the Greenway. In fact, my Lightning Circle had met his son, Leonardo d' Grange back then. In 580, the Count passed away, and Leonardo assumed his father's throne, forging an even tighter alliance both with the Greenway and with the Sisterhood. In fact, he actually married Sister Angelicano in 567.

During the Great Plague and invasion of the Centurions, Sisters Rosalita Bellini and Lucretia Botini brought nearly all of the Velona sector's Sisterhood to Fortress d'Grange. Half of them stayed on here, while the remainder continued into the Greenway. Over the years, Lucretia more than proved her worth and valor in defense and support of the Fortress. When it came time to expand because of the continuous population growth, the new huge tower was given to her to command, Fortress Botini. So strong has the alliance become that nearly all barriers between the local population and the Sisterhood have vanished utterly. United together as they have always been, this new eighth Sea Prince sector had blossomed and thrived. It was still expanding during the months that we were there; construction was ongoing on both the northern and southern sections.

Thus, I felt that here in d'Grange, finally Nature had restored the natural balance between men and women; both were treated as equals. This was also witnessed in the payment for services rendered category, where in the Sisterhood actually commanded slightly more for the same service. Interesting commentary, I thought.

Until 605, Count Leonardo d'Grange ruled. He and Sister Angelicano had four children. Count Laurence d'Grange, now fifty-three, had married Alana Ware from the Greenway. Count Laurence now ruled the city, assisted, of course, by the Sisterhood. Count Leo's older daughter, Leola, now fifty-two, had married Archellangelo Morelli. The youngest daughter, Lauren, forty-nine, had married Benidito Armono. The youngest son, Leroy, forty-six, had married Maggie Helmut from the Greenway. Yes, the Count had a fetish for children's names beginning with the letter 'L.'

However, when I learned these seemingly trivial details, one tiny name struck a distant memory. In my first lifetime here on Tarra, Roy and I had three children: Robert Roy, Ellen Sarah, and Sue Ellen. Sue Ellen had married a blacksmith, Al Helmut, but I never knew much more than that. Still, the last name rang a bell, but I had no way of knowing if this Maggie was in anyway related to Al Helmut or my daughter, Sue Ellen.

The next major event occurred after we had been here for two months. We had been playing four gigs a week for the last few weeks. That morning, a messenger from Count Laurence d'Grange arrived at our inn with a formal invitation to play an entire evening for his personal family. The Count was throwing a birthday party for his wife, Alana, and wanted to make the evening's festivities a memorable one for her. Of course, we accepted. I think even Sister Jolina was pleased with the invitation.

Thus, Thursday late afternoon, Sister Abrienda arrived with Sister Jolina in tow. Dressed in our finest performance clothes, we six began the long walk across town to the second tall tower. Abrienda explained that we would be playing in the Great Hall, located on the second floor. We were thankful that she also said that there was a minstrel's gallery in the hall. Actually, this was our first time inside one of these two, nearly identical tall towers. However, just as soon as we entered the main doors, we began to climb the spiral stairway built into the circular wall of the tower, so we didn't really see all that much. The second floor contained just this one room, the Great Hall, circular in shape, at least fifty feet in diameter. The minstrel's gallery was a raised platform three feet from the main wooden floor, but only barely large enough for all of us to fit. Of necessity, Fianna would be forced to dance on the main floor just in front of us.

Great tapestries hung at intervals around the walls and between the many windows through which the late afternoon sea breeze blew. Two pairs of great tables positioned at right angles to each other sat against the curved walls opposite the gallery, leaving a substantial open dance floor between us. The room was gaily decorated with flowers and colorful ribbons, and party favors graced all four tables. I presumed each of the brother's and sister's families would occupy a table. In addition, fifty lanterns provided sufficient illumination for us to see well, come sunset.

Once we set up and had Jolina properly seated with her instruments just where she wanted them, we played a couple of warm up songs. Again, the acoustics were fairly good in here, but a bit on the bright side I thought, perhaps due to the curved walls. Satisfied that Jolina didn't need her aid any longer, Sister Abrienda walked over to one of the tables, where she would normally sit when dining with the Count. We didn't have long to wait. Three trumpeters entered dressed in gay colors, with banners hanging from their instruments. They took up a position just in front of the gallery. I whispered what was going on to Jolina, who sat next to me.

Four different fanfares echoed loudly in the great hall as the four families and their children and guests entered, one family at a time, with the Laurence's family coming first. In all, close to thirty people, many being children and teenagers, were here to celebrate Alana's birthday. When everyone had been seated, they all sang a birthday greeting to her, while she smiled lovingly at the assembled extended family. Count Laurence then rose and said loudly, "As a special treat for you, my devoted, loving wife these past thirty-seven years, I present to you the latest rage about town, the Cymry Minstrels, all the way from West Reach! Joining them is our very own master musician, Sister Jolina Alwana!" Everyone clapped loudly and stared at Jolina, who did not have to see them all staring, fortunately. He then waved his hand as the signal for us to begin.

We played ballads and dance tunes for about an hour while they dined. However, I will say this, hardly anyone tried to talk over the music, preferring to listen and enjoy it. This I greatly appreciated, though one could hear the occasional, "But isn't she blind?" whispered among the children.

After we took a short break, the younger ones wanted to dance, so it was another hour of light dance tunes, some that we had learned from Jolina, some from our island. Fianna became the rage of the dance floor. Since she had no choice but to dance along with them, suddenly every boy in the room wanted his chance to dance along with her. She enjoyed herself immensely, though by the end of this set, she was quite pooped and really needed the break.

As the evening wore on, we began to play slower tunes, to wind the children down before bedtime. Naturally, we played our trademark lament, with Jolina playing the solo on the bass flute. She received a standing ovation for her performance. I had to whisper to her what the whole group was doing while clapping. I believed she actually blushed! After a few more ballads, inspiration struck me. I wanted to try out that lullaby that Willow Windsong had sung to me so many ages ago.

I stood up and said, "This song is a very special song once sung to me a long time ago. We give it to you on your special day." I really didn't know how properly to address the Count's wife, so I kept it general. I sat back down and took over on the bass flute. Jolina played her lute; Caitlyn, the dulcimer; Fianna and Fergus, on percussion. Slowly, that incredible lullaby that had calmed me down, brought me back from near insanity, began to echo though out the room. One by one the others joined in. It was a simple lullaby, made emotionally moving by our arrangement and style. It ended with me once more playing the melody on the bass flute, allowing it gradually to fade into silence.

The Count leaped to his feet, yelling "Bravo!" Everyone else clapped loudly, but I was looking at his wife to whom I had dedicated the song; it was her birthday. I was shocked to see what I saw. She was crying — no, I corrected myself, joy. Evidently, she had been moved by the lullaby. However, she was staring straight at me, her eyes drilling into mine, a very solid confront. Sitting at the table close to here was Leroy and his family, so that his wife, Maggie, was very close to Alana. And she too now stared intensely at me. I didn't know what to make of these women's reactions. Unlike Alana, Maggie had no tears, just an intense stare.

While I was watching the two women as the group applauded, Alana flicked her fingers in an unusual motion, a subtle, but intentional motion. *I've seen that before, but where?* Just as we were about to launch into a slow dance tune, it hit me! She was showing the secret hand signals that we druwid sometimes use when we're in a crowd and don't want to attract other's attention. She had to be a druwid! I flashed the proper reply almost involuntarily, so great had been all that training so long ago. It was just on automatic. Both Alana's and Maggie's eye brows raised, startled yet a second time. However, just at that moment, we began to play, and my attention went back onto music making.

Throughout the rest of the evening, I felt those two women's eyes on me completely. I was actually a little excited myself at having discovered at least one of the guardians. It was clear that she was either covertly or openly helping with the defenses of this town. After all, if this fortress fell, the Greenway was wide open to any invader from the south. It made sense, and I forgot about it and enjoyed playing music that the younger folks were enjoying, dancing slowly before us.

Finally, Count Laurence rose, raising his hands. "Enough, enough. I fear our musicians will play away the entire night! I want to spend a good deal of this night with Alana here." Everyone chuckled at his inference. Some of the younger children didn't get his meaning. A few teens whispered that he wanted to bed her, whereon, they said "eeuuuu," as young children often do. This was our signal to stop, and we began to pack up our many instruments. Interestingly, Jolina needed no help with hers, doing it all by feel.

Far more rapidly than they had entered, the children and young adults raced out the doors. Count Laurence, his arm holding his wife, along with several other adults came forward. He handed me a small pouch, our payment for services; I thanked him. He said, "Jolina, ah Jolina! What an incredible honor you have done me. The legends of your musicianship simply do not do you justice. I do hope you will continue to play music everywhere in d'Grange. If you every need anything, just send me word! You, all of you, are just fantastic. Thank you all for coming on such short notice." Jolina actually blushed; the happiness that shown on her face radiated in all directions.

She replied bashfully, "Thank you, Count d'Grange. My pleasure."

As he turned to leave, Alana separated herself from her husband, "You run along. I'll be there in a minute. I would like to have a private word with this marvelous birthday present you have given me." Cleverly, Alana and Maggie stayed behind.

Meanwhile, Sister Abrienda began helping Jolina off the gallery, saying, "We'll meet you outside. We go more slowly than everyone else."

Now that the place was nearly deserted, Alana gave me an eye motion that indicated she wanted the other musicians to depart before she spoke to me. She said, "Thank you all for such a wonderful evening. I shall always remember this birthday party. Good night." I nodded for the others to leave, which they did without me having to say anything further. Finally, it was just these two women and me left in the Great Hall.

"Who are you? That song is known only to a very few people on all Tarra! How came you to know that song, that lullaby," her voice was stern and commanding. I would have to answer, no doubt about that. Still, I didn't know either of these two women, though I could guess she trusted Maggie completely; she'd gotten rid of everyone else.

"Before I can safely answer, I must ask one small question." I lowered my voice so that no one could overhear, "Druwids?" Alana nodded affirmatively.

I then explained, "Someone very special to me sang that song to me many years ago. I think I was in Karka at the time. The song, her singing it to me, actually saved me from near insanity. It is a very special song for me."

Alana nearly fainted, clinging tightly to Maggie for support. "I, I only did that once. Elizabeth? Elizabeth Stanton?" she asked.

"Yes, that was my identity then. How can you know that? Only Willow. . ." It was my turn to have my legs go weak. "Willow Windsong?" Tears streamed from her eyes, as she nodded, Maggie holding her tightly.

Maggie took charge. "This is a shock for all of us, Bethany. We druwids have been looking for you for years now. We absolutely *must* meet tomorrow, privately."

I agreed; suddenly I would be able to get so many questions answered! I told them where I was staying and that we could have a private talk in my room. "We'll be there mid-morning. We'd better not talk any longer. Don't want anyone becoming suspicious." They quickly walked toward the door, as I picked up my many bags and headed out the side door to join the others who were waiting for me. I told them she just thanked me for that special song and that seemed to satisfy them for the time being. I dare not say more without first talking with Alana.

When we were back at our inn, Fianna finally opened the pouch and gaily announced twenty gold pieces. She positively insisted that Jolina take four of the coins. I was glad that Fianna was in charge of our finances, because she would not take no for an answer. Jolina left with four coins, although I saw her give them discretely to Sister Abrienda as they left. I suspect that this was the first time that Jolina had been able to contribute something financially to the Sisterhood, who had obviously been looking after her every need for several years.

As usual, Fergus took us to the bar section and bought us a round of ale to help calm us down. Mellowed out, we then hit the sack, more than a little tired, though proud of our achievements this evening. Fergus was out like a light, thankfully for me. I stared at the ceiling, pondering my incredible good fortune to have accidentally run into two active druwids. I speculated that they belonged to the same Circle. Then, I fully realized that this was Willow Windsong; the body that I had known so long ago had obviously perished, just as two of mine had. Yet, here as Alana, she still remembered me from so many years ago. I wondered if she, too, could remember everything from her previous life. I had so many questions that needed answers that I kept trying to hurry the night along.

Over breakfast the next morning, I explained that I needed to be alone this morning, and that some people wanted to have a private conversation with me. I suggested that Fergus take the girls shopping and see what ideas they could come up with for performance costumes when we finally began traveling around the Sea Princes. I promised them that I would tell them all that I could about the meeting when they came back for lunch. Hence, I had the place to myself. I tidied up, brewed a fresh pot of tea, arranged some bread on a tray, and then waited.

Right on cue, they arrived mid-morning, carrying shopping sacks, their excuse for wandering about the city, I surmised. I let them in and shut the door. After pouring them a tea, we three sat down and stared at each other for a minute.

"Do I call you Willow or Alana?" I began. "I find that it gets so confusing. I've been awfully fortunate to have kept the name Bethany each time."

"Alana, please. And yes I do too. I had forgotten so much about that lifetime, Bethany — is it alright to call you that? But you are a man?" She was confused as was Maggie.

I chuckled, "Join the club! I'm going by Ket Bethany. I prefer Bethany and my companions call me Bethany in private."

"It is most confusing. You have such long hair that any maiden would utterly die for, you know," Maggie added.

"It's one of my two vices," I replied, "long hair and the name Bethany."

"Well, we'd better get down to business first," Alana hurried along. "Maggie and I are part of the d'Grange Circle — Loremaster and Communicator," she added, nodding to Maggie and then herself.

"I can't see you being anything other than a Communicator," I teased. "You are one of the best."

She smiled at the compliment, "Sandy actually turned out to be much better than I, but of that later. To business at hand. We are keeping an eye on things here in secret, as you probably guessed. Our husbands don't know of our druwid connections — hence the need for some discretion. Things have really changed and changed for the worst. Honestly, we had all but given up hope of ever finding you or Alabaster ever again! I just can't believe our incredible good fortune of meeting like this. Whatever made you play that song last night?" I shrugged. I had no explanation, either.

"Okay, worry about that later. First, we sent the West Reach Circle to Nuadilan, as you requested, as Bethany Amir. Unfortunately, as the events played out, they got there too late to help you. Your daughter, Sarah, filled them in admirably. At Sarah's insistence, they all searched for you, but could find no trace of you. We all feared the worst."

I interrupted, "I was unconscious at the bottom of the ocean for several years. I got zapped by a Grey Creature." They nodded; it made sense to them.

She went on, "The All Greenway Circle saw the wisdom in what you were doing to counter what these Grey Creatures were doing. So for a few years, they continued in your footsteps, Sarah leading the way. However, not long after that, Sarah again sensed the presence of a Grey Creature walking among humans, and the West Reach Circle was able to confirm it. That was an invaluable piece of information to get confirmed, by the way. It has saved many lives since then. Anyway, it became abundantly clear that these Grey Creatures wanted to find out who was performing these special ceremonies and eliminate them. Hence, the West Reach Circle fled back to Mont Blanc, bringing Sarah with them. She's still there."

"Then, things took a horrible turn for the worst. We believe that these Grey Creatures discovered the druwid headquarters in Calgary. One night in 603, the complex was attacked and destroyed, along with the All Greenway Circle and several others as well. You can well imagine the panic that caused. Well, the remaining members of your old Lightning Circle decided that they had to find Alabaster or you. Honestly, we were all at a total loss on what to do. Doing a mind search over Tarra only brought ruin down upon them. They had only gotten started on their Mind Link search when the Grey Creatures detected them. Almost immediately, their aerial cars swooped down on them and all were killed instantly. We did get one piece of information from Sandy before she died. Alabaster is not in the Greenway nor anywhere further north."

I had tears in my eyes. My dear friends, my Lightning Circle, all had been slain by these Grey Creatures. She paused for a time while I wrestled with this horrid news. Sniffling, I finally said, "Go on."

"I'm afraid things only get worse. When you were Wid, the druwids peaked at four hundred one complete Circles: $1 + 1 + 7 + 49 + 343$. Ever since then, we have had two major problems. First, many bodies have grown too old or had passed away outright. For some reason, probably because of the Grey Creatures, we haven't been able to find suitable recruits, you know, beings that are outside their heads. Of late, we have become so desperate that we're training some headers, hoping that they can master some of the requisite skills."

"You are kidding? Headers?" I asked. Headers is our derogatory term for a spiritual being who is completely stuck inside his or her head.

"Yes, some are making the early grades, so maybe there is yet hope. However, there is more. Since around 603, when this disaster befell us, every time one of we druwids uses our powers to bring down lightning or fire and it is witnessed in public, shortly thereafter, I mean within days, that druwid is killed by the Grey Creatures. We are being hunted down like rats! Our estimate is that we have lost four hundred druwids to the Grey Creatures thus far. Our total number of active druwids is down to sixteen hundred, dwindling weekly!"

"We've lost eight hundred of us since 603?" I exclaimed, totally flabbergasted at these staggering losses. Both nodded. I swore a curse.

Alana continued, "Bethany, it only gets worse." I shrugged; how could it be any worse?

"The Greenway, as you knew it, is now gone, probably forever," she said calmly. My mouth dropped; I nearly fainted from the shock.

"It's the Axemen. They discovered easy pickings in the Northern Steppes. After the Galts had conquered the Arad and the Sea Princes, they had amassed vast amounts of wealth, so much so, that they became more or less non-mobile because of the sheer weight of all that gold. How can you transport tons of golden items? But the Axemen can't get to the steppes except through the Greenway. We've been invaded, though thus far they have stayed on a very narrow path, passing through our lands, mostly following the Elbe River and then the Bahn, that's the name we now call the paved road running from Calgary across central Greenway to Melantas on the border of the steppes. Yes, Melantas, which used to be the main Centurion headquarters, now is in the hands of the Axeman, who are using it as a staging area for their exploits into the steppes."

"It gets worse still. Because of all these factors and others that we cannot say with any certainty, the Greenway has now become politically divided into ten different kingdoms! Yes, ten men have carved up the land, calling themselves Kings of this and that. They claim to offer defense against the Axemen, and the people believe them, especially since we hardly dare openly to use our spells against the invaders. To do so spells death within a few days!"

"About six are actually relatively good men, trying to do their best. Two we have doubts about; two more are probably on the wrong side, allying themselves with the Axemen. However, druwids are adaptable. We are now maintaining a full Circle with each king, providing advisement as we can. Nevertheless, the situation is very grim indeed. I wish I could be the bearer of better news."

"But now things may be turned around! We have found you, Bethany! Long have we sought for either you or Alabaster. We need your guidance most desperately. When I reported our finding of you last night, I was ordered to bring you to Mont Blanc, but I replied, 'No one orders, Bethany.' So I am asking you, nay begging you, Bethany. Will you please travel with us to the only truly safe house in all the Greenway, Mont Blanc? We have often gone there, telling our husbands that we are taking a sightseeing trip into the Greenway. Yes, ever are the d'Granges and the druwids close allies. Our travels there raise no suspicions. Indeed, they are usually highly encouraged. Will you please come, Bethany?"

"Yes, but. I'm on a sacred mission to find Alabaster. When Grey Creatures zapped him, I made him a promise. He pledged me to come find him and help him if he were unable to contact me within thirty years. That time has long passed due to a miscalculation on my part because of my being zapped by that Grey Creature. I have perfected a new twist on mental searching that I can share with you, one that seems to eliminate the Grey Creatures finding me. However, and this is a big consideration. I am traveling with my sister and two very dear friends, my grandchildren from my last life and heirs to thrones; they are the Great Messiah Jes Amir's direct bloodline. We are all musicians and plan to travel around Tarra until I find Alabaster. There is just not any way I can go without bringing them with me. If I do so, they are very bright, knowledgeable young people; they will find out much about us. I can't possibly keep much of this a secret from them. However, if as you say, you are now training headers, gosh, I loathe that term, then perhaps they could be given some training while I am there? They would jump at just such a chance to learn. I need them to learn city survival skills and how to defend themselves."

"More than acceptable, Bethany. I will give you my personal guarantee that they will be informed as much as is responsible and trained as their abilities will allow. Can you leave soon? Time is of the essence I greatly fear."

"Yes, we were planning to play tonight for the dance. We can delay any other commitments. Would that work?"

"Thank you Wid Bethany!" Alana, er Willow, gave me a strong hug.

"You can tell me all about your adventures while we ride along to Mont Blanc.

"Say, there is one other thing, about Sister Jolina," I had a thought.

"I meant to give you my heartfelt thanks for salvaging her. Although Maggie and I tried several times, we couldn't reach her, but you did in no time at all! My compliments, Wid Bethany. After all, you are the Wid and we are not."

I smiled and explained, "Well, you know, Jolina is now back to making music really well. However, she still is terrified of her blindness. I was thinking, would it be possible for someone to teach her to use her other senses more fully and to even be able to use blind fighting to protect herself somewhat? I think that would completely put her back into the driver's seat in her life."

Alana commented to Maggie, "She hasn't changed in nearly a century! Still the kindhearted Bethany, rescuing people in dire straits. Your success with Isabel is now legendary, Bethany, and taught to every new recruit." I flushed. I hate being the center of attention. "Sure, see if you can bring her along. We'll do everything possible for her."

As they were about to leave, Maggie paused at the door and dropped another bombshell on me. Sheepishly, she said, "Bethany Stanton, you're my grandmother." My mouth waggled, I just rushed over to her and gave her a long, solid hug. "We can talk lots when we are on the trail," she said and dashed off to catch up with Alana.

I heard Alana ask, "Did you tell her?"

To which Maggie said excitedly, "Yes! Wow, after all these years, I get to meet her!"

"Him, now," she corrected Maggie. I chuckled, a little happiness among this horribly bad news. Inwardly, I was just a bit pleased that others found this just as confusing as I did.

When the others returned from their shopping trip around lunchtime, all three had that broad, sheepish looking grin on their face, a sure sign that they had been up to some mischief. However, as they saw the enthusiastic smile on my face, they momentarily forgot about theirs. "Who was here?" Fianna jumped in before the others got a chance. I guess my sister knew me pretty well by now.

"I have a tremendous surprise for all of you. I've just been visited by two Guardians, yes, two druwids from the Greenway. We have all been invited to the main Guardian secret fortress to spend some time with them! You get your wishes to meet Guardians! Lots of them, not just one or two. They've promised to train all three of you while we are there. We leave on Saturday morning. How's that for news?" I chuckled to myself as I watched their childish exuberance go wild.

"Whoopee! Unbelievable!" exclaimed Caitlyn. All this was beyond her wildest imaginations. I remembered my exhilaration when as a ten year old girl back in Uru, I went with Ellen, my mentor, to my first druwid celebration at the standing stones.

"Even me?" asked Fianna in disbelief.

"You bet, sis."

"All praise to Jehosa and the Blessed Holy Mother!" exclaimed Fergus, his usual composure evaporated. However, realizing what he had just uttered, he sheepishly added, "Oops. Sorry, Bethany."

"No offense taken, Fergus. I just had to surprise you all. Also, I have permission to take Jolina with us too. They will train her as well, if she wishes it. Isn't this just fantastic news? I've been out of direct contact with them for nearly a half century now. I am terribly excited about finally being able catch up on all the news. Pretty amazing indeed."

They chatted excitedly for quite a while, and I fixed us lunch as they gabbed about their incredible good fortune. Yes, for them, this was indeed a very fortuitous happening, and I hoped it would have far-reaching effects for many of my own personal, private reasons, which had nothing to do with the Guardians.

Only after we finished lunch did they finally realize I had made the lunch! Finally back to reality, Caitlyn said, "You'll never guess what we have been up to this morning." I couldn't and proudly, she continued. "If we are going to be traveling all around performing, we need some appropriate show costumes. You'll never guess what we found today! A seamstress from Cymry! Yes, right here in d'Grange!"

She went on to describe their lucky encounter. She had come over here to the mainland five years ago with her husband. Her clothing was definitely first class, according to both women. Hence, they were having fancy, official party dresses made for them, complete with the massive embroidery so typical of the Layamon region. Further, the seamstress knew a little about Tewdwr clothing and was making Fianna a similar matching dress only with the more subtle embroidery typical of our homeland. She actually had some tweed material available, so Fergus was having a dressy kilt outfit made so that his costume would be almost as good as if he had purchased one in the highlands.

"You'll never guess what we are having made for you, Bethany," Caitlyn continued, a teasing grin of accomplishment on her youthful face.

Fianna picked up their conspiracy, "Since you weren't there, we are having two made for you. One will be a fancy man's outfit, you know, the kind that we used to see when mom and dad took us to the big town twice a year. It'll match my new dress as well. We'll be a pair from Tewdwr, you and I. Best of all, she's making you a second outfit, just like mine. We figured that you might need to resume your female disguise, so this works out perfectly. If you need to, why you can switch disguises in a hurry. Isn't this just great?"

Laughing, I said, "You all have done very well indeed. Stroke of genius there, getting me two. I may yet need to travel in disguise, though I can't say for sure at the moment. It will be fabulous to be able to switch just like that. Well done indeed, all three of you."

"Well, you're going to have to come back with us to the shop this afternoon. We promised to bring you. You know, she has to observe you so that she can determine just the right embroidery pattern to use on your outfits, Bethany," Fianna added.

Just a bit embarrassed, I asked, "Won't she think it a bit odd that a man is having the dress made for him?"

"Not at all. We explained that we are performers, showmen. She understands how it is — you know, one person performing different roles on the stage. This way, you can go either way."

Later that afternoon when we four returned to her shop, I insisted that we pay for them in advance because I had no idea how long it would be before we could return to pick them up. Yes, she did study me for a time to get her impressions of me so that the special embroidery would match my beingness. What intrigued me was that she chose the very same designs that the seamstress had done way back last lifetime when I had gotten my first Layamon dress! The Wid in me began to wonder what lay back of this — surely not coincidence. I put this mystery on the back burner, hoping one day to find the answer to it.

Next, we had to talk to Jolina and convince her to come with us. I had no idea what to expect as we walked up to her room, following Sister Abrienda. We had already tracked her down and explained the Guardian's offer. Her comment was pretty much what I expected, "What a magnanimous, generous offer. Ordinarily, any Sister would jump at such an honor to be invited to the Guardian's training base. It is a fabulous offer. However, Jolina is blind and has been very difficult to handle. For years now, she mostly sits alone in her room, though we have all forced her to go for walks and such. Honestly, the change in her since you arrived is a miracle in itself. Yet to ask her to travel a long distance to a strange place with unfamiliar people, I doubt very much that she will consent to it. Don't get your hopes up too high."

As we neared the door to Jolina's room, she added, "Please don't moving anything around. She knows by feel just where everything is located. If you do have to move something, remember to put it back exactly where it was at, please." She knocked and the familiar voice of Jolina said to come in; we did. "I've some guests with me today; the Cymry Minstrels are all here to see you."

We entered a room that was pitch black, she, of course, needed no lantern and rarely, if ever, would open the heavy drapes that covered her solitary window. The only feeble light came from the open doorway. I spied numerous instruments neatly arrayed on a table in one corner opposite her small bed. She at least had a half dozen chairs available. She was sitting in one beside the table. The others were against a wall. We stumbled in and found a seat. "You forgot to light your lantern again," Sister Abrienda chided her.

"I keep telling you, I don't need it; it's a waste of good oil," Jolina dryly commented. Upon hearing us banging into the chairs as we took seats, she became embarrassed and apologized, justifying by saying that she seldom got any visitors.

"No problem, Jolina. I've come with some fabulous news for you. But first, I need to ask you if you know about the Guardians of the Greenway."

Didactically, as if repeating some history lessons she had been forced to recite, she said, "Yes, the Guardians and the Sisterhood have been the best of allies and our dear friends for nearly a century. It was their unselfish act back during the Centurion invasion that has changed the way women are treated throughout the Sea Princes. All praises go to Simon, Elizabeth, and their companions. Yes, I know about them."

"Good. This morning, the Guardians of the Greenway have asked me and my companions to come to their secret stronghold for a time, so that we may learn as much as we can."

"You've come to say that tonight will be the last time we play for a while?" Jolina commented. I did detect a slight note of sadness in her voice, which I took as a very good sign.

"Not exactly, Jolina. The Guardians have asked me to beg you to come with us. They wish to give you some personal training as well." I wondered how she would take this news.

She crumpled and held her head in her hands near her lap, moaning, "How *can* I? I am blind. I cannot see anything! I am completely lost outside of my room here. You have no idea of the horrors I go through just to get to the dance hall to play with you! Do you know what it is like even to try to eat if you cannot see anything? Let alone even using the chamber pot! How could I possibly do this?"

"Oh that part is simple," I tried to add a little levity to the situation. "We pick you up and plop you in a wagon and drive you there. That part is simple." She didn't much care for my light heartedness over her plight.

Sarcastically, she replied, "Sure that is the easy part. And then who will look after my every need once we get there? I am so utterly helpless."

"Well that is a load of bologna if I ever heard one!" I countered, pushing her slightly, unwilling to let her get away with that victim attitude. "You are one of the finest musicians that I have ever seen."

"Was," she interrupted me sarcastically.

"Bull! Are," I declared flatly. "We will get to play for the Guardians lots of times I expect. Undoubtedly, we will have an excellent opportunity to learn many of the songs and dances of the Greenway, a chance that any musician worth his salt would more than jump at. Look at me. You can't sit there and tell me that you wouldn't give your eye teeth to have the chance to hear and learn the songs and dances of another country, now would you?"

She did move her head in my general direction, which I took as a very good sign. "See, I didn't think you could resist. That lullaby that we played at the birthday party came from the Greenway." I added this as a hopeful enticement; I knew she liked it as well. "Look, Jolina, I don't care if you are blind, have gotten your nose on upside down, forgotten to wear your ears, or even if you forget to put your clothes on, if only you will play music and learn these new songs with us. You can even stand on your head if you want, as long as it doesn't interfere with your playing!"

My crazy concatenation of sillinesses had its effect. Jolina actually smiled for the first time since we arrived, at least I thought so in the dim light. I added jokingly, "Well, maybe we had all better make sure you keep your clothes on, it might be too distracting for the men." Everyone roared with laughter, even Jolina.

She said, "Are you sure I won't be a terrible burden to you all?"

"Absolutely not!" I exclaimed using that same attitude that Fianna often used on me, the "I know precisely what I am talking about" attitude. It worked on her too, just as it did on me.

Sister Abrienda chose this moment to say, "If you will go, I will take some time off of work. I am due for a vacation anyway. I will see if my children want to accompany us. They might not, however. Alica is boy-crazy at the moment; teenagers, you know how it is."

"You will? You'd come with me?" Jolina asked very much enheartened by her offer.

"Absolutely! Think of the honor we're getting: an invitation to visit the Guardians and learn from them! It's a fabulous offer, Jolina, a very high honor indeed!"

"Well okay then," she agreed meekly. "When are we to leave? What am I to bring?"

"We leave in the morning. We play the dance tonight and leave tomorrow. Bring all your instruments and leave the rest to us. We'll get some wagons so we can travel in comfort," I answered. I had been successful thus far. Jolina would come with us to Mont Blanc; this was a big first step.

That night at the dance, after we had finished, Sister Abrienda got everyone's attention. "I have an announcement to make. This will be the last concert these minstrels will be giving for a while. It seems that Sister Jolina and these minstrels have been personally invited to visit the Guardians in the Greenway, play for them, learn Greenway tunes, and get some personal training under the Guardians! I'm sure they will give us a special concert of new songs when they get back." The thunderous applause, whistling, yelling and foot stomping was deafening — all on Jolina's behalf, I surmised.

Jolina looked rather embarrassed, however, whispering to me, "I hope I don't let them all down."

"Spoken like a true musician," I replied. "You will probably do far better than we; you are so much better a musician." She smiled and I gave her a gentle hug.

Chapter 13 The Fortress at Mont Blanc

The next morning, we were packed and ready to go. Alana had sent word that we would be traveling in a caravan of wagons and that we wouldn't need our horses. Hence, we paid our innkeeper in advance for a month; she agreed that, if we were longer, she would hold the rooms for us; we'd make it right with her when we did return. All four of us sat just outside the iron gates of the inn, full of restless excitement, waiting for the wagons to pick us up. "I do hope they hurry up," exclaimed Fianna for the countless time.

Finally, midmorning a caravan of five wagons pulled up by us, accompanied by a dozen Sisterhood fighters on horseback. Additional Sisters drove four of the wagons, while Maggie preferred to drive herself. "Women fighters?" asked Fergus incredulously. He had not yet seen them fight.

"Look, the Count is sending his wife and sister-in-law off to the Greenway. You bet he is going to see that she is well protected. Besides, Jolina is also with us. So the Sisterhood has a vested interest in this convoy, hence the large group of fighters accompanying us. Honestly, Fergus, these fighters are perhaps the best on Tarra. I doubt that I could defeat one of them." He stared at them even more closely for the rest of the day.

One wagon held Jolina and another Sister, whose skill lay in preparing food while on the trail. Another wagon carried my group, while the fifth carried the supplies that we would need on our journey. "Would you care to join me for a while, Ket Bethany?" Alana requested after we got our bags piled into the wagon. I knew she wanted to talk privately for a while.

I climbed onboard their wagon. Maggie signaled to the Sisters, who moved on out in front of us, and we began to move slowly through the paved streets of d'Grange, heading toward the north gate. We said nothing until we had passed the gate and rode out onto the open dirt road that headed north toward the Greenway. I estimated that Mont Blanc was about seventy-five miles away, depending upon how winding the road was. We'd probably be four to five days en route.

Maggie began chatting excitedly, now that it was safe to talk freely, "You know, I have always wanted to meet you, Grandmother, er sir, er Ket. Golly, this is so awkward. I've been dreaming of a day such as this, and it's so confusing, sir."

I broke out laughing, "Yes, granddaughter, this is even more confusing for me than it is for you!" My laughter was contagious.

"Alana said this was going to be a mess, and she was right. Only, I'm supposed to get you all prepared for when you arrive. You have many of your relations to meet at the fortress. They decided they didn't want to shock you."

"Oh dear, this is going to be so utterly confusing. If we cannot hold a civil conversation without getting mixed up, then think what it will be like when we get there!" I fretted.

Alana pointed out, "It's mostly that everyone knew of you as Elizabeth Stanton. Only now you are this male, Ket, but you have such gorgeous hair — confusing is an understatement."

"I wonder if it would help matters if I dressed like a woman for a while? Then when you call me grandmother, it would appear perfectly acceptable. What do you all think?" I offered.

"Well, just between you and me, I'm only a Communicator, but I do think if you looked like a woman, at least for a while, everyone's conversations with you would go much better. That is, if you don't feel weird in a dress. Men usually do, that is," she added giving me a way out.

"No problem with that. I was forced to spend several months traveling around West Reach disguised as a young woman. A while longer is not a problem. Besides, my troupe thought it might be a good idea, me dressing like a female for some of our performances. They even went and ordered me a fancy dress to match Fianna's. However, Alana, I didn't bring any woman's clothing with me."

She chuckled, "I think we can take care of that. Come on back into the wagon with me." I followed her inside the tarp covered wagon and watched as she went through her trunks. She held up one of her spare dresses to me to judge the size. "This ought to work. Try it on. I'll move up front to give you some privacy."

A couple minutes later, I called out, "I think we have a slight problem."

She returned, gazed at me, and grinned. "You need to develop substantial womanly breasts, young man," she teased, and I laughed as well. She stuffed some rags inside and fiddled with the arrangement a bit. "There, that ought to do. Let your hair down too, while I fetch some slippers. Oh, your feet are much larger than mine. Maggie, can we borrow a pair of yours?" She hollered back for us to go ahead. A few minutes later, I looked quite like a woman indeed. I thanked her and together we climbed back onto the front seat, joining Maggie.

"How do I look?" I asked her. Her mouth opened wide!

"If I did not know better, I'd swear you were a woman! Honestly, already I do feel more comfortable chatting with you, grandmother." That settled it; for a while I would continue to wear dresses to lessen everyone's confusion as well as my own.

She gaily continued, "Well I'm supposed to break you in, orders you know, grandmother, so here goes. Since the tragic death of the remaining members of both the Lightning Circle and the All Greenway Circle, the Moon Circle is now in charge of Mont Blanc and the Guardians. You'll get to see all your children again. They are certainly excited about seeing you; I can tell you that! They lost you when they were very young. Ellen says that she can barely remember your face. Al claims to have no memory of you at all. Also, grandmother, you get to meet all us grandchildren; a lot of us are in the d'Grange Circle." I avoided asking her just how many that might be.

Merrily, Maggie continued, "And then there are all the kids from all your Circle members, the Pentons, Donegals, and Wilkins. They are dying to see you. In fact, John Henry, Misty Simone, and Lilly Elizabeth claim to remember you playing with them when they were children, though I expect the others were too young to remember you. Then there are all their children. You see, there are a whole lot of us living together at the fortress, all just dying to meet you!"

I laughed loudly, "Spare me all their names at the moment. How will I ever keep them all straight? I doubt that I will even recognize my own children. They were all very little when I last saw them. I guess I really had better wear these clothes. It's bad enough when you and I get confused. If there are this many of them, the confusion will be unmanageable." She laughed along with me.

I mused a bit, "Yes, Maggie, the only real regret I have is that I never did get back to the mainland to visit with my old Circle. I had always intended to do just that, but I was so busy running everything on West Reach. I guess that's not a good excuse. At least we did Mind Links and chatted several times," wishing my dear friends were still alive. I felt so old just now.

Undaunted, Maggie continued her mini-briefing. "There's been a lot of construction on Mont Blanc since you last saw it, I expect. Uncle Raphael, that's what we all used to called him, added dozens of new buildings. I bet you'll like them. Right now, I think there are close to one thousand people living in the complex."

"You're kidding me, Maggie?" I asked, recalling that when I last saw it, it might hold perhaps fifty.

"No, there are at least a couple hundred sisters living with us; they make up part of the thousand. That includes all the little children and trainees as well. You see, when the adults were killed by the Grey Creatures, that's something like four hundred according to John Henry, what to do with all their apprentices in training became a big problem, you know, with their mentors gone and all. Very traumatic for everyone. John Henry decided to bring the orphaned apprentices to the fortress. This way, one mentor can teach several throughout the day. It has been working rather well, or so I'm told."

She chatted on for some time. "Say, Maggie, just how old are you anyway, if you don't mind grandmother asking?"

"Thirty-five," she replied, "do I look it?"

"No, I was guessing maybe late twenties. One thing has been bothering me. Do you mind my asking personal things of you?"

"No, ask away, grandmother."

"Well, your marriage to Leroy. Did you marry out of love for the man or did the Guardians foist it off on you?" I planned to ask Alana the same question when I got the chance.

"We needed a second Guardian with the d'Grange family, just in case something happened to Laurence. I was the right age and was nominated for the job. Our meeting was arranged, naturally, though Leroy knew nothing about that. I flirted with him and got him interested in me, and he does truly love me. I'm rather fond of him, but I'm not really in love with Leroy. Don't get me wrong, my life has been truly rewarding. When I moved in there, the city had so little farmable land that they had to import nearly all their grain. Now, under my guidance, we've constructed almost enough terraced lands to support our own population, if only it would stop growing. I do get out and about the countryside nearly every day. Honestly, I have no complaints about it, if that's what you are worried about."

"Yes, I was. Back on the island, some young women have been force to marry real pigs. Forced marriages seldom work out. At least one of my grandchildren killed her own body rather than go through with a marriage to an awful man. Naturally, I was just a bit concerned about you. How about you Alana?"

"I'm too old to fuss about it," she chuckled. "No, it was pretty much the same with me. We desperately needed eyes in the d'Grange fortress, and I got chosen for the job because I'm a Communicator. It was easy to relay any news without raising the slightest suspicion. Like Maggie, Laurence dotes on me, as witnessed by my birthday party. It's been a good life with lots of accomplishments for the benefit of the d'Granges and the Guardians. I don't regret it, but I have often wondered what life might have been if I had ever met the love of my life."

"Okay, then I won't make anyone's head roll for these arranged marriages," I teased. They took me seriously, however.

"You wouldn't, would you, grandmother?" Maggie faced me with a startled look on her face.

"Actually, I would, if the marriage had been a disaster for either of you. Seriously, I'm not behind these 'marriages of convenience' at all. I only married the Great Messiah, Jes, because I was truly in love with the man and he, me. I only married Roy Randell because we were both madly in love with each other."

"Oh, grandmother, please go easy on John Henry. He's the highest ranking Wid around now, and he has been carrying the responsibility of all the druiwds on his shoulders. Yet, he is not half the Wid that you are, grandmother. Do you realize just how hard it was to replace you? I mean, after the Galts killed you. It was just awful, so I'm told. Sandy said it took over three years before poor old John Small was finally convinced to give it a go. He had a horrible time of it."

"Okay I promise. Say Willow, I mean Alana, do you ever get confused between this lifetime and the last one, like I am?"

She smiled. I remembered that smile. Okay, different body, but the same smile. Maybe it was her intention behind the smile. "You forgot that I never married last time. Willow never found her true love. My apprentices, all you youngsters — you were my children. Just between you and me, Sarah Jane tried her best to get me to understand this true love thing. It just never has happened to me. I'll be frank with you, as a Wid. Isn't a family really just a specialized, small group? Really, when it comes down to basics? Personally, I have never been interested in a small group; my goals and purposes as a spiritual being are so utterly focused on our group and all mankind here on Tarra, that family matters seem so utterly trivial to me, they just don't hold my interest beyond a few minutes. My own personal possessions, acquiring of property, wealth, and objects, like horses and fortresses and such — these never have entered my thinking. I have enough of the physical world around me to get by on and that is all that I need. I think Alabaster understood me."

"I do too, thanks," I replied. "We all have our own goals and purposes. It's terrific that so many of them overlap so we can have a group such as ours."

It was way past lunchtime, and Maggie called for a lunch break. After dismounting, I got quite a few stares from the Sisters, who now saw this lovely woman with long red hair. I hoped that Maggie or Alana would explain to them what was going on.

I certainly did just that to my troupe. Just as soon as Fergus and the others saw me, he teased, "Man, you just never know what Ket Bethany is going to look like. He climbs into the wagon as a man and we stop for lunch and here is this pretty redheaded woman."

Caitlyn teased, "My, what beautiful breasts you must have." Fergus roared. I did too.

Fianna just said that I looked good and that they were right in ordering that special dress for our performances. Over lunch, I explained my predicament. "According to Maggie, I've got dozens and dozens of my children, grandchildren, and those of my dear Lightning Circle's family waiting to meet me at the fortification. Every one of them thinks of me as Elizabeth Stanton. At least dressed this way, the confusion will be lessened, I hope."

Caitlyn comforted me by saying, "Yes, I can see that where being able to recall who you used to be and then running into all those children you had can be most confusing. I know that I would be so totally confused about it all that I would want to just forget the past." Suddenly she stopped short, with a strange, funny look on her face. There was more than an ounce of truth in her pronouncement.

"Yes," I probed, hoping she would vocalize what she had just thought.

"I think that I have just done that. I have an image in my mind right now of an old woman lying in bed. She's very ill; lots of children of all ages are standing around her, so many names to remember. Isn't that fascinating? So I forgot them."

"Very good, Caitlyn. Well done. Truth, nothing stops the truth, I always say. Come on. Let's get something to eat."

We joined the throng, which had gathered around the food wagon. The Sister was busy filling orders from our limited menu. Caitlyn and I were the last in line and had to take what was left. The Sister commented with a wry grin, "I like your new look." I smiled back. Caitlyn and I sat on a boulder together to eat our lunch.

At that instant, I felt, or sensed would be a better description, a cold chill come over me. "Grey Creatures!" I yelled the warning. Instantly the Sisters swept up close to the rest of us, encircling us, while facing outwards, swords drawn.

"Where?" cried Alana and Maggie, nearly in unison.

"Above us," I called out. All eyes gazed at the white clouds in the sky, but we saw nothing but a strange shadow moving high overhead. I seized the opportunity and called out, "Everyone, see if you can feel the enemy. I sense cold chills coming from up there. How about you?" I hoped that the Sisters could somehow feel our enemy as I did. We'd have more allies this way.

Everyone began whispering to one another, comparing what they might be sensing. I was greatly relieved and very encouraged that everyone present sensed something. Alana took charge and systematically recorded everyone's impressions of these creatures. Fortunately for us, it was now long gone, heading out over West Reach, if my guess was correct.

Ten minutes later, Alana finished interviewing the last person, Jolina. The consensus was pretty much the same: a cold chill or cold inhuman emotion or a chilling evil. Those were the most commonly found words to describe them. Alana issued orders to everyone to report to her immediately anytime anyone sensed them again. She returned to me, saying, "Well done, Wid Bethany. We have now even more people aware of how to spot them. Jolina said she felt them acutely and was more than a little scared. Isn't that interesting? I've got to take a few minutes and relay this to John Henry." She went to her wagon to concentrate on making the mental connection.

"That was really spooky, Bethany," Caitlyn whispered to me, even though there was no longer any need to be so quiet. "It is just like the feelings I always got when I was around dad's advisor, you know who. So that is one of these Grey Creatures!" I nodded. "Well, I do now feel a little bit sorry for dad. He's doomed, isn't he?"

"Yes, Caitlyn dear, your father, my son, doomed himself years ago when he let that creature gain entry into his life. I'm truly sorry, Caitlyn." We hugged each other until it was time to climb back onboard the wagons.

When we were once again moving, Alana said to us, "John Henry is terribly worried about our safety. He is sending an armed escort out to meet us at once. I tried to tell him the creature was heading for West Reach, but he ignored me. I'm sure that I would hate to have the amount of responsibility that man has!" I smiled. I knew what she meant, but I was soon to have all this and more.

Maggie continued relaying what she had been asked to tell me, presumably by John Henry. "Our fortress at Mont Blanc is now covered with numerous overlapping conjuring spells. When a non-druwid approaches the general area of our complex, they see simply the barren countryside. It has turned out to be very effective at keeping unauthorized people from discovering the fortress. John Henry says that there is some hope that it will also keep the Grey Creatures from discovering our fortress. Do think that is so, grandmother?"

"How can I say one way or the other without first having seen the fortress and examining the conjuring spells firsthand? From all of my encounters with these vile creatures, I would tend to think not. But then, perhaps they are not all-knowing after all." It was the best answer I could give. We chatted for several hours; for me, the time passed very quickly.

The Sisters knew this route well and had us make camp at a perfect location. We assembled in a U-shaped, small box canyon, one that was clearly defensible. A small stream provided fresh water, and there was plenty of wood not too far away. I was glad to stretch my legs and help my companions setup our campsite around our wagon. We all thought that having a cook along was one terrific idea, because we didn't have to bother with cooking, though we had little choice in the menu. Thankfully, the Sister made lots of tea.

No sooner had we all finished eating, when several Sisters sounded the alarm. Sure enough, that eerie, cold chill came over us once more. Again, it appeared to be high overhead and moving opposite from its path around noon. We presumed that it had not spotted us. Twice in the same day unsettled many of the women, so I helped Jolina bring some of her instruments to our wagon, and together, we gave everyone a short concert. That definitely lightened up the mood around camp. I felt confident that the creature was on some other kind of mission in West Reach and could have cared less about our small party camping here.

At the insistence of Alana, everyone slept in their clothes, in case we needed to make a fast get away. It was very early fall and the nights cool, so we four threw our blankets out under the stars, which looked splendid indeed. Naturally, Caitlyn and I snuggled close together, while Fergus and Fianna did likewise. For some reason, sleeping here beside Caitlyn felt so natural, so comfortable. I had no words for it, except it felt right.

The next day, I rode with my friends, and we chatted about the rough countryside. They pumped me for as much information as I cared to relate, especially about where we were headed and what they might expect. I sensed that all three were more than a bit worried about the upcoming training that I had promised them. It was the usual fear of the unknown. The day passed uneventfully, until late afternoon when the escort from Mont Blanc came galloping into view. John Henry had sent a hundred Sisters and several Protectors to escort us safely there. I knew he was overreacting and hoped that they all enjoyed going for the ride.

Mid-afternoon on the fourth day, the Landoc region was clearly visible stretching far off into the eastern horizon. Here was a barren land of rough rock, sparse grasses, few trees, and little water. Naturally, compared to the lush grasslands and forests just north of here, no one had ever bothered to settle this long, narrow stretch of land, which ran from the ocean all the way inland into the Northern Steppes. The Landoc was perhaps thirty to fifty miles wide, varying as it moved inland. At seeming random locations, a mountain would thrust itself up above the surrounding landscape. I say mountain, but its elevation was merely one to two thousand feet taller than the rest of the land about them. Mont Blanc was the first of a lengthy series of these mountains and only a day's ride from Calgary, the largest Greenway city.

Yet it was here in this desolate, out of the way location that I chose for us to build our fortress complex, back when we were all worried about the impending Centurion invasion. Raphael had been our master Planner and designer for the complex, constantly adding new features as his skill with stone masonry and construction increased. I wondered what the complex must look like now?

Then I spied it, sprawling across the summit area, nearly ten times larger than it had been when I was last here so many years ago. My friends could see nothing, the effect of the spell, I guessed rightly. I gave them a short lesson in observing the obvious, not what they expected to see. Sure enough, one by one, the complex suddenly appeared for them. All three were quite proud with their minor achievement as we steadily drew closer to the complex. Now I began to gape and stare as much as they were doing! Raphael had out done anything I could envision!

However, he wouldn't win any awards for consistency of building style. On the contrary, I could see from the wildly varying architectural styles, building to building, that he was more interested in learning and inventing numerous construction methods. I saw one Megalos type building with tall columns supporting the stone roof above, with no side walls, completely open to the air on all sides. I wondered what use this building would have. Winters here are cold and snowy.

In the far distance, I also spied several flocks of sheep, but nowhere could I see any farming fields. Hence, they still depended upon some trade for grain, the bread of life. I guessed sheep and wool were likely used for such trades. As we rolled up to the ten-foot tall outer walls that surrounded the complex, I saw hundreds of people standing and watching our arrival. I guess the arrival of the long sought Elizabeth Stanton was top news here. I felt very small and insignificant, and wished with all my heart that I wouldn't be the center of attention that I knew I was about to be. I dreaded it, but there was nothing I could do about it, save be as gracious as I could.

Two older men and one older woman, all likely in their sixties, stood just inside the gate, obviously the first people to meet me. Another older man, likely the same age, stood just behind these three. Alana pulled up on their left and motioned us to pull up on their right. It was an awkward moment for me, as we four climbed down from the wagon. I had no idea who any of these people were, yet every one of their faces was beaming with unfettered joy and happiness, lacking as yet a target for their attention. As if in answer to my prayers, Alana walked over to me and took my arm, pulling me close to the trio. She said, "Allow me to introduce you. These are your children, Robert Roy, Ellen Sarah, and Al Helmit. John Henry Penton is behind them. Kids — boy does that ever sound strange, you're all in your sixties — kids, this is your mother, Elizabeth Stanton, only in her third physical body, which is actually male, but she is appearing this way to keep the confusion minimized. Just ask Maggie here about the confusing mess. Oh yes, just call her Bethany, though she goes by Ket Bethany to outsiders."

I stared at my three children, greying, thinning hair predominating, while they stared back at a not quite fifteen year old boy dressed in one of Alana's dresses with flaming red hair trailing down her back to her rear. The mother in me swept in control of my body, as I rushed forward, tears of joy and happiness blurring my vision, my hands out stretched, encompassing all three as they did me. We had one very long hug, before stepping back to look carefully at each other. I burst out laughing. "This is so utterly unreal! You look like I'm supposed to look, while I look like you're supposed to look!"

The absurdity of the situation struck everyone and laughter could be heard coming from all direction. "Sandy has told me lots about what all you have done. I'm so proud of you three! Will you three please forgive me for not having gotten here years ago?"

"Of course, mom," Ellen Sarah exclaimed. "Sandy had kept us informed about you as well. Some of the things you have accomplished are unbelievable! How did you ever come up with that ceremony for those whose bodies have recently died that undid what the Grey Creatures had implanted in their minds? Do you have any idea just how effective that actually was, mom?"

I blushed. I'd never given that too much thought. I had just done it to help. "I guess I had better say hello to John Henry; he's the boss around here, right?"

"You bet, mom," Robert said, "he's our Wid." He looked at me and suddenly said, "You know you're totally right. It's so easy to look at you and call you mom. I know that your body is male; those breasts look rather fake.

But it is much easier to relate this way."

"I agree," Al added, "much easier mom. I sure am glad my daughter, Maggie warned me earlier. You can't know how glad we and everyone here are to see you at long last! John Henry, this is our mom, your mom and dad's best friend."

Still chuckling from the disparity of the ages between us, he opened his arms wide to give me a hug. "That was from mom and dad, Sarah Jane and Raphael. They made me promise them that if I ever came across you, I was to give you a hug from them."

"Thanks. I do miss them, John Henry. By the way, I can't thank you enough for having taken all those years out of your lives to help move all the Moon People out from their underground prisons into the light of the world. I had promised to help them, and you and your Circle did it for me. Thanks. Say, you have your mom's eyes and your dad's cheeks. Sorry I just see a bit of my dear friends in you."

"It was our pleasure to rescue them. But say, what do you think of all dad's work around here?" he gestured at the whole complex.

"Looks to me like he never stopped experimenting. Did he ever build two buildings alike?" I teased. John Henry laughed and said everyone always used to tease Raphael about just that.

He then said, "I've got another little surprise before you start in on meeting all your grandchildren and zillions of others." He waved his hand, obviously he had this all arranged. Out from behind a pillar stepped a lovely young woman in her mid-thirties. She looked at me shyly and with a twinkle in her eye.

"Sarah, is that you?" I exclaimed; we rushed to hug each other!

"Gosh, mom, it is so great to see you at long last. I have nearly gotten everyone around here killed just trying to find you! Looks like you picked up a Tewdwr body this time around. Red hair gives you away. Actually, it looks really good on you, except they tell me you have a male body?"

"Unfortunately, it's male this time. You know my passion for long hair, ah well. But dressing like this makes it easier for you to think of me as your mom or grandmother, doesn't it?"

"It sure does! How did you ever think of doing it?" Sarah pleaded to know.

"Alana, Maggie, and I sort of worked it out the hard way," I chuckled. "Say, you three, come on over here." As my friends joined me, I said, "This is my sister, Fianna. Can you tell we are related?" They all chuckled; matching red hair was a dead giveaway. No one else in the complex had such. "This is your cousin, Fergus, Ros's youngest child. This is my girlfriend, Caitlyn; your older brother's youngest, Sarah. Gang, these are my three children from my first lifetime here. Sarah is from my Amir lifetime. Hopefully it is not too confusing yet, but I know it will be so before long." Everyone laughed; they knew it would be so.

182

Sarah was delighted, "Greeting cousins, welcome to Mont Blanc! Gosh Caitlyn, the last time I saw you, you were just a little girl." Thus, the chatting began in earnest.

Slowly we walked into the main part of the complex, gaily chatting away. John Henry had already worked out how best to present me. Naturally, every druwid and apprentice just had to see me and at least shake my hand. I only really recognized Sarah. John Henry explained as we walked, "Bethany, what we plan to do is this. Each of your children is going to line up with their children, so you can be introduced with some faint chance of seeing who goes with whom. Next, all of the children of your Lightning Circle will follow suit. Once that is done, since there has been a lot of marriages between these families, on my signal, all spouses will join together so that you can get some faint notion of who is married to whom and such."

"Once we get through that ordeal, the Moon Circle will present themselves for your inspection, followed by the West Reach Circle, and then the d'Grange Circle. Once these have been presented, the others will be introduced in a large group. Doesn't that sound like a logical, reasonable way to go about this?"

"Yes, had I given this some thought, I probably would have done something similar. You know, I'm going to need a vast chart of names to keep this all even remotely straight. But that's what I get for taking three lifetimes to get back to everyone."

Yes, it took hours to greet everyone. However, when I finally got to meet Percival Penton, the West Reach Protector and husband of Sarah, I had to tell him, "Percival, I can't thank you enough for rescuing Sarah from the Grey Creatures on West Reach. I owe you big time for having done that for me. If there is ever anything I can do for you, you've only to ask!"

His reply was simply, "You already have. I married her! Sarah is the most loving, kind, intelligent, priestly woman I have ever known. She's the love of my life!" Sarah actually blushed at the unexpected comment.

I won't bore you with a recitation the list of my relations and those of my Circle's. Instead, I'll describe the complex, which was shown to us early evening, just after dinner. The name was still just Mont Blanc, after the mountain on which it stood. Now, however, the outer walls, some six feet tall, surrounded a circle a mile in diameter. Construction of all the buildings was stone; the only wood to be found was on the upper story floors. Raphael built it to last and with little maintenance. Two stables could house three hundred horses. In one cylindrical building all the grain and dried foods were kept. Four cisterns and three wells provided water at key locations. Rows and rows of ranch style homes abutting against each other housed the garrison and those Sisters who chose duty here. Another fifty smaller homes housed many of the families who lived here.

The most striking three buildings were the Great Houses and Watch

Tower. The two Great Houses had five stories each, housing the two Circles and their families along with meeting rooms, training rooms, and giant dining halls with kitchens and pantries. The centrally located Watch Tower rose another fifty feet above these two monsters and boasted eight stories. Its roof was dedicated to the study of the heavens. A barbican wall outlined the tops of these three buildings, so that an errant misstep would not result in a deadly fall. I soon learned that John Henry spent most of his time pacing circles on these roofs.

I was very thankful that John Henry allowed me the rest of the day to meet everyone and be slightly familiarized with the complex and its operations before he insisted on the "heavy" discussions with the Circles. In the later evening, we held a music concert for everyone outside in the amphitheater, which I learned was the name of the Megalos style building with no walls, only pillars. Jolina joined us and we played for nearly two hours. At once, I saw the cleverness and intention behind Raphael's design. Here was a public meeting place, which was not limited in the number of attendees. While the fortress now held close to a thousand people, because of the openness, folks didn't have to be within the building in order to hear and enjoy our music. However, unsure how the sound would carry, we mostly played on the louder instruments. I left no doubt in anyone's mind that I was in this lifetime at least a musician. Our concert was greatly appreciated, as indicated by the hour and a half that elapsed once we finished and before we four finally entered our private rooms for the night!

Since we hadn't had any private time with each other, before we turned in, Caitlyn and I went to my room, while Fergus and Fianna stayed in the girl's room. We hugged each other for some time, neither speaking. When I lovingly looked at her face, she gently avoided my gaze and pulled away slightly. "What's troubling you, Caitlyn?" I asked gently, something certainly was.

She fiddled with her dress for a time, gaining the courage to speak. "There are so many others here that are our age, you know pretty women who are Guardians like yourself or nearly so. I — I release you from your request to court me, Ket Bethany. So many of them would be so much better for you than I." She stared at my feet.

That was certainly true. I hadn't realized she would feel so inferior around so many knowledgeable druwids. I put my hands on the sides of her face, thumbs gently massaging her temples, which also insisted she meet my gaze. "Caitlyn, do you realize how weird this day has been for me? When I last saw my children, the oldest was three. Today, I see they are now old folks, and I didn't even recognize them. They see this not even fifteen year old male, their mother, dressing like a woman to avoid massive confusion while chatting, who they don't recognize either. I know virtually nothing about them; they, likewise — only the stories that have been told about me. At least Sarah I recognized, for not so much time has passed. She was sixteen when I last saw her. Of all them, I really can only relate to Sarah; I do yet have a strong affection for her. All these others that you met today are just strangers to me, Caitlyn, total strangers for the most part. Many of them I work with or will shortly do so."

"However, Caitlyn, I have eyes for you alone. You are the one lighting up my life, not these strangers. I have really fallen for you, dear, if you haven't noticed. I ought to be honest with you. Caitlyn, I think I'm in love with you." There I had actually said it! That wasn't so hard, I told myself. Her resistance melted, and she hugged me tightly; we kissed long and passionately. Only Fianna's knock finally interrupted that kiss.

The next morning after breakfast, Fianna, Caitlyn, Fergus, and Jolina were ushered away from me to get the first of their training sessions. I wished all four of them the best of luck. However, they were more than a little worried and tense. I guess I would be too, if I was in their shoes. Yet, I had total confidence in our teachers.

I was ordered to attend the Grand Council meeting, which was being held in the topmost room of the tall tower, far from any prying ears. Maggie was sent to fetch me so that I couldn't present the excuse that I had gotten lost, which I was considering.

Chapter 14 The Grand Council Meeting

I was slightly out of breath having climbed round and round the spiral staircase to this upper circular room. Everyone else was already present and waiting for me. The layout was readily apparent. Three very long tables were arranged in an equilateral triangle. Sitting around one side of the first table were the members the Moon Circle, sitting at the second identical table was the West Reach Circle, while sitting at the third table was the d'Grange Circle. Arcing around the far wall from these tables were two more, behind which sat other guests. In this way, every one of the three Circles could face each other. Clever arrangement, I thought, wondering where I was to sit. John Henry motioned for me to take the empty seat on his left, at the peak corner of the triangle. I would be facing all twenty-one of them, plus the onlookers at their table. I hate being the center of attention, but I knew I had to be so for the time being. Steeling myself, I sat down.

On my right going down the line were the members of the Moon Circle: John Henry Penton (Wid), Robert Roy Randell (Protector), his wife Misty Simone (Communicator), Henry Alabaster Donegal (Judger) his wife Ellen Sarah (Healer), Ellie Ann Wiklins (Loremaster), and Lilly Elizabeth Penton (Planner).

On my left going down the line were the members of the West Reach Circle: Jane Donegal (Wid), Percival Penton (Protector) [his wife, Sarah Amir Penton sat at the visitors table], Rodger Alan Wilkins (Planner), Willow Jane Donegal (Communicator), Russel Thomas Helmut (Judger), Mark Weatherford (Loremaster), and his wife Justine Weatherford (Healer).

Facing us at the third side of the triangle were the members of the d'Grange Circle: Tom Little (Wid), Alana d'Grange (Communicator), Maggie d'Grange (Loremaster), Jason Smallville (Protector), Al Smythe (Judger), Elisa Greentree (Healer), and Herbert Vine (Planner).

Against the wall at the observer's table were Sarah and six other Guardians from nearby Circles.

A giant map of the Greenway was drawn upon the floor in the center of the equilateral triangle of tables so we all could see it at the same time. John Henry stood and began formally, though I did detect some nervousness in his voice. "I call this meeting to order. We are honored to have with us today Elizabeth Stanton formerly Wid of the Lightning Circle. The first order of business must be a formal report by Wid Bethany of the results of the secret mission that Alabaster Benjamin Crowley sent her on so many years ago. While we know bits and pieces, which had been relayed via the Communicators, it is best that we hear the full report in person. Bethany. . ."

It was routine for any returning Guardian to brief the others on their return. John Henry maintained that tradition. An hour passed as I discussed my lifetime with the Great Messiah. I placed significant emphasis upon the true miracles that Jes had performed so there'd be no doubt that Jes had been special, likely the Son of God. I emphasized how Jes had managed to move a being, who was convinced that he was his body, out of his head with the full realization of his spiritual being nature. I also discussed how that observation very often changed the total outlook of the person for the better.

I spent some time detailing all that we had learned about the Grey Creatures, since everything we did from now on must take them into consideration. I spent considerable time detailing just how one could avoid being sucked into their energy trap in the Appian Way, essentially by not resisting its effect, which was rather difficult to do since that was one's immediate reaction: resist its pull. I discussed how Sarah and I had discovered that the Grey Creatures could walk among us disguised as humans and, more importantly, just how we could detect them. At this point, Percival asked me, "Excuse me, one detail. Is it true that when the creature in the aero car launched energy beams, not unlike a lightning bolt, you were able to actually deflect them as Sarah has claimed?"

"Yes, that's true. Their attack mechanism is energy based, rather like lightning. Remember that every one of us in the Lightning Circle was specially trained by Alabaster himself to be able to defend ourselves from other druwid attacks. I just used my old training that evening." Hushed gasps and hurried whispers echoed around the room. I realized that this bit of special training, which we had received, was not a well-known fact. I added, "To my knowledge, there are only nine beings that can perform this: Alabaster and his wife and the members of the Lightning Circle. It was the most difficult skill I ever had to master."

Percival asked the obvious next question: "Is this skill masterable by others, such as myself? If so, we may be better able to survive an attack from these Grey Creatures."

"I honestly don't know. It took me six months of daily practice to gain that skill under Alabaster's tutelage. He would be the best one to answer your query. I honestly don't know if I could teach it to another. I'm sorry, Percival." Next, I described in detail how a Grey Creature had become the close advisor to King Ahmad and the horrible results that came of that meddling. "Beyond any doubt, I'm totally convinced that these Grey Creatures are indeed meddling in our affairs, fomenting at the very least all these aggressive acts we have witnessed over the years. Their goals and purposes in doing so are, however, a complete mystery."

"Can we not amass a large group of the Sisterhood fighters and ourselves and raid their headquarters? After all, you just said that Jes Amir was able to severely wound one of these creatures," Percival asked. Again, I anticipated someone would ask this, probably the Protectors who loved a good fight.

"I appreciate your idea, Percival. However, if we rode against them with say a thousand of us, myself included, I can guarantee you that only one person would remain alive to close with them into hand-to-hand combat. The others would all be brutally slain miles from their lair." I paused for emphasis and added, "I believe I could deflect all their energy attacks and get my body physically close enough to attack them with a sword. However, the last time I was that close, one fist swing and my head was totally stove in. Thanks, but no thanks. These creatures are giants compared to us. Jes' sword strikes barely reached its knees. Guardians, we can't hope to defeat them with physical battles; we don't stand the slightest chance of success." I had to squash any and all ideas of actually attacking them directly. Such was utter folly.

"We must be patient and find another way to eliminate them. When I find Alabaster, I'll discuss some of my ideas to do just this with him. If he believes one of them has the slightest possibility of working, I'll spare nothing to implement it at once."

That then brought me to my current life and the aggression fomented by the Grey Creatures, which ultimately lay behind King Albert's attack on Cuch Glyn and the slaying of my parents and brother. I related why I had to disguise myself as a woman, fleeing along with my sister to avoid King Albert's revenge. This led to my searching attempts to find Alabaster. I clearly explained my alteration to the Mind Search technology. "To summarize, instead of expanding your awareness out over space, sensing the multitude of beings and minds, and then focusing in on the one you are trying to find, try this in reverse. Focus first on the specific being you wish to find, and then expand your awareness, senses alert for this single being and mind. I believe this approach is the best chance we have of not being simultaneously detected by the Grey Creatures. Thus far, they have not detected me while doing this repeatedly for the last few months." I finally finished my report, sat down, and took a long drink of water.

John Henry rose, "Thank you Wid Bethany. The selfish sacrifices you have made all these years has not gone unnoticed by us or not appreciated." As if this was a prearranged signal, everyone in the room clapped loudly and enthusiastically for several minutes. I accepted their acknowledgment of what I had done. In a way, it felt good to finally have all that acknowledged, for I could end cycle on all of that, moving on to the new challenges that lay ahead.

He continued, "As far as your personal pledge to Alabaster, we fully support your attempts. In fact, if there is absolutely anything that we can do to facilitate your search, you have only to ask. Once you have finished that mission, we would greatly appreciate your returning here to join us at Mont Blanc. In many respects, this is your home too."

"Next on the agenda is to fully brief you on all that has happened here in the Greenway since you have been gone. Once that is done, we beseech you to give us the benefit of your wisdom and advice on how to proceed." John Henry took it upon himself to do the reporting. Much of it was routine. I paid particular attention to the Axemen invasion, since this was one of the two currently pressing problems they were facing, that and the division of the Greenway into ten kingdoms. I found it interesting to learn that these Galt clans, who were nomadic horsemen by nature, were now utterly fixed in one location by the sheer weight of all their looted gold and treasures. Ironic, I thought. The Axemen were obviously not dummies, they had recognized the true situation in the steppes and had acted accordingly. It was highly unfortunate for the Greenway that the only real route for them to get to the steppes led through a portion of our lands. Hence, their invasion. Interestingly, they had never bothered to venture more than a few miles from the Elbe River, which led to the steppes. There was little or no gold or gems to be found anywhere in the Greenway, only farms, nothing to really interest these Axemen from Volksholm.

When he finished, I asked, "You mean that these ten so called kings just up and declared themselves the sole ruler of a portion of the Greenway? The inhabitants had no say in the matter?"

"Yes, none whatsoever," he replied.

"And the first action each took was to conscript villagers into their armies? Again, without the men's agreement to be a soldier in the king's army?"

"Yes."

I declared, "All ten kings are doubly doomed. All will sooner or later lose their heads!"

Maggie asked, "Excuse me, Wid Bethany. Why do you say that?"

"One thing I have observed in my extensive travels over Tarra is that all men and women place immense value on their power of choice in most matters. Whenever that power of choice is overwhelmed, suppressed, wiped out, put down, by whatever means, ultimately the person reacts with great violence and vengeance. Before they react, they behave mostly by being whatever they last were being when their power of choice was obliterated. For example, if the king conscripted a village baker against his will, that baker will go on being a baker, no matter how much they try to turn him into a fighter. He will resist thoroughly, and you'll see a baker on the battlefield, not a soldier. Throwing loaves of bread against cavalry is not very effective. I wouldn't give a copper for the longevity of these ten would-be kings. Do you follow me?"

You could have heard a pin drop in the room; everyone was listening intently to my explanation. I observed that not one of them had or made this observation. I was teaching them something fundamental about human behavior. Humbly, John Henry said, "Wid Bethany, what should we do?"

"First and foremost, Wid John Henry, I can find nothing at all that I would have done differently. You have taken brilliant actions in these matters. I commend you all on a job so far very well done." I knew that I had to acknowledge their efforts, not make them wrong, or all would be lost. John Henry visibly relaxed for the first time since I met him. Plainly, he was greatly relieved to hear from an outside, well-respected source, that his actions and decisions had been optimally thought out and done.

"However, there is one other action you ought to at least attempt. Percival and Sarah are the most likely candidates to carry this out." Both gave me a very startled look; I knew that none in the room had any idea of what I had just thought to try.

"If chaos and anarchy arise in all ten kingdoms, the very survival of this fortress is in doubt, right? You have to import almost all your grain and supplies, save that which comes from your flocks of sheep, right?" Everyone nodded affirmative, trying to see where this led.

"Maggie and Alana have said that not all ten of these kings are so opposed to the Guardians. Is one of those kingdoms close to here, our fortress?"

John Henry moved into the center of the triangle of tables to the giant map on the floor. "Yes, the Calgary region and the region directly northwest of us, these two are very closely allied with us."

"Okay, Calgary is too indefensible, too many ways the city can be attacked. Let's go for this one. What do they call themselves, this kingdom?"

"Southway," came the reply.

"Okay. The objective of this idea is to return the power of choice back to every individual in that region, including the self-appointed king there. First, by being very friendly to the king and every person in the kingdom, you go around pointing out the dire troubles that lay in waiting for them. Suggest that it is the right of every man and woman in the kingdom to have a say in who will be their king. Now, the clever part is that Sarah and Percival travel to every town and village, making friends with everyone. Once friendship is achieved, nominate Percival and Sarah for the position of King and Queen. Encourage the current king to campaign on his own behalf as well. Then when the time is right, hold a kingdom wide election. If you do it right, these two will be elected by a landslide. Next, you ask for volunteers to become soldiers in the army whose task is to protect the people in the towns and villages. Pay them well, treat them well, give them good equipment and training. In short, you make being a soldier a very popular and worthwhile career for young men and women, if they desire, to choose to do. I guarantee you that if you always act from the view point of allowing everyone the right to choose without any duress, your kingdom will still be standing when the others have long turned to dust."

For five minutes, the kudos and cheers and well-dones bounced around the room. At last, John Henry regained control. "Brilliant, Wid Bethany! I can see phase two already. Once we succeed in this kingdom, we move on to the next most likely one, and on and on."

"Precisely. I leave it up to you whom to choose to nominate for the rest of the king positions. Remember, always keep it light and cheerful and never use duress or force or threat of force. In time, everyone will react most favorably to you. Can we break for lunch? I have a starving teenager body on my hands." Everyone laughed and we broke for lunch.

The afternoon session was much shorter. First, they wanted to know how I managed to retain all my training, while having undergone two body deaths. They had just lost over four hundred druwids to the Grey Creatures. Normally, in previous times, the Guardians would find and assist the being who had just lost his or her body and help them get another baby body. Of course, they would be carefully monitored as the body grew up. Frequently, the druwid would need some retraining, because they tended to forget many things sometime after getting the new baby body. However, in the current situation, no attempts to contact those who had just lost their bodies were attempted for fear of instant retaliation by the Grey Creatures. I suggested that they experiment using the variation I had invented to look for Alabaster. This gave them hope of making contact with those that had been lost. Perhaps fifteen years down the road, those four hundred would be back in operation as Guardians once more.

Next, John Henry, very embarrassed, asked, "I hate to do this Wid Bethany, but you know the rules as well as I. Whenever a druwid returns in a new body, they often need retraining. I must ask you before your peers, is there any retraining that you need?"

"Well, yes. It seems that my powers of observing the obvious have partially taken flight," I kept it light. "I could use a refresher on this. In all these years, I assume that the healing arts have progressed. Considering the mission that I'm on, I ought to get up to speed on anything new about healing. Also, on this mission, conjuring may well be invaluable. I hate to admit this to all of you, but I never was very good at conjuring. I can do only the simplest of actions. You can forget fighter training. I know I have a male body this time, but I still hate swordplay! I simply refuse to learn sword play, sorry."

Maggie called out, "See, a woman in a man's body." Everyone roared with laughter.

John Henry probed a bit, "Nothing more? You still retain control over fire, lightning, and ice, for example?"

"Absolutely, lightning is still my forte." Again, laughter filled the room. I added, "I could use a good stout oak pole though."

"Okay then, I won't pressure you further, Wid Bethany. You are already moving on to my next question: What is it that we can provide you with to further the invaluable goal of locating Alabaster?"

"Why did I know you were going to ask that?" I teased; some chuckles were heard.

"Seriously, I could use some help. As you have gathered, my plan is to travel around Tarra, searching small sections at a time to avoid any chance of being detected by our enemies. What better way to do this than by being traveling musicians, troubadours? I have already proven the concept works. However, I could use some help. I would like to have my troupe learn as many songs and dances of the Greenway as possible, which gives us a greater repertoire, making us more believable. It would be great if we could have some gaily decorated wagons to travel with — I remember the wagons the traveling musicians had when my Circle first met them near Brownsville. I don't know if it's possible or not, but a few more musicians or dancers would greatly aid the disguise. Oh yes, I am utterly desperate for healing herbs and salves! Do you realize the abysmal state of healing outside the Greenway? Atrocious to say the very least!"

Alana interrupted, "Since they are first going to be crossing the Sea Princes and have to pass through the Velona sector, which is simply rife with bandits, more so than the other sectors, I would like to suggest that some Sisters go with them. It would be ideal if one of the Sisters was very familiar with the trails and towns. I think it also very prudent that we send along some other Guardians, Protectors or possibly those with good conjuring skills, since Wid Bethany suggests she isn't good with such spells. We all know that any caravan under the protection of the Sisterhood is rarely attacked openly." Her suggestions received unanimous agreement from everyone.

That night as I went to sleep, I realized that for the first time in thirty-three years I was going to have lots of help in my quest to locate Alabaster. Part of my own personal heavy burden in this area lifted from me. I felt much lighter, even more confident that eventually we would find him and help him out! I was no longer alone in my quest; I now had the full support of a group of my peers. What a change for the better.

That evening at supper, Sarah sat beside me and said, "Thanks mom for the incredible support for Percival and me. Did you know that I am an apprentice Healer? Of course, I probably won't finally pass until I am an old woman, but I keep doggedly at it."

"Well done indeed, Sarah! Well done. No, I didn't know that. Makes my choice of you two even better!" She beamed with pride. I was doing my small part to honor my pledge to Jes, that his children become kings and queens. Don't get me wrong, had these two not been entirely suited for this task, I would not have chosen them. It is just worked out that I was honoring my pledge too.

That evening, my three tired, sore, but exuberant companions finally joined me in our rooms. Theirs had been an exhausting day, full of surprises and challenges, which each had met. Caitlyn excitedly told me how she had actually learned to circle kick a sword out of an attacker's hands. Near the end of the practice, she finally had done it! Fianna talked on and on about how great it was to be learning how really to help heal someone. I suspected she saw the long range ramifications of such knowledge, ever the practical sister. Fergus, on the other hand, couldn't stop talking about the incredible benefits of observing your opponent in a fight. Yes, from my point of view, all these things that they gaily related to me were honestly just the barest beginnings of such skills. Yet, I recalled the excitement I had displayed when I had learned these things. I wondered how they would fare when they entered the city defensive skills portion of their training. Just walking down the main street of one of these large Sea Prince cities could well result in numerous attempts to pick your pockets.

I had not seen Jolina today. As I fell asleep, I kept wondering how she had fared. Hers would be the most difficult case to handle. I vowed to check up on her progress in the morning. I didn't have too, Alana caught me at breakfast, "Bethany, I hate to interrupt your training exercises for today, but I could use your opinion or help with Jolina. Tom, our Wid, suggested I go ahead ask you directly, without following the usual chain of command between Circles."

"Sure thing, I was just going to check on her progress. I didn't see her much yesterday."

"Let's go to my private room first, shall we?" I followed her to her room in one of the Great Houses. Compared to the other rooms that I had seen, Alana's was very sparsely furnished, probably because she spent so little time her. "I tried to reach her and get her mind calmed yesterday, but the resistance and confusion was just too great. She is all right when she is performing some activities, such as playing or working on defensive skills, which as expected, she found incredibly difficult." Alana found it difficult to describe just what was going on with Jolina, primarily because we have no words to discuss adequately mental things. She finally said that I should just see for myself. I followed her as she led me into the training room where the Sisters had brought Jolina a short while ago. I saw her sitting on a chair, hands in her lap, motionless, head slightly falling to one side.

"Hi Jolina. Bethany here. How are you?" I said softly, trying not to startle the woman.

"Fine," came the automatic response, though her head did not move, and she did not appear to me to be "fine." It was if I were talking to some social training response. How often do you say "Fine," when asked how you are doing by someone and you know perfectly well that you are anything but fine? Well, you may appreciate what I saw. In fact, her "fine" did not really answer my question. I made a mind connection to Alana. *She hasn't answered the question. I wonder how long it will be until she does?*

Yes, this is exactly what I ran into yesterday, Alana replied.

"How are you?" I repeated using the same voice quality as my first asking.

Instead of a rapid fire "fine," this time I got a long, "Ahhhh" that trailed into something not understandable. *We are making progress*, I sent to Alana.

"How are you?" I repeated once more.

"Ah, is that you, Bethany?" she muttered, turning her head slightly toward me. This still was not an answer.

"Yes, it's me, Bethany. How are you?"

This time I finally reached her and got a reply, "Not so good. This isn't going to work. I keep trying to open my eyes, but I can't see anything." She sounded hopeless, but not quite apathetic.

Alana sent me, *I see, you just keep asking the same question without varying it until you actually do get her to answer.*

"Tell me about it, Jolina," I asked. I had to find out what was going on with her if I were to have any chance of helping.

"Some days are worse than others; today is bad. I can't tell what is real any more. Kind of wish I had just died. This is a living nightmare," she said, breaking down at last into tears, holding her head in her hands. "They just don't know what it's like being blind," she sobbed.

"No, I certainly can't say that I have ever been blind like you, Jolina." Something she had just said struck me as curious and my intuition struck. "Jolina, let me tell you a story about myself and you see if it has any bearing on your situation, all right?" She nodded. "Some twenty or so years ago, I had a nice womanly body. I was in my forties. One night when the moon was half, someone hit me in my face with their fist, smashing in my head, and killing my body. Later on, when this body was born, whenever the moon was half, at night when I was sleeping, I would wake up terrified. It was totally black in the room. I couldn't see anything. Yet, I did see. My mind has all these pictures, images of begin chased by that man and having my face crushed by his fist. I would scream and try to get away, until my mom and sister would come, light a lantern, and shake me fully awake. Only when I could see the real room around me could I differentiate between the nightmare memories in my mind and the real room around me."

"That's kind of how it is with me, Bethany, only I can never wake up. I can never see the room. I can never tell for sure what is what anymore," and she cried once more.

I wished I were Jes and could just move her outside of her body, even perhaps curing her blindness while I was at it. However, that was just wishful thinking. Jes was long dead and gone. What if Alabaster was in similar dire straits when I did find him, continually reliving that nightmare with the Grey Creatures? What could I do to help him? I felt completely helpless, no ideas at all of what I could do if he were. I told myself, "Bethany, wake up! You have a perfect opportunity to experiment and try and do something that will help Jolina." I thought hard. I remembered that I had gone over and over my mental images of that frightful night with the Grey Creatures. I don't know how many times I relived them, but I do know that having gone over them so many times, often telling Fianna all about them, that now these images didn't bother me in the slightest — no more than images of my teacup at breakfast a short while ago. I wondered if the action of reliving them while telling them to another was beneficial? My gut feeling was that the telling of them to others was critical. After all, many people relived nightmares and they never did go away.

"Jolina," I took her hand in mine so she would have a physical reality of my presence, "I want you to go to the very beginning of what happened to you and tell me all about what happened to you. Tell me everything you see in these nightmare images. Will you do that for me and Alana? We are right here with you and my hand will hold yours all the time." I think that she did want to share her nightmares, her never-ending fears.

Meekly she replied, "Okay. I was having a fight with my husband. I hated him. We were arguing; he slammed a pot on the table startling me with its loud noise. I threw the pot back at him, and it hit him in the chest. He threw it at my head; it hurt, so I threw a flowerpot back at him, calling him a pig. He caught it. He said, 'Damn you bitch!' and threw the pot at my head. It hit me right in the eyes and shattered. Everything went totally dark. I screamed. I couldn't see anything. I wailed and flailed wildly around the room, knocking all sorts of things over. He slapped me in my face, yelling 'Stop it!' I couldn't. I couldn't see. Something hard hits my head. I think it is a long time later, I still can't see. I'm cold. I'm soaking wet. It feels like I'm on cobblestone streets. I think he threw me out of the house and left me to die in the street. I can't see. I just lie there and cry. I hear a soft woman's voice lifting me up, 'Are you hurt? Your face is a mess. Who did this to you?' 'I can't see!' I scream. She carries me somewhere. I hear voices, friendly women's voices. 'Drink this.' Nearly spilled it. I relax and fall asleep. I wake and scream, 'I can't see anything.' Someone tells me that I'm blind and will never see again. They tell me they are Sisters and will always look after me from now on. They ask me who I am and what happened. A while later, another voice says, 'It's done. I gave his head to Tur. We ransacked her house and brought all her things. I think she is that famous musician.' I sleep again. That's about all." Jolina finished up.

"Very well done, Jolina! I wonder, can you go through those images again and see if you can see more about what happened?" I asked. She ran through that night once more. What Alana and I both noted was that she began fleshing out the story, adding small descriptions here and there. Unable to resist, I Mind Joined with her and watched her progress. I noticed a key detail. Here and there in the images, there were black, blank places that she skipped over. When I had her go through it a third time, I noticed that some of these blank spots now opened up, and she could see those additional details. Fascinating, indeed.

Partway through that evening, she suddenly stopped, took my hand in both of hers, and laughingly said, "You know, when I was walking home that evening, before it all started, I decided that I had enough. I wanted him to leave me, move out, and get out of my life forever. I decided a big fight ought to do it. Boy, did I ever do it. What a silly thing to decide, and it did come true, didn't it." She continued to giggle over her silly decision.

I asked, "How do those memories seem to you now?"

"Oh," she said rather startled, "I don't seem to mind them anymore. That sure is funny, though. I feel lots lighter, Bethany."

"Well done, Jolina!" I thanked her. Now we were getting somewhere. "We are all immortal spiritual beings. What you were looking at was stuff in your mind. You, the being, are doing the looking. This here is your fleshly body," I squeezed her hand slightly. I wonder, can you now move out of your body's head, maybe a little ways in back of it?"

Her grip tightened on my hand, "Oh no! I'm holding on to it very tightly! I just know I will be lost utterly if I let go!" She chuckled again and added, "Gosh, Bethany, I don't know where that just came from! But I don't think I can do it."

"Okay, that's fine. Sometimes when I am outside my head," I relayed to her, "I can see things without using my eyes. That's why I asked. My vision when I'm outside and not looking through the body's eyes, is all blurry, and distances are totally screwed up."

"That must be exciting and maybe a little bit scary," she commented. "Say do see something yellowish in front of me." I looked around the room and suddenly realized.

"Wow. You are seeing the bright sunlight coming in your window!" I exclaimed.

Alana took over, "Good going, Jolina. Now see if you can also feel the sun's warmth on your face, hands, and chest. Can how does your front side feel compared to your back?"

"Oh, I see. I'm warmer here. Back is colder," Jolina replied.

"That's just perfect, Jolina. Now you are making good progress. Bethany, I can take it from here. I've kept you away from your training long enough. We three all learned something here this morning." I said goodbye, wished them luck, and left to go find my training session, rather late for it. Okay, I was very late for it; I got lost in the Great Hall for a while.

I walked into the room and was surprised to see ten young children present along with John Henry. "Come on in and take a seat. We are practicing observing the obvious. Now, who can tell us something about Bethany, who has just joined us to learn as you are learning."

One youngster piped up, "She is very late." The class giggled.

"Ah, now what exactly did you observe that tells you she is very late?" John Henry replied.

"Well, she just is. We all just saw her come in," he rationalized. Was I ever this bad, I wondered?

"Let's take it one step at a time. What did you actually see? No conclusions, just what did you observe?"

A girl answered, "Well, I see this woman with very long red hair, white dress, and brown shoes. But she's a man, isn't she? That's what mom said." Again, the children laughed a bit.

"We are starting to get there. Now, how do you know you saw a woman? How do you know you saw hair? How do you know it is long? How do you know it is red? How can you tell he's a man?" he needled them.

"Oh, I get it," another boy replied. "It's red because it's color is the same as my apple here." He held up his red apple so everyone could see.

"Very good. That explains the observation of red. Now how do you know it is hair that you are seeing? Could it not be a horse's tail attached to her head? What exactly do you see?"

"Well, if you want it that way," a lad said rather argumentatively, "I see long stringy things coming from the top, dangling and twisting downwards, some disappear at the shoulders. It's got to be hair, cause it looks like Julie's hair, only a different color and length."

"How could you determine that it is truly hair that you are observing?" he persisted.

One lad came over and pulled on my hair, "Ouch. Don't do that again!" I glared at him.

"So it didn't pull off, but could it not be horse hair tied tightly to her own hair underneath?" he asked.

"Oh I see. No, it can't. I see the oval shape of her head. See the hair starts coming out of it right where the flesh colored oval ends. If it were tied here in the front, I should see a gap or bump where the knot is at." Thus, the rest of the morning went. Actually, I rather enjoyed the session. I will admit it, I was very rusty at observing the obvious; I had fallen into the trap of rushing to conclusions far too quickly. I honestly needed this refresher.

The rest of the afternoon, I spent with the three Healers, going over the few new developments that I didn't know. Additionally, we put together a very workable healing pouch for me to use. Finally, I had all the herbs and salves that a proper healer is never without.

Over dinner, my companions filled me in on their day's training. Though tired and a bit sore from all the exercise and blows that they failed to dodge, all three were still enthusiastic about all they were learning. They were adjusting to the fast-paced routine. We could not spend the ten years that a child would need to master all the skills necessary to become a druwid Guardian. That was not our intention. When traveling through other lands and cities, it is prudent to know how to take care of oneself in likely situations that often arise, especially pickpockets of the larger cities. If my three friends could learn some street sense, we could more easily accomplish our dual missions of entertaining others and finding Alabaster.

However, after dinner, a man in his mid-twenties rode up to the complex, while we five were just getting setup in the open amphitheater once more to play for our hosts. John Henry brought him to me. "Excuse me Bethany. Here's someone I would like you and your troupe to meet. This is one of the finest musicians in Calgary, Edgar Elms. Edgar, these are the Cymry Minstrels form West Reach. Sister Jolina Alwana from Fortress d'Grange is playing with them. This is their leader, Ket Bethany. Don't ask why he's wearing a dress at the moment." The tiniest of smiles creased the lips of Edgar. Surely, this fellow had a bad case of melancholia, from drooping eyelids to the turned down edges of his mouth, even his unkempt hair announced to the world: here is a sad man. Even his clothes looked like he had slept in them for weeks.

I introduced the other members of our group, but that fleeting smile had long evaporated. Finally, he said, "I understand that you wish to trade songs with me, those of West Reach for those of the Greenway, Ket."

"Absolutely, we are getting ready to tour the Sea Princes and beyond and we need all the material that we can learn. We are just about to play for our hosts; you are welcome to play along."

"I'll listen. I presume you will play many dances. Nowadays, I only play laments and dirges," he drawled slowly. Even his speech was melancholic! Yet, he appeared more than a little surprised to see Jolina being helped into her seat, feeling the placement of her instruments. "I never expected to see Jolina play again. I *will* listen." He sat down on the stone floor about six feet right out in front of us, from where he could watch all of us closely and not miss hearing any note.

"Sour puss," Fianna whispered to me as I sat down and picked up my flute. That he was; however, his personality didn't matter if he could teach us Greenway songs.

Naturally, we played a number of lively dance tunes first. As the evening wore on, we switched to more ballads and then some laments. I was thinking of the children and their bed times — no sense playing lots of lively dance tunes just before they had to go to bed. Ah, ever the mother in me.

During the first part of the evening, I soon forgot entirely about Edgar, who sat like a frozen sitting statue in front of us. I could not tell if he enjoyed our playing or hated it, just no emotion at all. However, just as soon as we began to play our trademark song, Lyneth's Lament, with Jolina this time playing the bass flute, Edgar became highly animated, swaying to the shifting moods; he'd come alive! When the last low bass flute's notes trailed off into silence, he jumped up yelling "Bravo Jolina! Bravo!" making a bit of a spectacle of himself and slightly embarrassing her.

Each slow piece we played, whether sad or not, seemed to bring life to this young man. When we interspersed a ballad, he resumed his statue form. Weird, I thought, very weird.

When we finished, Edgar said, "Tomorrow we begin exchanging songs. I must know that lament first!" I smiled, figuring from his reaction earlier that he would want to learn that one. Edgar then ignored the rest of us and went over to Jolina, who was in the process of packing away her instruments. "Jolina, it is such an honor to hear you play once more. I had steeled myself against ever hearing you play again. You play like the nightingale in the summer, like the bluebirds of spring. Still, I have never heard your equal play in all the lands."

Jolina blushed slightly, "I remember you Edgar. Didn't we once play together at a festival? I think I was sixteen then."

"Ah, you remember me then, too. Yes, yes, we did. I still treasure those memories of playing with the master. I have practiced long and hard over the years, but I regret to say my performances still pale, compared to yours." I thought he was coming on to her rather precociously. Yet, she didn't seem to mind, so I didn't intervene.

"You are just saying that, Edgar, to please me. You know very well that I haven't played in five years, not since I was blinded. Now I play but can't even see where my fingers go; wrong notes proliferate." Good, I thought, she sees right through him.

"Remember what you said to me long ago? You said the notes are not what matter; rather it is the feeling, the emotion that you convey via the music, that is what matters. That comes from the heart."

"Touché," she smiled in his general direction. "I look forward to hearing you play tomorrow." A Sister helped her up and off to her room; I think she also thought Jolina needed rescuing.

John Henry caught up to us as we were trying to find our rooms in the Great Hall. "Hold a minute. I thought I ought to explain Edgar briefly. Sorry to have just sprung him on you like that. You see, a few years ago, he lost his loving wife and daughter in a tragic accident. Before that, he was a gay, optimistic man, full of life, whose music inspired the best in others. However, one evening while he was away playing, his wife and daughter went ice skating. The ice cracked and they fell into the bay and drowned. No one found them until the next day. That literally broke the man's spirit. He's been melancholic ever since. He does know his music, however. Besides, maybe making music with you folks might bring him out of his melancholia." I thanked him, for it explained a lot. I knew he was still carrying his grief on his shirt sleeve, so to speak.

Days stretched into weeks. One night Jolina actually came to my room on her own without anyone assisting her. "I can find your room all by myself," she explained excitedly. "Furthermore, I can feel you, Bethany. Look, she walked right up to me, stopping inches from me. I can sense your body heat and even the masses of the walls now! Steps still give me an awful time though," she admitted. I gave her a loving hug and congratulated her. She had accepted her blindness and was in the process of expanding her other senses to compensate so she could pursue her own goals in life.

Yes, we did learn two dozen songs and dances from "Sour Puss," which was Fianna's nickname for Edgar. On his behalf, he soon began playing with us on the slower pieces. Like Jolina, he had a solid feel for the music, could play well on his own, and most importantly, he could play proper ensemble. He added his lute and guitar to our sound, plus several louder double reed horns, all higher in pitch than Fergus's tenor shawm. Then, one night a messenger came carrying a large box for Edgar. "Gang, tonight you'll be blessed to hear the sweetest lament on Tarra. I had them bring me my bass shawm." When assembled, this instrument was huge; its sound was fantastic: low and nasally, and incredibly impressive! Yes, all of us were amazed at how well that instrument matched our songs. After that, we insisted he play it nearly all the time.

Maggie and Alana had returned to their home in d'Grange some five weeks ago. We were in our sixth week and I was getting restless to get on with my mission to find Alabaster. Hence, I finally announced, "Okay everyone, we've been here long enough. I propose that we return to d'Grange next week, give the Sisterhood one last concert as we promised, and then get on our way, heading down into the Velona Sector." My friends gladly accepted my decision, though I know they would have loved to stay on for years. All three had reached that point where they could fully appreciate the large amount of knowledge they did not have. It is a much better attitude than the man who believes he knows everything and is ignorant of his own stupidity.

However, it was my turn to be totally surprised, though, thinking back on it, perhaps I should have expected it. When she heard our plans, Jolina announced to everyone in no uncertain terms, "I am going to go with the Cymry Minstrels. After all, I now think of myself as one of them." Many tried to talk her out of it, citing the hardships of the journey. She doggedly stayed her course.

Finally, John Henry came to me with Jolina on his arm. "This is one stubborn woman, Bethany. I leave the call up to you."

"If Jolina wants to come along with us, I'm behind it completely," I replied.

"See, I told you so," Jolina teased John Henry. It was so good to see Jolina playfully teasing another; so much had changed while she had been here. I was pleased.

"Okay, you may go with them, Jolina. I'll have to make a few last minute changes, though. You know the Sisterhood will insist on giving you a large protection force; you're the most famous musician in these two lands," he teased her back. She smiled. It was good to see her smile again.

Naturally, when Edgar heard that Jolina was actually going to accompany us traveling all over Tarra as wandering troubadours, he begged me to let him come. Since John Henry thought the outing might do him some good, I consented, after he agreed to all my usual terms and understood that the ultimate purpose was to locate a man in dire need.

At last, we had made all the necessary preparations. Twenty Sisters accompanied us, all fighters, except two. The leader of Fighter Group One, as they called themselves, was Sister Adriana Socorro, a strong willed, middle aged woman, who was often trusted with the most difficult missions. She was a proven field commander and a no nonsense leader.

One of the two exceptions was a good trail chef, Camilla, who additionally looked after Jolina's special needs. The other exception, Felice Bugatti, was actually the daughter of Florencia Bugatti, the Sister who had accompanied my Lightning Circle across the Sea Princes. Flo knew the land like no one else I had ever known. Felice, now thirty-five, had followed in her mother's footsteps or as the saying goes, like mother, like daughter. Felice, or Fel as she preferred, would be our guide across the Sea Princes.

Additionally, John Henry sent along three Guardians, whose Circles had been broken by the intervention of the Grey Creatures, which had killed most of the Circle members. With the huge shortage of Guardians, it was impossible to replace those that were lost. For the first time in our history, broken Circles remained broken.

Alton Woodgrove, Protector Oak Circle, was twenty-five, well built, with medium black hair and eyes of the kind that seemed to penetrate you when he looked at you. His wife, their healer, had been killed. His three children, now in their teens, were staying at Mont Blanc.

Andre le'Goeur, Protector Waynesville Circle, was twenty-one, tall and blonde with blue eyes. He was in many ways a woman's man, a dandy; yet, his skill with the sword was something to behold.

Waverly Warwick, Communicator Waynesville Circle, was twenty-two with curly blonde hair, nearly yellow, with pale blue eyes. Unfortunately, her face was extremely plain, her nose, non-distinct, which didn't help her double chin and thin cheekbones. One could call her homely, but she had a dynamic personality. Everyone she met felt like this person was a true friend after just one short meeting with her. I thought it was a shame that she had not yet found someone to love her for herself, not her unfortunately poor comeliness.

John Henry asked me to reconsider my decision not to take along a Healer in case we should either find ourselves in great need or find that Alabaster needed skill beyond what we had. "No, please. You'll need all you have here. Besides, the Healer would probably have absolutely nothing to do or contribute for a very long time, assuming that I find Alabaster. Sending along a Healer would be wasteful of a Guardian. Besides, with four of us, we ought to be just fine in the healing department."

John Henry's gift of suitable transportation was perfect! Seven wagons had been built to my specifications and painted under my supervision. Yes, they all bore gay colors with many interlocking vines, ropes, and crosses indicative of the art style on Cymry. One wagon held the four of us. Another held Jolina, Felice, Camilla, and Waverly. The protectors usually rode their horses, but slept in a third wagon along with Edgar. The remaining four wagons carried our supplies, doubling as shelter for the Sisters during inclement weather. Two large draft horses pulled each wagon. Our horses, still back at Fortress d'Grange, would serve as spares. Additionally, the Fighter Group One insisted on bringing along another six spares for themselves. All of the spares were tied behind wagons for the most part.

While everyone busily began the lengthy loading of supplies into the wagons, Percival and Sarah came galloping into the complex. They had been out in the Southway Kingdom implementing my plan. "Mother, it is working brilliantly!" Sarah reported. "Everywhere we go, we are very nice and friendly to everyone. We haven't had even one person become hostile with us, not even the self-appointed king. Actually, if the truth be told, I think the King has been having many second thoughts about his power grab. There is a lot more to being King than playing at fighting. Anyway, we've rounded up support for the first general election for who should be King of Southway. With luck, it will be held in two weeks. Percival ought to be a shoo-in, but we are starting to campaign vigorously this week, visiting every town and village." We hugged, and I wished her good luck and asked her to have Percival or his Communicator keep me posted on how it turned out. Her husband was very proud of her. I could see it in his eyes and face.

The five-day journey to Fortress d'Grange was used as a shakedown trip, working out the optimum way to set up the wagons at night, tethering the small herd of horses, and all the other myriad tasks such a large group required. Unlike the Sisters who had accompanied the Lightning Circle so many years ago, these women camped with us and enjoyed our company; quickly we became one large happy group. In fact, by the fourth night, four Sisters volunteered to join our show and dance along with Fianna. Not to be out done, Andre gallantly asked to join the dancers so Fianna would have a proper male partner at times. I found it encouraging that so many wanted to get in on the act; our shows would be all the more believable, attracting no suspicion.

We spent a few days in d'Grange adding to our supplies and giving the promised concert at the Sister's large dance hall. All our newly learned songs we shared to rousing rounds of applause. Sister Jolina became the center of attention; word that she, too, had joined the traveling minstrel group had already reached here. Hence, absolutely every Sister had to come by and wish her well. All this appreciation, I felt, helped Jolina's self-esteem.

The last night before we left d'Grange, Captain Adriana came by our wagon with her maps. "Battle plans," she announced. "Time we go over the battle plans for tomorrow's journey," she stated very businesslike.

"Battle plans? We aren't in a war, Adriana, are we?" I teased. I saw that I could not win this one, "Okay, battle plans. Shoot." I got into the spirit of the thing. Our two Protectors joined us along with Felice, our expert guide. Together, we five set the pattern for nearly every night: we soon picked up the nickname the Planners. The first objective: to get to Velona by the safest route through this lawless country filled with bandits. I went along with Felice's suggestion that we get up onto the Paese di Dio as soon as possible, travel in total safety half way across the sector, and then head straight down the roads into Velona, minimizing the amount of time we would be exposed in the bandit country. Besides, the roads down the coastline from d'Grange to Velona were poor at best and constantly monitored by bandit groups seeking likely prey. I sincerely wanted my three companions to get an opportunity to see and experience the Paese di Dio, God's Highway.

Chapter 15   Into the Lawless Velona Sector, Sea Princes

November 1, 621 AH, our Minstrel Caravan pulled out of Fortress d'Grange, heading southward. Ultimate destination: Velona itself. The main track led ultimately to Velona, snaking its way precariously through massive boulder shields of rock from the craggy Appian Way peaks to our left. These very rugged foothills twisted their stony way down to the very ocean itself and then out into the waters, awaiting a wayward ship to crash upon them. Off the trail, even walking on foot was difficult; thick low-lying vegetation struggled for life among the multitudinous rocks, whose sizes ranged from three feet to a few inches in size, all loose, making footsteps treacherous. Obviously, great efforts had been made in the last twenty years to clear this small passageway large enough for wagons to pass, making an overland connection down to Velona.

This close to d'Grange, we were in no danger from bandit ambushes, because off the trail passage was nearly impossible. Slowly we picked our way along the trail. Occasionally, the lead riders would have to stop and remove some errant debris that had fallen or slid down onto our trail. Our progress initially was thus slow; we covered only sixteen miles the first day. Yet, around the time that we halted to make camp, we did meet one family of five who were walking towards the Fortress, immigrants we guessed from their tattered clothing and meager possessions. The three children looked to me to be half-starved. Captain Adriana invited them to spend the chilly night around our campfires and partake of our evening meal. As I watched her interacting with this destitute family, I saw a well of compassion underlying the steel-faced, field commander view that she presented to the world. My respect for her rose. Oh yes, I was back looking like a young man once again. The need for the disguise was gone for now.

The next day brought us a spectacular, though somewhat frightening view of the ocean. The trail edged its way to the very edge of a hundred foot sheer cliff. Far below us, we could hear the thunderous roar of waves crashing upon the boulder filled, narrow beach. To our left, the steep sided cliff rose several hundred feet to the top of a foothill. Only this narrow passage, eight feet wide, permitted passage on southward. Sitting on the wagon bench, yet another four feet higher and with no room for the slightest miscalculation, our progress slowed to a snail's pace. Adriana ordered seven Sisters to dismount. On foot, these women carefully led the wagons' horses along the passage, while we drivers mostly looked on and gazed at the fall to our right. Yes, it was very dizzying to look all the way down to the tumultuous ocean below.

On the third day, Felice, our guide, asked me if I wanted to ride ahead with her to help search for a route to the Paese di Dio, which the wagons could make. After two days of sitting on the cramped wagon seat driving the team of draft horses at such a slow speed, I was more than pleased for the change of pace. Together, we rode on ahead of the caravan for several miles before picking our way overland. "If I recall, there is an old deer track that just might do. Can you see it here in front of us?" she asked. I was certain that she was testing my skills!

"Yes, it's a very plain one, veers off to the northeast up there a ways. I think the wagons could make it this far," I replied.

She grinned, "Yes, you are right. Sorry, I just wanted to know for sure if you Guardians are as good as they say you are at following trails. No offense intended."

I smiled, "None taken. Actually, I think it a wise move on your part to gain certainty that someone other than yourself can see and follow these faint trails." After a time, I commented, "You know, I knew your mother, many years ago, Florencia. When I traveled with her, she had short blonde hair and blue eyes, but her face was worn with lines, looking older than her thirty years. As I remember, Flo was short and wiry, five feet tall I think. Her alto voice I found most intriguing. She really knew her horses all right, but Flo knew the land like the back of her palms. Someone said that she could navigate across the Lands of the Sea Princes with her eyes closed. During my time in her company, I knew that Flo knew more about the land and its terrain than any other person in the Sea Princes. Yes, your mother was one terrific woman."

Fel smiled, "Yes, that would be mom. She married later on, you know, and she taught me all she knew. However, Bethany, can I call you that? I mean, I still think of you as that young woman." I nodded, so she continued. "Mom told me endless stories about you and your friends. She thought more highly of you than she did of the Sisterhood, and that is saying something. Believe me when I say I'm incredibly honored to meet and guide for you just as mom did. I mean it!"

"I know we're in good hands. I'm very pleased to travel with Flo's daughter, too. From what I have seen of you so far, you are so very much like her that I sometimes start to call you Flo instead of Fel." She grinned.

"Mind if I ask you a personal question?" she asked, her face bore the signs of getting up the courage to ask me something that she was pondering for a long time.

"Sure," I said, wondering she had in mind.

"You are now a guy, so why do you have such incredibly long hair? Doesn't it get in the way? Don't you get teased a lot about it?" Ah, it was my hair once again!

"Fel, I have two vices. I dearly love long hair. I know, it gets caught in everything, takes forever to dry, and takes hours to detangle the mess sometimes. It can be a pain, that's for sure, but I just love it. You know, the neatest sensation is riding like the wind with my hair blowing behind me. And yes, I did get teased a lot as I was growing up. I mostly ignored it."

She smiled and asked the inevitable, "What's the second vice?"

"Bethany. I love that name. Just try to get your parents to name you that, especially when you're a boy."

She laughed, "How could they? It's a girl's name."

"Back in Tewdwr, customarily a person only has one name; they add the village name after it. I was Ket of Cuch Glyn. Naturally, I have changed it to Ket of Bethany, or Ket Bethany for short. Clever, is it not?" I teased.

She laughed once more. "If those are vices, then I wonder what drinking to excess or womanizing would be called?" she teased me back. After a pause, she confided, "My vice is I love to ride off across country alone, just as we are now doing — just like mom. I guess I do take after her. Ah, here we are, Bethany." She halted at a base of a fairly steep grade and gazed up towards the hilltop some two hundred feet distant.

"Here is why I asked you to come along. Do you think the horses can make it up this grade? If so, then once we get up there, I know the wagons can easily make it all the way onto the Paese di Dio."

I studied it for a minute. Yes, it was pretty steep. "I think the draft horses can make it. If need be, we can put the spare horses to work adding some extra pull. I can't wait to see the Paese di Dio once more. I just love it up there. God's Country, that's for sure. That was Flo's greatest gift to me, taking us to this sacred land." Memories of serenity came unbidden into my mind. Slowly, we returned to the caravan.

By late afternoon, the caravan itself arrived at this grade. Taking no chances, we hitched two spare horses to each wagon with two Sisters leading each of those. Slowly the straining horses inched the heavy wagons upwards. An hour passed going those two hundred feet! We camped just over the top of that hillside. Fel insisted that tomorrow night we would be camping on the Paese di Dio!

The next day, Adriana issued new orders to her women. While the wagons continued their upwards climb, led by Felice, they scattered around the countryside, collecting dry firewood. I explained to my companions that we were about to make the Paese di Dio and that there were no trees of any kind up there. We would have to bring along our own firewood or eat everything cold. I resisted all their beggings and pleadings about what this Paese di Dio was, saying only, "You must see and experience for yourself the Paese di Dio, God's Country." For the first time, I felt sorry for Jolina, for she would not be able to see the magnificent splendor that was the Paese di Dio, perhaps Nature's greatest wonder on Tarra.

True to her estimate, in the middle of the afternoon, my team gave a final lunging pull as our wagon finally made it onto the comparatively flat lands of the Paese di Dio! Here was a band of very low rolling hills that

206

steadily gained in elevation until they hit the rugged, sharply rising peaks known as the Appian Way. The Paese di Dio was a band about thirty miles wide, stretching the distance of the entire Sea Princes, hundreds of miles long. Not a single tree grew anywhere along its length. East to West, the rolling hilltops were never more than twenty feet above the basins. All the land was covered in a short, thick green grass, though many of the basins contained standing pools of clear, pure water. The elevation here was more than a mile high! Further, snows had already fallen at the higher elevations of the Appian Way, adding a brilliant contrast of color. Even Jolina commented that the air felt thin up here, thin and invigorating.

My three companions had never seen such breathtaking landscape and fell silent, gazing ahead at the breathtaking, serene beauty, and absolute stillness of God's Country. No one spoke a word as camp was made, fires lit, and dinner cooked. No one dared break God's Silence. Only while Jolina helped Camilla dry the evening's dishes, did Jolina break the silence, begging Camilla to describe the Paese di Dio to her. With all of her other senses more acute, Jolina knew this was a very special, nearly sacred place. Thankfully, Camilla whispered a lengthy description to Jolina, barely breaking in on the serenity of this land.

That night, Caitlyn and I slept on the ground snuggled up in our blankets gazing up at the heavens above. Here, the stars seemed so brilliant and so close that you could reach out and touch them. With her head lying on my chest, she whispered, "This is God's Country."

For three days, we traveled due east and met not a single person or animal, save the occasional field mouse. We also made very good time, traveling was easy and swift, though there were no roads or tracks to follow. Jolina broke the eternal stillness of the third night, our last, for the next day we' be heading back down into the dry gullies and valleys that led finally to the Med Sea hundreds of miles south of us.

Blindness had not kept this woman from experiencing the awe that was the Paese di Dio. The sound of her low bass flute began to float seamlessly into the experience. She was composing an original ode, which she later entitled, <u>Ode to the Paese di Dio</u>. I didn't know that it was possible to capture the mood and feelings of a place, but her music did just that! Further, this night we all learned something about this woman that we hadn't known before. Jolina was also a composer of music! In the ensuing days after this night, both Edgar and I learned to play Jolina's ode; like her, we played it solo on the bass flute. I was very deeply moved by this piece.

The next day, the wagons went down steep hills into the dry valleys of the Velona sector. If going up was strenuous, going down was almost a nightmare. Every second, I felt like I was about to fall forward off the wagon only to be crushed under its wheels! I decided right there that I did not ever want to be a drover! Going down steep hills on horseback was bad enough, but in a wagon, the experience was far worse. However, we all made it without mishap, much to my surprise.

Another day later and the spookiness began! Ahead we spied our first outlying small village with perhaps twenty buildings. The fighters rode on ahead to scout the village; we wanted no surprise ambushes. They waved the all clear signal, and the seven wagons rolled into this totally silent village. I saw no life anywhere, save us. The buildings looked rundown and in disrepair. Grass and weeds had already taken over the dirt streets of the village; vines nearly covered the sides of several homes. It was a ghost town.

Adriana commented to us, "Remember, the Great Plague claimed half the population of this entire sector, thousands upon thousands. There was no accurate count of the dead. Sometimes whole villages perished. Then came the Barbarian Invasion, the Galts from the Northern Steppes, who burned, pillaged, and ransacked what little had been rebuilt. Many of the nobles finally gave up on Velona and moved their homes and businesses elsewhere. Lawless banditry now rules in this sector, though we've heard that some nobles who didn't leave are trying to reestablish operations in Velona proper."

Scarcely daring to breathe, we passed on through this ghost village, preferring to make camp out in the countryside. Things were unimaginably different this time, compared to when I had first traveled the sector with the Lightning Circle so long ago. The extent of the damage caused by the plague was driven home to me. It is one thing to be told how bad it was while you are in the comfort of your own home and quite another to pass through a town whose population had become victims of the plague. None of us had ever witnessed anything like this.

However, ten miles further south, we encountered a village with people. Fellica Passe, it was called and was home for about fifty people, including children, very different from the number who dwelled here many years ago. Indeed, more than half of the buildings were in a state of partial collapse. Many had been torn down and their wood used to make repairs on the homes of the living. This was a rural farming community. Signs that it had once boasted extensive vineyards and olive groves were everywhere. Now, however, much of the land had been converted to crop land; sheep were pastured in several locations; chickens and goats freely roamed the streets, ducking out of the way of playing children.

As we rode into the village, many adults ran out to gather up the children, fully expecting yet another bandit raid. Finally, one man spied the yellow headbands and ventured out to speak with Adriana. "Sorry Sister, we mistook you for bandits. Welcome to our humble village. It has been long since we have seen your kind around here. I'm called Alfonso."

She dismounted and talked with the man, though none of us could overhear what was said between them. Shortly she waked back to my wagon and said, "We will camp overnight here. I told them we're escorting a traveling band of troubadours and that you'll play for them tonight in exchange for free use of the water well and some firewood. Acceptable?"

"You bet. Thanks," I replied.

Alfonso led us to the southern edge of the village, where most of the homes had been cannibalized for repair wood. Here we could make camp without interfering with the townsfolk. Yes, we had a wonderful time playing for these people; the enjoyment they had certainly made all this very worthwhile. I realized that this feeling must be what kept other troubadours at their trade, bringing unexpected joy and happiness to others. In my estimation, it was a most worthwhile goal, rewarding beyond measure.

Adriana also learned that the next two towns on down the line were havens for two bandit groups. Later after our concert, the planners met to decide our strategy for the next day. Adriana asked Felice if we could perhaps bypass these towns, but this far out from Velona, there were no other roads that we could take. Adriana vetoed my idea of bushwhacking our way around the general vicinity of the towns. She pointed out that the bandits would surely have outriders scouting the area around their safe havens. Did we want to play for a bandit group? We all agreed with a resounding, "No!"

In the end, no viable option existed; we would have to ride through the center of these two towns and hope for the best. I was beginning to see the incredible wisdom of having so many Sisterhood fighters with us. Adriana wanted to field as large an attack force as possible. Her orders were as follows: Fergus, Edgar, Wavery, Felice, Camilla, one other Sisterhood fighter, and myself would drive wagons the wagons; all the other occupants were to stay safely inside the wooden protective walls of the wagon. Andre and Alton would ride their horses along with the remaining eighteen Sisters. Felice, though not a fighter, was given the task of leading the seven wagons to safety, should we be attacked. Meanwhile, the nineteen on horseback would deal with the attackers. I hoped that it would not come to this.

Mid-morning of the next day, Felice called a halt; by her reckoning, it was time to take our defensive measures. The town was only a couple miles away. Quickly, we all took our assigned positions. As we then continued down the road, only we seven drivers were targets, sitting high on the buckboards. Our passengers were safe within the protective walls of the wagons. The riders moved out in front, taking the lead as we began moving once more.

As we approached this village, if the others we had passed were rundown, this one was a complete dump. Those buildings that I guessed were still in use were a patchwork quilt of mismatched, badly done repairs — something a child might do when building his first dog house all on his own without any guidance, skill, or proper tools. Additionally, refuse littered the street. Evidently, in this town, when one no longer wanted something or was finished with it, he or she would just toss it out a window or door. From the smell, I concluded these people never heard of a latrine or hygiene.

However, I ought to have predicted the sight before us; these were people who had lost complete and total respect for themselves, thus becoming hardened criminals.

Slowly, Captain Adriana led us onto the main, littered street; my wagon had just pulled alongside the first home, when I caught sight of men slinking out of side buildings, moving from the cover of one building on to the next — all certain signs of a staged event ahead. I observed the slight hand signals being passed from one Sister to another. Yes, they had spied them as well. I stopped worrying that perhaps these women had missed these subtle signs, concentrating instead upon where the confrontation might take place.

Based on the configuration of the buildings near the center of town and the wide central plaza and water well there, my guess was that would be the location. I wasn't wrong. Just as Captain Adriana pulled alongside the well, the last of our wagons pulled into the edge of the plaza. On cue, dozens of men stepped out of their concealed positions. An array of bows and crossbows were pointed at us. Their leader stepped boldly out toward Adriana, who raised her hand, signaling us to halt.

We were so close that everyone could overhear their conversation. The man said, "It is going to cost you ten gold pieces to pass through this town."

Adriana's reply was both loud and bold without the slightest hesitation or uncertainty in her voice. "There are no toll roads anywhere in the Sea Princes, certainly not here. If you do not stand aside, we will go through you. If anyone shoots at us, you have my sworn word as a Sisterhood member that I'll personally cut off your balls and let you scream before I cut off your head." Simultaneously, she signaled all of us to begin moving once more and kicked her horse into a walk. As ordered, my eyes stayed focused on Felice, her job was to direct the wagons, and I drove the lead one; where I went, the others would follow.

As we began moving, even though my eyes followed Felice, I had my attention on all those to either side of me who might decide to fire arrows my way. It was a tense few minutes. I saw a slight hesitation in the leader. I concluded that he would like to live another day; he obviously didn't want to tangle with a large band of the Sisterhood, even though the Sisterhood's presence in this sector had become minimal in recent times. I watched the men staring at us as we passed on by, rooted to their positions. Only after the last wagons had left the plaza and Adriana had circled around to watch for a surprise rear attack did the men begin to flood into the area that we had passed through, still watching the wagons recede from their view.

As soon as we left the village behind us, Adriana turned and rode up beside my wagon, saying, "They made the right decision."

I grinned back, "The reputation of the Sisterhood alone can prevent many fights. Well done, Captain Adriana." She returned my grin; she knew precisely what I meant. Immediately the talk between Caitlyn and Fianna was would these bandits try to follow us and sneak attack us during the night. I had to explain in detail just why the presence of a large band of the Sisterhood was sufficient to make these men back down, even when they had the advantage of both numbers and arrows.

We paused for lunch and then continued pushing southward. We arrived at the outskirts of the next village late in the afternoon. The physical condition here was equally as bad as the previous one. Without fanfare, we all took our assigned positions once more, before we began to enter the village. The layout of many of the Sea Prince outlying towns and villages centered around a central plaza and well. Half a century ago when I had visited here, small vendors and local farmers lined the sides of these plazas hocking their wares.

As we approached nearer the plaza, Adriana sent a flurry of small hand signals to her Sisters. Ahead, just past the well where the buildings began once more, a large barrier about three feet tall had been erected; sharpened poles protruded both inward and outward, rather like a jumping jack. Obviously, this was meant to stop any road traffic. I spied numerous men in the neighboring windows and on rooftops; many bows and crossbows were pointing down to where we would be forced to halt.

Nothing like a secret hand signal. While Adriana and the others continued to ride toward the barrier, Felice cleverly veered to the left, taking the last side street before the plaza. The intention was clear; the wagons would bypass the roadblock. Suddenly the voice of our Communicator, Waverly, spoke into my mind. *When the signal comes, place a wall of ice over the heads of our troops, anchored to the building on your left and to mine, which will be anchored to that one on our right. The men are going to do the same thing just beyond ours and will try to anchor theirs onto ours as well.*

What a diabolically clever idea! I'd never thought of combining spells like this. I watched carefully for the sign, even as I began my chant. I heard their leader from just across the barrier demand ten gold pieces for our passage. I heard Adriana's identical reply as before; evidently, she had this well-rehearsed. Unfortunately, this time the leader was a fool or had not had direct contact with the Sisterhood before. He gave an obvious signal for his men to open fire. Waverly's signal preceded it by mere seconds. She'd anticipated precisely correctly. As my spell triggered, anchoring solidly to the building and momentarily to hers, I wondered if she had done this combining of spells before.

Nearly a hundred arrows thudded into the ice sheet canopy above the heads of the nineteen riders. I knew that the ice sheets would very quickly collapse; they were not anchored at all well. No matter, at that same instant, one quarter of the riders, led by Adriana, cantered and jumped over the barrier into the group of fighters, completely disrupting their line. The remaining Sisters, as ordered, galloped out of the area of the ice, dismounted, and in pairs, began rushing into the buildings from where the volleys originated. I heard the resounding sounds of steel clashing on steel.

Now Adriana's plan might have worked except for one detail. As we rounded the corner, six fighters rushed to block our way. Felice, not a fighter, halted, and quickly backed up beside my wagon, unsure what action to take. I called out, "Those who can fight, hop off; let's take these men quickly. Fianna, you have the reins. As soon as we clear a path, drive on through before more men come to stop us. Felice, you lead them when it is safe to do so. Grabbing my new oaken pole, I hopped off and moved to meet these six fighters. Quickly, Fergus and Caitlyn joined me, one on either side. Waverly, in the second wagon, moved hers into a position where she could see what was going on and help if need be. She was the only occupant of this wagon and couldn't join us on foot.

"Caitlyn, your job is to protect our backs. Fergus, move over on my right a little further; Caitlyn, drop back behind us." No sooner had I said this than the six men rushed us. My pole was a flurry of action, whirling in and out and about, deflecting blows primarily, looking for an opening. Wham! I brought my pole directly on top of a man's head; he crumpled to the ground. I heard Caitlyn's dagger clanking upon a sword. I pivoted and delivered another solid blow to her opponent's head. Two down. A sickening howl followed Fergus's first kill.

Another took his place. Fergus began his second close quarters combat. The two remaining men tried various moves to get around the long reach of my pole. One made a poor attempt only to receive the full force of my pole in his stomach. Curling over, he fell to the ground, grasping his stomach. I move outward to deal with the last man. Behind me I heard the sounds of Caitlyn dispatching the three I'd knocked out. Fergus managed to disarm his opponent; the two men exchanged glances, and he fled down the street, running to save himself. We moved back to join Caitlyn, who had a terribly frightened face, her hands were shaking rather badly.

"I — I had to stab them. They were getting up and about to go after you," she tried to say. I could see that these were the first people she had ever killed. "I'm going to be sick," she added, rushed to one side, and vomited.

"Waverly, take care of her. I have to see what's happening back there. Felice, tie on to my wagon; drive mine on ahead out of town; then stop and wait for us," I took charge, just as a Wid would do so. Fergus and I headed back to the plaza.

I heard a hideous scream — a man's voice, thankfully. We entered the plaza in time to see Adriana holding the man's balls high in the air, before she beheaded him. It never occurred to me that Adriana was speaking literally. I thought she meant it figuratively! That scream pretty much sapped all the fighting will from those that remained. They dropped their weapons and surrendered to their Sisterhood opponents or merely fled the area as fast as they could run. Adriana walked to the well and washed herself clean, while her fighters began to report to her.

I sent a message to Waverly to bring the wagons back into the plaza. Casualties were starting to appear from inside the buildings. Quickly, I took charge, gathering our wounded into one area close by the well. "Adriana, get some water boiling, I don't care if you have to burn some of these buildings down, just get us some hot water." She hesitated, weighing tactical options, deciding as I had that we would be safe in the town now, at least for some time. She ordered a quick search of the immediate buildings.

By the time the wagons pulled into a semicircle around the well, I had all our casualties lying down or leaning against the well. Six women were injured, none life threatening, all with sword slices, primarily to their arms, legs, or chest. All would need stitches at once. For once, it was great to have three other healers with me. By the time we four druwids had gotten our healing pouches out and discussed what needed to be done to each, three Sisters carried a large metal pot of boiling water out of a building over to us.

We four set to work. An hour later, all six had been doctored and sported clean bandages, thanking us repeatedly for helping them. They usually did not have such immediate care, of that I was certain.

Adriana, seeing that we were finished, added her thanks and then gave us a formal report. "Thirty-three bandits are dead, including those four of yours. All buildings have been searched; all weapons found and properly destroyed, Sir. Our best estimates are that another two dozen escaped, perhaps more. There are some women and children in some of these buildings, but we have left them alone. I intentionally did not let my Sisters go after those that fled, though I ought to have. My reasoning is thus: let them spread the word of just what the Sisterhood does to those that attack them."

I couldn't help but laugh; she was so serious, so literal, and the message came through so loud and clear, "I'll cut your balls off before I behead you," that I just could not keep from laughing. "Very well done, Adriana. It's just that I didn't take your words to their leader literally! You meant what you said."

She looked at me as if I were a dummy. In total seriousness, she replied, "Of course, I always say precisely what I intend to do, doesn't everyone?" The Sisters around us, who overheard us, began laughing among themselves. I had a lot to learn about Captain Adriana of the Fighter Group One. She added, "A secondary mission of mine is to begin to bring back some lawfulness to the sector, as I am able. Those that fled are my messengers to others in this sector." I fully understood her motives now.

"Good job," I complimented her, while she thanked me again for helping her wounded.

Then, she asked, "Who do I thank for that magical barrier, which stopped all of those arrows?"

I deferred to Waverly, who explained that we four had joined forces to prevent their arrows from doing costly initial damage. Adriana thanked us all and explained, "I had expected to have fifty percent casualties from the rain of arrows. Still that left a significant margin for us to achieve total victory over these pitiful bandits who have no real ideas how to fight."

"That's incredible," commented Fergus. "You mean to tell me that even with say ten of your Sisters felled by arrows, the nine of you that remained could have taken on this whole gang of bandits? I mean, thirty-three dead; that's almost two or three for each of you!"

Adriana looked at him in disbelief, and then she realized Fergus was from West Reach and had never seen the Sisterhood in a fight before. "Yes, Fergus. These men were poor fighters. Out in the open plaza, one of my fighters could dispense with six of theirs, easily. Right?" she said to several nearby Sisters.

They all nodded, but one added, "We'd get six of them before one got us."

Fergus just kept on muttering, "Incredible! Incredible! Incredible!" The women smiled among themselves. Their thoughts were more than obvious to me, "Men!"

We did not intend to spend the night here in the village. Quickly, we prepared to move out. I insisted the three with leg wounds ride in a wagon so the stitches would not be torn. The other three were allowed to ride along beside the wagons.

Once we were rolling again, Caitlyn climbed up beside me. She wanted to talk. "I've never killed anyone before today. I felt just awful having to stab them. They were nearly helpless."

"That is a very good sign, Caitlyn. One never should enjoy killing another human being. You did the only thing you could. If you had a hammer or a pole, you might have knocked them unconscious again. Had you let them get to their feet, they would have tried to stab Fergus or me in the back. You did what had to be done."

"Yes, but I still feel awful," she replied.

"Can you imagine a world without these petty wars, where men would never think to kill another? I can. Somehow, I want to make Tarra into just such a place, only I have no idea how to go about it, save first get rid of these Grey Creatures. I'm sure they are inciting a lot of these petty wars."

"I'll back you all the way!" she exclaimed. "I hope we don't have any more fights."

"That's partly why Adriana was so brutal here, because she's sending a message to all the bandits. Honestly, it's a stupid man that attempts to fight a Sister! Once we're clear of the Velona sector, I'm sure we'll not likely be attacked again. The other sectors are drastically more civilized. Here in Velona, in all likelihood, it is only the Sisterhood which has the potential to bring back some semblance of law and order." I was wrong on this conclusion, however.

Chapter 16 The Gypsy Factor

The next day, we passed through another somewhat larger village, which had perhaps two hundred residents, eking out a marginal existence. We did not stop and play for them because we still could travel another half day. After checking on our patients at lunchtime, we agreed to let the Sisters with the leg wounds ride once more. Besides, we were tired of their constant complaining about not being allowed to ride again.

Adriana's own estimate agreed reasonably well with Felice's pronouncement that we were now about a hundred miles from Velona and the sea. I, of course, would believe Felice, but then I was slightly biased in her favor. We rode on southward until the middle of the afternoon, when Adriana called a sudden halt. I could see no signs of a town ahead. What I did see caused great wonderment.

Felice relayed Adriana's orders for the Planners to join her. Quickly, we joined her. We were on the crest of a low hill overlooking a small valley. Numerous campfires dotted the valley floor. Hundreds of gaily-colored wagons stood beneath the scattered trees. Horses were tethered in neatly arranged lines. Children were running and playing among the wagons, while women tended pots on the fires or were hanging out laundry to dry.

"I've no idea what we have run into," Adriana exclaimed to us, when we joined her. As yet, we had not been spotted by these people. It was the first time that I detected Adriana was unsure of how to react. This was something completely new, foreign to her. "What are they?"

"I've never seen anything like it," Felice added. I knew this was saying something significant. If Felice or her mother Flo had no idea of what these people were, they had to be new arrivals in this sector. "Look at their clothes, so gay," Fel added, obviously enthralled with what she saw. Four primary colors predominated, all bright shades: yellow, red, blue, and brown. Their dresses and pants were brown. Their shirts and tops tended to be one of the other three. Women wore a gaily-colored scarf around their heads, while the men wore similar colorful sashes around their waists. In no way did these people seem threatening, rather the contrary.

I realized that my druwid companions were deferring to me; I was still a Wid, though not theirs. I said, "Adriana, these look like foreigners to Velona. They probably know nothing about the Sisterhood. Why don't you let one of us make contact and see what's what?" Readily she agreed, this was outside of her experience and was more than willing to relinquish control.

Waverly commented, "Bethany, though entitled to because you are a Wid, perhaps it might be best if one of the Protectors acted as our spokesman. You will appear to them as a teenager."

"I agree, Waverly. Alton, how would you like to be our 'leader' as far as they are concerned?"

"Sure, but I've never seen anything like this either. Waverly, you let me know if I slip up or whatever, will you?" Alton replied. I knew precisely what he meant. If she spotted something, had a better idea, or spotted a goof, she'd mentally communicate it to him at once. Such was the value of a Communicator.

"Okay then, let's ride slowly down the road until we reach their position. We don't want to seem threatening, so how about having your fighters hang back and ride beside the wagons. Felice, Adriana, you ride up front with me. If any trouble comes, Felice, you high tail it out of there at once!" I could tell that Adriana was pleased that he kept her up front with him. From the look on her face, Adriana was still wide open for learning new things. In spite of appearances, she still had an inquiring mind. She was not just a brutal fighting machine.

As we prepared to move out, I said to Alton, "Probably language may be the biggest barrier here. If you can't understand them, let me know at once. I speak quite a few." From the look on his face, I realized he had not yet realized that, if indeed these were foreigners to Velona, they might speak a language that we couldn't understand. I suspected that he might be having second thoughts about accepting this task.

Slowly, our caravan moved over the hilltop and down toward their encampment, which I spied was actually at one of the crossroads. Recall, in these sectors, main roads angled out from the main city like spokes in a wheel. At periodic intervals of around twenty-five miles, circular roads would cross these spoke roads. This was one such place. Naturally, we were spotted the moment we appeared at crest of the hill. I watched their reaction. It did not seem hostile or threatening.

Rather the contrary. Children began pointing to our wagons, clustering together for a better view. Women paused in their domestic activities, moving to the sides of their husbands to watch as well. I spied numerous dogs running and playing or just panting beside wagons; they were completely ignoring us.

As we pulled up in the center of the intersection of the two roads, one man, his wife at his side, walked forward to greet us. I stepped down and joined Alton and Adriana. "Velcome strangers to the encampia of Bardia Zoreh. My wife, Reza." He spoke with a very strange accent, one I'd not heard before. Although his words were close to the Sea Prince dialect, they were not entirely so. Arad, perhaps, some of his diction paralleled that language.

"Well met, Bardia. I am Alton Woodgrove. This is Sister Adriana. This is Ket Bethany. We are the Cymry Minstrels currently touring the Sea Princes."

"Ah, no you wrong understand. Bardia just title — how you say, prince. Zoreh, calls me Zoreh." He shook Alton's hand firmly. "You have pretty sister," he said taking Adriana's hand, bowing, and kissing it, an action that surprised her no end. She nearly jerked her hand away from him.

"Er, no not my sister. She is part of a group of women called the Sisterhood, Sister Adriana," Alton tried his best to explain.

"Not *the* Sisterhood? No? Yes. We have heard much of this Sisterhood. I see it must be so; you bear a big sword," Bardia Zoreh commented.

"Ah, Ket Bethany. Such hair. Never has we seen such flames! So long. A man? Yes, I see must be so," he said as he shook my hand in his firm grip, comparing my attire and body shape to Adriana's.

Bardia Zoreh was perhaps thirty with jet black hair, closely cut, with eyes so black one could get lost in them. He stood around six feet, yet was thin and wiry. I spotted a strange curved blade stuck underneath his sash behind his back. It was perhaps two feet in length, very wide, quite different from any sword I had ever seen.

His wife, Reza, was a stunning woman. She stood a few inches shorter than her husband did, just as thin and wiry, with a full bosom that could not go unnoticed. Yet, her hair demanded my attention; she had black hair with a slight curl to it and was at least as long as mine was. Here was another woman who loved really long tresses! Likewise, she had black eyes and wore long golden earrings, at least six rings, and several necklaces of varying lengths. Rounding out her appearance, she wore many golden bands on her arms, all of which jingled as she moved.

Zoreh continued to try to understand all that Alton had said originally. "What is dis Cymry? Afraid I not know it."

"It is the big island north and east of here, some call it West Reach," Alton explained.

"Ah, zee big island. One day we go and see. Not today. Dis minstrels?"

"Musicians, troubadours, traveling musicians," Alton elaborated, trying several combinations of common words.

"Ah, zee, much like dis Gipsy. Zee play?" he asked.

"No, it's Ket's group. Cymry Minstrels is the name of his musical troupe," Alton hoped Zoreh would understand.

His eyes lit up, a broad smile revealed a missing front tooth. "Ah, Zoreh zee now. Yes." He opened his hands wide to us as he invited us, "Tonight you stay here at our encampia. Our guests. Gypsy guests. Later we play. You play. All dance. Have good time, yes?"

"You bet!" I exclaimed. "Thank you. I look forward to hearing your music!" I don't care whether Adriana wanted us to move on or not. I was staying. These people were very different. Their music promised to be equally so. I knew that all five of us musicians would insist on staying, listening, and playing in turn.

"Good! Good!" he shook my hand exuberantly. "You put wagons

somewhere. Make comfortable. I go tell others. Have food to share. Then make music and dance. Reza look after you." She smiled and nodded, while he rushed off to the others chatting gaily as he went.

While we returned to tell the rest of our party the news, Adriana warned, "I don't like eating stranger's food. What if it's drugged and we all fall asleep?"

"Now would be a good time to have a Healer here," Waverly pointed out. "Okay, Guardians, when food is served, do your best to check for poisons or drugs. If you detect something is amiss, then just raise your hand, and I'll contact you at once. We'll do our very best, Adriana, to make sure their food is safe." Adriana seemed somewhat relieved, though not completely.

We moved the wagons into our usual configuration, that of a circle. While the Sisters and our Protectors handled tethering of all our horses, Fergus and I managed to unhitch several sets of our draft horses. All the while, Reza hovered around me, watching my every move. At last, Reza said, "You take hair down before you play? We love see it. All Gypsies love see it. Never see red hair. You love long as Reza?"

I grinned at her, "You bet I do, Reza. Okay, I'll do it before we play." She grinned. I think that she would have loved to touch my hair and finger it, but she resisted the temptation, probably only because I was male. My sister did not fare as well. I spied Reza doing just that with Fianna's locks. Perhaps she was seeing if it was real.

Once we were settled in, Reza bade us follow her. She led us to a cluster of several wagons. "We eat here. You wait." Soon a dozen young women with long brown skirts and gaily-colored tops, though with significantly less jewelry adorning themselves, brought in bowls, plates, cups, and wooden utensils. Next, they brought us a feast, really, laying large plates piled with a wide variety of foods. Much of it was wild game, nuts, and the end of the season's berries. Fianna and I felt right at home with much of the menu, for it was remarkably similar to what we had gathered in the hills outside our village every week.

True to our word, we tested everything, but could detect nothing malevolent in any of it. Hence, we ate a wonderful meal, as far as Fianna and I were concerned. The others had never tasted at least half of the items before us, especially the wild game. Our friends found the taste of the meats rather strong or gamey, compared to the lamb they were used to eating. However, Fergus and Caitlyn compared some of it to venison, which they often had had back home. The delicious meal was topped with homemade mead, made from wild honey. Although the alcohol content was not that high, the taste was fabulous.

While we were finishing up, I noticed everyone was gathering around the large open space of the intersection of the two roads, leaving the actual intersection vacant. Each family carried one or two lanterns with them, and all were hung from poles, which they planted in the ground. Thus, the entire area was now well lighted. I estimated that there were about five hundred people gathered here. Next, a dozen men and women carrying all sorts of instruments moved over closer to our wagons. Bardia Zoreh spoke loudly, "Now we play. We dance!"

That was the signal. Their musicians began to play, while we listened intently. All six of us sat there gaping, eyes wide open. We had never heard any kind of music quite like this! Enthralling, fantastic, fast, and furious came the notes, but the scale was very weird. For our music, a song may have some notes sharped or some flattened, but never both. Yet with their music, always one note was sharp while another note was flattened. I believe this is one reason the music sounded so exotic to our ears, and so appealing and intoxicating. The rapid rises surged one's emotions to a fever pitch, while the cascading downward spirals felt like giant weights pulling on one's mind and body. As the musicians played, at least a hundred couples of all ages from the greying older folks to mere children crowded into the open space of the road intersection to dance and frolic with what seemed to our eye a wild abandon.

Their instruments consisted mostly of strings, recorders, and percussion. While they definitely had several varieties of guitars and what appeared to be a lute, the others we were not familiar with at all. They were played by pulling hairs tied to a bowed stick across the strings. In retrospect, these were possibly the forerunners of violins and violas.

Once we had heard a couple songs, Fianna pulled Fergus out to join them. I barely heard her voice say, "Just watch them, and follow as best we can!" I had no time to watch them, however, as Reza took my arm, pulling me into the undulating throng. I looked back at Caitlyn, but she was cheering me on, urging me to have a try. Already, she was tinkering on her dulcimer trying to pick out a note here and there, utterly fascinated with the sound and rhythm.

Reza was a good teacher, and quickly I caught on to the basic moves, which were just as enthusiastic and wild as the music. Occasionally, she would swing her head so that her long hair flew out in a giant circle, wrapping eventually around her neck. She encouraged me to do the same. Eventually, I liked it to something like a flinging hair fight, but it was immense fun.

After an hour of frenzied dancing, the musicians slowed the pace to what might be called ballads or laments. The dance motions were now subtle and much easier to master. I pulled Caitlyn out to join me, and we dance together for a while. At last, the music ended and Zoreh said, "Vee now hears the foreign minstrels. Shall vee?"

Quickly, we got to our instruments and began to play some of our livelier dance tunes, which were very different in sound from theirs. Of course, the younger gypsies quickly emulated Fianna doing her dances. Any fears that I had that they would not like our sound evaporated. They particularly enjoyed seeing Fianna doing the Crossed Swords dance. Following their pattern, we then settled into our slower pieces, including our trademark lament. This time, both Jolina and I played on our bass flutes, with Jolina taking the lead while I added subtle undercurrents. When we finished, the entire throng clapped and cheered. Some yelled, "They have gypsy blood in them." I wondered what they meant by that.

We played for well over an hour before Zoreh suggested that it was time to put the children to bed. Thus ended the most interesting night of music any of us six had ever experienced. While we put our instruments away, Camilla made us a small campfire and had water boiling for tea. We musicians sat around the fire and chatted about Gypsy music while sipping our tea. Presently, Zoreh and Reza joined us.

He began the conversation with the words we were dying to hear, "Vee stay here 'nother day. Swap music, eh? You like? Vee want to learn some your laments."

"Yes!" declared Caitlyn, unable to contain her enthusiasm.

"We would love to do just that, Zoreh. We're in love with your songs," I continued. "I think if I would let them, my friends here would stay with you for weeks!"

"Ah, is good then."

"Say, where do you come from anyway? None of us has ever heard of Gypsies. I cannot quite place your accent. It seems to be a bit of the Sea Princes, the Greenway, and perhaps a bit of Arad in there too," I changed the subject in an attempt to find out more about these interesting people.

"Gypsies come from Tarra. Gypsy is Tarra. Not from your countries," Zoreh attempted to explain. "Gypsy takes what likes from all languages."

"But where were you born?" I asked, trying to pin down some locale in which we might find more of these people.

"Yonder wagon," he pointed to his wagon. "Zoreh born there, as was Zoreh's mother and hers before her. Gypsy land is Tarra, all Tarra. Tarra provides for Gypsy."

"Do you travel around Tarra a lot?" Caitlyn asked, attempting to help me out.

"Sure, Gypsy sees all Tarra. Now seeing Sea Princes," Zoreh answered.

"But aren't you in danger from all the bandits here in the Velona sector?" Fergus wanted to know. "We just had a big fight with them recently. They wanted to rob us."

"No danger. Gypsy has nothing robbers want. No gold. No gems. No bothered by bandits." We must have looked rather astonished or perhaps they often got such responses from others they met. He continued, "Gypsy needs no gold. Too heavy to carry. Gypsy buys nothing. What Gypsy buy? Tarra provides all Gypsy ever wants. Gypsy free people."

My conversation got interrupted by Reza, who pulled on my arm saying, "Come. Reza tells your fortune. Come, come." She was so insistent that I followed her to her wagon. The inside of her wagon was crammed with things. Every available bit of space had been put to some use. Image taking all of the things you have in your house and then storing them somehow in a large wagon. Stuff hung from wall hooks and even from the ceiling. I had to duck to avoid banging my head on a cooking pot and some clothes. She motioned for me to sit at the tiny table just two feet square. A red cloth with melted candle wax droppings here and there covered its top. She lit two candles, which gave off a strange herbal odor. One other lantern near the entrance provided only a dim light.

"Reza tells your fortune. Reza never wrong. Give Reza your hands, please." I held them out; she took them in hers and closed her eyes, saying nothing for the longest time. I could smell the odor of her body mixed with wild flowers.

Finally, she said, "Ket Bethany, strange man-woman. Reza never sees such before. But Reza much afraid for Ket. Sees darkness in future. Reza tells anyway."

She opened her eyes and her black eyes seemed to pierce into mine. Without even so much as a blink, she said, "Ket on long journey. Seek man, but find woman. Find in desert. Ket go to Blue Women. Now Reza sees much danger. Ket makes choice. Reza says Ket not go south. Go north. Go north and Ket gets pretty blonde woman and many kids. Ket go south and no gets woman; gets death and darkness. So says Reza. Reza never wrong. Reza much afraid for Ket. Ket promises Reza Ket go north!" After a pause, she added, "Ket be gypsy in long time."

I've never had my fortune told before and hardly knew what to make of it. I will say that I was more than a bit startled. She knew I was on a journey to find someone. Spooky. Yet rest of it I took with a grain of doubt. To appease her, I said, "Thanks for the fortune and warning. I'll try to go north, not south. Thanks."

She smiled, but said, "You go now. Reza scared of what Reza saw. Reza needs sleep now." Hastily, I exited, banging my head into the pot. When I got back to our wagon, everyone had retired; only my three friends were waiting up for me.

"Well, how did the fortune telling go," asked Caitlyn. Fianna and Fergus were just as eager to know as well. I sat down beside them, leaning against the wagon wheel.

"Well, I don't rightly know," I said and repeated what she had told me as best I could, using her accent and words. Caitlyn giggled when she heard that I would get the blonde woman and have many children. Yet they all were very surprised with the rest of the prediction. Fergus talked first.

"How did she know that you are on a long journey?"

"Oh, that's an easy one," Fianna jumped in at once. "We're all

222

traveling around playing music and are far from our homes, if they know anything at all about the lands of Tarra like they claim. So obviously, we're all on a long journey. I think she was just saying the obvious and not telling his fortune."

"Aye, lassie, I think you're right," Fergus replied, giving her a loving squeeze. He was very proud of my sister.

"Well, the rest of it really is prediction," Caitlyn said flatly. "I guess time will tell if she's right. While you were gone, we learned a bit more about them," she continued, eager to relay her news. "It seems that there are quite a number of gypsy bands wandering around Tarra. Each band is led by a Bardia, a prince. From what we gather, I think there are at least ten Bardia, maybe more. There is some animosity between the bands, however. No one speaks very highly of any other band and tries to avoid them whenever possible."

Not to be left out, Fergus explained, "And they like to avoid towns when possible. Often, they aren't welcome by the villagers. Some claim that they have been called baby stealers, thieves, or worse. However, they claim they don't steal — just trade or borrow. Tarra provides is their motto. Adriana thinks it's prudent to keep a watch tonight. Two Sisters are keeping an eye on our wagons all night, so we ought to be safe." With that, we, too, turned in. Nothing happened during the night, however.

The next day, we checked on our six patients and found them healing nicely. Then, we intermixed with our hosts. The Sisters found themselves constantly in chats with nearly every adult in the camp. No sooner had one group finished chatting with them than another few would take their place. The gypsies were intensely curious about the Sisterhood, had apparently never met any before now, and were making up for lost time.

Midmorning, six of the gypsy musicians came over to us, and the sharing began in earnest. Both sets of musicians had to work very hard. For their part, the gypsies kept on trying to sharp one note while flattening another, which we continually had to correct them. Similarly, when we were learning, we all found it difficult to remember to sharpen one and flatten the other. In the end, by the end of the afternoon, both sets of musicians had learned a half dozen of the other's songs.

Needless to say, we spent another evening filled with music and dancing. Fianna and Fergus really picked up the dance steps rather well, planning to incorporate them into our show. When each music ensemble played one of the songs that the other had learned, the other musicians joined in as well, much to the delight of everyone.

After the concert, I asked one of the string players where he got his instrument. I was very keen on getting one and learning how to play it. Somehow, I wasn't surprised with his answer. "Made it. Vee make all our instruments. Vou want to see plans maybe?"

I could not pass up such an offer! I followed him some distance to his wagon, but noticed a Sister covertly tailing me. Adriana was taking no chances I surmised. His wagon was as full of stuff as Reza's! However, he had a larger working table, with various clamps and woodworking tools lining one wall. He produced a set of parchment skins and opened them up on the table, holding down the edges with small tools that were lying around. Here was a marvelous set of drawings. From them, I thought I might be able to make one. "What do you call these?" I noticed that he also had five more of them hanging securely on the back wall of his wagon. "If I had a copy of these drawings, I might be able to make me one and learn to play."

"Fidels. Vee can trade. What you got maybe I want?"

We walked back to my wagon and together, we went through my stuff. However, what ended up catching his eye was Caitlyn's old supple deerskin outfit she had worn when she was disguised as a young boy. When I asked her about it, she gladly allowed me to trade it for the plans. To my surprise, he also gave me one of his extra fidels. "Vee trade fair," he claimed. Caitlyn and I thought it was lopsided in our favor thought. I overheard him chatting happily with his wife about how she could take it apart and use it as a pattern to make more of them. The last thing I heard from him was, "Vee be much warmer in dees."

We awoke to a whirlwind of activities the next morning. The gypsy band was preparing to move out and folks were bustling about with last minutes activities. As I watched, I noticed just how efficiently they hitched up their wagons and was happy that they would be gone before we clumsily hitched up ours. We were still getting the hang of dealing with these large draft horses. These folks had it down to an art of no wasted motions! Even the children lent a hand, knowing just what they were to do. I guess if you spend your whole life living out of a wagon, you get good at such things as hitching up the horses. I wondered where they got their horses, trading what? I never got the chance to ask though. In less than a half hour, the gay colored wagons began to roll with everyone waving goodbye.

Camilla had our breakfast waiting and the others leisurely hitched up our wagons. Waverly came by to ask me if I had any luck locating Alabaster. "Nope, he is definitely not further up north from here or west. I checked all the way to the ocean last night." I did not tell her about Reza's predictions, however. I didn't place much faith in fortune telling. Soon we too were on the move once more.

Chapter 17 The New Velona

Twice more we passed through completely abandoned villages, one in the mid-morning, and one in the mid-afternoon. Felice knew that one of the large outlying towns was up ahead; we would make it by nightfall. However, Adriana suggested that we camp several miles outside of the town and make our passage through it in the morning when there would be ample light. The days were growing noticeably shorter and the night chillier. Winter was fast approaching.

Midmorning we entered the outskirts of Gabrellia, once home to several thousand, but now perhaps only five hundred. This time, we got an unexpected welcome, one I found rather shocking. First, from the general deterioration, we suspected bandits might occupy some or all the town. Yet, as we rode into the town, we spied five buckboard wagons, painted sky blue with a white cross on each side. To our right, a dozen men, most wearing blue clothing with a white cross emblazoned on both the front and back of their tunics, were jointly rebuilding a home. At least six others wearing tattered clothing were assisting, although they more often than not seemed to be getting in the way of the workers in blue.

We halted near the town plaza. Perhaps three hundred townsfolk were gathered there, all of whose clothes seemed equally poor as the workers we'd just past. However, the townsfolk were listening intently to a priest, again wearing the sky blue robes with white cross. I guessed the priest was in his late thirties or early forties; his robes hid much. Certainly, his curly hair and long beard suggested he still followed traditional Arad ways. There was no doubt in my mind that this priest was either from Juda Arad or that his parents were. Even his accent told me so as I began to listen to his words.

"Brethren, just as promised, the Holy Reconstruction of your town has begun this day. All praise to Jehosa. The Holy Church of Jehosanity of Zargarb, the mother church, has sent the Holy Church of Jehosanity here to assist you. You have already met the Holy Volunteer Workers, who have come to labor on your behalf, bringing their amazing, multi-talented skills to bear rebuilding your town, just as over these many years they have devoted tireless energies to rebuilding so many other towns all the way from the Zargarb Sector and now finally here in the Velona Sector. We of the Holy Church of Jehosanity desire nothing from you in return for our assistance in the rebuilding of your town and your economy. Not a copper please! It is the holy duty of every worshiper of Jehosa to strive to aid his fellow man, especially in these dark times. Just as in all of the hundreds of other towns and villages we have helped to rebuild, all that we ask in return is to be allowed to construct a Holy Church of Jehosanity in your town at a convenient place of your choosing. Nothing more."

So far, this sounded incredibly altruistic. A surge of pride flowed in me, thinking that all of Jes' preaching may actually be bearing fruit, fruit of which he would have been proud! The priest continued.

"Tur has long ago deserted you and your people, if indeed he ever existed. You have fallen, through no fault of your own, into a vile state of wickedness and sin. Ah that is ever mortal man's lot in life. You see, each of you has an immortal soul, a priceless thing, that which cannot die. Oh yes, these frail mortal bodies are subject to pestilence, sickness, and hungers. But your soul is immune to all these. When your mortal body fails, as they all must due in time, your soul may go to one of two places: Heaven or Hell. Let me elaborate. Jehosa reigns in Heaven, a place of eternal happiness, where all wants are provided, rich clothes, all the gold you desire, all this and so much more awaits your soul when it arrives in Heaven after the mortal flesh fails. Ah, but if your soul is not found worthy of entering the Gates of Heaven, ah, then where is it to go, you ask?"

"Souls found unworthy go to Hell, a place of eternal sulfur fires, so hot that it would melt a mortal body in but a few seconds. Oh, brethren, Hell is such an awful place for your precious soul to be condemned for all eternity! Because so many of Jehosa's children on Tarra have opted for the path that leads their precious soul into the very Gates of Hell, Jehosa, in his infinite mercy, sent his only immortal son to Tarra! Yes, inhabiting one our very own mortal bodies, the Great Messiah, Holy Son of Jehosa, came here to preach the path we must follow so that our precious souls may enter the Blessed Realm of Jehosa, when our mortal bodies fail at last. Yes, worthy people of Gabrellia, the Great Messiah has shown us the way to enter Heaven!"

"What must we do so that our precious soul may be allowed to enter Heaven you ask? Ah, very simply put, we must stop our sinning and repent our past transgressions. Yes, we all have committed little sins — yes, even I have been guilty. Have you never overeaten? Have you never had lewd thoughts about some woman or man? Have you never cheated at a card game or fudged a dice roll? I certainly have, I admit to you. Yet, these are not the sins that bar your soul from entering the Blessed Realm of Heaven. No indeed. The Great Messiah teaches us the ten deadly sins that condemn one's precious soul to the eternal fires of Hell."

The Great Messiah states in his Holy Decalogue:

There is no god but Jehosa.

Do not worship any other god but the One God, Jehosa.

Do not build statues of Jehosa, for Jehosa has no form. One may build forms of the Holy Son and the Holy Mother of the Son.

Set aside the Holy Day, Sunday, from your labors and worship Lord Jehosa upon that day.

Respect and serve thy mother and thy father, for they have labored long in your raising.

> Do not kill another who worships Jehosa.
>
> Do not steal from another who worships Jehosa.
>
> Do not commit adultery or lay with a woman before you are married.
>
> Do not lie to another who worships Jehosa.
>
> Do not desire another's house, possessions, or wife, if he worships Jehosa.

"These simple commandments as set down by the Son of God, if followed, will gain your precious soul entrance into Heaven when your mortal body succumbs at last. But what of those who have broken these commandments in the past, have sinned against Lord God Jehosa? Is his soul doomed to the eternal damnation of the Fires of Hell? Nay, even as the infidel Centurions crucified the Son of God upon the cross, he hath spoken of salvation, for he took the weight of all of your past sins upon him to that cross! All you need to do to have your past sins erased in the eyes of Jehosa is to repent those sins, accept Jehosa as the One God, and accept the eternal salvation offered by the sacrifice of his son, the Great Messiah. Accept this and your slate is washed clean of sin. You can start anew so your precious soul may walk through the Blessed Gates into Jehosa's realm, Heaven!"

"All across the Sea Princes, sector after sector, hundreds of thousands have cast aside the pagan Tur, accepting Jehosa as the One God, repenting their past sins, paving the way for their precious souls to enter the Gates of Heaven! Yea, these Holy Volunteers, the Holy Missionaries, you see laboring here are guaranteeing their souls will enter Heaven by giving unselfishly of themselves to aid those in dire need. Yes, today tens of thousands call themselves Holy Volunteers. It was these very same volunteers who entered Zargarb in its bleakest hour after the barbarians sacked the city, destroying half of the city. People were starving with no roof over their heads. In this time of need, the Holy Volunteers entered the city bringing food and supplies, helping to rebuild the city, one house at a time. You may say 'How come it took so long to get here to Velona?' My answer is a simple one. Between here and Zargarb, hundreds of thousands of people just like you were homeless and starving at the brink of death. But today, those people now have new homes, new jobs, and plenty of food, just as all of you will have here long before the spring comes!"

"Naturally, the Holy Volunteer Missionaries will be rebuilding the homes of those of you who do accept Jehosa as the One God and repent of your past transgressions, your sins. Naturally, they will be the first to get new homes as well as new jobs and the full support of the Holy Church of Jehosanity Northern Orthodoxy in Zargarb. If you doubt my words, journey into Velona. You will find your city has been greatly altered! Although much work still needs to be done there, you will find Velona a free city and thriving once more. We know that half of the Noble Houses chose to flee to Barcella, forsaking proud Velona. Yet, if you go to Velona today, you will see that all have not. The proud city of Velona is now run by the High Council of

Five. Four of your Noble Houses chose not to desert you in your time of need; they have stuck by you. They are now on the High Council of Five, gone forever is the House of the Prince and Tur. In their place, the worthy Noble Houses have given the fifth seat to the Holy Church of Jehosanity!"

"Finally, for those who wish to accept Jehosa as the One God and repent of your sins, I will conduct that ceremony here at noon. Until then, please consider all that I have said. Perhaps, elect one or more of you to ride to Velona and see for yourselves that what I speak is the truth. Until noon, I bid you thanks for taking the time to hear my words." He bowed to the crowd and backed away, leaving two dozen other priests to answer any questions.

I felt sick! What had happened to the preachings of Jes? How could this complete bastardization occur? I was fuming! For an instant, I thought about bringing down lightning upon all these men in blue and then charging throughout all the Sea Princes, doing the same! Twisted, altered, and outright lies, all of it! I was so angry, so upset, that I couldn't even speak! Thank god Caitlyn had the presence of mind to take the reins from me. I might have driven the wagon into this disgusting creature who called himself a priest!

I believe that Waverly also sensed the violent anger in my mind, for both Andre and Alton now stood beside my wagon here at the front of our caravan. We were impossible to miss; the Sisters had formed a tight circle around the seven wagons. I spied the High Priest moving our way. It took enormous concentration on my part to keep from slaying him instantly! Perhaps, Waverly was assisting me. I felt her mind touching mine.

When the High Priest drew close, Alton spoke, "Greeting Sir. We are the Cymry Minstrels, troubadours bringing music to towns and villages." I don't think even he expected the welcome he received.

Almost with a snarl, the priest said, "Your kind is not welcome in Gabrellia. We are trying to bring back law, order, and respect for fellow mankind here in this town. As you just heard, I'm attempting to get this bandit town to repent their thieving ways and become a viable asset to humanity once more. Your lewd music, frolicking, and cavorting will only just push them back toward their sinning ways. You're not welcome here. Please move on."

He looked at Captain Adriana and said, "You, fighter woman and your companions, would do well to repent of fighting and take up a worthy man, bear him many children, and fulfill your God given homemaker duties that you too may have your precious soul enter the Gates of Heaven. Please move on." He turned on his heels without another word, leaving both men aghast and Adriana fuming. She kicked her horse into motion, while the men ran back to their wagons. A minute later, the crowd of townsfolk looked at the rear of our last wagon as it moved on south beyond the plaza.

Presently, Waverly came running up to our wagon and leapt on board even though we were still rolling along. "Are you okay, Bethany?" My face was red with anger; my fists were clenched to the running board, nearly crushing the wood. My fingernails did leave permanent indentations in the wood, however. I still couldn't even vocalize a single word. "I'll ride a while with you," she said calmly. Poor Caitlyn was white with worry over me and was much relieved to have Waverly sitting beside us, even though we were a bit cramped with three on the front seat.

Adriana slowed her horse and came along side our wagon; she too was fuming. "Should we go back there and teach them a few things about life, Ket? I've a mind to give that Priest a good solid thrashing. The nerve of that man. It was the Sisterhood who entered Zargarb and did all the hard work, while those Arad men and priests just did normal construction. The nerve of that man!"

My anger gave way to tears. "None of that is what Jes Amir preached anywhere, ever," I sobbed. "He has perverted nearly everything Jes ever preached! Honestly, Jes did not believe anything that man said; you must believe me!"

Adriana saw my tears and calmed down, "We know, Bethany; all the Sisters know, really we do. We have always been in contact with the Sisterhood in all the other Sectors. We do know truly what actually took place. Let me tell you what that man was preaching today here is totally unlike what the real priests are saying back in Zargarb. Honestly, Bethany, many, many Sisters have converted to Jehosanity. As practiced in Zargarb, it is a good religion. But this man has made a complete mockery of it. So you don't have to convince either me or any of my Sisters. We know the truth, and it has nothing to do with what that poor excuse of a priest had to say."

If I could have hugged her, I would have. "Thank you, Adriana. Thank you. That means more to me than you can imagine!"

Just now, Felice pulled up on the other side of the wagon. "Well, are we going back to attack them?" she asked, though I couldn't tell if she was jesting or was serious.

Not answering, Adriana asked, "How far to the next town?"

"Half day ahead is another one. Three more until we hit Velona," our knowledgeable scout replied.

"Okay, then we will not go back and teach them a lesson. Let's see what the next town brings," Adriana ordered.

"Yes, ma'am," and Felice trotted on back ahead, leading us on down the road.

Alton now came trotting up where Felice had been; he'd evidently switched to his horse. "Everything okay up here?" he asked, a trace of worry in his voice.

"I've calmed down," I commented, wiping the wetness from my face. "I could have destroyed every last one of them, though." Then I realized that Waverly might know that when I was an apprentice druwid, I had once nearly gone insane, bringing down hundreds of lightning bolts to destroy those cavalrymen that I thought had just killed Ellen and my whole family. Probably this event was drilled into every new apprentice's head these days. Surely, Waverly, as a Communicator, must know about it. She probably was prepared to assist me just as Willow had done half a century ago. For her, I said, "Don't worry, Waverly. There isn't the slightest chance that I'll go insane and actually destroy all of them. I was just very, very angry and upset."

Waverly chuckled, "I suspected so, but I was not going to take any chances. Alabaster would have my hide when we find him if I did." We both chuckled.

Caitlyn chose this opportunity to add to our conversation, "Bethany, what that fellow preached back there is also nothing at all like how we practice Jehosanity back in Nuadilan , really not at all like that perversion he spoke about. I can see why you were so angry, Blessed Holy Mother. You were there through it all."

I gave her a hug. To Alton, I asked, "How could they have so altered Jes's teachings?"

"Glad you asked that! You see, Andre and I have been discussing this very thing. We have no vested interest in this religion, one way or the other. We know how terribly difficult it must be for you, having been his wife and all. So we've been working out a theory."

"Thanks, Alton. My skill as a Wid has been completely clouded on this issue. I do sincerely apologize for losing my temper utterly back there."

"Apology accepted, Wid Bethany. Really, though, you've nothing to apologize for; we are, after all, human beings first and Guardians second. Anyway, our theory goes this way. We know that for years now, this whole sector has been mostly abandoned, left to its own ways and means. The Sisterhood left long ago and only recently has been escorting convoys through here again. By all reports, Velona sector has degenerated into roving bands of bandits, eking out the lowest form of survival. The question is this: how does one bring back law and order to the sector? One could by using a total force of arms, that is one possibility. Another is to rebuild homes and businesses and re-establish a thriving economy so that the average person can make a good living once more. Perhaps, that is what the Church has in mind, bringing back the economy and stopping the fighting. Notice that we didn't see a single soldier or fighter back there in that town, not one! The Church is not doing it by force of arms, rather the opposite. Perhaps, that priest's silly balderdash was merely to allow many of those present to have a chance to start anew, to cease their banditry, and work toward more constructive goals. I think we can all agree that someone needs to re-establish law and order and get the economy going so that the folks can have a better life. Maybe this is one way it can be done."

I laughed and said, "Good god, Alton! Are you sure you're not a Wid instead of a Protector? That was excellent observations and reasoning; it's what I should have concluded and explained to all of you, not the other way around! Maybe I should give you the Wid position," I jested.

"Whoa, no way!" he laughed. "Being a Wid entails way, way, way too much learning for me. No way. Life's too short to learn all that a Wid knows!"

Waverly added, "We can see how effective their approach has been as we pass through the towns closer to Velona. I'd better get back to my wagons. Holler if you need me, Bethany."

"Thanks, both of you."

She nimbly hopped off and rejoined her wagon as did Alton, leaving Caitlyn and I to chat. Caitlyn commented, "Honestly, men! They think and insist that they know everything, when in fact they're ignorant. Men! Oops, present company excluded," she flushed, realizing that she had just included me in her diatribe. "One day that priest's lies will come back to haunt him," she prophesied. "You don't suppose that a Grey Creature has put him up to all this, do you?" she looked worriedly at me.

I shrugged, "Don't know. Probably not, if Alton is right, in his twisted way, he is trying to bring law and order into the bandit country, rather the opposite of the Grey Creature's goals that I've seen so far. I think that Alton may be right. Strong people like Adriana, who has the strength, will, and skill, just go in and establish order by their presence, enforcing it by swords when needed. They can directly control others as needed and are not afraid to do so. On the other hand, a weak person often uses veiled threats, coercion, and promises. All his lies are just a substitute attempt to make up for his inability actually to control others directly. When I was little, I remember my mother once offering to give me a cocoa if I would stop whining and crying about not getting my way . As much as I loved her, she just couldn't actually control me directly and resorted to subterfuge, which sometimes worked because I loved cocoa. If Adriana had been my mother, she would have just shut me up," I chuckled over the parallels.

"I see what you mean. You know, I really used to love, respect, and obey my father when I was a little girl, before he came under the control of that Grey Creature. However, when I lost respect for him, he completely lost his ability to control me."

"I'm glad that he couldn't or I'd never have met you," I gave her a little hug. "Besides, to control someone or something, one must have the appropriate knowledge of it and be willing to be responsible for it. Take this wagon here, if you had no knowledge of horses or how to drive a wagon, if you were unwilling to have much to do with the wagon and didn't like it, how well do you suppose you'd do trying to control it? You'd probably run it into a tree or off a cliff." She laughed at my analogy.

"You know, I bet that's what happened to dad. The Grey Creature simply blew away dad's willingness to be responsible for others and their lives and kept some key knowledge about others from him. That way, dad would be certain to fail to really control and thus make a complete mess of things." Suddenly, she fell silent. I turned to look at her.

She exclaimed, "That means if he really does wage war against King Albert, he will most certainly lose. Ashley's with him, so I'll probably lose my brother too," tears welled in her eyes. I put my arm around her. We rode on in silence for a time. Footnote: this explains why Caitlyn shed no tears when much later we heard the news that King Ahmad and his son Ashley were killed in January 622 at the Battle of Breagon. King Emil quietly moved his forces into Nuadilan and Amathon, extending his kingdom.

We camped some miles short of the next town unwilling to face what may lie ahead yet today. After the evening meal was served, Camilla asked me, "Say, would you care to hear about the real Church of Jehosanity and the Sisterhood's involvement from a mere cook? I'm writing a journal outlining some of our history. I've actually interviewed some of the Sisters who had a hand in it." Of course, I was very willing and almost as soon as she began, all the Sisters surrounded us to listen to Camilla as well. They already knew she was a good storyteller.

"It all began back in 586 just after the barbarians finally left the city of Zargarb. The Holy Disciple Bandar Dero founded the Northern Orthodoxy Jehosanity Church in Florintine Junction several months earlier. All around the outlying villages of that sector, folks were in dire straits; the barbarians looted, burned homes, and stole food supplies. Many were homeless and most were near starvation. Hence, Bandar began the Missionaries of Jehosa, one priest and six volunteer workers along with a wagon of food, supplies, and tools with which the workers could rebuild homes and businesses. However, the bandits thwarted their attempts to come to the aid of those in need, robbing them continually."

"Thus, Bandar came to the Sisterhood complex in Ranchero Paladina, run by Mother Sister Aminia Sciota at that time. She worked out a deal whereby the Sisterhood accompanied these Missionaries, safeguarding their passage. When the barbarians pulled out of the city, the Sisterhood and the church missionaries brought in wagon loads of food and healing supplies. Expecting chaos and disorder, Aminia sent Sister Fiona along in command of a hundred fighters. Sister Fiona then had only one arm; she had lost the other years ago to a man. Yet, Sister Rosalita, the greatest Fighter Group Leader in the Zargarb Sisterhood, had personally chosen Fiona, so you know she had to be good, even though she had only the one arm."

"Well, it was a good thing that Fiona was in command, for lawlessness prevailed in the utter chaos of the city. People were starving and some gravely wounded. No food was left inside the city. Had we not come when we did, all those in Zargarb would surely have perished. The nobles and prince did not return for another six months!"

"During those months, the Sisterhood and the ever growing numbers of Jehosanity Missionaries brought back law and order, rebuilding homes and businesses, fed the population, and even got the entire economy of the whole sector functioning once more, no small accomplishment, if I say so myself!"

"When the leaders finally returned, the nobles overthrew the prince, establishing the High Council of Thirteen to rule instead of the prince. They also insisted that the tradesmen have a representative on this council, so that their voice could be heard. However, since it was the Sisterhood who had restored the tradesmen back to life, they insisted one of us be on the council, representing them. Historically, when Sister Alicia took her position on the High Council, that was the first time in the history of the Sea Princes that women had a voice and vote in governing our land!"

Later on, the prince sponsored a clever campaign to murder those residents of Zargarb who chose to follow this new religion of Jehosa. Can you blame the ordinary folks for adopting Jehosanity wholesale? Ordinary believers of Jehosanity had come from all over the sector, donating freely their time and efforts to rebuild homes and businesses. They spent their own funds to buy food and blankets to give to those starving in the city and outlying towns. Such acts of human kindness and compassion for their fellow man have nearly been unheard of in the Sea Princes. Besides, the commandments that Bandar preached were very different from the ones we heard today. The major differences are:

Do not kill another.

Do not steal from another.

Do not commit adultery.

Do not lie to another.

Do not desire another's house, possessions, or wife.

Do unto others as you would have others do unto you.

Nowhere does Bandar or anyone else limit these to just those that worship Jehosa. And it was the last rule, I believe, that helped convince so many Sisters and others that this was indeed the true religion."

"Anyway, back to the murders. The prince paid spies to report on residents who converted to Jehosanity. He then paid dockworkers, who still adamantly believed in Tur, to murder them — not only men, but also women, mothers and fathers. I believe the total was well over one hundred murders. No one knew who was committing them. Once more Bandar Dero begged for the Sisterhood's aid in solving these crimes."

"Sister Calli was called upon to solve the mysterious murders. She had one of the most brilliant minds that ever a Sister had, though she had been horribly mistreated by her husband. Clever Calli solved it in no time, and, with Sister Alicia on the High Council, the Prince was brought to justice. The High Priest of Tur actually beheaded him, throwing his head out to sea!"

"So grateful was Bander Dero, that he prayed to Jehosa for a miracle to thank Calli and Fiona for all they had done to help the fledgling church. Here, I have very carefully researched this part. Yes, Jehosa created two miracles. Sister Calli was fully healed of her mental wounds, and Sister Fiona's missing hand regrew! I've talked personally with five Sisters who knew these two personally, and they all agree that her hand did regrow! Fully functional, just like she had never had it cut off!"

"Later on when the barbarians left Solamina, the Sisterhood and the Missionaries of Jehosanity both went to that sector's aid, with similar results. So you see, that so called priest back there was speaking nothing but lies and distortions of the truth. Without the Sisterhood, there would not be any Church of Jehosanity in Velona or anywhere else."

The Sisters clapped when she finished, more than pleased to have us hear their side of the story. Besides, I knew that most of these women wanted to know more about this new religion. Over the years, they had been going to the many Zargarb Grand Councils, where Sisterhood representatives of all the eight sectors met to coordinate their activities across the Sea Princes. There, they often held quiet discussions about the newly adopted religion that the vast majority of the women in those sectors had chosen. While Jehosanity had not yet come to Fortress d'Grange, many Sisters prayed that it would. They would join in an instant. Camilla answered a number of questions until it was bedtime.

Once again, Felice's timing was perfect, for we rolled into Alcalta mid-morning on Sunday. This town one was home to several thousand. The remnants of the massive expansion during the plague years were evident; the Prince had ordered the total evacuation of Velona, leaving only the plague ship anchored at the docks, a surprise for the invading Centurions. Thus, the tens of thousands of Velona residents had moved to these outlying towns, greatly enlarging their size. However, the quality of that new construction done in grate haste had been poor, and after this many years, the crumbling remains still stood on the outskirts of Alcalta.

Nearer the center, all signs pointed to a reconstruction binge of some magnitude! New homes and buildings were interspersed with quality repairs to older dwellings. The streets were clean of the trash and debris that we had encountered in the more remote villages earlier. All signs pointed to a thriving town. However, as we neared the central plaza, we spied the recently built Church of Jehosanity, towering over all other buildings in the town. It was three times the size of its neighboring dwellings, with a steeple that rose high above the town, a white cross at its peak.

Many people were walking toward the church as others entered. They all stopped to stare briefly at our slow moving wagons and riders. Presently, a priest wearing a sky blue robe with a plain white cross showing boldly across his chest walked out, heading our way. Once again, Alton took charge, climbing off his wagon and meeting the priest just beyond the Sisters, who had once more moved to encircle our wagons, just in case.

"Welcome to Alcalta on this the holiest of days. I am Deacon Amal Rashid," the middle aged man said in a friendly manner. I thought this sounded more hopeful.

"Yes, tis a fine day indeed," Alton replied. "We are a traveling band of musicians, just passing through on our way to Velona and beyond." He said no more, waiting to see how this man reacted.

"Ah, I gathered as much from your wagons. It is probably not wise for you to stop and play in Alcalta. My flock has turned to the Lord for their enjoyment and salvation and would not really appreciate your, shall we say, erotic dance music. Some of them used to be of a more unsavory nature before they accepted redemption and changed their ways. I would not want to see any of you harmed by their misguided loyalty to the Church and Jehosa. We are, however, just about to hold our midmorning worship services. You are welcome to attend and even repent and accept the eternal salvation of the Son of God."

What a clever way to say that our services were not wanted in this town. At least he was being very polite about it and not ordering us to leave at once.

He added, "Since you are musicians, perhaps you might like to attend our services just to hear our Sacred Music, the only music now sung in this entire sector. All sing praises to God in a pure unison of sound. All sing the same note — you know, purity of sound reflects the purity of the soul. If you know these Sacred Songs, you are more than welcome to lend your voices in praise to Jehosa. Mind you, keep to the purity of the single notes. If you will excuse me, they are waiting on me, I am afraid." He bowed slightly to Alton and headed back to his church.

Alton turned to us and asked, "Now what?"

Caitlyn answered, "Well, it wouldn't hurt anything for us to attend their service. We can listen to the music that their religion allows. It may prove worthwhile to us to learn them so we can fit in better when we get to Velona."

I grinned, "Spoken like a true musician. What say everyone? Shall we at least go inside and listen?" Everyone agreed, even the Sisters; however two stayed outside watching over our wagons and horses.

We walked inside and took seats at the very rear of this huge church. This chapel was fifty feet wide and at least a hundred feet in length, ending with a raised altar, behind which stood Deacon Amal. Behind him were two huge statues, nicely carved. One showed a man hanging from a cross; if I strained my imagination, I could see the face of Jes, barely. Kneeling before him was a statute of an older woman, presumably his mother. Her face looked up at him in great sadness.

The high slanted roof peaked at least forty feet over our heads. Great lanterns hung from the peak ridge beams. Pews were so numerous that I couldn't count them, only estimate the number of rows at likely thirty.

Hundreds of people sat facing their Deacon, but there was just enough room for us to sit unobtrusively at the very rear.

"Welcome one and all once more to the midday services. We are honored today with a band of travelers. Let us make them welcome in this Church of God. Let us begin by singing Psalm Forty-two, By the Blessed Stable He Was Born." The deacon was also a conductor, I noted as he spread his arms wide, as if encompassing everyone here. The song began.

Okay, this was hardly our style of music, but we listened, trying to memorize the basic melody. Several times, I heard Jolina humming along. Of all of us, she always picked up a new song the quickest. Soon, I realized that learning Sacred Music wasn't going to be very difficult at all. Each song contained only five notes, all sung in unison. On their behalf, I will say that the notes were chosen so that they echoed within this huge space, sounding pure and holy. Simple were their songs, yet there was that special quality about them. Occasionally, I detected patterns that were distinctly of Juda Arad origin; I had heard them as a child last lifetime. Yet, something about the childish purity of the sounds sent chills down my spine. Perhaps there was something about their church music after all. Certainly, these were not dances or laments. Still, the simplistic purity of the notes struck a chord in me and with my fellow musicians.

I'll not recount the sermon, however. You already have heard too much about religion, but I'll say this; there wasn't a single mention of the wife of the Great Messiah, Bethany Madelyn Amir, me, or the Holy Blessed Mother, as Caitlyn knew of me in that lifetime. Perhaps that isn't so strange, for the disciples were all highly jealous of me because their Great Messiah placed a far stronger dependence upon me than he did them. My opinion always seemed to matter; theirs often had not.

The Sisters, who didn't much care for the sermon either, also liked this strange music. On that we all agreed, it did sound "holy." At least from our combined viewpoints, it sounded sacred. Hence, we stayed in the town until late afternoon so that we could attend two more services. The Deacon explained that the church was not large enough to hold all of its members at one time, so he held four Sunday services. We had missed the early morning one.

By the time we rolled out of Alcalta, we had learned eighteen of their Sacred Psalms, at least well enough that we could now play them. Admittedly, out of doors, these plain songs without any harmony at all seemed to lose much of their spiritual quality.

Two more days and our caravan pulled up beside what had once been the Sisterhood training camp at the village of Portillio. Distant memories returned to me. It was here that the Sisters had whisked us to safety after Thomas had accidentally killed the beastly High Priest Horton Po, who was in the process of raping another woman. We had met other Sisters here and with their aid, begun our long journey across the Sea Princes. Only vaguely did I hear the orders to make camp for the night here, we would enter Velona in the morning.

Portillio had been long abandoned by the Sisterhood, evacuated around the time of the Great Plague, when they had discovered their Prince had loosened the plague upon the invaders. One night, the Sisters just up and left in secret, many moving to Fortress d'Grange and some on into the Greenway. Rotting ghost shells of buildings were all that remained of this Sisterhood training center.

The next day, we rode on into the once great port city of Velona. I was shocked to see how it had changed, mostly all for the worst. When I arrived here in May of 559 AH by boat, we saw a grand city of perhaps a hundred thousand people. At that time, Velona was neither the largest nor smallest of the Sea Prince cities, stretching inland for miles. Its docks could handle over three dozen ships simultaneously. Now, perhaps twenty thousand at most lived here. I spied two ships unloading at the docks.

Red tile roofs added color to the larger blue-grey stone buildings and brown adobe smaller homes. Very few buildings were actually constructed from wood, since all available wood was used to build and maintain their fleet of ships, now as then. Construction was occurring nearly everywhere we gazed.

The guiding principle appeared to be "Now is the golden opportunity to redesign the city." Four-fifths of the city had already been torn down. Enormous piles of red tiles, stone blocks, and adobe bricks lay neatly stacked at periodic intervals around the outer edge of what had been the outskirts of Velona. What remained of the city looked either new or in good repair, all close to the docks. The pale blue of the Med Sea contrasted sharply with the colors of the roofs and buildings. Off to the left, we spied the red brick roadway built by the Centurions when they had invaded so many years ago.

Also on this western side way down at the water's edge, I spied the beginnings of a giant wall taking place, as workers reused the stone from the buildings they had torn down. Some years from now, the entire city would be surrounded by a protective wall, which they hoped would prevent yet another sacking of their city. Next time, they would have defenses that would withstand a siege. I doubted the wisdom of that, however.

That the Church of Jehosa played a critical role in the rebuilding of Velona was more than evident. We spied a dozen of their enormous churches, their white crosses plainly visible even from this distant hilltop overlooking the city. I had to acknowledge the wisdom of Bandar. He'd taken advantage of the situation to build a huge number of churches in a very short space of time, ensuring the ultimate survival of his religion here in the Sea Princes. I wondered if he was still alive and if he knew how some of his priests were perverting the religion out in bandit country.

We were moving once more; Caitlyn had quietly taken the reins from me, allowing me to continue to reflect. She did grin at me and said, "Old memories, eh?" I gave her a little hug. We entered Velona from the northern main entrance. Gone was the old Velona I had known. Gone were the multitudinous plazas with the open-air markets with throngs hocking anything you could possibly want. Also gone was that spontaneous gaiety among the people. True, we passed several large construction gangs laboring with the heavy stones from the last few buildings being demolished. Somber, gaunt faces greeted ours, not unfriendly, just no emotion.

I knew our plans; we needed to pick up some food supplies and possibly a goodly amount of charcoal. This close to the Med Sea, virtually no wood, save olive trees, remained. Winter was upon us, and we needed charcoal to both cook and warm ourselves. Hence, we wandered the streets searching for suitable places to purchase what we needed. These details were left, of course, to Camilla and Adriana to work out; they had been here before, though not recently. Much had changed since they had been here as well.

We were about halfway to the docks when Adriana, in the lead, was stopped by two men wearing sky blue tunics, swords strapped around their waists, and bronze Centurion helms on their heads. Felice, who was riding beside us, whispered, "City guards." Though we listened, we couldn't overhear their conversation. I saw Adriana toss one guard a coin. After biting down on it, he put it into a pouch, tossed her back a token, and waved her to move on, which she did.

While her companions continued to lead the way, Adriana dropped back to let us know what she had done. "Found us a place we can camp. For a gold piece, we can camp at the city park. It has the only grasslands left in the city and it has several wells. I was informed that we aren't to hold any outdoor concerts, unless you are playing the Holy Sacred Music. Otherwise, we may come and go as we please. Oh yes, he also warned us against going too close to the docks at night; there are some really roughnecks there who often cause trouble. We will be stopping shortly to get supplies at a warehouse close to the docks. With luck, we can get everything at one place."

Everyone told her thanks and well done. I had an uneasy feeling that I could not shake. The last time I was here with my Lightning Circle, events in the city had caused us to flee for our lives. I hoped nothing like that would happen on this trip. Five minutes later, we pulled up beside a large warehouse with a sign over a set of very wide doors, large enough for wagons to pass through. It read Vitorrio, which I assumed was the name of its owner; this was the shipping warehouse of one of the ruling nobles. Inside, this enormous space, crates lined walls ready for shipping, while workmen were busily crating recently arrived goods and unboxing others.

It felt good not to have to be in charge, just to be a lowly gopher for a change. Most of us were kept busy carrying bags of charcoal and food sacks back to the wagons. Adriana was most efficient at purchasing supplies. I gave her the twenty-five gold pieces to pay for the goods, which she at first refused, but I insisted.

Ah hour later, we arrived at our designated camping ground, the city park. What a sight! When I was last here so long ago, these were the grounds of the Church of Tur! I recalled the iron fence that surrounded the huge church complex of buildings. All that, the buildings — all were gone. No trace remained. Grass grew where the church had stood. Evidently, the Church of Jehosanity had wasted no time in removing the last traces of Tur worship in Velona!

While there were a number of others using the park when we arrived, they all moved away from us, staring at us. Not unfriendly, just overly cautious, I surmised. We set up camp and Camilla began to cook. I whiled away the time by telling all that wanted to listen about what Velona had been like a half century ago, when it was a thriving city five times as large as it now was.

Once the early supper was finished, Alton and Andre announced that they were going for an exploratory walk to the docks. "If any news is to be found in this city, the docks will be where it is at. After all, didn't the guards caution us against going there? Must be a better reason." I knew I couldn't talk them out of it and wished them good luck. Waverly added, "Try not to get into any trouble. We really don't want to have to come rescue you two." The Sisters roared with laughter.

Honestly, we musicians were incredibly bored. We weren't allowed to make music; yet nearly every night we would at least practice some. Even Jolina was restless, until a Sister took her arm and led her on a stroll around the park. At sunset, we found ourselves having to bundle up from the chill. Even if it snowed this early in the season, I knew that it would only be a light dusting, not the feet of snow that we sometimes received in the Greenway.

Following the pattern being set by Jolina, Caitlyn and I also took a lengthy stroll, as did Fergus and Fianna. Interestingly, Edgar, who had sat at his wagon staring after Jolina and the Sister, finally got the nerve to go join them. I spied him taking Jolina's other arm.

We were some distance from the others when a young man nearly completely hidden by a cloak that he had pulled up around his head came up to us. "Excuse me," his voice betrayed his youth, "are you gypsies?"

"No, troubadours, traveling musicians," I replied, sensing an emotional letdown from this stranger. Evidently, he had been hoping that we were.

"I'm sorry. I mistook you for gypsies, you know, the wagons and all, strange clothing." Then, his mind registered the rest of what I had said and he added, "Traveling musicians? Does that mean you will soon be leaving Velona?"

"Yes, we had intended to play our way across the Sea Princes, entertaining folks. However, apparently, we aren't welcome here and will be leaving in the morning," I said truthfully.

He glanced fearfully in all directions and then said pleadingly, "Will you allow another wagon to join yours as you ride out of the city tomorrow? Please, I beg you; it's a matter of life and death. I will pay you." He pressed a money pouch into my hand.

I handed it back, "Keep your money. You have more need of it than I do. What is going on and why do you need to leave with us?"

Continuing to glance in all directions, he explained, "I'm Gregorio. Some of us want desperately to get out of Velona, to escape these religious fanatics. I'm an artist and my wife, a sculptor. We can't find any work any longer, except to make church icons as dictated by the Deacons. We'll be killed if we do otherwise. We want to leave, but have been told that we are being watched and will be killed if we try to leave. I hope we can have our wagon join yours and just leave quietly in the morning, before they get wise to us. If you have any compassion for your fellow artists, you must help us."

Caitlyn whispered into my ear, "You've just got to!"

However, I had already made my decision, "Sure, it might be smart if your wagon joined us in the middle of the night so you are here when we move out."

"Oh thank you! Thank you! You have saved our very lives." Just then, he spotted a shadow and hastily decided it was time for him to make a fast exit. I kept my eyes on the shadow, but it turned out to be only a dog. This man certainly was scared.

"You did the right thing," Caitlyn said as we continued our walk. "We just have to help him out. How oppressive this version of Jehosanity is! I hope all the cities aren't this way." We continued our walk and then joined the others at the wagons. I explained what I had done to the others. Adriana said that she would have her Sisters be on double watch during the night in case any trouble arose.

Much later, the Protectors returned, smelling of ale. I surmised that they had a good time while learning the news. Alton got Adriana and us together, "I've a surprise for you. When we leave town in the morning, we're going to have an extra wagon going along with us." Another one I thought? From the looks on our faces, Alton didn't quite know what to expect.

"You see, we heard lots of tales in the pub down close to the docks. Not everyone is happy with the sudden religious fever that has swept through this sector. Some claim that they've only replaced one tyrant with yet another tyrant. All is not a happy religious community, as the Deacons would have us believe. Apparently, if you're too vocally against this new church, you're liable to go missing. The dockhands listed off nearly twenty of them who are nowhere to be found anymore; they just disappeared in the night."

"Anyway, to the point, this place here, the city park, used to be the headquarters of the Church of Tur in Velona before it was torn down and turned into a park two years ago. There are still folks around here who believe in Tur, especially the mariners, who have a vested interest in fair seas, and many of the dockhands. Now the only surviving member of the Po family, who used to control the Church of Tur, sharing power a long time ago with the Prince, has contacted me. She wants to leave Velona with a wagon of priestly artifacts. You see, when they were raising the old Church here, she would poke around late at night, salvaging what remained of their holy artifacts. In the process, she found a secret chamber underground where the real treasures of the Church laid hidden for nearly half a century. No, it is not piles of gold coins or gems. Rather jewel encrusted holy symbols I would call them. I saw a few of them; she showed us. Magnificent works of art, really. If the current rulers discovered them, they will be dismantled and melted down. Already, five other church artifact that the workers found raising the old church here have met that fate. She is desperate to save what remains. I've taken the liberty of telling her that she could come along with us for a while. I should have checked with you all first, but, she was so pretty and so insistent," his voice trailed off.

"Sure, I'd say this is a worthy purpose. It's one thing to bring in law and order and re-establish commerce, and quite another thing to suppress and destroy another's religion and beliefs," I replied. "I'd of done the same thing."

Alton seemed relieved. He added, "I've told her to bring her wagon here midnight, when no one is likely to see her."

"Good thinking, she can join the other wagon that I've let join us around then too," I popped my surprise on him. It was his turn to look mystified. "The church is suppressing local artists, forcing them to only create works for the church and nothing else under pain of death. I've allowed an artist couple to join us for a time too. He's supposed to bring his wagon here in the middle of the night as well."

Her hands resting on her hips, Adriana gave us a stern look in the dim lantern light. "I let you go off for a short while, and you invite half the world to join up with us!" It was half said in jest, half serious. I couldn't tell whether she was upset with us or not. She went on, "Look, gang. If the authorities in this city find out about either of these two, we might have to fight our way out of the city and this sector! Ever think about that? You are risking my Sisters. I ought to have a say in it."

"I'm sorry, Adriana," I said, "You are absolutely right. We should have asked you first before committing to doing it. Forgive us?"

She smiled, "Yes, I think I would have done the same. Men!" She turned to notify her companions of the latest addition to our group. Nevertheless, as Wid, I shouldn't have done this without consulting her. I did feel ashamed I wasn't doing my job. I resolved that from now on I would, starting now.

I got the two Protectors and Waverly together. "Look, we shouldn't risk our Sisters any more than we have to. Both of these new wagons could cause us a whole lot of grief. I think it is prudent that we pull out of Velona just as soon as they both arrive, right in the middle of the night. Probably only a few night guards will mark our passing. Then, should trouble arise later on, we would be out in the open. No innocent bystanders could get hurt." They agreed with my analysis, especially because we would be free to use our druwid spells out in the open, and I walked over to Adriana to explain. She was greatly relieved to hear my plan, thinking it very prudent indeed.

We hitched up the horses a little before midnight, to avoid tipping our plans prematurely. We hadn't waited long before a wagon slowly moved up the street toward us. One cloaked person sat on the open buckboard. "I'm here," a woman's voice spoke to no one in particular; she was unsure of whom to speak.

Alton and I walked quickly to her wagon. "Elona, this is our leader Ket Bethany. Ket, this is Elona Po, the last of the Po line in Velona, I'm sad to say." Alton offered her his hand as she dismounted. She was about the same age as Alton, with blonde hair and brown eyes. Yet, the bags under her eyes and their redness told me quite a lot about her. Long had she been worried and under intense stress and strain; plus she was probably sad about having to leave her ancestral home as well. Yet, she had no choice but to leave. I hoped she wasn't also leaving a family behind.

"Pleased to meet you, Ket," she said very politely. The other Po's that I had encountered so long ago had been very nasty fellows. It was nice to see that not all Po's were that way. Even in the dim lantern light, I could see her staring at my long red hair, which I usually just had tied in a simple ponytail at night.

"Yes, I'm from Tewdwr, West Reach. Red hair is very common there. Plus both my girlfriend and I like really long hair," I added trying to be as plausible as possible.

"Well, it sure is long and red," she commented. "I'm so glad you are helping me out. Did he, did he explain things to you? I know I'm putting you all at great risk by helping me out."

"Yes, he did. I think it is commendable of you to try to salvage what's left of your heritage. Perhaps in another city, you would be welcomed and could once more have your treasures seen and worshiped by followers of Tur. Say, do you need any help driving your wagon?" I asked, suddenly thinking she might not have much experience at it.

"I can manage. I got this far on my own. Perhaps you could have someone check the harness over and see if I got it all hooked up right. I've only done this once before." Instantly, two Sisters began a thorough inspection, and they make a couple of minor adjustments.

While they were examining the harness, another wagon pulled up.

This one had a canvas cover so that one couldn't see inside. Unlike Elona, who only had one horse hitched to her wagon, this one had two. From the depressions left by the wheels in the grass, it was substantially loaded.

Alton and I walked over to the new arrival. The same young man sat on the buckboard, partially covered by his cloak. A canvas flap blocked our view inside. "Hi Gregorio," I said. "We've decided it might be smart to leave town right now. Are you all ready to go?"

"Yes, thank you ever so much! Where do you want us?"

I got Adriana's attention. When she came to me, I asked, "What marching order do you want the wagons to follow?"

Two minutes later, we began to pull out onto the deserted street. Felice led the way riding just in front of our wagon. Behind me, came Gregorio's wagon. Next came Fergus followed by Elona. The remaining wagons brought up the rear. Cleverly, the Sisters and the two Protectors encircled us so all angles were covered. Only the clopping of our horses' hooves broke the stillness of the chilly night. Indeed, before we finally left the last outer building behind us, we had passed several night guards, who seemed to take little notice of us. We headed out onto the Centurion built road that closely paralleled the Med Sea coast, heading toward Barcella, the next large Sea Prince city and sector. Miraculously, we were not followed. How different this time was compared to my last exit from Velona.

We were on the road built by the Centurions. For once, I was thankful for their handiwork. These master road builders had lowered the crests of hills and raised the depth of valleys, making a road that was smooth and nearly level. Even with our heavy wagons, we made far better time than we had on the dirt roads leading down into Velona.

However, the next day, three riders came galloping out from Velona along the Coastal Road, as it is now called. It was more than obvious that they were looking for our guests. As soon as they spied the two different wagons, they hurriedly reined in and rode swiftly back toward Velona. I couldn't tell whether they were after Elona or Gregorio, however. It mattered not to me.

When we halted for lunch, giving the horses a much needed break, we discovered that Gregorio had brought his entire family of five and all their possessions. His wagon was laden with artist tools, as well as the expected pots and pans, and three children, the oldest of which was five. At my suggestion, we hitched one of our spare horses to his wagon to ease their burden, especially if the enemy returned in force.

Adriana caught my attention during lunch, and I joined her for a private walk some distance from the wagons and others. "You are picking up on our secret hand signs fairly well, Bethany. I'm worried about those riders. I'm going to have two Sisters drop back several miles and keep a rear lookout."

"I agree, Adriana, that would be very prudent given the

circumstances. Since we are now out in the wide open spaces, if they attempt to attack us, let us Guardians respond first. Only if they get past us should you commit the Sisters to the defense. I just don't trust this entire sector. First, bandits are rampant, and second, these religious fanatics are not much better. I just have a bad feeling about the situation, so I agree. Let's have as much warning as possible." She relaxed; the stress she was under lessened, as she found out that I felt much as she did.

"Are you sure you aren't a field commander?" she teased me. "You sure have the intuition of one." I took that as a compliment, though it was merely just observing the obvious as far as I was concerned. As we packed up and prepared to continue, two Sisters rode back down the road toward Velona. I explained to the other Guardians what they were doing and my plans if we were attacked, and then the wagons rolled on once more.

Around two in the afternoon, the two Sisters came galloping at top speed toward us. Adriana immediately called a halt. Alton, Andre, and I joined Adriana, as she walked up to the two dismounting Sisters, whose horses were panting heavily, lather flying in all directions. They had been ridden hard.

"About three miles behind us, something like fifty cavalry riding hard. Be on us in maybe ten minutes or so," came the report. Instantly, Adriana took charge. She thanked the two for their warning and began a quick survey of the land about us, looking as I would have for the most defensible location at hand.

"Let's move off the road, put the wagons in a circle on that hill crest, force them to charge uphill to meet us," Adriana ordered. I concurred and quickly we issued the orders to the others.

Immediately, Gregorio began wailing that he had brought doom upon us all, but I told him to shut up. Now was not the time for recriminations. I added, "I knew this might happen before I accepted your request. Besides, it could be Elona Po they're after, not you and your family. Now get your wagon into the circle and stay put." He shut up and followed the orders the Sisters were continuously giving out, arranging the wagons in a tight circle atop the hill.

"Adriana, how do your Sisters prefer to fight: on foot or from horseback?" I asked.

"On foot," she replied, just as I had guessed.

"Okay, you deploy your forces to protect the wagons as you see fit. We Guardians will stay on horseback and see what we can do to prevent even one cavalryman from getting past us." She nodded, though I knew she didn't think much of my plan. What could a couple Guardians do to stop a charging cavalry force? I didn't bother to explain.

I gathered Alton, Andre, and Waverly together for a brief conference. "Waverly, you are to stay back at the wagons and handle any emergency healing that arises. We need to know that someone is looking after those who may be wounded. Until your healing is needed, feel free to spell away," we both grinned at that last.

I continued, "Alton, Andre, we three are going to ride halfway down to the road and stop them from gaining the hill and attacking the wagons directly. Use any and all spells you may desire. I see no reason not to let lose everything at our disposal. Agreed?" Both men grinned broadly, knowing I had just given them the okay to blast away full throttle, something which they had not done in a long time.

Just as we were mounting up to head to our designated position, Elona Po, white faced, walked up to us. "I'm terribly sorry I have brought this doom upon you. I am a Priestess of Tur by inheritance and perhaps by training. I will help as I can." I wondered what that meant, "perhaps by training," but there was no time to inquire.

"I knew that this might happen when we agreed to escort you. Both Alton and I considered it before we agreed, so don't fret about it. We knew this might happen. We are prepared for them. It is probably best if you stay with your wagon and help Waverly with any healing that may be needed. Okay?"

Her face crimsoned. I had touched something. "I — I never had the chance to learn that aspect of being a Priestess, but I will do as I can. I, er, I ah, can sort of do some other things. I will try to hold my position and protect the other wagons, Ket. Thank you." She hastily turned around and headed uphill to her wagon.

Alton mused, "Strange woman. I wonder what she meant by all that? Sounded fishy to me." We rode the short distance to our designated spot and sat waiting for the cavalry to arrive. I glanced over my shoulder to inspect the hilltop defenses. The remaining horses were corralled inside the wagon circle so no matter what happened, we would not lose them. The Sisters, swords drawn, formed a semi-circle around the wagons facing us. However, I noticed Elona Po standing tall on top of her wagon. She had pulled her cloak back, revealing her long blonde hair and face. Evidently, she wanted the attackers to make no mistake about her identity. I wondered if this meant she would sacrifice herself so the others could survive. Strange woman indeed, I thought, echoing Alton.

Two minutes later, we saw the oncoming riders, galloping at top speed our way. When they came within a half mile, they reined in, horses dancing wildly about as their leaders surveyed our defenses. Then, the unexpected occurred. One rider raised a white flag attached to a pole and rode slowly our way, a sign of parley. "Damn, not what I expected," I commented.

"I'll go see what they want," Alton offered.

"No way, if they want a parley, it's the Wid's duty. You Protectors stand at the ready in case of treachery. I once died attempting to parley with and insane leader. I'll not make the same mistake a second time; you may count upon that. See, we'll meet quite out of bow shot range." I kicked my horse into a trot, giving the two no chance to countermand my order.

Slowly I rode toward the approaching man. We met half way between the two opposing forces. From his demeanor and his ornate tack, I guessed that he was the leader. My guess was not wrong. We halted facing each other, and he spoke first, "I am Velona's Captain of the Guards, Hildaldo Corri. You have committed two treasonous offenses against the Holy Church of Jehosanity of Velona. You are ferrying two traitors out of the city, one Elona Po and an artist family. You will return with us to Velona to face charges of high treason or die here on yonder hill. Your choice. Personally, I hope you choose to fight." He snarled visciously at me. I could tell that my long hair offended him and that he thought I was effeminate and easy prey.

"Number One: it is you and the vile creatures who call themselves priests that have totally butchered the holy religion of Jehosa. Number Two: if you do not turn around and leave us alone, every last man in your party will be slain. We show no mercy to vile traitors of Jehosa. Your choice. Personally, I hope you choose to fight." I countered with as much of an anger tone as I could muster, emulating his own pronouncements right back at him. Considering I had a big hand in this religion via the Great Messiah, such was not hard for me to do.

For the briefest instant, the Captain was taken aback with my words and intention. However, his military training kicked in, and he said with a snarl, "So be it. I will personally cut off your head!" He neck reined his horse violently around and cantered back toward his lines, expecting me to do the same. Instinct suggested otherwise. I continued to face him.

He'd not gone but a few hundred feet, when he whirled about and let lose an arrow toward me, expecting to shoot me in the back as I rode back to my side. I simply caught the arrow mid-flight with a quick hand motion, broke it in half in my hand, and dropped the pieces onto the ground. Then, I cantered quickly back to my Protectors. I had sent the message I had desired. I wondered if that man had ever seen someone effortlessly catch an arrow in flight. If he had, then maybe he would think twice before committing his action.

Alton ordered me, "Now you follow our orders. Get behind your Protectors. When they get close enough, I'll drop fire on the left flank; Andre, the right; Bethany, the center. Prepare. Fire only on my order." Together, we began our chants. I felt adrenaline surging in my veins, far more intense than I had ever felt it with a female body. I wondered if this was unique to male bodies, but had no time to consider it further. I made sure my pole was at the ready, should any get by our fires. I still refuse to use swords in combat.

The seventy-five cavalry spread out in a single orderly line. Then, with a hand signal, they cantered uphill toward us, swords gleaming in the bright sunlight. "Now!" ordered Alton. Simultaneously, three huge sheets of blazing fire appeared above the riders and promptly dropped on the unsuspecting riders, burning exposed flesh at once, lighting fires on clothing and leather, and singeing horse hair. Yes, I would have rather spared the poor animals, but under the circumstances, there was no other way to stop this many. I didn't want the Sisters to bear the brunt of this attack because of our decisions.

Wails of pain from man and beast filled the air; riders fell flaming onto the ground. However, these were not the ordinary cavalrymen that we faced. No indeed. Two dozen of the lesser effected, merged their line, and continued closing up the hill. There would be no time for a second fire blast. In seconds, they would be upon us in close quarters combat. When they were within thirty feet of us, suddenly a giant wall of fire arose between us and them. Some fifteen-foot tall flames sparkled and crackled along a line some fifty feet long, like some gigantic flaming bed sheet! "What the. . ." I exclaimed in total surprise; never had I seen a fire spell used in this way! I looked at Alton and Andre; both looked at me in complete surprise! None of us had done it. We turned to look back at the wagons, half expecting to see Waverly chanting away; perhaps this was her contribution. But no, she had her mouth open in complete disbelief as did we!

Then, I spied Elona standing tall upon her wagon; both her hands raised high over her head, chanting away. This was Elona Po's doing. Had I ever underestimated this woman! "Quick, this gives us another chance to blast them!" I ordered. Simultaneously, we launched three more sheets of fire above the startled men. Through the flaming wall, we saw everyone falling off their horses, rolling on the ground in a valiant attempt to squelch their burning hair and clothing.

Adriana now ordered her forces into the action. The Sisters raced downhill to join us. Anger still surged through my veins; male hormones are much harder to control, I noticed. As they reached me, I ordered, "Mercy killing; leave none alive." Like a wind, the Sisters carried out my order. I calmed down and looked at Alton and Andre. "We can't let one of them report back that Guardians were involved nor can we afford to cure seventy-five badly burned men in such intense burn pain." This was just justification on my part. I knew it, but there was some truth in my pronouncement.

Alton commented, "Remind me never to mess with you, Wid Bethany!" Both men chuckled and joined the Sisters.

A few minutes later, Adriana came up to me and asked, "Pretty amazing indeed, Bethany. Now what? Should we just leave their bodies for the vultures?"

"No, they were soldiers following orders, no matter how culpable. We are civilized. We should at least bury their bodies. Any horses that may survive, we should care for; then let's just turn them loose and give them their heads. The horses may choose freedom from man or return to their stables. It is the least we can do for the animals."

"Agreed. I'll see if I can find a suitable spot where the digging is easy. It will take us some time to bury this many, however," Adriana replied and went off in search of softer ground.

"While she is looking, we should have a word with this Elona Po," I suggested. We three rode up to the wagons. She had already gotten down onto the ground and had pulled her cloak over her head, hiding as much as she could. I motioned her to come over to us away from the others looking out of their wagons, cheering and thanking us. Waverly joined her, and we five congregated out of earshot from the others.

As Wid, it was my responsibility to lead the interrogation. "Elona Po, thanks for that incredible assist." I thought beginning with a good acknowledgment was the proper place to begin.

"I thought that it would stop them from reaching you and give you time for another volley," she said timidly, unsure of her footing. "I, I just couldn't kill them, however," she said apologetically.

"You did very well indeed. You were quite right; without that diversion, we would have had to fight them hand-to-hand. This way, none of us is injured. Nice thinking, Elona," I attempted to set her mind at ease.

I continued, "However, Elona, I do have some questions for you, as you probably are expecting." My voice was serious.

She said a brief chant and replied, "Now I shall know if you speak truthfully or not. You must understand my position. I'm the last surviving heir of the founding fathers of Velona. There are none left in the Prince's line, and only I remain from the Po line. Rightfully, Velona should be under my rule; it was my ancestors who founded and built the city. When you met with their leader, what did he say?" She spoke with a steeled determinism that I had not yet seen in this woman.

I decided the best way to proceed was the truth. Quickly, I repeated what the Captain had said and my reply, which did bring a smile to her face. She replied, "You speak truthfully. I must ask one further question before I can answer your questions. Are you all Guardians from the Greenway? Remember, I can tell if you are lying," she added resolutely.

I couldn't see any reason to withhold our identities from her at this point. However, there was the small matter that Thomas had killed Horton Po when my Lightning Circle had been in Velona some fifty years ago. Could she be holding some kind of blood feud with us? His son had hired some bandits to hunt us down and kill us afterwards. Yet, she had created that diversionary wall of fire after she had seen us bring down fire. If she had wanted revenge, she could have brought it on top of us. "Yes, we four are. We are on a secret mission and in disguise. Our mission has nothing to do with Velona or anything to do with Jehosanity or the Sea Princes, if that is a concern of yours."

She couldn't conceal her excitement upon hearing my confirming words! A huge girlish grin appeared on her face, and she totally relaxed for the first time. "All thanks to Tur! I thought so when I saw you bring down the fires! I'm very, very pleased to meet some other Guardians at long last!"

I stared hard at her and suddenly realized this woman was not inside her head, but rather positioned somewhat back of it. Who was she anyway? What did she mean other Guardians? All I could think of to ask next was, "How did you learn to create that wall of fire?"

She grinned sheepishly, "I knew you wanted to ask that. That's why I had to be sure to whom I was speaking first. Luigi taught me, my foster father who saved my life countless times." Seeing our startled faces, she added quickly, "I think he used to be called Luigi the Net Maker a very long time ago."

Fifty-year old memories came flooding into my mind. Luigi had been our Guardian contact in Velona, when my Lightning Circle had first arrived in the city. "I see I ought to explain a little," she added. "You have to understand that many of my relatives and those in the Prince's line have done some rather nasty and downright evil things. That's why Tur took their lives in the end. You must also realize the utter chaos that has thrived here in Velona for nearly a half century. When the ill-thought out plague hit the village in which most of my Po relatives were living, many of them died. I was born during the barbarian invasions. My parents were killed when I was six and my elder brother took the throne of Velona's High Priest of Tur and ruler during these lawless times. That invasion caused massive chaos and loss of life everywhere. When I was six, I was standing on the streets of Velona beside the bodies of my parents who had been hacked to death by the Galts. I too would have perished except for the intervention of Luigi, who was then around sixty-eight years old. He took me away to his net shop and then through a secret passageway. We escaped by small boat up the coast and then headed inland to a village north of Velona, out of harm's way."

He raised me as his daughter, though I know that I was really the daughter that he never had. He told me about his wife being killed so many years before. That's how old Luigi became my foster father. He looked after me and really for the most part raised me and taught me many, many very useful things. I am afraid that I let him down many times, just not getting it right. Yet, I did manage to learn how to create magical fires. When I was fifteen, Luigi passed away, and I moved back into Velona, staying at the Church of Tur with my brothers. Of course, my brothers never would let me learn much of anything about the priesthood — you know, women are not supposed to be the High Priest. However, I kept my eyes and ears open and even spied on them."

"Luigi taught me to observe and stay in the background out of sight. Knowledge is wisdom, he always said. He told me a little about the Guardians of the Greenway and that I should ever keep an eye open for one of them, but none ever came. Still, I did as he taught me. Overhearing my brothers, I learned how to chant the Detect Lie spell, and I learned most of the ceremonial scriptures and rites. Somehow, I survived all the disasters, which have befallen Velona all these years, including the ransacking of the Church by the bandits. I escaped by using a secret passage; my brothers perished. However, I couldn't stand in the background when these vile Deacons of Jehosanity began melting down the Church of Tur's historical treasures. I had to act. I have built up many supporters among those who still believe in Tur. Mostly they live down near the docks, and they have given me some measure of safety these last dozen years. For years, I have kept a sharp eye out for other Guardians, but until now, none ever were in Velona that I could see anyway."

"Luigi always said that if a Guardian should come, I was to offer them all the aid I could give them. Unfortunately, it seems to be the other way around yet again. I owe you my life. Yet, once I have brought these treasures to safety, I will repay my debt, as Luigi would have me do so. So I do pledge," she stated determinedly.

"Incredible, Elona," I replied, more than a little surprised with her revelations. "We need to discuss all this in greater depth, but not now. We need to help get all the dead buried. I'll just say this; it sure is a small world. I knew Luigi. When I first came to Velona over fifty years ago, he saved all of us. My group owes him a big debt, so consider our help repayment for his aid back then. I will explain more later on, but let's go help the Sisters."

Indeed, Adriana had found an excellent location for the mass grave, the remains of a quarry, which the Centurions dug, mining for the paving stone of the roadway. Still, it took us nearly an hour to drag the remains into the pit and then cover them up. We had no more than finished this ghastly chore and were walking up the hill to the wagons when Felice shouted a warning. She had been assigned look out duty while the rest of us were on burial detail. Everyone rushed up to the wagons and looked where she was pointing.

Here, the Centurion roadway was less than a mile from the Med Sea. Just off shore, a Sea Prince ship rode at anchor! A purple pennant fluttered in the wind; all its sails were stowed. We could see a tiny rowboat moving slowly toward the shore, coming straight at us. Our gaily-colored wagons were plainly visible to these mariners. "What do we make of this?" asked Adriana. "One rowboat doesn't seem like much of a threat."

"Hey, they are coming for me!" exclaimed Elona. "That's our secret signal, the purple pennant. They must have a very urgent message for me! I must do down to the shore and meet with them."

"You're not going alone," I declared, and Alton seconded it. Alton helped her up behind him, and we three rode on down to meet the rowboat. I left Andre in charge, just in case there was additional cavalry on their way. It took us only a few minutes to reach the white sands of the beach. I thought it was a particularly beautiful beach. We waited a few more minutes before the small craft finally pulled up on to the beach before us. Two sailors had brought one messenger to speak with Elona.

"Hail and well met, Josquin," Elona greeted the middle aged man, who climbed out onto the white sands. He bowed in reverence to her.

"Hail High Priestess of Tur. All praise to Tur that we have found you in time! We've been searching for you all day. I've come to deliver two warnings to you. The Deacons of Jehosanity are enraged at your flight from Velona and have ordered out nearly a hundred of their finest cavalry to chase you down. They ought to be arriving soon, we estimate. The ship's captain has said that he will risk banishment from Velona by giving you safe transport from here to Vito, if only there is yet time to load the Holy Relics onto his ship before the cavalry come."

"Thank you, Josquin. All praise to Tur. The Holy Fires of Tur have protected us from the cavalry. Yes, they got here about an hour ago. None survived. We've only now just buried the last man. None of us are hurt, not even a scratch," she replied.

"All praise to Tur and the Holy Fires! This is most encouraging, High Priestess! It shows just how weak this false god actually is! Wait until the others hear about this unexpected turn of events!" Josquin couldn't conceal his elation over this miracle news. Yes, in his eyes and very likely all the remaining followers of Tur, this was a divine miracle.

"You mentioned Vito. What about Barcella?" Elona got him back on track with his messages.

"Yes, the second message. Our spies have learned that already the Deacons have sent outriders to Barcella, who will get there long before your slow wagons. He has ordered your immediate arrest and seizure of your wagon of treasures! It is very unsafe to be discovered anywhere in this sector. You know how close their ties are. Hence, we have all agreed that you should flee to Vito, it being the closest safe city at this time. As I said, the ship's captain has said that he will risk banishment from Velona by giving you safe transport from here to Vito." I watched Elona closely as she heard this bit of news. She looked shocked and a bit dismayed. Evidently, she had counted upon finding safety and sanctuary in Barcella.

I interceded on her behalf, "Can we have a few minutes to discuss matters?" He agreed and I signaled Adriana and Felice to join us. As soon as they reined in and dismounted, I told them the news. "It is an awful lot to ask the captain to risk banishment. Felice, any way we can somehow travel through the rest of Velona and Barcella sectors without attracting too much attention?"

Alton added, "Look, we need speed. How about hitching some of our spare horses to the other wagons so they can cover more ground faster without straining themselves? We could even travel extended hours when the risk of ambush is low." I noticed that Alton glanced at Elona to see how she took his suggestion.

Felice drew a sketch on the sands. "Here is Velona, Barcella, and Vito. Here is where we are now, just outside Velona. About seven miles ahead is a small town with a rim road beginning there. We follow it to here and then at the next spoke road, go north to the next rim road, and then again north on the spoke all the way to the Paese di Dio. From there, absolutely no problem except the winter snows may become too deep if we take too long to pass. Already there is snow there, but it should not be too deep just yet. If we can push the horses to make fifty miles a day, we should arrive in Vito in six or seven days, barring any unforeseen difficulties. Look, they are expecting us to flee to Barcella. They will not be expecting us to go north, and certainly not to travel the Paese di Dio at this time of year. The zig-zagging will tend to throw them off our true destination."

Alton exclaimed determinedly, "There, see, we can do it. Elona, we can get you safely to Vito without the horrible sacrifice of the ship and her crew." Again, he gazed at her.

His words ought to have been my pronouncements as Wid. However, I let it pass, saying, "I agree with Alton. For everyone's safety, we should take this slight detour. Speed is of the essence, so let's make use of every horse we have. Adriana, do we have enough tack to hitch the spares to the wagons?"

"I brought quite a bit, just in case, but I'll have to go check on that. If not, perhaps we can purchase some in one of these towns that we pass through or else just make do," she replied, relieved that we were going to bypass further trouble in Barcella.

"I don't know what to say," Elona gushed, taken completely by surprise with our genuine attempt to help her and her followers. "You would go that far out of your way for me?" Alton enthusiastically said so. "Well, I hate to force an entire ship to go into exile because of helping me. I accept. Let me go explain things to Josquin." She returned to her follower and told him of our plans. I let Alton remain to bring Elona back to the wagons, while the rest of us returned to start getting the extra horses hitched up.

A half hour later, by various unorthodox means, all our spare horses were lending their efforts to pull the wagons. The most limiting factor on our speed now was the plodding nature of our heavy draft horses pulling our musician's wagons. Just at suppertime, we entered the small town and turned left onto the rim road, which arced north and eastward, somewhat back the way we had come. To further confuse matters, we traveled all night long, passing through several towns during the night, where we continued our strange zig-zag pattern of roads. Every few hours, however, we rotated wagon drivers so that they could warm up and eat a cold snack.

When we finally stopped briefly at sunrise, Alton then checked the clothing of our guests. While Gregorio and his family had plenty of warm clothing — they had brought everything they owned with them — Elona was ill equipped for this journey. Alton donated a number of his spare garments

252

to her and helped her fix up a tarp over her wagon to provide slightly more protection from the early winter cold. Everyone was dead tired from having traveled all night, so we wasted little time getting some needed sleep for a few hours before starting on our journey once more.

We had passed through the heaviest bandit country during the dead of night and our prospects for further trouble diminished with every mile we made. Evidently, our ruse worked, for no cavalry ever found us. For six more days, we pushed the horses hard and long without any mishaps.

After we had recovered from traveling all night that first night, I had Elona come ride with me so that we could get to know each other better. I knew she must have many questions that she desperately wanted answered. It was time well spent. Luigi was right; under better and proper circumstances, Elona was indeed prime druwid material. I could not fault him for having taken her as his apprentice; he had given his life in our service and cause with almost no thanks for having done so. However, her training had ended far too soon; under the right circumstances, she could well become another renegade druwid! Still, I had no right to force her into additional training. On the other hand, she was a practicing High Priestess of Tur, and her priestly ideals did indeed act as a check and balance upon her fledgling druwid powers, especially her command of fire spells. She couldn't use her fire spells to attack another, only place a barrier and give her opponent a choice. This she had demonstrated to my complete satisfaction.

Yes, I did have to explain a bit of my history to her so she could understand just how it was that I knew Luigi. She had me tell her everything about him and the help he had provided us. In fact, she had me relay it twice; she was committing it to memory. I sensed a deep love between her and Luigi, that of a father and daughter. Curiously, after she returned to her wagon, Alton stopped by and pleaded with me to relay all that she had said, as well as my observations. He agreed with my conclusion that being a High Priestess tended to counter her half-training of druwid skills. Alton seemed to be paying special attention to Elona, more so than I would have predicted. I wondered why.

At last, we rolled across a unique stone bridge, the likes of which my old Planner, Raphael, would have greatly admired! In typical Centurion design, the arched stone bridge spanned the Jonquin River that sliced across the southern road that led directly down and into Vito. About five miles further along, we rolled into the town of Litorio, a small town, perhaps a hundred miles north of Vito. For once, our timing was better; it was nearly noon. Coming down from the Paese di Dio, most of the other villages we passed through during the nighttime hours. A quick estimate suggested there were perhaps a hundred stone buildings with the familiar red slate roofs, smoke clouds curling upwards in the frosty air, contrasting sharply with the light dusting of pure white snow.

Yes, there was a single Church of Jehosanity here, its white cross standing high above all other buildings, but only this one. As we entered the town along the paved road, which went straight on through it, we spied a rather large inn. We stopped and Alton entered to check it out. We were in luck! They catered to road travelers, and yes, our music would be most welcome here! Hearing this, I splurged and spent five gold coins for rooms for everyone along with a good hot meal and warm bath. I received kudos from all quarters, especially Elona, Gregorio, and his family.

However, the Protectors and several Sisters had to carry the ten precious crates from Elona's wagon inside to her room. None of us wanted to risk leaving them outside. Still, Adriana posted a continual guard over all the wagons and horses. The afternoon was spent using all the hot water the kitchen could make, baths all around — most welcome, I might add. I felt like a new man, squeaky clean, for a change and didn't mind my hair taking the rest of the night to dry out.

Just as back home, word that we would be playing at the inn this evening spread quickly around town. Just after supper we assembled in the main room that served as both pub and diner. Already the place was filling up. We had not played in nearly a week, and I found that I really wanted to make music! We played to a packed house for over two hours, thoroughly enjoying ourselves. From our point of view, this was more like it. At last, we were sharing music with others. Although religion was never discussed, it was apparent that things were much different here in the Vito sector.

Our spirits raised, we hit the road the next day, heading for Vito, the city. We played at two more inns along the way, and nearly every evening we slept in a relatively warm bed instead of the cold wagons. The night before we were to arrive in the city, Gregorio came to me and said, "You are really quite good musicians. You should at least drop by the Artist's Guild in Vito. You might find other musicians there. I have a friend who moved here last year, while the getting out was still good. I'm sure he can introduce you to the Guild. From his letter, I understand the Guild has a large number of members, you know, artists, sculptors, and musicians, too. I have never been to Vito, but we can ask around and find the Guild easily, I should think. Ket, my wife and I really feel that we owe you something for having helped us escape and bringing us all the way to Vito. She has suggested that perhaps you would accept a portrait of you and your girlfriend, maybe one of Fergus and Fianna too. What say you? I would only need to find a studio or borrow one for a few days — that is, if you are going to stay in Vito long enough. I would really like to give you back a little something."

Exchange, good old exchange. We had helped him out of a tight situation, and his sense of pride, self-worth, demanded that he give something back in return. I had rejected outright his money pouch, and now I was positive I'd done the right thing in rejecting money; he had a large family to support. "If we end up staying long enough, I think that would be a perfect gift, Gregorio. Thanks. I'll let Adriana know that we're to inquire about the whereabouts of the Artist's Guild. She'll get us there."

Chapter 18 The Month in Vito

On January 7, 622 AH, our caravan rolled into the outskirts of Vito, home to eighty thousand people. I had never been to Vito; we'd bypassed it when I was last in the Sea Princes a half century before. However, with only a few exceptions, Vito appeared as Velona had so many years ago. A thriving commerce center, the docks were huge, able to accommodate ten ships at one time. Sprawling outward for miles, laid out in a giant semi-circle, the town held countless grey stone buildings with typical red slate roofs. The streets were laid out like spokes in a wheel with curved side streets appearing periodically, typical of the Sea Prince cities. One just had to get used to curving streets and alleyways.

Although it was now winter, still people crowded the streets, bundled up against the chill winds from the Med Sea. Ah, the open markets thrived here, just as they had so long ago in Velona. Even as we rode in from the north, two fundamental changes were strikingly obvious. First, a ten-foot tall wall of grey granite outlined the western half of the city; the eastern portion was still under construction. A giant gatehouse perched high over the roadway, as the well-traveled road entered the city. Great gates with reinforced iron hung open. They would not be shut at least until the remainder of the outer wall had been finished. Surprisingly, there was no toll to enter the city and no guards posted at the gate.

The second obvious feature was the dozen Churches of Jehosanity. One could not miss them, for they stood taller than any other buildings with their white crosses reaching for the sky, as if symbolically attempting to touch Heaven. This secondary main roadway built by the Centurions ran straight through the city joining up with the lengthy east-west roadway that traversed the entire length of the Sea Princes. Other than the radiating spokes, the east-west coast road was the only straight east-west road in the city; all the others were curved, like a wheel rim.

Periodically, larger squares appeared, all occupied by the thriving open-air markets and food venders. As we drove past the first of these many markets, I spied several members of Vito's Sisterhood, as did Adriana. She stopped and introduced herself and received several sets of directions. She came back to me to report, "We should stop at the Sisterhood inn. Sister Alvira says that they could easily accommodate our large party. It is expected that I, at least, do so."

"Great. Sounds fine with me. I would feel totally safe sleeping in a Sisterhood run inn."

"Good, I thought so," Adriana quickly flashed a few secret hand signals and added, "Okay, she is off to let them know that we are coming. I have the directions for the Artist's Guild and the sole remaining Church of

Tur. Both are more or less on the way to the inn. Shall we drop off our guests as we go?"

"Well done, as usual, Adriana, lead on," I validated her.

The Church of Tur was located very close to the docks and warehouse district; one side of its compound bordered on it. Only the mariners and those closely related still worshiped their sea god. Here, we bid farewell to Elona, who thanked us profusely for all we had done. She asked where we might be staying and I told her. She then veered into the lane leading to the churchyard gates, waving to us. Elona was nearing the end of her quest to restore the holy relics, and her relief was plainly visible on her smiling face.

Ten minutes later, we halted before an enormous square building with more windows than any other that we had seen so far. Here, we said farewell to Gregorio and his family. I promised that we would stop by in a few days and see about the portraits. Another ten minutes and we approached what had to be our destination — the inn run by the Sisterhood. In fact, it was more like an entire complex! Over the plain doorway that opened onto the same road that we had entered the city upon — the Centurion made road — was a large painted sign of a beautiful young woman wearing a yellow headband. Below her feet was a single word, 'Inn,' in large block letters. The main structure was two-stories tall, U-shaped. We were actually facing the bottom side of the 'U.' Clearly, this inn could house hundreds of people at a time.

The center of the 'U' was a courtyard garden, which at this time of year saw very little use. Just behind the courtyard were the kitchens and pantry buildings, all dwarfed by the main complex. Behind these two buildings was a long, two-story building, the stables, with a haymow on the second floor. We had too many wagons for the stables to handle and were allowed to park the seven out in the unused courtyard. I learned later on that the big square building just across the alleyway was the Sisterhood Dance Hall.

I accompanied Adriana to make the initial arrangements. As I stepped inside, I was overwhelmed with what I saw. A red carpet led up to the manager's desk. All along the short corridor and going down the two long hallways to my left and right were paintings! Not just crude ones, these were extremely realistic and very well done indeed. On the desk was a small marble statue of a young Sister; the gold colored lantern sat upon her head. The manager said, "Greetings Sister." When she saw me she said, "And Sir or Madam as the case may be. Such red hair, so long." I said Sir, and she continued, "Welcome to the First Sisterhood Inn of Vito. How may we assist you?"

Adriana explained, "I'm Sister Captain Adriana Socorro of Fortress d'Grange. I'm here with twenty of our Sisters escorting the Cymry (West Reach) Minstrels and a party of Greenway Guardians as they tour and play throughout the Sea Princes. We have seven wagons," she continued to enumerate our size and needs.

"You've certainly come during the right time of the year. We can easily accommodate your every need. The dead of winter is our off-season, you know. How long will you be staying? I ask because we have special Winter Monthly Rates, most affordable." She outlined the deal; it was so good that I couldn't say no. I handed over twenty-five gold coins before Adriana could get to her pouch. She chuckled at me, but I know that she appreciated my gesture.

The manager added, "You are in luck, Captain Adriana. Both Mother Sister Carmina Bunne and her Fighter Group Leader, Ellen Els, are staying here for a few weeks. I'm positive that both of them will want to meet with you as well as with the Guardians. Both were at the First Grand Council at Zargarb, you know, and met personally with the legendary Sandy and Simon Donegal, Guardians from the Greenway. Also, the Sisterhood representative on the High Council of Seven, Sister Belinda Bertonelli, most definitely will want to speak to all of you as well. She often stays here during the winter months. And would these minstrels be a'wanting to play, perchance?" My exaggerated nod was all the encouragement she needed. "We hold dances as often as we can in the dance hall out back. You are welcome to come and play as often as you like. There are so little activities in the winter time, you know." I asked her to send someone to my room with details and specifics. We left her smiling from ear to ear; we had made her day in many ways!

Our rooms were all in a row at the end of the west wing, indoor side, first floor. This way, we had easy access to our wagons. While we men began carting the various sacks and packs and instruments into the rooms, Caitlyn and Fianna went off to explore our new surroundings, hoping to find the way to the dining room. By the time that I had our gear stowed — Caitlyn and I were now sharing one room, while Fergus and Fianna, another — the two women return, excitement radiating from their eyes. "There is a public hot bath over in the east wing. It's heated up once a day. It's free. Guess where we are going tomorrow morning after breakfast?" Caitlyn exclaimed.

"Same place as Fergus and I are going," I teased her back, "to the hot bath!"

"Well, there are more women here than men, so if you are going in with us, you are just going to have to smell like lilacs as well!" she teased back.

"That's infinitely better than I smell right now," I ended the tease. She couldn't disagree with this point.

We then organized our many packs and sacks, making the small room more like a home, since we were going to be living here for a month. However, we had no more gotten stuff arranged, when a maid knocked on our door with the news that, since so many of us just arrived, the public hot bath would be heated and ready for us in a half hour. "Yippee," chorused the women.

Quickly, we got out our cleanest clothes and prepared to head to the bath. In the hallway, out came everyone else. Not one of us wanted to be left behind. We made quite a sight as our large group, chatting gaily, marched down the long hall, across the even longer main floor past the manager's desk, she waved as we passed, and all the way down to the end of the eastern hall. In warmer weather, it would be far faster just to cut across the courtyard, but none of us wanted to dash across there; it was cold outside.

The bath was large enough to accommodate thirty-six at one time, so we nearly filled it completely up. Everyone peeled off their dirty clothes and eased themselves into the warm waters. Yes, the water was scented with lilacs, but we didn't care, though the women, of course, did.

There was only one slightly awkward moment, when the Sisters undressed. They were very unused to being seen naked in front of men. Many had scars from fighting or worse on their bodies. I defused the potential embarrassment, by saying, "Wow, look at all the beautiful women. Guys, we are outnumbered ten to one." Everyone laughed as Caitlyn and I slid into the warm water, followed at once by everyone else. While the Sisters paired up helping each other wash their backs and such, Caitlyn and I followed suit, while Fergus and Fianna paired as well.

Fianna and I were the last ones out, quite some time after the others had gotten out, dried off, put on their clean clothes, and left. I helped her get her hair manageable once more and she, mine. She was very pleased to see that her hair was now only slightly shorter than mine was. Together, we walked back to join the others, a very happy brother and sister.

When we arrived back at our rooms, a Sister was waiting for us, ready to arrange for our playing. Since I had taken so long, Edgar had already worked out the arrangements, but was waiting for me to give them the final okay. We would play every other night, but not on Sunday, their Holy Day. In return for playing each evening, we would receive a gold piece. I realized that this alone would pay for half of the cost of our staying here! We accepted, of course. Tomorrow night would be our first gig.

However, the next morning's meetings brought something wholly unexpected for us to do. At breakfast in the large dining room, a messenger brought us a request, really an order, for us to meet with the head of the Vito Sisterhood and their representative on the ruling High Council of Seven. News travels fast within the Sisterhood. Shortly after breakfast, Adriana led us into a smaller side room, just off the dining room. Alton, Andre, Waverly, and I accompanied her. Three women were already there awaiting us. Two were very old with thinning grey hair streaked with white, one was much younger, perhaps thirty.

All stood and warmly greeted us, "Welcome, welcome indeed! I am Mother Sister Carmina Bunne, the leader of the Vito Sisterhood, for what seems ages now. This is my Fighter Group Leader, retired mostly, Ellen Els," she introduced the other older woman. These two had worked together for close to a half century and had seen some of the most enormous challenges and changes ever to face the Sisterhood and women, in general, here in Vito. "This is the Sisterhood and tradesmen representative on the ruling High Council of Seven, Sister Belinda Bertonelli."

The two older women, in their middle sixties, definitely looked their age, with wrinkled hands and age lines on their faces. Yet, they still had vitality of life in them. In contrast, Belinda was still youthful looking with shoulder length, light brown hair, with cute bangs in the front ending just above her eyebrows. She wore a blue dress accentuated with brown, the most favored color combination in Vito. I was drawn both to her penetrating hazel eyes and to her face, both of which radiated supreme self-confidence and intolerance for lies. I suspected she could see right through most fibs or distortions that others on the High Council may try to foist off on them.

After introducing ourselves, Sister Carmina said, "Please sit down. I won't presume that you know all about events of the past here in the Sea Princes, so I will tell you a bit of our history — why it is that I so very much wanted to meet you." She related the tale of our Lightning Circle's passage across the Sea Princes over a half century ago, described from her point of view anyway. She particularly emphasized the role that Simon had played in precipitating the beginnings of massive changes in the way women were treated throughout the Sea Princes. "Can you imagine my joy and happiness when Simon and Sandy both came to the First Grand Council in Zargarb?" She went on about all those days, expressing what an honor it had been to actually meet and shake hands with them.

"So you see why I just had to meet you all. Four Guardians, here in Vito." She then asked what I had anticipated she would most want to know. "It is my duty, my obligation to the Sisterhood, to have to ask you this." She seemed rather apologetic about having to ask. "Are you here on some business that I should know about? Something that might impact the Sisterhood in any way?"

Even though I was just a teenager, not yet fifteen, it was my position as Wid to speak, "No, Sister Carmina. You may rest assured that if our coming had anything remotely to do with the Sisters, we would already have sent word to you. No, we are on a mission to find one of our own Guardians, who has gotten himself into some kind of trouble; just where he is at, we don't know. Under the guise of being troubadours, which we really are, we are traveling about Tarra in search of him."

"Thank you, Ket. You understand that I was obligated to ask you. I didn't mean to seem like a prying old maid."

"No problem, I know you had to ask. I would have done the same thing if I were in your shoes." I made her feel at ease.

Smiling, she asked, "Such amazing long hair, red too. Do all the men on your island have such magnificent hair? You are so young, too. Yet you seem to speak for these older Guardians. And what a strange last name,

Bethany. You know, I could not help but recall that the Simon's leader was also called Bethany; she, too, had very long hair, I am told. Coincidence perhaps?" She had a wry smile, but I saw that her companions both were equally curious about these points.

Trusting implicitly the Sisterhood, I replied, "This body comes from Tewdwr, West Reach. Yes, flaming red hair is the most common hair color there. You may have noticed my sister, Fianna; hers is just like mine, except hers is a little shorter." I had it tied in a simple ponytail, but it flared out wide and full at its ends — I had just washed it last night, and it always was rather bushy afterwards. "Honestly, just between you and me, I just love really long hair. I did get teased a lot about it while I was growing up."

Everyone chuckled and Belinda commented, "Some women around here would just die for hair like yours." More laughter followed.

"Seriously, to answer the remainder of your questions is more problematical. I really don't want to deceive you or tell you untruths. The Sisterhood has been our finest allies for over a half century now. What I am about to tell you, you may choose to disbelieve or not as you see fit. We are all immortal spiritual beings that inhabit for a time these mortal bodies. When the body passes away, we just go find ourselves a new baby body and start life anew." I paused to observe their reactions.

"You speak much like the deacon of the Church of Jehosanity here in Vito," Belinda commented.

"If you can accept this concept, then perhaps you will intellectually understand what I am about to explain. You aren't wrong about Bethany. I'm she of whom you spoke, but that was two mortal bodies ago. When I first came here to the Sea Princes, I was the leader of the group. Sandy and Simon were two very good friends of mine. We were very close. This lifetime, I chose the last name, Bethany, both because I really like that name and because so many still think of me as Bethany. I still remember nearly everything that has happened to me all these years, even though I've had several bodies now. Yes, these three Guardians still think of me as a leader. Hence, I am speaking for our small group." Adriana gasped; she had no idea that I was *that* Bethany!

"How do you remember things from your previous life?" asked Ellen.

"Doesn't everyone?" I teased, knowing most people chose not to do so. "Seriously, think about it for a moment. What would be the last memory one would have of your pervious lifetime and mortal body?" I paused a moment and added, "It's death. Deaths are often rather traumatic, are they not? And you suddenly lose your body, all your possessions, all your loved ones. Kind of makes it a bit of a nasty thing to want to remember, doesn't it?"

"I wonder," Ellen commented, "You know I have always had these pictures in my mind of an old man who raised, trained, and loved horses. Then, one day, he fell off the fence and smashed in his head. That's all I have ever seen. I've loved horses all my life, good with them. Do you suppose?"

"More than likely," I grinned at her. She grinned back.

We all chatted for perhaps another half hour, and I found them just as fascinating to talk to as they did us. Unfortunately, I then opened my big mouth once too often and asked, "So Belinda, how are things going with the High Council? Is this method of government working out satisfactory for everyone?"

Suddenly, her demeanor became deadly serious. "How strange you should ask this question!" Instantly, all four of us were fully alert, and even Adriana looked up and stared at her fellow Sister. This was news.

"This isn't going to make any sense to you at all unless I back up a bit. Here goes. Yes, for quite some time now, the High Council of Seven has been working fairly well, governing the sector. Given enough time and discussions, problems always seem to have worked themselves out for the best for all concerned. Until recently, I think everyone has been satisfied with the High Council."

"There must be a but," I interjected.

"Yes, it all began about two weeks ago. There are seven of us on the council, one from each of the four noble houses, the prince, the church, and myself, representing the tradesmen and the Sisterhood. One of the nobles on the council, Hermino Vitali, is the problem. Several years ago, he took over his father's position. Antonio Vitali is in his seventies and rather feebleminded, and at last, his son took over his position. Hermino is twenty-five and rather handsome. He's married and has a loving wife and three children. Unlike some of the other nobles, he used to be well liked. He was always seen strolling around town with his wife in his arm. They went everywhere together. You'd see them at concerts, building dedications, even at church services."

"About two weeks ago, all that changed. He stopped going to concerts and has not officiated at any of the usual dedications that he used to perform. He was one of the better-liked nobles before two weeks ago. No one has seen him in the company of his wife for over two weeks now, but that is not the problem. For the last two weeks, he has been lobbying the High Council to form up a large army and head to the Northern Steppes to take back what the barbarians stole from Vito! Of course, no one else wants to do that, but I am afraid he has been relentlessly talking to the other members of the council and has gotten two members convinced that this is what we should do. One more vote and the measure will pass!"

"But there is more; I have had Sisters watching him last week. He has also been going to the local pubs every night, inciting all who will listen that they should demand the High Council form up an army to take back what was stolen from us by the barbarians from the steppes! Half of the dockworkers are now backing him up, putting even more pressure on us four holdouts. So I ask you the question that has been burning in my mind:

can a man change so completely in such a short time? Is this possible? Is it possible to go from a person who seems to have the welfare of his people in his heart and mind to a warmonger — almost overnight?"

Waverly, Alton, Andre — all stared at me. I knew they were passing this question on to me, the Wid. "Belinda, it is possible for someone to experience something horrible, such as battlefield butchery, and then go insane or crazy or have a drastic personality change as a result. It takes an awful lot to cause such a wild swing in a person's behavior. Something traumatic must have happened to Hermino two weeks ago."

Belinda looked glum, "We've had no battles here for years. With the coming of the Church of Jehosanity, violent crime has dropped to all-time lows. Absolutely no calamities have happened here for years now. What else could possibly have caused this and can it be undone?"

"I cannot image," I replied truthfully. She looked positively crestfallen; she had placed so much hope on us. My heart melted. "Say, we're going to stay here in Vito all month. While we're going to play many gigs at night, we have absolutely nothing to do during the days. What would you say to allowing us to investigate this matter and see if we can figure out what has happened and perhaps help to set it right again?"

"You would do that for me?" she asked almost not believing her incredible good fortune.

"Hey, it is a good mystery. Otherwise, we're going to be very bored all month. Sure, it will give us something constructive to do."

"Oh how can I ever repay you? Thank you! Thank you! I'm sure that Carmina and I will place all our resources at your disposal. Anything you need, just ask. Oh thank you!"

"Yes, the Sisterhood thanks you, whether or not you succeed," Carmina added. "I will place the entire Sisterhood here in Vito at your disposal."

"Well, I guess the first thing we need to do is meet this Hermino or at least see what he looks like, where he lives. Will it be alright if we interview his family without his knowing about it?"

"We have a lunch council meeting at noon on Saturday at the Pig's Inn. Our meetings are always open to the public, and there is a small observation gallery set aside for concerned visitors. You could come, see him, and hear him. Would that do for starters?"

"Noon it is!" I replied. Actually, I was a little excited about having a real mystery to solve.

"I'm sure we can arrange for you to meet with his wife. In fact, she is likely to come tonight to hear you play; she's never missed a Sisterhood dance in two years. I'll see what can be done to get you introduced to her. In fact, I'll assign one of my assistants, Sister Felicia, to act as your guide around the city. It can be a bit confusing for newcomers. She'll be at your disposal all the time. Thank you again!"

As we walked back to our rooms, Waverly insisted, "Since I don't really have much to do at the moment — you are all playing and such — why don't I take charge of the interviewing? A woman may feel more comfortable talking about sensitive issues to another woman, Ket. Besides, I'm bored too," she grinned.

Andre added, "And I'll keep an eye on her. Alton can watch over the minstrels. Now we all have something to do."

"Okay, but be careful and keep me posted." I couldn't keep them from having something to relieve their boredom. The day passed altogether too slowly for all of us.

Right after supper, we began setting up our instruments for the big dance at the Sisterhood Dance Hall, which was a very large building, though not tall. The smaller rear section held a small kitchen where the drinks and party treats were prepared. Several Sisters were already in the kitchen making their preparations, anticipating a large turnout. Even though we had not yet gotten fully prepared, people began arriving. Sister Felicia, a woman of thirty, brought a pretty younger woman up to meet us.

"Excuse me minstrels, but I want you to meet Mrs. Luzi Vitali, the wife of the High Council member, Hermino Vitali." She had dropped enough proper names on us so we couldn't possibly mistake this woman for the one we needed to question. "She is a strong supporter of the Arts here in Vito."

"I'm so pleased to meet you. Felicia tells me you have traveled all the way from the island of West Reach. My, such a distance! Allow me to welcome you personally to Vito and to say how thankful we are to have minstrels come to play for us. There are so few good troubadours around these days. Probably because the barbarians killed so many, and the younger ones just do not have the skills well learned as yet." She would have rattled on even further, except for two things. One, she suddenly spied my long red hair and then Fianna's. Secondly, Felicia tried to cut her off so that she could introduce us.

"This is the minstrel's leader, Mr. Ket Bethany and his sister Fianna."

"I am so please to meet you both! Such incredible hair. I've never seen such a vibrant red before, and so long! Do all the men where you come from have such magnificent long hair?" she asked, holding out her hand for me to kiss gallantly.

"Pleased to meet such an ardent Arts supporter, Mrs. Vitali," I replied. "We come from Tewdwr, West Reach. There, our hair is as common as blonde is here. And no, I just like mine long." I then introduced the other members. However, she was very surprised to meet Jolina and could not get over the fact that we had a blind musician with us. Apparently, that was a novelty here.

Cleverly, Felicia then introduced the woman to Andre and Waverly, explaining to her that these two and Alton were acting as our managers. Waverly cleverly moved the elegantly dressed woman away from us so she could begin to make friends with her and allow us to continue setting up. By the time that we were ready to play our first round of dance tunes, the place was packed. I later learned that three hundred people had come, a slightly larger crowd than normal. However, so successful was our first performance that every time we played here after this, the place was packed to capacity; nearly four hundred came to hear us every other night. We became an instant hit in Vito.

As you might expect, requests for additional performances at other establishments soon came pouring in to Alton, who actually had to become our manager! Within a few days, we were soon booked every night of the week, except their holy day, Sunday. It's hard to say which music was the most popular. The older women loved the ballads and laments. The younger folks preferred the fastest dances. Everyone desired to hear songs from more distant lands. Yes, we musicians had a ball every evening.

Later that night, Waverly filled us in on what she had learned from Luzi Vitali. She was very thankful Felicia was with her because our mastery of the Sea Prince dialect was not that great, just the basic five hundred word vocabulary. The Sister proved invaluable to Waverly. "Essentially, what Belinda told us is true. One Friday night, her husband failed to come home after work. All nightlong she worried something dreadful may have happened to him. He's never failed to come home, though sometimes he worked late. However, when he did, he always sent a messenger home letting her know so she would not worry. From all she said, he was a loving, considerate husband and father. However, he did show up on Saturday morning, smelling of ale. He was totally changed. He refused to talk to her, just changed his clothes. He even ignored his three children and left within a half hour, saying something about some business to attend. Ever since then, he shows up every few days, again only to change clothes. He has not spoken more than ten words to her in two weeks, let alone give her a hug or kiss. She is beside herself with worry and doesn't know what to make of his horrible change."

"I did find out some other details that I'll check out tomorrow. It seems that ever since she has known him, every Saturday morning he goes fishing with his best friend, Julio Termino. However, Julio came by to see if he was sick or something. It seems he had not shown up to go fishing for two Saturdays now. This gets stranger the more I find out."

I suggested, "After you check with Julio, see if you can find out what his usual Fridays consisted of, you know, where he goes, what he does, what route he travels, things like that. Perhaps we might get some clues if we can backtrack his normal routine. You know, maybe he visited a particular pub, and when he left, he was a different man. We need more clues."

She laughed, "I'd say we need a whole lot more clues! So far, this city seems very quiet to have caused someone to break down this way. Strange."

The next day, we could not help her out. Gregorio came by. He had obtained some temporary studio space and wanted the four of us to come for our first sitting. The man was very insistent and excited as well. Just after lunch, Alton, a Sister acting a guide, and the four of us walked to the Artist's Guild — the impressive large building with the enormous number of windows that we had seen when we first entered Vito. The walk, though chilly, was entertaining. We passed through numerous open-air markets in the various plazas we passed.

Answering our knock on the door, a door boy asked who we were and what we wanted. I learned that only artist members of the guild and their families were allowed inside or those that had an appointment. The young lad, perhaps twelve, was expecting us and had us sign in a visitor's logbook. Quaint, I thought. Then, he led us down a long hallway to a stairs. We passed by over a dozen paintings that I thought were fabulous. Some were scenes of harbor life, some were ships at sea braving storms, and some were portraits — very realistic and lifelike. We climbed up four sets of stairs to the top floor. A beaming Gregorio was there to meet us.

"Such a studio! I never imagined I would get to paint in such a magnificent studio! Come; let me show you around as we go to my small spot. I picked one by the window so we can have good light." Essentially, we were in a converted warehouse type room, about two hundred feet square. Enormous stone columns supported the roof, but these were the only "walls" in the space. Many other artists were at their easels and took no notice of us as we passed. The place smelled of linseed oil and paints. Each artist had a portion of the room in which to work. Paintings were everywhere in all stages of completeness. He estimated that at least fifty painters worked in here, though seldom at the same time.

His corner was actually that, a corner location with windows on two sides. He had two large three-foot square canvases on two easels ready for us. Admittedly, his supplies looked very meager compared to the others that we had just passed by. Soon, I discovered that I didn't like posing for a portrait very much at all. For two hours, Caitlyn and I had to sit on a box holding a pose without moving much. Sure Gregorio teased us, chided us, and did everything he could to help us sit still. It didn't help that Fianna and Fergus also teased us, but we vowed to get even, their turn was next. Four hours passed eternally slowly. We were thankful that he said that we wouldn't need to come back for a couple days for the next sitting and that the next ones would be much shorter!

On our subsequent trips to the Artist's Guild, we had become rather well known as great troubadours, and we were given a tour of the entire guild. I found there was a tremendous amount of talent among these artists. However, only a tiny fraction of their potential was being tapped. The problem was one of remuneration for their works. Currently, the best paying commissions were for the Church of Jehosanity, doing items of a religious nature, the precise final product closely dictated by the church. Rare were the commissions that paid sufficiently for the artists to make ends meet. Hence, they stifled their abilities in order to make money or they went hungry or worse. The compromise most artists had made was to do the paying, straight-jacketed pieces for the church and then on the side paint or sculpt their truly artistic creations. They appreciated my prediction that one day they would be handsomely paid for making true works of art.

Waverly's next report was even more interesting. She had spent several hours chatting with Hermino's close friend, Julio Termino. Indeed, Hermino's complete absence from their weekly fishing outings was very unusual. These two had been friends since childhood and had been fishing every Saturday for years. For Hermino suddenly not to show up twice, without even so much as a word, had Julio more than a little concerned. "Something must be terribly wrong with Hermino. Perhaps he was hit on the head while he was walking home, and his memory was altered. That can happen I'm told," he'd suggested.

She went on, "Even more interesting is that Julio ran into Hermino in the pub one night last week. Hermino completely ignored him! Wouldn't even say hello. All Hermino did was try to convince others there that they had been wrongly robbed by the raiding barbarians and that they should pressure the High Council to enlist an army, attack the barbarians in the steppes, and get their money back. From what Julio said, he certainly found many ears willing to listen and agree with him."

"I've got my work cut out for me," Waverly continued. "I am now going to go on the theory that sometime while walking home, Hermino was attacked and probably robbed. There are cases where someone takes a nasty blow to the head and loses their memory, wholly or in part. That could account for it. Andre and I are going to try to ascertain his last known movements that day and see if we can retrace his steps. Perhaps a clue will arise."

I thought that it was a plausible idea and told her that I thought she might be on the right track. Our curiosity was now sufficiently roused that we were looking forward to that High Council luncheon meeting where we could see Hermino in person. On the other hand, no one had reported seeing any kind of wound on his head. His wife did not see anything out of the ordinary about his physical appearance. Still, this was the only theory we had at the moment.

Until the day of the High Council meeting, Waverly and Andre went about their painstaking research, interviewing any likely prospects, attempting to piece together the normal movements of Hermino before he changed personalities. Meanwhile, we found ourselves working with a dozen local musicians. Word of our unique sounds and songs spread throughout the city. Naturally, many Vito musicians wanted to learn some of ours, trading some of theirs. Most of the afternoons were now filled with jam sessions, which we all enjoyed immensely.

Finally. the day of the High Council meeting arrived. All six of us musicians headed across town to the Pig's Inn. Jolina insisted on coming along, if nothing else than to aid in making our appearance at the meeting more plausible. We three couples walked arm in arm, Edgar leading Jolina. I'd noticed the sober-faced Edgar had been paying more attention to Jolina than before. They had often had long private talks. I was curious what they discussed, but thought better of outright inquiring. Although it was cold, we chatted; our spirits were high, enjoying the sights of this large city. Following Belinda's instructions to the letter, we entered a side door that led directly to the balcony, which overlooked the main dining area. Actually, the balcony was only ten feet wide and covered three sides of the large room. From the rugs on the floor to the rich tapestries and elegant tables with gold plated, to the fancy lanterns that only dimly illuminated each table, I concluded that normally the nobles and their families dined up here.

We had barely walked inside when Jolina gasped, stifling a shriek. In a blind panic she attempted to flee, nearly knocking over several tables and chairs. She broke free from Edgar and flailed her arms around panic-stricken in a wild attempt to flee. I literally moved my body into hers, grabbed on to her tightly, and pressed her in the right direction to the door. She continued to muffle her shrieking, thankfully, or everyone in the place would have been looking at us. I managed to get her safely outside, where the cold air hit her face.

"We are safely outside, Jolina. What is the matter? What's going on?" I asked as calmly as I could muster. The others followed us outside and arrived just in time to hear her terror stricken answer.

"There is one of those evil creatures in there — like the ones that flew over our heads when we were traveling to Mont Blanc! I don't want to go back inside. Take me home, please," she begged mournfully.

I was dumbfounded. We had only gotten inside, and I hadn't even had the chance to look down at the assembling council. Yet, Jolina had sensed the Evil Creature's presence long before I. Obviously, her training had indeed heightened her other senses! "Edgar, you lead Jolina back to the inn. Fergus, you take Fianna and Caitlyn. I'm going to duck back inside and see for myself."

"Aye, laddie. I want no part of that creature. I'll see they all get back safely," Fergus replied. From his tone, I could tell he was very glad I had suggested just this, though I knew that if I had asked him, he would have gone back inside with me.

"I'm going with you, Bethany," Caitlyn bravely protested. "Someone's got to watch your back." I couldn't talk her out of it, and there was no time to stand around arguing about it. As the four began walking as fast as Jolina could safely manage, she and I ducked back into the inn and crept stealthily onto the balcony, scarcely daring to breath.

She followed one step behind me. Moving very slowly, I edged my way to the railing and looked down at the assembled council. All seven had arrived and were being served their lunch by three waitresses. None was looking towards the empty balcony. From Belinda's description of the seating order, I stared at what must be Hermino Vitali. I felt the cold, evil chills down my back, trickling all the way down my legs. Even Caitlyn felt it; her legs began nervously twitching. I'd seen enough. Carefully we backed up, making very sure that our motion didn't attract the attention of the council members below us. Thank goodness for the low light level here in the balcony! As soon as we got safely outside, Caitlyn put her arms tightly around me for support; her legs nearly gave out. We stumbled along like two drunken men, heading back to the inn.

A few minutes later, we caught up with the slower moving party. "Jolina, thank you for alerting us all. You probably saved our lives back there. Thank you!" I highly validated her. I didn't want her dwelling on the fact that she fled in terror, rather I wanted her to feel that by sensing it and warning us, she had done a very good action. Her face showed me that I was right in doing so. It changed from being a grief stricken victim to one of meek pride.

"Well, now we know why Hermino has been acting so strangely," I said. "He's not Hermino, but one of the Grey Creatures disguised as Hermino. Brother, do we ever have a really *big* problem on our hands!" We walked to the inn without saying another word.

I sent Edgar to the dining room to fetch us all a stout ale. I needed a relaxant just now and figured the others did too. I summoned the three druwids into my room and told them what had just happened. Waverly spooked! "Damn, if he finds out that we're on his trail, he's going to come after us and slay us! I've brought doom to us all!"

Alton attempted a bit of bravado, "It has to get past we Protectors first, Waverly." However, once he had said it, he regretted it. She looked at him with a look that could kill. He realized that one fist swing would be the end of him. Thankfully, Edgar arrived with two pitchers of dark, stout ale, right on cue.

One beer later, I began to feel its relaxing powers seeping through my limbs. I calmed down, as did the others. Waverly finally said after a loud belch, "Okay, now what do we do? We can't just tell Belinda that she has an evil Grey Creature in her midst! No one would believe us!"

"You are right. Let's get everyone together. We need all the bright ideas we can muster," I concluded. A few minutes later, everyone crowded into my room, bringing their pitcher and mugs. For an hour, we discussed what we could do about the situation. Everyone present agreed that we could not just tell Belinda the absolute truth of the matter. It was just too wild — an alien creature disguised as a human. We just wouldn't be widely believed, though we estimated we could manage to convince Belinda. All the others, such as the other High Council members, would only think us mad, crazy, or suffering from hallucinations.

For an hour, several of us suggested all sorts of ideas, including myself. None was really workable. As time wore on, our suggestions got wilder and wilder, including putting on a public display of attacking him with lethal swords so that everyone could see that he was not harmed, forcing him to act to kill us. Yes, I said the ideas only got wilder!

Good old Jolina! She quietly said, "What happened to the real Hermino? Aren't we forgetting about him?" I stared at her; we had indeed!

"Jolina, I could kiss you!" She definitely flushed. "Yes, she is absolutely right. We have forgotten all about the real Hermino. Look, supposing we could find him. What would the Grey Creature do if suddenly the real Hermino came walking into the council meeting declaring that the creature was an imposter?"

Caitlyn cautioned, "Of course, the real Hermino might well be dead. Yet, that could work too. We bring his dead body into the council room. Everyone can see that there cannot be two Herminos."

"Yes!" I cried. "Either way, we expose the creature. Now all we have to do is find the real Hermino, alive or dead. Ideas?"

Now the ideas became far more well-grounded; we all were on much more familiar ground, so to speak. Some thought that he might well have been killed and his body dumped into the ocean. Others thought that his head might have been smashed so badly that he would not be recognized. I pointed out that his wife reported that he was wearing the same clothing when he finally returned home that he, the real Hermino, had put on the day earlier. The obvious conclusion was that the Grey Creature had taken all of his clothing and accessories. That meant that the real Hermino was probably naked, alive or dead.

Waverly commented that if anyone of us had known him, then we could have done a mind search and located him, just as I was doing for Alabaster. Unfortunately, none of us knew the man, so the easy way was totally out.

"We must make use of what Waverly has already discovered," I thought aloud. "She has determined pretty much his normal habits. Perhaps we ought to retrace his steps that night after he left work and walked home. If this had only just happened, we might be able to find signs of a struggle, where it occurred. Unfortunately, it has been almost three weeks now. Still, I think that is our best avenue to follow."

"What if the creature sees us poking, nosing around," Jolina quietly added. "It could easily kill us all."

Alton answered her, "We'll just have to do our searching when we know he is tied up elsewhere, like at a council meeting."

"Hey, laddie: how about when he's at the pubs inciting others to war?" Fergus suggested.

"Well, that means we can do it just about any night," I concluded and then realized that we were giving concerts nearly every night. I was not going to let the three of them go off on their own looking. Say, tomorrow is Sunday. No concerts. Let's do our searching after dark tomorrow," I suggested.

"Well, I'm coming," declared Caitlyn, "though I may not be any good at finding him. I can at least watch your backs." Everyone began insisting that they were coming also. I tried to explain that I dared not risk all their lives, but none bought my plea.

Even Jolina, who declared, "I'm coming too. I seem to be able to sense them sooner than the rest of you." How brave Jolina actually is, I thought to myself!

"Absolutely, Jolina! Your job is critical; alert us if the creature is anywhere nearby!" She smiled, even though I knew she was terrified inside. It's the mettle of the man, or woman in this case, who does what's needed, though terrified of doing it. I noticed that Edgar was holding her hand.

For another hour, we discussed things to bring along, methods of observation, realistically what clues might still be observable, and so on. Then, it was time to eat and get ready for the evening's dance performance. Honestly, our music was very off this night, and we played poorly, barely able to keep our attention on what we were doing.

When I finally crawled into bed and snuggled up to Caitlyn late that night, she made an astute observation, "He is probably still alive. Why? Because if this creature gets his way and gets the Vito council to go to war, he is not going to want to stick around play Hermino forever. He cannot up and just disappear. Everyone will wonder what happened to Hermino. So Hermino is likely alive somewhere. Either that, or his dead body is being preserved somewhere so that the creature can have it found, when he wants to disappear." I thought that was brilliant reasoning, and I told her so. She snuggled up tightly to me.

Sunday night just after dinner and full dark, we six and the three druwids pretended we all wanted to go for an evening stroll. Adriana, though suspicious, was not too concerned about our safety any more. We knew our way around town reasonably well, we all had improved our language skills, and we were in a better neighborhood not known for much crime. She bade us have a good walk. There was still the occasional person in the streets, so we pretended to be out on a walk and headed to Hermino's office building, which was a few blocks from the Pig's Inn.

Waverly then directed us along the most likely route that Hermino would have walked on his way home. Her conclusions were based upon the descriptions provided by six of his friends and associates. We walked the mile and a half from the office to just outside his front door, finding nothing. Undaunted, we turned around and retraced our steps, looking even harder. "Laddie, how are we supposed to see anything in the dark?" protested Fergus when we arrived back at his office once more. He was not alone with that sentiment.

"Let me think a moment," I asked. *Observe the obvious, Bethany!* I told myself, relaxed, and reflected back over our path.

"You know, there is only one block where someone could be ambushed. All the rest of the way along here, there are so many pubs and other establishments that are open at night that it would be very risky to attempt an abduction. Someone might come out of the inn or pub and accidentally see the whole thing. Only that one block. Let's have another look, okay?" For the third time, we began walking the route.

"Bethany, you are right. Look, there is an unlighted back alleyway right here in the middle of the block. Looks like two warehouses with this tiny alley between them. I wonder what's down the alley? Shall we have a look see?" suggested Waverly. We cautiously headed down the narrow passageway, only eight feet wide, just barely wide enough for a wagon to pass. Presently, we reached the end of the alley and stood upon a wooden fisherman's dock. Some thirty feet ahead was the Med Sea. This wharf was built on heavy timbers sufficiently high enough that waves could never break over the platform. Just ahead, we spied over twenty small fishing boats, either tied up or pulled entirely up onto the dock, awaiting the return of warmer weather.

I had a flash of memory just then. When I had visited Velona nearly a half century ago, our druwid contact in the city, the net maker Luigi, had shown us his secret get-away. In one room of his shop was a trap door in the floor. A wooden ladder led down to the actual shore below his shop. I remembered the awful stench and utter filth that was down there, when he showed us where he kept his small boat that he could use to make his getaway, rowing on up the coast a ways.

"Gang, I think I have an idea," I pronounced. "Look around for a trap door in the deck floor. There ought to be a way to get down to the actual shore below us. It is probably awfully stinky and filthy down there. What better place to hide something that you do not want found? No one in their right mind would go down there unless it was a dire emergency of some kind."

Everyone scattered and began looking diligently for a way down below. In daylight, our task would have been much easier. Even a full moon would have greatly aided us. However, tonight the sky was overcast, and snow was on the way again. Still, we searched. I was just about to suggest that we give it up and try it in the daytime, when Alton whispered, "Wid Bethany has done it again! There is a trap door here." He pulled it open, revealing a dark, three-foot square opening into utter blackness.

"We should have brought some lanterns," said Fergus completely disgusted to have gotten this far only to have to quit because we could not see a thing.

"What an awful smell!" exclaimed Jolina, holding her nose. The pungent odor of rotting fish assaulted our nostrils.

Instantly, four blue lights appeared in Alton's, Andre's, Waverly's and my hands. Together, we positioned them over the black hole. The others made various comments, and Edgar explained what was going on to Jolina.

Jolina then shocked us all, "So that is what I am seeing. I can see their blue lights, very strange! Rather pretty aren't they?" I gasped; she could see our conjured lights! Later on, we would have to explore this with Jolina!

Fergus protested, "We are going to stink something horrible, laddie, if we go down there!"

"Only the four of us will go down; we have the only lights. Jolina, you are the rear alerter. Let us know the instant you sense anything, all right? The rest of you, guard our rear. Besides, if we find anything, we're going to need lots of help getting him up this ladder. It looks like it's about twenty-five feet to the ground."

"What if someone else comes along?" asked Edgar.

"You couples kiss and pretend you have stolen away to a quiet place to make out," I said without thinking.

"Who am I going to be kissing?" inquired Caitlyn.

I barked, "Oh, Fergus, pretend you are entertaining two women!" Caitlyn giggled. We four began our descent, Alton leading the way. I went last. Fortunately, the ladder was still quite solid. Still, it was quite a drop, should one lose their grip. Once on the ground, we did a quick survey. We were still a ways from the actual water, though at high tide, we could see that the water would be up to where the ladder was. Refuse covered the entire sandy beach, rotting heads of fish predominated, the fishermen's refuse pile, I presumed. We moved further inland, carefully searching for anything out of the ordinary.

The shore gradually rose higher and higher as we moved away from the sea, until at last only a narrow space lay between the beach and the bottom of the deck above our heads. There just wasn't much down here, except several rotting remains of long discarded fishing boats. This was indeed just a garbage dump.

"This is futile," commented Andre, "there is nothing down here."

As if to dissuade him, Alton began turning the rotting hulks over. Waverly joined in to help. Andre just watched them. Suddenly, Waverly commented, "Hey, this one is heavy. I can't seem to overturn it." Quickly, Alton joined her and together they rolled the remains of the fisherman's boat over. A body wrapped in many blankets rolled out of the boat!

All brought blue lights to bear at once. No doubt about it, we had found Hermino. He was naked, tied up so securely that he could not move, and gagged twice. He was unconscious, but his body temperature was dangerously low. I spied signs of dehydration along with starvation. His blankets were soaked with excrements long dried. But he was alive!

273

I relayed the news to the others, who could not help by let out muffled cheers, and all crowded around the trap door, trying to see. Carefully, Alton and Andre lifted up the unconscious man and carried him to the ladder. Meanwhile, Waverly concentrated and made a mental connection to Adriana.

The men were discussing how to get him up the ladder, while Waverly finally said to me, "I've let Adriana know. She is sending a number of Sisters to help us at once and will have the hot bath ready by the time we get him back to the inn."

"Good thinking," I complimented her as we watched helplessly, while the two men struggled to get the man up the ladder. It took them nearly twenty precarious minutes to lift him up to a point where Fergus and Edgar could reach him and pull him the rest of the way up. Once the four of us were up, we shut the trap door. Just then, we spied a dozen Sisters running down the alley towards us.

They had brought even more blankets. After wrapping him further, we turned the last one into a lift. With six of us holding on to the edge of the blanket, we could easily carry him. Off we went, moving as rapidly as possible. The Sisters had their swords drawn and led the way back to the inn.

Twenty minutes later, we slipped into the back door of the hot bath. All the way back, I had been thinking this thing through. We must not have our actions known to anyone beyond the Sisterhood. If the fact that we had found him and uncovered the Grey Creature's intervention, then our lives would certainly be forfeited, for it would hunt us down as we traveled. This was not mere speculation on my part. Given that they had already hunted me down and killed my body last lifetime, it was a certainty they would do it again. There was too much at stake for everyone. As we entered the bath room, I said, "Okay gang, here is the situation. No one, absolutely no one outside the Sisterhood, must know of our part in this. From now on, only Sisters may be seen with him. The Sisters will have to claim that they discovered his body and rescued him. Of course, we are going to have to work our healing magic on him, but use conjuring so everyone, including Hermino, sees just another Sister in here."

"But you have worked a miracle," Adriana protested.

"If the evil creature discovers that Guardians were involved, we are as good as dead!" I replied sparing no politeness. "Look, sometime later on when this all blows over, then you may give us credit. Just not now." She felt better about it, but I knew her intrinsic sense of honor dictated that she not take credit for something she had not done. My pronouncement had given her a way to retain her honor.

"Ah, I see, just like the Simon-Simone thing! Right. I follow you. I have already sent for Belinda. Is he really alive? Will he recover?" she asked.

While I was explaining the situation, the other three druwids had begun to examine our patient. Seven blankets were undone, revealing a tightly bound, naked body. They set to work cutting him lose from the ropes and removing the dual gags. His tongue had swollen enormously; dehydration was severe, though it was apparent that the creature had forced some liquids down his throat several times, because dried remains outlined the blanket that had covered his face. Gently, Waverly slid his cold body into the warming waters. The four of us quickly washed off the stench, stripped, and entered the water as well. Carefully, each of us thoroughly examined Hermino and then compared our findings. Frostbite had begun to take hold of his fingers and toes, but three of us suggested the appendages might survive, but would have to be monitored often. Waverly insisted that we begin to get warm fluids in him as soon as he was conscious enough to swallow. Adriana left to get the chef to make a gallon of chicken soup for him.

We were all rubbing the circulation back into his limbs, when Belinda, pale from the shock of the news, came running into the bath, quite out of breath. She'd run here all the way. Aghast, she stared at Hermino's unconscious form, not grasping what had happened. While I continued rubbing his arm, I began the lengthy explanation, ending with, "So you see, the creature that is pretending to be Hermino is an enemy of the Sea Princes. Very clever plot — kidnap one from the High Council, disguise yourself as him, and set about your goal of getting the city-state to take those actions which would ultimately destroy it."

"Good god!" she exclaimed, as the complete picture of the last three weeks finally made perfect, if not terrible, sense to her. "Will he live?"

"Too soon to tell," Waverly answered.

"I've got to let everyone know at once!" declared Belinda. "If he should die," she did not finish her sentence; her voice fell silent.

"I know, Belinda," a sudden thought struck me. "Why don't you call for an emergency meeting of the High Council tomorrow morning? Tell them that the emergency meeting will be held here at this inn, and that immediately afterwards, the West Reach Minstrels will play a special concert for the High Council. When they are all here, bring them into this bath and let them see Hermino for themselves. That ought to shock them sufficiently to immediately see the truth of the situation, whether he lives or not."

"Won't that be placing everyone on the council and those here in grave danger? Might this imposter try to take revenge on us all?" she asked very concerned about the consequences.

"I don't think so. If the imposter killed off the High Council, he would lose the connections and knowledge of the personnel currently running the city-state. I suspect he will be very angry, but I don't think he would try to wipe everyone out, because it's not in his best interests, whatever they may be. Nevertheless, it would perhaps be prudent to have a large number of

Sisters in the immediate vicinity, a measure of security, you know."

Belinda agreed and rushed off to work out the preparations, sending messengers to notify all the council members. Adriana did the same, rounding up all available fighters for the morning meeting. Carmina and Ellen also dropped in to see Hermino for themselves and to thank us repeatedly. We also filled them in on the plans for the next day. "Such vile treachery!" declared the leader of the Sisterhood. Carmina added, "We should arrest this imposter; try him for high treason."

"As much as he may deserve it, I believe it would be wise to see how he reacts and act accordingly. No sense in getting a lot of Sisters killed just to apprehend this vile creature," I suggested. "Who knows how powerful this one may be. He may even use poisoned blades or worse." I attempted to give her some justification for not ordering her Sisters to attempt to apprehend the creature. His fists alone would slay anyone of us instantly with just one hit. I had visions of the bath being littered with the bodies of hundreds of Sisters.

"Vastly more importantly, you must send word of this whole situation to the other cities so that they can be alert for a similar plot against their High Councils. You may well be helping to expose others in the other cities. That is far more critical than apprehending this single culprit." She bought my line of reasoning and headed off to her room to prepare seven duplicate messages to be sent to all the other cities.

For two hours we worked on Hermino, getting his circulation going, warming his body slowly back to normal. Eventually, he regained a groggy consciousness. At once, Waverly began spoon-feeding him the warm chicken soup, primarily broth at the start. Once his tongue began to return toward normal, she added small bits of the meat as well. Literally, she sat up all night with him; only toward morning did she finally get some sleep. With the help of the Sisters who continuously hovered around ready to help in any way, he was carried to a room close to the bath. Several volunteered to sit and watch him sleep.

At breakfast, Belinda arrived with a bundle of clothes she had picked up from his wife, who had insisted on coming with her. The poor woman was nearly beside herself with grief and worry and just barely had come to terms with what had happened. Only when she was allowed to peek in on her sleeping husband did the magnitude of the situation finally sink home in her mind. She'd been taking care of an imposter these last three weeks, worrying and fretting over a total stranger! She thanked Jehosa that she had not actually gone to bed with this total stranger masquerading as her husband!

Next, Waverly examined him again, once she wiped the weariness from her eyes; she only had two hours sleep. His body temperature had dropped again slightly. Several Sisters once more carried him back into the hot bath, once it had been reheated. Besides, Belinda was planning to bring the High Council here to the bath to see him. While his wife and Waverly hovered over him, the room became a flurry of action. Fifty Sisters filed into the room, taking guard positions along all the walls, swords at the ready. Outside the rear door, another fifty took up similar positions. Ellen inspected her troops and made minor adjustments.

Once more, I reiterated to Ellen that the Sisters were not to attempt to attack the imposter unless he attacked them first. I found that getting this across to the warriors was exceedingly difficult. Every one of them fully intended to capture this imposter, despite orders to the contrary. Although it took some doing on my part, I finally felt that I had their agreement to wait and see what the imposter did before committing themselves to a battle that I knew they could not win.

Slowly time dragged on, every spoonful of soup that his wife got down him seemed like a major step forward, as we all waited for the arrival of the council. Finally, a Sister relayed a signal that the group was nearing the main entrance of the inn. We four Guardians, made doubly sure that our conjured spells made us appear as just another Sister. We pressed as far back as we could, trying to stay out of the confrontation. This had to seem to be between the Sisters and the High Council. Jolina and the others were in the large dining hall, setting up our instruments. I doubted very much if the concert would be held, under the circumstances. Nevertheless, if the council still wanted us to play for their lunch, we would.

The advance signaling of the Sisterhood reminded me very much of the Guardians. Everyone in the bath knew when the group had entered the inn, when they made the turn down the right wing, and even when Belinda opened the door to the bath. She said, "The vital situation that has forced me to call this special session is just inside the bath. Please follow me." In walked six other men behind her, single file, with the Hermino imposter last in line.

"My god! What is this? What is the meaning of this?" called out the first council member to see Hermino in the warm waters, his wife still tending him. One by one, the men gasped, totally startled, and shocked to see a duplicate Hermino in the waters. They all turned to stare at the imposter, as if he had some explanation. From the bath, Luzi Vitali said, "This is the real Hermino Vitali! That man is an imposter!"

Now a normal human suddenly and unexpectedly having his cover blown would have several possible physical reactions, one of which would be some facial reactions, perhaps a flushing of cheeks. I watched his face and body intensely, looking for telltale signs. I saw none! He merely looked at the man in the water, looked at the men staring at him, their mouths gaping, and let out an inhuman roar. Well, it sounded like a roar that a bull might make.

In a flash, the imposter shoved his way forward, knocking all the High council members, including Belinda, into the water. He swept past the line of Sisterhood fighters, who didn't even have time to react to his incredibly swift movement! He smashed his fist into the wall near the back door. Debris flew wildly about the new hole in the wall; I'd say the creature was indeed angry, assuming they could feel human-like emotions. He didn't bother to open the door. Barreling his whole body into it, the door wrenched from its hinges as he forced his way outside, where another bunch of Sisters were waiting.

These too had no time to react; he shoved his way through them, knocking several aside as if they were pieces of paper. We heard another loud grunting noise while he paused fleetingly, as if deciding where to go next. He then streaked down the street, knocking over a random person here and there. None of the Sisters outside could believe a person could run as fast as this imposter did. Several Sisters had to be helped back onto their feet.

Chaos reigned for the next few minutes; the flabbergasted council members were helped out of the bath; questions flew left and right with abandon, though answers remained few. Some called for the Sisters to hunt this traitor down and behead him. Others thought this was far too dangerous, given the speed and ferocity that they had just seen. A few asked why the imposter was even doing the impersonation, suggesting he had been after the Vitali fortune.

Belinda finally restored some order, "May I suggest we dry off the council members and meet in the designated room. I believe that I can answer some of these pressing questions. Meanwhile, will some of you see to the needed repairs to that wall and door?"

Carmina and Ellen issued orders for just that. Additionally, Ellen took the initiative, "I will send out a hundred scouts to make sure the imposter has actually fled Vito."

However, I suspected the Grey Creature was likely well on his way back to its secret fortress high in the Appian Way, hopefully, with the diabolical scheme completely foiled! Of course, I had no way to know if this was indeed the case.

A half hour later, the dried-off men, wearing some spare clothing that the innkeeper scrounged up — none of which was to their liking — assembled in the meeting room. Hot tea and biscuits awaited them. Lunch was slightly delayed. Belinda began her lengthy explanation, beginning with the startling personality change that caught the attention of the Sisters in the first place. She briefly described the gathering of information that Waverly had done, assigning it authorship to another unnamed Sister. Next, she described our search for Hermino and how it was that his hidden body was discovered, once more alleging a team of Sisters had done it.

"Given the circumstances, I would like to make a motion that every item that has been passed by the High Council during the last three weeks be voided and a new vote on each taken, perhaps including Hermino, if he survives. Perhaps the Vitali House will assign someone to take his place at least temporarily," Belinda proposed. It was immediately seconded and passed unanimously.

"Next, I would move that we write up fully what has happened here, paying particular attention on how we detected this imposter, and route this to all of the other High Councils in the Sea Princes. Who knows if there is not an imposter in Zargarb even as we speak," Belinda stated. Once more, it was instantly seconded and passed unanimously. At this point, the meeting was interrupted by four women serving the fancy lunch.

When the meeting adjourned an hour later, the Sisterhood received a glowing public proclamation for meritorious and distinguished service for Vito. The proclamation was posted at fifty prominent locations around the city. Belinda also claimed that this proclamation was also politically motivated, because the High Council was letting the citizens of Vito know that a diabolical plot to ruin the city had been foiled by the High Council, since Belinda was a member. Still, I thought this was yet another indication that women in the Sea Princes were gaining the respect they deserved. Yes, we did not play for the High Council; they all wanted to head home to change clothing; none were in any mood for music.

While the council met, we guardians also met, trying to answer the major question: should we tell the Sisters here about the Grey Creatures? Certainly, the d'Grange Sisters knew about them; they had experienced their presence flying overhead at least. Here, however, the Sisters would not have direct observation to rely upon, save only the inhuman exit the imposter had made. In the end, we decided that the three ought to be fully informed and let them determine what, if anything, should become common knowledge. Once the council meeting adjourned and we found out that we did not have to play for them, we Guardians met with the three leaders. Yes, it was a somber meeting, filled with what seemed far out ideas to these women. Whether or not they believed us, I really could not tell.

After all, suppose someone began telling you about strange alien creatures that lived in the tall mountains at the edge of your country. Would you believe such without direct observation? I left them with a parting bit of wisdom. "Look, observe, that is the key. I certainly do not expect you to believe what we have been saying. Instead, keep your eyes open. Observe. One day, you may see something that will convince you one way or the other. You may also send messengers to Fortress d'Grange, because they have already experienced these creatures."

Belinda's final comment was, "I shall push the High Council to get the remainder of the outer walls completed this spring. Perhaps the barrier wall will help keep them at bay." Since we knew that they often flew overhead, I knew that this was a futile method to keep these evil creatures out of Vito. People often clutch at straws, however.

At our next dance concert, we met yet another interesting pair of musicians, Arturo Coglicelli and his wife, Donatella. As the packed house began slowly departing and we were packing up our instruments, these two came up to the gallery. "Well done indeed! Your fame is not unfounded," exclaimed Arturo. Both he and his wife had long, thick, slightly oily black hair, and piercing coals for eyes. His neatly trimmed goatee and wide mustache contrasted with his olive-colored skin. Donatella wore her hair long down to the middle of her back and wore a heavily pleated, colorful dress with black dancing shoes. He introduced his wife and himself.

"This is my wife, the Dancing Master, Donatella. I am Arturo Coglicelli, Fiddle Master. Together, we are the famous duo Exotica. Perhaps you have heard of us?" Unfortunately, we had not.

"Honestly, no we haven't," I said. "We're rather new here." I introduced the others of our group. However, we were actually staring at them, for they didn't look at all like the usual Sea Prince residents that we were accustomed to seeing. Of course, they were staring at us likewise. Okay, it was a rather awkward moment, which I defused. Smiling, I asked, "I can't help noticing that your skin and hair are not blonde like the others here in Vito."

Both laughed, and Arturo commented, "Aye, and such red hair, so utterly long. If it weren't for your clothes, we would easily mistake you for your sister. But yes, we are part of the tiny minority in this sector, the Alain. Our ancestors came here aboard Sea Prince ships long ago from the Southlands. Most of us live in the outlying towns, not here in the large city. We prefer more open spaces, if you grasp my meaning. So cloistered here in Vito."

"Yes, we know what you mean. We are from Tewdwr, West Reach. Our village has perhaps a hundred of us, so a place like Vito is overwhelming. Glad you liked our music."

Donatella smiled and said, "Yes, indeed. We've never heard much of what you played and found it intriguing. I dearly loved your crossed swords dance, Fianna. Impressive!" My sister beamed proudly. She added, "We couldn't help but notice, Fianna, that you are using some castanets. Our people brought them here to Vito long ago. However, I can tell that you really don't know how they originally were intended to be used. Yet, your use is indeed novel and added greatly to the show. Good improvisation, that's for sure. Also, we could tell that you must have encountered the gypsies. You are playing some songs in their style. They, of course, got it from us."

Fianna asked, "We only recently got them, but there was no one to show me how they are supposed to be used. I just fiddle with them as best I can. Glad it works. Do you know how they are supposed to be used?"

The huge grin on Donatella's face was more than a sufficient answer. "Got time for a jam session?" she asked, nodding at Arturo.

"You bet!" We all exclaimed.

"I always carry my fiddle around with me. Give me a few minutes to get ready," he explained and began undoing his carrying case.

Donatella said awkwardly, "I don't want to seem like a busy-body, but doesn't Jolina see very well? I'm sorry, but we were both more than a little curious about her."

Laughing, Jolina commented, "Nope, I can't see a thing." She added curiously, "that you all can see." I knew this was a reference to our magical blue lights. Again, my curiosity rose, but once more, now was not the time to question her about it.

To my surprise, Edgar jumped in at once, "I look after her. I am her eyes. Jolina is the greatest musician in the d'Grange Sector!" I also noted there was a bit of life, of excitement, in his voice, a spark I hadn't seen before in his melancholic outlook. His was a subtle change, but a change, nevertheless. Further, was that a smile I detected, though fleeting, on her face?

"Incredible! Your keen sense of mood is just fabulous, Jolina. My sincere compliments," she replied.

"Ah, here we go, just got to tune it slightly," Arturo broke in on the conversation. "What shall we play for them, my love? Your call."

"I want to see your dancing and the proper use of the castanets," put in Fianna earnestly.

Donatella replied with a smile, "The Alain Wedding Jig, it is. I need the exercise," she added, though I did not know what she meant. We all found out at once.

Arturo began playing a slow, solemn strain on the low string. Donatella slowly paced graceful, exaggerated steps onto the dance floor. Almost asynchronously, the sharp clapping sounds from the castanets echoed in the nearly empty dance hall. She was not hitting the beat uniformly, and the effect was engrossing, totally ear catching! Then, almost without warning, he slid onto the middle strings and the pace became hectic. She danced and twirled, adding her percussion sounds that were now in synch with his rhythm. I could now see why she wore a dress with so many pleats. As she twirled around, her dress expanded, flaring outward revealing her muscular, shapely legs. Yes, the music and dance was spectacular to say the very least!

Poor Jolina! It was the first time I had seen her crying. Edgar did his best to try to describe Donatella's intriguing dance to her. I could see that she desperately wanted to see but could not. Inspiration struck. I conjured my blue light and placed it near the dancing woman. Because the dance hall was still illuminated by all the oil lanterns, my small addition of blue was not particularly noticeable. Suddenly, Jolina exclaimed, "I can see her! Edgar, I can see!"

Fianna just had to join Donatella on the dance floor, trying to mimic her moves. Even Caitlyn got into the spirit of the dance and joined Fianna. To my utter surprise, Jolina had Edgar help her onto the floor as well, and soon she too was mimicking the fleet-footed moves of Donatella. Fortunately, only Arturo noticed Jolina; his wife was too caught up in her dance to take full notice of the blind Jolina copying her motions. Only when the dance finally wound down did she grasp the significance of Jolina's actions. As they ended, we cheered, "Bravo! Indeed!"

Out of breath, Donatella gasped, "I thought she was blind?"

"Somehow I can see the blue light of Bethany's," she replied. "You are the best dancer that I have ever seen or heard about, Donatella!" commented a beaming Jolina, with Edgar taking her arm. He too was smiling, a first for him.

"Bethany," exclaimed Fianna, "we just *have* to learn how to do this dance! Please!" She looked at me with begging eyes and then at Arturo and Donatella. "Please!" she pleaded with the three of us.

Laughing, Arturo replied, "Ah, we thought you just might! Only if you can teach us that crossed swords dance."

"Aye, laddie, no problem. We can teach you that highlander's dance in no time at all," Fergus broke in; it was his homeland's dance, after all. "But it really needs the bag pipes to sound proper."

"Well, I have got a fiddle from the gypsies, but I still don't have it learned at all well," I added. I can see that I have an awfully long way to go to even get the basics of that instrument learned," I added.

"Say, can I see the fiddle? I'm a good judge of their quality," Arturo volunteered helpfully.

Since it was back in my room, we finished our packing and headed back to our rooms, our two new friends in tow. I got out the fiddle and gave it to Arturo. I watched him carefully as he inspected it closely first and then played on it. "Mediocre," was his final pronouncement. "Say, on Monday, I'll take you around to Fidelio Giovanni. He is the very best fiddle maker in all the Sea Princes for my money. I think once you play a bit on one of his you will feel and hear quite a difference. The fiddle is a difficult instrument to master and nearly impossible on one such as you have here. Yes, you can play acceptable gypsy music on this one, but you will see what I mean."

"Thanks!" I replied.

"Say," broke in Donatella, "we are giving a show every night for the next three weeks. I know you're heavily booked, but you're welcome to come and hear us. Perhaps during the daytime hours we can get together and swap songs and dances. Once this three-week gig is up, we'll begin our yearly springtime tour of the outer towns and villages. We take our wagon and travel all over this sector during the spring and early summer. Then again we do it all over in the late fall and winter. Honestly, now is probably the best time for us to spend time together."

I looked at the others who were grinning and had my answer. "You're on. While we were planning to leave around the first week of the month, since it is still rather cold, we can stay a few weeks longer before we hit the road as well." We all chatted for another hour before our two new friends left for their inn.

Monday morning, Arturo and I entered the quaint shop: Fiddles Only, Proprietor and Maker: Fidelio Giovanni. We were the only customers in the small storefront, perhaps twelve feet square. His workshop in the rear adjoined his tiny storefront. Odors of resin, polish, and wood permeated the room. Tapestries hung at various locations on the walls, which Arturo said adjusted the acoustics properly. Lining one side was a display case filled with five gorgeous looking fiddles and twenty bows. Middle aged, Fidelio had the typical Sea Prince look, blonde hair with blue eyes. He had long fingers and wore an apron covered with wood dust, resins, and polish.

From the first moment I saw him, I could tell I was in the presence of a master craftsman, a maker of very fine instruments. The pride in his work and his enthusiasm for the fiddle showed in his every pronouncement. Quiet and soft-spoken, this man knew how to make quality instruments whose sounds were unparalleled. Arturo had me try all five; admittedly, my skill was poor, yet I could both feel and hear the difference between one of these and my own fiddle. Then, as if on cue, Arturo played one of them. I think the two men often did this when a potential customer was in the shop, a master musician demonstrating the master instrument. When I left the shop, I was less one month's inn wages, but the proud possessor of a Giovanni fiddle!

When we finally packed up our wagons and rolled out of Vito heading northward, the light snows had all but melted. It was the last week of February. During this time, I had not sensed the presence of Alabaster anywhere around here. Further, because of our long delay in Vito, I had expanded my search pattern northward, staying clear of the mountains of the Appian Way where the Grey Creatures dwelled. Hence, as we headed north, our plans were abbreviated to traveling only up to the second crossroad before heading further eastward. Of course, these crossroads were like the rims of a wagon wheel, it would eventually curve us back to the Med Sea and the Centurion built paved roadway that headed on into the Bonilla Sector.

Chapter 19 Moving Right Along

We halted for the night some twenty miles north and west of Vito, camping just off the road in valley close to a large vineyard and olive grove. Spring was still a ways off and the night was chilly. Slowly, we got back into the groove of camping out. Sister Camilla, the chef, began her preparations for the evening meal, while the rest of us handled the horses and collected what firewood we could find, which was not much. Lanterns were lit and several charcoal cooking fires were started. Groups gathered around a small bonfire to warm their hands.

With nothing much to do, I gazed at our small troupe. Alton had been acting reserved all day long, but I had not asked why. I sensed that something was wrong, well, not wrong exactly, just not quite right. Then, it hit me! We were too many. Quickly, I counted our number. Yes, we definitely had one extra person with us!

Alton noticed me counting, so I guess my action was rather obvious. "Er, I'm sorry Wid Bethany. I should have consulted you first."

"We are one too many," I replied certain of my count.

"Yes, you are right," he blushed and seemed ill at ease. "I guess I ought to have known that you can't put anything by a Wid. I've allowed her to come along with us."

"Allowed who?" I replied, growing exasperated with his stalling. "Out with it!"

"Elona Po. I've got her over there with that group of Sisters, trying to be as inconspicuous as possible."

"What?" I replied, neither angry nor upset with him, just significantly curious. Why wouldn't he have just asked me?

His face flushed, "She does have a debt of honor to repay us from her point of view. Without our help, she would still be stranded in Velona or dead from the cavalry. She deserves a chance to help us somehow." I put on one of my stone faces that said I did not believe this was all of it, but yes, I could see that argument.

He mumbled something and added, "She is a half-trained druwid. We owe it to her to see to the finishing of her training, as much as possible. After all, it was Luigi's decision to train her. What would happen if she goes rogue on us and we had neglected the chance to train her otherwise? It would be our responsibility, now wouldn't it? I have decided to take her on as my apprentice, that is, until she makes her choice on which advanced path to follow." My stone face did not waver. True, we really should at least find out what she did and did not know and judge what ought to be done next.

His face really reddened and I knew I had him. "Okay, so I have fallen in love with her. Now are you satisfied? It's taken me a very long time to get over the loss of my wife and child."

"Thanks for telling me, Alton. You are right in allowing her to come with us for all three lines of reasoning. You should have cleared it with me before hand, that's all. However, I can see your methodology. If I refused, it's hard to send her back after we've already traveled this far." He gave me a silly look, and I knew I really hit the mark this time. "Okay, you ought to formally introduce her to the other Guardians as your apprentice. Have you considered where she is to stay?"

"Right, I will do so as soon as I let her know it is okay. She can share my wagon, if you all don't mind," he smiled happily, greatly relieved that I had not taken him to task for this breech of etiquette. While he went to relay the news to Elona, I gathered Andre and Waverly for the special introduction. However, before Alton returned with Elona, I clued them in on what was about to happen. From their reactions, I suspected all three had been involved in this deed, though I didn't press them as I had done Alton.

When they joined us, Elona had a big smile on her face and stood at attention, as if this were a military organization. Alton said formally, "Fellow Guardians, let it be known from this day forward that I have taken Elona Po as my apprentice druwid, and I will be responsible for her training until she chooses her area of specialty." That is all that needed to be said, short and simple, yet more binding than one could imagine. Our word was our honor and law. It also gained Elona the complete respect from all druwids everywhere, as befitting any other apprentice druwid.

"Elona, welcome to our group. Your situation is most unusual. Let me explain. Normally, when we accept an apprentice, that person then begins a ten year period of intense study. Assuming the person passes all the tests along the way, then they are initiated as a full druwid Guardian and assigned to a Circle of Seven, their very own Circle. However, in your case, Luigi left us no clues about what he has taught you and what you have mastered. It would be a great sin on our part not to cover fully all that must be learned. So what we'll be doing is teaching you as if you are a raw recruit. However, at each stage, we'll consult with you first; if you believe you already have that skill or knowledge, we can just give you the passing test. If you pass, then we'll skip that portion and move on to the next. I should think that within a week or so, we ought to be able to have a good grasp of what you do know already and what you don't."

Elona relaxed completely; her fears and anxieties melted. "Oh thank you! I was worried about this training. Luigi taught me quite a lot, but until now, I had no idea if I had really learned enough. I know I just couldn't do some of the things he asked me to attempt."

I smiled, relieved that she was taking this so well. I added, "Usually, in the later years of training, once the basics every druwid knows has been mastered, the apprentice is then asked to specialize in one of seven areas or skills. The Protector is a master at fighting; the Healer, in the healing arts;

the Communicator is able to use their mind to communicate across vast distances using telepathy; the Planner is a designer of buildings and such as well as a good mathematician; the Loremaster knows about plants and animals and nature; the Judger is a highly skilled arbitrator amongst men and also a conjurer; finally, the Wid is forever learning, in search of knowledge, truth, and wisdom. Very few ever attempt to become a Wid."

"Great! Luigi explained these positions to me accurately then," she said, confident that she was beginning on the right track.

"We are not a full Circle of Seven," I continued. "We are on a special mission and have two Protectors: Andre and Alton. Waverly is a Communicator. I am a Wid. Unfortunately, we do not yet have access to a Judger, Healer, Loremaster, or a Planner. Those weren't needed on this mission. However, don't let this concern you. If you eventually choose one of those paths, arrangements will be made, so don't worry about that."

"How soon do I have to decide?" she asked, slightly concerned that such a decision was eminent.

I chuckled, "Not for some time. We must get you fully trained up to the point where you need to make that choice. You can have all the time you need when the time comes, so please don't worry at all about it. It's not something that one rushes into. I see that the others are beginning to turn in for the night. I'll be brief. We're on a secret mission to find someone who is badly in need of our help. You do not know him, and we don't know what body he may be occupying now or even where on Tarra he is located. Hence, we are being a band of traveling musicians, which justifies our traveling nearly everywhere in search of him. I will know when I find him, on that you can count. Until we know what it is you already know, it would make no sense to go into more details, because you might not have the slightest idea what I was talking about. I'll say more at the appropriate time. Fair enough?" She agreed and we all returned to our wagons for some needed sleep.

When I snuggled up with Caitlyn, she asked timidly, "Should I volunteer to become your apprentice, Bethany?" She'd evidently kept her eyes and ears open, perhaps a bit too much.

"Nah, I'm more than happy with you just as you are, Caitlyn, my love. Guardian Luigi had already begun Elona's training many years ago before he died and left the task unfinished. She's like a wild card, and we don't know what she knows and doesn't know. We really are obligated to make an attempt to finish what Luigi started," I explained.

"Good, I don't think I want to spend ten years studying from dawn til dusk, but I would, if that's what it would take for me to be with you," she added.

"To be with me, you just have to be yourself, Caitlyn. I'm in love with you as you are." I gave her a hug and a loving kiss as we settled down for the night.

286

The next day, I chose to ride my horse for a while and chatted with Adriana and Felice. Adriana commented, "One thing I learned from our stay here in Vito is that the banditry problem has nearly vanished from this sector. That's something I thought I would never live to see, mind you. It's all due to the influence of the Church of Jehosanity here in Vito. I think the key was the ability of the Deacons to find work for every able-bodied person. This turn of events will make our passage through the sector much simpler indeed, almost boring."

I chuckled, "Nothing about this trip has been boring yet!" She and Felice laughed along with me. Yes, it felt good to have a horse underneath me once more, if only I could canter away for a while. As far as my search for Alabaster was going, with all the time we spent in Vito, I had thoroughly searched all three sectors we'd passed through three times now. I was utterly convinced that he was not in the Velona, Barcella, or Vito sectors, only four more to search.

The days passed slowly, however, and we did play at two additional inns along the way. Finally, the rim road we were traveling met its opposite member in the Bonilla Sector. Now instead of traveling south by east, we were traveling north by east, following the arcing road round fifty miles from the city of Bonilla. The plan was to follow the rim road until we reached the spoke road directly north of the city and then head due south to the city. Once the city had been searched, we would retrace our route one spoke further east and rejoin this rim road until it connected with its counterpart in the next sector. This way, I ought to easily be able to search all the sector for Alabaster with the minimum of wasted time.

After the first week of intensive training and testing, we four had a good feel for Elona Po and the difficulties faced by Luigi. The crux of the matter lay in her undying, complete belief and faith in her God Tur. She accepted without question any datum that was anyway related to religion, biased in favor of Tur. The result: a kind of blindness in which a person cannot observe the obvious. Instead, they see what they want to see or imagine or wish or hope to see. Luigi never managed to break through this sightless barrier with Elona Po. If we could not, she was doomed to failure as a druwid and would never be able to progress much farther that she already was. The result: she ought to be at that stage in which she chooses a specialty or concentration of study. However, she had far too many holes in her education, holes in which her blind faith hid the real truth from herself.

Hence, for a week, we allowed her to discuss and ask questions that would enable her to make her choice for a specialty, while we four attempted to come up with a remedy — some way to break through her fixed ideas centered or based upon religion. I knew better than to discuss religion with her. Then, I hit upon the crux of the matter. In order for anyone to learn about anything new, they first must discover that there is something there to be learned and that they don't already know it. With Elona, her fixed, preconceived ideas led her to believe that there was nothing there to learn or if there was, she already knew all she needed to know by simply believing in her God Tur, that it was his divine will or wish for the outcome to be as it occurred. This we had to crack.

Our first opportunity came rather unexpectedly at the second village we came to in the Bonilla Sector. We had set up camp at the edge of the village because they didn't have an inn capable of holding our large party. It was late afternoon when a frantic young man came up to us asking to speak to our leader. When he was brought before me, nearly in tears, he begged, "Please, it's my wife. She is giving birth to our third child and something has gone horribly wrong! The midwives have sent me to ask if any among you have any skill with childbirth. If any of you do, I beg you please try to save my wife and child, please, I beg you!"

What a fortuitous event, I thought. "You are in luck. We have four among us who have a good deal of knowledge and skill in healing. I am Ket Bethany."

"Oh thank you, thank you! I'm Georgio and my wife is called Lenia. Please, come quickly," relief gushed from his entire body. Quickly, I sent for the others and Elona, while I grabbed my healing pouches. Within two minutes, Alton, Andre, Waverly, Elona, and I hurried after the frantic Georgio.

"She's been in labor for over a day! The pain is horrible. She used to scream, but now she is so quiet," he explained as we fast walked after him. Shortly, we entered his small grey stone home in the village. We entered the front room and the odors of various herbs assailed our nostrils. The midwives were doing all they could for the poor woman. Both came out of the bedroom when they heard us entering. "Marianna and Bethilna," Georgio introduced the two middle aged women.

"She's this way," Marianna gestured and we crammed into their bedroom. "The baby is backwards and cannot get out. We've tried everything we can think of, but nothing has worked." I glanced around the room and could not help noticing a small altar to Tur. These people still worshiped Tur. Perfect, I thought to myself. Rapidly, we four examined the young woman and verified the diagnosis was indeed the correct one. It was.

"Elona, these people worship your God Tur. Here, take a look at this woman's situation and then we will compare notes." She took this as yet another observe the obvious test, which she rapidly did. Once she had finished and agreed as well with the midwives, I then asked, "Okay, Elona, what would you do here?"

"Oh that's easy. We pray to Tur. If Tur deems us worthy, the baby and mother will be fine," she replied almost on automatic, as if some mental circuit was talking to us.

I saw both midwives gasp and knew that I had Elona right where I wanted her. Turning to Marianna, I asked, "What would you say to Elona's suggestion?"

"She has not got a bat's brain! If we do nothing, both Lenia and the child will die. That is as certain as the grapes will ripen this year!" Wham, that frank and honest reply hit Elona smack in her face, which became red as a beet. I wished we had brought a healer with us, but I would just have to make do with the four of us.

"Marianna, I agree with you completely. We must get the baby reversed if possible. Elona, observe!" I gave her that order with total intention; she couldn't help but observe. "Boiling water?" I asked. Georgio soon came back with a steaming pot. While he was fetching it, I conferred with my druwid companions. Between us, I had the most experience with childbirth, so I elected myself as the one to make the attempt, guided by the suggestions of the others.

"It's too late to try different body positions. I'm going to have to go in there and see if I can swing the baby around physically." Carefully, I tied my long hair back out of the way, took off my shirt, and washed my entire arms in the hot water. While they were still wet, I began the process. Using their hands, Waverly and Alton monitored my progress and offered directional suggestions. Poor Lenia, weakened as she was from her lengthy ordeal, fainted as my hands entered her. She had already torn and was bleeding somewhat; Andre was kept busy wiping away the blood. Thirty tense minutes later, the baby slid out into my arms, alive and kicking.

"You have a fine son, Georgio," I relayed, "he's doing just fine." I need not have added that last, because his crying was readily apparent to everyone, who cheered. While the midwives and Alton cleaned up the baby, Waverly, Andre and I cleaned up Lenia and examined the amount of damage that her body had suffered. If her womb had torn, she could die of internal bleeding very quickly. This I carefully explained to Elona, who looked very pale and peaked at the moment. Waverly knew what I needed to do next and found a lantern, lit it, and brought it close so that I could see inside.

"Elona, here, you have a look. Does she have any tears? Is she bleeding internally?" I ordered. She knelt down beside me, a hand over her mouth, straining like mad to keep from vomiting. I was pushing her nearly to her breaking point, but I had to crack through her fixed idea barriers.

Faintly, she muttered, "No, I don't think so."

"Good, we agree on that point," I complimented her. "No internal bleeding."

"But all this blood?" Elona added. "She's torn."

"Right, we need to sew her up a bit. Marianna, what would happen if we just leave Lenia like she is now?"

"She will probably get a horrible infection and die," came the aghast reply. I had asked only for the benefit of Elona, giving her an outsider's view, which was the same as ours.

"We are all in agreement then. Okay, let's do it," I added, knowing that Waverly had already sterilized my needle and thread. She handed me the threaded needle. "Observe what I do, Elona." Again, it was an order that she could not fail to obey, so strong was my intention.

Using the tiniest stitches I could manage, I sewed up the two-inch tear rather nicely. Yes, I know that Sarah Jane could have done a much finer job than I did, but I did not have the luxury of her presence. She had been the finest Healer I had ever known. Once I finished, I let Andre finish wiping her clean, while Waverly applied some of our herbal ointments that promoted healing and kept out infections. When we were through, she looked nearly normal. Waverly then waved a small vial by Lenia's nose, and she regained consciousness.

"Congratulations Lenia, you have given birth to a fine son. Both mother and son are doing just fine," I reported the news to the weakened woman. Alton placed the baby with its first diaper in place and wrapped in a warm blanked beside the young mother. Tears streamed down her cheeks, as she held the infant to her bosom. As if on cue, everyone quietly gathered our gear and went back into the front room, leaving Georgio and Lenia alone with their new son.

While Andre cleaned me up, Elona ran outside. I knew what she would be doing, but she had controlled her body during the critical phase. That was the important thing. Meanwhile, the midwives chatted with us, calling us great healers and such. We imparted our orders for Lenia's care for the next few days and told them we'd be staying around for another day to make sure Lenia was on the road to full recovery. Both women greatly appreciated this gesture.

Just as we were leaving, Georgio came out to thank us repeatedly. He said apologetically, "I really don't have much money, but I will gladly give all that I have to you. You have saved my wife and son!"

"Save your money, Georgio. Your family needs it far more than we do. Besides, you have already given us something far more valuable to us," I replied. His blank look told me he had no idea what I was talking about, so I added, "You gave us a chance to educate our apprentice, Elona. For us, that is a very great payment indeed. Thanks. If you need us, we'll be camping where you found us tomorrow as well." He shook our hands enthusiastically as we finally left.

Elona, looking awful, was already back at our camp. The aroma of supper filled the air around our wagons, which suited me fine. I was suddenly very hungry; however, food was the last thing Elona wanted to see just now. However, I made her drink some honey laced tea and saved some supper for her to eat later on, once she had recovered somewhat.

Once I had eaten and Elona finally consumed the tea and had recovered somewhat, I asked her, "Okay, I know that was rough on you; you did very well this afternoon. However, I must now ask you, what did you observe?" From my stern tone, she knew that what she said was important, rather like a test.

"If we would have done nothing but pray, both would have likely died. I can see that now. I don't know how you did it, but you got the baby's position changed, and he came out very quickly after that. I didn't know that you could sew up that tear like that. Will she really be all right? I mean will she really heal up properly? Can she have more children?" Elona said in a rush.

True, she hadn't answered my precise question, but she had seen that her fixed ideas would have resulted in the loss of both patients. Her reply told me that she had seen that there was something here to be learned and that she would now be very amenable to learning about it. I answered her, "Yes, to all three. There is always some small chance for an infection, even with all of our precautions. However, in all likelihood, she and her son will be just fine; she will heal and be back to normal in a few weeks. I see no reason why she can't have all the babies she might want. We'll educate the midwives on how and when to remove the stitches in ten days' time; we can't stay here that long. So, yes, our actions saved both today. Now then, how about answering my question: what did you observe?"

Alton glanced at me. I didn't need telepathy to know what he wanted to say but didn't. I was being very hard on Elona. Still, it had to be done. For an hour I kept her at it, until she gave me a complete and proper recital of what she had actually seen. When she finally finished, she had nearly answered one of her own questions: how had I done what I had done. Thus, in the end, she had converted her own observations into the basic knowledge of what had been actually done to the young mother to correct the problem. Elona accepted her first true lesson in the art of healing; we had finally broken through some of her religious barriers. Further, Elona was totally aware of what had happened. She was now also fully recovered and starving. Alton took a smiling and confident Elona off to warm up the supper I had saved back for her.

When they were gone, Waverly commented, "That was an incredible session you just did for Elona! I can see why you are indeed the Wid! I never could have done that or even seen the need. I would have just let her sleep on it and worked at it in the morning."

"By then, it would have been too late for proper assimilation," I explained. "By finally telling me precisely what she had observed, she also got a lesson in healing. She can see what we actually did do. Had we waited, we probably wouldn't have gotten the conversion of observation into the lesson."

"Well, you can see why I'm not the Wid!" She and Andre both laughed. "I do agree, I think finally we have broken through her barriers to learning. Well done, Bethany, well done indeed."

"My sentiments exactly," added Andre. "Do you think Alton will forgive you, though?" he added half in jest. I smiled and went for some more tea, and to find Caitlyn and fill her in on the afternoon.

Over after dinner tea, Caitlyn commented, "Bethany, you know what is just a bit strange with this town?" I admittedly hadn't noticed anything. Smiling with a minor observational coup on me, she went on, "No Church of Jehosanity. None. Only one small Church of Tur. You know, I think that this is the first town we've entered that did not have one of those tall churches with the big white cross at the top, prominently displayed." We speculated on why this might be before we crawled into our bed in the wagon under many covers; it was still late wintertime.

The next day, we checked on our patients and found both were doing well. Since we could not stay here for days, I instructed the midwives on how and when to remove the stitches. Also, I told them that if there was further trouble or complications, to send someone after us, outlining our intended direction of travel, on down the spoke road into Bonilla. Early afternoon, we headed on down the road once more, anxious to get to the large city, which was still a couple days away. Adriana pointed out that at least three different bandit gangs had spotted us but thought better of tangling with the Sisterhood; they just let us pass their positions. Threat of a superior force was more than enough to ensure our safe passage.

As we drew closer to Bonilla, old memories of the Sisterhood there came back to me. I wondered what had happened to Sister Janisseko Botellio, their leader, who I'd met over a half century ago. Probably she had long passed away by now, for she was an older woman when I had known her. I faced the prospect of dealing with total strangers in this city. However, I trusted implicitly the Sisterhood. On the day that we expected to make Bonilla, around noon, Sister Felice, riding up front, called a halt. "We've got company coming our way," she relayed back to us. I got down on foot and walked to the front of our group, joining Adriana and several others. I could see a band of Sisters riding towards us.

When they drew close, I counted twenty Sisters in their party, all fighters from the collection of weapons each carried. Their leader dismounted and greeted Adriana, "Hail Sister. I am Fighter Group Leader Leda Furstio of Bonilla. We have had news of your coming, and Reverend Sister Janis Botellio sent us out to ensure your safe arrival. No troubles with bandits I see?"

"Thanks for the welcoming party. Yes, no troubles, though three sets marked our passage, but thought better of attacking us. I am Sister Adriana Socorro of Fortress d'Grange. Our guide here is Sister Felice Bugatti," Adrianna replied. Next, she introduced us in turn. When she got to Fianna and me, I found all twenty of them staring at our hair.

"The messengers were not wrong," Leda explained still staring at my hair. "It really is fiery red and so utterly long! Do all men wear their hair this long in West Reach?" she asked what was probably on all twenty sisters' minds.

Smiling, I replied, "No, maybe half this length is common. I just love long hair, sorry. Yes, red hair is most common in Tewdwr, that portion of West Reach when my sister and I were born. How far is Bonilla? Will we make it there yet today?" I deftly changed the subject.

"Be there by nightfall. You'll be staying at the Sisterhood-run safe house, I assume," she answered, remembering her orders.

"Sure thing, if you have enough room for us."

"Aye, that we do. A hot bath awaits us," she grinned and remounted. We climbed back onto the wagons, continuing the slow, boring journey into Bonilla. Very late that afternoon, we crested the last hill before the city and got our first sight of this expansive city, which lay only a couple miles downhill from us, nestled in a sheltered bay of the Med Sea. The low, red sun light reflected off the whitecaps at sea. Smoke from thousands of chimneys curled into a greyish smoke cloud over the city. The barren tops of five sailing ships could be seen at the docks.

What caught my immediate attention was the ten-foot tall grey stone wall that entirely surrounded the city, a giant semi-circle, roughly seven miles in diameter. Periodic gate houses allowed entrance. Sister Leda yelled to us, "Your entrance fee is waived, compliments of the Sisterhood." I wondered what that fee might be and filed that question away to ask later.

What a gate house! Two towers rose on either side of the enormous iron re-enforced heavy wooden gates. A second story joined both towers forming a ceiling over the entranceway. I spied numerous arrow slits in the side walls and trap doors in the ceiling above me as we drove our wagons through this entrance. I hated to guess what might come down upon us if we were attacking enemies. More than apparent was the new philosophy of city protection; two sackings of the town within a half century certainly changed the nature of the city defenses!

New construction was everywhere; evidently, the barbarian's sacking had been too thorough. Much had to be rebuilt. However, this definitely was one way of dealing with slum renewal, I thought, perhaps not the best because people's power of choice had been overridden. Yet, from all signs I could see as we rolled along the cobblestone streets past the new stone homes and buildings, Bonilla was prospering at this point in time.

However, one new feature that had not been present some fifty years ago when I visited the city was the city guards, dressed in blue and brown outfits. Nearly every intersection boasted at least two of these heavily armed men. I wondered if they had a crime problem or a population control problem.

Caitlyn beckoned me out of my reverie, "See what's still missing, Bethany?" I flushed; no, I had not seen what was missing. She playfully poked me in my ribs, "No Churches of Jehosanity. No towering buildings with the white crosses. I haven't seen a one all this time, and I have been looking for them, naturally. I wonder what that means?" Neither of us had any answer.

A slow hour passed as we ambled our way along towards the inn, which was located on the far eastern edge of the city up close to the barrier wall and a smaller gate house exit. I assumed this would allow them to exit rapidly if need be, sharp contrast to the Sisterhood inn in Vito. When we finally drew up outside their inn, once more, I was amazed at its size. Their inn complex sprawled, filling an entire city block!

The entire complex was surrounded with a seven-foot tall wall of stone; no one could see inside the open areas easily. The main inn itself was a two-story building with numerous windows, but the sleeping rooms were all relatively small, each one holding two Sisters and their meager possessions. A long hall divided the building in half, with sets of rooms on either side, so yes, it was a very long building, but rather narrow. Just behind this main building was a huge courtyard where fighter training was held along with other more social functions. A huge stable paralleled the main inn, only on the other side of the block; the two large buildings were separated by the courtyard. Along the eastern side, a smaller, one story building housed the bath, kitchen, dining room, and pantry. Fully five hundred Sisters could be housed here at any one time without overcrowding, along with their horses. Yes, it was an impressive operation.

This time when we entered the main doors to make our arrangements, their leader, Sister Janis Botellio, and their High Council representative, Sister Talla Harmunio, were there to welcome us personally. I wasn't surprised to see them; the Sisters relayed information faster than any other group I'd ever met, save only we druwids, of course.

"Welcome to Bonilla, Ket Bethany," she began, "I'm Mother Janis Botellio, leader of the Bonilla Sisterhood. This is our High Council representative, Sister Talla Harmunio. I believe you have already met our Fighter Group Leader, Leda Furstio. This is our former Fighter Group Leader, Sister Winea Uno." We shook hands formally, and then I introduced our group, one by one. Nevertheless, from the corner of my eyes, I could not help noticing all the women present were staring at our long red hair. Before they could ask, I gave my usual explanation about it, and they chuckled and seemed amused about our hair.

"We have rooms arranged for you already. However, it is time for dinner. Would you care to join us for dinner now or would you prefer to get settled in to your rooms and perhaps take a bath before dining?" she asked.

"I suppose that we ought to make use of what light is left and get our things out of the wagons and moved into our rooms before we dine," I replied.

"Fine, I think we shall just delay our dining for a short while, until you can join us. I'll send along some Sisters to help you unload and get your wagons and horses properly serviced. When you are ready, you will find us in the dining room," she replied. I could tell that she wanted to meet with us at the earliest opportunity, and I went along with her wishes. Quickly, we were led to a side gate in the tall wall, and we led our horses and wagons into the secluded courtyard. Thirty Sisters arrived to lend a hand, and together we made short work of this mundane, but necessary task. Less than a half hour later, our band strolled into the spacious dining room.

Most of the Sisters had already eaten, though some fifty still lingered, likely to get a close look at us, I surmised. The four of them sat at a rather large table and motioned for us to join them. Adriana's group sat at several smaller tables nearby so they could overhear the conversation. First, we dined on roast lamb with dumplings. We had our choice of wine or tea; most of us chose tea. Thankfully, they held their conversation to a minimum while we ate.

When the dishes were cleared and we sat back sipping our tea, I asked, "I couldn't help noticing your last name, Botellio. Are you any relation to Janisseko Botellio? I knew her a long time ago."

She nearly jumped out of her seat, so surprised was she, "Yes! She's my mother, though she has passed away some ten years now. How could you. . ." she faltered.

Oops, I had done it again! I spent the next few minutes explaining about immortal beings and bodies and how I had been here some fifty years ago. Just to make sure that she knew I wasn't fibbing or making it all up, I described some of my adventures with Janisseko, how much I had really liked her, and how greatly she had aided my Lightning Circle back then. "You're — you're the same Bethany?" she exclaimed almost in disbelief. Yes, I had said enough personal remarks that could only come from someone who had known her mother. She relaxed somewhat, saying, "You had to know mom, but I don't know anything about spirits or past lives. I'll just accept you as Ket, is that all right?"

"Absolutely perfect," I tried to put her and the other Sisters more at ease. Again, I wished that I knew what Jes Amir could do to show them that they were spiritual beings, perhaps moving them outside of their heads. Once more, I regretted not having pressed him harder for that information.

"Well, I guess I ought to get to the business at hand," Janis sighed, sipping tea. "I must ask this, you know, since you are all Guardians and such. Are you here to help us out in some way? Is there some danger that we need to be aware of? We got the message from Carmina of Vito telling us of the near disaster that was prevented there. Are we in for some similar calamity?"

"No, we're on a secret mission of our own that has nothing to do with the Sisterhood or your country. We are looking for a lost Guardian who is in dire peril. Since we don't know just where on Tarra he is located, we are using the guise of traveling troubadours to search. Yes, we are good musicians and will give some concerts here, if you like." The Sisters heaved a big sigh of relief. I suspected that they had been fretting that something horrible was about to happen. Now the mood around the table lightened very noticeably.

Caitlyn took this chance to ask, "Say, I noticed that there are no Churches of Jehosanity around here. They were all over in the other sectors that we passed through."

The Sisters all laughed as if this was immensely funny. "Okay, I should explain a bit of our history, Talla, their Council representative answered. "We are proud of the fact that we here and also those in Pieta learned from experience. You see, we had the benefit of watching what happened in Zargarb in the aftermath of the barbarian invasion. The Prince, priests, and all the wealthy nobles fled to the southern islands to wait it out, taking their great wealth with them, and leaving the populace to face their doom. They waited until they were certain the barbarians were gone for good before they returned. However, the nobles there, like here, have had entirely enough of this city sacking, and they rebelled, ousting the two leaders, the Prince and High Priest, substituting a High Council in their place, though those two have a seat on the council. The Sisterhood also occupies one seat, so we have a vote for the first time in history! However, the plight of the people in Zargarb was dire; starvation ruled the day. That's when the opportunistic Missionaries of Jehosa stepped in, aided by the Sisterhood. Yes, together, we saved the people and restored the city to some semblance of normal. Thus, when the wealthy finally arrived, the rebellion of the nobles worked out well."

"The only thing that we objected to was the sudden discarding of our religion, our god Tur, and the universal adoption of this Jehosanity. Therefore, during the wintertime when the barbarians were not to be found in the Sea Princes, our nobles met with Prince Vassilli and the High Priest. They even sent word to us to send a Sisterhood representative. To make this shorter, they agreed that once the barbarians had left Bonilla and Pieta, everyone would return at once and rebuild quickly, giving those Missionaries no chance to come into our sectors and destroy our religion! Old Vassilli was wise, he foresaw that if he didn't change the way the sector was governed, he'd be overthrown just as the other Princes had. Therefore, he created our High Council of Eleven and even gave the Sisterhood a seat on it. Thus, there was no rebellion, and we worked together once the barbarians left the city."

"The end result is that we have successfully kept these Jehosanity people out of our sectors and kept our religion in tact! Even today, the priests of Jehosanity know better than to set foot in the Pieta or Bonilla sectors. We've already killed a dozen who have tried to infiltrate our sectors, mostly in Pieta, however. By the way, the old Prince has passed away; his son, Prince Armando Vassilli has taken his place on the council."

"Hasn't this damaged the unity among the Sisters?" I inquired. "We know many in the other sectors really do believe in Jehosa and not Tur."

"We never discuss religion," explained Janis. "If we did, then, yes, we would have deep divisions. Only when the Sisterhoods are united have we ever stood any chance of gaining acceptance. Believe me, we will do nothing to lose that now! The vast strides we have made are almost beyond belief, though I will admit that many of the youngest Sisters find it hard to believe how badly women were treated a half century ago."

"Ah, that is understandable," I acknowledged. "However, I'm not so sure that their Priests ought to be killed. Have they retaliated? Might a civil war between sectors result from this?" I speculated aloud. War and fighting never solves any problem, only creates far bigger ones than were there before. "Say, I couldn't help noticing that there are city guards at every intersection now. Is there a significant crime rate? Didn't the Sisters used to provide security?" I continued to probe, thought I didn't quite know what data I was really after.

Talla answered me, "Ever since the reconstruction began in earnest, the crime rate has become very low, mostly the occasional pick-pocket. No, the Council decided to employ as many people as possible. Our philosophy is if a man has work, he will not resort to crime. In addition, they are on the lookout for anyone preaching Jehosanity in the streets. We have outlawed open preaching of that religion. You might be interested to know that we have made a pact with Pieta. Together, we are pledged to keep Jehosanity out of our two sectors by any means possible. Further, Pieta has already raised a substantial army, just in case the Jehosanity priests attempt an all-out invasion."

This riled me no end. The worship of Jehosa had nothing to do with invading other lands or forcing itself off onto other peoples. If Jes knew about this, he would sure come back from the dead to set things straight! Talla went on, "Additionally, the city guards are there to control the population as needed."

"Ah, you have some new idea of the meaning of control of which I am not aware," I replied sarcastically. "Look, control is just seeing that something gets done that benefits everyone, the person, the family, the group, all mankind, the realm of plants and animals, and even free spirits. The second that you come down from that by using threats, forcing another under duress or sword point or fists, you are simply stating that you cannot control that person and are now using force to get your way. That is not control but bullying at the very best. Ordinarily, none of us has any resistance to being controlled by another or controlling another. However, when someone abuses that, we develop an unwillingness to be controlled and the downward spiral begins." I could tell from her quizzical expression, she did not understand me.

"Look, suppose that you had a small child and that you saw them reaching for a pot of boiling water on the stove. You would not hesitate to control the child's body and get him out of the way. That is good control or really just control. On the other hand, saying you will do this or else I will punish you is not control at all but using force and duress to get your own way. The more that you do it to a person, the more the person will resist you and eventually will become very uncontrollable. Actually, even to get to the point of threatening him with force, you are in effect saying that I can no longer control him, therefore I must force him to bend to my will, which is not control at all." Now I had reached them; all women were thinking about their respective situations.

"I say all this because there is a fundamental principle here: the individual must be given some power of choice over his life and matters. Look, before the High Council ruled Bonilla, you had no representation in the governing of the sector whatsoever, right?" They enthusiastically nodded. "How did you feel? You see, you had no power of choice at all. Now compare how you all feel with the present situation with having a representative on the ruling council?"

Talla chuckled and replied, "Ever so much better! I see your point indeed. Now we have some power of choice over the governing of our city, whereas before we had none at all. Yes, things are going vastly better now. You speak wisely indeed!"

"Ah, good. Now the next step is to give the average person in the street some power of choice in the governing of the city as well. Then, you would have a totally stable city and need no guards to enforce anything."

"Hum, you know we could do that within the Sisterhood, Janis," commented Talla thinking aloud. "We could hold some kind of election for who is to hold our High Council seat. I know you chose me because of my skills and abilities. Wouldn't it be even better if every Sister had a say in who was going to represent them?"

Janis didn't like the idea so well, "Yes, but. What if they elected someone who was ill equipped for the job? That person could wreck everything we have won almost overnight!"

"You are very right, Janis," I validated her. "If you wanted to do this, you would have to educate the Sisters so they knew what skills were needed in their representative. Otherwise, they would have nothing on which to base an intelligent vote. Further, you might limit the elected representative's term of office to say two years. After that, elections would have to be held once more. This way, you could get a poor choice out of office more quickly. These are just some ideas, mind you. However, look at what you are both doing almost instinctively. You both saw at once that doing something like this would increase the power of choice among all Sisters and that this is a very worthwhile thing."

Janis commented slyly, "I suppose my position ought to be voted upon as well." Everyone roared with laughter. She added, "Ket, we will think upon what you have said and see what may be done. I do like the idea of greater power of choice myself. I don't know why we did not see it ourselves."

"Back in our lands," I elaborated, "the people of the towns and villages are in the process of electing someone to be their ruling King and Queen. The candidates are out meeting with all the people they can so that everyone in the land knows who they are and what they are like. Thus, the people will elect their ruler. In contrast, in other nearby sectors, one man had unilaterally proclaimed himself their king and ruler. All does not go so well in those sectors. Time will tell how the experiment in the power of choice will work out. Thus far, it is very promising."

Waverly took the opportunity to inquire, "By chance has Bonilla been raising an army of its own, like Pieta has? I'm just curious."

"Not as such just yet," Talla explained. "We are still behind Pieta in terms of general recovery from the barbarian invasion. We only got the outer protection walls finished last fall. The High Council has voted to begin the creation of a garrison force to protect and man the walls in the unlikely event of another invasion."

Waverly smiled and looked straight at Talla, "One small piece of advice I'll give you. Make the job of city protection soldier a lucrative, well-paying job. Do not force young men into guard duty; rather make it seem like a good, well-paying, worthwhile job. Then, equip and train them well. If you do so, you will never again be overrun by barbarians. Force them to do it or poor pay or ill training and the walls will not protect you as you hope."

"I see what you are driving at," Talla commented. I could see that she had never considered this before and grasped the significance of Waverly's advice at once. "You know, the biggest hurdle is how to pay their salaries."

"Well, if they are there to protect everyone in the city, then everyone in the city should contribute towards their pay," Waverly pointed out. She asked, "By chance is Pieta paying its new soldiers well and making it seem a worthwhile job for its citizens to do?"

"Er, no," Janis answered. "I've heard that they have filled the ranks with conscripts, men forced to serve two years at a time. There has been a lot of grumbling and complaining by the younger men in the pubs, which we have overheard. I, too, see what you are pointing out, Waverly. We practice just that here in the Sisterhood, always have. Our fighters have the highest honor and respect among our Sisters, and are paid well. It has been one of our long-standing successes. Talla, make just such a proposal to the High Council for us, will you?"

"Absolutely!" Talla replied enthusiastically. "However, I can see that if we follow this plan, then we should never totally depend upon Pieta's soldiers in any way. They'll be no better than the Prince's forces have been during the Centurion invasion and the barbarian invasion."

Waverly smiled and agreed, "You've got my point precisely. No better than the past."

"Dear me, it is getting late," said Janis apologetically, "I'm sure you all want to take a hot bath and get settled in, and here we are keeping you from it."

"No apology needed," I replied smiling. "Say what about playing some dances for you?" We spent the next few minutes setting up several performances and then it was off to the hat bath!

In the bath, Elona swam over to me, a worried look on her face. Caitlyn and I were washing each other. "Excuse me, Ket, but can I ask you a question? I dared not ask it in front of all the Sisters." I consented, wondering what it was.

"Do you think that there will be a religious war between the followers of Tur and those of Jehosa?" she asked me directly.

"Elona, I just do not know enough about the ulterior motives and the personalities of those in charge of running the Church of Jehosanity around here in the Sea Princes. I honestly cannot say one way or the other. Yet, I'll be honest with you, Elona; it wouldn't surprise me to see a civil war break out between these two religious groups."

"I was afraid of that. That's what I kept thinking all the time they were talking. A civil war between sectors is coming. Can we prevent it?" she asked. Both she and Caitlyn stared at me anxiously waiting my reply.

"I just don't know. Perhaps as we travel through these other sectors we will gain more information. I certainly do not want to see these people fighting among themselves. Now go get Alton to wash your back," I teased, as Caitlyn began to do mine. She needed no further encouragement.

"She's not a dummy," Caitlyn whispered to me when Elona was out of hearing range. "Do you suppose that there is a Grey Creature behind this, you know pushing both sides toward a war, like they are doing with my dad?"

"You may be on to something there, Caitlyn. It certainly has that smell. You know, for any two people ever to come to blows, to have a violent disagreement, it always takes a third person behind the scenes to create it. Men do not inherently desire to fight other men, but if there is another person in the wings telling each how bad, how awful, the other is, and that they just have to do something about it, fighting can occur. The real challenge here is to find out who that other person in the background that is fomenting the civil war actually is and to expose him or her."

"I see," she answered but continued to think. "You know, I bet that other person is not in Bonilla, but rather in Pieta, because it appears that Pieta is moving much closer to war than the folks here are."

"Astute observation, my love. Precisely." I validated her and she gave me a warm hug. Unfortunately, I felt a swelling that my pants usually covered. I flushed, still not used to this male body! She felt it as well and gave me a coy, flirting look, which only made matters worse. We two were the last ones out of the bath.

We played numerous dance concerts over the two weeks that we stayed in Bonilla. The people were friendly and greatly enjoyed our music. However, I found no sign of Alabaster or anything else of particular interest to us. Following our plan, we next headed outward from the city on a northeasterly spoke road, intending to travel about fifty miles before we took another rim road, following it until it intersected with another rim road from Pieta. That was our plan anyway.

Chapter 20 Caitlyn's Observations

As we rode along the rim road leaving Bonilla, at least three bands of bandits approached us but thought better of tangling with the Sisterhood. I complimented Adriana for battles not fought. She had a good laugh at my jest. Prudent indeed were we for bringing along the large Sisterhood escort. Things changed somewhat when the rim road intersected its counterpart in the Pieta sector. Felice had unerringly brought us just where we had intended to be.

As we approached the junction of the two rim roads, Felice and Adriana halted our convoy. Up ahead, I could see a dozen well-armed men with relatively new brown uniforms with sky blue accents. Clearly, these were not bandits. I walked up to join the two women who were speaking with one of these men. "They claim to be Pieta Military Guards and insist that they inspect all our wagons. It seems that they think we may be some of those Jehosanity Missionaries trying to sneak into their sector," Adriana quickly brought me up to the present in their conversation. "I explained who we are, but they won't take my word for it."

"I am Ket Bethany, leader of the West Reach Minstrels, troubadours. We are traveling across the Sea Princes at the moment, playing various inns."

"Sorry, it matters not whether I believe you, and I am inclined to believe you," the man said diplomatically, "but we have our orders. We must search all incoming wagons. If you are musicians as you say, then you have nothing to hide, and you can be on your way very soon." I could tell he was trying to make this as acceptable as possible. Certainly, he did not like to have to be doing this searching either. He clung tightly to his justification of "just following orders."

I could see no reason not to accommodate their wishes; why get started on the wrong foot, so to speak. "Just be extra careful. We have a lot of delicate instruments in the wagons and one blind musician." Six men dismounted and left their crossbows on their horses and followed me back toward my wagon, which was first in line. Caitlyn felt uneasy as they began nosing around our wagon. "What do these missionaries bring with them in their wagons?" I asked, curious as well as trying to make polite conversation.

"Heck if I know," laughed one of the young men doing the searching. "Looks like you have a lot of instruments in here; yours is okay." They moved on to the next wagon. While we walked he added, "They usually come in sky blue painted open wagons, not these high topped kinds. You obviously live in yours. Just a formality, you understand."

After looking into every wagon, though they acted awkwardly around

Jolina, they waved an all clear signal back to the others. Together, we walked back to the front of the line. "Have you caught many of these Jehosanity missionaries?" I asked.

"No, not here on the border of our ally, Bonilla. However, I hear that those on the eastern side have caught a dozen trying to sneak into our sector and killed every one of them. I got stuck out here on this rim road, and I'll never see any action," he lamented. He was a very bored man.

"Couldn't we be spies?" I asked their leader, when we all got back to the front. I was just a little peeved at this inconvenience.

"Nah, you've got the Sisterhood protecting you. Hence, not spies. If they weren't here to vouch for you, why, that would be quite another matter, one for the Prince to adjudicate. Here, show this to the other guards you encounter," he added, giving Adriana a funny looking coin. "It means that you have already been searched and allowed entry into Pieta Sector; that way you'll not be bothered with another search later on."

"Jeesh, how many checkpoints do you have? Are these missionaries that much of a threat to Pieta?" I inquired.

"Plenty, exact number is a secret — sorry can't say. Well, they took over all the other sectors except us and Bonilla, so they must be quite a threat, I reckon." I did not press the issue further; they mounted up and moved out of the way, so we did likewise, eager to put some distance between them and us. I did not like what I had just witnessed. What had become of Jes's religion anyway? Pieta and Bonilla both felt threatened by the missionaries of Jehosanity. How could this possibly be? I had no answers.

Now the early spring rains began falling. Each day it rained, fortunately always a light rain. Slowly the road turned into mud lanes; had we not had draft horses pulling the wagons, we would have had to stop and wait until dryer weather returned. True, we could have traveled along the Centurion paved stone coastal roadway, but then we would not be able to keep up our appearances as traveling musicians visiting each sector. It would look more as if we were just passing through.

We played at several inns on our way towards Pieta. Actually, we again followed the rim road until we reached the north-south spoke road that led straight down to Pieta. Yes, at each junction between spoke a spoke road and a rim road, Pieta guards were on duty. The strange coin displayed by Adriana did allow us safe passage without additional wagon searching. Actually, twice we had to wait in line because the guards were searching ordinary wagons, locals carrying produce and supplies between the towns. Hence, the only conclusion I could reach was that even the local people were being suppressed by this overly aggressive action. Eventually, the locals would rebel against them, I concluded.

Agila was the name of the town of about one thousand folks here at the crossroads, where the rim road met the north-south spoke road. More out of curiosity than anything else, I asked Fergus to gather some information for me. He was a natural at pub chatter and could easily get the local folks talking away. On a break between sets, he got a pint of mead and worked the men at the bar. I sat close enough so I could overhear his conversation, mostly.

"Aye, laddie, we sure do see all those guards at every crossroad. Young lads, all of 'em," Fergus began innocently. "From 'round 'ere?"

Belching one older man replied, "Yep, they come and force our young men into their guards. Don't pay 'em much either. We need them young, strong hands to mind the fields, tend the grapes, and olive groves. But what can you do? War's going on with them nasty Jehosanites over in Solamina and Zargarb. Heard tell twenty-five of 'em were caught sneaking into Pieta. Killed every one of 'em too." More belching followed.

Another man continued the gripe session, "Yeh, and they stopped my wagon yesterday! Can you believe that. Young Antonio, he knows me, 'just foll'rin' orders he says.' Hogwash I says. They's going to shoot me with them crossbows if I didn't stop! You'd think they's knowed a Jehosanite when they sees one."

"Doesn't sound like a war to me, laddie," Fergus replied. "Wars are armies fighting armies. Do these Jehosanites have an army ready to invade here?"

"Aye, some say they do, but I says if they did, where's it at anyway?" the man belched once more.

His companion added, "Yeh, but banditry's long gone. All these blasted guards put an end to them scourge. Least we donna have to worry 'bout bandits robbing us no more. Some goods come from it all, I says."

"Aye, laddie, does seem a good benefit. Don't take kindly to bandits myself either, though musicians 'taint got much to be stolen. Guess if the army does come marching through here, you all get to head into Pieta, safety behind the wall?" Fergus queried.

"Never make it! If we ever sees an army, we'd be dead long 'fore we could ever get way down there. Besides, they 'taint got room fer us all," he replied and belched once more.

His companion added, "Don't du us much good way up 'ere, now does it?"

"Aye, but ye're fergetten that they take over a third of our crops now. Says they's storin' it in Pieta for safety, should an army come thru 'ere. We jest have t'r get down to Pieta to get re-supplied is all."

"I says they's jest dining royally at our expense, that's what I says," the belching man put in, once more sounding off.

I gave Fergus a sign that indicated we needed to play our next set, so he excused himself, and we climbed back onto the stage, which was very small and very crowded with we musicians. I thanked him for a job well done. He merely said, "Laddie, they said just what I would have expected them to be complaining about. Weren't you expecting all that he said?"

"Yes, but something tells me that I needed to hear it firsthand."

The next day we began our slow journey straight south toward Pieta. Certainly, the villagers enjoyed our music and begged us to stay on a few more nights. It was plainly obvious that our music gave them great relief from the drudgeries of their lives. I truly wish that we could have stayed longer, but I had a pressing assignment with still no trace of Alabaster. We had not gone five miles before a large party of Sisterhood fighters, riding up from Pieta, hailed us. Once more, that we had been expected was the only possible conclusion. Again, I marveled at the speed and accuracy of the communication lines among the Sisterhood. However, I also wondered just how the Sisterhood would deal with a potential civil war between the different sectors. How could each group remain neutral?

A few minutes later, Adriana rode back to my wagon to relay the news. "We've got an escort of fifty Sisterhood fighters this time. I wonder why so many? Anyway, we are to try to make Rosalinda by late afternoon, and you can play at the Boar's Head tonight. However, the next and last town before Pieta, Encinda, is off limits to us. We are allowed only to pass through the city, and then only under the protection of these Sisters. I could get nothing further from them concerning Encinda, but something is most definitely going on there. Guess we will just have to wait and see. Acceptable?" I nodded; she signaled the Sister, who motioned everyone to get moving once more.

"I'll bet there is an army around Encinda," Caitlyn predicted. I gave her a hug and agreed. It did seem likely.

We did arrive in Rosalinda in the late afternoon, just as predicted. Evidently, we were considered "people of great importance" by the Sisterhood here in Pieta, because when we arrived at the inn, our accommodations had already been arranged beforehand. Additionally, there was a room for everyone, including the fifty Sisters from Pieta; we had nearly every room in the inn! I could not help noticing that our rooms were entirely surrounded by rooms occupied by the Sisterhood; they would be protecting us even as we slept.

While we were unloading our gear, Adriana brought a Sister over to meet me. "Fighter Group Leader Alice Augato, this is their leader Guardian Ket Bethany."

"Quite an honor, sir," Alice exclaimed in a mellow alto voice, as she shook my hand firmly. Alice was a knock-out blonde! I estimated she was perhaps thirty years old but extremely fit. Her muscles were solid but not overly large, and she was my height, though trim. I could not help but notice her firm, large bosom, pale blue eyes, and flush cheeks. Yes, she was more than an attractive woman indeed. I felt that embarrassing bulge swelling in my pants once more; damn, I hate male bodies.

"Very pleased to meet you as well, Alice," I answered. "Thanks for the escort. It was becoming tiresome being stopped at every road junction by the guards. We certainly don't have to worry about any bandits with so many of your able fighters with us."

She smiled a completely disarming smile. I could tell that she often used her good looks to defuse tense situations. I immediately liked this woman; why fight when there were obviously other methods available? "We've effectively eliminated the bandits in the Pieta Sector. It is very rare that we are honored to have Guardians visiting Pieta. We owe you so much that we will take no chances whatsoever with your safety within our sector. I do love your hair, by the way — so long and so red! May I?" she asked, wanting to touch it to convince herself that it was indeed real. She ran her hands through it coyly as my bulge grew enormously.

"Yes, never have cut it. Most of us in Tewdwr, West Reach, have vibrant red hair. I just like it long." She smiled and I added teasingly, "really long."

Just then, Caitlyn joined me, carrying her dulcimer. Quickly, I put my arm around her slim waist and said, "This is my fiancé, Caitlyn. This is Pieta's Fighter Group Leader Alice Augato." Caitlyn smiled, leaning her head on my shoulder; her hands were entirely filled with her large instrument. Nevertheless, all three of us got her intention: This is my man; keep your hands off him.

"You certainly do have an unusual man, Caitlyn; take good care of him. I just cannot get over his hair! Impressive. Well, I have lots to attend to. We can talk more when we get to Pieta. We'll catch your concert tonight; bye for now," and she turned and headed back outside, probably to ensure that the horses were properly handled.

As Caitlyn and I headed toward our room, I commented, "Wow, what a knock-out!"

"I noticed your bulge, Bethany. Don't go getting any ideas now," she teased me back. "Yes, she sure is attractive," she conceded. I gave her a reassuring hug.

We had a bit of free time before dinner. Elona took advantage of it and came knocking on our door. "Excuse me, but I have made my choice of specialization." I bade her to sit on the edge of our bed and explain. Yes, this was perhaps the most important decision she had to make, one not to be treated lightly.

"I've looked everything over several times now. I've decided that I want to become a Protector, if that is all right with you," she added hastily, half expecting me to veto such a request.

I didn't expect she would desire to be a Wid or a Communicator or a Planner for that matter. I had half expected she would want to become a Judger or perhaps a Healer, given her pronounced priestly bent. "You've considered this carefully, Elona?" I had to avoid any appearance of invalidating her; it had to be her choice made for appropriate reasons and desires.

"Yes, I am the last of the Po's. I know I should've gotten married a long time ago, but I never could find any man I could trust or tolerate, let alone love. I even thought about joining the Sisterhood, but gave that idea up because it would mean leaving Velona forever. The Sisterhood has practically abandoned that sector and for good reasons. But then I met Alton. I — I," she flushed and her embarrassment grew.

"You've fallen in love with him, am I not right?" I helped her over the awkward moment.

"Yes," she relaxed knowing that I knew her heart. "We want to get married one day and have many children. His children are already grown up and on their own. Since there will be more Po's as a result, I want to be able to provide the absolute best protection I possibly can for them as they grow up. Being a skilled Protector will give me the best chance to see that our children make it."

Yes, on the surface, this sounded completely plausible and quite sincere. Yet, something, call it intuition if you desire, told me there was something even deeper to her request. She was still a Po. "Elona, this is a totally honorable approach, one I certainly would bless. Yet, is there not still some desire on your part somehow to regain what you've lost in Velona? I mean your heritage is that of the founding fathers, is it not?"

"Well, yes, that too," she added, unsure of herself. I knew instantly that there was indeed more to her choice than what she had said thus far. I said softly, "Yes," encouraging her to elaborate.

"Our sector has become so corrupt that the average person can barely stand to live there. If there is any way that I can correct the situation, I am obligated to make the attempt. Being a Protector can only aid me, but frankly, Bethany, right now, I don't see any way to rectify the mess in Velona. It appears that the sins of my founding forefathers have turned Velona into a hell-hole with no way out." Moisture swelled in her eyes. The image I long carried of the man's head being cut off and tossed into the ocean when I first arrived in Velona over a half century ago came back vividly in my mind.

"Yes, the sins of your forefathers are quite huge indeed. Elona, where there is yet life, there is still hope for the future. I grant my approval for your choice. Given your circumstances in life, I completely agree with your choice. May you find the inner strength to make your choice a reality. Hard work and many pains and bruises you have chosen, yet, in the end, you may achieve your goal of becoming a Protector like Alton. Go now and tell him that I have approved. He can begin your training as soon as he desires."

She looked up at me; elation overrode the tears. Elona almost could not believe what she was hearing. "Oh thank you, Bethany, thank you!" She bounded out the door to go and tell Alton. I looked at Caitlyn, and she, me. Together we smiled.

"You know, it would be quite something if Elona could somehow regain control of Velona and turn everything there around, making it a great place to live," Caitlyn expounded. "Though like she says, I have no idea how she could do it either." We kissed and then headed off to find dinner.

Two days later, around noon we closed upon Encinda, a town boasting some two thousand people originally. From the crest of the hill just north of the town, we could see clearly that far more than that were here. Just east of the town proper and occupying nearly all the olive groves there was an island of small tents. Men and horses clustered in small groups, nearly as populace as the olive trees! A secret no longer, Pieta had indeed raised a sizeable army!

For security reasons, Alice led us off the road and onto smaller tracks, passing way west of the town. We passed through olive groves, vineyards, even past small homesteads, before rejoining the road south of Encinda. Thus, we only had this fleeting glimpse of their army and could not tell their numbers or their equipment. *This does not look good,* Waverly placed into my mind as we rolled along. Even Caitlyn was very quiet as we detoured around the town.

That night we camped out in the open and by noon the next day, we arrived at Pieta. The city had grown considerably since I had last seen it, perhaps by thirty percent. The grey stone hemispherical barrier wall was now the most prominent feature as we paused to view the city from the last hilltop before heading down the long valley to the Med Sea shore. I counted at least ten ships currently parked at the large docks. Already the many vineyards in the fields all around the city were sprouting the new green growth of spring. Occasional flower fields caught my eye, likewise, Caitlyn. "Picturesque," she commented.

Entering the city was much the same as Bonilla; two great gate towers spanned either side of the huge iron re-enforced doors. The same second floor overhang had many trap doors through which unspeakable things could be dropped on any door smashers. Numerous arrow slits on the side walls spoke of a determined effort to keep siege armies at bay. An entire squad of guards manned the entrance. Because of our escort, we were rapidly allowed entrance without even being questioned. I wondered how much difficulty we might have had if it were not for the presence of our Sisterhood escort.

As we rode slowly along the crowded streets, throngs of people were shopping or working. Pieta was indeed a bustling city, full of activity during the day. Estimates suggested that one hundred fifty thousand people now made Pieta their home. By far, Pieta was the largest city I had ever seen. As with Bonilla, most of the buildings were new. Once again, the barbarian invasion had resulted in massive destruction of extant structures. It was simpler to level everything and start over, according to some master plan. I did notice that they allowed for some expansion room on the northern portion of the city. Currently, it held a many-acre park, where grass and flowers were greening, as it was nearly spring. Several times, we had to move off to one side to allow other wagons and carts to pass by our convoy.

We continued down to the main coastal road, built by the Centurions a half century ago when they invaded. Here, we were so close to the sea, that we could smell the salt air. Turning right, we headed westward toward the outer wall, stopping just short of that grey stone barrier. Once again, the Sisterhood had built their city complex as close to the wall as possible and close to a city gate. Easy access, I presumed.

Here, the complex occupied two city blocks! The two-story inn was huge and could hold close to seven hundred residents. Behind the imposing inn was the typical courtyard, entirely enclosed by a seven-foot tall wall. The Sisterhood still preferred privacy. I could tell that one large section was setup to train their fighters. The stables were the largest I had ever seen, housing easily a thousand horses at one time. We easily were able to store our wagons and horses in it. I wondered how much work it was to fill the hay mow for the winter; such would be a full time job for many hands. On another side was their community building with a very large dance hall where we were told that we could play anytime we wished.

We all entered together, and as I expected, the leaders were waiting to greet us, welcoming us to Pieta. Again, Sisterhood efficiency. Since I was the male with very long red hair, Mother Sister Mandi had no trouble deciding whom to address first, though she could not conceal her surprise at the reality of my red hair. "Greetings and welcome to Pieta. I am Mother Sister Mandi Zorio. This is the High Council representative Sister Allia Gatti. You've already met our Fighter Group Leader, Sister Alice Augato. Ah, here she comes now. We would like to extend a warm welcome to all of you to our inn and to Pieta. Rare indeed are we hosts to Guardians. Please, consider your stay on the house, but do play as many dances as you desire." I shook their hands and then introduced our party, beginning with Sister Adriana and Felice.

With the formalities over, Mandi said, "By now you realize that we must hold a private meeting with you. I expect the other Mothers have done similarly. However, let's get you all settled in first. Once you've unpacked, a Sister will show you the way to the dining room. Let's have tea or wine." Of course, I agreed and we were led to our rooms. This time, we were assigned what had to be the royal reception or perhaps the wedding suites. All were spacious and full of amenities that we had not yet encountered, including a very nice desk and mahogany chairs. Tapestries depicting mariner scenes decorated the walls. Even a marble statue of a Sister sat on a pedestal near the door. About a half hour later, we four Guardians along with Adriana were led down the lengthy hallways to the dining room in the adjacent building.

Periodically along the hall, fresh spring flowers spread their flagrance as we passed by them. Indeed, this was the nicest Sisterhood inn that we had encountered. The huge dining room, which could seat probably five hundred at one time, currently held only three other occupants. Mandi waved and motioned us to join them. We did so and tea and muffins were quickly served.

Mandi Zorio was thirty-five with light brown hair. Her skin had a slightly olive hue to it. Hazel eyes framed an oval face. She was not overly attractive and was surprisingly short, just five feet tall. Her body was not what was impressive, rather her keen mind. Alice Augato, the fighter, had changed from her traveling clothing and was even more attractive in her brown dress, outlined with blue, which matched her eyes. She smiled at me as I sat down. My guess was Alice was barely thirty. Allia Gatti, their council representative, was a tall woman, six feet, though fairly skinny. She wore her blonde hair shoulder length, quite differently than most Sisters, who opted for an easy-care short style. She had black eyes and wore a bit of makeup that accentuated her features. However, she paled in comparison to Alice. Rather, she opted to appear as acceptable to the High Council male members as possible, which I thought was a rather wise move on her part.

Having sat through this several times before, I began by explaining our mission and that it had nothing to do with the Sisterhood. Mandi smiled, saying, "I see you've been interrogated before, just as I suspected, or predicted rather. Thank you. Yes, I did need to know this. We have received a number of messages from the easterly Sisterhoods, relaying what you have done and the urgent warning about imposters. Let me thank you for having exposed that imposter. All of the Sisterhoods benefitted from your aid. Allia and I have carefully reviewed all that has gone on here for some time; we can find no suggestion that there is an imposter acting to destroy Pieta, thankfully."

We then chatted about the imposter situation and its ramifications. I asked about their recent history. Allia explained, "We saw what happened to Zargarb and Solamina in the aftermath of the barbarian invasion. Wisely, Prince Pietro Almarino and High Priest Alfredo Fedora acted in the best interests of Pieta. Even before the barbarians came here, they set up a High Council of Thirteen, even including a Sisterhood representative. The bargain to relinquish power to the Council was that each member must provide an equal share in the survival of Pieta. The nobles readily agreed to that stipulation. Before the actual invasion came, the Sisterhood stockpiled a large amount of supplies that would be needed once the invaders left. All of us were determined not to let these Jehosanite religious fanatics gain a foothold in Pieta by offering help. The Church of Tur even secreted away many of its priests in Sisterhood safe houses, ready to come to the aid of our citizens once the barbarians left. In the end, it all worked out just perfectly. We were able to save ourselves without any outside aid. Bonilla did likewise."

"But you are now afraid of an invasion from Jehosanites from Solamina?" I queried, asking the question bluntly.

Allia looked at Mandi, unsure how to respond. Her leader stalled a moment, and then said, "I'm sorry. I didn't want to bother you with our internal affairs. You probably have more than enough of your own problems." She cleverly was giving me a polite way out.

"The Sisterhood is one of our oldest allies — certainly the most trusted ally. We could not help seeing a rather large army outside Encinda. Guards are at every crossroad we encountered. Security seems awfully tight — tighter than I have ever heard about. Something must be threatening you. We would really like to know the true situation here. Perhaps we may be of some assistance. I can see that a civil war may be close at hand, and I am very worried about how the Sisterhood can survive as a whole. I hope you do not go to war amongst yourselves."

"Damn, you are good, Ket Bethany," Allia replied. "You have already cut to the quick of the matter. Yes, we are in a devilishly nasty position here. For years now, we have been building up an army with which to stop an impending invasion from Solamina and their Jehosanites. We've already caught a fair number of their missionaries trying to infiltrate the Pieta Sector. They have been dealt with severely, in hopes that those in Solamina will get the message to leave us alone."

"It hasn't worked, however. Am I right?" I replied.

She chuckled, "Observant you are. No, it hasn't. That's why there are so many watching all the intersections."

"And you only have one vote on both Pieta's and Solamina's High Councils?"

"True, we have tried our best to get both councils to see reason, but to no avail."

Waverly asked, "How is it that you know that Solamina is raising an army to invade Pieta? Surely, the Sisterhood representatives on both sides know what is going on via the High Councils. Sharing military secrets can be viewed as treasonous by both sides."

"You have hit the mark quite closely," Allia acknowledged. "Both myself and my Solamina counterpart Renata Bleu know of every detail of the arming of the two sectors. Obviously, we continually veto all such motions, but they are passed anyway. We have told both High Councils that should war break out, then the Sisterhood will remain neutral and will not fight for either side. Still, they know that we share information. This has caused us a great deal of worry and speculation. What if they make plans behind our backs so that we cannot relay the information? Hence, we have got many Sisters out doing actual spying just to make sure that we really do have accurate information on which to base decisions."

Mandi added, "You are right. Come a civil war, the Sisterhood may well be doomed, trusted not by either side and attacked by both armies.

Some suggest that this is ultimately their plan — a way finally to get rid of the Sisterhood. Unfortunately, I am of that belief — that this is just another scheme to get rid of us because the Sisterhood has become so powerful in the eyes of the nobles and the Prince."

"I noticed that both your complex here and your counterpart in Bonilla are located by the wall, ready for a fast exit. I might even suspect that you have a secret tunnel under the wall for just such an eventuality," I speculated. All three women turned crimson.

"How did," Mandi began, but never finished her sentence.

"We will not tell a soul. I promise. That is just what I would have ordered built, if I were in your shoes," I added. No one spoke; an awkward silence fell.

"I will be honest with you. I have some knowledge of this new religion," I broke the stillness. I explained about immortal beings inhabiting bodies once more, elaborating until I felt that these three women grasped my meaning. Next, I described my mission last lifetime, when I was the wife of the Great Messiah. I went into detail about the original religious beliefs, pointing out how strict following of such a code was undoubtedly behind the generosity and willingness for so many Arads to come to the aid of the desperate folks in Zargarb and Solamina. "Back then, I think their motives were twofold: come to the aid of their fellow man and to spread their religion to others, building churches in exchange for their aid. Overall, I support their having done so. The alternative would have been to watch thousands starve to death or worse."

"However, that was then, not now. Passing through Velona, I saw how corrupt the religion has become, little more than a means to control a wild population by coercion and force. Free will and power of choice have vanished from Velona completely. Not good at all. Admittedly, we have not yet been to Solamina or Zargarb, though they are next on our journey. Hence, I cannot say what their situation actually is right now. Back in Vito, all seemed to be going well, however. We saw no signs that they wanted to conquer other sectors," I finished up.

Waverly added, "Remember Sisters that for two groups to fight a war, there has to be a hidden third person working behind the scenes to foment the necessary hatred to go to war. Man desires to get along and prosper. War never solves any problem; it only creates others. In the end, both sides lose. Look at the current Galt situation, for example." The Sisters were unfamiliar with this idea, and Waverly spent ten minutes going into detail and giving some examples.

"You mean that when my husband and I split up, we split because of the interference of some other person?" asked Mandi, almost in disbelief.

"Well, did you and your husband get along well just before you decided to get married and shortly thereafter?" Waverly inquired.

"Well, yes, but I think it was just puppy love. We were too young, really," Mandi answered.

Undaunted by her excuses and rationale, Waverly asked, "When things started to go bad, was someone telling you bad things about your husband? Perhaps that he was cheating on you or that he was worthless or no good or a wife beater?"

"Well, yes, come to think of it. His mother — she always came to visit me. She claimed I was like a daughter to her and that she wanted to protect me from her son's violent temper." Mandi became silent as other similar memories flooded into her mind.

Waverly said softly, "Precisely. I'd bet a pot of gold that she also ran you down behind your back to her son. Did she approve of your marriage when you first announced it?"

"Actually, no, she was angry with him, saying that he was marrying beneath him. Damn, she was the one who actually broke up our marriage!" exclaimed Mandi. The relief she felt was apparent to all present, and she broke out into a laugh as well. "Damn her anyway. I should have seen that one coming!"

"That's what a third party can do," Waverly continued. "Within the Guardians, we have certain people who are highly trained to be able to spot these things and find them out. Unfortunately, we did not bring one of our Judgers along with us this trip. We didn't think we would need one."

Andre, who usually was silent at these meetings, spoke up for the first time. "Gang, I wouldn't be surprised at all to find one of these 'imposters' behind this impending civil war between Solamina and Pieta. Sisters, you have our word that we will use what skills we have to see if this is indeed the case. If so, perhaps we can completely prevent this nasty war from ever happening." He looked at me, realizing that I, as Wid, should have made the pronouncement. I nodded my approval, setting him at ease. I was pleased that Andre finally added something to the conversations.

"You would do this for us?" asked Mandi, not believing her good fortune.

I replied, "Certainly we will. Please don't get your hopes up too high. We only have limited time to spend in Pieta, but we will do our utmost to track this all down. It is also in our own interests to help our allies in their times of need. You have our word as Guardians on this."

She smiled, "Thank you from all of the Sisterhood! I can see that you are aptly named, Guardians." We all chuckled over that one.

We adjourned to make some plans. Mandi placed the entire Sisterhood at our disposal, naturally. In our rooms, I decided, "Okay, Andre, you are in charge of this investigation. Waverly will be your assistant. Also, get Elona actively involved; I think that this would be a great learning situation for Alton's apprentice." He grimaced and protested that he was only a Protector, but I did not let him off the hook.

Alton commented, "That'll teach you to open your mouth, Andre.

Bethany should have made the pledge. Serves you right." We all laughed good-naturedly. After Elona was brought into my room along with the other members of the minstrels and Adriana, we explained the situation fully. Even Caitlyn agreed with Andre; she felt sure that a Grey Creature was behind this whole mess. However, none of us knew exactly how we would be able to find that out, let alone explain it to the Sisterhood.

First, Andre carefully explained the theory behind what we were attempting to do. Waverly added several examples to help make it clear to the others. Once they all understood, Jolina commented, "I'll bet there is a Grey Creature behind this." We all laughed and agreed with her. I marveled at how readily non-druwids could grasp this basic principle of life. Even blind Jolina had.

Andre declared, "Okay, we will need to interview many people to find out what they have heard from whom. We need a set of standard questions to ask. Suggestions? We can revise them as we get more information in on the situation." We discussed this issue for an hour, trying any number of questions out. In the end, we decided to keep it as simple as possible, because we'd have to interview a fair number of people. We decided upon three initial questions:

Who told you that the Church of Jehosanity or its missionaries were bad or evil?

Who told you that the Jehosanites were planning an invasion of Pieta?

Who told you that an army was being raised in Solamina intent upon invading Pieta?

Of course, if a name was mentioned, the follow up question was "What was said?" Based on these, Andre and his helpers would survey as many relevant people as possible. Once that was complete, we would then tally up the names found. Of course, the name most frequently found would then become the target of our investigation. Andre and his team faced a lot of legwork as well as persuasion; they would have to interview each of the thirteen council members as well.

Next, we headed for the bath, supper, and then the dance hall. It was time to entertain the Sisterhood. After all, this time our stay was "on the house."

During the next week, we managed to play for a dance every night, much to the delight of the women here. However, we soon became besieged with requests to play other gigs. In part to facilitate Andre's investigation, we arranged to play a special concert for the nobles and their immediate families. Allia arranged this one for us. While the clothing was vastly fancier and more expensive and jewelry, prominent, the nobles and their families enjoyed our music just as much as the Sisters did.

During the long days in which we had very little to do, Caitlyn, Fergus, Fianna, Edgar, and Jolina began taking long strolls through the city. We were repeatedly told that crime was very low these days, and there were city guards on duty at every intersection in any event. Since I was tied up working with Andre, doing the massive tabulations, I gave them the go ahead to take their daily walks. However, I insisted that a couple of Sisters should always accompany them, just in case.

One day as they were strolling along the bustling street, Caitlyn said, "You know, I want to help too, but there seems to be nothing we can do."

"I agree with you," Fianna replied. Jolina put in her "Me too."

"Lassies, I do too, but you know Ket; we better leave this in their hands," Fergus protested slightly. "Besides, what do we know about finding the guilty party?"

"Well, I always think that men are motivated by money, at least many that I've seen," Caitlyn said flatly. "Present company excluded," she giggled. "Who stands to benefit from a civil war between Solamina and Pieta?"

Various ideas flashed by the group before Jolina commented, "Those who make the weapons of war."

"You are right, Jolina!" exclaimed Caitlyn. "I should have thought of that. It's simple, really. Those who make the weapons stand to benefit by selling loads of them to the army. I wonder who around here makes all the swords and bows and arrows?"

"Crossbows, too, lassie," added Fergus.

"Gang, since we are going for a walk, what say you to seeing if we can find all of the weapon makers and do a little sleuthing of our own?" Caitlyn suggested.

"I'll let you know if I sense a Grey Creature," Jolina offered.

A few questions of passersby later, the quintet entered Horton's Weaponry Shop. Dozens of swords lined one table, while various bows and crossbows hung from wooden pegs on one wall. Again, this was only a small storefront; the real workshop occupied seven times this space adjacent to it. Another display held numerous daggers and knives of all shapes and sizes. Wiping his hands, Horton entered from his shop. "G'day to you all. What are you interested in seeing? A petite dagger perhaps," he said, eyeing Caitlyn and Fianna. "Say, aren't you the famous troubadours that have been playing dances the last couple days?"

"Aye, laddie, we be part of them, West Reach Minstrels," Fergus replied.

However, Caitlyn had no intention on being sidetracked from her self-appointed mission. "Our fathers back in West Reach are kings and are trying to raise an army to kick the Axemen off the island. They've already built a town up north, stealing our wood. We are interested in seeing about how to go about equipping an army with swords and bows and such," she explained.

Horton smile, "Well, I'd never have guessed that one. Rather an expensive proposition, equipping an army. For example, I've made those swords you see there. Each one sells for ten gold coins. Bows are five."

"Wow," exclaimed Jolina, "I see what you mean. Is it hard work to make a sword? I'm blind but curious nevertheless."

"If one's life depends upon a blade, there's no accepting an inferior product. It takes me about a week to make a good one — one you can depend upon in a fight," Horton replied.

Caitlyn smiled coyly and asked, "So what if we wanted to purchase say a thousand swords and perhaps five hundred bows, with sufficient arrows of course. How long would that take? I mean when we arrived here, we could not help noticing that Pieta is fielding a sizeable army itself just north of here."

"Observant are we," Horton teased her. "Seriously, I couldn't accept such an order; it would take me years to fill it."

Frowning, but not put off, she replied, "Well, Pieta's army surely has swords. If you can't make that many, where could we go to place such an order?" She put the provocative question at him directly, but did not expect a true answer.

"If you want to buy in bulk like you are suggesting, you should go to the New Barq trade representative over on Vino Street. The Centurions are good for something, if it's a quantity of weapons that you want. I'm sure they will ship them to your island. Heck, we Sea Prince merchant's motto is 'We ship anything anywhere,'" and he chuckled to himself, proud to have gotten his favorite joke in on these strangers.

On a whim, both Caitlyn and Fianna purchased a pair of small knives that fit nicely in their boots. Then, the group headed off in search of Vino Street. A half hour later, they paused outside a very small shop; the neatly painted sign read: New Barq Trade Goods. The five entered.

The room was barely ten foot square. A table with four chairs facing a single chair dominated the room along with a giant map that showed Juda Arad and the Sea Princes. Behind the single chair was a scroll case with several parchments neatly stowed. A bronzed skin man in his late thirties sat in the single chair, sipping a cup of wine and smoking a pipe. In a definite accent, he said, Lucius Thalax, at your service. I'm sorry, but I've only four chairs. How may I be of service?" He wore a curved, well-tended moustache and had very greasy hair.

Caitlyn did not trust him the instant she heard his voice; she felt ill at ease. Nevertheless, she explained about wanting to see about the purchase of a thousand swords for her father, the king. "Yes," Lucius said, "we may be able to do business. We can supply that many in say a month's time. Would they need to be transported to West Reach? If so, we will have to add shipping costs to the sale. I can give you a good discount on a thousand at one time, though the discount is larger if you wanted say five thousand."

"Aye, laddie, now that would be a sizeable army to eradicate the Axemen from our shores," Fergus helped Caitlyn. "How much for each would that be?"

"If you got say one thousand, the base cost would be five thousand gold coins. Shipping from New Barq to West Reach would add another hundred to the price, guaranteed delivery, mind you. On the other hand, if you wanted five thousand, we would need a couple months to prepare that many, but the total price would only be ten thousand. Shipping would still be just another hundred." He fiddled with his moustache, knowing that they were not really going to lay down that kind of money.

"Say, we are new to Pieta. Where is this New Barq anyway?" asked Fianna. She had no idea at all how far this place was or where it was located.

"Right here," he smiled and pointed out the only port city in Juda Arad. "We built New Barq over the ruins of Al Barq, which was destroyed years ago in the Barbarian Invasion."

"Golly, you must have a huge weapons factory in New Barq to be able to make that many in such a short time," Caitlyn observed.

He laughed, but it sounded more like a sneer. "The weapons are made all throughout the Southlands and Megalos, dear lady. True, a few are made in New Barq, but most come from further south. There is no finer blade in all Tarra than a Centurion made blade. Fergus was about to take issue with him, because he felt those made in the Highlands were vastly superior to the one's he'd seen here in the Sea Princes, but he thought better of it.

Instead, they thanked him for the information and left. Outside, Jolina commented, "I may be blind, but I get an awful creepy feeling when I am around that man. I do not trust him. What did he look like?" Edgar attempted to describe him for her.

"Well, now at least we know something," Caitlyn summarized as they walked back to the inn. "The Centurions are the ones supplying the weapons in quantity here in the Sea Princes. I'll bet anything that Solamina is getting theirs from the same people."

"Aye, lassie, I'd bet anything they do," Fergus agreed wholeheartedly.

Fianna frowned; she'd just remembered something her brother had said a long time ago. "Bethany once told me that there are some other really bad, strange monsters living way down south doing pretty much the same thing to the people there that the Grey Creatures are doing here. You don't suppose," her voice trailed off.

"Suppose what," asked a confused Jolina, who could not see the pained and confused expression on her face.

"You mean there are more of these aliens around?" asked Caitlyn.

"Aye, we should talk to Bethany about it, right away, if we can," Fianna signed. The group soberly went in search of me.

When they found me an hour later, Caitlyn explained what they had done and had found out. "Fianna tells me that there are other evil alien creatures down south. Could they be behind bringing in all these weapons?" she asked.

"Yes, I deserved to be kicked in the butt," I replied. "I've been so caught up with these Grey Creatures, that I completely forgot about those mantises out in the Red Desert."

"Okay, I'll do it," Caitlyn said playfully, as she punched me in my rear. Everyone laughed, letting off their fears in the process.

I explained to them all about the enormous praying mantis creatures I had seen so long ago. "It's like the two groups manipulate countries into wars and then siphon off the spiritual beings, when their bodies get killed on the battlefields. However, why should one rival group be funneling weapons to their opposite's armies?" On the surface of it all, it did not make sense to any of us. We chatted about the situation for some time, but with no further solid conclusions.

Chapter 21 The Imposter Strikes Again

Two agonizingly slow weeks were required for Andre to conduct the survey properly. We just could not walk up to members of the High Council and ask them these very sensitive questions. Obviously, their army and plans for its use was an off-topic subject, especially for visitors from West Reach. Cleverly, Andre made use of Allia to survey these critical people. Actually, it took several days to define accurately which people out of the hundred thousand plus that lived in Pieta we should survey. Opinion leaders and those in power were the likely choices, but Andre also included several innkeepers and tradesmen.

Finally, the challenging task of sorting out the results was at hand. Surrounded by piles of parchment notes taken, we four Guardians, Elona, and Allia began to summarize them. Essentially, we were looking for those names that appeared most frequently. Two days later, we finally had the mess summarized. However, Allia's comment spoke volumes, "This cannot be; I guess your theory doesn't work."

We all stared at the final parchment with the tabulated results. The number one person to whom the majority had responded telling them how bad things were was Allia herself! "Look, I am definitely *not* trying to start a war!" she protested very defensively.

"No one is saying that you are," I tried to calm her down. "Look at the runner up, one Lucius Thalax. Caitlyn said he is a Centurion trader who sells arms to Pieta. Is that correct?"

"Well, yes, he is our primary contact person, but he has only half the count that I do," she continued to protest her innocence. The others looked completely baffled.

Elona said, "Well, we must have made a mistake somewhere, that's the only explanation."

Suddenly, I gave a little laugh, "Of course! Of course! I ought to have seen this without even doing the survey! Of course, it does make perfect sense." Everyone stared at me, and Allia was about to slug me. Well, at least she made a fist.

"Actually, these results are the very best possible result for all of us, including Pieta itself. Don't you see?" Obviously, none did. "Look, the border between Solamina and Pieta has been fairly closed for years now. The average trader going back and forth has brought little real information back with him. We don't have to deal with some evil person spreading lies to everyone here in Pieta. On the contrary, all the critical information has been funneled solely and only through Allia here, with some help from this Lucius Thalax person."

"But I'm not a traitor!" Allia fairly screamed at me.

"No you are not. In effect, you are innocent. The key, critical question for you, Allia, is how have you gotten the information that you have been sharing with the council?"

"From the Sisterhood messengers that we send back and forth to Solamina," she declared, as if that ought to be plainly obvious.

I smiled, "Yes that is precisely what I had assumed all along. I should have spotted this two weeks ago. You can kick my butt." I glanced around to make sure Caitlyn was not present, remembering what happened the last time I so declared.

"But," Allia started to say and then thought better of it.

"How do you relay such critical information, Allia, by written messages?" I asked.

"Oh no, that would be far, far too dangerous for everyone. Think what would happen if someone intercepted it — though everyone knows that the Sisterhood spans across all of the sectors and is not loyal to a single city-state. Nevertheless, we would never take such a risk as a written message. We send dispatch riders with a verbal message to deliver. I don't know the details. I just prepare my message and speak it to the next available dispatch Sister, and she takes it from there. When a dispatch rider arrives, she comes to me and speaks the message in private. I then relay it to those that need to know."

Grinning, I replied, "That is precisely what I predicted you would be doing. Now do you all see what I am hinting at?" Again, blanks stares came my way.

Elona ventured a guess, though, "Are you saying that their messengers are somehow at fault?"

"Suppose for a moment that some evil person, whose goal was to bring about a civil war between Pieta and Solamina, somehow got on this absolutely critical communications line. That person could color every message that was exchanged between the two Sisterhoods. Obviously, now that the Sisterhood has a High Council representative in every city, they would be obligated to share that information with their respective councils, who would then act upon that information. I think it is a perfect setup for someone who was trying to bring about a war."

"Wow! I can see it clearly now!" exclaimed Elona. "Now it does indeed make complete sense. We ought to have seen it at the beginning, before we went and did this whole survey thing."

"Are you saying that we have a traitorous Sister in our ranks?" protested Allia.

"I highly doubt that, Allia. I've never heard of any Sister ever being disloyal to the Sisterhood, but then I don't know all that much about your organizations. I would just be completely taken aback if one were, however."

She felt vindicated and it showed clearly upon her face, whose color now returned to normal. I continued, "Now our task is touchy. Without raising any alarm, we need to find out precisely how the message system actually works and who is involved — all the details. From that information, we may be able to work out what to do next. Need I point out that at this point in time, this should be kept in the strictest confidence. Not a word beyond us and perhaps Mandi and Alice, agreed?" Everyone did, though I knew I was going to have a hard time not telling my friends and sister.

"Okay, I will fetch those two. I'm sure one of them can fill us in on the messenger details," Allia said. She left to find her two leaders. We cleaned up the massive paper mess while she was gone. In less than ten minutes, she returned with Mandi and Alice in tow.

I quickly explained our findings and what that meant. Both women were nearly dumbstruck to find out that the Sisterhood was somehow involved. "What we need now is to know the precise workings of your messenger system," I said calmly.

"It's a relay system," Mandi began. "We station several Sisters at key locations, one is always nearby Allia, naturally. She sends and receives the most messages by far. Yet, Alice knows the details; that is her responsibility."

Alice explained that a dozen Sisters were assigned to the messenger service, rotated as needed. When Allia needed to send a message, she contacted the Sister on duty, told her the message, and got her to repeat it until she was satisfied that the messenger had it memorized. Next, that Sister would ride up the northeast spoke road for fifty miles, and then take the rim road southward until she got to the last village, Brindle, which lay on the border of Solamina and Pieta, though it was still in Pieta proper. Brindle was also directly on the great east-west coastal paved roadway that the Centurions had built some fifty years ago. Just a few miles further down the paved road, she took Solamina's rim road that similarly intersected the coastal road. Finally, a few miles up that road was a village called Halibut. There, she would find her Solamina counterpart and relay the message to her. Once she was satisfied that the other rider had the message memorized, she would return, while the other rider would follow a similar path up the rim road, and then down a spoke road into Solamina. If there were a dire emergency, the riders would save time by taking the coastal roadway directly.

"So at least a dozen Sisters make this ride into Halibut?" I asked, wondering how so many could be a part of the subterfuge.

"Oh no. Usually only Sister Mia makes that long ride, because she is one of our best riders and fighters. She has never been intercepted nor molested along the way. She is a no-nonsense person," Alice explained. Then, she added, "I would trust her with my life. She ought to be above suspicion!"

"Ah ha!" I exclaimed. "Now we are getting somewhere! One rider delivers all the messages."

"Well, two actually," Alice explained. "Sister Abrianna is stationed in Brindle and it is she who is met by the Solamina rider when a message is coming from them."

"So someone from Solamina meets Abrianna in Brindle?" I asked. She nodded affirmative. "Does Solamina follow the same pattern? That is, with two Sisters making the runs, one from Solamina outward, and one from Halibut outward?"

"Now that you ask," Alice said rather surprised, "I don't know. I always just assumed that they ran their messenger service as we do. It would make sense to do it that way. I cannot see how they could do otherwise, unless they relayed the message to someone always stationed in Halibut. Now what do we do?"

"We think," I replied and did just that. I needed a way to find out if the messages were in fact being altered somewhere along the way, and if so, narrow it down to as few Sisters as possible — all without raising any red flags that something was going on. "We must be very careful not to alert anyone what we are doing. I have an idea."

"Suppose that we send someone that we completely trust to Solamina and have them explain what we are attempting to do. Simultaneously, we will send a specific fake message both ways, and then wait and see how that message comes through. I suspect that both messages will arrive somewhat altered for the worse. This way, we can either prove or disprove our theory."

Andre spoke up, "Let's send Felice and Adriana. Neither is from Pieta or Solamina. This way, neither side will be suspicious of the sender."

"Good idea, but will they risk this potentially dangerous mission?" I asked.

"Have them take the coastal road, it's faster and safer," Alice replied. "I'm sure if you explain how serious this is, they'll not hesitate to do it. They are, after all, fellow Sisters."

"Now we need a message, one which is harmless enough. I certainly don't want to cause a war to break out, but one which could be suitable altered," I said, thinking quickly. We discussed several ideas among ourselves.

"How about this," put in Elona.

Our army is finishing its basic training and is getting ready to deploy into the field. If there are no signs that Solamina/Pieta is massing its army on its border, then our council will recommend that they be deployed in scattered locations throughout the entire sector.

"Brilliant! If an army is so scattered, it is effectively useless," I exclaimed. "That would also be a signal for peaceful relations. Yet, it could be altered in any number of ways. Excellent, Elona." She beamed; the apprentice had made a good contribution.

"Consider it done! I'll go get Adriana and Felice," Mandi replied, confident this message would be just perfect. A few minutes later, she returned with a pair of mystified women. Neither had expected to be called into this very private meeting.

I had to explain to Adriana and Felice, "Essentially, we now suspect that the messages being relayed between the two Sisterhoods, Solamina and Pieta, are being altered somewhere along the lines of communication. What we want to do is to send a special message both ways and see if it is altered. That means we need to alert the counterparts of Mandi and Allia of what we are doing so they can play their parts. The trouble is, if the message does come through altered for the worst, then those Sisters may take matters into their own hands. Above all, we do not, I repeat, we do not want to alert whoever is doing the alterations that we are on to them. Hence, even though they may have an overwhelming urge to do something about it, they are to take no action until they hear from us."

"It sounds good from this end," Adriana replied, fiddling with her hair. I could tell she had some problem with my idea. I encouraged her to say what she was thinking, and she continued, "Well, you have to look at it from their viewpoint. A couple Sisters from a far distant sector come riding in saying all this. Would you be inclined to believe them and go along with them? If I was in their shoes, I certainly would not."

"Ah, the fatal flaw in my plan," I commented, realizing that she spoke with a good sense of reality on them. "Ideas?" I threw it open to all concerned.

Felice asked, "Does the Sisterhood in Solamina already know that some Guardians are making their way across the Sea Princes and will soon visit them? You all were expecting us when we came. Would it be a safe assumption that they would also have gotten word as well?" Now that was a good question. Mandi explained that they had passed that information on when it had come several weeks ago. Since then, she'd had a couple queries relating to us and had already sent word that we were in Pieta.

Andre jumped in, "Well, that settles it. I'll go along with Felice and Adriana. Certainly, they will believe me. I can coordinate things."

Mandi scratched her head, "I hate to be sexist, but you are a man. Any man seen going into our headquarters is going to raise a red flag, if you follow me. Could you possibly send Waverly instead? She can go disguised as a Sister and would not raise any undue attention."

We all looked at Waverly, who replied, "After all, I am your Communicator. I can relay at once what is going on there. We can stay in touch easily."

"Okay, Waverly, you may go. Just be extra careful," I added. "When you have taken off down the coastal road, Allia, you send the message in the usual way. Waverly, Adriana, and Felice ought to be in Solamina long before the message arrives."

"One minor detail," broke in Felice, "it's been a very long time since I was in Solamina. Could you possibly send along another Sister who is more familiar with the Sisterhood there? I don't want to get delayed because of whatevers."

Mandi nodded, "Point well taken. Yes, Alice, send along someone to act as guide. How soon can you be ready to travel?"

Adriana answered, "Give us an hour to make preparations. Is that soon enough?" I admired the efficiency of these women. A few minutes ago, both were probably relaxing, enjoying their free time and the next, they were off on a mission.

While the others headed off to make the arrangements, I continued, "Let's assume that the messages do get altered for the worst. Assume as well that Solamina uses two Sisters on relay as you do. Then, that leaves us with four women who could be doing the alterations."

Elona added, "But since the messages are getting altered both ways, two of the four must be involved, doesn't that make sense? Would that not imply that there are two of these Grey Creatures involved? After all, one is always in Solamina, while the other is in the border town of Halibut. Or vice versa, if it's Pieta Sisters doing the alterations. Or it could be one from Pieta in Brindle who alters it when it comes from Solamina and one in Halibut who alters it when it comes from Pieta. Or could these creatures actually be monitoring things in the two cities, passing along the altered messages when they ride out to the two border towns?"

We all got a good chuckle out of this pile of "or's." I suggested, "We could eliminate the Sister here in Pieta to whom the message is relayed before she rides to Brindle simply by being sufficiently close to her when the message gets delivered to her."

"Wouldn't Jolina be the best one qualified for that task?" asked Alton. "She does have an uncanny knack for sensing them far better than we. Just look what happened at that inn council meeting."

"True, but then look how she panicked when she did," I countered.

"Well, she was not expecting to meet one then. If we asked her to help this time, she would be alert for it and probably would not react too badly," Alton countered. "But we had better also ask Edgar; she never goes anywhere without him anymore."

"Okay, you can go ask her," I yielded, "but for heaven's sake, don't insist or push her into doing something she doesn't want to do." He agreed and left to find her and Edgar.

You should have seen the look on Jolina's face when she, Alton, and Edgar came walking into our room a short while later. Proud, pride, worthwhile, these do not do her justice. She said, "I'm terrified of these creatures, but I really want to help. I know I am more sensitive to their presence than anyone else, probably because you are not blind. Edgar will be with me, so I should be okay. Besides, Alton said I don't even have to be close to the two conversing Sisters."

"Thanks, Jolina, you are an incredibly brave woman," I

complimented her; the others chimed in similarly and Jolina's face shone brightly. Since she was risking her life for us, I felt it only proper and right that she should know what we were attempting to ascertain. I filled her and Edgar in on the details, knowing that I would also have to tell my sister and fellow musicians as well. So much for keeping a lid on our plans.

Shortly, Adriana came by to say farewell and that they were now heading out of town. Allia gave them another half hour to get clear of the city proper. Meanwhile, two Sisters led Edgar and Jolina out for a walk. These two did not know our plans, but were told where to take them: close to the stables, where the messenger who would ride to Brindle would receive the message from Allia, relayed to her by other Sisters. Timing was critical, so we gave them plenty of time to get into position so Jolina could sense if there was a Grey Creature nearby the stables.

At last, Allia sent for her messenger and gave her the message to be delivered to the Sisterhood in Solamina. From behind a partly opened doorway, we all listened in and heard the Sister repeating the message several times until she had it down pat. She gave a brisk salute and left to go find the rider at the stables. We rejoined Allia, who said, "So far so good. She has the message correct. Now we just have to wait."

"How long?" I asked.

"The message should be in Solamina in four days. Waverly's group should be there in three or less, depending upon how fast Adriana pushes them," Allia replied.

"How can we wait four days?" I exclaimed, and we all chuckled. Every one of us wanted to know the outcome right now! After all, if the messages were being altered, we really had a problem on our hands!

An hour later, Jolina and Edgar returned. She'd sensed nothing at all, and we all gave a big sigh of relief. In fact, she had been close enough to hear the message; she swore the rider woman had memorized it correctly.

"Well, then, that eliminates one of the four," declared Elona. "That leaves three to go."

Over dinner, I explained in detail what we had done in Vito, rescuing Hermino from the clutches of the Grey Creature. Of course, Mandi and the others had already gotten word of the imposter being exposed, but had not known of our part in it. She commented, "I might have known that you Guardians would have been behind it. I found it hard to believe that the Sisters in Vito did all that by themselves. I certainly could not have done it. Now it makes sense. Yet I do see the need for secrecy — rather parallel to the Simone-Simon historical situation, isn't it?" We grinned.

Later on when I had filled Caitlyn and the others in on what we had found out from the survey and the test messages, Caitlyn commented, "Now don't you think you should check out this Lucius Thalax person? Perhaps he is one of the Grey Creatures, though I did not feel ill when we were around him and Jolina did not react. Nevertheless, he is second on the list for spreading dire news. After all, the Centurions now have dealings with all the different sectors. What better way to set one against the other than through him?"

The next day, we spent making inquiries about Lucius Thalax. Various Sisters were contacted, and we slowly pieced the sketchy data together. He had arrived in Pieta some five years ago and opened up shop. All manner of trade goods to and from the Southlands were funneled through him. At first, mostly wine and olives were sent south in exchange for additional food, spices, iron ore, and coal. Gradually, year by year, more and more of the trade was in weapons of war. This past year, armaments comprised nearly one hundred percent of the trade with the Centurions!

We learned that three light skiffs routinely sailed back and forth between Pieta and New Barq, delivering his newly made orders back to the Southlands. The actual merchandise was always shipped in the large sea worthy Sea Prince vessels. I pointed out that to date we had no knowledge whether the mantises could disguise themselves as humans and walk among us. Considering their vastly different body shapes and enormous sizes, I doubted that they could. However, they certainly could implant thoughts and ideas in someone's head. Of that, I had firsthand knowledge from a half century ago, when I was in the Red Desert.

Conclusion: if the mantises were also involved, finding out their part would be a vastly more difficult challenge than the imposter Greys. In truth, I had no idea how we might do just that. Caitlyn did not like my ignoring of Lucius Thalax and so took matters into her own hands several days later when we were all wrestling with what to do about the altered messages.

At dinnertime on the fourth day, Waverly made mental contact with me and relayed the message as received by the Solamina High Council Sisterhood member, Renata Bleu. The message was:

Pieta's army is finishing its basic training and is getting ready to deploy into the field. They are going to deploy all along the border with Solamina as a warning for Solamina not to do anything brash.

"Damn!" exclaimed Mandi.

"Well, that explains a whole lot!" said Allia.

"I wonder what the return message will be," I commented. "See, Allia, you have been vindicated completely. You have been fed false information, and the High Council of Pieta has acted on it, which they naturally ought to have done."

"Yes, all well and good," she retorted, "but now how do we explain all this to the High Council?"

"Don't do anything yet," I quickly advised, "we don't know the full story."

"Argh. We wait another four days!" she exclaimed in disgust.

Waverly notified me Renata had just sent the return message. Hence, I relayed this small bit of news. Yes, we would have to wait another four days, but none of us expected anything but an altered message to arrive. The crux of the problem was what do we do about it now? How do we expose the plot? How do we repair the damage done? These were monumental problems, I thought.

Unbeknownst to me, Caitlyn and her group made another visit to Lucius Thalax. Later she told me what she had said. All cheery, she told him, "Well, looks like there is not going to be any civil wars around here. Have you heard the latest news? They've signed a treaty wherein missionaries from both churches will be allowed to travel freely throughout both sectors. Isn't that just great news?"

Once she had delivered the news and bought a knife for me as a present, they left. However, they hid out and spied on what he did next. She observed that he took a parchment scroll down to the docks and delivered it to a man on one of the fast sailing skiffs, which set sail almost at once. "So you see, Bethany, he is not in mental communication with mantises. He is sending ordinary messages back to someone in New Barq."

Okay, so I gave her a hug and a lot of credit. I even had her explain what she had done to the other Sisters, who were likewise pleased to find out that Lucius Thalax simply sent ordinary messages back to New Barq. He was therefore a vastly smaller problem that could be later handled. However, little did we know how wrong we were at this time.

Four days later, the return fake message arrived. I Mind Linked with Waverly just to be doubly certain of the original message. Like the one we had sent, this one read nearly the same, suggesting that Solamina was about to deploy its army along the border with Pieta, clearly an escalation of the hostilities, which, if followed, would bring the two sectors much closer to an all-out civil war! What to do about it all was quite another problem indeed.

Since Jolina's observation ruled out any alteration of the message as given to the dispatch rider, then only three possibilities remained. Our dispatch rider altered it or one or both of those from Solamina did the deed. All of us found it very hard to believe that one or more Sisters would have sold out the Sisterhood! Yet, on the surface of it, such appeared to be the case.

"What happens when the rider is ill or indisposed?" I asked. "Do you send a substitute rider?"

"Of course," Mandi replied, "but she is seldom ill."

"Well, I can see no other way but for us to go and see if we can find out what is going on," I concluded. "We do have the perfect cover, troubadours traveling across the Sea Princes."

"I'm going as well," insisted Mandi, "and I'll bring along several hundred fighters. We'll put a stop to this at once."

"Whoa, hold on a minute," panic crept into my mind as I saw hundreds of Sisters being killed by a Grey Creature. "Let's think this through a bit. Suppose that you really do have two traitors in your midst. If you suddenly arrive at those villages, the women will be tipped off that the masquerade is up. Further, if it is the Solamina Sisters who are doing this, wouldn't you going into Solamina territory be viewed as an act of aggression by some? It might start the war we are trying to prevent. Besides, we'd never be able to find out just what has been going on there. On the other hand, if the Grey Creatures are somehow involved, one of them could easily slay all of your fighters." The Sisters uniformly looked downcast and angry, frustrated that there was seemingly nothing to be done.

"We need to move secretly and quietly and not raise any suspicion until we find out what is going on. Once we know, then we must find a way to let everyone on both sides know what has been happening, defusing the aggression if at all possible," I suggested solemnly.

Mandi settled down, assuming her proper leadership role, "Forgive my outburst. You are right, of course. My temper got the best of me for a minute."

"You have every right to be angry. I certainly would if I was in your shoes. Let's all put our heads together on this one," I said diplomatically.

Alton suggested, "Bethany, I think you're on the right track with us visiting those towns. We certainly can detect the presence of any Grey Creatures. If they aren't involved, then the only answer must be a pair of traitor Sisters, at which point the Sisterhood could become actively involved in bringing them to light and justice."

"Hold on a minute; we're forgetting that we have Waverly with Solamina's Sisterhood right now," I suddenly saw the genesis of an idea forming. "I think the very first action ought to be some direct, one on one communication between the two Sisterhood leaders and us."

"You mean we should go to Solamina?" asked Mandi not believing what she was hearing, after I just vetoed her heading off to Solamina.

"No, I had something else in mind. Please, why don't you go get us some tea and biscuits; give me a few minutes of total quiet? I want to contact Waverly." I got a fair number of strange stares. Waverly was over a hundred miles away at this point. Yet, the Sisters did as I asked.

Once they had left, Alton whispered, "Mind Link?" I nodded. I relaxed and expanded my awareness, concentrating upon reaching Waverly. She was very easy to make contact with — she was a Communicator.

Waverly, I want to try to make a Mind Link between the three leaders here and their counterparts there in Solamina so they can discuss the ramifications of this mess directly. I think our minstrels traveling on to these two key outlying towns must be the first step in unraveling the mystery. However, on the off chance that the Grey Creatures aren't involved, it would be prudent to have two Sisterhood fighter groups nearby. Somehow, we must get the proof of what has been going on and make it very visible to both High Councils, somehow. How — I've no idea yet. Is such a Mind Link going to be possible? I can help on this end.

Now that is a brilliant idea, things are getting nearly uncontrollable here. When both messages came through vastly altered for the worse, it was all I could do to keep the Sisters here from going after their two messengers! Let's give it a try. I'll round up Mina, Ali, and Renata. Contact me when you are ready on your end. I agreed and broke contact.

"It's on," I grinned at Alton, Andre, and Elona. Soon, the Sisters returned with their arms full of hot tea, cheese, and biscuits. While snacking, I explained what we were going to attempt.

"One of the skills of our Communicators is mental telepathy. We can make the connection between more than just the two of us. When we do, it is called a Mind Link. Waverly is going to join their three, Mina, Ali, and Renata with us. However, I forgot to ask who they were, sorry. I assume you know who is who?" Mandi nodded. "I will join us here with Waverly, and all of us will be able to communicate with each other."

Allia looked upset and frightened, "But I don't know anything about telepathy. How will we be able to talk?" I'd forgotten how strange telepathy must seem to those for whom it was just a fairy tale.

"Relax, it is the simplest thing. All you need to do is think your thoughts and the others will hear them. If you get too disoriented, just go ahead and speak the words aloud, but that is not necessary. Alton, you make sure we don't get interrupted." He nodded as he assumed his role of Protector. I went on, "Now let's just get nice and comfortable. It doesn't hurt a bit. Only the thoughts you think or speak are going to be heard. By the way, who are Mina, Ali, and Renata?"

"Renata Bleu is their High Council rep, my counterpart," Allia quickly said. "Mina Lia is their Mother and Ali Bastia is their Fighter Group Leader."

"We should explain fully what we have done and the conclusions we have made thus far. Okay, relax time." I shut my eyes and expanded my awareness slightly. I detected the faint pull of Waverly, for she had kept some slight attention on me all the while, making our rejoining very easy for me to do. I would have my hands full maintaining contact with those here with me. I easily found Alton, Andre, and Elona and connected with them. Next, one by one, I added the other three Sisters into the link.

This is amazingly fantastic, so utterly intimate! thought Allia. The others, including Elona, who had never experienced a Mind Link, had a very similar reaction. I was grateful for Waverly maintaining our original connection, because I easily latched onto her and was aware of another three minds there with her.

Bethany here, I've got Mandi, Alice, Allia, and three other Guardians connected with us on this end. Perhaps, I should speak first and bring everyone up to speed. Just don't all try to talk at the same time or this will become a mess! Slowly, I began to relay all that we had done thus far. Next, I let Mandi verify all this with Mina, just to make sure both leaders were aligned together.

Mina was furious that in all likelihood two of her own Sisters were actively betraying the Sisterhood. I expected that reaction. However, chatting in a Mind Link was a great convincer; I was certain that all would now follow our orders and not charge off and do anything rash or stupid, destroying any chance of bringing this into the light of day. I made sure that both representatives saw how utterly crucial it would be to get the evidence needed to convince the High Councils that they had been used for several years now.

Finally, I got all parties to agree to go along with my current plan. At last, we all said farewells and we broke the link. Naturally, the three Sisters thanked me profusely and just had to chat with me about their experience. True, I had shared some key druwid actions with outsiders, but had I not, then the Solamina Sisterhood may well have acted on their own, botching our chances. Elona's comment was shared by all, "That was *so* intimate!"

The next morning, my initial plan began. Alice took Adriana's place as our Sisterhood leader, and she brought along two of her top fighters with her, one of which was thoroughly familiar with the back roads around the Pieta sector. It was very hard to replace Felice I discovered. Meanwhile, Mandi and a hundred Sisterhood fighters headed down the coastal paved roadway. Rather than leaving in a large group, they left in small groups of five, scattered over several hours. Their task was to move into position south of Brindle.

Over in Solamina, Mina and Ali were doing the same, accompanied by a hundred of their fighters. Meanwhile, Renata took Waverly, Felice, and Adriana to meet casually the dispatch rider stationed there in Solamina. Nothing more, just meet her.

Waving goodbye to our new friends, our gaily-painted wagons rolled out of Pieta, heading on the northeast spoke road, actually following the path the dispatch riders would have taken. Our destination was Brindle. We had not gotten more than five miles out of town when I got a message from Waverly. *She's not a Grey Creature! I don't understand this but she is just a young woman.* Waverly was very confused; could we be completely wrong about all this? I reconnected from my end and told her to get back to the Sisterhood inn and await further orders.

Next, I relayed the news to our party and then made contact with Mandi, telling her the unexpected and strange news. That they may be dealing with a traitor Sister radiated from Mandi's mind.

Alton's dry comment was simply, "Perhaps the other Solamina Sister is our Grey Creature." He sounded hopeful.

Two agonizingly slow days passed before we spied the outskirts of the small village of Brindle. Cradled in a small valley surrounded by vineyards and cork trees, Brindle was home to perhaps five hundred people at most. Roughly circular in shape, the village had around a hundred buildings of various sizes. Some were well maintained, but others looked like they had seen better days. Alice had told us beforehand that the size of their local inn could not accommodate our large party. Thus, we made camp at the western edge of town.

While the others went about the task of setting up camp, Alice led Alton and me into town to locate Sister Benia, the dispatch rider. The Sisterhood had purchased a very small cabin near the eastern edge of town. Here was where Benia or her replacement would stay, awaiting the next message from Solamina. As expected, she answered Alice's knock on her door.

Benia was only about twenty years old, young and wiry, but not very good looking. She had an ugly scar on her left cheek. I suspected that was the result of a love affair turned sour; Alice had alluded to her deformity. "Hi ya," she said cheerily. "Wow, Alice, you all the way out here! Breaks the boredom; come on in."

We did, and Alice introduced us, "I'd like you to meet Ket Bethany, the leader of the troubadours from West Reach and his companion, Alton Woodgrove." We shook hands, but she gaped in awe at us. Even stationed out here, she knew who we were, Guardians.

"Wow! Wow!" she kept saying, all the while fussing with her hair; she'd been napping, and it was a little messed up. "I can make some tea. Got a little wine, if you'd rather. Sorry, only got two chairs here. No room for more." Indeed the one room cabin held a cot, a wardrobe, a table, two chairs, and a small stove for cooking along with several cabinets where food was stored. Pots and pans lay scattered about and more than a few were dirty. Benia was evidently lax on doing the dishes.

"We'll pass on tea, Benia," I apologized, "the others are setting up camp just outside the village. We are going to play at the inn tonight, and we wanted to personally invite you to come and listen."

She was delighted. From her enthusiasm, I could see she was one very bored young woman. I guessed that she would sit in her cabin for days before a message might come. Only then could she get into action, only to return later on to more days of utter boredom.

When we rejoined the others at camp, absolutely everyone crowded around us to hear the verdict. "She's a fine young woman," I said to the hushed group. Everyone had the same thought, "It has to be the other one in Solamina at Halibut."

Once we had our dinner, we then carried our gear to the small inn. Quickly, we saw that the entire town could not get inside, so we did the next best thing. We played our concert on the front porch, turning it into an evening the town would never forget.

When we got back to our camp and wagons, everyone looked at me, with Alton voicing what everyone was thinking. "Well, now what do we do? Alice says that Halibut is only a few hours from here, and we should be there by noon tomorrow. So what do we do when we get there and detect that the Sister is really a Grey Creature?" From the nearly unison nodding of heads, I could tell this had occupied their minds all evening.

"This message situation has been going on for years. Each of these messengers spends the vast majority of their time either waiting out here in a border town with little to do or in Solamina, where they must still be readily available at all times. Alice, how frequently are messages sent back and forth this way?"

"Oh I'd guess perhaps once a week at the very most would be the norm. However, there have been times when a flurry of messages went back and forth for a few days. Why do you ask?" Alice wondered, as did everyone else.

"Look at Benia's situation. She sits around her tiny cabin all day and all night long waiting for the messenger to arrive. I don't know about you all, but I would be incredibly bored, with so very little to do. Alice, how about the Sister on duty in Pieta, the one who rides here bringing the message? What is her life like?"

"Pretty much the same; she has to be on call all the time. When she goes to the market, she must let another know precisely where she is heading and where is going to be, just in case a message comes down while she is out. We do have another take her place so she can attend a dance now and then," Alice replied. "Why?"

"Okay, suppose that you are the Grey Creature masquerading as one of these dispatch riders. How would you like being stationed out here with nothing to do the vast majority of the time? Personally, I could not stand it. Nothing to do. Boring beyond belief. See where I am going with this?" Blank stares confronted me.

"Could, could the creatures somehow know in advance when a message is to be sent and then intercept them?" asked Elona, trying to grasp at any explanation that might fit my synopsis.

"That would mean, Elona, that we ought to find that all the dispatch riders are simply are intercepted at some point on their journey, right?" Okay, I was using her, but also I was allowing her mind to formulate the obvious extrapolation from her original statement.

"Yes, it would. When they are riding, in the process of delivering the message, they must be somehow intercepted. But how do these creatures get the message out of them and then implant a false message without the Sister being aware of it all? That would be implied from this, would it not?" Elona bit her lip, thinking hard, imagining various possibilities, all of which were beyond her normal imagination, beyond the imagination of nearly everyone who was here, except me. Even my Guardians did not really know of what these creatures were capable. I did.

"When we get to Halibut and meet their relay messenger tomorrow, I predict we will find a normal Sister, one who is just as bored as Benia is here. Okay, I'll tell you my theory on what has been going on here," I relented. "Mind you, it is just a theory based upon what we have observed firsthand. My guess is that we are dealing with a single Grey Creature, probably living in Solamina disguised as someone who is probably not an important person, so as not to raise suspicions as they were in Vito. He knows the precise route these dispatch riders take; they always travel the same route and arrive at the same destinations. The weakest link is: how does he know when a message is to be sent or that one is coming in to Solamina from Pieta? Ignore that detail for now. Somehow, he spots the messenger, intercepts them. I suspect that he reads the message from their minds and then plants an altered message in its place. Finally, he somehow blanks out the entire meeting from the consciousness of the rider, sending them on their way."

"You mean that these women have been hypnotized somehow?" asked Alice. "Now that would seem to make sense to me. I've seen some hypnotists doing parlor tricks, and the victim doesn't even know he's following their orders and directives. I can understand now how this might be possible. The imposter could easily plant a suggestion so that the rider would not remember the interception at all. Makes some sense."

Elona asked the key question I knew someone would be asking, "Does anyone know how to 'un-hypnotize' someone? If so, we could really find out what has been going on from the poor riders."

"That is Waverly's next assignment," I grinned. "I maybe a Wid, but I'm not a Communicator; this is definitely her area of expertise, but this is getting ahead of events. Tomorrow we must meet this remaining Sisterhood dispatch rider. If she is just a Sister, then we'll move into the next phase of this operation. If by some chance I'm completely wrong in my deductions and we run into a Grey Creature imposter, we'll keep right on going, trying not to do anything to bring attention to ourselves."

Everyone seemed to accept my judgment in this matter. The relief that the other Sisters felt knowing that thus far three out of the four riders were perfectly okay was more than evident. Yes, had the two turned out to be Grey Creatures, things could get very messy and bloody quickly.

Midmorning the next day, we rolled into Halibut, a small outpost on the border of Solamina and Pieta, population even smaller than Brindle. Here, the craftsmen produced quality wooden casks for food storage or for wine. Barrel makers were sitting outside their shops working away carving, shaping, and steaming wooden slats as we rode into the village. Here, folks waved, smiled, and even stared at the gay wagons. Alton announced who we were and that we would be playing a concert on the steps of the inn this evening. Naturally, this statement brought a great deal of conversation among the folks of Halibut.

Once we made camp, again at the edge of the small village, Alice led us to the Sisterhood cabin, located at the very edge of the circle of some thirty buildings. She had gotten directions from her counterpart during the Mind Link the other day. Again, we knocked on her door, and another young woman, around twenty with light brown hair cut short and overly large big blue eyes opened the door. "Message? Oops, I guess not. Come on in Sister."

Alice, Alton, and I entered her small cabin, which was very similar to Benia's cabin. As she walked over to the two chairs, I noticed that she had a limp in her left leg. She noticed me noticing it, "Dad broke it. Got drunk; beat me; I left him. May his bones rot in his wine. Sorry, I only have two chairs. Alice you take one." She left the other chair for us men to fight over, while she sat down on her bed.

Once more, Alice did the introductions, only this time mentioning that we were Guardians; she had no idea whether our presence was widely known within the Solamina Sisterhood. Interestingly enough, we weren't! "Gosh, real Guardians? The miracle workers? In person?" she replied flabbergasted and shocked.

"In the flesh," I smiled in reply. "Very pleased to meet you, Sister Lonia. We are actually also traveling musicians from West Reach. Tonight, we're giving you a concert from the steps of the inn. I wanted to extend my personal invitation for you to come and hear us play."

"Wow! Me? Sure, sure!" the excitement shone from her eyes and face. Then it darkened, "I'll bet anything that a message comes through, and I'll have to spend the night riding to Solamina. Be just my luck!"

"Nah, don't think so, Lonia. I think you are going to have a nice night of it all. I bet you are a good rider and very knowledgeable with horses."

She smiled, "Of course. I'm one of the best riders around. I'm light as a feather, and I know horses. You know, it's like they and I can communicate with each other, not like people. I don't really get along well with people. But with horses, why, we are kindred spirits; we ride free as the wind. There is nothing like a fast canter in the wind up a hill and down again. We move as one being, my horse and I. Nothing better in the world than a good horse ride. That's the one thing I dislike about this job, though. I so seldom get to ride anymore. Though I do sometimes steal away for a night ride, of course, when I don't think there is going to be any messages coming, you know. I mustn't miss a message, but then I really do miss going for a ride. I've got three horses of my own here, two mares and a stallion. One day, I am going to be a breeder of fine horses, so I rather have my start here. One of the mares is due to foal later this spring. If I raise her and train her well, I may be able to sell the colt and use the funds to begin my stables, you know, buy a higher quality mare. The stallion is very good, has great conformation, and stamina. He and I just love to ride just as fast as we can go."

Yes, Lonia was starved for someone to talk to! I finally got a word in, "We share the same love, Lonia. I just love to canter across the green fields back home, with my long hair flying behind me. Nothing can beat that sensation!"

Alton broke in, "Say, I can see that you two could talk about horses all day. Ket, we really do need to get back to the others and get our instruments ready and such. We've promised them all a concert. We wouldn't want to disappoint them. After we're all set, you can come back and chat with Lonia all you want." I knew he was teasing, but he was also giving us a graceful way to make our exit without alarming Lonia.

As we left, standing beside her open door, Lonia called out, "Oh please do come back, and I can show you my horses." I waved and said I would like nothing better.

Back at our camp, I relayed that Lonia was not a Grey Creature imposter. Everyone was relieved. At least for the moment, we were safe. Of course, everyone wanted to know what we were to do next, Phase Two as I had called it. I was secretive, okay, so I wasn't sure what to do next. I hadn't worked out the details yet. I bought some time by taking a time out to contact Waverly who was still in Solamina.

After explaining what I had observed, I asked her about hypnotism. She replied in her teaching mode, *A hypnotist literally stops someone's attention and fixes it solidly. He is not really controlling that person, just fixing the person's attention so hard that the only thing that is real is the hypnotist. Usually, it is done by swinging a bauble in front of the person's eyes and having him fixate his attention on the bauble. Based on what you have seen, those are the only two possibilities that I can ascertain: they are traitors or they are being hypnotized somehow. Interestingly, Bethany, the rider here in Solamina, Jenia, is also overly talkative similar to your Lonia. Probably that is because of their relatively boring isolation for long periods.*

That settled it. I asked her to relay my next request to the large group of Solamina Sisterhood fighters just south of us. At the same time, I contacted Pieta's group. Riding hard, three days would be needed before my next phase could be implemented. It was crucial that nothing about what we were planning should leak out to anyone. However, when the Fighter Group Leader of Solamina, Ali Bastia, arrived clandestinely, I had to do some explaining to everyone. It was imperative that Ali's presence here not be known to Lonia.

Hence, I gathered everyone together for a secret meeting. "No one is to know that Ali is here with us. She is Lonia's boss. It is vital that Lonia not know that Ali is here with us, so Ali has disguised herself and will pretend she is one of the many d'Grange Sisters with us. Shortly, we are going to have another message for Lonia to deliver to Solamina. All along the route, the several hundred Sisterhood fighters have fanned out and hidden themselves. The objective is simple: let's just observe what actually happens to our message as it is delivered. Ali and I will be accompanying Lonia. She and I have been talking a lot about how we love to ride like the wind, so it'll not be hard for me to convince her to let us tag along. What Lonia will not know is that every so often, a pair of Sisterhood fighters will also be watching us. Once we have passed by, then they will close in from behind, just in case trouble later develops. Also, our minstrel caravan will also move out along the same route, though obviously the wagons will be going much slower. The whole purpose of phase two is simply to observe what happens to the message. Thus, it is vital that the observers not be observed, if you follow what I am saying."

"Brilliant!" "Great idea!" "Why didn't we think of this?" were among the catcalls I received from everyone when I had finished. In two days' time, a "dispatch rider" came galloping up to Lonia's cabin. Conveniently, I was sitting on her porch chatting about horses with her. "Hiya, Lonia! Got one for you. Ready?" She stood and began to concentrate. "Pieta reports that one half of the army is being deployed on the Bonilla side against possible trouble from them."

The two women repeated the message several times until Lonia had memorized it perfectly. The other dispatch rider from Pieta then mounted and began her return trip home. While Lonia was quickly grabbing her supplies and gear, she asked, "You still want to go for a long fast ride, Ket?"

"You're on!" I exclaimed enthusiastically. I didn't have to fake this part; I hadn't been on a fast horse ride for far too long. "I'll bring along one of the d'Grange Sisters to look after me once we get to Solamina. She can follow along behind us." Lonia said this would be a fun trip, and I hastily exited to get my gear and horse. Also, I had to issue the final orders.

I found that Ali had already gotten my horse and our gear ready for the trip. She smiled as I complimented her for her thoughtfulness. Ali was thirty-five years old and a veteran of many skirmishes. She was a no-nonsense person with an alto voice that commanded the attention of others. Her athletic build spoke of many hours of training all throughout her life. She was now dressed in borrowed d'Grange Sisterhood clothing; and I used a conjuring spell to make her facial appearance look quite different to Lonia.

Five minutes after Lonia had gotten the message memorized, we three mounted up and kicked our horses into a full gallop. Ali, following my orders, stayed somewhat behind us. Purposely, I had undone my ponytail knot and let my hair fall normally behind me. Now riding like the wind, my hair flapped and fluttered behind me like a blazon red banner. Okay, so I'm a bit vain about my hair flying in the wind. Lonia looked over at me, commenting, "Looks cool! You do like to ride fast! Well, I have always liked to do it. I just can't ever seem to get enough of it. Bonnia here, she loves it too. See how she is stretching out with her front hooves? She is almost as fast as a real racehorse, though I have never entered her into any races, mind you. Perhaps I ought too? What do you think? Yours is keeping up. That is a good sign. If you can't keep pace, I have to follow orders and let you follow as you may. I have this message to deliver, you know. Should I race her?" She finally paused enough for me to answer.

"Sure why not? Is she wins some, then her foals would be even more valuable, don't' you think?" Oh no, I had just opened the door for Lonia to chat endlessly on the monetary value of her possible foals! She did in a seemingly endless stream of conversation for several minutes. At last, she decided that we ought to be quite for a while and just enjoy the fabulous ride. Whew!

After a while, she slowed the pace; the horses were well lathered and needed a respite. Periodically we raced ahead and then slowed. That was the pattern for the next two days. She rode well into the night, claiming that she had to reach Wilkin's cabin, the halfway point. The cabin was just off the road, well hidden in a thick grove of trees. If one did not know it was here, one would miss it. Lonia knew precisely where it was at, even in the dark. I could see why she made an excellent dispatch rider. Once inside, she lit a small oil lantern and together, we all took care of the horses, giving them a good rubdown. Lonia brought a bucket of clear, cold water from a little stream that ran just behind the cabin. Finally, we three went inside and fixed a light supper. Ali kept very quiet and tried to stay invisible in the background. I helped by asking Lonia questions, which kept her chatting gaily with me.

Lonia was up and at it before first light. As the sun rose, we were off once more, cantering down the dirt road. I marveled at the dewdrops sparking reddish in the early morning light. Yes, I knew I could have one great time just being a dispatch rider, as long as there were plenty of messages to relay, mind you. Lonia said that we would make Solamina before nightfall. Yes, we were covering miles rapidly!

While we were riding, I kept one eye pealed for the Sisters who were supposed to be hiding along the route. Several times, I did spot them, though Lonia, occupied somewhat by chatting with me, failed to see them, thankfully. I didn't know what she would do if she saw any Sisters hiding beside the road, and I didn't want to find out. We rode hard all day.

Around three in the afternoon, we were drawing close to Solamina. I could see faint traces of smoke high in the sky in the far distance. Here, the trail was surrounded on all sides by many olive groves. Occasionally, we would pass by a farmstead proper. Suddenly, without any warning, Lonia reined in her horse. She ceased all conversation with me and did not answer my questions. "What's up? Why are we slowing down?"

I watched her carefully and even moved slightly ahead of her so that I could see her face clearly. Her eyes told all! They had some far-away look in them. Lonia was barely aware of the universe around her! I whispered to Ali, who had come up close to see for herself, "She is in some kind of trance."

Off to the side of the road was a rundown, abandoned old barn, nearly ready to collapse. Obviously, it was long unused by anyone. Lonia walked her horse up to the barn and dismounted, leading her horse slowly inside. We two followed from a distance. Far off, I heard other Sisters moving in as well. Whatever happened, it was comforting to know that we were not alone. We two stood in the doorway watching Lonia. She tied her horse to a pillar and began digging in the dirt floor beside another pillar. Soon, she produced some kind of metallic object. She pushed a button on it and a red light started blinking. She laid the box-like object down on the ground and sat down on some rotting hay, eyes closed, waiting. Quickly, I had Ali take our two horses outside and hide them some distance away.

Meanwhile, I crept into the barn looking for a place where Ali and I could hide and not be seen. I knew that someone, a Grey Creature most likely, would soon be coming. Ali rejoined me, and together we crawled underneath some hay in a back corner, likely out of the way of Lonia. Only our eyes were visible, but with no internal light, the late afternoon slanting rays of the sun coming through the open barn doors would not illuminate us at all. We held our breaths and waited.

About a half hour later, a strange looking man quietly walked into the barn. I immediately sensed that cold chill down my spine! He was a Grey Creature disguised as a human. I felt involuntary trembling coming from Ali next to me, but I dared not whisper a comforting word. My fingers found hers and grasped them. That was all the reassurance I dared give her.

The man walked to the blinking box, did something to it to stop the blinking. Evidently, it was some kind of signaling device. He spoke in a cold chilling voice, "Lonia, repeat the message you are to deliver." She did so mechanically. He paused a moment, thinking about how to alter it, I assumed. Next, he said, "You will forget this message. You will forget this message."

Sounding a thousand miles away, her voice replied, "I cannot remember the message."

"Good. Here is the message you are to deliver in Solamina. Pieta reports that the entire army is being deployed to the Solamina side against a possible attack." He repeated it several times and had her repeat it several times. Then, he said, "You will not remember anything about this barn. You will not remember meeting me. You will sleep for another ten minutes. You will lead your horse out of the barn. You will mount your horse and begin to ride to Solamina. When you feel the air on your face, you will wake up and feel completely refreshed and ride hard to deliver your message." Once more, he repeated it several times. Without another word, he turned and left the barn. We could not see where he went. Once we thought he had gone, we two quickly scrambled out of the hay and barn. Ali brought our horses back, and we prepared to meet Lonia when she came out of the barn.

Slowly, still fogged out, Lonia led her horse out of the barn, mounted, and began to ride once more. Then, suddenly, she woke up and gaily declared, "I guess the horses are cooled down enough. Let's ride like the wind into Solamina!" Smiling at me, she cantered off. I kicked my horse and followed her; Ali was right behind me. From the corner of my eye, I also saw that during this delay time a large number of Sisters had gathered and were now preparing to follow from a distance.

The cool, late afternoon breeze calmed both Ali and me down. The cold, emotional chill from the creature finally left us. Soon we saw the outskirts of Solamina moving our way. When we came up to the gatehouse, Lonia called back, "I'll see you all later on after I deliver my message, if I can. Cya. Thanks for the company!"

We waved as she passed through the gate and into the city. Ali, disguised as a d'Grange Sister, handed the gate man two copper coins. As we approached, I briefly chanted a conjuring spell; those that watched us enter saw two similar looking women. I dared not let them see my long red hair; it would be a dead giveaway. The gateman nodded and we followed after Lonia. However, Lonia was completely out of sight.

Throngs of people crowded the streets as we meandered our way through them. Ali regained her composure, but was more serious than I had ever seen her be, "Follow me. This is the worst business I have ever been involved with — we must go to the secret safe place. I will bring the others there as fast as possible!"

She led me to the southwestern edge of the city where the coastal paved roadway from Pieta entered Solamina. Once more, the Sisterhood had built their new inn adjacent to the outer wall, only a defensive distance from the wall proper so that men could man the walls in times of siege. This time, Ali handed her horse over to a Sister in the stables and bade me do so as well, highly unusual. The unwritten rule is that the rider of the horse is responsible for its handling and stabling. Quickly, she led me inside and into the basement, avoiding most of the Sisters, who were out in the courtyard chatting with Lonia and interpreting her message. She walked me up to what appeared to be a side wall with a gorgeous tapestry hanging depicting a maritime scene. She felt for something just behind the hanging. I heard a grating sound and assumed a stone secret door had just opened. She pulled back one edge of the tapestry to reveal a black hole.

Several lanterns hung nearby, ostensibly to keep the storage room visible. She took one off its hook and told me to follow her. Ducking behind the hanging, now I could see steps leading downward. Out of curiosity, I counted them as we descended and the cool air of an underground chamber touched my senses. Forty-two steps, perhaps twenty feet underground, we arrived on level ground. I saw a tunnel running off in both directions. We headed westward down the tunnel. I guessed that when we had gotten beyond the walls, a large cavernous room opened before me. Across the space, I spied the tunnel continuing on, probably to a secret exit far from the walls.

The chamber was filled with dried foods and numerous blankets, a perfect hiding place, I thought. Ali said, "Help yourself to whatever you want to eat. Water's over there. I am going to round up everyone I can find. I'll bring Waverly here as well. This is incredibly serious business," she repeated herself. She lit several lanterns for me and then made a hasty exit, saying, "I apologize for wetting my pants, but that man scared the heck out of me. I've never done this before. Sorry. I must change." Even in the dim light, I could see her face turn scarlet with her confession.

"I won't tell anyone about it, Ali. Such a reaction is quite common. I'll make myself at home." She forced a smile and left, her footsteps echoing down the long tunnel. I felt suddenly very isolated! In part to get my bearings, I took one lantern and began to explore the chamber and its contents. I discovered a latrine against one far wall and even a small stash of swords and bows with quivers of arrows. A small treasure box, though locked, jingled with coins inside. I realized that this would make a great place for the Sisters to hide out from trouble, as well as a place to regroup and exit Solamina with money and supplies. Certainly, these women attempted to think of every possibility. No one else would look after them, I realized once more.

Bored, I fixed myself something to eat and then lay down to nap, waiting for others to arrive. Arrive they did, singly and in twos, Sisters slowly began arriving. Waverly and those who had accompanied her to Solamina arrived first, speaking in hushed voices. She spied me and said, "Ali is gathering all the leaders from both cities. Everyone should be assembled here in perhaps an hour. I take it the result was very shocking. I've never seen Ali so shook up. Several of her associates made similar comments to me on my way down here."

"Yes, shocking, but only the truth sets one free. Both Sisterhoods are now in the process of learning the horrible truth of what has been happening to their communications. What has me even more worried is that both sets of High Councils have believed their reports and have acted upon them all these years. What is this going to do to their credibility on their respective councils?"

"I've been thinking that one over for days now. It would be unfortunate for the Sisterhoods to lose face and trust after working so hard all these years to gain it. I wish there was some way we could lend them a hand with this," Waverly said sympathetically.

"I feel the same way, Waverly, that's why I have been going purposely slowly and have gotten both sets of leaders nearly together in space and time. I am still not certain what the next phase should be, though I know that they are going to insist on some action be taken immediately. Any ideas about undoing the hypnotism?"

"Well, some people are readily hypnotized, while others can be, but only with difficulty. Others, not at all. I doubt that you could be hypnotized, Bethany, and probably not myself either for that matter. Obviously, both these young women were easily entranced by the Grey Creature, but then perhaps it has some other technology that induces trances in the best of us,

340

who knows," Waverly began educating me on the subject. Hypnotism, I had never had time to examine before now.

I relayed to her all that I had seen and heard. "Knowing what happened, how easily orders were implanted in her mind, could you not hypnotize her and plant different commands?" I asked.

"That depends first upon whether or not I could actually hypnotize either of them and secondly whether my implanted commands would be powerful enough to override those of the Grey Creature," she answered.

"You know what? This is utterly incredible, but I just realized that we know virtually nothing about the human mind! We know a great deal about our fleshly bodies and the material universe. We know something about ourselves, spiritual beings, well a little bit at least, but nada about our minds and its operations! That would make a fascinating study."

Waverly laughed, "Leave it to a Wid to come up with a new area of study right in the middle of a major crisis!" We both laughed, which released some of the tension I was feeling. What action we took next lay squarely on my shoulders.

An hour later, Ali joined us and said that everyone who could come was now here. From Pieta, Mandi and Alice sat beside each other on some blankets. From Solamina, Mia, Ali, and Renata sat similarly perhaps six feet from them. Andre, Waverly and me sat facing both groups, while Felice and Adriana sat off to the side of us. Waverly had established a Mind Link to Allia back in Pieta and with Alton and Elona, who were riding along in our minstrel wagons on their way here.

Ali began, "All praise goes to Ket Bethany. Without his insight, the shocking truth would never have been revealed. Ket, I'll begin at the beginning and relate what I saw. If I misstate something, feel free to jump in immediately and correct me, okay?"

"Please, just call me Bethany, and sure, go right ahead."

I admired Ali. She had been scared so badly that she had wet her pants, though she didn't mention this detail in her narration, naturally. Still, she took her time and described all that had happened carefully and in good detail. I only needed to add a bit here and there. I could see why she was their Fighter Group Leader, for she missed nothing of importance, although frightened nearly to death. Periodically and predictably, the Sisters gasped at what she related, nearly as shocked as we had been.

When she finished up, Mandi cursed, "This means that everything we had heard about Solamina has been twisted and outright wrong. Worse still, we shared all this distorted information with the High Council who acted upon it. No matter what we do about it, and we certainly must do something drastic about it, we are doomed. Who will believe us anymore when we report situations to our Council?"

Mia interrupted her, "Same with us, Mandi. Everything we have heard about Pieta we have duly reported to our High Council, which acted accordingly. We are in just as bad a position as you are in; we are doomed!"

"Our credibility has been utterly shattered!" put in Ali. "No one will believe us after all this comes out." Alice, her counterpart, seconded that observation. Renata, the Solamina Council member merely cried; large tears of utter failure streamed down her cheeks. It was she that no one would ever believe again; her career as a Council representative was utterly ruined. Though Waverly said nothing, I suspected Allia was having similar thoughts and reactions, her career would be destroyed.

Finally, Mia asked the most germane question that I knew would eventually be coming, "Who was that man anyway? Should we launch a manhunt for him? Capture and try him for high treason?"

Now the time had come for me to talk openly, "Mia, that was another of these 'imposters' that we warned everyone about, only this time instead of posing as a High Council member, it is probably just some unimportant man who lives somewhere in Solamina. Lacking any better term, we call that imposter a Grey Creature." I then had to go into a lengthy explanation of these creatures, telling of their giant body sizes and incredible strength. I also related how one of them had slain my body last lifetime, just to re-enforce my next statement.

"Hence, under no circumstances should we attempt to capture it. Such an action, though highly warranted, would be the height of folly. If it desired, it could slay every one of us before we could even slightly wound it!"

In their eyes, I could see this creature rapidly becoming an ultimate weapon — that is, something that can utterly end our lives, but over which we can have no effect at all, a recipe for doom. "While we cannot possibly damage it or slay it, we can expose it. I mean we can cast the light of day upon what it has been doing and completely undo all the damage it has inflicted upon both sectors. Believe me that alone would be dealing it a terrible blow! Several years of its constant work would be instantly cast aside. Yes, I suspect that will be sufficient punishment of itself."

"As I see it, there are more phases to this operation." Now I had their undivided attention. Eager eyes stared at me, measuring every word I now spoke. "Phase three is to expose the creature and end its meddling. Phase four is to learn what has, in actual fact, been given out as false information to both sides. Then, based upon that, phase five is to correct the damage done. Finally, phase six is to come up with a method of delivering messages that cannot fall victim to a similar plot in the future. I already have worked out phase six; that is the easiest one, and you, too, have probably already thought of preventative measures you can take. Yet, we must take these in proper sequence. Next up is exposing the imposter."

You could hear a pin drop on the stone floor. I continued, "I've already figured out just the way to do this, expose it, without unduly endangering the Sisterhood members. However, just remember, our part in all this, even the very presence of Guardians here, must be kept a total secret for the time being. If not, our lives will be forfeit in all likelihood. Just look at what they did to me last lifetime. We all would be dead before we ever got to Zargarb. Before I continue, I need you all to make us that promise; leave our part in this out, at least for a few years anyway."

Mandi nodded, adding, "Oh I get it. Just like our predecessors did with Simon-Simone. Yes, you have the sworn word of all Pieta." Mia spoke likewise for Solamina. Hence, I could continue. "The key is the simple fact that I now have a strong force of Sisterhood fighters from both sides here at the same time, along with your key leaders." I outlined my plan. Quickly, everyone present agreed that it should work well and not unduly endanger any of us.

When I finished, Ali asked enthusiastically, "Can it be implemented tomorrow?"

"Absolutely, the sooner the better," I grinned back at the smiling Sisters. However, deadly serious, I added, "But you must do this precisely the way I tell you to do it. Otherwise, we Guardians' lives as well as yours are very likely forfeited. This imposter is nearly superhuman in strength and who knows what weapons it might have to wipe us all out." My footnote of dire consequences did not go unheeded.

Early the next morning, I checked with Alton to see where our caravan was located. His estimate placed them perhaps another day out from Solamina. If my plan went very wrong, Alton was ordered to pick up the pieces as best he could for both sectors. Bitterly, he complained that his position as a Protector demanded that he be at my side. Yet, he also knew that he was the main Guardian left to protect the rest of the musicians and the Sisters traveling with us. Though grumbling, he accepted my orders.

Around nine, the Sisters led me on down their escape tunnel. Behind a distant hill, the tunnel ended; its entrance cleverly hidden by many boulders. From here, one could not be seen from the city, and it was sufficiently far away from the walls to be behind the front wave of assaulters. About a quarter mile further northwest, the Sisterhood kept a small ranch. Here, we found our horses waiting for us. Already, the several hundred Sisterhood fighters from both Pieta and Solamina had gathered, making last minute preparations, checking their swords and bows. I hoped and prayed that neither would be needed!

Ali gave the order to move out. Silently, everyone moved into their marching order locations. We Guardians rode on up to the front with Ali and Alice. Even Adriana could not be kept away from this confrontation. We rode mostly northward and within a half hour reached the abandoned farmstead with the nearly collapsing barn. Carefully, we looked for signs of the imposter's presence or anyone who might get in the way. Thankfully, the road and the farmstead were deserted. Two Sisters rode on down the road toward Pieta; their role was to stop anyone from coming down the road accidentally running into our large force and the imposter.

The two field commanders, Ali and Alice, quickly deployed their forces. All moved off into the olive groves and surrounding lands, totally encircling the barn area. Within a few minutes, we could see no trace of these hundreds of women fighters. Next, those us that remained painstakingly wiped away the telltale hoof prints so that the place looked deserted. Next, Andre, my Protector today, and I took our positions underneath the molding hay, far back from the spot where yesterday I had seen the imposter working with Lonia. Our job was to observe only, though we both knew that, if the imposter chose to attack the Sisters, we would instantly join the fray.

Finally, Ali and Alice shook hands, and then they burrowed into the stinking hay, hiding themselves fairly close to where the action ought to be. Confident our preparations were the best we could manage, I made mental contact with Waverly and set my plan into action. Renata called for a messenger to relay a message to Pieta, and at once, that Sister rushed out of the inn, heading for the stables and the location of the Solamina messenger, Rencina. Within two minutes, the dispatch rider had the message memorized. Meanwhile, other Sisters had saddled her horse, so Rencina leaped into her saddle and galloped out of the stables into the streets of Solamina. Waverly sent me a mental message that Rencina was off and running. I whispered this to Ali and Alice. We knew that in less than a half hour, the dispatch rider would be here as well as the imposter. We waited.

Gosh, I had forgotten just how much I hate waiting! For a while, I could hear my heart thumping, and I began to panic, fearing that the Grey Creature could hear my heart! Then, I remembered how frightened Ali had been yesterday and hoped that she would not wet her pants today. All she needed was to be utterly embarrassed in front of her troops. Yes, all sorts of wild ideas flooded into my mind, including the thought that this might be the last day of this young body's life! Memories of the gypsy's fortune telling came back: yes, I would have many babies with the blonde woman, Caitlyn.

The eternity, which lasted a half hour, came to a sudden ending. We heard the arrival of Rencina's horse, heard her dismount. Carefully, we four moved the hay slightly so that we could see her better. The zombie Rencina slowly walked over to the pillar, scratched some dirt away, found the metallic box, and pressed the red button on it. In the dim light, we could see a red light flashing silently. We waited. While Rencina waited in a hypnotic trance, we four waited in fear. Everything depended upon these Sisterhood fighters not losing their concentration, not yielding to the terror and fear emanating from the Grey Creature.

This second eternity seemed even longer than the first. Yes, at any instant, I could call the whole thing off, and we could all leave before the imposter arrived. Still, I steeled my nerves and hoped the others could do so as well.

At last, we heard footsteps coming slowly toward the barn, faint, but sure. Then, framed by the morning sunlight shining behind him, the old man we had seen yesterday appeared once more. He slowly walked over to the blinking light and switched it off. His cold voice asked, "You are under my control. What is the message you are to deliver?"

That was the appointed signal. I felt the hay in front of us move as the two Fighter Group Leaders stood up and revealed themselves. I kept both my fingers on both hands crossed and held my breath. Her voice nearly faltering, Ali said coldly, "Solamina Fighter Group Leader, Ali Bastia."

Right on cue, Alice added, her voice almost catching in her throat, "Pieta Fighter Group Leader Alice Augato."

Just outside and having received my mental signal, the hundreds of Sisterhood fighters came out of hiding, slowly riding their horses up closer to the barn. The sounds of so many horses were unmistakable. So far, all was according to my plan.

Ali spoke next, "We know what you have been doing to our messages and dispatch riders for the past several years. Your treachery ends today. Both Sisterhoods are fully aware of what you have done and are in the process of undoing all the damage that you have caused."

Alice added her part, "There will be no civil war between Pieta and Solamina. Your plot is ended. Leave now and our fighters will not attempt to stop you." I had insisted on this bit just in case the arrival of the hundreds of fighters outside hadn't been heard by the imposter.

Barely a minute had passed while the two brave, though frightened, women said their speeches. I dare not breathe. How would it react? He turned and saw a large number of mounted Sisterhood fighters had taken up positions just outside the barn doors, bows pointed his way. I knew that he would be utterly unconcerned about any rain of arrows; he was likely impervious to them. It was the sheer numbers that I had counted on to force him to keep his retaliation in check.

He smashed his fist into the heavy timber supporting a section of the barn roof. The timber splintered as if it was kindling wood! He let out an unearthly bellow, likely an outburst of inhuman anger, assuming these creatures had such an emotion. Snatching up his signaling device, he whirled on his heels and walked determinedly out of the barn toward the fighters. They were under orders not to attack unless attacked first. The imposter waved his hand in a sweeping motion, causing an enormous gust of wind, which literally shoved a number of horses closest to him out of his way. Riders and horses went sprawling onto the ground. Still bellowing like some angry bull, he began running down the road toward Solamina. I say running, but no human could run as he did. The Sisters who were not splattered on the ground saw him run faster than a horse at a full gallop! Even if they had wanted to stop him, they would be unable even to catch up with him!

Inside the barn, our problems only began! An ominous creaking sound came from the roof. Bereft of one of its main supporting timbers, the sagging roof began to collapse! Rencina was still in a trance, standing motionless beneath the falling roof. Instantly, both leaders rushed toward her and bodily carried her out of the barn. Andre and I raced right behind them. Just as we passed the barn doors, the roof fell rapidly, crashing to the ground, bringing with it the four sides of the barn as well. A giant cloud of dust and debris flew outward, covering us all. Choking and coughing, everyone staggered and moved further away from the mess.

The collapse of the barn broke the shocked silence of the large group of fighters. "Did you see that?" "No one can run that fast!" "How can this be?" "Wow, the whole barn fell down!" Various similar comments flew back and forth between the women. Meanwhile, others began to assist the dozen women and horses who had been knocked to the ground and out of his way. One horse had broken its leg; two Sisters had broken limbs. Mostly, though it was bruises and nasty bumps.

I ordered Andre to assist the injured Sisters, while I went to examine Rencina, who was still solidly in her trance! Ali was waving her hand before her eyes and even lightly slapping the unfortunate dispatch rider on her face, all to no avail, as I walked up to them. I knew that I needed Waverly's assistance immediately. However, even a Mind Link with me would not be enough. "Let's get her on her horse and get her back to Waverly as fast as we safely can do so. I don't think she will come out of her trance as we ride. It is an awfully deep trance." Okay, I admit I had never seen anyone in such a trance, so this was mere speculation on my part. Since slaps had not brought her out of it, my pronouncement was accepted.

Accompanied by a hundred fighters, Ali and I headed back to Solamina, leading Rencina on her horse. Andre stayed behind to help set the broken arms and legs. The remaining fighters helped him and would escort them all back safely a little later on. As we rode, I complimented both women, "You played your parts just perfectly. Very well done indeed! We've ended the treachery and have avoided a nasty confrontation as well."

"Yes, but did you see him run? How can that be?" broke in Ali.

"Incredible! I wouldn't have believed it unless I'd seen it with my own eyes," added Alice. "You are certainly right when you say it looks human but is totally inhuman!"

"I know. You both did very well indeed. Congratulations on ending the treachery!" I continued to validate them.

"Yes, but did you see what he did with just a wave of his hand? Knocked horses and riders aside as if they were leaves!" Ali continued to vocalize her shocked amazement.

"I guess you are more than right, Ket," Alice sighed. "Had we tried to fight him, we would all be dead. I mean, it is just downright unbelievable!"

"You can say that again," exclaimed Ali. All the way into the city, both women vented their fears, observations, frustrations, and worries. Behind us, I could hear the other women engaging in similar conversations. Yes, after today, several hundred more people knew something about the power of these Grey Creatures, even if they had not seen what they really looked like.

When we finally rode up to the Sisterhood complex and inn, Waverly was there to meet us at the stables. Renata Bleu, Mandi, and Mia were also there, eager to hear the wild stories the others were telling them — all speaking at the same time. Using this as a distraction, Waverly and I led Rencina into the inn and to a quiet room that Waverly had already prepared for us. "Leave her with me, Bethany. You go see to the others. I'll let you know if I need any help."

I left and joined the others. Renata looked at me; her facial expression spoke the words for her, "Are they speaking the truth?" For the benefit of the two leaders and council representative, I quickly recounted what had happened. Hearing it from me, they began to believe these incredibly wild tales!

A little while later when Andre and the remainder of the fighters arrived, bearing the wounded Sisters, the leaders had even more solid evidence that what we had been saying had in fact occurred. "Let's go get some tea and work on the next phase," I suggested. Accompanied by Andre and the leaders of Pieta and Solamina Sisterhoods, we went into the inn to relax and discuss the repercussions of our actions.

"First, you probably ought to send a group of fighters to fetch Lonia here as well. Caution them that when she gets to the collapsed barn, she is likely to go into a deep hypnotic trance. If so, they are to gently bring her here as fast as possible," I suggested. At once, Ali went to issue the orders.

Once things had settled down a bit, I began, "Okay, the next phase, as I see it, is to find out what lies have been told between the two sectors. I think that the best way, short of Waverly somehow being able to undo the hypnotism of Lonia and Rencina and finding out directly, is to have you leaders try to recall all the messages that you each received during say the last couple of years. Obviously, what was received was not what was sent. I'll take notes for you and attempt to document the major alterations that have occurred. Our objective is to document the most significant lies that have been spread between Pieta and Solamina. Later on, we'll worry about what to do about them." The women most definitely appreciated not having to worry just now about how the damage would have to be repaired. Thus, I still had time to work out ways and means for the Sisterhood not to lose the confidence of the two High Councils or the tradesmen they also represented.

"Well, we were told that the Jehosanites thought that our worship of Tur was pagan and had to be eliminated in favor of the one true God," Mandi started the discussion.

Chuckling, Mia commented, "I actually sent something like the worshipers of Jehosa believe that Jehosa is the one true God. Since any and all help from Tur and the followers of Tur was noticeably absent after the barbarian sacking of the city, it was the duty of every good Jehosanite to come to the assistance of those in Pieta who were in need."

"Well, that certainly altered the message," I snickered as I jotted them both down. Thus, three hours went by very quickly. Soon, it became clear to both sides that every time a message was sent, the imposter had perverted it into something sinister and threatening, which was precisely how it had been perceived by the receiving Sisterhood. All alterations lay in the direction of having both sectors create a large army and then going to war with each other, which already had come perilously close to fruition.

By the time that the leaders had finished, both had become very close friends. Nothing like airing dirty laundry to bring people closer together. Never before had these two been so friendly toward each other; they now had a mutual bond of having been deceived by their common enemy. Yet, to rectify the damage that had been done required more thought on my part, though I promised them I would outline my ideas after supper. "Before we break for a while, I have one suggestion to make regarding your future dispatches." All the women suddenly gave me their undivided attention. "There are two actions you can take. One, never use the same route twice in a row. Vary the routes somewhat, make any possible interception of your riders more difficult to achieve on a routine basis." From their "sure, sure" looks on their faces, I knew that they had already thought of this one and probably were making plans to implement using alternate routes in the future. "Secondly, send critical messages written down on parchment, but written in a secret code. If the message was intercepted, it would be unreadable without knowing the code that would unlock the dispatch. Let me show you an example of what I mean." I had Mia dictate a sentence that she might place in a dispatch. I dutifully wrote it down, letter by letter on a scrap of paper.

"Next, you need the special code to use both in enciphering and deciphering the message. For example, let's use 'All dogs have white feet.' I write that down, but notice I omit any duplicate letters." I wrote down: A L D O G S, and so on. "Now, you write out the alphabet and then write this series of letters just below the alphabet, letter by letter. The way it works is every time the letter B occurs in the dispatch, it is replaced by the L. Every C is replaced by the D." Quickly, letter by letter, I rewrote the message Mia had dictated to me. When I finished, I said confidently, "Now here is the actual message you send with the dispatch rider." I showed them the confusing jumble of letters. It looked to all eyes as a random pile of letters, complete gibberish! "When you receive this, Mandi, you write out the alphabet and then place the known code below the letters. One by one, you take each letter in the message and see if it has a replacement letter. If so, use the substitute; if not, use the original letter." In short order, the original message Mia had made up reappeared on the fourth line below the original series of gibberish.

"Notice that both of you must know the special code. Further, prudence dictates that the special code be periodically changed. It only needs to be a short, easily remembered sentence."

"This is pretty slick," exclaimed Mia, excited about the possibilities now that she had seen it working. "It is simple and not easily cracked without the code sentence."

"I like it!" put in Mandi. "Always before, we rarely sent written messages out of fear that they might be intercepted. However, this offers us great protection. Let's do it!"

"Absolutely, but we must keep the number of Sisters who know what the code currently is to a minimum: we two leaders, our Fighter Group Leaders, and our High Council reps," added Mia. I sent them off to work out their first code sentence and how to deal with periodically changing it. Meanwhile, I wanted to check on the progress, if any, that Waverly was making with Rencina.

I found the room she was using and quietly slipped inside, hoping my presence would not adversely affect her work. Waving her fingers, she signaled me to join her out in the hallway. "You want an update, I reckon," Waverly whispered to me, I could tell she was rather exasperated, if not downright frustrated. I nodded that I did. "Well, she is in the deepest hypnotic trance that I have ever heard about — that's for sure. I know I can bring her out of it any time I desire, but I've avoided doing that thus far. I'm trying to determine what its effect has been on her well-being and whether I might be able to re-establish this trance later so she could be interrogated. I assume they want to have her thoroughly questioned about all the alterations of messages she was told to relay?"

"Not exactly," I relieved her of much of her worries, "I've already had the two leaders document the most significant messages as received and then as sent. So at this point, both sides know pretty much all the most important lies that have been spread by the Grey Creature. I think that we can safely omit having to have her knowingly relate each and every alteration the imposter gave her."

"Well, that is indeed a big relief. I have come to the conclusion that if I give her the command that she will remember all the incidents that have happened to her while she was hypnotized by the imposter, she may suffer serious mental side effects, such as feeling totally unworthy, that she has betrayed the Sisterhood, and worse. I looked for but have not yet found any suicide command should the imposter be found out. You know, he could have made such a suggestion, 'If you are discovered, you are to immediately kill yourself,' you know, something like that. Fortunately, I don't think such has been installed by the Grey Creature."

"Wow, I had not thought of that! We might have gotten her rescued only to have her take her own life! Good thinking, Waverly," I validated her wise insight.

"What I have been wrestling with the most is whether to implant the command that when she wakes up, she will remember all the times she was hypnotized — you know, that she can now recall all that she was told not to recall. The truth is always better than a lie, but will the truth totally overwhelm her? That's what I have not yet determined, if it is even able to be determined. We know so little about the human mind, yet we all have one and use it daily. Interesting, is it not?" Waverly commented.

I replied, "My suggestion is to tell her that she has been hypnotized by the imposter, ordered to relay wrong messages, that she is not to blame, and that there is no fault on her part. I'm sure that Mia does not plan to punish her in any way."

"Yes," Waverly cautioned, "but in doing so, am not I then guilty of implanting other thoughts into her mind? Anything I say is going to be taken very literally. I mean if I say she will have to go to the bathroom, she will do so at once, whether she needs to or not."

I pondered this for a minute, before replying. "Okay, I still think it best to have her know the truth about what has happened to her. Just be as gentle on her as you can. Make sure she is convinced that none of it has been her fault in any way."

"Okay, you are the boss, but I'm inclined to think this is the wisest course of action to take. Say, what about Lonia? Shouldn't we help her out as well?"

"Sisters have gone to fetch her. However, I told them to expect that when she gets close to the collapsed barn; she will likely fall into a deep trance. If so, they are to bring her here directly and as fast as possible," I explained.

"All right. I'm going back in and do it. Do you want to watch?"

"I suspect it will be better for her if there are less people around when she comes out of the trance, don't you think so?"

"Yes. I'll bring her to the dining room when I have her stabilized." Waverly cautiously and quietly slipped back into the dimly lit room.

A half hour later, Waverly brought Rencina out of the room. Her face was wet from tears. From the wetness on her shirt sleeves, I knew she had done a lot of that and with good reason. Though I had never met her, she did seem rather quiet and remote. My eye glance at Waverly brought a response, "She's accepted what has happened and wants to meet with Mia and Ali right away, before she sees anyone else."

"Okay, you two stay here and I'll bring them to the room," I replied and ran off in search of the two leaders. It took several minutes to find the two women, and as we headed back, I explained what Waverly had done, cautioning them, "Be extra gentle and careful with her. She knows just how damaging her actions have been. We don't want her to feel like she is to blame for all this in any way." At the door, I knocked and Waverly told us to come on inside.

Crying great floods of tears, Rencina, without waiting for either woman to say a word, blurted out all that she had been forced to do by the imposter. At least she rattled off a fair number of them, anyway. Mia gave her a long, solid hug, patting her lovingly on the back as if she were her daughter. "There, there now," she said, "you were entrapped by the imposter. No real damage has been done. We found out about it all in time. Cheer up, Rencina; we have just invented a brand new way of sending the messages. Next time we send a message via you, it will be written down in a secret code; never again will you have to be put through this torture. If someone intercepts the written message, it will look like gibberish. Here, I brought a sample of what it looks like. I thought you might be interested in seeing it."

Rencina looked at the test message we had encoded a little while ago. It was just seemingly a random series of letters on the page. "This means something?" she asked incredulously.

Mia handed her the translated message. "Wow, no none will be able to figure this out. Thank you. I feel ever so much better about being the dispatch rider now. I was going to resign, you know. After all, I have been completely undependable for years now."

"Oh no you haven't!" the stern voice of Ali spoke up. "You have been completely dependable and indispensable, for that matter. You always got the messages through no matter what. It's not your fault that the imposter chose you to attack, if that is quite the right word for it."

"You mean that I'm not fired?" asked Rencina, who could not believe her good fortune.

"No way, Rencina! We need our messages to get through now, even more than before. There is none better than you and Lonia. You two are nearly impossible to replace. I'd promote you, but then who would take your place?" She jested. It took Rencina a moment to get the tease, but then she grinned for the first time today. Definitely, the woman was on the recovery side of the ledger, I concluded.

"Let's all go get some dinner," I commented, the growling in my stomach was becoming annoying. With the tensions gone, we all headed toward the dining room, where Rencina would have to face all of the other Sisters. I hoped that would also go well.

Two more days passed before my minstrels finally got here, rolling into Solamina mid-afternoon. The band of Sisters brought Lonia in earlier that same morning; as we guessed, she was in a deep trance ever since she passed the destroyed barn. By the time the wagons arrived, Waverly had Lonia handled and on the road to recovery.

During these two days, I decided to put the last phase into operation. Discussing the situation in depth with both leaders and council representatives — Allia Gatti was with us via my Mind Link with her — we decided on the following approach. Both reps were to relay that the Sisterhoods had just discovered another imposter, who was feeding both Sisterhoods false and outright lies about the opposite sector. They were to explain that the Church of Jehosanity did not have and never did have any hostilities toward those who worshiped Tur. However, and here was the saving grace for the Sisterhoods, in effect, the lies had brought about a very beneficial result: both sectors now had a force which could be used to defend and man the newly constructed walls around the cities as well as actively patrol the sector, keeping banditry to a minimum. I had them point out that in this respect, these two cities were several years ahead of the other sectors. Further, there was some concern about the Axemen of the north. Certainly, these barbarians had been invading the Northern Steppes, where the Galts, who had last invaded and sacked the Sea Princes, lived. Thus, a new threat lay just on their borders, so having a defensive army equipped and trained was now a great benefit to both cities.

Both leaders and reps readily took to my ideas. After a good deal of embellishment, they agreed to bring the matter before the respective High Councils the next day. Later reports from both representatives, Allia and Renata, told of their complete success. Instead of having their respect lowered to all-time lows, quite the opposite occurred. They were praised for thwarting another dire plot by the imposters. However, both Councils wanted the Sisters to redouble their efforts to capture these imposters and bring them to justice. While they agreed to do so in principle, we all knew that this was impossible to bring about — they'd seen too much of the imposters and knew they had no chance of doing so.

Thus, when our wagons finally rolled up beside the Sisterhood inn, I was elated to see my fiancé, my dear friends, and sister. It was time to make music once more. I was more than ready just to play music! This, to everyone's delight, we did for the next two weeks. However, I detected no sign of Alabaster in the Solamina Sector.

Chapter 22 On the Way to Zargarb. . .

May Day 622, we had resolved, would be the day that we would depart for the Zargarb Sector, continuing our mission to find and rescue Alabaster. A couple days before our departure, Mia and Ali requested that we Guardians meet with them; they wanted to share some information about events in Zargarb that we should know about before we entered that sector.

When we four plus Elona were sitting in the nearly deserted dining room, cups of tea at hand, Ali somberly explained, "Zargarb has been dealing with a very serious problem for a number of years now. Since you are about to enter their sector, we need to explain why you will very likely be challenged at some point. However, we have notified the Sisterhood there of your coming, so perhaps it will not be as bad as I describe. Well, maybe you, Mia, ought to describe it to them. You know I get so angry and frustrated talking about it."

Mia smiled; that was the difference between these two women, the leader and the Fighter Group Leader. "After the barbarian invasion has come a new kind of invasion, a thieving-political invasion. They call themselves the Old Man of the Mountain. It is a sect as far as anyone has been able to ascertain, reputedly religious in nature, but we doubt that based upon what they do. Essentially, they are a bunch of murderers and thieves. One of their representatives comes to a town and tells the leader to give them such and such, often gold and food supplies. If the leader refuses, the representative leaves and simply disappears. Sometime later on, a townsman, funny, it is always a man, walks up to that leader and kills him, usually with a well-placed dagger thrust, sometimes poisoned. The assassin calls out silly things, like 'All praise to Allah' or 'Take me, Allah. Now I am worthy.' Invariably, the townsman who just killed his own leader is slain, either by the townsfolk or by his own hand if the defenders delay too long in attacking the assassin. A little while later, that same representative shows up back in the town making the same demands, threatening to slay another leader if their demands are not met."

"Essentially, every town and village in Zargarb lives in utter fear that they will be next. The High Council has ordered the representatives deaths, but that has done nothing to stop them. At this point in time, every convoy going into or out of the sector is being stopped and searched. Lord knows what they are looking for. Word from their High Council has been very vague about this, and our Sisters there are just as baffled. Thus, it is likely that you will be stopped and searched, perhaps several times before you reach Zargarb proper. I've requested that the Sisterhood there provide you an escort, but as yet they have not replied. So far, Solamina has been lucky; no Old Man of the Mountain representatives have shown up here."

Although we pressed them for additional information, this was all that they really knew about the situation. Obviously, they had been preoccupied with other threats to give it much worry. We thanked them for alerting us in advance, and we relayed the information to the others in our rather large party.

On May Day, we rode out of Solamina, heading northeast on the spoke road, following our usual passage out of a sector. With an arm around each other, Caitlyn and I sat on our buckboard. It didn't take much effort to drive the two draft horses. By now, both knew what they had to do, plod along after the Sisterhood leaders out in front of them.

Ah, the flowers! The yellow sunlight on the fields of wild flowers was indeed picturesque, even romantic, we two thought. I longed to lay with Caitlyn out among the fragrant fields, basking in the warm spring sun. We compromised, arms around each other, gazing as we passed the many fields on either side of the dirt road.

Yes, the next four days were heavenly! Although we gave two more concerts at a couple of villages, mostly we chose to camp out among the bounty of spring in Solamina. However, after dinner, I was asked to assist in the training of Elona — specifically, be her sparring partner. Alton had reached that point in her training where she needed to learn to catch objects coming her way, such as arrows or quarrels. He had tried for a week to teach her how to do this, but had failed miserably. Somehow, Elona just could not get the hang of what she was to do. She kept insisting that it was impossible to react that fast. We both knew that she was merely insisting on her rightness, not observing and acting. How often have we done similar — insisting that we are completely right, without even looking or seeing that we are wrong?

Hence, I began sparring with her so that Alton could closely observe her and attempt to assist her somehow. Elona handled a sword well, that I discovered in the very first session with her. Yes, she easily could out-duel me with a sword, a fact that was not lost on her. Rather, she took a good deal of pride in completely besting me with a sword. However, when I then switched to my favorite weapon of choice, a simple wooden pole, her smug look vanished; repeatedly, I managed not only elude her thrusts and whacks, but also I succeeded in knocking her feet out from under her. We kept at it that first night until she could hold her own against me and my pole. Yes, she learned how fairly quickly, but then this was just more sword training.

The second night Alton wanted me to get more into the catching or snatching of objects. First, we gave her a short demonstration. Alton threw a spear at me, which I caught. Next, he shot arrows at me. Here, I demonstrated the two techniques, deflection and snatching, explaining deflection was the easiest and safest. Snatching was the most humiliating for the shooter, however. While she watched, she kept on insisting that this was impossible, this in spite of the fact that she was seeing me do it right before her eyes. Now, I saw what Alton was facing. He gave me a forlorn look, suggesting HELP!

Sometimes, inspiration strikes. I made a crude ball out of a bunch of socks. "When I throw this ball at you, Elona, you are to deflect it with your hand. To the right or left, I don't care which, just deflect it." She insisted that anyone could knock a sock ball out of the way. I tossed it at her several times and she proved she was right by easily deflecting it. I grinned, I knew now that I had her! "Okay, do the same thing with this small stick." I pitched a small one-foot long piece of firewood her way.

Again, she deflected it, but not without uttering "Ouch! That hurt when it hit me."

"Deflect it, not hit it," I suggested. Again, I pitched it her way. A few more times and she got good at moving it out of the way, rather than smashing it out of the way. "Notice how hard you need to touch it in order to move it out of the way," I called out. Soon she realized that it took merely the lightest tap for her to alter its path so that it wouldn't hit her.

Next, I graduated to a long pole, similar in nature to a spear, though I didn't say this to her. "Oh, this is easy," she declared. The pole flew even slower toward her than the stick. We kept at it until I was pitching the pole as hard as I could at her, as if it were a spear.

"What's the difference between that and a real spear thrown at you?" I suddenly pounced upon her.

She had a rather silly look on her face for a moment before admitting, "It hasn't got a sharp, metal point."

Caitlyn easily remedied it. Using her new knife that she had purchased in Pieta, she whittled a nice point onto the end of the stick. Once more, I began throwing it at her. However, this next time, I threw it lightly, gently, and slowly her way. I saw her flinch at once. This one had a point! We kept at it, and by the end of the evening, she no longer flinched when I threw it as hard as I could at her.

The next night, I repeated the process, only this time, I moved even closer to her. However, I did have to back off and throw gently a normal pole so she could get her reflexes honed to this shortened reaction time. Interestingly enough, by the end of the session, I was throwing a real spear at her, although from a distance. She continued to deflect them nicely. Alton never failed to give her praise at her successes, and she felt elated by the end of the evening.

The fourth night, I explained how demoralizing it is to an opponent when you simply catch their thrown spears, dropping them onto the ground. Catching is much harder than deflecting. Thus, I began with my sock ball and slowly moved up. By the end of the evening, she was catching the wooden spear that Caitlyn had made the night before. Of course, the real test would come when I threw a real spear at her. Yes, we were making progress now, although arrows would take far more work. I recalled how long and hard I had to work at deflecting and catching arrows before I really had the confidence to be able to do it well.

Naturally, Caitlyn and Fergus wanted to learn this art as well. However, I promised them both that I would take all the time that was needed once we finished our mission. This, they both accepted. Later Caitlyn confessed that she spoke without thinking clearly, "I would be too embarrassed to try it out in front of all these people. I'm glad that you are making us wait until later. But don't think I will forget about it!" She added that last playfully and we kissed warmly.

The next day, we forded a small stream that separated Solamina from the Zargarb sector. I signaled Adriana to hold up a minute. On the Zargarb side, I spied numerous signs of recent horse traffic; Adriana and Felice did as well. Together along with Alton and Andre, we examined them carefully. Bandit gang was, of course, in the back of my mind. The consensus was that the tracks were two days old; dung piles provided a convincing argument to the time line. We guessed that the riders were some kind of patrol force, since they did not cross the river, but returned from whence they had come, the direction we were headed.

Thus alerted, we resumed our journey, following the Zargarb rim road, which here went nearly northeast for a time. Once more, my plan was to follow the arc until we reached the north-south spoke road; then head due south into the big city. As we rode slowly along, Caitlyn pointed out the terrain was different in this sector. Indeed, Zargarb was drier than the other Sea Prince sectors. After all, it bordered the semi-arid desert land of Juda Arad, where water was a scarce commodity.

Late afternoon, we began a slow descent down a long hill into a small town. However, a dozen cavalrymen lay between us and the town; they were riding in a tight formation out towards us and would run into us within a few minutes. Hastily, word of the cavalry approach was spread to the wagons. We bunched the wagons somewhat closer as we continued toward the town and riders. Soon, the riders, having spotted us as well, halted in front of Felice and Adriana, who had no choice but to signal the rest of us to stop.

Their leader, not yet twenty-five and with his first command, spoke, "Hail Sisters. Zargarb Home Guard here. I'm Corporal Zagutti. As you know, all wagons entering the sector have to be searched for signs of the assassin representatives."

"This is a troubadour music group all the way from West Reach, the West Reach Minstrels. We know nothing of these assassins or their representatives," Adriana replied.

"Nevertheless, ma'am, we have our orders; we must search every wagon," the young lad overly enthusiastically countered, signaling his men to dismount and begin the search. Since there was no point in arguing the matter, Adriana shrugged towards me and I nodded my assent.

Two men not much older than me came up to our wagon. Caitlyn and I had to step down so they could climb aboard. "Please be careful; we have a lot of valuable musical instruments in there," Caitlyn said haughtily. She didn't like this invasion of our privacy.

"Looking for people, ma'am," one of the young men answered her. He then called out, "Clear." Both men slipped back onto the ground, moving to the next wagon. We climbed back onboard.

Caitlyn spoke to the leader, who was still in front of our wagon, "What do these assassin representatives look like?" Good question, I thought and whispered that to her. She smiled.

"We aren't sure," came the reply, which, of course, only infuriated Caitlyn further.

"Well, if you don't know what they look like, then how are you going to know if we have one inside our wagon?" she retorted back. The man's face flushed.

He stammered, "We'll just know, that's how." Caitlyn let out a huff as if to say "stupid."

She asked, "And how many of these assassins have you found so far? Should we be worried about an assassin trying to kill us?"

"Well," he finally spoke truthfully, "actually, we've never found any, but it's not likely we would find any out here. They come from Juda Arad, so they get intercepted in the eastern half of the sector. You are perfectly safe from the assassins, ma'am. They only kill town leaders who don't give them what they want. Now, I keep saying we ought to follow them, when they are leaving with the spoils from a city. You know, find out where they go, and then launch a big assault on them and wipe them out. That's what I'd do. But then, the generals, they don't listen to me. One day, when I'm a general, I'll get to do things properly."

Caitlyn had made the mistake of urging him to talk, and now she could not get him to stop. Somehow, the man felt if he said enough words, then she'd forget about his ignorance on what these assassins actually looked like. She, however, didn't.

However, the men returning from searching the last of the wagons stopped him. "All clear, sir! They can move along now." Hastily, the corporal repeated the words, telling us it was okay to continue into the town. Caitlyn was going to tell him about our possibly playing a concert in the town's inn later this evening, but then thought better of it. Adriana signaled us to move out, while the cavalry mounted and continued on westward back the way we had just come.

Around four in the afternoon, our gaily-colored wagons rolled into the town of Escari, home to perhaps five hundred people and at least a hundred stone buildings, all in good repair. Kids were playing in the streets, but they stopped to stare at us. Even the adults on this main street paused to watch our wagons roll on by. Adriana was looking for an inn, though she doubted any would be large enough to accommodate our group. As she pulled up in front of the Dew Drop Inn, a Sister was sitting on the porch whittling on a piece of wood. She jumped up as soon as she saw us.

"Hi, are you the folks from Solamina? The troubadours?" she asked, her eyes wide with excitement.

"Sure are," Adriana replied with a broad grin.

"I'm Sister Becca, I've been ordered here to wait and watch for you. Been here for several days now. I really didn't think you would be coming this way!" She was a young woman, perhaps eighteen, with typical light brown hair and blue eyes. Becca was not overly cute, but not ugly either. "As soon as you get here, I'm supposed to ride like the wind to get the main Fighter Group. They are to escort you into Zargarb."

"I'm Sister Adriana from d'Grange. This is Sister Felice, our tracker. What a shame you have to leave just as we arrive. Couldn't you spare a couple minutes so you can at least meet everyone." She now lowered her voice, "Especially the musicians all the way from West Reach?" As I dismounted and helped Caitlyn down, I overheard Adriana and could tell she was teasing poor Becca.

"Sure you can delay a couple minutes," I went along with her. "Hi, I'm Ket Bethany, the leader, and this is my fiancé Caitlyn. We are from Cymry or West Reach as you call it here."

"Wow! Such incredibly long red hair! You are a guy, right?" she exclaimed, her eyes opened wide.

Caitlyn answered for me, "All the guys have red hair where he comes from, a place called Tewdwr. What have you been carving?" Both of us noticed she was carving an eagle perched on a stump out of a foot long block of wood. Further, it was nearly done and the likeness was very realistic. She was a good carver.

"Oh, I just see things in pieces of wood and try my best to get that image out for everyone to see. An eagle is perched in this discarded piece of a main mast," she replied modestly.

"That is really good work, Becca. Do you ever sell them when you get them finished? If so, I'd like to buy this one, when you get it done," Caitlyn said and meant it.

She blushed. "Sometimes. It'd be an honor, miss. Sure thing. One day, I hope to have saved up enough money so I can afford my own shop in Zargarb, but that day is a long way off. That's why I always take these silly remote assignments; they pay more."

"Deal!" proclaimed Caitlyn. However, the others had dismounted and joined us, so more introductions were needed. Yes, she was very surprised to see that Fianna had very similar red hair, and she cleverly guessed that she was my sister. Bright young woman, this Becca. However, she did have a job to perform. Quickly, she gathered up her carving and headed for her horse.

A minute later, we heard her galloping out of town, heading on down the rim road.

Alton went into the inn to see about arrangements. As we surmised, the inn could not house us all, but the innkeeper was very pleased that we would hold a concert here this evening. While he sent messengers out on the streets crying out the message, we remounted and rode to the eastern edge of town to set up camp for the night.

Yes, we played for these people for nearly three hours. Men, women, and children, nearly everyone in the town turned out. Most had to stand or mill around outside the inn, however. We were the major event of the spring for these people. Times like these made me really appreciate just what we were doing for the average person in the Sea Princes: the sharing of music and dance with others. In a way, I would hate to have eventually to end our journey.

After our concert was over and folks headed for their homes, one man wearing blue priestly robes stayed around us watching as we packed up our instruments. When we were finished, he spoke quietly to me, "Sir, might I have a word with you." From his clothing, I made the assumption that he was with the Church of Jehosanity. I told the others to take off; I'd be along shortly, though Alton did hang back, keeping an eye on me. Protectors.

"I am Deacon Balturi of the Escari Church of Jehosanity. Let me extend not only my thanks but also that of the Church for donating your time and skill to play for our town. Giving selfishly to others is a holy commodity, alas not found so readily in men. Yes, you brought fine music to them. We are all very thankful. Secular music is so very scare these days since the gypsies have stopped traveling around our sector. Probably because of the trouble we've been having with the assassins. However, I noticed you accept no exchange for your concert, save the occasional beer. I would like to extend a more formal thank you by inviting you and your musicians to attend tomorrow afternoon's mass. In doing Jehosa's work, we've found that people greatly appreciate, shall we say, sacred music sung and played during our mass. Music helps to lift one's soul to greater heights. If you and your fellow musicians would join us, then we can return the gift of music by letting you hear some of our sacred music. Mind you, you will not hear the lively dances. But something tells me that you would appreciate our sacred music, it is not so distant from some of your laments. If you can attend, it is at two o'clock."

"Thanks, I'm called Ket Bethany. We're not in a rush. I think it would indeed be interesting to hear your sacred music. Thanks. Looking forward to it," I replied, thinking what a vast difference in the Church's outlook toward troubadours he held. It sounded much more promising.

"Great, see you then," he replied, genuinely pleased that I accepted his offer; he shook my hand and left for his home. I joined up with Alton, who had overheard the Deacon.

"Guess we are going to have a listen," he teased me as we walked to the eastern edge of the town where we'd set up camp.

"I figured it would give the Sisterhood here more time to get to us. I certainly want to avoid trouble. I didn't like being stopped and searched today. Perhaps if they are escorting us, we can avoid that hassle." He smiled; he liked my reasoning.

At two the next afternoon, we filed into the large stone church, the tallest building in Escari, its white cross perched high atop the roof, symbolically reaching toward heaven. Actually, our entire group decided to attend, and we filed into the rear of the church. I must also admit I was curious about how Jes Amir's teachings were being followed here in Zargarb, the closest land to Juda Arad. Stepping inside the church, I was pleasantly surprised. A lush red carpet led from the nicely carved oaken doors, past all the pews, and on up to the altar. On the side walls, enormous paintings depicted various holy scenes, some of which I thought I recognized. Back of the High Altar was a giant mural depicting that last meal we and the ten disciples had shared, when Jes pretended to have risen from the dead. Curiously though, I found that I, his wife at the time, was absent from the mural! I looked closer, there were the ten disciples surrounding Jes. Faintly in the background, there seemed to be another unidentified man. Ah, they had either purposely altered me into a man or dropped me completely out of the picture. Interesting.

Caitlyn and Fergus chatted about the similarities to their churches back in West Reach, as well as pointing out differences. She was more than a little annoyed that the Holy Blessed Mother was nowhere to be found in any of the paintings. Perhaps a hundred people gathered for the afternoon mass. The majority was women; the men were still at work. As the Deacon slowly walked up to the High Altar, a dozen dressed in choir robes solemnly marched in and took their place behind him.

The sacred music was sung entirely in the Arad language, all of which I understood, but most of my companions did not. Ten psalms were sung. However, the sound was most unusual. No harmonies, everyone sung the same note, only an octave or two separated the voices. "Perfect pitch," Jolina whispered. Indeed, the notes were pure without any ornamentation or embellishment of any kind. Yet, the sound did have an uplifting quality to it, so much so, that I too felt far more reverence than normal. It was "holy music."

The actual mass I found boring, entirely similar to what we'd all heard before. We had planned to stay around afterward to thank the Deacon, but our Sisterhood escort arrived and ordered us to follow them at once. I simply called out my thanks and that we had to go. The Deacon smiled back.

Outside, some fifty Sisterhood fighters surrounded us, all mounted, all armed to the teeth, all with saddle bags that were overflowing or at least well-stuffed with gear. One unusual looking, middle aged woman whose skin was a shade more yellow than her companions was the leader. "I am Fighter Group Leader Lenkova Pazzio. I am charged with your safety here in the sector. There has been some trouble in Zargarb, and Mother Cecilia Amalio has ordered me to take you temporarily to our secure safe house in the northern part of the sector. Your safety is paramount — her orders. We need to get moving right away." Her names rang a distant bell in my mind. Where had I heard those two names before?

"I am Ket Bethany, the leader of the West Reach Minstrels. Pleased to meet you. Trouble you say? What kind of trouble? We are rather used to that," I commented, all the while trying to place those names! I knew I ought to know them. She looked at me rather queerly, and it was not my hair, for a change. Yes, she did notice it, but that evidently took a distant second place.

"Cannot say out in the open like this. I'll explain once we are on the road," she replied in a very no nonsense way. She was used to being supreme commander, that I could tell. Then she added, "Strange things, names. Once upon a long time ago, there was another Bethany who came to the Sea Princes. She was a powerful Guardian from the Greenway, way up north somewhere over the Appian Way, I'm told.

"This way," I replied as I walked back toward our camp, though I obviously did not need to show her the way, she'd already checked on our camp before finding us in church. Lenkova, Lenkova, that name echoed in my mind. "There once was a Lenkova born to a very powerful fighter here in Zargarb, Rosita Armino was her name," I continued talking aloud. It had come back to me now, all the stories that my old, dear friend, Sandy had told me.

Lenkova, who was walking by my side leading her horse, froze utterly mid-stride. Startled, she asked, "How did you know that? Yes, I am she. You speak of my mother. Did you know her? No, that is impossible; you're just barely of age, if that."

This, of course, caught the attention of the other Guardians, who also had heard of Rosita and her children by the barbarian invader Mikhailovich Strokova. By agreeing to bear him two children, she had kept the entire Sisterhood in all the sectors free from the barbarian attacks! As usual, I had opened my big mouth once too often. Yet, I had to answer her. "Ride beside my wagon for a while and I will explain. Yes, I am that very same Bethany of which you know." I at least had to tell her the truth, even though she looked completely shocked and nearly in total disbelief.

With the assistance of the fifty additional Sisters, we were able to break camp in record time, hitting the road in less than a half hour. True, Lenkova complained about us using slow draft horses, which slowed our pace considerably from what she desired. I could tell that she was used to speed in emergencies such as this, though I had no idea what kind of emergency would compel the Sisterhood leader to whisk us away to a safe house, very distant from the city.

Lenkova requested that we keep the wagons in a tight formation. Her guards took up positions around the twenty Sisters who had accompanied us all the way from d'Grange. Adriana was a little put out by having her authority suddenly usurped, but had no choice except to go along with the heightened security measures. No longer guiding us, Felice dropped back to chat with our cook instead. We rode in silence for about five miles, before turning north on to a spoke road; there, we headed north instead of south toward Zargarb.

Finally, Lenkova dropped back to ride alongside my wagon. "I've had another thought about your draft horses. Can they pull these heavy wagons cross-country?"

"Sure, if a wagon can pass, they can pull it," I replied, confident of our horses.

"Okay, then I'm changing plans. We make a bee line for the safe house; it'll save days off our travel time." She rode ahead to issue the new orders. Satisfied with her marching order, she once more dropped back beside me. "Okay, Mister Ket, you have some tall explaining to do." I sighed, indeed I did.

I'd explained this so many times now, that it was becoming routine, we being immortal spiritual beings inhabiting for a short while these mortal bodies. I explained briefly about my first lifetime as Elizabeth Stanton, leader of the Lightning Circle and followed that with a short discussion of my last life as the wife of the Great Messiah. I told her how I had talked at length to Sandy and Simon after they had returned from the First Council of the Sisterhood. It was from them that I learned of Rosita's monumental sacrifice to save the Sisterhood. I also related the small amount of information she had told me of Rosita and Antonio's incredible rescue of her two children from the Galt encampment just after their father had been slain near Sud in the Southlands. My objective in all this was to let her know the little that I did know and to allow her some opportunity to put how I knew this into some kind of perspective.

Simultaneously, I took the opportunity to examine this beautiful woman. She was thirty-four, but looked twenty-one, slim at the waist with strong arms and legs. Her skin had a slightly yellowish hue making her remarkably attractive. She had shoulder length, straight black hair that shone in the sunlight, making her one of the few Sisterhood fighters I'd seen who did not cut their hair short. Yet it was her eyes that caught my attention and more than once; they were sky blue — so unusual they commanded your attention; one could not help but notice them.

When I finished up, she replied, "Well, you sound an awful lot like the Jehosanites. I don't know anything about spirits, but I do know what's real: bodies. Lacking anything to the contrary, I must accept that you speak truthfully. With four of you Guardians in this caravan, I can see why Cecilia

— she's our leader — I can see why she is going to these extreme measures to ensure your safety. I admit that at first I thought it was a total waste of time to send me personally on this assignment. I told her so, still she insisted. I must say that I am both impressed to be in the company of four Guardians; and also I'm honored to be your escort, though I still don't believe my presence is really needed."

"I take it that you are a very accomplished fighter and a good leader," I surmised and suggested in the same breath.

She smiled for the first time, "Well, yes on both accounts. I've never been beaten by man or woman in a fair fight yet. Perhaps that is only because I've never faced anyone who is particularly good. I'm well respected, if that is what you mean." You can tell when someone is uncomfortable talking with you. Even though I got a smile from her and reasonable conversation, still, I sensed that she was forcing herself to chat with me. Perhaps it was her body language or the way that she really did not look me in the eye. Good riders do not need continually to watch where they are going; the horse is intelligent, not prone to doing dumb actions. She exuded reticence to talk freely with me; that was my conclusion. Now that I'd answered her questions sufficiently, she excused herself, "I must really see to our path." Lenkova nudged her horse forward, joining those in the lead, leaving me with more questions about her.

"She sure is pretty," Caitlyn commented after she had moved on forward, "and really sexy looking, don't you think?"

I laughed, "Yes, nothing passes your observant eyes, my love. You noticed the bulge in my pants, eh?" She punched me in my ribs.

I went on, "Yes, beautiful, sexy, rather an exotic appealing woman."

"Did you notice that she seemed very reluctant to talk with you?" Caitlyn asked. "It sure seemed that way to me. Yes, she answered your questions, but I could tell that she was or felt very uneasy in doing so. But then she is in the Sisterhood; no telling what some man has done to her, though I don't see any major physical scars. Her clothes could be covering them up. Haven't all the Sisters been somehow abused by men? Isn't that one of the main reasons for the Sisterhood, to provide a safe-haven from abusive men?"

"Historically, yes. Fifty years ago, I couldn't find a single Sister who didn't bear some deep scars, physical or emotional ones. However, Caitlyn, I thought that in more recent times, a job in the Sisterhood had become an acceptable avenue for employment, not just for the abused women. Somehow, I can't see Lenkova allowing some man to harm her, at least not physically. There must be something more behind it. However, we may never find out if it is very personal."

Shortly, we needed all of our driving skills. The Sisters led us off the road out across the countryside. The topography in this sector consisted of tall hills with a well-defined ridge line and deep valleys. These women knew well the lay of their land. Cleverly, we angled one way and then another, always maintaining approximately the same elevation as we meandered in and out of one valley system and another. Via Adriana, we learned that three days hard travel would get us to their safe haven in the far north of the sector.

We made camp that night in a secluded valley; Lenkova risked allowing us to have several small campfires, though they were limited to cooking our dinner. However, she positioned our wagons far closer together than we normally would have placed them. Her fighters then encircled us, bedding down on the periphery. Any attackers would have to get through them before they could engage either the Sisters from d'Grange or us. What kind of danger were we in puzzled me as well as everyone else, including Jolina. Needless to say, we were not allowed to practice our music.

After dinner, Cailyn and I took a stroll around the campsite, primarily out of sheer boredom. When we came upon Adriana and Felice, I stopped and asked, "Adriana, have you been able to get anything out of these new Sisters? Like what the supposed danger actually is all about? Lenkova seems reluctant to talk to me."

"I've been making discrete inquiries from some of the others. I'm just as curious as you are. All are a little hesitant to talk freely about it. Perhaps they are just as much in the dark as we are. At least they agree that another assassin demand has been made down in Zargarb, but why that should affect us here so far to the north is beyond me. They also alluded to the possibility of Axeman raids coming from the Northern Steppes, though I deem that very unlikely. After all, aren't they interested in stealing all the gold from the Galts who stole it from the Sea Princes several years ago? Makes no sense to come down here, at least to me. The Sisters also referred to the Pope's Holy Paladins, whomever they may be, something about their crusade for holy relics and possible attacks against the Church of Jehosanity here in this sector. All in all, I sure am glad that d'Grange is snuggled up against the Greenway. All we have to worry about are bandits from the Velona sector coming up north towards us. Pretty tame."

"Thanks, that is far more than I had learned from her. Good going, Adriana," I said very gratefully.

"Oh one more thing, about Lenkova, her compatriots said that she rarely talks to men and that the chat with you earlier today was one of the longest any of them have ever seen her do. I pressed them a bit about why. All I could find out is that Lenkova detests men in general. Does that help any?" Adriana asked, knowing it only raised more questions.

I gave her a fake teasing laugh, saying, "Sure helps a lot." All three of us laughed.

Adriana added, "At least a couple said that she keeps pretty much to herself and doesn't talk about her personal life to hardly anyone."

"Well," Caitlyn commented, "that rules out me trying to get her to open up." Adriana agreed with her.

By the end of the next day's travel, we encountered the primary north-south spoke road that led on up to their safe house at North Point, a cave complex only a few miles from the Paese di Dio, God's High Country. We made camp just off the road, only this time a host of guards were posted at all times. Many people traveled this road; hence, we needed to be very alert for trouble — that was the explanation we were given. The good news was that by the end of another day's travel we should arrive at North Point. The bad news arrived while we were eating our dinner.

Munching on a leg of lamb slice, I heard the distinct sound of galloping horses coming towards us from the north. In a flash, the Sisters dropped their plates and silverware, and rushed to arm themselves. As a protective measure, I asked my party to fall back to the wagons in case of trouble, while we Guardians joined forces with our twenty d'Grange Sisters. Long dark shadows covered the road; the sun was nearly setting in the west. However, I could see the shapes of two riders coming down the road from the north, galloping at top speed.

Lenkova fanned her troops out in a V-shaped net, leaving a hole for the riders to pass by at the bottom of the V. In seconds, the riders drew near enough to see the array of Sisters, bows raised in defense. To my surprise, the riders frantically reined in, raising large piles of dust from the sliding hooves of their well-lathered animals. "Hail Sisters. We're looking for Lenkova. Anyone seen her or know where she might be?" called out one of the riders, a young girl probably not even fourteen. In the dim light, I could not see either of them all that well, but I'd say her companion was even younger, maybe twelve.

I did see Lenkova step out into the road, however. Unfortunately, the messengers now kept their voices so low that, from this distance, I could not make out what they were telling Lenkova. Yet, whatever they said, it was short. A minute later, the two young women wheeled around and began riding hard back the way that they had come. I heard Lenkova issue a loud curse, and she stomped her foot hard on the ground, as she reluctantly turned to return to our encampment. I guessed that the news was not good.

You can tell when someone is pondering a situation. Lenkova obviously was doing just that, as she slowly walked back over to the camp, her head bowed low, looking at her feet perhaps, though it was not that dark just yet. I saw her make an exaggerated arm gesture. At once, all her troops scurried up close to her. For an instant, I considered whether we should join them. However, at that point Lenkova looked up, with a look on her face that suggested she had reached a decision. Another arm motion brought all them rapidly towards us. I motioned for all of our party to gather close to me as well. Something was definitely wrong.

With a sigh of disgust, Lenkova said loudly, "Just got word that Axemen have invaded our sector way up at the northeast corner." Many gasps came from her audience. "It's worse. They appear to be heading in the general direction of North Point." Major gasps resounded and all sorts of curses as well. "As you know, it is only lightly defended; all our children are there. We have no choice but to abandon our current assignment and ride hard to intercept them." Cheers resounded as the women heard that pronouncement. I realized that these women would fight to the death to protect their most vulnerable. "It's worse," she added, and at once, the noise evaporated; you could hear the crickets singing. "The estimate is they are five hundred strong; we're fifty — well armed, but only fifty." She added that last to drive home her point. They were going off on a suicide attack, outnumbered ten to one.

She turned to face me, "Under the circumstances, North Point may not be the safest place for you to go. I release you from that order. If you will just follow this road, it will eventually take you straight south into Zargarb."

I replied calmly, "Thanks, but no thanks, Lenkova. As I understand it, all your young mothers and your children are housed at North Point. What kind of an ally would stand by in such a situation? Not us. We're going with you. I'll send Adriana along with the wagons to North Point. If the Axemen get by us, at least there will be twenty strong, able fighters to help defend them. Besides, four of us have healing skills, which will undoubtedly be greatly needed."

A protest began to swell up in Lenkova, unused to having her orders altered, I wagered. However, Adriana added, "Count us in as well."

Not to be left out, Fergus and Caitlyn said, "And us too, Laddie, we can fight too."

"Now wait a minute, someone has got to drive these wagons, Jolina, and our gear to North Point. You all can't come," I protested this time.

"I'll drive your wagon, Bethany," Felice volunteered. "Edgar drives his and Jolina's; the cook, hers. We only need a few more drivers."

"Right! Let's see, if we add our numbers to Lenkova's, the odds drop to only five to one. Much better if you ask me," Adriana said decidedly.

"Now wait just a minute!" Lenkova nearly shrieked. "I'm in charge here. I say who goes." After her outburst, she calmed down a bit, "I'm under orders to get you all to safety. Originally, that was North Point, but things change."

I knew what she was about to say; her mind was fairly screaming it at me. I interrupted gently, "Yes, you are in charge, Fighter Group Leader Lenkova. Yet, I bid you not to forget that we, from the Greenway, are your sworn allies. Do not cast away like grains of sand what aid your closest allies may provide. Even the d'Grange Sisterhood is an ally. We all are." Suddenly, I spied the button that would collapse her protest. "Please do not shame us by rejecting our aide, such as it is." I emphasized the word shame. Magic, that word slammed home to her; her mind recoiled, and all of her resistance melted away. She could think clearly once more.

366

Quietly, she said, "Five to one does sound a whole lot better than ten to one. All right. This road leads directly to North Point. You can't miss it, even in your sleep. Honestly, between here and there, nothing should bother you. Those two teenagers rode all the way down and saw no one else on the road. Hence, I'm willing to gamble your wagons should have a safe passage to North Point, assuming you're still willing to gamble on leaving them unprotected." I nodded my agreement.

"Okay then, all those that wish to ride into battle, pack up at least two day's rations and plenty of water. Let's ride within the hour. If your draft horses are up to it, I would prefer them to continue northward for much of the night as well," she said.

Instantly, the camp became a flurry of action, with our poor cook fielding numerous requests for two days' rations! First, my group hitched up the draft horses and saddled our spare riding horses. Once more, I was very glad that we had the foresight to bring them along. Less than an hour later, seventy-seven of us waved goodbye to the few who remained to drive our wagons to North Point. I had already given my sister a big hug and kiss. She would be driving Fergus and her wagon all by herself.

As we waited for the order to begin our nighttime northerly ride, Elona asked, "What are these Axemen like? How do they fight? I've never seen any."

Moving so that Fergus, Caitlyn, as well as Elona could hear my answer, I replied, "They are usually very heavyset men, several hundred pounds at least. Thus, they aren't agile and nimble, and rely on brute force. None of us can stand before them; we'd just be bowled over by their sheer weight and momentum. Never give them a chance to use that brute force against you, that's the secret to defeating them. Use your agility and speed wisely."

I continued, "Waverly is going to be in charge of emergency aid to the wounded. Hence, she must be defended while she is helping the fallen. Fergus, you and Caitlyn are in charge of sticking by Waverly's side. Where she goes, you go. Your job is to defend her at all costs so that she can do her rescue tasks."

"Aye, laddie, that does seem to make good sense. You have my word. I shall defend her with my life," Fergus declared solemnly, but also enthusiastically.

"Me too," Caitlyn said meekly. "Perhaps I will be able to help Waverly as well."

Chapter 23 Battling the Axemen

Lenkova mounted up and turned in her saddle to look upon all of us, her troops, one last time. "Mister Ket, will you ride up here with me for a short while? I have things I need to discuss. Okay, move out!" she barked. At once, we broke into a canter, though I pressed my mare harder and moved along side of Lenkova.

"Please just call me Bethany," I said.

"But that is a girl's name," she finally said what she had been thinking for some time.

"Well, I'm a girl really, only I've got this male body at the moment. Want to swap? Yours is very sexy," I teased her, hoping she wouldn't take offense.

She looked at me seriously for a moment, "Is that possible? Swapping bodies?"

"Dunno, sometimes I sure do wish it was easily done. I'd trade this one in a flash if I had the chance. Do you realize how much trouble I have been having trying to adapt to being a male? But I've flatly refused to cut my hair!"

"But then you like the company of men over women?" she asked. I immediately filled in the unspoken thought.

"Strange at this may seem, no. I am deeply in love with Caitlyn and will marry her when my mission is finished. I don't quite get it either. I would normally look at handsome men, but this body knows what it is after, if you follow my meaning. I'm still adapting to trying to be a male. Sometimes I do slip a bit, but that isn't what you wanted to talk about, right?" I added trying to change the subject. My cheeks felt quite red, though it was now so dark she could not see them, fortunately.

"No I wanted to discuss tactics. I don't know what all you really do know about us, as fighters. We are primarily defensive fighters, not offensive ones. Don't expect us to charge into battle. We let the battle come to us, if need be."

"Same with us. We Guardians try to avoid open battle if possible. If unavoidable, we try to defend at all costs." I thought a moment, wondering how much to reveal to her. Yet, she was in charge and ought to know. "You are lucky that you have four of us and an apprentice along. We have certain nature spells that we can command, such as bringing down fire from the sky or lightning bolts, though we need some clouds around to do that. Weather wise, I don't really know what it's like around here, not well enough to predict at least. Any storms brewing?" My favorite weapon is lightning bolts, naturally.

"Magic? Then, those stories we have been told are true! You can strike down someone with a bolt of lightning?" she asked incredulously.

"Just between you and me, yes, lightning strikes are my specialty, but we need some clouds."

She glanced at the sky. "Probably get some clouds rolling in within a couple days. This far inland, it rains usually once a week. Down on the coast, it's another story. The Med Sea brings in rain much more frequently. Only the larger storms move this far inland, and then only in the springtime or winter. Summers around here are hot and dry."

"Thanks. One final question for you, Lenkova, how soon do you estimate we might encounter the enemy?"

"We'll be in North Point for breakfast. Based on what they said, we will ride due east until we encounter them, probably two more days at the very most. Why?" she asked.

"Brilliant! We have enough time then. Excuse me. I want to talk to the other Guardians. We are going to ensure that we have a cloudy sky at hand when battle is joined," I hastily explained.

"You can control the weather?" she asked, her eyes nearly popping out of her head. She was taken completely by surprise with her own conclusions based upon what I had just said.

"Yes, but it takes time. And time we seem to have." I dropped back, leaving her to mull over what I had said. I quickly explained what I'd learned to Andre, Alton, Waverly, and Elona.

"I didn't know you can control the weather!" exclaimed Elona. "When do I learn how to do that?"

"Tenth year," Alton hastily explained to his apprentice. She sighed knowing that she was a long way from that.

During the frequent rest slowdowns, we four did our chants, re-enforcing them every opportunity we had. If indeed we had a couple days, very likely we would have pulled substantial clouds our way. With the four of us able to use lightning bolts, that should go a long way toward evening the odds.

Also during one of the rest periods, Lenkova told me that we really just had to hold or delay them for a week at most. By then, hundreds of the Sisterhood fighters would have been mobilized and rushed to the defense of North Point. Perhaps, Zargarb would also send some of its cavalry. Plus, there was always the chance that the High Council would also act.

By morning, we did arrive at North Point, however, we did not stop because a rider had come telling us the bad news that the northeastern-most town, Brancella, had been overrun by the Axemen. We had no time to delay here at the safe haven. Women and children stood outside, within the stone courtyard surrounding the caves, waving to us as we rode up to them and then veered due east. I learned that Brancella was home to about five hundred folks and was two days from us. Unfortunately, because of the steep ridges and valleys, we could not travel in a straight line, but were forced to take a more roundabout route.

One day out from Brancella, several battered Sisters were on foot, making their way towards North Point when we ran into them. They had been stationed in Brancella and gave Lenkova a full report. Two days ago, the Axemen surrounded the town and came smashing their way into the town, killing anyone who offered any resistance. After forcing their way into each building and not finding hardly any gold or silver or gems, they then raped most of the women and took fifty slaves, women and children. The distraught Sisters described how the fifty were shackled together and were being force-marched away to the east, probably to be taken back to where the Axemen lived in the far north.

When the Sisters heard the news about the slave taking, vehement curses arose all around me. Waverly properly bandaged the three wounded Sisters, and Lenkova sent them on their way to North Point. Seeing an opportunity to speak with her, I said, "Lenkova, we now have two missions: stopping the Axemen and rescuing the townsfolk. Correct?" She grinned and nodded, though she looked at me with some curiosity. Perhaps, I was getting closer to melting the ice between us.

We rode on. Late the following afternoon, we were riding up the side of a steep valley, covered with low brush. The skies had darkened considerably all day; our joint attempt at pulling in the storm clouds was working well. As we crested the ridge, the noise of the advancing Axemen caught our attention. At once, everyone dismounted and concealed themselves.

Lenkova came over to me, "Time to have a peek at what we are facing. Care to come scouting with me? But only if you can move silently," she added.

"Absolutely," I replied. However, Andre insisted where the Wid went, so went his Protector. Lenkova grumbled but led on anyway. Slowly and quietly, we three crept to the ridge line and peered over into the adjoining valley. About a mile away coming down the down side of the next ridge came the enemy forces, smashing, thrashing the underbrush out of their way. "Noisy bunch," I whispered in jest.

Now it was time I used my keen powers of observation. What exactly were we up against? Memories of the fights I had with Axemen raiders last lifetime in West Reach came into my mind. I whisked them out and cleared my mind, focusing solely on what was visible here and now. After several minutes, Lenkova broke the silence, whispering, "They are like wild bulls. No organization to speak of. Five hundred is a rough estimate. Look how they have something like fifty out in front of the main mass. I wish we had brought more arrows with us. We need to exploit that weakness. Take down the leading fifty and retreat before the main mass can get to us. Let them send out another fifty and take them out. Should work until we run out of arrows. Rather hard targets, though. They wear bits of metal on their arms and legs and chests. Only get one shot. They all have those round shields, which they will bring to bear to thwart a second volley. Damn, I wish we had more arrows!"

Andre spoke up, "We concur with your assessment. These guys are brutes of men — every one of them must be between two and three hundred pounds, and all are at least six feet tall, a bunch of giants. Woe to any of us who must try to stand and hold a line against them. One of those guys could push me over like I was a feather!"

Lenkova looked at Andre as if she had never seen him before. A sudden thought raced through my mind: was Andre succeeding where I was failing to reach Lenkova? She commented, "Good that you see it as I do. We must get back and prepare to hit them when they climb this ridge." Quietly, we three made our way back to the others. As we approached the group, she added, "My compliments. You really can move silently."

Andre replied, "And the same for you. We didn't expect you'd be able to move so silently through the brush. Well done." She again looked at him in the eyes. Was it Andre's natural charm with women?

Hastily, Lenkova outlined her plan, even as the first sprinkles began falling on us. We positioned all the archers, fifty of them, along the ridge line. Standing back, the remaining twenty or so held onto the many horses. Waverly and her team were ready to go into action should one of us get wounded. Alton, Andre, and I positioned ourselves uniformly along the line of the archers; we would let loose lightning strikes and guard against any of the Sister's positions from being overrun, giving them time to retreat. Lenkova cautioned every archer to aim for the head and to conserve arrows; make each one count.

I took up a position on the left flank, Alton, the right. Andre decided to stay close to Lenkova. Slowly and quietly, with rain sprinkles falling on us, we crept up to the ridge line to wait. The lead group was now crossing the small trickling stream that flowed down the valley toward the Med Sea. Her group of fighters was well trained. Without the need for orders from Lenkova, each Sister around me began detailing for her neighbors which Axeman would be her target. Clever. This way, two or three would not be shooting at the same target. Fifty archers against fifty Axemen. This sounded hopeful at least.

The real problem lay in the size of the actual targets: their heads. Any shot elsewhere stood a good likelihood of merely bouncing off the armor bits. Further, in all likelihood, a second volley would be fruitless because they would use their shields to protect their heads. I will admit that this time there was so much going on that I forgot that I was waiting and you know how I hate waiting.

Now they were so close that I could hear their heavy breathing as they stomped their way up the rather steep slope. At this distance, I realized that Lenkova didn't plan on a second volley; there wouldn't be time for that.

My respect for her command grew.

When the lead men were about a hundred feet from the ridge line, Lenkova gave the signal. Fifty arrows whizzed at nearly the same time. At once, she barked, "Fall back." Everyone hastily began running back toward the horses. Looking along the line, at least thirty of these men would not rise again. However, the remaining twenty began shouting and issuing orders in a language I did not understand. As I began running with the Sisters beside me, I saw the Axemen charging up the hill to come after us.

We were halfway to the line of horses when the first of the remaining twenty or so men came charging over the ridge line, racing down towards us. They may be giants of men, but they still could run. Yet I sensed Lenkova had further plans. She had wanted to dispatch the entire fifty lead scouts if she possibly could. I heard her order, "Half archers at horses, half swords line protection." I didn't know what she had planned, neither did Alton or Andre. Thus, when twenty-five Sisters drew their swords and formed into a straight line awaiting the advancing Axemen, we three naturally fell in behind them.

A peal of thunder reminded me. I concentrated and found my black energy mass above me and put a small line between one charging man and the energy cloud. In the next instant, a surge of lightning followed that path, sending the man flying through the air, dead on impact. Alton and Andre followed suit. I hoped that the Sisters would not try to break this charge of "giants" because they'd only be bowled over. I needn't have worried.

Just as the burly men reached the women's formation, that formation seemed to give way, falling back and to the left. The move was unexpected and took the Axemen by surprise. That was the instant the women struck. Flying circle kicks landed upon heads, while in the follow up swing, their swords struck into flesh, wounding arms and legs and necks. The charging men stumbled behind the line of women who quickly reformed their line, only now facing the opposite direction, away from the line of horses and archers. Again, the burly men charged into the women, expecting to melee with them, where their brute strength would allow them to vanquish these amazon fighters instantly. I will say this for the Axemen, they were not stupid.

Now alert to the giving way tactic, they did not fall for it this second time. Indeed a wild melee began with the Sisters slowly giving way, retreating up towards the ridge line and away from the horses and safety. Using my pole, I managed to knock two men out; a nearby Sister cleanly finished the job for me. A sword fight actually lasts mere seconds before one or both are wounded. With close in fighting like this, we could not use our lightning bolts. However, Alton and Andre did not share my distaste for swordplay. On the contrary, they seemed to relish a good fight.

Three minutes later, the skirmish was over, not an Axeman still stood. Rapidly, I watched as the uninjured Sisters hastily went from body to body slashing throats to ensure none lived. Andre commented, "I've got two!"

"Ha, three here," Alton teased back.

"Four here," Lenkova momentarily caught their enthusiasm.

Meanwhile, Waverly and I rushed to the five wounded Sisters. We had to get them to the horses and put some distance between us before the large mass of Axemen could reach us or all was over. The Sister I assisted had a bad leg wound, so I just carried her to the horses. Alton and Andre each carried another two Sisters, while Waverly, Caitlyn, and Fergus helped the other two. By the time that we were all mounted, a massive wave of Axemen crested the ridge, screaming and yelling in their wild language. At that instant, Andre's illusion fired. Even as we began riding off, looking back over our shoulders, we saw that first wave of men falter, even stopping for a moment, staring in utter disbelief at us.

Once we were a safe distance away, Lenkova asked Andre, who was now riding beside her, "What was that all about? Why did they stop?"

Andre chuckled. "It was what they thought they saw that made them pause momentarily." Cleverly, he waited until she insisted on knowing more, before saying, "I just made up a little illusion there. They thought they saw five hundred Sisters riding off. The sheer numbers that they thought they saw caused them to delay. Not long, mind you. I'm sure when they examine our tracks they will revise their estimates downward." She gave him a strange look, I noticed.

We stopped over the next ridge line. Quickly, we five began working on the wounded, with Waverly tending the worst casualty, the large leg slice. Elona took care of the least wounded as best she could, her healing skills were still in the apprentice stage, and she had to ask Alton for help occasionally.

While we were thus occupied, Lenkova set up the next attack. Adriana volunteered five of her Sisters to take the positions of those that were wounded, keeping our firepower at fifty arrows. Lenkova thanked her profusely, promising that her five would not be called upon to stay in the melee line. She then took up her observation point. The rain now began descending in earnest.

"Damn, just what we don't need right now and no boiling water," cursed Waverly. By the time that we had finished sewing and bandaging our patients, ignoring boiling water and procedures that we normally would have followed, Lenkova was signaling the approach of another wave of the Axemen. For safety's sake, I had one of our Sisters begin leading the five wounded Sisters back toward North Point. We all took our positions once more.

This time, the enemy had donned their fighting helms, metal hats with huge horns protruding out the sides, fierce looking, but non-functional. Additionally, all carried their shields at the ready. Andre commented, "Well, they are still following their same basic pattern, fifty way out in front of the main mass."

"Typically men!" commented Lenkova to him.

"Say, since it is really storming now, if some of them get struck by lightning, why, it would not look suspicious. How about letting us launch a few volleys before you shoot your arrows?" She hesitantly agreed after he insisted that the Axemen would not be the wiser about our action. Before Lenkova gave the order to fire the volley, we had electrocuted a dozen of them. At least one, however, stood up afterwards in a daze, stumbled around the hillside, evidently unharmed.

This second attack felled only twenty-four of the oncoming enemy. With their helms and shields, they were much harder to hit. Once more, we found ourselves facing fourteen charging Axemen when they finally reached the hilltop, charging down towards us and our small lines. During the brief melee that followed, I dashed up and down my section of the line, using my pole to save Sisters who got into trouble. As I spied a Sister being overwhelmed, my pole found its mark, deflecting the killing axe strike, startling the opponent, or temporarily stunning him, all just long enough for the Sister to get out of the way.

In the middle section, Lenkova ran into trouble. She slipped on the soaking ground and fell down. A burly Axeman rushed toward her intent on severing her head. At the last second, Andre's blade sliced into the man's chest from the side, and he fell down onto Lenkova's upward pointing sword. "Thanks, owe you one," she said as she wrestled the heavy man off her legs. A short while later, Andre was trying to help another Sister who had taken a bad cut to her arm. However, he didn't see the Axeman closing from behind him. Lenkova's blade first severed the man's arm and then his head.

"Thanks, we're even," jested Andre, and he continued to help the wounded Sister to her feet. She then ran toward the gesturing Caitlyn for aid, bleeding profusely all the way. Three minutes later, the fourteen were dead. We had suffered three more casualties, all arm and chest wounds, but two were in bad need of care, bleeding rapidly.

Time was precious. The main mass of Axemen would come charging our way in only a couple of minutes. Waverly cried out, "Use tourniquets for now." Quickly, we did just that. We barely got them all mounted when the front line of the enemy crossed the ridge line. This time, Lenkova watched Andre intently as he chanted his simple illusion. Fascinated, she watched the leading wave of burly men falter for a moment, long enough for the Sisters to make their hasty exit unhindered.

This time, we rode for a half hour, moving two ridges over. By now, the rain was pouring down. All were drenched, but it had the benefit of washing the blood off us while we worked. Again, without boiling water and proper techniques, we did our best to staunch the bleeding. We knew we would have our hands full redoing nearly everything once we could get them dried off, water boiling, and the proper lighting and herbs at hand. Now we could only hope to keep them alive long enough to get that chance.

Cleverly, Lenkova has asked one Sister to remain behind at the first ridge line. Her job was to report when the enemy got to her position, but to flee as fast as she could when they were sufficiently close. By the time we had finished up, that signal had already come. We joined Lenkova back on the front lines once more. "How about giving us some time to deal with this next bunch?" I asked. Besides, I was getting more and more angry with these infernal Axemen. With so many of her troops already seriously wounded, she agreed. The plan was for the group now to move out, heading for the next likely attacking position, while we four stayed behind to do our best to stop some more of them, reducing their numbers by attrition.

I must admit it was rather spooky when the group mounted up, leaving our four horses tied securely to some low brush. We four lay on the ground at the ridge line peering off into the distance, looking for signs of the oncoming enemy. Rain fell in sheets now, lightning crackled all around us. Deafening rolls of thunder echoed across the countryside. It was so dark that we could barely see. Finally, Andre called out, "I see one over there." We commenced our long-range attack. We estimated that during the next few minutes that we had hit perhaps fifty men.

However, at the end of our barrage, the Axemen decided on their own that the elements were against them. We watched as they retreated and sought shelter from the torrential rains. Since there was nothing more we could do here, we slipped and slid down to our horses and headed off, following the clearly visible tracks in the growing mud left by the others.

"This is not so good," Andre commented between peals of thunder. "We're leaving an unmistakable trail any idiot could follow." We all agreed, but I could think of nothing to alleviate the trail we left.

Soon we caught up to the others. Lenkova had purposely not set a fast pace, enabling us to join them more quickly. "Got about fifty more of them, but they are calling it quits, retreating, seeking shelter from this storm. Wish we could too," I yelled about the noise of the thunder.

She yelled back, "We absolutely must get across the creek up ahead. There's a cave complex we can use just on the other side." A half hour later, we re-crossed the little creek that we had originally crossed only hours ago. However, to my utter amazement, the creek was now a raging, swirling mass of brownish waters. "Barely in time," she yelled. Yes, it was very tricky crossing, more than one horse lost its footings and nearly spilled its rider. Yet, luck was on our side, and we all made it safely across. She yelled at me, "An hour from now and no one can cross it. It will be over a horse's head deep! Come on."

The Sisters knew where they were headed. An hour later and much further north and at the end of a valley system a gaping black hole appeared.

We dismounted and led our horses inside. Now the problem was lighting; no one could see; we were all more than drenched. Suddenly, five blue lights appeared, providing enough light for us to see to get inside safely. The cave had three side chambers. In the pale blue light, which the Sisters continuously marveled over, we positioned all the horses. Another chamber had some dry wood stacked neatly in one corner, along with some food and blankets. Evidently, they sometimes used this cavern and kept it supplied for emergencies, just as we druwids did with our shelter cabins in the Greenway.

Waverly at once set to work on making a fire. Again, you can imagine the general amazement as a wall of fire suddenly appeared above the stacked wood and slowly settled down upon it, igniting the wood. Quickly, the Sisters used the fire to light a dozen lanterns, and we extinguished our pale blue lights. Elona felt proud that she had contributed here as well, and she had Sisters chatting with her about how she could make that light. "Okay, bring the eight wounded here close to the fire. Get water boiling. Guys, get out all our healing packs. Now we have got to do all this over and do it properly or they will all die of infections or worse!" She used her take-charge voice, and we obeyed implicitly. This time, Elona became the common gopher for we four doing the surgery, though we let her do the final bandaging as we moved on to the next victim.

Meanwhile, the other Sisters cared for the horses and prepared a hot meal for us all. Personally, I lost track of the time, for the tedious work seemed to take forever, before Waverly stood up and stretched out her back, saying, "Okay, Elona, bandage away. That's the last of them."

Tired, we joined the Sisters for the hot meal, more than glad they had fixed it. We were so exhausted that we would have probably just laid down and slept instead, too tired to fix our own meal. Lenkova said seriously, "I don't know how to thank you for fixing up our wounded and for everything. You were right; your help is invaluable. Thanks from the entire Sisterhood."

"That's what allies are for," I replied, too tired to say much more. While they chatted, we ate and quickly fell asleep. Tonight, we were safe, but tomorrow was another day. At least three hundred fifty of the enemy still lay somewhere out there behind us.

We awoke to a dark grey day. The intense storm, which we had nudged our way, had past, leaving the dark, ominous sky. The danger of the flash floods was now gone. Our patients, though in some pain, were all on their path to mending. However, seven of the eight should not be moved for several days. The eighth offered to stay behind and look after the others. I knew the decision that Lenkova must now make: should she leave these comrades behind and hope that the enemy forces would not discover this cavern complex or should she risk their healing by having them try to ride all the way back to North Point.

Andre, too, knew what she must have been pondering, as he watched her shapely form pacing back and forth near the entrance. He approached her and said, "You know, I could cast an illusion over the entrance here and make it appear to be part of the hillside. Only someone who knows this is the entrance would be able to find it. Would that help out?" Of course, he already knew that it would.

"You can *do* that?" she asked near disbelief, wondering if he was teasing her. He chatted awhile longer before concentrating on making his chant. He took her arm and walked her outside; everyone watched them; the eavesdropping Sisters muttered something quietly among themselves, but I couldn't hear what they were saying.

From the expression on her face, I knew she was very shocked to see that the entrance hole was simply not there. She moved her hand through the illusion into the opening. For a time, she was speechless. Immediately most of the Sisters had to go and see for themselves. I smiled, remembering the first time that I had witnessed such illusions, when I had been an apprentice so many years ago. I also knew that the effect would wear off in a few days, if it wasn't renewed periodically. Still it offered these women a greater margin of safety. However more significantly, when the rest of us left, we would have to find a way to hide our tracks. Illusion or not, the trail of seventy horses would lead anyone right into the cavern complex.

Interestingly enough, this was precisely what Lenkova pointed out. Her solution was to have everyone leave, leading their horse following as closely as possible the trail made by the person in front of them. That way, the trail to be hidden would be as narrow as possible and more easily covered up or scratched out.

Next, we ate a hot breakfast, not knowing when we would get the chance to eat again. That finished, one by one, we left the cavern. After we were a mile away and on rocky ground, several Sisters went back on foot to cover over the narrow signs of our passage. While five Sisters worked on this project, she sent out ten scouts in a fan-shaped manner, spreading outward towards the east, looking for the enemy's current location. Before we really could make any firm plans, we had to know where the Axemen currently were now located and where they were heading. At best, we hoped that five miles separated us from them.

An impatient hour passed before the riders began returning. Their main force had been spotted roughly where they had stopped to find cover from the deluge yesterday. Several scouts reported that the main encampment had large fires burning; they were still drying out. However, two groups of their scouts were out on the prowl about a mile from the main force. One had gone slightly north; the other, south.

Lenkova suggested a plan of attack that I would have chosen, which I found interesting. She divided our forces in half. Each headed to intercept one of these scout groups. The idea was still attrition, eliminate them a small bunch at a time, again by taking them by surprise. The Axemen were not quiet men, part of their code was to let their enemies know that they were about.

Andre accompanied Lenkova, while Alton, Waverly, and I went with the northern group. This time, Adriana commanded our forces, since our group consisted primarily of the d'Grange Sisters. Adriana followed the same tactics that Lenkova had used yesterday. We positioned ourselves on a ridge line ahead of their forward movement and waited for them to get within range. We three let loose several volleys of lightning strikes, while the Sisters let their arrows fly. The dozen men had no chance at all. We mounted up and headed back to the rendezvous point completely successful and without any mishaps.

When we arrived, Lenkova's group was waiting for us. They'd dispatched another dozen men. With the outlying scouts out of the picture, we rode closer to their encampment. Anyone could have found them, smoke from their crackling fires rose high into the dark sky. Their loud talking was hard to miss. Still, we were cautious and were rewarded with spotting several guards positioned some distance from the main group. Now the question became what do we do next.

She teased me by saying, "I know what you men would do about now — charge into their camp and melee the lot."

"I cannot disagree with you Lenkova," I whispered back, "I've seen too many try just that. Usually, there is a huge loss of life."

"No, we will bide our time until they once more move out and again pick off their advance men. However, only fools would fall for the same trick a second day, but we will see," she commented. She did not have a very high opinion of these men; neither did I for that matter. We waited patiently until noon. Finally, dried out and bellies full, the men broke camp.

"Damn, they are not as foolish as I had hoped," Lenkova commented as they moved out, heading our way. This time, they traveled en mass; they did not send out a scouting party of fifty to check what lay ahead. Clearly, they had learned their lesson from the day before. Naturally, this made our task all the harder, even though we had made a dent in their numbers.

Lenkova's next trap was sprung when the large mass of the enemy began climbing up the side of the ridge behind which we were hiding. One Sister, lying on the ground with a branch hiding her face watched their progress and gave the signal when they were within killing range. As a group, all the Sisters suddenly rose up, took aim, and fired one arrow. Four lightning bolts followed in quick succession. We immediately dashed to our horses and rode off as fast as we could go. Still several return arrows flew wildly around us. Yes, they too had bows, just not the proper occasion in which to utilize them.

Three more times we utilized this same tactic; three more times we rode like the dickens to escape the hail of return fire. A crude estimate suggested that we had eliminated at best another hundred of the Axemen, maybe less. After we rode away from the third surprise attack and halted to regroup, Lenkova now faced a new problem. We were mostly out of arrows; there were not enough to go around for a forth surprise attack. Still we had the horses, which meant a whole lot in this situation.

One solution, which was rejected out of hand, was to return to North Point to get more. The delay would only bring these men closer to the safe haven. While we were resting and grabbing a bite to eat, I vocalized my thoughts aloud, "Has anyone got any ideas why these Axemen are so utterly intent on heading due west? The lucrative cities lie far to the south. There is mostly nothing but tiny villages this far from the coast. What can they possibly gain by going this way? Do you have a secret gold or gem mine out in these hills somewhere?"

Everyone laughed. Lenkova smiled, saying, "Don't be silly. We have no gold mines out here, only a few small villages. I cannot see anything of any value whatsoever that would attract an army to come this way. It is a complete and utter mystery, but then, they are men. Lord knows what goes on in their minds!" More than a few women laughed heartily at her poke. Someone catcalled out, "Sex." Everyone, including us, roared with laughter, breaking the growing tension.

"Seriously, gang, we are out of arrows and they are not. That precludes us riding up like cavalry, taking a whack at them, and riding off before they can hurt us. They'd wipe us out in a hail of arrows. We've got to try some other tactic, though what is eluding me at the moment," Lenkova honestly confessed to everyone.

While we were talking, a scout came back to report that the numbers of the main body seemed substantially fewer. Hence, Lenkova ordered several more scouts out to verify the observation. Crafty, this leader was; she also sent four scouts out mostly north and south of our position. Had she not had the foresight to do this, things might have gone far worse for us. A half hour later, the first of these returned. Indeed, the main body now numbered barely a hundred strong. Lenkova became very worried indeed, pacing back and forth. She needed more information on what exactly these burly men were planning and doing.

A short while later, the other scouts returned nearly panic-stricken. A large force of the Axemen were running westward both north and south of our position. "Damn, they are trying to flank us and encircle us!" declared Lenkova. Both groups were about two miles from us; the main group, but one mile.

"We have a choice," Lenkova announced to all of us. "They are trying to encircle us and finish us off. If we stay here, we are going to be surrounded and that is unacceptable. We could ride on further west and hope they later on take a different strategy with us. We could go back to North Point and resupply arrows, but that will take at least a day or two, bringing the enemy even closer to our children. However, the first choice is suicide, and the second and third violates our goal to delay them until more forces arrive." There didn't seem to be a viable choice.

Lenkova continued, "They are slowly moving our way in a giant, square-bottom U shape. We can use that against them. What I propose is dangerous for us, but might work. Let's ride west and south and position ourselves such that the leading men of the southern line of Axemen runs into all of us. Instead of a wall of men, we have only one or two coming at us at a time. Obviously, we must defeat them rapidly, because eventually, their main body of a hundred strong will come upon us. If we are forced to do battle with those, in due time, the northern bunch will finally join as well, probably overwhelming us. See, I said it was a dangerous plan."

Undaunted, one Sister piped up, "How about making our stand on Heart Break Hill? The southern bunch is heading towards it."

She smiled, "Yes, that's where I propose to make our initial stand. What say you all? It's your lives that I am risking." Cheers and "Let's do it!" resounded from her troops. Certainly, this leader was very well respected; these Sisters would follow her anywhere, I surmised.

"Okay," Lenkova grinned, "let's do it. I want three pairs of scouts out. One to monitor the main central body, the other two monitors the northern spur. When the group you are watching gets sufficiently close to Heart Break, come on in and join us. No heroics, scouts; just give us as much advance warning as possible."

We mounted up and headed southwesterly. One Sister explained to me, "It's called Heart Break Hill because it is a steeply sided hill in the shape of a heart, mostly, and there is no water to be found for miles, hence the break part." We both chuckled over its symbolic name.

Not quite an hour later, we began climbing up a very steep hill covered with the familiar six-foot tall brush so common in this northern portion of the Zargarb Sector. Yes, the horses labored hard to climb the hill, so I knew that men on foot would definitely be at a major disadvantage attacking upwards. At the top of the roughly five hundred foot, mostly level hilltop, the brush was stunted, only growing a couple feet tall, probably from lack of moisture. However, only by walking the perimeter of the hill could one ascertain it was heart shaped.

We rode to roughly the center of the hill. There seven grey, lichen covered stones stood in a circle. Can you imagine the shock of us druwids upon seeing one of our Standing Stones out here in the middle of nowhere and not even in the Greenway? Yes, we were shocked. Memories of that other set of Standing Stones back in the Highlands of West Reach that Fergus had shown us came back into my mind. Seeing this set of Standing Stones raised a number of powerful questions, for which none of us had the slightest answer.

Lenkova thought the stones made a perfect place for us to tether our horses. We left them saddled and ready for a fast get away, should the battle go too ill for us. Waverly decided that near the stones would be a good location to place her first aid station. She along with Fergus and Caitlyn prepared the healing supplies in anticipation of their desperate need. The rest of us spread out along the eastern edge of the hill and began the long wait for the leading edge of the southern flanking Axemen to arrive. This was going to be a very nasty battle — I held no doubts that many of these Sisters, even us, may not see another dawn. Once more, Alton, Andre, and I positioned ourselves with roughly one third of the fighters. Andre was at the side of Lenkova, I noticed, and I was not surprised. I joined my group north of her, while Alton stayed with those south of her. Elona chose to stay with Waverly and assist those in peril. In hindsight, her action probably saved the day for us.

The waiting was interminable. I think I speak for all of us. Risky was an understatement. Several hundred of these burly fighters could easily overrun our position. If we were encircled, we could not escape without fighting our way through their masses. If we were totally tied up in a melee here on the hilltop, how could we retreat to get to our horses, let alone escape? The men would be right on top of us. The plan called for the enemy men to come towards our position in one's and two's, which we could easily handle. However, if they were smart, they would simply flow around the hill and wait until all their forces arrived before attacking, at which point our doom was certain. Yes, I was beginning to wonder if I was about to fail Alabaster yet once again!

On the positive side, the heavy clouds persisted, and we druwids could easily use lightning to assist. We also decided that we might also safely use fire, if pressed; the recent heavy rains might prevent raging brush fires. Still, the plan, better than the alternatives, was fraught with peril; we knew it and so did the Sisters. Nevertheless, in the back of my mind, I continued wondered what motive these Axemen had in so relentlessly coming in this particular direction. It made no logical sense to me.

Lenkova insisted that we make good use of the brushy cover on the hilltop. Consequently, we all were ordered to lie down and conceal ourselves from view. Only she and four others stood plainly visible to anyone approaching the hill from below. Her idea was simple; convince the enemy that only a few were defending the hill so that they would attempt to engage them. If they saw a whole line of fighters on the hilltop, logically, they would hold their positions, wait for others in their forces to arrive, and then charge up the hill, overwhelming the few defenders. So yes, her idea did make sense to me; trick them into committing a few men at a time. However, very quickly they would catch on to our subterfuge.

I heard Lenkova chatting with Andre, who was standing beside her. "If we had days to prepare, why, we might be able to roll boulders down upon them, unleash caldrons of boiling oil, hails of arrows, and the like — maybe even erect some physical barriers to halt or slow them down — to say nothing of making some shield covers to protect us from their rain of arrows like my mother once did. Alas, we must make do with what we have."

Andre replied, "From what I've seen, Lenkova, you are a brilliant defensive field commander. I, for one, would not want to go up against you, even when you are not as prepared as you might like to be! You have one additional factor aiding you, us. Four Guardians. I promise you we'll do all we can to assist."

She smiled at him, and I could see that she met his eyes, "Thanks."

"But what we just do not get is why? Why do they come this way when everything of any real value lies far to the south? Why head due west near the edge of the Paese di Dio? To the four of us, it just makes no sense at all. Are we missing something?" he asked.

She sighed visibly, "This far north there is only a handful of tiny hamlets, really, a few hundred people at most. Shepherds are up on the Paese di Dio, of course, not many though. The only real thing of value is North Point, where our pregnant women stay, the children are raised, and those that need special care dwell. That is of value only to us."

"How about even further west, say in Solamina? Anything of note there?" Andre pressed her.

"Sorry, I don't know much about that sector. I've never heard of anything there," she replied. "No, it doesn't make sense to me either, so I just write it off as another example of the silliness of men's reasoning. What else could it be?" she said defiantly. After a pause, she added, "Mom and dad are there, in North Point. I must stop these barbarians. Both are very old, and well, you can imagine the worst."

"I understand," said Andre, and he put his arm on her shoulder. Interestingly, she did not force it off her.

We waited in silence for nearly an hour before we heard their approach. Like noisy wild pigs trampling through the underbrush, the Axemen stumped their way westward looking for us or more likely maneuvering to encircle us. When the lead pair finally neared the bottom of the steep hill, we could see them at last and they, us. For a brief instant, stares were exchanged, while the sounds of others coming up behind them broke the stillness of the land.

They fell for the bait; the two charged up the steep side of the hill, huffing and puffing, waving their battleaxes threateningly. The four waited calmly close to the edge of the hill for the struggling men to get close enough to attack. The sweeping arcs made by the large battleaxes, of necessity, forced the four slowly to move backwards, precisely what Lenkova had intended. When the enemies' backs were exposed, two more Sisters sprang from their cover and attacked, catching the two off balance. While their attacks did little but startle the men, the four in front seized the opportunity to strike fatal blows. Two down. Only seconds passed.

However, the others now charging — if one could call their mad scramble up the steep slope a charge — saw the surprise move. Thus, they would not be so easily fooled. Slowly but surely, a steady stream of burley men appeared on the hilltop. More and more Sisters came out of hiding to combat the new arrivals, until at last, we were all involved in this life and death struggle. Early on, over a dozen Axemen were slain. Now, five minutes into the wild melee, the going proved far tougher. Two Sisters took axe cuts and crumpled to the ground. Others rushed to prevent the enemy from finishing off their victims. Meanwhile, Fergus and Caitlyn did their job. Fleet of foot, both rushed in during those seconds when the other Sisters were valiantly keeping the Axemen from lopping off the heads of the two wounded Sisters. They reached them and physically pulled them back out of immediate danger and over to the standing stones. There Waverly and Elona set to work on them at once, rapidly binding the wounds to prevent blood loss. There was no time to do much else, because more were taking wounds.

Ten minutes into the melee, I was tiring and knew that the others were as well. In slow motion, I saw Lenkova stumble and watched her unable to avoid the down swing of her opponent's axe. She took a nasty cut to her thigh, only her rolling motion saved her from instant death. Andre stabbed the man through his heart while his axe was still on its back swing. He tried to help her to stand, while still parrying with the man who was originally attacking him. How he could do both at once was a miracle. However, she could not stand. I saw Fergus rushing towards them as well as another Axeman. I grabbed a stone and threw it at the Axeman who was attempting to intercept Fergus. While it only gave him a solid knock on his helm, it did distract his attention to me, and he changed his path, heading for me.

I'd had enough of this close quarters combat. Mechanically, I reached out and made that fine line connection from the running man to the dark clouds overhead. Nature did the rest. Wham, the lightning bolt eliminated him. I found myself now with no immediate opponents. Thus, I retaliated using my favorite weapon, lightning bolts. I dropped all those that were not too close to our people. In just a few minutes, only a dozen men remained fighting close to the Sisters. I glanced back at the standing stones and was shocked to see twenty Sisters lying on the ground just inside the stones. Poor Waverly and Elona could not keep up.

Another minute later, five more were transported to the stones, but the melee had temporarily ended. Hundreds of Axemen bodies lay strewn around us, littering the hilltop. At this point, two Sisters, the center scouts, came galloping up the hill side, yelling, "The main body is nearly on you! They are trying to surround the hill!"

The unspoken order was implemented without Lenkova uttering a word; she was in too much pain and fading in and out of consciousness. We retreated to the stones, intending upon getting everyone on horseback and making a hasty exit. Because nearly a third were wounded, by the time that we had gotten several situated on a horse, the Axemen had arrived and began launching a rain of arrows wildly upon the hill, hoping that some in the rain of death would find their marks! It would have proved deadly, except that Andre and I reacted simultaneously with the same spell. Clustered so tightly together and beneath the tall stones, we both created a wall of ice propped upon the tops of the stones!

Both of us were rather surprised with the result of our spells. The ice walls ended up being twice their normal dimensions. As a result, everyone, including the horses, was completely covered with the ice canopy. Hundreds of arrows bounced off or stuck in the sheets of ice overhead, just seconds after the ice appeared! Four volleys of arrows were thus avoided, miraculously no one was struck!

Alton, Andre, and I now took matters into our own hands. Alton called out, "Fire time." Each of us created a horizontal sheet of flames in the air just over the edge of the hill where we could hear their charging footsteps. The flames shot skyward momentarily before they fell with increasing speed toward the ground. Once more, we three were dumbfounded! Our sheets of flames were twice their normal size! We heard screams of pain and terror and knew it was being effective. We created another set, slightly offset from these, covering more of the unseen approaching enemy. Again, we had huge walls appear, though fewer cries from its victims. In essence, we were mostly guessing where the as yet unseen men were located coming up the hillside. Unfortunately, just then the other two pairs of scouts came charging up the hill from our rear, screaming, "The northern bunch is nearly here. There is only a narrow space open to flee!"

Flee? We could not, not without abandoning over a third of our companions. Alas, we really had no choice but to hold our ground here at the stones. Sisters carefully got the few wounded who were on horses back off them and safely onto the ground again. Everyone bunched the wounded close together at the center of the stones, side by side. All the horses were tied to the rear stone in a big mass, completely beneath the now melting ice sheets. I yelled to Waverly, "Keep the sheets above and around the horses!" I depended upon her not only to save the wounded but to keep the horses as safe as possible. Without horses, once this was over, we would be in dire straits! That assumes, of course, any of us were still alive to use the horses.

Grimly holding their weapons, the remaining Sisters moved out, encircling the stones, preparing to defend to their last breaths. Now, we saw our doom coming. Simultaneously from all sides, the Axemen, some showing signs of their encounter with our flames, reached the hilltop. Hundreds surrounded us on all sides! Now Elona acted. Whosh! She created her flames. Remember, she has always been opposed to using flames to attack another human being. Her flames formed a vertical flaming circle thirty feet tall surrounding the stones and the wounded and the horses! Again, the sheer size of her wall was more than double what it should have been, but I had no time to try to figure out why.

As the men charged toward us, we three let loose more falling flames. However, these men kept charging anyway, some burning and falling to the ground mid-step. A handful of Axemen began firing arrows into the thick of the melee, caring not if they hit their own men as well! It was all or nothing with these crazed men!

Inside the cylinder of fire, Lenkova regained consciousness and witnessed the melee going on around her. She spied an Axeman aiming an arrow toward her and Elona, who was standing over her. She watched as the arrow took flight coming right at Elona. The apprentice reacted, and she caught the arrow, which would have pierced her chest. With a look that could kill, she stared at the shooter and merely dropped the arrow onto the ground. She had learned her lessons well. The man stood aghast staring at this woman standing tall within the cylinder of flames. He never saw the sword thrust from a Sister who plunged her blade into his chest while he gaped.

Me? I just went ballistic. When I get angry, I mean really angry, you know how I react. I just snapped. As rapidly as I could, I formed the faint line of connection between man and energy cloud and moved my attention to the next man, knowing totally and completely that Nature would respond. A second at most maybe per man? I had no sense of time whatsoever. I just looked at the next man, made the tiny, faint line of connection to the dense clouds above me, and put my attention on the next man beside him without waiting for the result. Others told me afterwards the cacophony of thunder was enormous and deafening. So powerful in fact, that nearly all fighting ceased, as everyone attempted to cover their ears from the noise! Me, I heard nothing but music to my ears. I did not even recognize the fact that I had entirely gone around the hilltop in a circle pattern. I saw a body; I made the connection, saw the next body, made the connection, saw the next body, made the connection, saw the next body, made the connection. On and on and on and on and on and on. I did not discriminate between standing bodies or those lying on the ground. I vaguely recall slowly turning round and round as my attention went from body to body.

STOP BETHANY! THEY ARE ALL DEAD! STOP! Words screamed into my mind. I felt the overwhelming urge to keep right on going and did so. ***BETHANY! STOP! PLEASE STOP, BETHANY! THEY ARE ALL DEAD! STOP! STOP!*** Stop? Why? These animals masquerading as men did not deserve to live! Actually, I recall that I could not see too well. I saw all the kings's men and Galts around me and wondered where Alabaster and the renegade druwid Erline were. No matter, we had thousands of Galts to slay. A tiny part of my consciousness said, *this happened over fifty years ago; this is not now.* I blinked and the hilltop came back into view. ***FOR GOD'S SAKE, STOP BETHANY!*** Screamed in my mind. I shrieked back *Why?*

They are all dead. Stop, please, stop.

Who said that? Erline? No she isn't here, can't be her. Alabaster? No, I am trying to find him. Who? Oh, Waverly. At last, I paused briefly to see if it was Waverly. In that instant, my eyes focused upon the hill around me. Destruction lay everywhere; the chaotic arrangement of charred bodies formed no discernable pattern to my eyes. More importantly, none moved. I saw no motion and *that* finally allowed me to pull out of it. I blinked and collapsed upon the ground, utterly and completely exhausted and drained. Faintly in the back of my mind, I feared that I had already killed all of our valiant Sisters and felt a huge surge of guilt sweep over me.

Some awful smell assaulted my olfactory senses; I jerked my head away from it, and awoke to find Waverly waving a tiny vial of skunk excretion in front of my nose! "Are you all right?" she asked; her face was white as a cotton sheet — all the color completely gone. Her eyes seemed to be twice their normal size, which of course could not be, just my imagination. I sat up.

Around me, only Waverly was standing. To my complete relief, I saw many Sisters sitting on the ground, obviously alive. I had not slain everyone! Thank god for that! However, as I slowly gazed at the faces all staring back at me, including Alton, Andre, Elona, Lenkova, Caitlyn, and Fergus, every last one of them appeared to me white as sheets. "I can't see too well," I muttered, "you are all white." I added, "Everyone is white," as my gaze focused on nearby Sisters.

Finally, Andre, good old Andre, spoke up, "Remind me *never* to cross Bethany! Good god!" He gestured around the battlefield. His levity became contagious. Many gave a fearful chuckle, agreeing with him.

"Why are you all white?" I asked stupidly, wondering if something dreadful had happened to my eyes.

"Next time, can you please give us some advanced warning when you are going to go ballistic on us?" Andre continued to tease me. Many others suddenly laughed outright, relieving their own tensions. In jest, he added, "And can you also provide ear plugs? That would be most helpful. Can any of you all hear me?" he teased further. Everyone roared at his jest. He'd taken their private thoughts and vocalized them playfully, allowing the shock and terror to be relieved in everyone.

"Strange, your faces now are starting to have some pink in them," I muttered to myself.

"Well, you certainly gave us all a dreadful scare, Bethany!" Waverly said sternly, braving attempting to act severe with me in an attempt to get me to see what had been done.

I muttered, "Oh," and began to look more around me. Devastation lay all about.

Elona helped bring me fully back. "Say, I caught my first arrow! I did as you said, Bethany, just stared back at the shooter and dropped the arrow on the ground. You should have seen the look on his face!" Finally, her words sunk in, and I smiled.

Lenkova, though in great pain and weak, managed to utter an order, "Situation analysis please before I pass out." At once, her troops sprang into action. They were now back on familiar ground, so to speak. So few of them, however, actually moved about, only ten. Ten out of all our people had not been injured in some way. Miraculously, none of us druwids, Caitlyn, or Fergus had sustained any significant injuries. The ten quickly reported to Lenkova, who was slipping back into unconsciousness. "No more Axemen seem to be around. Horses spooked but okay. Sixty are wounded. What do we do now?" Unfortunately, she passed out and could not issue her orders.

Instead, Alton and Andre took charge. "Ah, Adriana, you are still with us. Good. You take charge of these other nine. Clear us a path so we can eventually ride off this hill. Make sure they are dead. Search them if you deem it appropriate. The rest of us, let's get going on at least stopping all the bleeding. Waverly, you get the most seriously wounded. Caitlyn, you and Fergus lend we five a hand as we need it. In fact, take Elona and make a quick survey of the wounded. We need to have those hurt the worst tended first."

An hour later, we had everyone's wounds wrapped tightly to stop blood loss or rather slow it down. We had to get them to some shelter where we could do a proper job of healing. Immediately, we thought of the cavern complex where the others were staying, recovering. Luck was with us, one unwounded Sister knew the way. I will point out that anyone of us four druwids could have retraced our route back to the cavern, but we would have had to take far more time doing it. Indeed, it took all of us working constantly to get so many wounded onto horses. Some were unconscious and had to be tied to their mount. In the end, each of us ended up leading three other horses behind us as we rode slowly back to the cavern.

At dusk, we finally rode up the familiar isolated valley and into the illusion, which obscured the entrance. Once inside, we got several fires going and brought all the pots of water to a boil that we had with us. Each of us five druwids allowed one other person to act as our aide, fetching and assisting as they could. Those who were left made some strong tea and supper for the rest of us.

How long we sewed, applied healing salves, and wrapped bandages, no one could say for sure. It was pitch black when we finally finished the last woman. Two Sisters had died from massive bleeding; there was nothing we could do to save them. The other's wounds were about equally divided between arm, leg, and chest wounds. Each wound generally took quite a lot of stitches to sew up, because battleaxes leave large wounds from their big blades, often cutting to the bone. Caitlyn's final comment to me — she had been my assistant the whole time — was, "Dawn's coming." All of us then collapsed on blankets, exhausted.

When I awoke, it was night, and I grew confused, until Caitlyn explained that we had slept through the entire daytime. She estimated that it was about nine pm. During our lengthy sleep, some of the other Sisters had arisen and tended those in need. They had fetched more firewood and had tea and warm food awaiting us. I ate hungrily, and then we all began our close inspection of all our patients. We were very fortunate that only two women needed further care. Their cuts had been very deep and required reopening of the wounds, deep cleansing, and even more careful re-sewing, if their limbs were to be saved. Several hours later, the tasks were finished; we had all conferred and worked together on these two. Since it was dark, we all once more laid down to sleep.

This time, we awoke to sunlight; our biological clocks were finally back in synch with Nature. After eating and inspecting everyone, Andre called for a conference. I already guessed what he had in mind.

"Gang, we are out of bandages and healing supplies. The food is almost gone. Water is dangerously low. Nothing left for the horses to eat. None of the proper meals for all these recovering wounded. Tis grim indeed. However, all that aside, there remains those captured townsfolk to rescue. If we delay too long, they will likely be out of our reach, unless we wish to launch an expedition into the Northern Steppes. There is what? About ten of us that are not in bad shape. Here's what I propose: Alton and I will take two Sisters with us, who can guide us to that village from which the slaves were taken. From there, we will pick up their trail and rescue them, bringing them safely back to their town. Meanwhile, dispatch another two Sisters back to North Point, requesting immediate assistance here. The rest can stay here tending all the wounded," Andre finally finished, having enumerated each of these on his fingers, making sure he'd not forgotten something.

Most of his suggestions I had already decided ought to be done, except for his racing off after those who took the slaves. Before I could reply, Lenkova's voice came loud from behind us, where she was lying on a blanket. "I'm coming too, so make that five of us."

"You are in no condition to travel!" Waverly broke in adamant in her view. "You'll only rip out the stitches and bleed to death along the way."

"Then, patch me up so I won't. It's my responsibility to rescue those villagers, and I aim to see it through," retorted Lenkova, just as adamant as Waverly. Both women glared at each other, each determined to have their way.

Andre stepped in, "Ladies, how about a compromise?" Yes, he had a way with women. "Let's see if she is able to mount and ride. If so, let's see if she can keep up. If her wound reopens or she cannot keep the pace, she returns at once. You are of no use to anyone if your body dies, Lenkova."

"Well, if she will promise," Waverly backed down from her stern stand.

Reluctantly, Lenkova gave her word. She also suggested who should go with us and who should return for help. While the four Sisters and our two men began gathering up what they would need, I scrounged through all the remaining meager supplies, forming a care package. "Here, I've given you a good deal of the remaining food because we ought to be re-supplied long before you will be. In addition, I stuck in the last of our bandages in case her wound opens up. Keep Waverly informed of your progress please."

"Yes ma'am," Andre teased me back. Lenkova gave us a queer look, not grasping his tease. We both caught her stare, and Andre explained, "Well, sometimes he acts just like my mother. Besides, he's had more experience with female bodies and temperaments than males, like me. It was just a jest, nothing more."

She grinned and got the joke. "Honestly, with that hair, anyone could be fooled," she half teased and half meant it.

"By the way," Lenkova added, "I really need to thank you for saving all of our lives back there on the hill. I would not have come back from this trip. On behalf of the entire Sisterhood, thank you all for your aid. I will admit that when I first met you, I had many reservations. After what I think that I witnessed on Heart Break Hill, I can honestly say you are incredibly powerful allies, if not gods!"

The mention of its name brought back an important question that was in the back of my mind for days now. "Lenkova, before you go, do you know who built those standing stones on the hill? Or when they were put there?"

She shrugged her shoulders, "Nope, as far as I know, they have always been there. Maybe my mother knows. You can ask her when you see Rosita. If she doesn't know, maybe she can try to find out for you. Is it important?"

"Thanks, I'm just really curious, that's all." She was struggling to get to her feet. She had taken an axe cut to her upper left thigh; from the grimace and clenched teeth, I knew she was in great pain just trying to stand. Without drawing any attention, I slipped my arm under her left arm and provided just enough lift to take the strain off that leg. Standing now, she glanced at me, and I slipped away, as if nothing had happened. For a fleeting second, she intentionally looked me in my eyes. I accepted her acknowledgment, perhaps the ice between us was thawing. However, I did accidentally pick up her thought, *A man would not have done it like that.* Encouraged, I whispered to her, "Avoid trotting. It will rip the stitches."

She whispered back, "I thought as much. Thanks for the warning." Andre was motioning that they were ready to leave. Without another word, she gingerly walked to her horse; the five slowly walked them out of the cavern complex. The two who were heading back to North Point also left right behind them, claiming to everyone that they would be back in two or three days' time.

Waverly, Elona, Fergus, Caitlyn, me, one Zargarb Sister, Gallia, and one from d'Grange, Myra, were the only ones who did not have any wounds to nurse. The six of us had to tend to the nearly sixty wounded Sisters. We had six who were in critical condition and would require frequent observation. Ten, including Adriana, had relatively minor wounds and could be counted upon to help out, as long as we did not overly tax them. Waverly had thought ahead; the six critical patients were grouped together so that one person could easily keep an eye on them. As the silence came after the departure of the two groups, she motioned for us six to move closer to the entrance away from the wounded; she obviously wanted a conference.

In low tones, she said what I was expecting, "Okay, we are in a tough situation. At this point, we can't feed anyone — hardly anything's left. We can't do anything for three days. Also, we need water; if any need further surgery, we must have water. And we've used the last of the firewood."

As Wid, I ought to be taking charge. However, Waverly was doing a great job of keeping things going and I told her so. The others agreed with me, and she smiled appreciatively. I said, "Okay, Waverly, you are in charge of watching the critical patients. The rest of us — we are going to have to become providers and fast. Water, firewood, something for food. Oh yes, and something for the horses to munch on; they are getting a bit edgy. Caitlyn and I'll go in search of something edible for us. Elona and Myra, you lay in a stockpile of firewood. Gallia and Fergus, you are in charge of fetching water and something for the horses. I figure Gallia knows this area the best, so she may have the best chance of finding both. Waverly, if anything comes up, just mentally contact us." Everyone agreed and we all set off on our tasks.

Caitlyn and I climbed the ridge under which the caverns lay to get a better sense of what the surrounding lands might offer in the way of edibles. "It's pretty bleak," she finally verbalized what we both were thinking.

"Yes indeed. Well, if we still had any arrows, we might be able to hunt some rabbits," I mused.

"Or even a deer," she added, thinking of all those who would need feeding soon. "But we are out in the middle of nowhere, and it is a pretty bleak landscape. Not even berries to pick. No nut trees either. It sure is different than home," she commented, a slight homesickness in her tone. I thought her pronouncement was an understatement. Her eyes brightened, she exclaimed, "I bet I know where we can get something!" I grinned her way and she explained, "The Axemen's camp. They must have brought a lot to eat along with them. There were hundreds of them, and from the size of them, they must have had large appetites. We only need to visit what's left of their base camp, wherever that may be." I gave her a hug of appreciation. She had a great idea.

We quickly got our horses and brought along two spares hopefully to carry back supplies. "If there is a base camp, Caitlyn, I will find it," I declared optimistically, though I knew that this would be a challenge in observation. We rode south for several miles until I spotted the signs of the passage of the flanking men. "Now we back track and follow the path that has the biggest signs of trampling, where the majority of men passed by. This way," I explained. We rode a couple miles to the east before turning north once more.

"There is something," Caitlyn whispered. Indeed, ahead, though mostly concealed by the brush and trees, was a small tendril of smoke curling and rising in the air.

"They may have left some men, like cooks, back at the main camp," I cautioned. "Let's sneak up on it and see." We rode a short distance, dismounted, tied the horses securely, and slowly made our way to the smoke's origin. Indeed, in a large, man-made clearing lay their base camp. It was deserted. The smoke was coming from the final embers of a long dying fire that once must have been a large bonfire indeed, judging from the fire ring of stones around the ashes. More importantly, packs of stuff, cooking pots and pans, large water skins, and chests lay all around one side. The ground had been trampled by the milling of hundreds of heavy men.

The remains of several deer carcasses showed that we were not the first visitors here; at least one bear had his fill before we arrived. "So much for the fresh meat," I said. Next, we began a thorough search. We found boxes of dried lentils and legumes and tied four of them to the packhorses after I brought them into the camp. On further searching, I found a prized box, "Well, I'll be. Look at this: Greenway tea! It's been a long time since I had any of this!" Caitlyn smiled, knowing how much I loved a good hot cup of tea.

She added a small box of salt to our growing stash. We thought about bringing some of the water skins back with us, just in case, but they smelled so rancid that we thought better of it. Then, Caitlyn found a pack that was stuffed with dried fish. "Now we are in business!" she declared. "All this ought to hold us over, don't you think?"

I agreed and we mounted up and retraced our route carefully. It would not do to get ourselves lost out here. An hour plus and we re-entered the cavern complex with our prizes. Inside, we saw that the others were equally successful. A cooking fire was blazing, water boiling, and a huge pile of wood lay stacked against a wall. Fergus commented, "Hi laddie, good to see you got back. Next time, you get to go for the water! Do you know how hard that was? Why, we had to make ten trips, and those buckets got very heavy. If it weren't for Gallia here, we'd never found any."

Teasingly, I replied, "Well, then, wait til you see what we brought back. Anyone care for some quality hot tea? Perhaps some fish, lentils, and legumes?"

"Laddie, you jest me. Where could you find that around here? We're miles and miles from the sea and any general store."

Caitlyn began unpacking our horses, while I displayed my treasure box of Greenway tea. Waverly came to inspect our food supplies and could only say, "Well, I'll be! How on Tarra?"

Caitlyn smiled and said, "Compliments of the Axemen. We raided their main base camp, although a bear was there first and took all the fresh meat. Will all this do?" She, of course, knew very well that it would feed a small army for days.

"Congratulations go to everyone," Waverly exclaimed. "Well done indeed. Now all we need is a good chef to begin cooking."

"Lassie, that leaves me out," Fergus quickly bowed out. I did as well, never having been a good cook even when I had female bodies, let alone this male one.

Gallia, getting in on the ribbing, said, "Men! None knows the first thing about cooking. You'll probably have us try to eat the dried lentils! If someone helps out, I'll cook," Caitlyn volunteered, though she was not much of a cook either.

An hour later, everyone ate their fill or as much as Waverly would allow them to eat. All we lacked from a perfect meal was some bread. With the chores done, we all sat around the dying fire sipping our second cups of hot tea.

Waverly said very seriously, "Bethany, I would like some explanations of what exactly happened on Heart Break Hill. I've been putting it off because other things were far more important to handle. Now we have idle time. It seemed to me that you almost went renegade on us with those lightning bolts. I mean you were killing the same men for the fourth time! I thought I could never get you to stop!"

Have you ever had some conduct of yours of which you were not proud, yet no one mentioned it for some time? Just when you had it pushed nicely out of your mind, they bring it up? "Let me tell you a story," I began. I described our wagon ride to Karka, with my family and Loremaster Ellen, well over fifty years ago. I was a young girl and apprentice druwid with only a few years training. During the thunderstorm, the King's cavalrymen ambushed our wagon, firing quarrels into all of us. I thought I saw my parents, my brother and sister, and my teacher, Ellen, die in the attack. I described how I became one with the black energy masses and clouds of the storm and began to bring down lightning upon these wicked men.

Totally untrained and unskilled in doing this action coupled with the emotional shock of having seen everyone I loved get killed, I had nearly gone insane, lashing out the only way I could, firing lightning bolts from the sky. I described what I had done and how the Communicator Willow had finally helped me regain my sanity. I saw that Elona was listening to my every word, which was a very good sign.

For the benefits of the non-druwids present, I described what could have happened to me, permanent insanity. Next, I moved along in time to when as Wid, I was attempting to parley with the King Randolf, who had made a treaty with the Galts. I rode into a hail of arrows instead, dying instantly when one pierced my head. I described how Alabaster, Erline, and I proceeded to eliminate at least a thousand evil men that day, raining down lightning bolts everywhere. I explained how Alabaster was able to help me keep my cool and not go completely berserk or insane.

"You see, in crisis situations of great magnitude, I definitely run the risk of going berserk in my attacks. Yes, on the hill, when nearly everyone was wounded and hundreds of the enemy were closing in for the final kill, I did go berserk once more. Yes, you may call it temporary insanity, I won't protest. Literally, I just turned on some kind of automatic response, bringing down a bolt on each man, turning round and round as I went after every enemy fighter. However, you are right; it took control of me. I didn't even see that they were all dead. Did I really hit them each four times?"

"Yes you did," Caitlyn said meekly. "I was really afraid for you, Bethany. You had me really, really scared for a while there. You didn't seem to hear anything we were screaming at you. The noise from all that lightning was totally deafening. We had to cover our ears!"

"Waverly reached my mind at long last. Thanks for persevering, Waverly. I heard you, but it took such a very long time for me to respond and somehow shut that automatic response thing down. I really am so sorry that I frightened everyone."

"We have no right to complain, Bethany. Every one of us owes you their life. If you had not done that, we'd all be dead right now," Waverly countered.

"Elona," I said, turning this into a learning situation for the apprentice, "with great power comes an even greater responsibility to use it wisely. Temptation is always present. I am particularly vulnerable to abusing that power in such situations. Three times now. I am sane and alive *only* because dear friends came to my rescue. I am capable of such destruction that not even my long training can sometimes control. As you gain power, learn well how to master it, as I know you already have with your circles of fire."

Elona grasped what I was saying. However, since we were now discussing the attack, something had been bothering her and she took this opportunity to ask, "Master, I do have one question to ask, if I may."

"Just Bethany, please, I am no one's master," I teased.

"You know that I do not feel right in bring fires directly down upon the enemy as you all did during the battle. I use the flames to protect instead. I think I do it for the very reasons you suggest. I know my own skills and limitations with the flames. Yet, on that hill, my circle of flames was at least twice its normal size. I have never been able to make such huge walls of flames as I did there. It has been bothering me. Do you know why that was so?”

"You know, Elona, I had the same thing happen and have been wondering about it ever since. Actually, all three of us had our sheets of flames appearing more than twice their normal size. To my knowledge, that has never happened before to any druwid. This definitely is a mystery. I love mysteries that I can unravel and obtain the truth. At the moment, I do not even have the slightest speculation why that happened, only that it did occur to Andre, Alton, and me. And now you too. Strange indeed. When there is time, it is a mystery that I intend to solve.”

"Alton has told me that standing circles in the Greenway are holy places and that you conduct ceremonies there,” Elona continued exploring for more information on these circles.

"True, they are actually astronomical observatories. The stones tell us when the first day of spring and winter actually are, along with midsummer and midwinter. Usually, we celebrate there four times a year, if we can, but at least at the two equinoxes,” I elaborated, knowing that she was pumping me for more information. "However, to the best of my knowledge, no druwid built them. Alabaster, the founder of the druwids, once told me that he discovered these stones and worked out their purpose of being a calendar. I've often wondered just who built them and why.”

"Who lived in the Greenway before you were there?" she kept at it like a dog with a bone.

"Don't know. I've no idea," I was truthful.

I think that she realized she had exhausted what I knew about them and changed the subject slightly, "What about all the dead? I mean we can't just leave all those dead bodies lying all over Heart Break Hill, can we?”

"No, we would never do that. I don't care whom the person was that died, common human decency dictates that their remains ought to be buried. Otherwise, they pose a severe sanitary problem, you know, rotting, stinking corpses. Such can even pollute streams from which we drink. However, there are so many dead and so few of us that I planned to wait until the reinforcements arrive.” I wanted to change the gruesome subject and added, "By the way, congratulations on catching your first arrow shot at you in combat. Well done.”

She grinned proudly, just as I had done so many years ago when I had first accomplished this difficult feat. "I just got very mad at them for trying to hurt those who were wounded and out of the melee,” she rationalized. Yet, there was some truth in what she said. Necessity levels can raise what we can do, if the need is great enough. I think that both she and I shared a mutual understanding of what impact dire need can have on our actions.

Around the middle of the third day, outside our cavern complex the thunderous sounds of many horses coming up the valley echoed in our ears off the walls. Gallia, after a cautious peek out of the entrance, gaily announced, "Relief has arrived!" Many Sisters managed a cheery "Yeh!" Shortly, several people entered on foot, leading their horses.

In the lead was an older woman, grey hair cut short indicated a Sister, her face lined with wrinkles. She walked with the stiffness of old age. Handing her reins to an equally elderly man, she barked commandingly, "Where is my daughter? Is she all right?"

The ten of us were standing in the center of the complex, behind us nearly seventy women still lay on their makeshift beds of blankets, though many had sat up to see who had come. Gallia answered for us with only the tiniest delay; evidently, she was used to taking orders from this woman, "Fighter Group Leader Lenkova went with four others to free those villagers who were carted off to become slaves of the Axemen. They left over three days ago. She has a bad battleaxe cut on her left thigh, but she absolutely insisted that they take her along with them, ma'am!" She emphasized this last part.

The woman seemed beside herself with worry and concern, but the elderly man spoke soothingly, "Isn't that just what you would have done, dear?" She glared at him and calmed down.

"Right as usual, Antonio. I most certainly would have gone, even if they had to tie me to the saddle." Surprised at her own remark, she hastily looked at Gallia and said, "She wasn't tied to the saddle was she?"

Gallia giggled slightly, "No, ma'am! Bethany subtly helped her up onto her horse so no one would notice how much pain she was in. Bethany was the one who said that if she was fit enough, she could go. Waverly didn't want her to even stand up." As she spoke, she pointed each of us out to Rosita.

Now the woman turned her attention full on me. I was the one responsible for letting her severely wounded daughter go galloping off after the others. She looked sternly at me and said, "Ma'am, you let her go with a bad leg wound?" More than a few of the wounded Sisters chuckled in the background.

I answered, "If she doesn't trot, she shouldn't pull the stitches out. I had sewn her up fairly tightly, figuring she would try to do more action sooner than the others. I left strict orders with Alton and Andre that, if she showed any bad signs, like stitches pulling out, she was to return here immediately. As you can see, she is not back, so all must be well. However, if you want, Waverly can make contact with them and double check on her current condition."

Rosita flushed, color returning to her worried, pale face. My voice had given me away. "I'm sorry, sir. It's just that your hair is so utterly long, and she called you Bethany." More Sisters chuckled in the background.

Smiling broadly, I replied, "Think nothing of it. I had to masquerade as a woman for a time before arriving here in the Sea Princes. Besides, I have a passion for long hair, and my name has been Bethany for several lifetimes. However, this is the first male body I've had, and I am still trying to get used to it, not all that successfully, I might add." The Sisters chuckled even more. "Seriously, Waverly will make contact with them and see how she is doing."

"By the way, we should introduce ourselves," I went on, seeing that over fifty other Sisters by now had walked into the cavern. "I'm the leader of the Cymry or West Reach Minstrels, a Guardian from the Greenway. This is Waverly, also a Guardian. This is my fiancee, Caitlyn." I continued with the others present, including Adriana.

She then replied, "You will be glad to know that the others and your wagons all arrived safely at North Point without incident. I'm Rosita Armino Pazzio; I used to be the Fighter Group Leader for Zargarb. This is my husband, Antonio." He smiled and nodded at me, though he still stared at my red hair. "She is my daughter, Lenkova," she explained and continued the introductions. At last she asked, "Okay, what is the most urgent thing we need to do for you? So many wounded. How large was the force anyway? I didn't believe Edara; she said at least five hundred Axemen."

"We never did a proper count. Their bodies still lie where they fell, unfortunately. We have our hands full here and no way to bury that many," I replied. "However, five hundred may be a low count. I'm sorry that we couldn't save two of your Sisters, though. Their wounds were so bad that they died almost instantly. To answer your question, though, our horses are in the worst shape just now. While we've been able to water them, we've not been able to feed them much of anything for three days. Perhaps you can see to them first."

Immediately, twenty Sisters leapt into action and began leading our horses out of the cavern. Rosita asked, "Edara said that you had no food or bandages?"

"Well, yes, when we sent Lenkova off to rescue the villagers, we sent along with them most all that remained of both, just in case her wound opened up. However, Caitlyn and I found the Axemen base camp and confiscated some of their supplies. I do admit everyone here is tired of dried fish, lentils, and legumes. If you have brought bandages, we sure could use them right now. We really should redress all their wounds."

Now the remainder of the Sisters went to work, unloading boxes of supplies. Once we had water boiling again, we three began to make our rounds, tending to each of the many wounded Sisters, changing their bandages and such. Rosita followed us from patient to patient, observing the condition of each woman. She finally commented, "You have worked a miracle here. At least half of these women ought to have died from their wounds, while another quarter should have lost a limb or two. If I had not seen this with my own eyes, I would not have believed it! All that I have heard about the Guardians pales in comparison to this!"

Gallia overheard her and called out, "This is nothing. Wait until you see Heart Break Hill!" Twenty some other Sisters backed her up. "We'd all be long dead if it wasn't for Bethany."

I blushed. I hate being the center of attention. Rosita's eyes seemed to burn into the back of my neck. I muttered, "I got angry and went a little insane, but I managed to save them."

"Just what did happen on Heart Break Hill?" she asked pointedly. "Edara told me a wild and unbelievable tale." Gallia took this as an opportunity to retell all the events since we first found the Axemen. With all the others around the room adding in bits and pieces to her story, interrupting her every so often, Rosita finally got an accurate picture of what had happened. Still, she found it hard to believe.

When Gallia finished, Rosita explained, "By tomorrow night, around five hundred fighters should be getting here. I sent word everywhere for Sisterhood help. The last word I had was that they had assembled and were planning on riding through the nights to get here as fast as possible. When they get here, I want to go see Heart Break Hill for myself," she declared.

"Can I go with you?" asked Elona.

"Sure," she replied. I volunteered to go as well. I wanted to examine the standing stones more carefully. It took us most of the afternoon to care for each of the wounded. Waverly gave a dozen permission for light activities, and they gladly got up and wandered outside, chatting with their newly arrived friends. No doubt, they were elaborating on the details of their great battle.

This was as good as anytime, so I requested, "Rosita, er, everyone, what we Guardians have done here must, I repeat, must remain a secret for say a year. Rather like the Simon-Simone situation some fifty years ago. If our part in this becomes widely known, our secret mission is doomed and our lives will likely be forfeited. So please, keep our part in all this a secret." She agreed and made sure that the word got out. Funny, how easy it is to get someone to agree to keep something a secret, especially when you are allowed the appearance of having accomplished what someone had.

Meanwhile, other Sisters had cooked us up a hot, refreshing dinner, and we ate our fill. Sitting around the dying embers of the fires drinking the fancy Greenway tea, we began to chat once more. Rosita asked, "I don't know if you know who I am. Guardians Simon and Sandy greatly aided me a long time ago. Have you heard of them?"

I smiled, "I was their leader, Bethany. They were my dearest friends. Yes, even though I had another body located in West Reach, Sandy filled me in on all that they had seen and heard during their visit here. She told me all about the heroic actions you took to save the entire Sisterhood in the Sea Princes. I don't know if I could have had the heart to have made the sacrifice that you did, Rosita."

"You're — you're *that* Bethany of which they constantly spoke of?" she asked more than a little surprised.

"Yes, I was the leader of their Circle, the Lightning Circle." I didn't think her eyes could open any wider. "But it looks like things actually turned out far better. How long has Lenkova been with you?"

"Oh, ever since the children's father was killed down by Sud in the Southlands. Antonio and I snuck into the Northern Steppes, found the children, and stole them from the Galts. We got married and we've raised them. He and I have two other children as well. He's always treated both of them as if they were his. Antonio's been a good father. Yet, all did not work out for the best, I am sad to say. Her brother, Illanovich, just did not like our lifestyle. He hated shepherding, wanted nothing to do with the Sisterhood. When he was sixteen, he up and left, though he did say that he was going back to his father's land, the steppes. Since then we have had no word from him. I don't even know if he is alive or not. On the other hand, Lenkova has been a fabulous daughter. She took after me, but you have already seen that. In fact, I think she is a much better Fighter Group Leader than I ever was, although I continually worry about her safety."

"She has the total loyalty of her troops," I commented, adding, "and she is the most brilliant defensive field commander I have ever seen. During the days of the battles, every one of her decisions was precisely what I would have done; only she came up with them ten times faster than I could have. She was totally committed to seeing that the Axemen did not penetrate to North Point. By the way, both she and I have been wondering why the Axemen were so totally intent upon marching due west way up here in the Sector. It makes no sense. Do you have any idea what they might consider so valuable that they would risk everything to go this way?"

Rosita shook her head, "It has me baffled as well. There is virtually nothing of value way up here, save a few shepherds and their flocks. It's largely uninhabited."

Elona chose this moment to ask her curious question, "Say, Rosita, do you know who built those Standing Stones on Heart Break Hill? We're wondering who made them and when and why and what they might be used for."

"No idea, child. I came across them when I was a young girl exploring these wild lands. They were deserted then, no villages for miles. I guess it is just a mystery," Rosita replied. Elona's face sank.

A thought struck me, "Say, would you mind if I asked you a personal question about Lenkova? If you think it is too personal, why just say so." She nodded and I asked, "When we first met, she was very cold and aloof towards me and the other men with me, yet she got along well with Waverly. Has something awful happened to her?"

She sighed, "No, you are right. She detests men; I think that is the right word for it, ever since she was a little girl. She only loves and respects her father, Antonio; he's the only man. We've talked about it some. I think a lot of it has to do with who and what her biological father was. She believes that he was evil and insane to have done what he did. Further, she blames him for abandoning her in favor of his sister and making war. In other men, she sees him. Hence, she detests men. I can understand her though. In many ways, she is as I used to be before I met Antonio here. We both firmly hope and pray that one day she will meet the right man and all that will change. Unfortunately, it hasn't happened yet."

Antonio added one thought, "There are some good men around, but she just has to find them and meet them. We all have some bad aspects; we are not perfect. I am afraid Lenkova looks at each man and sees the imperfections and never sees the good."

Such wisdom from a shepherd! I wholeheartedly agreed with them, but then Waverly pulled me away from the chat. It was time that we made our rounds for the night, examining all our patients once more. Once that was done, Waverly then relaxed and made her nightly mental contact with the two Protectors. A short while later she took Rosita, Elona, and me aside, "Alton reports that they have today picked up the trail left by those leading the captured villagers. They are being forced to walk on foot and have left a clear trail. Tomorrow they will begin to catch up with them. He estimates that they may likely overtake them somewhere in northern Juda Arad. Lenkova is holding up fairly well; her wound is still on the mend. Via Alton, she wants me to tell you, Rosita, not to worry, that she just had to see this through, and that you would understand. Before I break the connection, is there anything you want me to relay to Alton to relay to Lenkova?"

Without thinking much about it, she said, "Tell her that her mother does worry and to be careful. Oh, and yes, I would be doing the same thing." Waverly smiled and relayed what she said to Alton.

Then, Rosita realized how this conversation must have been happening, via mind contacts. Again, her eyes opened wide. "You can really talk with this Alton, even though he is days away from here?"

"Yes, it's not easily learned. I spent ten long years learning how to do it," Waverly explained, hoping to put it in some kind of perspective.

"I just never realized just how powerful our Greenway allies actually are," she commented.

I added, "The only problem is that there are so few of us. That's always been our biggest barrier, too few. It takes ten years of constant study to know and be able to do what we do. That's such a long road to follow." She nodded agreeing wholeheartedly.

The next morning, Waverly decided another dozen could begin to carry out light activities. With all the new arrivals and those whom she had given the same permission the day before, why, the cavern became quite full of chatting women, moving about. There were more than enough hands to handle all the chores. Yes, I definitely felt the pressure of these past days lifting from my shoulders.

Sure enough, midmorning, a large number of Sisterhood fighters arrived, though they did not attempt to all enter the cavern; we were crowded already. Gallia and several others whom Waverly allowed saddled up to go with the armada to inspect Heart Break Hill and the other smaller battlefields. The dead had to be buried.

As promised, Caitlyn, Elona, and I went with Rosita and the armada. Fergus refused to go. I suspected that he felt that if he went, being a male, he would be obligated to dig graves all day or lug the stinking corpses to their final resting places. He wanted no part of either task, so he quietly stayed, claiming he needed to protect Waverly.

As we were saddling up, I whispered to Elona, "Let's do a quick test. Conjure your blue light and place it on your saddle. I'll do likewise. Caitlyn, you notice just how bright and large each is. When we get to the Standing Stones, we'll do it again and compare the results. I have a theory about that place." We did so and she carefully observed each of our lights. Then, we hit the trail with close to five hundred Sisterhood fighters, all armed to the teeth this time.

Even though Rosita was retired, the lieutenants insisted on verifying every order that they gave with her. Old habits die hard. Still, the ride to the hill began pleasant enough. The dark storm clouds had entirely gone, and a crystal-clear blue dominated now. The warm day felt refreshing after so many days hovering the semi-dark caverns. For a time, our spirits rose.

However, as we came within a mile of the steep sided hill, the stench of rotting corpses reached our noses. One needed no guide to find the battlefield. I also realized that I was about to confront the aftermath of just what I had done there days ago. By the time we reached the fire-scarred edge of the hill, we all stopped and tied cloths over our noses to help defeat the stench. Charred bodies and electrified ones lay scattered around the hill, concentrated of course on the eastern approach to the hill proper. We urged our horses up from the western side roughly following the same route we had used to leave carrying all our wounded fighters.

As we reined in at the standing stones, no one spoke. Everyone just stared, hardly able to believe their eyes. Dead and decomposing Axemen lay everywhere just beyond the stones, often piled on top of each other, hundreds of them. No one spoke for several minutes, as eyes stared this way and that, minds trying to grasp what had happened. Only then did Rosita turn and stare directly at me. As if on cue, all five hundred of her fellow fighters did the same. Hearing what had happened from Gallia was one thing, but the mind could not grasp such, for it seemed too unreal. Here was the shocking evidence. By all conclusions, every one of us should have been slain utterly. The number of enemy was so great that there could not be any other outcome. Yet, we were all alive with only two actual casualties. I muttered, "I had lots of help from your fighters and my friends." I didn't expect them to believe that and they didn't. True, during the lengthy burial process, some were found to have died from wounds inflicted by the

Sisterhood fighters, but most were badly burned or electrocuted.

"Are you sure you are not a god?" asked Rosita.

"No, just a man who'd fare far better with a woman's body — a man who had a bout of temporary insanity," I replied, rather sick at my stomach at seeing the magnitude of my destruction that day. I hate fighting and now I hated it even more. What a waste of human life. Still, the Axemen did not ever attempt to parley or discuss why they were here, why they wanted to destroy poor villages and cart away the villagers as their slaves. I resolved that in the future, I would try harder to find ways to communicate with enemy forces before unleashing such wanton destruction upon them.

"My daughter really does owe you her life! As well as all the others in the cavern!" exclaimed Rosita, as she finally comprehended the full magnitude.

"That is what allies are for, to help out," I answered meekly.

"One of you is worth hundreds and hundreds of us," she proclaimed. Many of the other fighters around her nodded their full agreement with her conclusion.

"Unfortunately, there is only one of me. I only know of two other Guardians who might have doled out this much destruction in such a short time. No, our Guardians normally can't remotely approach this kind of destruction." I had to make sure the record was straight on this detail. I could not have these women thinking that any Guardian they met could deal out the kind of destruction that I had done.

Gallia described the locations of the previous spots where we had attacked the advancing men. Riders were dispatched to each location to ascertain the situation there. Meanwhile it was all hands on digging a massive burial pit. Obviously, with the sheer number of dead to be laid to rest, putting them into one massive pit proved the easiest approach. Once the hole had begun to appear, others began to search the fallen bodies and then drag them to the hole, dropping them in. A small amount of dirt was put on each soul, symbolically defining his final resting place. We had just assumed that burial was the Axemen's preferred method, although it could have just as easily been that of cremation.

At the end of the very long day, the final estimates placed the tally at five hundred thirty-three dead Axemen; two dead Sisters. Bear in mind that this was only a good guess; we had no intention of digging up the graves that the Axemen had made some miles from here, where those that we had slain by arrows had been buried, just to get an accurate count. I did hear some comments from some of the fighters around me, "Ten to one! Can you believe that?"

While this gruesome work was going on, we three were not allowed to help dig. To some degree, we were still held as gods or at the very least their saviors and thus spared the manual labor. We used our time wisely, migrating over to the Standing Stones. Elona commented, "I am pleased that you are humbled and anything but proud of your accomplishment here. That is most honorable. Tur, I'm sure, is pleased by your actions, Bethany." Her priestly nature was asserting itself.

"No, anything but that, the slaying of so many men is nothing to be proud of. It is truly sad that I could find no other way," I replied. "But now let's explore these stones while we have the chance. Let's do the blue lights again. Are you ready Caitlyn?" Once more, Elona and I conjured our blue lights. Even though we were outside in broad daylight and our base test earlier this morning was inside the caverns, the difference was spectacular. Our lights were twice as bright and covered twice the area!

Elona's observation was a good one, "Is it the stones, is it the location, or is it a combination of the two? How do we determine which? We cannot very well dig up and move these stones! Each must weigh a ton!"

I thought about her questions seriously for a time, before I realized there might just be a way. "You know we are failing to observe the obvious! If our druwid attacking spells and conjurations are somehow re-enforced and doubled in size and effect here, then it makes logical sense that all our other skills may equally be enhanced. Let's sit down here inside the circle of stones, close our eyes, and see if we can perceive anything." Thus, we three sat down beside each other, closed our eyes. I opened my mind and awareness. I found that it was trivial to make a Mind Link with Caitlyn and Elona and so did. We joined and observed as one.

After a time, I moved way up above my head and began to see as a spiritual being, not using the body's eyes. Normally, when I do this, space becomes rather distorted, and I am a very poor judge of distances. A mile could be a foot; a foot, a mile, if you follow me. However, today, I could see the hill around us as if I were standing high above it looking down upon the hill! Because of the Mind Link, the others did too. Soon, all three of us were floating high above our heads, looking downward at the women bustling about, digging, searching bodies, and so on.

Caitlyn and Elona both had the identical thought, "I really am. I'm not my body, I'm way up here!" I realized that for the first time, I had done something similar to what Jes, the Great Messiah, had done for others!

Suddenly something unexpected became completely visible! All at once, we three saw some kind of enormous energy field lines flowing up and out of the ground beneath us. To us, it appeared cylindrical in nature, force lines flowing nearly vertical up from within the circle formed by the Standing Stones. Some distance above us, they flared out in all directions into a giant cylindrical arc rising high into the sky. Where they then went, we could not see. We now had no doubts whatsoever about how our spells had become so enhanced. It was some force coming from Nature herself that chose this spot to burst forth!

Observing more closely, where the radiating flares of energy were heading, I discovered that a large number of them were actually heading north and west toward the Greenway, which had a relatively large number of these sites. I saw one heading nearly due west, very likely heading for West Reach! Some went south and a few went further east. It was an incredible discovery, to say the very least. Further, with our senses so wide open, as I gazed down one beautiful arc of energy heading southeast, I felt the dim presence of Alabaster!

So shocked was I at that discovery that I opened my eyes and broke the Mind Link, startling the others. "Alabaster! I sensed him! That way. We are getting closer to him! More importantly, we are heading in the right direction!" The spell thus broken, we three discussed what we had seen for quite some time. We had discovered a new aspect of Nature, that of Tarra itself. She radiated energy fields! No wonder we had considered these places "sacred," although until this moment, no one had known why. I wondered if Alabaster even knew this detail. I suspected he might have.

At this point, our chances for further discussion ended. Sisters needed a place to pile the confiscated weapons and items. The clearing by the stones was the only available spot. We volunteered to stack and sort the stuff that the Sisters were bringing over here. By the end of the long day, we had amassed around three hundred battleaxes, all in good repair, those that were not were buried with the fallen. Also, close to a thousand gold coins had been found along with a number of gem stones. A hundred serviceable bows were salvaged along with a small supply of arrows. Fully three hundred fifty well-made knives were also retrieved. I wondered what would become of all this stuff, but never got the chance to ask.

At dusk, this very tired crew finally arrived back at the cavern area. Most made their camp outside. Inside, we found that Waverly had allowed even more of the wounded to begin light activities, and the place was now abuzz with activity. Odors of a luscious supper hung heavy inside; I found my stomach was indeed growling, more than ready to partake of their hospitality.

After dinner, Waverly again held council with the Sisterhood fighter leaders and Rosita. "By tomorrow, I think that all but a dozen of the worst cases can safely ride back to North Point. These twelve, however, cannot yet be moved — probably not for at least a week yet. Unless you can transport them by wagon."

"That's great news indeed. I'll organize a party to lead the wounded back to North Point in the morning then. It does appear that the entire band of Axemen has been stopped. However, now that the dirty work is done, I will send out a large number of scouts, fanning out over the entire area, just to make sure that there are no other roving bands somewhere out there in the wilds of our sector. I did send ten fighters on to the village today, riding hard. I hope that by tomorrow at the latest they can join up with Lenkova. I'll send another couple dozen tomorrow. Do you think that will be enough?" asked Rosita.

"Probably. The latest news that I have from Alton is that they are closing rapidly on the slavers. He expects to make contact tomorrow. Andre, Alton, and Lenkova all agree that there cannot be more than six Axemen leading the slaves. He thinks that they can easily handle them. Oh yes, I'm supposed to tell you that her wound is not healing as well as it should be, mostly because she is being so active. Alton says not to worry; it will probably heal just fine when she gets back and stays off of it for a while."

We could tell that Rosita wanted to say, "See, I told you so! It isn't going to heal." However, she bit her lip and did not say what she was thinking.

The next day, the ingenuity of these Sisters surprised us all. Gallia asked Waverly to come outside to inspect something, but she would not say what. When we followed her outside, a large group of Sisters were standing beside a horse. Behind the horse was a pair of long poles, wickerwork crisscrossed them, forming a bed. Gallia asked, "Can those badly wounded fighters be safely transported this way? We would go very, very slowly. We cannot get a wagon in here, but we can get these out."

"Well, I never thought of this!" a surprised Waverly commented, as she closely inspected the device. "Yes, it might just do. Can we give it a try?" Everyone volunteered to be the guinea pig, but Waverly herself took the first ride. Lying on the contraption, two Sisters tied her securely to the device. Then, they led the horse a ways down the valley and back again. Her well-done pronouncement was welcomed with loud cheering from the gathered Sisters. Gallia supervised the hasty construction of eleven more and our departure plans were changed. Yes, the dozen women were more than grateful to be moved out of this dark, damp cavern. To sleep in a real bed was their fondest desire right now.

Around ten that morning, the party headed back toward North Point. In case of trouble, a hundred fighters accompanied us. Rosita and Antonio rode back with us, while the other four hundred headed off in many directions to carry out their orders and tasks. I did notice that when we had finally vacated the caverns, a fresh supply of food, blankets, hay, and firewood had been left behind for future needs.

Chapter 24 Respite in North Point

In the middle of the afternoon, Waverly announced loudly for everyone to hear, "Alton has just reported in: they have rescued the villagers. All are safe, none injured. They're now leading them back home." To Rosita, she added, "Lenkova is doing fine; Alton refused to let her enter the combat; he made her guard the horses. She protested, but went along with him." She laughed long and hard, imagining the look that her daughter must have given Alton!

Two days later, we arrived safely without incident at the North Point complex. I got the longest, strongest hug from Fianna that I had ever experienced. She was very glad I was back with her and safe. However, after the welcome, she said, "Gosh, you stink. You have dried blood all over you and your clothes. You need a bath!" Everyone roared with laughter; we were in desperate need of a good bath and clothes washed. That was an understatement!

The clever Sisters had diverted a nearby stream, channeling its waters into a bathing pool. During the summer months, all bathing was done outdoors here in this pool, which could hold thirty at one time. Everyone pitched in to wash the wounded women first, Waverly and I hovering over them, making sure the bandages did not get too wet. The smiles on their faces told me how grateful they were for such a small luxury as this. Two hours later, we ten finally got our turn. While many helpful hands saw to all the laundry, we soaked for quite a long time. Fianna was kind enough to tend to my hair, which by now was quite ratty and tangled.

Later that night, refreshed and well fed, the minstrels finally got a chance to play once more. For two hours, we entertained the women and children. I was surprised to find that there were over a hundred children of all ages here. I think they enjoyed the music even more than the adults did. We promised to play for them every day that we were here. Besides, Waverly insisted that we stay until the dozen worst cases were well on the road to recovery. Additionally, we couldn't leave until the others returned from the rescue mission.

Thus, the next week was like a continual vacation for us. Here, all cares and worries melted away. Children ran and played outside all day, while women did perfectly normal chores that one would expect. At North Point, life doled out no stress whatsoever. That, of course, was what was intended for this place of refuge. One day, Antonio took Caitlyn and me up onto the Paese di Dio to see his many flocks of sheep. So yes, it was a week's vacation for us all.

A week later, Alton, Andre, Lenkova, and the other Sisters, who had accompanied them, arrived at North Point. All were loudly cheered for their accomplishments. Of course, Rosita gave her daughter a big hug, but from the horrible limp, everyone knew that her leg was not healing. Without further ado, Waverly had her whisked off to the bathing pool, stripped, and cleaned up. Next, she re-stitched the entire wound, because many had ripped out, leaving an ugly mess. There was also slight touch of infection that Alton had spied and begun treating. Hence, Waverly dutifully worked on Lenkova. After an hour, she finally put the last of our salves on it and bound it up once more. "I hereby order you to stay off that leg for at least a week!"

Upon hearing her orders, Andre nodded, picked her up in his arms, and carried her back toward the caves. Everyone began laughing. Honestly, no one had ever seen Lenkova allow a man, other than her father, to pick her up. Yet, she was smiling and giving him orders about which way to go inside the complex. I found that very interesting indeed. So did Rosita and Antonio; both looked at me with a questioning look on their faces. I could only shrug a "Who knows?" Later that night, gossip spread like wildfire, "She actually kissed him!" was repeated over and over as the news spread among the Sisters.

The week passed swiftly, as we tried to get our own goals back on track. Foraging for herbs replenished our used supplies a little. The Sisterhood managed to replace our supply of bandages. Most days, we practiced our music and always gave a concert each night. Although I was itching to get going, Waverly insisted we stay until all the wounded were well on the road to recovery, because she hinted that the healing arts here were in their infancy.

Near the end of the week, over half of the fighter group returned to North Point both to update their leader, Lenkova, and to get further orders. They reported that three other small bands of Axemen had been found in the eastern wild lands roaming at will. About two dozen fighters had been in each band. Had, because the Sisterhood fighters proceeded to eliminate them. Speculation was rampant over the reasons for the presence of the Axemen this far south of the steppes, but that was all it was, mere guesses. No one had any hard evidence of their purpose.

During that week, Alton could not be separated from Lenkova, who was confined to bed rest; he sat at her side. The two always seemed to be discussing something. However, once she had received the reports, she sent for the rest of us Guardians. "You've heard the reports, I assume?" We said that we had. "Okay. I've received word that you may travel south to Zargarb, but I am supposed to brief you. Zargarb is under three threats at the moment. The first one, you have already seen. No one actually expected the Axemen to invade the Zargarb Sector, although there was some speculation they might. Hence, we had sent Sisters to all the outlying villages most likely to see them first. Other situations seemed far more dangerous at the time, which is why it took so long to mobilize our counterstrike group; they were on assignment elsewhere.”

“Our Council rep, Alicia, insists that the assassins of the Old Man of the Mountain pose the most serious threat to us. Naturally, I have disagreed, but that's behind us now. She told me she would fully brief you on them when you get to Zargarb. The other situation is much more problematical; it's religious in nature. Mind you, I am not a religious person, but many Sisters are. I've asked mom to brief you on this one, since she was directly involved, ever since the arrival of the Holy Missionaries of Jehosanity, right after the barbarians left our city in ruins.” A sudden surge of violent anger arose in her, and she spat on the floor. “Curse the barbarian father of mine; may he rot in the fires of hell for all time!” Vehement anger flooded out of this woman, taking us by surprise. We were all mildly interested to strongly interested in her briefing, but the sudden outburst of such hatred caught us by surprise. An embarrassing silence filled the room for an awkward moment.

Like a war hammer, it struck me — I knew what lay behind Lenkova's personality and outlook on life. Now was not the time to deal with that, so I said politely, ignoring the nearly psychotic tantrum, “So is Rosita coming here to explain or are we to meet with her later?” While the others were fumbling with their own reactions to her anger, my question brought her out of it almost as suddenly as she had gotten into it.

“Yes, she should be here shortly. I have often teased her saying, 'You've got religion.' You know, just to annoy mom. Honestly, she knows a lot about it firsthand.”

“What do I know a lot about firsthand?” came the voice of Rosita, who had entered this section of the cave complex looking for us and her daughter. She had bits of chicken feathers on her arms; a good guess was she was helping the cooks with today's meals.

“Jehosanity and their problems that threaten us,” Lenkova replied. “I told them that you will brief them on the situation. You know how I am about dumb religious things,” she added rather snidely. Her mother ignored the barb.

“Well then, I suppose I ought to begin at the beginning, hadn't I?” she said, and we followed her lead and sat down on the cold floor. I suspected this might take a while.

“Well, after the barbarian invaders left our sector” — Lenkova spat on the floor again but Rosita ignored it — “everything was in shambles. Our nobles and the prince were somewhere safe on the southern islands in the Med Sea, along with all the money. The economy was wiped out, along with the vast majority of homes. Half of the city population had fled to outlying towns, but there they fared no better. Within the city proper, people were slowly starving to death. The Sisterhood, we had some small stocks of supplies and were arranging to get them to those most in need.”

“But then out of the blue comes Archdeacon Bandar Dero, only then he was just Father Dero. It seems that his people, he came originally from Juda Arad, had also known the same suffering as we; the barbarians sacked their country the year before. Anyway, his followers say it is their duty to mankind to assist those in need. To that end, he formed up wagon groups consisting of a priest and six volunteer workers, the Holy Missionaries of Jehosa they were then called. These volunteers traveled to the towns and villages and brought the folks supplies, helping them rebuild their homes and businesses. However, with so many starving, banditry was running rampant. Somehow, they had to eat too was their justification. Anyway, he made a deal with the Sisterhood — we provided the escorts, and they, the aid. Of course, we added our own aid to theirs. In short, together, we selfishly came to everyone's aid in due time."

"It took a while, but we got law and order restored and restarted the economy and actually had things going fairly well, when the nobles and the prince finally returned. That's when the nobles rebelled and formed the High Council of Thirteen to rule the sector instead of the dual Prince-Priest leadership of the past, which had failed to protect Zargarb from sacking twice. Alice was the duly elected Sisterhood representative, as you know, representing the tradesmen and us."

During this time, I was carrying Lenkova and had appointed the one armed Sister Fiona to take my place; she was a superb fighter and deserved the chance to show that she could do it. Now this is important, for it will explain much to you about many of us and our religion. During this recovery time, as the missionaries built their new churches in Zargarb, our people began converting to this new religion in droves. Then, suddenly, over a hundred of them were murdered, one by one. It was a great mystery, and Bandar came to us seeking aid. One of our Sisters, Calli, loves to solve mysteries, but she had been so badly mistreated that she was psychotic and hardly ever said a word. Yet, she solved the mystery, and with the help of the one armed Sister Fiona, they brought the guilty Prince to justice. They had done an incredibly fantastic job of it."

"Now here comes the critical part. Bandar Dero then prayed to the Son of the great God Jehosa, known as the Great Messiah, to heal Calli's psychotic insanity, and one armed Fiona was holding on to her. Fiona had to because Calli often went insane in the presence of men, you see. His prayers for healing were answered! Right before our eyes, he performed a pair of miracles for all to see! Yes, the insanity was fully cured! But the shocker was Fiona's hand — it regrew, if that is the proper word, right before everyone's eyes! Good as new, as if she had never had it cut off! As the word of that miracle and the Sister Fiona's obvious new hand spread, can you imagine how that convinced so many that this was truly the work of God, the one true God?"

"Like a wildfire, this new religion became our religion all throughout the sector. Yes, there are still a few who worship the old ways of Tur, but they are few, and we all live in peace."

Just then, I made the fatal mistake of replying, "Yes, I was with Jes Amir, the Great Messiah, that night when he healed her. He told me about it. I can't tell you how glad I am to hear that some of his disciples and my friends survived the sacking of the Arad, have spread his teachings, and are acting as Jes would have wanted. In Velona, it is the opposite. If Jes knew what they were doing there in his name, he would turn over in his grave!" Memories of the butchery of his teachings that we experienced while in Velona came back into my mind, I was reminded of them by her story.

When I stopped, you could hear a pin drop in the caves! A number of other Sisters had dropped by to listen to Rosita retell the tales once again. They never tired of hearing them from one who had actually witnessed much of it. I noticed that not only was Rosita staring at me, but also more than a dozen others. Yet once again, I had put my foot into my mouth.

I did not need to have her say "How is this possible?" or any of the dozens of other incredulous questions. Although I had already explained about immortal spirits when I told them about my first lifetime as Bethany Stanton, I had not told them about who I had been last lifetime. Fortunately, the teachings of Jehosa were well known to my listeners. Thus, in principle they could grasp what I was saying. "You see, in my last life, the mortal body that I had before this one, I was Bethany Madelyn Amir, the wife of Jes Amir, the Great Messiah, and the mother of our children." I had just dropped a bombshell.

"He-she's right," spoke up a timid voice. "She's the Blessed Holy Mother, as we call her back in West Reach." I turned around to see Caitlyn along with Fergus and Fianna standing quietly at the very back of the room. Obviously, they wanted to hear what was being said as well.

As they grasped the significance of this, suddenly all the Sisters knelt on their knees and began praying toward me. I was very embarrassed, "Please, please, none of this. Do not worship me. That was last lifetime, not now. Please." I suddenly realized the full danger. If word leaked out that Jes had not died on the cross as the disciples believed and had risen from the dead, it could destroy everything! I put my finger to my lips as a signal to Caitlyn and to Fergus, who was about to say something as well. I quickly added, "Yes, even as far away as West Reach, the teachings of Jehosa have spread. We have many churches of Jehosanity there. So Rosita, I do indeed know full well that what you are telling me is the truth. Truly, it was a great pair of miracle — of that, there can be no doubt whatsoever."

Lenkova did not take my pronunciations at all well. I realized that she had spent her entire life down grading them, attempting to make nothing of them. She had to, in order to retain some semblance of her own self-worth and sanity. I would deal with her later. I desperately needed to get Rosita back on the right track. "So, Rosita, how has all this become a critical problem here in Zargarb? It sounds like everything worked out perfectly.

Oh, and *do* go back to sitting please!

"Oh, well if you wish me to," she hesitatingly sat back down. The other Sisters took their cue from her and did likewise, though they stared constantly at me. She continued her narrative, "Well, at this point in time, the Church of Jehosanity Northern Orthodoxy as it is called is very well established, as I was saying. However, Archdeacon Bandar Dero has discovered that another disciple, Pope Yazi I, has established yet another version of the church all the way down in Megalos, if you can believe that. They are called the True Church of Jehosanity."

"The two versions of the church definitely do not get along. In fact, for years now, the southern church has sent what are called Holy Paladins of Jehosa up into Juda Arad. Supposedly, they are searching for Holy Relics of Jehosa, items touched and blessed by the Great Messiah, the Son of God. Whether they have ever found any, none here can say. Except that if some are found, they would have been taken at once back to the church in Megalos."

"Not to be outdone, our church has sent several expeditions into the Arad as well. One group returned with the actual cross upon which the Great Messiah was crucified! It is the church's most prized possession! Well, they brought back three of them, I think that they are still trying to ascertain upon which of the three our savior was placed." I felt slightly sick at my stomach. Worshiping crosses. I told Jes that what he was doing might not work out as he had planned, but he had overruled me on this one. I had visions of the priests fighting over a lousy piece of Centurion-made wood.

"Pope Yazi I somehow heard of our discovery and has demanded that the crosses be turned over to his Holy Paladins and brought to the True Church of Jehosanity. Archdeacon Bandar Dero has, of course, flatly refused all such demands. Since there are a relatively large number of Holy Paladins scattered around the Arad, it is presumed that at some point they will try to take them back by force, starting a religious war."

"Good god!" I exclaimed passionately.

"Yes, you see why we are so worried. The High Council has sent a good deal of its defensive cavalry to Florintine Junction, where the mother church is located, just in case of trouble. The Sisterhood was also asked to send forces and to provide scouts. More than a few are widely scattered throughout that area, looking for advance signs of a congregation of these Holy Paladins, which we think will be the first step toward attacking the Church. Any questions?" she finally finished her lengthy briefing.

"Damn that Yazi! I never liked him in the first place, and he detested me," I muttered, remembering the actual hatred that he always displayed against me.

"If you would like me to try to arrange a meeting with the Archdeacon, I still have some pull. I might get it arranged," Rosita asked. I knew that she was thinking that, if I was the wife of the Son of God and traveled with the disciples as they taught at Church, I might want to renew an old acquaintance or more.

"Thanks, Rosita. However, not at this time. We are here on our own critical mission to find one of our own Guardians, who has gotten himself into some very serious trouble and needs rescuing. That has to take priority. Perhaps once we find him and assist him, I can return. If so, then I will take you up on your offer." I hoped that I was being gracious enough in declining. The absolute last thing I wanted to do now was confront the disciples! If they should find out about Jes's deception, there was no telling what the ramifications of that might be!

"Okay, just let me know. It is the very least I can do for all that you have done for us and my daughter here," she replied very sincerely.

I needed the subject changed slightly and asked, "So what's your best guess about these Holy Paladins attacking the church in Florintine Junction? Any chance that they will also head for Zargarb itself?"

"Will it rain sometime this week?" she said rhetorically. "I'm sure of it, but Lenkova still believes that they will think long and hard about starting a religious war. I know that she thinks that there could not be anything sillier than going to war over religions, particularly those who are in what is supposed to be the same religion, the worship of Jehosa. However, I've met more than one fanatical person in my lifetime. I'm sure that they will try something, such as a midnight raid on the Church there. Now if I were Bandar Dero, I'd move the Holy Relics, if they are truly valuable, down into one of the many churches within the walls of Zargarb. In case you didn't know, since you were last here, we've built a strong defensive wall around the city now. It's fifteen feet tall and twenty thick. We all hope and pray that we never need to test its strength. In case of trouble, we even have a plan for folks in the outlying towns and villages to run for the safety of the walls. A quarter of the enclosed space is in open parkland where they can stay in an emergency."

Lenkova chose this point to interject her strongly felt opinion, "You mean to keep folks in, don't you mom. The walls keep people inside, as well as outsiders from getting in — works both ways. And just how often do we have barbarians trying to get in anyway?" That last was said sarcastically.

While Rosita ignored her daughter's remarks, I addressed them, "I'm with you, Lenkova. I love the freedom to come and go, the freedom of spaces. If I were to live in a walled town, particularly if I had to pay to regain entrance, I would feel like a kept rat!" These words which I pronounced so lightly here this day would one day come back to haunt me, but that is another story for another day.

At this point, the meeting seemed over. Lenkova's chilling comments ended it. One by one, those who had stopped to listen went on with their chores. Rosita thanked me once more, and she too went back to the kitchen. Finally, only Andre and I were left beside Lenkova, who was still lying on her bed, allowing her thigh to heal properly. He leaned over, gave her a kiss on her forehead, and excused himself — nature called. Alone with her, I saw that the anger and disgust she had minutes before vocalized had still not left her. Looking down at her, I felt the urge to do something to help this brave woman, who had done so much for the other women here. I wished more than once that Jes had shown me how he had been able to heal by placing his hands upon the person. Yes, I'd observed him do this on many occasions, but I never did get any inkling of what he actually did, only the results, a healing of mind and soul.

Lenkova was not about to let go of her anger. "You've traveled widely, more than I. Haven't you seen plenty of men who do nasty, evil actions? You must have seen plenty. You keep saying that you are all keen observers. You must have seen tons of really evil men, right?"

Part of me wanted to set the record straight, particularly about good and evil. Often what we see as evil, from the viewpoint of the doer seems good. Much like the original attitude of the Centurions when they invaded: bring law and order, writing, construction of roadways and public bathhouses, better hygiene, and more to the savage peoples of Tarra. If you have to slay many of their men, then to rebuild their population rapidly, rape their women so that new children can one day help with the rebuilding. However, have you ever tried to express reason and logic to an angry man, or woman in this case? Because they are in anger, they are not listening to what you have to say; they're simply trying to stop everything. I resisted my initial urge to explain about good and evil just now.

Instead, I replied, "Yes, Lenkova, in my years and travels about Tarra, I have seen much of what you would call evil actions." Her face displayed her vindication! I continued, "Yet, women are just as guilty of these actions as are men. Doing bad actions are not the sole province of men." I had acknowledged her, and I could see her anger subsiding, a very good thing indeed.

Antagonistically, she explained her innermost feelings, "Take my bastard of a father, for example." I knew I was now getting close to the crux of her mental turmoil that she had struggled with all her life. "No one in history had ever attacked, slaughtered, pillaged, and conquered so many lands, so many people as that bastard did. He goes down in history as the biggest bastard of all time! He even had the audacity to extort rape out of my mother, ransoming her for the Sisterhood. What kind of a man, a father, would do that? And he expected *me* to be raised by him? Ah! Had he not been slain by the Centurions down by Sud, when I would have been old enough, I would have stabbed him in his heart! The rotten slime ball!"

Again, I resisted temptation, saying only, "Yes, Mikhailovich Strokova has gone down into the pages of history, no doubt about that! As I understand it from Sandy who helped your mother make the arrangements with him, he bedded your mother because she was the only one who could ever stand up to him in a fight. Hence, he thought that the offspring from such a union would provide unconquerable, superhuman children. Everyone knows that's a lot of wishful thinking."

She chuckled rather antagonistically, "You got that right! Illanovich, he was a wimpy child, whined a lot if he didn't get his way. But a superman, ha, anything but that. Just between you and me, he ran off when he was old enough because, here, he couldn't get his way. He didn't want to earn it — only just have it given to him because *he* was Mikhailovich Strokova's son. Around here, no one cared, except in a derogatory way. He ran off to the steppes a long time ago. I would lay odds that he is long dead now."

"Yes, you see how wrong Mikhailovich's reasoning actually was. People often see and think what they want to see and think, not what is," I replied acknowledging her.

Finally, she opened the door for me by asking, "Do you really believe that you are not a body but a ghost?" Yes, she was now becoming slightly bored, bordering upon some slight interest in our chat.

"Yes, and I think I can make you see it too, because you are a very keen observer, are you not?" She nodded and I had her full attention. "Okay, can you pinch your good leg?" She looked at me rather incredulously, but did, saying "Ouch." I went on, "Okay, that is your physical body, no doubt about that. The body is but one part of us all. Now can you get a good picture of your horse in your mind?"

She closed her eyes and a smile crossed her face, "Yes. Love them. Such freedom we share together."

"Good. Now that was not a real horse you had there, right, but just a mental image or picture of one, right?"

"Well of course! A horse weighs a ton — just a picture of my horse."

"All right. That is the second part of man, the mind. It's full of pictures; some are memories of past things; some are imaginings of future things, but always it is used to solve our problems; perhaps we think with the mind." She nodded and I popped the killer question, "Now, Lenkova, who is looking at the picture of the horse?"

"I am," she said glibly. I did not say a word, just watched her, and waited as the full realization hit her. "Me, I am doing the looking."

"That's you, the personality, the immortal spirit, the ghost as you called it, the soul."

"I never thought about that before," she replied thinking hard and yawning.

"Do you have memories of your childhood?" I asked, setting her up for my next action.

"Well, sure, I remember lots of things," she replied.

"Well, I do too. Also, I can remember who I was last lifetime, where I went, what I did. Well, I must admit, I can't recall what I ate for breakfast on such and such a day. Only the key, more important things can I easily recall.

I suspect that if I sat and dwelled on it long enough, I probably could remember what I had to eat. But who cares? That information is beyond trivial. I can remember all that I did in the short lifetime before that, when I was being Bethany Stanton, just like you can remember your horse."

"Wow, I think I'm beginning to understand," she said in an interested tone.

"Now of course when it comes to remembering one's last lifetime, one major thing can get in the road of doing so. Think about it, what would be the last memories one would have of a previous lifetime?" I gave her a minute to make her own conclusion.

"Well, assuming this all to be true, why, then that body's actual death would be the last memory, wouldn't it?" she exclaimed.

"Precisely, if it is a particularly painful death, would you be inclined to remember all of that or would you prefer to just forget about it all?" I offered.

"God, my thigh hurts bad enough right now; I sure wouldn't want to experience it all over again. I'd try to forget it. Oh, I see what you are getting at!" she yawned heavily.

After a moment, she said rather sheepishly, "You know, ever since I can remember as a little girl, I have had these pictures in my mind of a man doing terrible things, just before he got killed."

I simply encouraged her further by saying quietly, "Yes."

After a long pause, she said very timidly, "You know, I think I was a Galt barbarian in Mikhailovich's army last life. I was killing, raping, and looting with abandon. Then, I smashed into a villager's home. The young man tried to defend his wife and baby by pointing a wooden pitchfork at me. The look on his face when I ran him through with my sword was horrible! After raping his wife and stomping on the head of their baby, I left, but I felt thoroughly disgusted with myself. I went on to the next house to trash, but I just stood there doing nothing and let that shepherd run me through with his wooden pitchfork. I had to end it. We were killing ordinary people just like ourselves!"

Again, I just said, "Yes," encouragingly.

After a pause, she exclaimed, "Good God! No wonder I have hated men all my life. I've been tormented by my own actions as a man!" She burst out into a giddy, hearty laughter, so hard that her thigh hurt in protest from all the motion. She added mid-laughter, "I've been making Mikhailovich my scape goat for what I did. I don't know what you just did, but I feel so light, as if the weight of the world has been lifted from me!"

"What's been going on?" teased Andre, who had returned to find Lenkova laughing very hard.

Smiling, I replied, "I'll let her tell you all about it. I'd better check on some other things." Yes, I was making an excuse to leave those two alone.

Later that night, Rosita came to the small cordoned off section where

414

Caitlyn and I were staying. "I just wanted to personally thank you for the miracle that you did for Lenkova! Word of it has spread all over North Point now. Her lifelong animosity and anger toward men has utterly vanished. To us, it is a miracle indeed. Thank you so much!"

I blushed, muttering, "My pleasure, but she did all the work of it herself." I suddenly had visions of these women now worshiping me!

Caitlyn added, "Well, he-she was the wife of the Great Mesiah."

"I guess some of his Holiness has rubbed off on you," Rosita concluded.

"Yes, Jes was a great person and healed many in his father's name, Jehosa," I added, hoping she would take the hint to assign the miracle to either of them.

"Thanks again. We will all pray and give our thanks to Jehosa and his Holy Son." She hastily excused herself, since Caitlyn and I were previously snuggling with each other.

The day before we were to leave for Zargarb, Andre came to us and announced sheepishly, "There is something that you all must know. I have asked Lenkova to marry me. That is," he hastily added, "once our mission is finished and you are all heading back home. I have decided to remain in Zargarb as the Guardian watchdog. I foresee this as a hotbed of trouble and want us to have eyes and ears in the thick of it all. That is, assuming you'll allow me to do so," he added looking at me.

"Congratulations," I smiled, though we had all seen it coming for some time now. "Yes, you have it, once the mission is done. I agree, Zargarb may be the latest hotspot, and having one of us here may prove invaluable." Andre actually shook my hand in thanks.

A week later and accompanied by a heavy escort of Sisterhood fighters, our caravan finally rolled into Zargarb without incident.

Chapter 25 Episode in Zargarb

Spectacular, impressive, nearly beyond belief was the walled city of Zargarb! Yes, it had grown considerably since I had last been there and now boasted a population of nearly two hundred thousand! Its numbers were enlarged considerably by those fleeing Juda Arad, looking for a better life. It's docks could handle three dozen ships at one time, according to the Sister who was leading our large group safely to the city. The city wall was nearly a perfect semicircle centered upon the docks from which the lifeblood of the city flowed. As usual, the streets that ran east-west were curved, paralleling the walls, while those running north-south were straight like the spokes of a wheel. The curve of the arcs was small over the space of a city block, which was about three hundred feet long and sixty deep. Since the shape was semicircular with spoke roads heading outward from the docks, to avoid a sector being longer than three hundred feet near the outer wall, many of these spoke roads were not through streets, that is, they did not run the entire depth of the city from the docks to the wall. Rather they often dead-ended in an arc street.

The Sister explained that there were three residential areas of the city, each containing some hundred blocks of homes, nearly two thousand. The wealthy nobles and their families lived in the western area; the merchants and trades folk, the middle area; those from the Arad, the eastern area. Further, the warehouse district surrounded the docks for easy access to ships. Further, three additional areas had been established, these lay close to the northern arc of the wall. To the west were housed the City Guards; to the east, the Sisterhood complex stood; in the central area, a vast wide open space devoted to grass provided a place to house others during an emergency siege, as well as room for future growth and expansion.

Six enormous gates allowed entrance to the city. The two-storied guard towers on either side of the six gates provided a solid defense should someone attempt to assault the gates in a time of siege. Our caravan rode through the one closest to the Sisterhood complex on the northeastern side of Zargarb. Of the six gates, only this one was operated and controlled by the Sisterhood, manned with their fighters. Hence, we were allowed into the city with no fuss or entrance fee.

Most all the buildings that we could see as we approached and entered the city were constructed from stone with red tile roofs. A consistency of design and color was clearly visible as were the numerous Churches of Jehosanity, whose white steeple crosses often stood taller than any other building in the city. All told, there were twenty-five of them.

The explanation that we were given for the segregation into sections within the city was this was what the people desired. The many immigrants from Juda Arad desired to live close to each other, likewise with the nobles and their families. Tradesmen also found living close to the business district more conducive to their needs. Hence, the city was built around these guidelines. However, I had my doubts about just how well all this segregation would eventually work out on the stability and quality of life. On the other hand, nearly every building in Zargarb was new or nearly completely refurbished. The Galt sacking had the side benefit of urban renewal on a citywide scale.

Caitlyn loved the wide-open green park area in the very northern portion of the city adjacent to the Sisterhood section. As we rode down the streets of their own section, I marveled at the sheer size of it. They owned close to one hundred buildings! Many of these they rented out to those in need as a way to help folks get a new start on life. Hence, many from the Arad first settled here. Later on, as they found employment and began to earn wages, most moved into the Arad section.

The actual Sisterhood complex dwarfed all the others we had seen, however. Theirs occupied four city blocks. Two inns, a huge kitchen and pantry building, a bath, and an enormous stable were the primary buildings. A totally enclosed courtyard doubled as a practice field and a formal gardens. Additionally, they had three buildings totally devoted to the stockpiling of goods for emergencies. They estimated that they could feed the entire city for a month if need be. Never again would they sit by and watch so many in their sector starve. What amazed me was that they were slowly enlarging everything; their goal was to be able to provide for a three months' emergency. Later, I learned that the Zargarb Sisterhood numbered nearly ten thousand women and their families!

Upon our arrival, dozens of Sisters came out of the stables to handle our wagons for us, while they insisted that we go take care of the registration process. We rated five-star service it seemed. Hence, our group followed our guide into the main lobby. Plush would be an understatement. Carpeted floors led to the main desk; tapestries depicting scenes from the history of Zargarb adorned the walls. Bronze lanterns provided a warm illumination giving one a comfortable, cozy feeling. Marble and granite statues graced alcoves in the hallways near the sign in desk, exquisitely done. Some were historical Sisters, some fictional representations. One that caught my eye was the two Sisters standing on the hill fighting legions of Centurions! I could see the strong likeness to Guardian Isabel, who had been one of the two who had led the Sisters in that historic battle so many years ago. Yes, I was impressed with the Sisterhood inn.

The Sister who ran the desk bubbled with enthusiasm of our arrival. "You are to be given the rooms reserved for nobility. It is the highest honor we can provide." As I reached for my money pouch that Fianna had handed me, yes, I still had her in charge of the minstrel's finances, the Sister replied, "Oh, no. Put that away. Your stay here in Zargarb is on the house, our compliments. Once you have seen your rooms, porters will help you carry all your things from the stables to your rooms. After you are settled in, just pull on the red rope in your rooms. An assistant will answer the ringing bell and come to you. Her job is to assist you in any way that she can to make your stay here completely worry and care free. Our bath will be heated and ready for you just as soon as you are settled. Finally, once you are clean and presentable, our leaders would like a private word with you Guardians."

I thanked her profusely. However, she leaned forward over her desk slightly, and adding, "Let me be the first to welcome you to Zargarb. It is such an honor for us to provide your room and board during your stay. In fact, you are *the* most important people that have graced our inn to date! By the way, you two," she indicated my sister and me, "I just love your hair! Although it has been described to me, frankly, I just did not believe their stories. So red, so long! Personally, I love it!"

None of us were at all used to the royal treatment that we were given. Sisters carried our many sacks and packs for us, though we insisted on carrying our precious instruments ourselves. The rooms were carpeted, spacious, and elegantly furnished. Caitlyn's comment spoke for us all, "Golly, in here, I feel like a queen or something!"

Two hours later, we five Guardians were led to a private dining room where we met with the Zargarb Sisterhood leaders, less of course Lenkova who was still back at North Point recovering from her thigh wound. Red carpet, bronze lanterns, sculptures, tapestries, mahogany tables, and chairs — such was the private diningroom, seating two dozen at most. One table contained a silver tea set with silver platters laden with rolls, honey, and cheese. Only two women were present, waiting to meet us. One bade us serve ourselves, which we did and joined them. "Thanks for the tea; it's really a good one," I complimented them as we four took the four chairs opposite the two women.

"I'm Sister Cecilia Amal, the leader of our Sisterhood here in Zargarb," she began. Cecilia was matronly in outlook and age, at least forty. Streaks of grey had begun appearing in her otherwise brown hair. She was a short woman but not overweight. Her voice was steady, commanding, and almost motherly in tone.

"And this is my right arm, Sister Alicia Madriosa, our High Council Representative from the very beginning." She was perhaps fifty-four years old; her hair was grey. Lines of age creased her face, but gave her an elegant look to accompany her keen eyes and sensibility. Her greatest talents lay in both being able to detect when someone was not telling the whole truth and in being a negotiator par excellence. Her reputation, impeccable; her record for bringing sense and balance, for bringing the High Council to formulate optimum solutions to Zargarb's many problems, was legendary in the city. No other woman was as well respected by the common man as Alice. Every tradesman trusted her judgment implicitly; she'd proven herself to them repeatedly.

"I assume that your business here in Zargarb does not concern the Sisterhood," Cecilia continued, "or the other Sisterhoods would have sent word. Correct?" I nodded. "So then, let me give you our most sincere thanks for going so out of your way to help with the Axemen. When the initial reports came to us, I must admit I thought that they were greatly exaggerated. True, I've never known Lenkova to exaggerate, so I assumed overly enthusiastic others reporting were the culprits. However, when the tallies finally arrived, we just could not believe it! Lenkova went up against the Axemen at ten to one odds! She and all of her fighters should have been slain; yet only two were lost. Unbelievable, so we owe you so much. Please, your stay here is completely on us. We cannot thank you enough. If there is anything that you need or even desire, please let a Sister know."

"Thanks, Cecilia. We'd like to play for some dances, if that's okay with you," I replied.

She grinned, "Yes, we had heard such wonderful tales of your playing. You are so young, but I'm told that the man with the long red hair is their leader — the Guardian's leader that is. My, but your hair is impressive. The younger folks would enjoy your music every night, if you'd let them. We have a large dance hall; name your night or nights. I'm sure we can accommodate. Are all Guardians such fine musicians?"

"Er, no. We're all individual people with different skills. I really enjoy making music. These three and our apprentice are definitely not musically inclined," I chuckled as they shook their heads collectively "No!" I continued, "Actually, we are just passing through, looking for one of our Guardians who has managed to get himself in a lot of trouble. We don't even know where he is located, but we are getting close to finding him, I think. We plan to stay here perhaps a couple weeks, if that is acceptable to you kind folks."

"Absolutely fine. If there is anything we can do to help you find your missing person, you have only to ask," Cecilia volunteered.

She toyed with her teacup and stopped, looking me in the eyes. I could tell that there was something she was debating to say. I nudged her a bit, "Looks like you have all sorts of nasty situations with which to deal. The Axemen for one and these Holy Paladins from Megalos for another. We've found it strange that the Axemen were so intent on pushing westward toward North Point. Even Lenkova and Rosita were baffled. Do you have any ideas what they might have been seeking?"

Obviously, this was not what she was debating telling us, for she stopped fiddling with her teacup and looked at me once more. "No, I am afraid that we here are just as much in the dark as everyone else. Mind you, we have spent hours discussing it, but no one has the slightest ideas why. As far as these Holy Paladins, thugs, I call them, are concerned, I seriously doubt that they will attack our churches here in Zargarb. Nevertheless, we and the High Council have taken their threat seriously and have taken precautions." Again, she looked back at her empty cup.

"Lenkova also said that you would brief us on the third problem, something about the Old Man of the Mountain, she said." Bingo, this was what she was debating. She looked straight at me.

"Would you mind listening to the situation and perhaps then sharing your wisdom with us regarding it? I have no right to ask you. You have your own mission to perform. It is just that the problem continues to grow, and quite frankly, I do not know how to deal with it."

"Certainly, we are your allies. We'd be more than glad to offer our wisdom," I replied putting her at ease. "Besides, we have a couple weeks to spare."

Greatly relieved, she said, "Again, thank you all so very much. I will let Alicia fill you in; she is more knowledgeable about it than I am. I just try to run the Sisterhood, Alicia deals with these larger matters of state. Alicia. . ."

Alicia grinned, "Have some more tea. You are going to need it. You asked for it," she jested. Loving tea as I do, I obeyed at once, grinning along with her.

"For years now, we have been plagued by these assassins of the Old Man of the Mountain. Although only in recent years has the problem gotten out of hand. I'll be blunt and frank. One of their representatives appears in one of our towns. He, always a male, delivers a message or ultimatum really to, say, the mayor of a town. He demands gold, food, sheep; demands vary. If the mayor does not comply within a month, then shortly after that some man from his town walks up to him and kills him. Of course, the killer is immediately slain by the mayor's guards. A few days later, the representative shows up once more making the same demands. Their extortion has proven lucrative, for who can resist for long? Of late, the demands are becoming more grandiose, more expensive. A few weeks ago, one of the members of our own High Council received the threat! We've tripled the guards around him and are hoping for the best."

"The High Council has sent out guards to every town and village with orders to stop and search every wagon. I was out-voted on this decision. I'm afraid the leaders are panicking over this. We've no effective way to deal with this problem. Can you offer any insight? Have you faced similar extortion plots?" Alicia asked.

"No, we met one of those guard groups as we entered your sector. That's the first we've heard of it, really. But to be of any real help, we need to know far more about it," I answered honestly.

She beamed. I could tell that I had just said the magic words for which she had been hoping. "So very like Sandy and Simon you are. Well, I am prepared. Cecilia, send for Calli while I tell them about her, please." Cecilia quickly got up and left the room, while she continued. "We have been blessed with Sister Calli, a woman whose mind is the keenest that I have ever known. She positively thrives on solving a good mystery. I don't know if you know much about our history, but Sister Calli was pivotal in solving the Hundred's Murders, as we now call it. For her aid, the Son of Jehosa, the Great Messiah, actually healed her as well as her helper, Sister Fiona, of the one hand."

"Yes, we are all very familiar with that — Simon and Sandy told us all about it," I volunteered, but quickly hoped that Alicia would not ask about the age disparity or the time line of this. I really did not want to get into a discussion about my previous lives just now. It was too dicey, because Calli and Fiona were the two that Jes had healed late one night. He did it from our bedroom. This was too close to the truth, that Jes did not die upon the cross, which if known, would tend to destroy the fledgling Church of Jehosanity. I was not prepared to destroy said church at the moment.

Cecilia entered almost at once with Calli, leaving no doubts in my mind that both of these women had fully intended to have Calli discuss this matter with us. Their problem was how to get the issue raised without seemingly putting us on the spot, had we not wanted to listen or had we had other pressing matters of our own with which to deal.

None of us had seen Calli, but we had all heard Sandy's description of her, only now she was much older. Calli was a thin woman, perhaps five-five and one hundred twenty pounds. Her blonde hair was now streaked with white, befitting her fifty-five years. While Sandy had told us that her hair was quite curly and cut short like all of the Sisters, that was then. Calli had let her hair grow, and it was as long as mine was! She had full lips and breasts of which Caitlyn would be more than envious. Cecilia introduced Calli to us, and we to her, pouring her a cup of tea as well. Meanwhile, Alicia pulled a third chair over to their side of the table for her, and Calli sat down between them.

All the while, she never took her eyes off my long red hair, which I had tied back in a simple ponytail. I'd just had a bath, and it was still wet, making a long wet line down the back of my shirt. Still, as it dried, it began its usual flaring out at the bottom. "Very pleased to meet you Guardians from the Greenway," Calli said, adding to me, "I'm so please to meet another who also treasures really long hair, though I must admit I never thought it would be a man who did. Nevertheless, I have filed away that fact, who knows when it might prove useful." I smiled back at her; she was precisely correct in her observation.

She continued at a great pace, "Alicia has told me that I'm to tell you all that I know and have concluded about the Old Man of the Mountain mystery. I keep telling them that I have it all solved, but they don't believe me. Am I to understand that you wish me to tell you what I know and have deduced? If so, then perhaps you will help me convince them that the mystery is indeed solved."

I chuckled, "From one hair lover to another, yes, Calli, tell us all about it. If, as you say, you have it solved, I'm excited to hear all the details. Spare us none. That way, we can better advise you. Will you mind if we interject a question here and there as they form in our minds?"

"No, I can handle many separate trains of thought simultaneously."

Alicia roared with laughter; Cecila chuckled. Alicia interrupted, "She's not kidding. I once saw her dealing with ten different problems all at the same time. She solved them all too. Calli is positively an amazing woman. Go for it Calli; you have a willing audience. She's fond of saying that we don't listen or take her seriously some of the time." I detected a bit of a situation between these women on this point. Calli smiled and ignored the barb.

"Okay, then here goes. Now then, we must begin with the facts that are widely known here in Zargarb. To date, there have been ten extortions with one in progress. The first of these occurred in 595 in Florintine Junction. The mayor's assistant was slain before three dozen sheep were given." She continued to rattle each of the other nine off, rapid fire. "Finally, Arturo Caligli of the High Council has received the latest extortion threat. He is to deliver six hundred gold coins or face assassination; he has a little over a week remaining to hand over the money."

She talked faster than any person I have ever met, but paused to catch her breath before launching into the next explanation. "Now then, these are just the ones here in Zargarb. However, for even longer they have been extorting towns and villages in Juda Arad. I have now documented fairly completely three hundred and five known attempts, all eventually successful, I might add."

I could see she might now launch into a description of every one of these attempts, and quickly asked, "Sister Calli, you are amazing. Perhaps we can speed this up by having you explain your solution to the mystery. By the way, how do you remember all these facts?"

"Oh, I never forget a fact. I remember everything I've seen or heard. I think it is just a knack that I have for it. Anyway, if I describe all the remaining facts, we would be here far into the night. Before I give you the solution to the mystery, let me say that I have done extensive research on the puzzle. We have had one hundred thirty-five thousand six hundred forty-two people from Juda Arad either immigrating to Zargarb or passing through — that I know about, mind you. I have interviewed seventy-five thousand eight hundred fifty-one of them personally. Just added another man this morning. Just wanted you to know that I know what I am talking about in this puzzle. Now then, where was I, oh yes, the solution."

"There have been two Old Man of the Mountains. We are now dealing with the successor to the first one. Both leaders are of Arad lineage; both are quite religious. They are currently living in the very high country of the Kathas Mountain range up in the northeastern portion of the Arad, about fifty miles east of where the old Qaam fortress used to be; Al Tarm was its name before the Galts sacked and destroyed it. I have their location pin pointed to within a circle of some twenty-five miles. Their population is now around three hundred fifty men, women, and children, give or take twenty. That's the range I have deduced. When they are ready to extort another town, they send in a spy, always of Arad lineage, to scope out their victim. Never do they request more than what could be paid, mind you. They then kidnap someone from that town and transport that person to their fortress. Drugs are used to keep the person they've kidnaped from being conscious of the entire travel. This could only be Dragon's Breath Extract, made from a plant that is found only in the high country of the foothills of the Kathas Range. Once the victim arrives at their fortress, he is very likely drugged using hashish, wined, dined, and given a small harem of beautiful women to dote on. He is told that he is in heaven. Once they determine that the hapless victim finally believes this, he is then re-drugged, given orders that, if he slays so-and-so, when he dies he will be worthy to re-enter heaven and live as he was living, surrounded by the luxury and women. Still drugged and unconscious, he is then brought back to the town, where he is awakened and reminded of his task. He does the assassination with glee, desiring only to return to heaven. There, I believe that about sums it up. Mystery solved compliments of Sister Calli!" She beamed with satisfaction.

I was speechless, so were my friends. Indeed, if her deductions were correct, she had outlined their entire operation! "Calli, this is the most remarkable piece of deduction that I have ever heard of, simply incredible!" I validated her. Alton, Andre, and Waverly likewise had only kudos for her, which she accepted graciously, but we all knew that she took this as the highest praise, since it came from four Guardians.

She replied, "Oh, it was easy. Anyone could have done it, if they only took the time to reason it all out. Of course, now you will want to see just how I reached these conclusions, right?"

Grinning, I answered, "You bet! Let's start with how come there are two leaders."

"The first extortion that I have been able to document occurred in 588 in a small town in the Arad. These plots have been occurring ever since then, so that makes it a span of thirty-four years. We know that most of the younger, fit men died during the failed rebellion and the Galt invasion, which followed immediately. Thus, the first Old Man was likely an older man. Lifetimes being what they are, it seems likely that the original founder has passed away and one of his lieutenants has taken his place."

"This is supported by the nature of the extortion demands over time. Originally, all requests were for food and other living supplies. In 601, the demands began including gold, silver, and gems for the first time. I suspect that this is the influence of their new leader," she stated.

I commented, "I see, yes, that does seem most reasonable. The Arad lineage is likely because the first and most frequent extortions were located entirely within Juda Arad and that all their representatives who have come to Zargarb have been Arads. How about the religious sect part?"

"That's an easy one," she gaily answered, "Except for the last dozen years or so, I have never met any person from the Arad who was not a deeply, devoutly religious person. Originally, as I understand it, the people belonged to one of four different sects, differing in their ways of worshiping Jehosa. Since this group formed right after the barbarian invasion, it makes sense that these were still deeply religious people. Of course, today, all that has changed; Juda Arad has become a barbarian land, where banditry is the only way the poor folks can survive any more, what with all of the destruction they've had, continual invasion from the Holy Paladins, and the Old Man assassins group, and so on. Even the Axemen have explored some of the northern portions of the country, I'm told. Considering the location of the group, I would hazard a guess that these people were probably originally from the Qaam sect, though I do not have enough information to state that as a known fact. It's just my suspicion."

"Amazing, Calli, it seems so simple when you point out the salient data," I replied. "However, how on Tarra did you deduce their location as being in the very high country of the Kathas Mountains, fifty miles east of Al Tarm, and even determine it to within a circle of some twenty-five miles? This seems incredible."

Calli smiled again, "Oh that was the easy part."

"You've got to be kidding!" exclaimed Andre.

She decided to play with us. I could tell that playful look one gets in their eyes when they suddenly decide to have a little amusement. "At Florintine Junction, there was a one month delay before the assassination. At Musgrava, one month and one day. At Gregorio, one month three days. At Zargarb, one month six days." She rattled off many other places and durations. "At Jerilum, two weeks." Dozens of towns in the Arad followed rapid fire. I suddenly hoped she wasn't going to recite over three hundred of these! Fortunately, she finally stopped and said, "Given these as samples, what does this suggest?"

Ah, she was mentally testing us! This incredibly bright woman had just turned the tables on us, so to speak; we were now under her scrutiny. I thought fast. I wasn't about to let her win this mental game. If she could work it out, so could I. She had given us a clue: places and durations. "Well, if the person being extorted decides not to pay up, then they have to have some local person in place ready to do the assassination. Since the assassinations come shortly after the refusal to pay, the person drugged into doing the deed must have already been processed and be physically near the town. So it is just a mathematical problem after all. You simply plot out how far one might go in two weeks from Jerilum. Combine that series of locations with one month from the Junction and all the other three hundred or so and it should yield the common locus from which the trips all radiate. Brilliant thinking, Calli!"

"Darn! I thought I had you all on that one," she chuckled. "You catch on rapidly. Yes, I've kept accurate records of all the known extortion attempts and plotted them. The only variable is I don't know the precise speed of travel in the Arad. From what I know, watering holes are critical and often dictate how far one travels on any given day. It is mostly a desert region, very short on water. I made some guesses here and that accounts for the twenty-five mile radius of uncertainty. I did personally examine one of the assassins after he was killed. I found definite traces of Dragon's Breath Extract on his body. He also still smelled of hashish as well, and his clothes reeked of it. A little visiting with our Arad settlers provided me with where it grows naturally in the Arad. It also correlates very nicely with the location deduced from the travel times."

"Calli, you amaze me utterly," Andre complimented. "But there is one thing I still haven't figured out. How is it you know there are about three hundred fifty there?"

Grinning again, she explained, "Well, to figure out the population and how they are living and also correlating with where I have them located, you must review what their extortion demands have been through time. I'll spare you the details. Initially, what was wanted was simple necessities for survival, food, clothing, and hand tools. Given the volume, I estimated perhaps a hundred people had to be supplied. If they really are way up in the high country, if not in the mountains proper, they must have a great need for grains, vegetables, and such. From what I have learned of the mountains, very little could be grown there. Hence, the town, if we may call it that, depends for its survival on these extorted food products. No extortion and they die of slow starvation. If you observe the pattern over these past thirty years, the total volume collected during any one year has been steadily growing. Given that volume, one can make an educated guess of how many mouths they are feeding. Every time I get more information, I redo that year's calculations. I am confident that their numbers have not yet reached four hundred. They would need more food supplies."

"Well, Calli, I support all your deductions. You are an amazing person indeed!" I acknowledged her. Cecilia and Alicia now seemed very sure of themselves, that Calli had reached the proper conclusions and "solved" the mystery. "I guess the only remaining question is what can be done to stop the Old Man of the Mountain. I assume that you have made some plans, Cecilia?"

Smiles evaporated. Calli answered for her leaders, "Well, actually no, as a matter of fact. I think that they only half-believed me, and then there is the problem of having to cross the entire width of the Arad. It is a desert and water is scarce. If you do not know where the watering holes are located, you can easily perish. Plus, the whole land is pretty much lawless; banditry is commonplace. Besides, the Holy Paladins are roaming around there at will, to say nothing of the Galts and Axemen. Even though their numbers are small, it would take an army with many supplies to make that journey safely. So while we really do know all about them, there is not much we can do about them. Right?" She looked to Alicia for confirmation.

"Yes, Calli is right. There really isn't much we can do about them, unless you know of an army for hire," Alicia added that last in jest.

Cecilia added, "We certainly do thank you for hearing Calli out. We really did need to have an outside opinion on her deductions. Yes, we believe her, but with you four in agreement with her as well, then I can consider it conclusive."

"Our best defense, I feel," Alicia continued, "is to surround the intended victim with a lot of Sisterhood fighters, making it very difficult for the assassin to succeed. That's the policy the High Council has decided to put into effect."

I knew that she was looking for my opinion or at least validation that the Council had done what it could. "Unless there is an unseen army around here, I think your plans are the best, all things considered."

"Thanks. Well, we have taken up a lot of your time. I think we ought to let you get back to your friends and your mission," Cecilia said, ending our lengthy meeting.

Naturally, we retold much of this to our friends later that evening. Then, it was concert time. That night, we played for the largest crowd to date. Well over five hundred attended our first dance. During the next two weeks, the attendance grew well beyond capacity of their hall. Yes, we felt our music was very much appreciated by the people of Zargarb.

Because of the size of this city, I spent nearly two weeks carefully searching for Alabaster. From the observations we made at the Standing Stones atop Heart Break Hill, I suspected Alabaster was still more southeastward. If we followed this glimpse of him, we would be heading into the Arad next, at least southern Juda Arad.

We Guardians spent considerable time discussing our options. It hardly seemed fair to thrust our twenty d'Grange Sisterhood fighters into the lawless Arad. They would be completely unfamiliar with everything including the language and terrain. Of those in our party, I was the only one who had been in the Arad and that was in my last lifetime. After all these years, probably much had changed, so I could not rely solely upon my prior knowledge of the land. Besides, we were entering the Arad during the incredibly hot summer months. We all knew that a single goof could result in death from heat stroke and lack of water, should we miss finding a water hole.

While we were dealing with ways and means of entering the Arad, Caitlyn, Fianna, and Fergus did quite a lot of shopping. They had acquired two sets of Arad clothing for every member of our group, including the

Sisters from d'Grange. Why? Caitlyn took to heart my descriptions of the heat there and just how cool the light robes and headpieces were compared to our woolens, leathers and linen clothing that we all had. Hence, she made it her personal mission to see that we were all properly clothed for the journey. For their efforts, we did heap praise and thanks upon them.

As our departure date neared, Caitlyn asked, "Well, have you decided to hire a guide yet?" This was one possibility that we had discussed on several occasions, though we had not yet acted upon it.

"Well, no, dear," I replied. "It keeps coming down to being able to trust our lives to a stranger who has no allegiance to us or our mission. If we get attacked, for example, the guide might flee for his life, leaving us in the lurch."

"You still think you can't remember the watering hole locations well enough?" she asked.

"No, I would really hate to depend only on my memories from last lifetime. I keep saying that things may have changed during all these years," I answered truthfully. Yes, if it were only me, I would take that gamble, but I could not if our whole troop went.

"So what are you going to do?" she asked in a rather pedantic way, impatient for me to make a decision, one way or another. I shrugged helplessly; she grinned and gave me a hug. "You'll figure it out; you always do."

Just then, we heard a commotion in the hallway of our inn and stepped outside our room to find out what was happening. Dozens of Sisters were engaged in a discussion, which we could not help overhear. "Yes, I tell you I saw it. The assassin tried to get at Arturo Caligli. Ten Sisters tackled him before he could stab him. Yes, the dagger was poisoned. Well, at least it looked that way to me. I saw stuff dripping off it, and it wasn't blood. It was black." Another voice said, "Lenkova's got the situation well under control."

She mentioned the magic word, Lenkova. What was she doing here in Zargarb? She was supposed to be up in North Point healing, bed rest and all. While Caitlyn got the rest of us together, I interrupted and asked one of the Sisters to take us to Lenkova at once. Soon our large party was running through the streets toward the noble's section. All ready news of the attempted assassination had begun to filter through the crowds in the streets. A half hour later, we were stopped by a line of Sisters, blocking entrance to one of the numerous market areas where two major streets met. Because several Sisters were with us, we were allowed on through the line.

Up ahead, a crowd of Sisters, swords still drawn, was hovering over a body. The slightly yellowish skin of Lenkova stood out. "Lenkova," I hollered out, "We heard that your forces got the assassin." The fighters moved back so we could get to her and observe the body.

"Hi Bethany, Andre, everyone. Yes, my tactic seems to have worked out well, except for the poison. Gina took a cut from the blade and is not doing so well. Perhaps you could have a look at her? Please? Just don't touch anything until Calli gets here and does her thing. I've already sent for her."

We four rushed over to Gina who was definitely beginning to show signs of poisoning. The cut from the dagger was just a simple slice, which normally would not even need stitches. However, she had become weak and nauseous, slumping on to the ground. Others had propped her up against the side of a building, but she looked like she was starting to lose consciousness. Waverly said, "Mandrake. Suck as much as you can out of the cut, Bethany. I'll go make a strong stimulant. Andre, get some plaster to assist in the sucking, once Bethany has gotten what he can out. Time is against us." She wanted to treat this as if it were a viper bite, I concluded, and set to work, sucking and spitting. After about ten minutes, I too began to feel slightly ill and had Alton continue in my stead.

"Here, drink," Waverly thrust a mug of super strong tea in my hands. I began to drink, though it tasted awful. Within a few minutes, I felt it reacting with the small amount of poison that I had absorbed through my mouth. My heart was actually racing from the combined effects.

Poor Gina had to be slapped hard back to semi-consciousness so that Waverly could force the liquid down her. Andre came back with a bag and, while Alton stopped and sipped the tea, Andre applied a heavy plaster to the wound. It would tend to suck any poison still near the area into it as it dried. A tense hour passed before Waverly gave her permission for Gina to be moved back to the inn, where she could watch over her constantly. As they carried her off, she had recovered consciousness and mumbled a bit with her fellow Sisters who were carrying her.

"That was close, Lenkova, but I think Gina will be all right. I will go back with them and watch over her until she is completely out of danger. See you boys back at the inn," Waverly said cheerily.

"Once again I am in your debt, Waverly. Thanks for saving Gina. It was her fast reactions that foiled the attempt on Arturo Caligli," Lenkova replied and the two women gave each other a hug.

During all this Calli had arrived, and we wandered over to where she was carefully examining the body and grounds. Seeing us, she commented, "One month and six days. See that blackish stain on his moustache? Have a smell of his clothing."

We cautiously did. "Dragon's Breath Extract?" I asked and she nodded. Hashish was clearly detectable. He had evidently been smoking a rather large amount of it fairly recently; its odor permeated his clothing.

She continued, "The assassin is from the Zargarb sector, not an immigrant from the Arad. Probably twenty-five years old, give or take. Very poor, down on his luck, I'd say. Look at all the patches on his shirt and pants. Not much left there to patch in places. Shoes worn out, holes beginning. Too poor to afford a few coppers for a new pair. Now comes the hard part, trying to identify who he is. If we can find someone who knows him, we might gain additional clues about how he was abducted and when. Surely, someone among our two hundred thousand must know him."

Just then, an artist that she had sent for arrived. "Sister Calli, another sketch?" the young lad of nineteen asked. Clearly, he had done this before.

"Yes, as life-like as possible. Once you have it done, get it Okayed, and then make twenty copies. Bring them to the inn and pick up your gold piece. Thanks, Benotelli," Calli smiled at the young man. He quickly set to work. Turning her attention to the dagger lying off to one side where Gina had knocked it out of the man's hand, she said, "Queer dagger isn't it? Not made here in the Sea Princes, I don't believe."

Indeed, the dagger was specially made for assassinations. Its blade was shaped like several "S's" which provided a greater surface for the poison to adhere to. Further, I spied a plunger mechanism in its hilt. A small button, which fit one's thumb nicely, was at the very top. Inside the handle, a vial contained the poison. Thus, when one stabbed one's victim and had his thumb on the button, the force of the blow hitting the target would move the button downward, forcing the poison out and down the blade rapidly. We conjectured as to whether or not the poison flow would commence if the blade missed entirely.

"It is certainly lethally ingenious," I commented.

Calli chuckled, "That it is, that it is indeed. Notice that the hilt is too small for a man's hand, forcing one's thumb to be positioned over that button which injects the poison. Yes, this has been well-thought out by some diabolical mind somewhere."

Several Sisters came running up to Lenkova, "No sign of that assassin representative anywhere, boss. Per your orders, five hundred are now scouring the city. If he is still around, we'll find him. He cannot get out of the gates, that's for sure."

Lenkova scowled, "Not unless he uses a disguise or waits until dark and goes over the wall. There are lots of ways out of the city if you really need to exit secretly." She spat on the ground, "If I get my hands on him, he'll wish he had been the recipient of that dagger!"

Since Calli was finished with her observations, Lenkova issued her final orders, "Once Benotelli has finished, search the body, but I doubt you will find anything. Then, deposit it outside the gates on a cemetery slab. Maybe his relatives will turn up. If not, he'll get a pauper's grave in two days." Turning to us, she added, "Walk you back to the inn?"

Andre put his arm around her, and she led her horse with her free hand. He said, "You were supposed to be bed resting."

"And miss all the excitement?" she played with him. "No, it is healing just fine. Based upon Calli's deductions, I got here last night, expecting just such an attempt today. She was correct with her timing. Isn't that just incredibly amazing? Sorry about the bed resting, but I've had my fill of that, but you all can look at it when we get to the inn. I'm sure it is healing just fine. It is a little sore though when I walk too much."

Without a word, Andre whisked her up onto her horse in one sweeping, gentle motion. They still held hands as we walked slowly back to the inn. During the long walk, my heart stopped pounding from the effects of the poison, and my strength returned gradually. After we arrived, Waverly took a break from watching over Gina in order to examine Lenkova. She promptly removed the stitches and pronounced her well on the road to recovery. Thus, the Fighter Group Leader felt vindicated on personally coming on down to Zargarb. She did not mention that she had left North Point nearly a week earlier!

That night, we had dinner together. Sipping our tea afterwards, Lenkova said, "I heard that you are soon going to head into southern Juda Arad, is that correct?"

"Yes, I believe that we are getting really close to finding the one we have been looking for— I have a hunch that we are within maybe a hundred miles from him," I replied.

"I thought as much," she answered. "So have you got your guide yet?"

"Well, no not yet," I said, and Caitlyn poked me playfully in my ribs.

"Good!" Lenkova stated flatly.

"Huh?" I reacted. This was not what I expected her to say.

"Well, I am coming too, and I will bring our guide," she quietly laid her bombshell upon us, with a tone that implied the matter was no longer open for discussion. "Look, I have already cleared it with my boss, Cecilia. I'm supposed to be on a healing vacation for a month. Riding along with you all would be a nice vacation, don't you think? I'll be off my leg most all the time, you see, so it all works out perfectly. I'll be bringing another two dozen fighters with me, two of which are Arad immigrants who know the land well. Honestly, this is the very least we can do for you after all that you have done for us." She lowered her voice and her cheeks reddened, "Besides, I didn't relish being away from Andre that long." Andre flushed as well.

"Are you sure that your absence from Zargarb is acceptable with Cecilia?" I asked. "I sure do not want to be pulling you away from more critical matters."

"Yes, we are all sure," she replied, as I suspected she would. Still, I felt uneasy about taking borrowing their Fighter Group Leader for so long. "Who is your replacement?"

"Mom," she answered, with a grin. Everyone laughed.

"Okay, then. I accept. However, I'll have Waverly contact Cecilia once every day to make sure that you're not really needed back here. Do I have your word that if you are needed here, you will return at once?" Reluctantly, she did agree. I hoped that I would not have to hold her to this promise.

"When do we leave?" she asked. We chatted a bit about the arrangements and decided that June 15 would be ideal, giving everyone enough time to stock up and get ready. Her two scouts advised her to bring along an extra wagon, whose purpose was to carry nothing but extra water, just in case. They also suggested that we bring one and a half spare horses for each member of our group. This necessitated bringing along yet another wagon to carry extra grain and fodder, just in case. We were heading out into a desert land.

The day before we were to leave, we received an invitation from the Archbishop Bandar Dero to come and visit with him, to view the church. Via the father who delivered his message, Bandar had heard wonderful things about our music and wanted to thank us on behalf of the church. For some time, I debated whether I should go. Caitlyn convinced me, "Look, it would be an affront to the church, which has obviously been of invaluable and good assistance to the people of Zargarb. Perhaps they do not even know of the atrocities being committed in behalf of their church back in Velona."

"Yes, but, but they must not know about the worship of Jes and his wife back in West Reach — at least not in too much detail. As far as they know, Jes died on a cross at the hands of the Centurions in Jerilum. They mostly despised me or even hated me, his wife. I think that they have totally forgotten about us. I prefer to keep it that way for now. But you are right, dear; it would be a bad affront to the church not to at least show up to accept their thanks."

With a Sisterhood escort leading the way, Fergus, Caitlyn, Edgar, Jolina, Fianna, and me, accompanied by Alton, Elona, Waverly, and Andre, made our way midmorning across the city to the largest Church of Jehosanity in Zargarb. Yes, I felt very ill at ease; so many things could go so very wrong. I fidgeted with my hair, my clothes, anything within reach. In contrast, my fellow musicians were carefree and quite cheerful, fully expecting to get additional recognition for our bringing of music to the common folks. I hoped and prayed that this would be so.

An hour later, we paused beside the mother Church, which occupied an entire city section. The huge stone church with its enormous white cross was the tallest building in Zargarb. It was an impressive, yet simple, non-pretentious building, unlike what was to come in later centuries, but that is another story. A knee-high stone wall demarcated the church and its accompanying buildings. As our party arrived near the main entrance, a priest was there waiting for us. "Greetings West Reach Minstrels," he said widely to all of us, unsure who the spokesperson was, me really. "Welcome. If you will follow me, the reverend Archdeacon Bandar Dero will see you in his rectory, that smaller residence over there." He pointed to a non-descript stone building off to one side.

"Our living quarters," he explained. "I am Pastor Philas Al Mare. I've been conducting most of the masses these days. I must warn you, the Archdeacon is very old and in frail health. He spends a lot of his time sleeping. Please do not feel affronted if he should suddenly doze off while seeing you." This news I found more encouraging, for he was not likely to delve too deeply.

Philas was quite talkative, "You see, while he is the supreme leader of our church, the daily operations have been taken over by four other Deacons. Those four live here along with Bandar. I'm sorry to say that three are currently out of town, church business, you see. Deacon Pilate is still here, but I must apologize on his behalf; he has asked me to tell you that his is rather under the weather today and cannot leave his room. He's old as well. So it is up to me to show you around. Ah here we are," he said as he graciously opened the door, motioning for us to enter.

No sooner had Jolina set foot inside the entryway when she stifled a shriek, turning it into a choking sound. We'd seen her reaction before, and we knew instinctively what that meant! As we all turned to look at Jolina's incredibly pale face — her shaking hands trying to hide her face — I quickly explained, "I'm so sorry, Pastor, Jolina has also not been feeling well. Probably we should not have brought her along with us. Edgar, would you please walk her back to the inn? Maybe take a couple Sisters with you, please? We'll be along shortly. I'm so sorry, Pastor." I sounded as propitiative as I could be.

"I understand. I do hope she will be all right. Bit of illness going around the city these days. We all have bouts with it," Philas sympathized. Edgar, arms tightly around Jolina, carefully led her back outside, accompanied by two Sisters. The rest of us turned to follow the Pastor, who led us down a narrow hallway. The entrance and the hallway were plain, mostly unadorned, save one large sculpture near the end of the hallway. It was a statue of Jes upon the cross, done exquisitely in white marble. While I thought less of the meaning, the workmanship was first rate. Philas caught me noticing it.

"That is a likeness of the Holy Son of Jehosa, dying upon the cross at the hands of the Infidels. It was carved by the greatest artist in Zargarb, Michaello, son of Hermino. He only has the one ear, you know. Ah, here we are." He stopped by the last door and knocked gently. An aged, soft voice said to come in.

Inside the very modest room, with only a bed, desk, and chair, was Bandar Dero, sitting on the chair, blue robes draped over him. Yes, he was very old indeed, his hair nearly gone and what little remained was white as new fallen snow. He'd gained a little weight about the middle since I had last seen him so very long ago — either that or his arms and legs had grown thinner. Still, I recognized him. Of all the ten disciples, I had liked Bandar the most; he'd always been civil to me and our children.

"Welcome minstrels, welcome. I am Archdeacon Bandar Dero. I have heard such inspiring things about your music. I can tell you that you have raised the spirits of so many of our younger folks. I just wanted to thank you all personally for your generous gift of music. I understand that you have been playing all across the Sea Princes and for little or no pay. It is so very rare that we see such altruism. And you have come so far, West Reach it is said. Is this so?"

As our leader, I had to face him, "Yes, Archdeacon. We are mostly all from that island and a long way from home. I am Ket of Cuch Glyn and this is my sister, Fianna."

"Such red hair! My, I've lived a long life, but never have I seen such red hair," he actually brightened up slightly, looking closely at our hair. I continued with the other introductions of the musicians, and mentioned that two were not present, Jolina having become ill. Then, I introduced our managers, the other four Guardians. By the time I finished up, I could tell he was about to doze off in his chair.

He suddenly remembered something and jerked himself awake. "Pardon me, I find myself so very tired and yet it is but morning. Yes, as I said, I wanted to personally thank you all and give you this. Please accept this small token of gratitude for all your playing throughout all the Sea Princes." He handed me a pouch. As I accepted it, his head drooped and he was asleep in his chair. Mechanically, I passed the pouch on to Fianna.

Very quietly, Philas said, "He has fallen asleep. If you will follow me, let's not disturb his holy sleep." We tiptoed out of his room, and the pastor reverently shut the door. A minute later, we were back outside the rectory. "If you will follow me, I will give you a brief tour of the church." We diligently followed him.

Inside the church, again, nothing was pretentious. In fact, it bordered on the austere. Yet, it was huge, with a great vaulted ceiling at least thirty feet over head. The rows upon rows of wooden pews could seat seven hundred worshipers at one time, according to Philas. What impressed me most was the artwork in and around the High Altar. On either side of the altar were two magnificent, life-sized statues of Jes and what was supposed to be his mother. Across the entire back of this area was a huge wall mural of the Last Supper, when Jes returned from the dead to deliver his final sermon to the disciples. Indeed, I did recognize all their faces. Naturally, I looked to see if I was in there, Bethany Madelyn Amir, his wife. All the disciples were in their proper places. Yet, I was always on his left at these formal meetings. In the mural, there was a figure in that position, but it was not recognizable as man or woman, more like someone serving the meal. Ah well.

"And over here is where our choir stands and sings the Holy Psalms during the masses. If you have time, you are more than welcome to come and hear the Sacred Music. It does send chills down one's spine; it is so holy," Philas continued. Soon the tour was over. There really was not much to see. The Church of Jehosanity Northern Orthodoxy retained its humble roots as true as they could to Jes's teachings, altering only what they had to, making it acceptable. Even though I knew how badly they had altered Jes's teachings, particularly about having a soul from being a soul, I still found that I respected what Bandar had actually accomplished in his long lifetime.

As we filed out and said farewell to Philas, I expanded my awareness slightly and felt that cold chill of a Grey Creature, lurking somewhere inside the rectory. It had to be masquerading as Deacon Pilate. Quickly, I dropped my senses to normal, hoping this slight touch had gone unnoticed.

All the way back to the inn, the sole topic of discussion was the Grey Creature and what it was doing in Zargarb, posing as a religious leader of the church. Speculations ran wild, particularly once we caught up to Jolina and Edgar, who had been walking slowly waiting for us to rejoin them. She had recovered from her sudden fright, and once more, I complimented her for her incredibly good senses and timely warning. Yes, she held her head tall the rest of the way back to the inn.

Once we had returned, I sent word to Cecilia, Lenkova, and Alicia; we just had to have an emergency meeting, and I would have to tell them about this imposter. While we were all sitting around in our room waiting for word of when we could meet, Fianna finally examined the pouch's contents. She shrieked as she dumped a handful of gems into her lap! We gaped, while Jolina felt them with her fingers. Later, Fianna had them evaluated by a Sisterhood gem cutter and announced that we had nearly a thousand gold pieces worth of gems. Bandar had really been incredibly generous to the West Reach Minstrels! I knew without a doubt that he had been totally sincere and genuine in his words with us this morning.

We met later that afternoon with the three women. They had already heard about the previous two imposter encounters in the other sectors, so I did not have to do an awful lot of explaining. All three were shocked to discover that they had one of these imposter creatures in their midst, as if they did not already have enough to worry about! However, after a lengthy discussion, none of them had detected any adverse actions traceable to Deacon Pilate. Our immediate conclusion was whatever it was doing, it was doing it within the church and not to Zargarb proper.

Cecilia had the final words, "We will assign a number of Sisters to keep an eye on him discretely from a distance and see if anything about his activities can be discerned." Since Waverly was going to keep in contact with Cecilia, she promised to relay anything that was learned about his actions. For sure, no one would trust anything that this deacon proclaimed or even said. I hoped this would lessen the impact of whatever it was trying to do here in Zargarb. I guess what bothered me the most was having no idea whatsoever of what he was trying to do masquerading as a deacon. The only possible thing would be some kind of involvement in this confrontation between the two rival Churches of Jehosanity. If the mantis creatures had a hand in Pope Yazi's church, then perhaps this creature was keeping watch over this church. Why? Your guess is as good as mine was at the time.

Chapter 26 Alabaster, At Last

With a small herd of horses, nine wagons, and close to fifty Sisterhood fighters, we rolled out of Zargarb on the 15th as planned, taking the coastal paved road eastward for a time. The Centurion made road closely followed the Med Sea coast, angling on down to New Barq, the rebuilt town of Al Barq, which was totally destroyed during the barbarian invasion long ago. Even with the draft horses, we made good time on the road. Two days later, we entered the cedar forests at the very southern edge of the Zargarb sector. These magnificent trees grew here and extended a ways into the Arad to the east of us and for a good deal of distance on south into the Arad, ending some twenty miles from New Barq.

Since none of us, save myself last lifetime, had ever been in a cedar forest, the experience was novel. We paused for hours smelling and strolling about the woods. While the others were examining the sights, memories came back to me. Jes and I had passed through these very trees, escaping from a band of Galts on horseback. They'd attempted to kill us, and I was forced to bring fire down upon the ten attackers. I remembered our fearful flight through these very woods. However, now was not the time for memories. With a good deal of effort, I cleared my mind and sought the general direction to Alabaster. I could tell that we were getting much closer to him and pin pointed the direction that we must travel to reach him.

I took Lenkova and the two Sisters, Mara and Kesha, aside for a brief conference. "We need to go in that general direction. If my memory serves me right, we can get through the forest here easily, and there's a north-south track on the other side. Still, we need to go mostly southeast, not south. Ideas?"

Both of these women were lifelong, close friends, who had immigrated to Zargarb several years ago. A roaming band of Galts had slain their husbands, while they were forced to watch, and then both had been raped. Their two older sons, who were around ten, had protested, and were killed as well. To avoid further degradation and starvation, they left the Arad bringing their remaining four children with them. I discovered that these women knew well the southern half of the Arad. Mara was more talkative to men, and she answered me, "Yes, you are right. How do you know about that less well-traveled track?"

I did not want to get into my past lifetime or explain about being the wife of the Great Messiah just now. "I can recall some things from a previous life," I kept it simple. Both women seemed to accept my explanation at face value. Mara went on, "We can go perhaps twenty miles due south on that path. However, as you must remember, it is mesa country. One cannot just go southeast because of the steep mesas along the way."

"Yes, I forgot about that. Well, every time we get to a spot where we could move one mesa further to the east, let me know. and I'll make a decision whether to go east or continue south. How's that?"

"Not so good. Some valleys lack water holes for extended distances. We could run into serious trouble if we end up missing them," Mara cautioned.

"Very true. Promise me that you will let me know if, by veering another direction, we may run into just such an eventuality, all right?" Both women agreed.

Kesha nudged Mara, who added, "You are also aware of the vipers and scorpions in the Arad?"

"Oops. Yes, I am, but I doubt that any of the others are," I answered, feeling how ill prepared I actually was. I should have discussed all these details with the others before we even set foot in the Arad. Hence, I called everyone together for a short meeting.

"As you know we are close to the border of Juda Arad. Once we enter that land, be exceedingly careful when on foot. There are many very poisonous vipers around and scorpions. Every time you go to put on your boots, please shake them out. You never know what will come falling out of them. Scorpions and other critters love those nice dark holes. Please be extra careful." This caused a bit of a stir, especially with Jolina; Edgar was quick to guarantee he would be her eyes in these matters.

Lenkova volunteered, "Normally, I would send out scouting parties ahead of us to avoid any surprises, you know bandit traps and such. Here, however, we only have Mara and Kesha who know the land. It would be folly for me to send out one of the others. Yet, I don't want to put either of those two out on point alone. If anything should happen to them, we're in big trouble. Bethany, since this is your expedition, I defer this matter to you." She had cleverly placed the responsibility squarely on my shoulders, having said what she would normally have done.

"Since I'm the one who ultimately must lead us to Alabaster and since I knew well this land, albeit more than twenty years ago since I was last here, I'll ride point, taking Mara with me as well as two others. This is a land of mesas. Let me explain. Coming from the east towards the west, the land slopes upwards for some distance. At the peak is the mesa top. However, on the western side, the mesas drop so sharply downward that one cannot climb them at all. The western sides form a natural barrier to all travel. Hence, we must choose our routes carefully if east-west travel is desired. North-south is not a problem; one just follows along the natural valleys between mesas."

"What I am driving at is this. From a mesa top, one can see for a very long distance, especially north and south of that mesa. Hence, there is no way one can practically avoid being spotted by someone perched on top of a mesa, which is usually several hundred feet above the valley floors. If one wishes to travel with a good chance of not being detected, different tactics must be used from those in the Sea Princes. Here, one must travel the back ways between mesas where there are no villages and settlements — off the beaten track, so to speak. However, finding sources of water then becomes critical. Part of the reason that there are some areas, particularly in this southern section of the Arad, that have few to no settlements is just that, lack of a watering hole. We are depending upon Mara and Kesha to make sure that we don't head off in some direction where there is no water for a long distance."

"I'll ride point, but we will not be more than a mile ahead of the rest of you. Actually, there is no point in being further ahead; correct me if I am wrong on this detail, Mara, Kesha." Both women agreed with me completely.

"No point, the wagons can be spotted from a far distant mesa — sometimes ten miles away," Kesha added.

"Dust storms, don't forget those," Mara appended. I encouraged her to explain. "During these dry, hot summer months, sometimes the winds pick up, and we get dust storms. They can be so bad that all travel is impossible until the winds die down. Grit gets in your nose, mouth, everywhere. Being caught out in the open in one is very bad. Kesha and I can usually tell when one is coming; we'll alert everyone in plenty of time."

"Okay, I suggest we change into our Arad clothing and robes. Once we clear this cedar forest, we will be out in the wide-open spaces of the Arad. I know you'll all feel much more comfortable in these loose fitting, light clothing during the daytime. Nights get surprisingly cold though," I cautioned. We proceeded to change from our Sea Prince clothing into these light robes and head wrappings. A half hour later, we were finally ready to continue our journey, leaving the paved road, bushwhacking across the cedar forest.

For a while, Lenkova and Adriana joined Mara and me riding point. Both leaders wanted to see firsthand this new arid landscape. For a time, we followed an old logger's track, made by the dragging of heavy cedar logs out from the deep forest down to the road. The route we traveled seemed very familiar to me. Then, I realized I was actually following the route taken by Jes and me when we fled the Arad to Zargarb so long ago. About an hour later, we halted at the very edge of the cedar forest at the very same spot where the charging Galts had ambushed Jes and me!

I couldn't help myself from commenting to my three companions, "Wow! It was right here that the ten Galts came charging down this narrow track from up north that way. As soon as they saw us, they attacked, firing many arrows our way. I was protecting the children. Boy, my memories of that day are sure vivid!"

Lenkova and Adriana stared off across the countryside. It was hilly and sandy where we stood beside our horses. About ten miles to the east, two tall jagged edged mesas could be seen, with a valley between them in which one could travel eastward. We had only two choices here: go south along the track or head east to get into the next valley system over. I sensed we ought to head east and consulted with Mara, who agreed with my call.

Meanwhile, Adriana had been walking around this little clearing at the forest's edge. "Well, I'll be! Hey, gang, take a look here," she pointed to the ground. Sure enough, the remains of several arrows lay partially embedded in the ground and a tree. Dry rot had long ago set in, a slight touch and the shafts disintegrated in my fingers. Everyone chuckled over her find.

By now, the caravan of wagons and riders joined us, and I explained which way we were heading — mostly eastward following the faint track. We four then rode on out in front. Five quiet miles passed slowly, we dared not get too far out in front of the others. Lenkova commented, "You know, Bethany, that there has been a good deal of horse traffic over this track recently?"

"I'm not a super judge of it, but it certainly looks like it, coming and going, right?" I deferred to her expertise. She agreed.

We rounded a bend; the hillside obscured our view until we had completed the bend. We pulled up quickly. Just ahead were some twenty men wearing sky blue tunics with white crosses on both their front and back sides. All were big men and heavily armed. They were currently taking a rest stop. I spied one man urinating onto a nearby bush. Their bronzed skin gave them away, though their voices, which followed, would also have.

One man, their leader I hazarded a guess, said, "Well men, looks like we have a mini-harem here. Only one young lad. How about some afternoon sport? Take the lad out." Unfortunately for the women, they spoke in the Centurion or Megalos tongue. However, I speak basic Centurion and fully understood his orders.

I spoke hastily to the three, "They mean to attack us and rape you three. Mara, ride fast back to the convoy and warn them." Since I spoke the Prince's dialect, the Holy Paladins didn't understand what I said. However, Mara's sudden about face and cantering off back the way we had come told them that we either understood them or knew that these men were a threat. However, his men rushed to grab their crossbows. Adriana and Lenkova managed to get their horses partially turned before two fired at me.

Since I knew they planned to shoot me, I was ready for them. The first quarrel, I deflected with my left hand; it thudded into the sand off to my left. The second, I simply caught with my right hand. Using my fingers, I cracked the shaft in half, dropping it to the ground, all the while, staring straight at the two shooters. I said slowly, "Don't get me angry!" As I spoke, I quickly chanted. Just as I turned my horse around, a wall of ice suddenly appeared behind me, standing between the group of men and me. I kicked my horse into a canter and followed the others. Both Adriana and Lenkova looked back at me and saw another dozen quarrels thud into the wall of ice, which slowly fell over onto the ground. That delay was all that we needed. Galloping away back around the bend, we could no longer be seen, and thus these men couldn't shoot us in the back. However, we could hear them kicking their horses into action, but now we had a good head start on them.

Galloping away, Lenkova called back to me, "I didn't know you spoke Centurion."

"Yes, I can speak the basic language, though not fluently."

I heard her mutter to Adriana, "Why does this not surprise me?" I grinned.

A couple minutes later, we arrived at our caravan. Only moments ahead of us, Mara had reached them and delivered the warning. Already the wagons were beginning to form a defensive circle; Sisters were circling wide around them to from up a defensive perimeter. I galloped up to our wagon and yelled for Caitlyn to hand me my pole. We had about sixty seconds to set up a defense before they came charging into view. I yelled, "They want to slay the men and rape the women. Let's use that against them. Guys, ride to my side and stay close. Use ice walls to stop quarrels. Sisters, take care of those that get by us."

Fergus, Alton, and Andre galloped up to me, and we rode a short distance out in front of the circling wagons. A fair number of Sisterhood fighters dismounted, slapped their horses into the center of the wagon circle, and formed up between the wagons and us, though the wagons were still trying to form their tight circle around our large number of spare horses and those of the Sisters. The thundering hoof beats of the twenty were heard just before we spied them rounding a slight bend. Instantly, they reined in, surveying the unexpected situation. Their leader called out very excitedly, "Men, we have hit the jack pot! Each of you gets three women! Take the four men out first. Charge!"

Once more, they kicked their horses into an all-out gallop, waving their swords at us menacingly. Alton muttered, "Idiots! Three ice walls in a row, if you please. Now!" Understand, our walls of ice are just thin sheets, perhaps an inch thick. In this heat, the ice melts rather rapidly. Further, without solidly anchoring of said walls, they simply slowly fall over, smashing into the ground. Alton's strategy was simple. Since these men were charging full speed toward us, their forward momentum would defeat them as they crashed into these walls. True, the sheets would shatter, but not before dislodging the riders. Always with charging cavalry, the advantage goes to their forward momentum. Alton's idea was to remove their advantage, making them fight in place.

As the lead pair of charging men closed to forty feet, three walls of ice suddenly appeared immediately in front of them. Wham! Wham! Wham! Horse and man smashed into the nearly invisible barriers. Six men and their horses went down in a mad jumble of wildly flailing limbs. The remaining fourteen managed a crash stop, several trampling and stumbling over their fallen comrades. The falling ice sheets hit the ground hard, raising sand and dust clouds briefly partially obscuring the attackers, adding to their confusion.

We four rushed forward, stepping over and around the fallen. My pole knocked the nearest rider off his horse; I moved on towards the next one. Behind me, I heard Sisters coming up fast and knew that they would finish off those on the ground. Andre dashed about, attempting to fight one man, while dodging the sword swings from two others. Alton, on the other hand, took an entirely different approach, one that I would never use.

With the advantage to the rider over one on foot, Alton continued to level the field. Instead of attacking the rider or parrying with him, he cut the horse's throat with his sword. Horse went down; its rider was forced to meet him on foot. His superior swordplay quickly dispatched the Holy Paladin, effective, yet sickening, as far as I was concerned. Three minutes later, it was all over. Their leader had stayed well back of the melee line. As he watched his eighteenth man fall, he screamed out, "Bitches! I'll bring the entire Legion down on you. Revenge will be sweet!" He and his other man hastily galloped off heading northward.

We stood catching our breaths, surveying our situation. Waverly called out, "Wounds?"

I had a couple of small cuts, as had Andre and Alton. Nothing serious. None of the Sisters had been harmed at all. While Waverly examined each of us and bandaged the cuts, Lenkova asked, "What did he say when he left?" I quickly repeated his verbal tirade.

"Well, they were sure poor fighters, these Holy Paladins," Lenkova commented. "How many are in a Legion?"

"One hundred," I replied. "I sure hope that there are not that many close by!"

"Damn! That many? We should be heading out fast! Double damn. How are we ever going to hide our passage? With all these wagons and horses, we are going to leave a trail that a blind man can follow!" she added, thinking about the problem.

Mara broke in, "May I suggest that we take the next valley up ahead that leads southward? It is an isolated valley system because there is no water for a long distance. Perhaps we can hide our trail. The ground is dry and sandy. A sandstorm would wipe out our passage."

"Excellent, Mara. Make it so at once. You heard her; get those wagons moving now! Adriana, out in front, take several with you. Halt when you find that southern track. You ten, come with me. You ten, search those bodies, break their weapons. Action time, ladies," Lenkova barked.

A flurry of action swept around us, as Waverly continued her first aid. Adriana, Mara, and a couple others galloped on ahead towards where we had first encountered this band. One by one, the wagons began to roll once more, with many Sisters bringing along the many extra horses. Ten began swiftly searching the dead bodies, confiscating what might be valuable. I heard swords snapping and turned to watch as one sister stuck the blade over a rock and dropped another heavy rock onto it while her foot held the pummel securely to the ground. Snap, the blade broke. One Sister came up to me and said, "Found this. Book of some kind. You take it and see if it is worth keeping." I stuffed it into my saddle bag and mounted up, Waverly had finished with me.

By the time the ten Sisters had finished, Waverly had as well. We all mounted and followed the wagons. Lenkova insisted that we do so. I turned to watch what she was doing until I rounded the bend and could no longer see her and her small band. They were cutting large branches and tying them to their horses with bits of rope. Soon they came up behind us. The dragging branches raised a large dust cloud behind them. "This will help hide tracks," she said, "not too effective, but it is a start. Think you all can whip us up one of those dust storms? Now would be a good time for one."

Alton replied, "Sorry, I would if I could, but I've never seen a dust storm. I don't know what one actually is."

I have, but one does not command weather on short notice. On the contrary, it takes time to force a major change in the weather patterns. To our surprise, Kesha, who had stayed back, said softly, "I think you might just get your wish. The conditions appear right for one. I can tell better by evening. I'll let you know, Lenkova."

I wondered what she meant. The sky was a crystal blue, not a cloud in the sky. Normally, in summer, one might see a few high cumulus clouds on occasion, but certainly, no appreciable rain would fall during these hot summer months. Hot it was, in the low nineties just now.

Fifteen minutes later, we caught up with the slower moving wagons. Impatient, Lenkova took a group of ten back the way we had come to examine how effective their brush dragging had been. While the land was sandy and dry, still there was no hiding the fact that a number of wagons, along with numerous horses, had just passed through. On the positive side, the dragging had sufficiently messed up the horse hoof prints that one could not tell how many horses went this way. Nevertheless, she and her crew dismounted and began experimenting with different ways to hide the deep ruts left by the wagon wheels.

Ten miles ahead, we reached a minor junction of valleys between four mesas. The eastward track we were following headed on east. More importantly, I saw that the valley to our right, heading south did not have any well-marked track leading down it. Obviously, no towns lay in this direction, which meant no water for some distance. Down this one we went, following the lead of Mara. We passed beneath the sheer sides of the mesa off to our left, to the east. Small shrubs dotted the valley floor along with many boulders of various sides. Great care was needed to drive our large wagons along this valley floor. Mara did her best to pick out a traversable passage. However, progress was painstakingly slow.

Lenkova finally rejoined us, "Well, on foot, we can fairly well hide the wagon ruts. We've hidden them for a mile up to this valley and on down to this point." She was sweating profusely, as were her ten companions. "This heat is nearly unbearable!"

"Make sure you are all drinking lots of water," I replied, "heat strokes are common out here in the Arad, if you are not careful." She spat on the ground in disgust. I could tell that her first experiences of the Arad were not being particularly good to her. By late afternoon, everyone was drenched with sweat, including our horses; we had been pushing them steadily all afternoon without any rest periods. The temperature soared into the low hundreds. I estimated that we were a good ten miles down this deserted valley. No signs of any watering hole could I see, but then I did not expect to find any.

The sun was ruddy red, low in the western sky just above the distant mesa top far off to our right, when Mara called a halt. She and Kesha chatted briefly before she announced, "Look at the sun. See that orange glow there below it? Feel the gentle breeze on our faces?"

Cheers arose, but for the wrong reasons. We all thought that the breeze was most timely and refreshing, cooling down horse and man. Mara cried out, "No! You don't understand. That is a dust storm forming. By nightfall, it will be upon us. We must find shelter at once!" I looked around at the incredibly barren landscape. Shelter? Where? Boulders, shrubs, sand, gravel, and a rugged side of a mesa. Mara and Kesha took charge, without waiting for orders from Lenkova! They rode on ahead and returned in minutes, "This way, hurry," Kesha called out.

Shortly, we saw the two dismounting behind a huge slab of mesa, which had fallen off the steep side a very long time ago. With a struggle, we managed to pull all of the wagons behind the slab. We were sandwiched between the slab and the sharply rising mesa cliff. Next, following Mara's urging, we positioned the horses close in with the wagons, tails facing the slab and the approaching dust storm. Mara asked me, "We all should be in shelter. Could all of us fit inside the wagons to wait out the storm?"

Quickly, Caitlyn and I re-arranged our gear so that as many Sisters could join us as possible. Twelve crowded into our wagon alone. The others followed suit. A half hour later, as the sky darkened rapidly, everyone was huddled inside the wagons and the flaps pulled down. Because we were so cramped inside, we dare not light a lantern; hence, we huddled in the darkness waiting the storm's arrival.

Just a few minutes later, howling winds whirled around our position; biting sand pounded upon the wagon sides. Soon, dust began to seep into the cramped insides of our wagon. Following Mara's advice, we wrapped our headscarves over our faces to help keep from inhaling volumes of the fine dust particles. I hoped the horses would not be terribly harmed, but there was nothing I could do for them if they would have been.

Time passed endlessly, the fury of nature continued relentlessly outside. Eventually, I dozed off. The next thing I knew, daylight shone through small cracks in the wagon. One by one, everyone stirred and struggled to get out of the wagon. Muscles were so cramped that each of us experienced a good deal of pain just trying to do such a simple thing. We stretched and looked at the world around us. Now we had only tan horses; yes, every horse was tan, the color of the sandy ground around here. Dust and sand covered wagon wheels nearly half way up to the axles! Oops. We looked funny too, our clothes were also tan in color.

Caitlyn's comment spoke for us all, "What a mess!"

Camilla, assisted by two others, got out the cooking gear and built a small charcoal cooking fire. While they made breakfast, we began cleaning out the wagons, while others rubbed down the horses. Neither chore was more than begun when Camilla had our breakfast ready. Grumbling, we knew that we would spend at least a half-day cleaning up before we could continue our journey.

Over tea, Lenkova commented, "Well, our tracks have been nicely obscured. I don't think that the Holy Paladins will be finding us anytime soon. Bethany, I thought that the Centurions were great fighters. That bunch yesterday were fools."

"I agree, Lenkova. I can tell you from personal experience that those paladins are nothing like the real Centurions, not even remotely close in skill. Still, if they bring a hundred down on us, we will be hard pressed. We got lucky yesterday; no one was seriously injured."

"Ah, then I will withhold judgment on Centurions until later. Say, how is it that you speak their language?"

"My Lightning Circle actually visited Megalos a half century ago. I learned it then and haven't forgotten it all."

"I see. Those ice walls certainly helped. I've never seen a better arrow barrier. Even though they did not hold up against the charging men, it did break their charge for us."

"Alton takes all credit for thinking that one up. I would have never thought of using our spells in that manner, but then, he is the Protector and I am a Wid. We have very different viewpoints on combat."

Kesha heard us chatting and interjected a bit sarcastically, "Well, you see for yourselves just how nasty men are — they see a woman and immediately intend on violating her. They only have one thing on their minds. Bastards, all of them." Her face crimsoned as she glanced at me, and added quickly, "Well, perhaps not all men."

"They are probably totally insecure and have such an incredibly low opinion of themselves that it is not funny. Eventually, they will pay for what they now do, only pay in spades. Kesha, one day they will realize just how bad they actually are being and then go on a total withholding of themselves from all women. I've seen it happen with one of the Great Messiah's ten disciples. In fact, he is their leader down in Megalos, calls himself Pope Yazi I. He has gotten to the point where he now has to hate all women, no matter how good and great that woman might be. He is completely blind to all women and cannot even see them."

"Yes, but then he is free to commit even worse atrocities on women," Kesha countered.

"Yes, but I've known of some women who are just as bad," Lenkova interjected her thoughts. "Take Zdlenka, the sister of my despicable father. I heard that she planned all the attacks and killings. I've even heard she resorted to horrible physical torture of merchants just to gain information. She cut off a trader's fingers, if you can believe that."

"Well, you know I think it is sort of a slow death as a spiritual being. Look, if you or I did something awful, our immediate reaction is not to say anything about it to anyone, rather to withhold it from others because we're not proud of it, or are embarrassed, or feel very guilty about having done this bad thing. Now look at what happens when we do just that. Don't you feel like you are more distant, more separated from those that you did it to — far less close to them. That's just what happens when you try to withhold it from them. Also, since you need to be somehow right, you then tend to find fault with those that you harmed. If you can do so, then doesn't it make your bad actions seem to you to be far less bad? Take those Holy Paladins yesterday. I feel awful because we had to kill most of them. Right at this moment, I want to put a lot of distance between them and me. If I'm allowed to say what bad fighters they are, how terrible their plans and actions towards you women were, why, then isn't it more acceptable that I helped kill so many of them? You see, we naturally try to lessen the scope and impact of what we have done. It is a natural response."

I felt like I was doing well with this so I continued. "Now suppose that we keep on finding ourselves doing the same bad actions, over and over. Would not we eventually conclude that we could no longer withhold or keep ourselves under control towards these people? Can you imagine the state of mind of a person who finally concludes that he can no longer control his own actions? Pretty pathetic. If their actions were toward the opposite sex, then they would no longer be able to experience sex, families, or love of another. Think of all that life around them that they would have shut completely out of their lives. This is what I mean about the slow death of a spiritual being. If they kept it up, eventually, they would exist solely and only for themselves. So much for the six other areas of life, families, groups, mankind, animals, plants, the physical world around them, even other spiritual beings. In my opinion, such a life is hardly worth living."

Lenkova added another comment, "I can see what you mean. I did some despicable things last lifetime as a man. This lifetime, I was violently against men, trying to stop all men. I had confused my own actions as a man with other men. I was making all other men guilty of what I had done. You are very right, Bethany. Look at me — look how old I am! Until now, I have denied myself all men and thus something as beautiful as a family, children, and love. Thank Jehosa for Andre!"

A tear trickled down Kesha's cheek, "I had all that, and then men took it all away from me!"

"I understand; it is a huge loss. You fight back and start over again. Don't let a few evil men ruin the rest of your life. Get a new love and enjoy a family once more," I encouraged her. "Show those evil men that you cannot be stopped by their bad actions! Don't succumb to their wickedness."

Her grief abated and she became quite testy, "Yes, that's easy for you to say! How am I going to do that?"

I got a bit bored and said, "I know; it is so hard to find the right man."

She got slightly interested, "Well, I guess I would actually have to go out and meet some men, wouldn't I?"

"Yes, I suppose you would at that. What a chore. You realize there must be a hundred thousand men in Zargarb, ignoring the rest of the sector!"

She began laughing, "That is a lot, isn't it? Well, I really don't like beards on men, so I can eliminate a whole bunch right away."

"Eliminate who?" asked Mara, who had just walked up, catching her last pronouncement.

"Bearded men, silly. You know I've told you I hate that fuzziness." Suddenly, Mara and Kesha began chatting about how best to go about finding the right men for themselves. Lenkova took my arm and pulled me away from them, leaving them to enjoy themselves.

She gave me a little hug and whispered, "Thanks. I've never seen her laugh."

Caitlyn spied me and called out, "Hey you, get in here and help me clean out this filthy wagon, or you won't have any place to sleep tonight!" She was teasing of course, but I climbed in to our wagon and lent her a hand with it.

After lunch, everyone was as clean as we could manage. Rather, one might say that we were as dirty as before, but felt better about it. We knew that a real bath was only in the far distance somewhere. Hence, we headed on south, down this valley. Near sunset, we came to the end of this mesa and could veer eastward once more. No sign of any watering hole did we see, nor for the next two days.

The third day brought us to a small hamlet of fifty people. Ten adobe homes surrounded a small watering hole. Fig and date trees dotted the perimeter. A flock of sheep grazed on the far side of the hole, while six children played in the open area on this side. We traded an evening of music for the restocking of our water barrels. We had used nearly half of our supply that we had brought with us. Had we not had the foresight to bring a wagonload of water with us, we might all be skeletons lying in the dust by now.

Since Mara and Kesha now had a good feel for the general direction that I wanted to travel, they asked about the town that we would get to, if we continued on east and south, Al Mareka. "It's all thieves and bandits now," the village elder explained. "But you have enough fighters with you so you may get by them." It didn't sound good, so we bypassed that larger town, going some twenty miles out of our way, again down mostly unused tracks where there were no watering holes.

Slowly another week passed uneventfully. We met mostly vipers along our way and one shepherd tending a nearly starving flock of sheep. Lenkova kindly shared some of our water with him and his twenty sheep. We continued on another day until we arrived at a very isolated watering hole in south central Arad. A single home snuggled up close to the small puddle of water. Ten tall fig and date trees surrounded the area. As we rode up, the three young children, who were playing outside, quickly ran indoors, while a man and woman came out. The man carried a sword, and the woman held on to him with her arms.

A glance at the two of them told me quite a lot. From his skin color and build, he was a Galt! Seeing his horse grazing behind the house helped confirm it. She, however, was a native of the Arad. Both looked rather fearfully at our large group. Lenkova, riding point, called out to him, "Hello. We're traveling musicians, just passing through. We didn't even know there was a water hole out here." She was attempting to be friendly; she also knew that he was a barbarian from the Northern Steppes.

"Hello. Karmanski Zolgoti. Out of way. No towns here," he spoke very broken Arad. His tone varied from fear to concern, back and forth, which I thought very strange. Most definitely, the woman was afraid.

Since our wagon was first in line, just behind the few point riders, I could see and hear their exchange. I knew a very little Galt, but decided to try, "Greetings. I am called Ket, the leader of the West Reach Minstrels. We've come a very long way and have been playing for the towns and villages along the way."

He brightened up. My accent and grammar construction must have sounded better to him than his command of Arad. "Ah, musicians, yes. You speak my language, not so good, but better than I do hers, I'm afraid." However, Lenkova and everyone else up front turned to stare at me; none of them understood a word we'd just said.

He continued, "Are you lost? No towns way out here. Al Tith is over that way about twenty miles near the Centurion road," he explained.

I grinned and had a plan, since it was roughly the direction I wanted to go anyway. "That's where we're headed. We thought we were taking a short cut back there. We ran into some trouble with the. . ." I fumbled for words; I had no idea how to say Holy Paladins in Galt. "The, ah, soldiers in blue with the white crosses on their shirts."

"Ah, yes. Bad men. Fear them. No short cut, but you are close now. Where is West Reach? I've not heard of it," he replied. I sensed his fear abating, leaving mostly concern in his voice.

"It is a big island off the west —" Oops, I didn't know how to say "coast" in his language, so I improvised, "side of the Sea Princes, beyond Velona, out in the big water." I also didn't know "ocean" in his language. Perhaps, they did not have a word for it, since the Northern Steppes had no large bodies of water remotely close to it.

He shrugged. West Reach was not in his reality. Since it was already late afternoon, I asked, "We've got our own food and water with us. Could we camp nearby here for the night? If so, we can play our music for you and your family in exchange for letting us camp nearby."

"I will ask Juli. If she says okay, then it is okay with me." The two spoke a few words, a smattering mixture of Arad and Galt; evidently both made compromises in language. "She says okay, so okay." I quickly explained everything to the others, and we drove the wagons beyond their small homestead into the rough countryside. With all the horses, I didn't want them making messes where the children might be playing. Quickly, all hands pitched in to setup camp. Some handled the horses, some built the fire circles for the charcoal cooking fires, some worked on making the meal for our large group, a few had latrine duty. For a while, the five of them watched our activities from just outside their house; certainly, this was an event for the children. During it all, his wife must have ducked back inside to fix their supper; I saw a thin smoke tendril rising from the chimney.

Around dusk, dinner finished and bedrolls out, we musicians gathered around, preparing our instruments. Caitlyn was a bit testy; sand had gotten inside the sound holes of her dulcimer and was doing its best to avoid being shaken out. Finally, we began to play. At once, the family came outside and up to our lanterns to watch and listen. After the first song, both Karmanski and Juli completely relaxed. We were what we said we were; I suspected that both had their doubts until now. When Fianna and Fergus did their dancing, joined by a number of the d'Grange Sisters, the children just had to join in as well, though they had no idea how to dance. Yet, their huge grins and laughter spoke volumes. Even their parents were smiling and laughing when we finally finished a couple hours later.

While Juli ushered her children off to bed, Camilla brought us a large pot of tea, and we shared it with Karmanski. "Thank you for playing. The children just loved it. They've never heard music before and are not likely to again for a long time. All three will not forget this night; neither will my wife nor I."

"Our pleasure," I replied. "It brings us happiness to bring a little happiness to others in the world."

"Ah, I know about happiness. Juli is happiness," he seemed to want to talk, so I nodded encouragingly. They were an unlikely combination, an Arad woman and a Galt man. "We are out here where no one comes just to stay alive. You see, many years ago, I was part of Czar Strokova's mighty invincible army. I am ashamed to say that we plundered and pillaged all throughout the Arad. I was way down south when the invincible army was routed in the middle of an enormous storm. I lost everything, my horse, my sword, my supplies, my unit, my friends, everything. I crawled away from the slaughter in the mud and rain. On foot, I walked north all the way from close to Sud, it is called. Long time. My feet were bloody. I ate roots and bugs I could catch with my hands. When I finally crossed over into the Arad here, I was nearly a dead man. Still I struggled through the desert, but became lost. No water for days. Finally, I could walk no more and fell to the ground. I expected that spot to be my final resting place."

His wife came out and snuggled up to him. "Juli, she found me lying like a dead man in the dust and sand, just outside of Al Tith, where she lived. We had sacked her town three times; we had killed her young husband. Yet, Juli gave me water, cleaned my bleeding feet, dragged me into her home, and even fed me. Perhaps she didn't know I was a soldier."

She butted in, "Yes, I knew, but you were dying. You were not being a soldier then. So I helped you."

"Well, it took me weeks to recover. I couldn't walk for the longest time. Still she nursed me back into a healthy man. During all that time, I finally realized something I had not really known before. Juli is a person, just like me. Sure, her skin is different; she speaks a strange language, but she is still a living person. When I got well, I made a decision. I could continue on my way back to the steppes. There, I could rejoin what is left of my clan. Yet, all that is there is a mountain of gold. I could be wealthy man, sitting on the gold piles, or I could stay here with Juli. I stayed. We married now."

Juli had her arm around the big man. She took the opportunity to elaborate further, "Married, we are both outcasts. The Arads in my village call me bad names, spit on me, and will not even talk to me anymore. Some of his people came by once, and they called him names too. We are both outcasts now. Makes no sense to me. I knew of this water hole, and we just moved out here after that. Almost no one comes this way; there is no water, as you know, on up that valley. Now we have three fine sons and all that we can want."

He added a final thought, "Juli and the boys are worth more to me than all the gold in the steppes!" Okay, so I had a tear in my eye when he finished; there was lots of dust everywhere after that dust storm.

"Al Tith is not a good place to go," Karmanski added. "Young Arad men rob many travelers. A band of men from my country are also somewhere nearby; they are still looting what they can. Then there are these nasty Blue Shirts from way down south, they are the worst, really. They have no respect for life at all. If you go into Al Tith, you be very careful. You have so many women with you that you will attract bad men like flies to a dung pile."

"Thanks for the warning. I think we will give the Al Tith a wide berth. We've already had one run-in with the Blue Shirts; I hope we can avoid them in the future."

"Yaw, avoid Blue Shirts," he agreed. Both yawned and we all broke up for the night. The next day when we finally began to roll onwards once more, all five stood and waved us goodbye.

Based upon what he had said about the town, Mara was quite glad that I ordered us to go around that town. Again, Lenkova rode point along with Mara and two others. Slowly the arid, bleak landscaped passed by. Around two in the afternoon, we reached the great paved north-south road, built by the Centurions. It ran right down the middle of Juda Arad. We were halfway across the country.

More importantly, I sensed that Alabaster was now very close; perhaps we were within miles of reaching him. Lenkova, Mara, and I discussed our path as we halted beside the deserted, but paved, roadway. "We are very close now. Over that way a few miles maybe," I pointed southeast.

Mara explained, "There is a mesa between us and where you are pointing. How about risking traveling down the road, until we get around to the south side of the mesa, and then head off east. That ought to put us about where you are pointing."

Lenkova cautioned, "Could be risky indeed. I suspect the Holy Paladins and Galts probably use this road a lot."

"Arads won't use it," Mara added. "We'd only be on it for less than an hour. We could send scouts out ahead of us some distance."

"Okay," Lenkova agreed. "It will save us a lot of time, especially since you say we are really close to him now." She issued a number of orders, and a dozen fighters galloped off down the road, while we pulled the wagons onto the road. Ah, yes, smooth riding! Such a wonderful sensation! To say nothing of our speed, we covered the five miles in a little over an hour. When we pulled the wagons back onto the rough dirt track once more, I regretted it had been so short!

The Sisters enjoyed riding way out in front of us, so when we began heading east down the valley between the mesas, the dozen continued to do so, joined by Lenkova and Mara. Since we were now very close, Caitlyn suggested I join those up front. I gave her a big kiss and gladly mounted up to join Lenkova. However, right behind me came Alton, Andre, Waverly, and Elona. I guess we all had the same idea at the same time; none of us had used telepathy this time.

We rode on for several miles, and the sun was low in the western sky when we heard screaming and yelling up ahead of us. I was concentrating on keeping a tenuous contact with Alabaster and felt sure that the noise was coming from his location. I ordered a full charge to find out fast what was going on. I had visions of finally finding him only to lose him to some bandits! Just as we rounded a hill and curve in the track, we saw twenty Holy Paladins standing on the ground wresting with two women. Actually, wrestling with one of the two; she was screaming, as they were attempting to rape the pair.

Half of her clothes had been ripped off, but she was not fighting against those who were trying to force themselves on her. Rather, she was begging and pleading for the men to leave the other woman alone. Her companion was muttering strange words, waving her hands just as if she was preparing some druwid spell, but the words, as we drew close, were utter gibberish. I yelled as loud as I could, "Leave those women alone!" We nineteen came galloping towards the group of men.

Lenkova barked to me, "Defensive only!" Turning to her Sisters, she called out, "Form standard line." I knew what she meant; the Sisters were not an offensive attacking group. Instead, as I had seen before, they would dismount and let these men charge into their hastily formed line.

I notified Andre and Alton, "He's one of those women. Protect them at all costs." There was no further time for words. All reined in some hundred feet from the Holy Paladins who were also rushing to form a melee line. Hanging onto my pole, I leapt from the saddle, joining with Andre and Alton. We were acting as a spearhead for our side.

Behind me, I heard Waverly order Elona to help her grab the horses and prepare to help her assisting any that were wounded. I caught a fleeting smile from Lenkova when she also heard Waverly. She wouldn't have to use one of her fighters to handle our horses.

When the men saw that we were primarily women and were not charging cavalry, their hastiness relaxed. A tall man with some braids upon his chest grabbed a hold of the screaming woman. He yelled encouragement to his men, "What have we here? More women. Go easy on them, and there will be plenty of sport in bed tonight!" With one hand, he held a vice grip on the upper arm of the woman, who had now stopped screaming. The man who had been ripping the clothes off the other one tried to do the same thing, but she kept wiggling and struggling, waving her arms back and forth, calling out nonsense.

Since I needed room, Andre and Alton spread out on either side of me. Actually, I was at the point of our defensive line, several feet ahead of the others. Somewhat behind us, the Sisters spread out so we couldn't be flanked. The fighters in blue rushed into us. My pole was a whirl as I carefully watched my opponent's moves and countered. My follow up swing usually connected. Both Andre and Alton tried their best to stab at those I dislodged while they were fumbling and recovering. Twice they were successful, but usually, they had their own hands full, parrying, and thrusting at their own opponents.

I heard the clank of steel upon steel and knew many of the Sisters were defending against the onslaught. For once, the odds were even up at the start. However, as I upended my third opponent, I realized these men were much older than the younger ones we fought earlier. Indeed, these were seasoned veterans, and I suspected they were ex-Centurions! I managed to stun another one.

Meanwhile, well over half rushed into the line of Sisterhood fighters on either side of us. Typical of their style, they gave way to the forward momentum of the rushing men, doing their best to dodge the thrusts and slices thrown at them. At the last instant, each woman attempted to pivot on her left foot, allowing their right to swing in a big arc, coming around, and smashing the opponent in the back of their heads. If the Sister didn't lose her footing and if the opponent was caught off guard or knocked ajar, then the Sister plunged her blade into the back of the opponent as he moved past her position. In a sudden life and death melee, this is a lot of if's. Four Centurions fell because of this initial tactic. However, these men wouldn't fall for the same action a second time.

As a preventative measure, as the charging line of Holy Paladins moved past the initial line of the women, Elona raised her fire sheet barrier, placing it between the melee and Waverly, herself, and the horses. Her idea was to discourage any of them from continuing their rush and next attacking them. Of course, she could raise and lower the edge that touched the ground so they could pull wounded Sisters back to relative safety. During this initial charge, though four men went down, three Sisters also failed to dodge totally the sword thrusts and were wounded. Cleverly, the Sisters reformed their line with their fallen behind them, hoping Waverly and Elona could somehow get to them. Waverly circled wide to the left, while Elona did the same to the right, each hoping to get around the combat to reach one of the three wounded Sisters.

Their tactic worked partially. While Waverly managed to get behind the Sisterhood lines, a Holy Paladin moved to cut Elona off, forcing her into combat and the melee. Had she been a tenth year Protector, I would have had no worries about her safety, no more so than I did for Alton or Andre. However, she was not! The sudden fury of the man, coupled with his sneering, condemnation of her skills, evaporated her training. She barely could manage to parry his deathblows and retain her sword. From the corner of his eye, Alton saw her dire plight. An anger rose in him that I have never witnessed before. With a violent smash, he ended his half-minute duel with the Centurion who was on him, whirled to look at the back of the man hacking and slashing at Elona. He muttered a chant that I didn't recognize or have forgotten if I did know it. Wham! Some kind of energy beam shot through the air, colliding with the man's head.

Shocking was the scene; even Elona cried out in terror and dismay.

Where the man's head had been was now empty space, filled with a small fountain of up-rushing blood. Slowly what was left of the body slumped to the ground. She stared at the headless form and then at Alton. She saw another rushing to plunge his sword into Alton and that brought her out of her shock. "Behind you!" she screamed. He whirled and stuck out his sword at waist level. The Centurion took the blade in his belly. As Alton turned around, he saw the look of total surprise on the man's face, before it faded into lifelessness. Violently, he pulled his sword out of the falling body.

Three more Sisters were down, and Waverly was kept busy rushing from one to another, trying to stem the flow of blood as a first step. Elona ran to join her, duplicating her tourniquet actions. Fortunately, only five Centurions remained standing; two were back holding onto the two women; three were battling with us three Guardians. We heard the sound of galloping horses and knew the rest of our group was rushing to our aid. Their leader saw them coming and screamed, "Back off, or I'll cut her throat!" The other man put his sword against the still struggling other woman, following suit.

At that moment, I knocked my man out with a good pole thrust to his private parts. He went down. Alton and Andre forced theirs to back up, and they decided to retreat to where their leader was standing. Alton's eyes still radiated violent anger. He dropped his sword, which instantly startled me; he would be defenseless if they came at him again. He called out, "Andre, take the one on the right." He chanted briefly, raised both of his hands high over his head and then threw them down as if he was throwing daggers at the leader, whose sword was up against the woman's throat.

Thud! Thud! A sickening squishy sound resulted, as a pair of black rod-like sticks appeared protruding out from the man's eye sockets, where his eyes had been. Now I recognized the spell. I had only seen this one used once before. Well over fifty years ago, when I was a little girl of six in Uru, the Galts had raided out village. Loremaster Ellen had gathered us at the center of the village and placed walls of ice and of fire encircling us, preventing them from reaching us and harming us. Their leader finally broke through and tried to kill Ellen. She reacted using this same spell; two rods appeared to fly straight into his eyes, blinding him permanently.

Here, however, so great was Alton's anger, that his rods had gone clear through the leader's head, stopped only by the inside back of his skull. He died instantly. Andre's likewise. The remaining Sisters pounced upon the two remaining men, slaying them, while one stepped beside me and jabbed her sword into the heart of the man I had knocked unconscious. The battle was over by the time our help arrived. We were also very out of breath.

Waverly took charge at once, "Get fires going. Boil lots of water. Elona, go get all our healing pouches. Get us some blankets to lay the wounded on quickly. Here, let's get them organized by the seriousness of their wounds. Put the worst over here." I was so exhausted that I couldn't have moved the wounded, even if I had wanted to do so. Many fresh hands began to do the work. Several took charge of dragging the dead men out of the way, making a pile of them, and then stripping them, searching for anything of value.

Caitlyn, dear Caitlyn, she and Fianna brought a water bucket and cups around to those of us still standing. I drank heavily and thanked her. Two Sisters carried a pair of blankets over to the two women we had rescued so they could cover up their near nakedness. Alabaster! I'd forgotten all about him in the rush of things. I walked over to the pair and said, "You are safe now. We are your friends. We are here to rescue you." I looked at the one I felt certain was Alabaster's new body, and added, "Alabaster, I'm Bethany. I finally found you!"

She muttered, "Martha, we must make room for Bethany and her companions. They are due here any day now. I went for a walk in the snow and nearly fell in the pond. Why are the chickens laying their eggs in the daytime? Not now, Martha, I am counting. Ellen, you do what you think best and we will back you all the way. A storm's coming, I do love storms, la-di-da-di-do. Roy, Bethany is dead. Dead is Bethany." Her voice finally trailed off into silence, as she wrapped herself in the blanket and rocked back and forth on the ground, like a small child.

The other woman hastily said, "Please don't hurt her. She doesn't understand much. Allyah is not right in her head. Thank you for saving us," she added. "I'm Yannah Muffti; she's my older sister. Please don't hurt her; she doesn't understand much."

"I'm Ket Bethany. I have been looking for her for a very long time. I believe I can cure her of her madness. Yannah, you're now in the safest hands on all Tarra. These are Sisterhood fighters from Zargarb, and we're from the Greenway, far up north. You are now very safe indeed."

She stared at the women as if she had not seen them before. "Really? Sisterhood all the way out here?" I nodded and she did relax. I saw the tenseness in her body completely drain away. I headed back to help with the healing.

"How bad are we?" I asked Waverly, who had just stood erect for the first time, stretching her back.

She looked at me and said, "Damn, you're hurt too!"

"What? Where?" I hadn't felt anything. She pointed to my right arm; my shirt was torn and blood soaked. "Probably just a scratch," I replied. Ignoring me, she tore my shirt away to have a look at it. It was on the back side of my upper arm, so I really could not see it.

"Okay, over there, get in line. It isn't bad, just needs some stitches. We have three on the critical list. Seems nearly everyone has some battle scar from this one."

"Well, I can help now. You can fix me up later on. Let's get going," I replied. Alton, I saw, was in the middle of the line with wounds in three places, though none life threatening. Andre and Lenkova each had a pair of cuts as well. I joined Elona and Waverly; we had to deal with the three critical ones first. Following Waverly's orders, I tended to the Sister whose arm was cut to the bone; a tourniquet had temporarily stopped the bleeding, but the main artery had been severed. I wished my dear old friend Sarah Jane was here. She had once sewed up one Sister nearly as badly wounded as this one was. Since I had helped her, I attempted to do what she had done.

Using the tiniest needle and thread that we had, I managed to reconnect the large artery. An hour later, the wound tightly bandaged, I released the tourniquet and prayed my work would hold. I held my breath for several minutes, not daring to breath, as if the mere force of my breath might somehow bust the stitches. For now, it did seem to hold, no major gushing of blood occurred.

Waverly, on the other hand, was having a devilish time with the worst case. The Sister had taken a sword thrust through her chest. Massive internal bleeding resulted. In order to save her life, Waverly attempted what only a Healer should try: she cut the woman's chest open, revealing the wounded organs, and tried to sew them up. She was only half done when I finished with my first Sister.

Meanwhile, Elona, following Waverly's orders had managed to get a serious leg wound sewn up, saving the leg. Now we moved down the line to those in less trouble. Only we discovered that Alton and Andre had already handled over half of them. They've patched each other up first and then set to work on those with the smaller wounds, mostly serious cuts. Naturally, Andre first sewed up the new wounds on Lenkova's right leg and left arm. She grittily commented, "Now I have balanced scars, one on the left and one on the right. Just don't you *dare* tell me I need two weeks of bed rest!" Andre was too tired to jest back.

Thankfully, with four of us now working on the lesser wounds, in another hour, we had them all patched up. I was the last to get sewed up; once more, I had completely forgotten about my own cut arm. Alton did the sewing on me. Only then did Waverly finally rise. "Well, I've done all that I can. In hindsight, perhaps we should have brought a Healer with us. I've used a Mind Link back home and tried to follow the Healer's directions as best I can. I've never tried to cut someone open before. It's lots harder than it looks. So many things inside the body. I wonder what they are all used for?"

"Will she live?" asked Lenkova.

She shrugged her shoulders, "Your guess is as good as mine. If I had done nothing, she would be dead by now. She's still breathing, so that's positive, I guess."

"Again, I cannot thank you enough for saving our lives," Lenkova said sincerely. "Have you found the person you have been looking for? I thought it was a man."

"Well, yes. We've finally found Alabaster, only now he has a woman's body," I answered truthfully.

"But she's crazy?"

"At the moment. I said I knew he or she was in trouble. If we can get her somewhere that is safe, peaceful, and quiet, we can see if we can cure his or her insanity." Of course, I had no idea whether this was possible or not, but I had to keep up appearances and not show my disappointment. With the Grey Creature situation escalating out of hand, I desperately needed to talk to the old Alabaster, the wisest man I have ever known.

Yannah Muffti strained to overhear our conversation. She heard enough to rouse her curiosity. "You can cure my sister?" she asked me, a great longing in her eyes.

"He or she was or rather is a very great friend of mine. He got this way because of trying to help me. I'll devote the rest of my life to getting her back to normal. I pledge this to you Yannah. Only we have to first get everyone to some safe, quiet place, where we cannot be disturbed."

"You go to see the Lady in Blue, too. That's where I was taking Allyah, when these bad men stopped us. Blue Lady gives everyone sanctuary at the Grey Havens with the Holy Order of the Blue Servants of Jehosa. You take us there, and we will be safe, only safe place in all the Arad."

"I'm sorry. I don't know anything about this Lady in Blue. Originally, my plan was to rescue Alabaster, er Allyah that is, and take him back to the Greenway, where she would be completely and totally safe from any harm," I replied. "At the moment, we dare not travel until our wounded have healed enough."

Lenkova broke in, "Look at how much trouble we had getting this far, Bethany. We are now more than half way across the Arad. Going back the way we came is going to be risky."

"Aren't we forgetting something?" Waverly broke in; she'd just joined us, teacup in hand, her first real break from all the nursing. "Alabaster. Shouldn't we have a look at how she is doing? Yannah, is your sister physically well?"

"Oh no. She is very sickly. Something is wrong, but I don't know what it may be. I hoped to find some help from the Lady in Blue. It is said that she can heal. I prayed to Jehosa that she might heal Allyah."

"That settles it, boys! Yannah, we four are great healers ourselves. I'm going to have a look at her. Let me look first, guys, she may be very edgy around men," Waverly ordered. I knew she was right. How had I forgotten even to check her out? I guess it was the strain of having to do so much emergency work on our Sister friends.

"Yes, how do you know that? She is often terrified of men," her sister replied.

Waverly walked over to where Allyah was still lying on the ground on her blanket. In fact, during all this time, she had not moved from the spot where she had been forced to the ground by the paladins. As she approached the young woman cautiously so as not to unduly frighten her, she heard her mumbling nonsense sentences, bits of dis-related, old conversations. "Hi, Allyah, my name is Waverly. I am here to help you get your body well. May I take a look at how you are doing?"

"The first birds of spring are here, Martha; oh how I wish my wife was here to see them. I am not well, I fear. Heal me. Before you go, there is one thing that I must tell you." She paused, having forgotten what that thing was. Waverly realized she had actually answered her question, only in a rather roundabout way.

"My, you are overly warm. Fever. Something is wrong." Carefully, she looked for any physical injuries, beginning with her head, half-hoping to find a head wound, which might account for the insanity factor. Finding none, she went on down her body, asking if it hurt here and there.

"The horses are all accounted for, father. Can I play now? My feet hurt. Come on; throw a lightning bolt at me; I must learn to deflect it," Allyah's voice continued muttering, but Waverly did not understand what she was saying.

She checked her feet and exclaimed, "Good gods! Badly infected feet." Then, she got a whiff of something else. "Yannah, have men had their way with her before?"

Yannah, near tears, answered, "Yes, four times now. I couldn't protect us from all the vile men. Is she bad?"

"Allyah, can the other healers come and look too? They are men, but they will help you, not hurt you. I need their opinions if I am to help you."

"Will you look at all the green? My love, I dearly love this land, let's make our home here. Not hurt me. Okay. Ride, ride like the wind; don't look back. Ride!"

We took that as a yes and slowly joined Waverly, who whispered, "Feet and womb. High fever. What do you think, Bethany? You've had more experience with this kind of infection than I have had."

Allyah muttered, "Ducks are swimming in the pond now. Do you think it will snow? Bethany. I know you. Have you come for me? Erline must be classified as a renegade druwid for now, there is no other choice; but mark my words, one day she will help save us all."

"Yes, Alabaster. I am here. I've come for you. I promise I will help you," I replied, choking back the tears. We three examined her body, even more gently than Waverly had done. We did not want to upset her any more than necessary, if she was terrified of men mistreating her.

"Mother, I don't like spinach! Thank you. I knew you'd come. Martha, I am a bit old for this, but would you care for this dance around the stones?"

"Perhaps she is just delirious from the fever," Alton offered.

While we were discussing this as a possibility, Yannah dashed our hopes, "No, she has been like this since she was born; our mother said so. After they killed mother, I've been looking after my older sister. She is all I have left. They have killed everyone else. Please save her."

"Daddy, I want a puppy like William has, please daddy. . ." her voice trailed off. She fell unconscious.

"We have the water hot once more," Lenkova notified us, hobbling on one leg toward us. "My god! Her feet. Oh, no!" she saw the infection in her womb and nearly gagged. She quickly turned away and hobbled back to her Sisters and the fire.

"Alton, Andre, you each take a foot. Bethany, you and I get this mess. Where do we even start?" It was the first time that I heard Waverly become so disheartened. I knew that this was far beyond her or my healing skills. When my Lightning Circle had found Isabel, it was our Healer, Sarah Jane, who actually managed to save her life from the massive womb infection that Isabel had contracted.

"Mind Join with the best Healers back home. Have them tell me what to do," I ordered. She was very willing to follow my lead on this one. I remembered that Sarah Jane's first action was to clean out the womb, so I began with that. Taking a rag, I soaked it in the kettle of boiling water, and pulled it out with a stick. Once it cooled slightly, I began wiping.

I felt the mental tug as Waverly's Mind Link formed. I sensed many others were now with me. *Ellen Sarah Stanton Donegal here. Justine Weatherford here. Elisa Greentree here.* Four more announced their presence. Waverly had hooked up with seven of the best Healers in the Greenway.

I sent, *Look through my eyes.* I was prepared for their reactions and had steeled my mind from any startled jolts. Good thing that I had. The number of "Oh my gods!" were numerous.

Ellen Sarah recovered first, *What supplies do you have?* I let Waverly discuss that with them, while I continued the basic cleansing action. I knew that all seven would be heartbroken to hear how poorly equipped we had become. We've already used up nearly everything we had most recently acquired.

Finally, *Ellen Sarah sent, Mom, I'll guide you through this. Trust me. Sarah Jane taught me well.*

What I wouldn't give to have Sarah Jane here with me now!

I know, but her new body is still too small. The others are conferring, and I am passing along what we all agree is the best thing to do. Okay, now here we go. Time passed ever so slowly for me. While the others back in the Greenway could see what I saw, I wished that they could also take over control of my body — just go ahead and perform the operation with it. The sun was setting in the west when I finally finished and Waverly broke the connection, but not before Ellen Sarah sent, *Very nicely done, mom. I couldn't have done better myself. Contact you tomorrow. By the way, everyone says very well done on finding Alabaster.*

Alton and Andre had long ago finished their part. They had lanced the worst parts of the infection, drained out the puss, sterilized everything, and nicely bandaged up her feet. Both were waiting silently by the campfire, along with Elona, Lenkova, and Yannah.

The Sisters had already made camp and disposed of the dead bodies in a mass grave. Additionally, they had confiscated all twenty horses, claiming that there were of good breeding. Caitlyn brought me some supper and I ate hungrily. However, now my shoulder was indeed hurting from the sword cut, and I was more fatigued than I had been in a very long time.

"Well?" Andre asked the question on everyone's mind.

"Too soon to tell. We've had the seven best Healers in the Greenway working together on this. I just followed their orders. However, the consensus now is quite optimistic, though there is some question as to whether she will ever be able to bear children. They messed her up pretty badly. The Healers say that if the fever breaks, she will likely mend. However, we shouldn't move her until the fever breaks. And how are our other patients?"

Several Sisters overheard me and called out in a chorus, "We are doing just fine. Thanks!" One Sister came over to Yannah, "Here, we found some clothes that we think will fit you. Give these a try. You can change over there behind that wagon. The men can't see you there. Bethany, here," she handed me a dress, explaining, "Camilla sewed this together after dinner. It's for her sister. None of us brought any dresses with us, and yours are way too fancy. We figured you needed her wearing an open dress so you can see." Her face flushed; she did not finish her sentence; she didn't have to, however.

"Many thanks. Yes, it will be perfect. You are very observant Sisters. For some time now, we will need to be able to watch over her personal parts. Once she is healing nicely, I'm sure she would rather wear something more practical." She grinned sheepishly and returned to her companions. Waverly took the dress over to the unconscious Allyah and removed the rest of her torn clothing, replacing it with the relatively crude dress, which was actually ideal for our needs now.

I was so tired that I excused myself and crawled into our wagon. Caitlyn was there waiting patiently for me. As soon as I managed to get inside, she had my bed ready. As I lay down, she gave me a long massage, saying, "Very well done, my love. I knew you could do it." If she said more, I didn't hear it. I was asleep.

The next day after breakfast, we inspected our patients. Most were well on the road to recovery, save those who were more seriously wounded. Waverly's patient was still critical, occasionally coughing up blood, not a good sign. Allyah's fever persisted; we four decided that it might be somewhat less than the night before.

Once the inspections were done, a Sister came up to me and handed me another small book. "We found this on the leader. We can't read it, but figured you might."

I thanked her and joined the others around the fire for a mid-morning tea break. "Yannah, can you tell me more about this Lady in Blue that you were talking about yesterday. Where is she located? How far?"

"My mother said that shortly after the barbarian invasion, word began to spread about the Lady in Blue and her Holy Order. Mom said that the Lady offers sanctuary to anyone who is in need, even men, though not many. While I was growing up, I saw quite a few women in our village become so desperate that they just up and left, saying that they were going to seek the sanctuary of the Lady. So a week ago, when a gang in our village came and raped us one more time, I had had enough. I packed all that I could carry and led my sister out of the town, Al Tith, late one night. We've been walking on foot ever since. I am very sorry that I don't know exactly where the Lady in Blue's Grey Havens is located. I only know that it is high up in the foothills of the mountains, down near the southern border with the Southlands. I've been told that all you need to do is get close to them, and they find you. I do hope that is so."

"Well, it sure seems to be a lot closer than going back the way we came," I added.

Mara commented, "More importantly, there are not very many towns way down here in the southeast Arad, not large ones anyway. Long ago when the Infidels came, most migrated further north. There are some small villages with good watering holes. If we don't run into any more problems, we are probably ten days from where she is suggesting this Grey Havens might be located."

"Okay, then that settles it. When it is safe to travel, we make for the Grey Havens," I decided. Everyone was relieved. Considering all the trouble we had thus far encountered, Lenkova wanted all her Sisters to be in top shape for the return journey. That included herself, for she was still hobbling because of the pain in her other leg.

"Yannah, can you tell me about your life and your sisters? You see, if I know what all has happened in your lives, it may help me heal your sister's mind."

She was more than willing to tell me everything in hopes that somehow her sister might be made well in the head. Yannah was the youngest in her family of five. In addition to Allyah, she had an older brother. Her mother told her that Allyah was not right in the head, and that Jehosa would one day help her to become right once more. Until that time, it was our duty to look after her, since she could not do much for herself. Indeed, she had spent her childhood looking out for and after her older sister, who could barely be trusted to go to the bathroom properly. She saw it not as a chore, but as a fun game; she and Allyah played many games together. All was well until three years ago when a roving band of Galts attacked their village, and their father was killed defending his family and home. While life had been the barest survival when her father was alive, now it was a challenge just to put one meal on the table at night. Her son worked at whatever jobs he could find in the village, acting as the man of the household.

Last year, some Arad roughnecks got drunk and tried to have their way with the three women. Her brother died trying to protect them, just as her father had. Now things deteriorated; often there were only scraps for supper. Yannah stepped in and did many odd chores for bits of grain to help feed the three. She took in wash, watched over children, anything that she could barter for precious food. Then, a short while ago, the blue coats came to town and raped all three women; her mother died trying to protect the two girls. That's when Yannah decided to seek sanctuary with the Lady in Blue.

She explained that Allyah always answered your questions, but seemed to surround the answer with dis-related statements. She encouraged me to treat that as a game. Then, her strange behavior would not be bothersome. When she had finished her brief life's story, I promised her that she would never again go hungry and that her sister would always receive the very best of care, whether we received sanctuary with this Lady in Blue. Indeed, Camilla, our cook, hinted to me that Yannah ate like there was no tomorrow for the first few days.

Later that idle afternoon, I remembered the small book that the Sister had given me. I remembered that they had given me another one, which looked an awful lot like this one sometime ago. I went back to our wagon and found it buried under some dirty clothes. Since I had time to kill, I examined both of them. Can you imagine my shock when I read their titles written in the Arad hand? The Gospel of Jamal Mazra, Disciple of the Great Messiah and The Gospel of Amar Tarabulus, Disciple of the Great Messiah. Both were one of the two copies of the original works, hand-copied line by line by the scribes at Qaam. I recalled how Jes Amir had requested that each disciple take the time to write down all his teachings from their point of view and then make two copies in case the original was damaged. Somehow, these Holy Paladins had uncovered two of these original copies. Historically, these would be invaluable, especially to the true worshipers.

I showed them to Caitlyn and Fergus, both of whom were tremendously excited about them. "Laddie, can you read them to us?" he begged.

"Please," begged Caitlyn. Well, I really had nothing much to do, so I decided to give it a go. However, before long, all the Sisters who worshiped Jehosa gathered round our wagon, listening intently. Each felt they were hearing the holiest of words. Jamal had been a messiah prior to becoming a disciple, which meant he was a freedom fighter and warrior. Amar was a fisherman, and I appreciated his renditions far more than Jamal's. His were more down to earth and practical, untainted by any hidden agenda of driving out the Infidels, the Centurions.

Actually, to my amazement, these two had reasonably well documented what had occurred during those years. True, there was a bit of a fighter's slant present, along with disappointment that Jes had not come to slay the Infidels, at least from Jamal's point of view. Nevertheless, when compared with what we had been hearing preached by the Church of Jehosanity, these tales were noticeably different. I had a strong hunch that somewhere far down the road in time, these documents would be of immense value. I was not wrong, but that is way ahead of the story.

When I finished, I gave these two to Caitlyn and Fergus, who intended to take them back to their respective churches as a Holy Treasure beyond measure. Both of them realized just how valuable these two original gospels really were. Both they and the Sisters grew even more excited when I explained that originally, there were ten different gospels, one written by each of Jes's ten disciples. Naturally, I was highly encouraged to find a copy of the other eight.

By the third day, everyone was getting very restless. The temperatures during the daytime rose into the high nineties. Nights were, of course, chilly in this desert land. Further, we were but a few miles from the main, well-traveled north-south paved road. Anytime we expected trouble might find us. Making matters worse, another dust storm hit us on the third afternoon, making a mess of all our bandaged patients. Every wound had to be re-cleaned the next morning. Hence, we decided to get moving, after taking care of our patients.

Allyah's fever broke that morning; she was out of any immediate danger, though weeks would be required for her to heal fully. We still had no idea if she would be able to bear any children after she recovered. Our other seriously wounded Sister had stopped coughing up blood, but was very weak, slipping in and out of consciousness. Waverly was pessimistic that she would survive, and so allowed us to begin traveling once more. However, we no more than got the dirt cleaned out and the horses hitched, when a teary-eyed Waverly announced that her patient had died.

We solemnly buried her with honors. Lenkova put her hand around Waverly, "You did your best. I know. I watched you. Thanks for trying; no one else in our organization would have even tried. A tribute to your skills are the rest of us. So many of us are still living when we ought to be dead or minus limbs."

"I know, but I so wanted her to make it," Waverly cried. We all did.

Our solemn group finally began to roll once more. Mara had cautioned us that our water supply was getting dangerously low, another reason to get moving. She estimated that we could resupply at a watering hole somewhere south and east of our current position. Because none of us knew just where this Grey Havens was located, by mutual agreement, we headed for the southernmost portion of the Arad, planning then to head straight east into the mountains.

During the heat of the afternoon, we moved past the current mesa and then turned south down the valley between two more. As we neared the end of the valley, I recognized the landscape. I'd been here before with Jes. If my memory was right, a small village lay in the crossway between the four mesas; Fakir, was its name.

We rolled into the village of fifty adobe homes in the late afternoon. The buildings roughly encircled the large watering hole, which really was a small pond fed from an underground source of water. However, something else was going on here. We could see probably most of the adults in the town milling around the central plaza by the water. Only one horse was there, and it was still saddled. No one took any notice of us. I kept the wagons back in case we needed to make a fast getaway. Lenkova, Mara, and me, accompanied by ten fighters slowly walked up to the crowd.

Someone was saying, "But we don't have that many sheep anymore. You took so many the last time. If we give you another twenty, we will have none and die. You might as well just come in and assassinate us all."

A sneering voice answered, "It is your choice. You can pay us the twenty gold pieces or else we take twenty sheep."

"But you took the last coin that anyone in the village had last year. Between the Infidels, the barbarians, and you, we've nothing left except the rotting clothes on our backs. You want my tattered shirt?" The man began removing it in protest.

The cold, covert voice replied, "You've heard the Old Man of the Mountain's request. How you meet it is of no concern to me. I will be back to get your answer in three weeks' time." He turned on his heels, and the crowd parted, allowing us to get a good look at him. He was walking directly towards us on his way to his horse. He was dressed in very fine linen robes with rings, gold, and gem encrusted broaches. His moustache and beard were neatly trimmed and well oiled.

I was a bit furious with the extortion I had just heard. I acted a bit brashly. "Sir, may I have a brief word with you?" He stopped, holding onto his reins, which I took as a sign to continue. "I presume that you are a messenger from the Old Man of the Mountain." He gave a half bowing nod of his head, as if it were somehow reverent to acknowledge the Old Man. "I have just arrived. I have a message for the Old Man. Tell him that I know where he *is* and that I will soon be coming *for* him, to put an *end* to all this assassination business. Thank you."

The man's eyebrows rose noticeably. "You are not from the Arad? Are you threatening me?"

"No, I am not from the Arad. No, I am not threatening you. I am telling you to tell the Old Man that I am coming for *him,* and I will put a stop to all of your extortion and assassinations once and for all time. Just tell him that."

"And who should I say you are? I'm sure he will want to know," he said with an incredible sneer that sent chills down my spine. I could well imagine him calculating my assassination.

"Tell him that I am and always will be the right arm of Jehosa's Son, the Great Messiah. Tell him that Jehosa is not pleased with what you have done. Thus, he has sent me, the Long Right Arm of Jehosa, to put an end to this madness," I answered. I knew that I could not refer to any location in any country or to any directly traceable person. They would most certainly seek instant retaliations. So I kept it figurative. After all, when Jes was traveling and preaching, I was his right arm in many ways. I had not really planned on going after these assassins, but I figured it was high time that they had something serious to worry about — that not everyone was going to lie down and take their extortions. It was time that they worried seriously. Besides, the cryptic message would give them much to ponder. I bowed slightly, a certain signal among the Arads, that this conversation was over, that I would say no more. Courtesy demanded he nod, which he did rather reluctantly. He mounted and rode out of town heading west. I guessed he would use the paved roadway to return to the far north of Juda Arad.

Then, I had another idea, "Sir, excuse me sir," I got the attention of the man who was doing the talking for the village. I didn't know if he was their leader or just a protestor. "My party is somewhat low on water. May we spend the night at the edge of your town and fill our water wagon from your hole? If so, I will pay you twenty gold coins for the water. It is only fair; water is precious here in the Arad. Some might go so far as to say that water is its life blood." I took that passage directly from one of their prophets that I knew last lifetime.

Shock and disbelief met my gaze. All the adults gasped. Finally, the man exclaimed, "Truly thee are the mighty Right Arm of Jehosa. Yes, yes. Take all that you need!" I had just given them a way out of this extortion attempt, given them some more time to try to get their lives going.

I walked to Fianna's wagon; she already had them counted out. Grinning, she handed them to me, whispering, "Well done!" I grinned back, gave them to the man, and bowed in the traditional Arad manner. He returned the bow.

When I got back to the others gathered around the line of wagons, I said, "Okay, some will get our water wagon filled up. The rest of us will make camp on the other side of the town. No one is to say one word about whom we are or where we have come from. If these people learn even one shred about who we really are, the Old Man will surely find out, and the Sisterhood will suffer assassinations like mad or worse. No one speaks a word about who we are or the name of any town or village anywhere." Lenkova backed me up on this one!

Later on while we were all together eating dinner, compliments of Camilla, Lenkova asked the question now on everyone's mind. "Bethany, are you really planning to go searching for their lair and attack them?" Instantly, everyone, absolutely everyone, stopped what they were doing and listened to what I would answer!

"No. I just wanted to give those people a dose of their own scare tactics. You know, make them fret and worry for a change. There is always a remote chance that they will stop extorting and assassinating people, if they think that Jehosa has sent someone after them. Besides, you know I hate violence. I'll fight to defend, but I always try reason first, when possible. Who knows, maybe this will bring their leader to his senses." I chuckled, "Besides, I gave them a good allegory to sort out. I expect that Calli would be able to determine just who I was from what I said to him. Since these are religious people, perhaps if they reason it out, they might desist in further extortions." Everyone relaxed; I suddenly realized that most thought that I had been serious and would soon be heading north to attack them.

Later that night when Caitlyn and I were lying beside each other in our wagon, she said, "You know, I have already figured out what you meant by the Right Arm of Jes. You are the Holy Blessed Mother, was always with him, and was his right arm, according to all our teachings. I'm worried that if I figured it out, so will these assassins."

"Perhaps not. You see, they have already dismissed all traces, or nearly so, of the wife of the Great Messiah from their lore. No, only those who follow the true teachings will have any chance of figuring it out. I assure you that these assassins, even if religious, have long forgotten all about his wife. Then, again, they might just figure it out. Even so, they will have no idea of my current identity. Well done on figuring it out, dear. I had to think fast and that was the best I could invent." She gave me a hug and we kissed.

The next day, I resisted all attempts by the grateful townsfolk to pump me for information, my plans, and such. Yes, they were most grateful for their timely rescue and wanted to share what meager food they had. In the end, I accepted a basket of dates, saying, "Jehosa is proud of you. Continue to follow the Decalogue and the teachings of the prophets and the Great Messiah." Again, I bowed, signaling the end of the conversation. They did likewise.

Quickly, we moved out, heading further south. Later on, Alton came up to me on his horse; I was driving our wagon. "May I have a word with you, Wid Bethany?" Gosh, he sounded very formal! I motioned my head toward Caitlyn. He said, "She is welcome to listen." I agreed.

"I've been thinking all night about what you said to that assassin representative, especially the part about you were coming to put an end to it. Personally, I would like to do just that, but we all know that it would perhaps take quite an army to get there and do the job."

"Yes, I think we are all clear on that," I replied, wondering what he really wanted to say. He was beating around the bushes with me. "Out with it, please." I pushed him slightly so that he knew that I knew that he was stalling.

"Well, Sir, there might just be a way to put them out of business, so to speak — one that does not require taking an army across the Arad to get to them. I've given this a lot of thought. If what Calli has deduced is correct, that they are in some fortified position very high in the actual mountains and not just on a hilltop of the foothills, there is one possible tool in our arsenal that might work to our advantage."

"Alton, please, just say it!" My mind raced over our skills and nothing came to mind. I hadn't the slightest inkling of what he had concocted.

"It's a Protector-only spell, Sir," he continued to hedge.

"Yes," I encouraged, still having no clue.

"Suppose that the very earth began shaking violently. In the mountains, why, it would bring any fortress crumbling down. I've talked with Andre, and he, too, believes that we can do it, with both of us joining forces, so to speak."

"You mean you can cause the very earth to quake?" asked Caitlyn in complete disbelief.

"Mind you, we have only done it to a small extent while practicing and learning how to do it. Neither of us have ever done it for real; it is a most powerful action, often with devastating results. It's not as if we can go outside of town and shake the earth; it would damage the buildings in the town. But we think that we can do it, and we wanted you to know that we are very willing to give it a try, should the occasion arise. I mean if we ever do get up north and ever do by chance come across them."

"Thanks for telling me. You might just have something there, Alton. I will keep that in mind. However, I have no plans for going north or for searching them out. I've only just found Alabaster, and we have got our hands more than full trying to figure out how to help him, I mean her, over her insanity."

Caitlyn interjected, "Remember what the gypsy said: 'You go north; you have blonde woman and many fine sons.'"

We both laughed and I said, "Caitlyn, you don't forget anything do you?"

She laughed and replied, "Not when you are involved in it."

For three more days in the sweltering heat we moved due south. I swore that the temperatures reached well into the hundreds! Our progress was slow, and heat stroke was present, particularly with the horses. However, the mesas now appeared far less tall and the towns less frequent. At last, we reached the great river that divided Juda Arad from the massive Southlands. There was still sufficient water for us to refill our wagon, though just barely. In the spring, the river was wide, though shallow. By midsummer, it would be nearly dry, and midsummer was rapidly approaching.

We camped beside the river two nights and one day; it took us that long to refill the water wagon! After that, we headed due east, following the bank of the river for the most part. The going was rougher, though, because of the hills, which further within the Arad, turned into the mesas. Four days later, we could see the distant green foothills of the Kathas Mountains rising before us, a most welcome sight for us, especially those from the Greenway. The next day, we rolled onto the green grasslands of the foothills.

Now the going became more difficult for the wagons. True, the baking temperatures abated, but now large boulders often blocked any straight-line path we might take. Constantly, we had to maneuver these large wagons carefully around obstacles. Also, we were now steadily climbing, each hilltop rose higher than the previous one.

Lenkova rode point. Midmorning, she halted the caravan and beckoned me to come have a look at what she found. I stepped down and walked to her. "Trails, lots of them," I commented as we met.

"Yes, glad you can see them too. I was worried that I would have to point them out to you. From the signs, I would say that these are horse trails, not deer or sheep trails," she observed.

"Absolutely. I agree, many horses have been going across these grasslands in various directions. Look at all the crisscrossing paths!"

"If I read this right," she continued, "they all seem to come from or head in that general direction. Perhaps we should head that way as well. What do you think?"

"Well, I've never heard of wild horse herds in the Arad, but that may just be old information. It certainly seems plausible that if we head that way we may find some habitation, a village perhaps. If so, maybe we can get some directions to this Grey Havens place. Lead on." She grinned, glad that we agreed so completely. All that day we continued on east, hour by hour we gained in altitude. The grey rugged peaks of the mountains grew steadily larger and more vast and imposing by the hour.

In the late afternoon, we came across a natural water bowl. A trickle of a stream coming down from the distant mountains filled up the basin before it overflowed and trickled on down the hill. It was a natural place to camp for the night. Also, many horse trails radiated out from it. Clearly, this was a primary watering hole for a great many roaming horses, though we had not seen any thus far.

Sometime later at dusk, while we were eating our supper, a Sister called out, "Look there!" Just north of us, some twenty-five horses stood about a half-mile away watching us. Purposely, we had made our camp on one side of the basin only. Lenkova insisted that we allow access to any horses that might show up to get a drink. After all, we all thought that this was their place, not ours. I imagined the horses must have been trying to decide whether it was safe for them to come down to drink or not. Our huge string of horses probably convinced them to try.

We watched as one by one they walked slowly toward us, ignored us for the most part, and took long drinks from this natural pool. Our horses whinnied quite a lot and some of these newcomers replied as well. I wondered what they were telling each other. Then like specters in the night, they quietly walked back the way that they had come, only breaking into a canter when they were some distance from us. Free spirits, these horses seemed to me, wild and free, though remarkably tame around people. Most curious, I thought.

The next day we continued pushing towards the mountains, covering some five miles until around ten am, the most curious thing I have ever witnessed happened. As we crested the next shallow hill, there stood twenty horses, obviously waiting for us. One, a large stallion, kept motioning a direction with his head. Suddenly, I realized that it was trying to get us to follow him! "Follow that horse!" I called out to Lenkova.

"I was just about to suggest that very thing. It is like the horse is trying to tell us something," she yelled back to me. We veered slightly to the northeast now. Around noon, we were reaching the end of the foothills. The rugged, tall mountains rose alarmingly steep only a mile further east from our location. Still the horses kept leading us toward the mountains.

Finally, we could see some kind of grey stone buildings in the distance, cradled up against the steep side of this mountain. "I think we have found the Grey Havens," Lenkova called out. If so, I could see why it was so named. Soon, we could see a fair number of people moving about and knew that if this wasn't the right place, there would be someone to ask.

As we approached, still led by the horses, we could see quite an establishment! The undulating hills had hidden much from view until we were this close. Several large flocks of sheep grazed on the grass to the north of the complex. Fields of crops dotted the landscape out in front of the buildings; each field had a low stone wall around it. Just to the right or south of the buildings, a small stream came cascading down from the high mountain behind it, forming a natural watering basin from which the stream trickled on down the foothills until it reached that pool by which we had last camped. People were working in the fields as well as watching over the sheep.

Lenkova spied a wagon-worn path leading up to the stone complex between the stream and the southernmost building. Instinctively, she headed this way; the horses seemed contented in our choice of path and stood like motionless statues, watching our caravan slowly close the distance. The air was clear and cool way up here at the very edge of the foothills. More than a mile high, the air was thinner as well. Still, the green grasslands were impressive, especially having just come from the near desert below with its oppressive summer heat.

Lenkova and Mara dropped back even with our lead wagon, which I took as a signal that she would let me do the talking. As we drew even closer, the herd of some twenty horses moved on up closer still to the buildings and then stopped, waiting patiently for our arrival. "Most unusual horses," I commented. Caitlyn and Lenkova agreed; neither had ever seen horses act this way before. We drew even with the first of the cultivated fields; a man waved to us and we waved back. One by one, others in the fields waved hello as well. Finally, the rutted path curved toward the first gray stone building. There standing waiting for our arrival stood a man and a woman. Surprisingly, the large black stallion that had been giving us orders trotted up to the woman, who patted it lovingly and said, "Okay, Big Boy II, you can go and play now. Thank you." He neighed once and trotted to the other horses, and they all cantered off out over the green lands.

We halted before the pair. The man in his fifties was definitely from Juda Arad; from his long brown beard and hair, I guessed Qaam or Amirite sect. He wore sandals and a lose fitting white robe of the kind often worn by their prophets. She, also in her fifties, wore a blue linen dress with deer hide moccasins. Her hair and face demanded my attention, however. Long, straight, silky black hair flowed down her back; yes, hers was longer than mine was! Her eyes were like shining black coals, piercing to one's soul. Her skin was most definitely yellowish, much more so than Lenkova's. However, she was stunningly beautiful, even at fifty-some years of age. I guessed she had to be from the Northern Steppes and thus a Galt! They each had an arm around the other. He spoke first, "Welcome to the Holy Order of the Blue Servants of Jehosa at Grey Havens."

She added in a soothing voice, "Do you seek sanctuary here?"

Chapter 27 The Grey Havens

I answered, "Yes, we seek sanctuary — well at least for a while, though perhaps one in our party may wish to stay longer. We've many wounded who need time to finish healing, and we have one special woman whom we wish to try to heal. I guess maybe it would be temporary sanctuary, if there is such a thing."

She replied quietly and formally, "Sanctuary is hereby granted."

He added, "Permit me to introduce myself. I am Prophet Emil Al Amir. This is my wife, the Lady in Blue." He bowed in the typical Arad fashion, while she merely nodded her head slightly.

I needed to do our introductions. "Gosh, our introductions are going to be a bit of a mess. If you get too confused, stop me. First, I'm the leader of our group, the Cymry Minstrels. We are troubadours from West Reach, or Cymry as we call it — the large island just off the coast of Velona in the Sea Princes. I am called Ket Bethany, but I prefer just Bethany. This is my sister, Fianna; my fiancé, Caitlyn; and Fianna's fiancé, Fergus from the Highlands of West Reach. This is Edgar from the Greenway and Jolina from Fortress d'Grange. Though blind, she is the best musician in their sector. Edgar is a famous musician in Calgary, Greenway. Together, we make great music."

Since neither interrupted me, I continued, "These are Alton, Andre, and Waverly, all from the Greenway; and this is Elona, the Priestess of Tur back in Velona and apprentice of Alton." Oops, I slipped, mentioning apprentice! I hurried on, hoping they wouldn't notice it. "We have been escorted by the Sisterhoods of both d'Grange and Zargarb. This is Sister Lenkova, the Zargarb Fighter Group Leader. This is Sister Adriana, Captain of the d'Grange Sisterhood Fighter Group One. Adriana and her Sisters have accompanied us all across the entire Sea Princes, while Lenkova and her Sisters has graciously accompanied us across Juda Arad."

"We came here because we were searching for someone, and we found her. She is called Allyah, but she is gravely ill and cannot walk at the moment; she is the one we must find a way to heal properly. Her sister, Yannah, ah there she is, she had seen enormous tragedies in her life and probably would like to stay here on a more permanent basis. It was Yannah who suggested that we come here, after we rescued the two of them from the clutches of some men intent on having their way with them." I tried not to make the description sound too horrible for Yannah's sake.

"In exchange, we can either pay you folks or we can give you all concerts as frequently as you desire or some combination. At this point, I know that we are an very large group to suddenly show up on your door step, and you may not have the space to house all of us. So if we are too large for you, would you allow us to camp nearby a source of water? We're all used to camping out in the open." There, I figured that about covered it.

Emil laughed, "Did you get all that, dear?"

She grinned, "No."

Still smiling, he continued, "She has already granted you sanctuary here. We must admit we've not had such a large group come visiting, as you suggest. We do have a large stone building that houses livestock during the wintertime. At the present, it only needs to be cleaned up a bit. I think that all the women could fit comfortably inside. We do have about a dozen guest rooms, which you are more than welcome to use as well. Probably your wounded would be better off in these rooms."

She added, "Sanctuary means that here you are safe and that your needs will be met, within reason naturally. However, if you wish to make a monetary donation, that would be greatly appreciated; it will help purchase additional supplies, should such be necessary. Long has it been since there has been any real music around here. I know I speak for everyone when I say that we would love some evening concerts. Perhaps the livestock building could also double as concert hall? We don't have a building that could hold everyone who would want to listen."

"Great. We can also play outside under the stars. Then everyone could bring a blanket to sit on and enjoy the evening. We've played for kings and nobles, but we honestly prefer to play to ordinary people, Lady in Blue," I replied. Actually, she had not yet given her name, so this was a subtle hint in that direction.

She smiled; your heart would melt if you had seen such a smile. "I can understand that perfectly now. Once, I would not have."

Emil added, "You are most welcome to attend church services as well. We hold them every Saturday afternoon, that is, if any of you are followers of Jehosa."

"Thanks, some will certainly enjoy doing just that. Currently, there is no prophet or religious teacher of Jehosa in Fortress d'Grange, and many of those Sisters would like to hear more about your religion. Many of the Zargarb Sisters are members of the church there. Back in West Reach, we also have many churches of Jehosa, which are well established," I explained.

A slight anger rose in Emil, "Ah, pity for those of you from Zargarb. Bandar ought to know better. I am afraid that he had made a travesty out of the teachings of the Prophets of Jehosa, even those of the Great Messiah himself. However, his alterations are nothing compared to the perversions done by the disciple Yazi, down in Magalos!" I could tell that he was particularly annoyed with Pope Yazi I.

Yet, he calmed down at once, "Ah, but you have worship of Jehosa in West Reach. That I did not know. So far away! I would love to know more about that."

"Oh that is easy," Caitlyn exclaimed; after all, this was her area of expertise, along with Fergus. "A large number of people from Juda Arad have immigrated to our island, making new homes and lives for themselves. My own church was founded by the wife of the Great Messiah herself; we call her the Blessed Holy Mother. And Fergus' church has a lot of prophets who came there from the Arad. Both he and I have been rather disgusted with all the alterations that have been done elsewhere in the Sea Princes. We would really love to attend your services; yours must be far closer to the original worship." Caitlyn suddenly wondered if she had said entirely too much and glanced at me with a worried look on her face. I noticed that both of them noticed her glance at me.

"Sure, we would be honored to have the opportunity to hear the word of God here," I hastily said, hoping to defuse anything. The man and woman looked at each other, although no words were spoken, I felt that they somehow communicated something.

The Lady in Blue warmly said, "Enough talk. You have been through a dust storm and need to clean up as well. Behind the livestock building you will find our bathing pool, which we use during the summer. Let's get you all settled in and cleaned up. Then we can talk more. We seldom get such interesting visitors, as you seem to be. At the evening meal, I will spread the word that you will be giving us a concert of music say tomorrow night, if that is fine with you. After you have dinner, let us all meet and talk long into the night. Until then, our sons and daughter will help you get settled in." She waved her hand, and three came walking out from a nearby building.

"This is Amin, our eldest. He will help you with the livestock building. This is Fakir, he can show you where to stable your horses and park the wagons. This is our daughter, Lenka, she can show you to the guest rooms and help with things indoors. If you have any questions, just ask them, I'm sure they can answer them all. Until this evening's meal, I bid you good day." She nodded and he bowed in the Arad manner. Arm in arm, they walked back inside another building.

Several of us followed Lenka inside to see the dozen guest rooms. Though small, all were comfortable and would sleep two of us. Three rooms were designated for us musicians. Two more for the Guardians. Lenkova and Adriana agreed to share a room. The remaining we used for the worst of our wounded, with Yannah and Allyah sharing a room. Once this was decided, we rejoined the others outside at the livestock building.

It was huge and would more than accommodate the Sisters, who had already begun to fix up half of the space into living quarters. Honestly, it did not need much cleaning at all. The pool out back would allow about twenty to bathe at one time. I suggested that the Sisters use it first, which they immediately accepted. Normally, they expected that we would have used the bath first. Quickly, they headed off to make use of it before I changed my mind.

Fakir explained to me, "We have the wagons parked here off to one side out of the way. Currently, the horses are crowded into the corral. If I might ask, do you plan to stay here for several weeks? If so, I would like to suggest that you turn your horses loose and let them wander about the countryside, grazing as they might. When you need them, the Lady in Blue can have them rounded up in no time. She has a way with horses. Besides, they probably will love to meet our horses. She has well over five hundred at her beck and call out there across the foothills." Fakir was about twenty-eight years old. We learned that he was married and had two young children. His brother was also married and two years older than him. His sister was married and two years younger than himself.

Lenkova and Adriana were reluctant to turn all our horses lose, so we kept six stabled in the corral, just in case. The rest were allowed to wander off freely in search of good grass and companionship of their own kind. We hoped this was not a terrible mistake. As we watched them trot off, I asked Fakir, "Say, I don't recall hearing your mother's name. Should we just keep on calling her Lady in Blue? It sounds rather awkward."

He smiled, having heard this question many times before. "Mom's a very private person. A word of advice, don't ask her any personal questions." That was all that I could get from him. Strange, I thought.

Time passed rapidly, we carried the wounded inside to their new quarters, emptied the contents of every wagon so that the sand and dust could be thoroughly removed, and then bathed. Caitlyn and several others also began a laundry detail; many sets of clothing needed to be washed. Interestingly enough, the Lady in Blue quietly examined each of our wounded, though she said nothing. Before we knew it, it was time for dinner. Lenka came to fetch us to her mother's table, while Amin notified those in the large building. I noticed one detail: these people ate in shifts. There was no way to feed so many people at one time. Hence, the community meals were done in shifts of fifty at a time. Periodically, Prophet Emil would excuse himself to say grace for each new group after they had taken their seats.

The meal was plain but nourishing, nothing fancy, but filling. Yet, everyone talked among themselves, sharing ideas and thoughts. I could see that this was a very contented community of people. Mostly the men were concerned about raising larger crops and building more stone buildings. Women worried more about making warm clothes for the winter. No one ever mentioned any kind of hostilities from the outside world. It was as if this community was totally isolated from the cares of the rest of the world far down below.

Once the lengthy mealtime was finished and the dishes cleared away, our hosts brought out a large pot of tea. I presumed it was time for a serious chat. Emil began, "You have given us much to ponder during the day. My dear and I seem to have a rather large number of questions to ask you. Mind you, here in the Grey Havens, we have a firmly established policy. No one has to say anything more than they choose to freely discuss. If we ask a question that you would prefer not answering, please feel free to say so. The Grey Havens is a sanctuary; you would not be here if you did not need a safe place, even if only for a brief time. Although we may be curious about certain things, you are under no obligation whatsoever to say more than you desire to say. We only ask that what you do say is the truth. Our doors are open to anyone who needs sanctuary. Yes, we even have given such to several Centurion soldiers a while back. Dear, you may go first."

She smiled at him and looked at Fianna and me. I knew what she was about to ask. She did not let me down. "I can't help noticing you have such long hair and so red! Is it real? How is it that a man loves such beautiful hair? I know it is such a pain to detangle and to dry. Your sister's is nearly as long as yours."

Grinning, I answered, "Fianna and I come from Cuch Glyn, a small fishing village in Tewdwr, West Reach. There, bright red is the most common color for hair. So yes, it is real. You have me though. I do have two vices. One is that I just love long hair; I can see that you too love it as well. I particularly love to have it blowing behind me when I ride like the wind across the countryside. It's always bushy like this after I wash it. She's been trying to get hers as long as mine. I think she has about made it now." Fianna and I grinned at each other.

The Lady in Blue smiled back at both of us. I knew that she also enjoyed riding like the wind. "Okay, I give up. What's the other vice?" she asked playfully.

Darn, I had put my foot in my mouth once more. "Er, I dearly love the name Bethany. In our village, we don't have last names. I am just Ket of Cuch Glyn. She's Fianna of Cuch Glyn. Since I have this male body this time around, I just couldn't figure out any other way to be called Bethany, unless I sort of adopted Bethany as a last name." There I had given an honest answer, without having to dive into past lives.

She commented, "There is much in a name. Bethany. Even in yours, Lenkova," she said looking straight at the woman. "Bethany is such a strange name around here, yet it holds much power. Are there many Bethany's in Tewdwr?" Lenkova gave me a strange look, wondering how on Tarra she had just entered the conversation.

"Er, no, Bethany is not a Tewdwr name. I don't think anyone is called that anywhere in West Reach, at least I've never heard any others with that name," I replied wondering where this was leading.

"And yet you prefer it," she commented. To her husband, she said, "Okay, your turn."

"I'm going to change my question, dear. I want to follow up his answer, if you don't mind. Bethany is a strange, yet powerful name. You say you love that name, but it is not known in Tewdwr. How is it that you decided that you had to be called Bethany? Forgive my unlimited curiosity."

He was a prophet. I knew I was on thin ice. However, I had my own questions. His last name was Amir, the same as my married name last lifetime when I was the wife of Jes Amir. Probably there were hundreds with this very common surname in the Arad. Still I was curious. "We are all immortal spiritual beings who inhabit these fleshly bodies for a time. I know who I was and what I did in my last two lifetimes before this body, though I cannot pierce that veil of blackness before those lives. In each of those, I was called Bethany. Yes, I had a female body twice before. This time I have this male body and, quite honestly, I am still trying to adapt to it. Caitlyn can vouch for that detail." Caitlyn grinned, but said nothing. "So I just naturally respond best if someone calls me Bethany."

Emil grinned, "Why is it so often the case that one answer seems always to lead to yet another question? Again, I remind you that you need not answer if you do not wish to. Yes, we followers of Jehosa are very familiar with the fact that we are all immortal spiritual beings, attempting to regain the great realm of Jehosa from which we were all cast out so very long ago. Around here, however, so very few can recall any former lives, that we prophets have such a hard time convincing them of their spiritual nature. It is a great pleasure to speak to one who is aware of what they really are. If you don't mind my asking, what were your sir names before?"

Why did I just know that he was going to ask this question? "Before I answer you, might I ask you a short question?" He chuckled and agreed, eager to get his question answered. "Amir. Are you anyway related to one Jes Amir, who died quite some time ago at the hands of the Centurions?"

His facial expression answered for him. Even the Lady in Blue looked surprised at my question. "How could you know? Yes, Jes was my cousin. There is great power in names."

"Okay, then I can answer you truthfully. I first was Elizabeth Stanton, Bethany for short. Last lifetime, I was called Bethany Madelyn Amir. I was Jes' wife. I apologize for never having met you. Honestly, Jes was so worried about bringing down the wrath of the Infidels upon his family that he never did introduce me to his relatives, outside his immediate family."

Emil's face turned ashen. Hastily, he asked, "And one of the twelve disciples was called Raul?"

Darn, he was testing me! "No, there were only ten: Amar, Hamah, Jebal, Rafha, Jamal, Ismail who was the darn traitor by the way, Bandar, Dez, Abu, and Yazi, whom I detested as much as he detested me. I told Jes not to accept Yazi, but he vetoed me on that one. In fact, he only overrode my suggestions with Yazi and Ismail. Six were messiahs; the others were a fisherman, a shepherd, a moneychanger, and a blacksmith. Actually, I got along best with Dez Madan, the blacksmith. Yazi hated women. I've heard that he has formed a Church of Jehosanity down in Megalos, and I fear for the safety of the women there." Little did I know just what an understatement this actually would prove to be, but again, that is for another time.

Emil relaxed and the Lady in Blue seeing this did likewise. I had satisfied him that I was who I claimed to be. He commented, "This is a Holy Day, Bethany. I believe you, for only a few of us know that Dez and Bethany were good friends. Even Bandar has written your part in the life of our Great Messiah out of the history books."

"Tell me about it! I know, we visited his church in Zargarb before we set out for the Arad. He has had some magnificent paintings made, depicting our Last Supper. All of the disciples have a fair representation in the painting, but I have been relegated to a minor, non-descript figure in the background. I thought it somewhat amusing, if not sad."

"I've always claimed that Bandar has perverted our religion. This is even more proof," he exclaimed, that anger swelling in him once more. I realized that there was some animosity between the two. Could they have met sometime during these years?

"My turn, dear," the Lady in Blue broke in, deftly giving her husband time to regain his composure. I think that she didn't like religious arguments. "I couldn't help noticing all your wounded. Some are indeed very serious. Had someone around here suffered such grievous wounds as they, many would not have survived or would have lost the limbs that you have saved. The only conclusion possible is that you are a great healer. If indeed you used to be the wife of the Great Messiah, it is said that she too was a great healer."

"Oh, I had a lot of help. Alton, Andre, Waverly, and even Elona. They all did as much as I. Of us, Waverly is the best, in my opinion," I didn't want her to think that I was the lone healer. Then, I thought better of what I had just said and thus implied.

She looked at me with those jet black, piercing eyes of hers, and coyly said, "I won't be distracted from my original question; I'll get to that in a minute." It was a tease. "Might I ask how is it that they came by these wounds? I know virtually nothing about this Sisterhood, only rumors of abominations, of amazon women. You do not look like abominations or amazons to me."

"Twenty of us came upon two dozen of Yazi's Holy Paladins — boy what a complete misnomer that is — anyway, these men were about to —," I looked at Yannah.

"Just say it," she declared miserably.

"They had ripped the two women's clothing nearly off and were about to have their way with them when we came along." I looked at Yannah and said, "No, I won't say it. You deserve better." Now looking back at the Lady in Blue, I said, "The two dozen now lie in a grave. Unfortunately, try as we might, we just couldn't save one Sister's life. She lies buried along our trail here. While I can give a summary of the Sisterhood, I think that Adriana or Lenkova is far more qualified to answer."

Lenkova hastily deferred to Adriana, who was more than happy to discuss the Sisterhood. She told of their origins, of how women had been so badly mistreated, less than second-class citizens. These survivors of male brutality banded together for survival. Over the years, they had developed into the best defensive fighters in the land — they had to just to stay alive. While not every woman learned to fight, many did. Others took on supporting roles so that all Sisters could live a decent life. "Some fifty years ago, all that had changed when the Guardians from the Greenway came through the Sea Princes. Bethany here led them. It is a matter of historical record how they managed to get the Centurions to force better treatment of women in the Sea Princes. The Governor stated that if a woman had her tongue cut out, then he would see to it that the Prince had his cut out as well. That forced a dramatic change in our treatment by men."

"May I interrupt," Emil broke in. "We've heard a strange tale about a one handed woman named Fiona whom Jehosa actually healed by re-growing a hand. We thought this was pure fantasy."

"No," Lenkova answered him. "She has passed away now, but I knew her when I was a very little girl. Her husband had cut her right hand off in a drunken rage. After her meritorious services to the Church of Jehosanity, Bandar Dero prayed to Jehosa and the Great Messiah. And yes, a miracle did occur. Her hand regrew. I shook it on any number of occasions. That is factually true. It was indeed a miracle." Thank heavens she did not mention my part in it!

"Hum, maybe Bandar has been doing something right? Could I have been so completely wrong about him all these years?" Emil wondered. "Indeed, a miracle long after Jes passed away. Most interesting! Pray continue."

I broke in with, "All of us have done both things of which we are proud and things of which we are anything but proud. I ought to know." The Lady in Blue gave me the queerest look. Not until later on did I grasp its meaning.

Adriana continued her description of the Sisterhood's history. "I joined up because my husband continually beat me. One day, he forcibly raped me. I vowed no man would ever do that to me again! I cut off his balls and joined up with the Sisterhood. Every one of those women here with us — every one of them has suffered physically or emotionally at the hands of men. Most hide their scars well. We do not openly talk about them." I was shocked to hear what had happened to Adriana. I had had no idea about her mistreatment.

She then went on to discuss what had happened after the barbarian invasions and how many of the sector's had rebelled against the priests of Tur and the Princes, taking over the reins of rulership by forming the High Councils. She described the horrors of the aftermath of the barbarian invasions and how the Sisterhood had come to the rescue of the common man.

Lenkova added many details since she had witnessed much of it in Zargarb as a young girl. Adriana described how the tradesmen had insisted that a Sister be on the High Councils to represent their interests. "So now for the first time in our history, we outcast women have a vote and a say in our government. Yes, we have come a very long way. We owe much to our strongest allies, the Guardians of the Greenway." She looked at Alton, Andre, Waverly, and me.

Lenkova added, "So you see in our Sisterhood, the Fighter Group Leader is responsible for the entire safety of the Sisterhood in that sector. Captain Adriana is second in command in her sector. If we should falter — well, so many lives depend upon us. Take my mother, for example. Rosita, during the barbarian invasion, she and her fighters — she was the Fighter Group Leader before me — she actually stopped and held off the barbarian leader and his forces. She made a sacrifice that saved the entire Sisterhood in all the sectors. She bore that bastard's children so that he would leave us alone." Lenkova was on her pet peeve once more and was quite animated and livid in her pronouncements.

What she did not see was what I did. The Lady in Blue's eyes watered, and she turned ashen for a time. Evidently, Lenkova's discussion made quite an impression on her. "Look, over a month ago, the darn Axemen sent five hundred plus fighters into Zargarb, heading for the location where we raise our children and our safe house for those who are trying to recover from the atrocities committed upon them by men. I took fifty of my fighters and our Guardian friends, and together we eliminated every one of them! Just crossing the Arad to find Bethany's friend we were attacked without any reason or provocation whatsoever by twenty-five or so of these so called Holy Paladins, Unholy Bastards would be a more accurate name. They didn't say anything to us, except that they desired to rape us all. They charged into us and we defended ourselves, eliminating all but two, who were cowards and fled the battlefield. Then, we came across those that were attacking these two young women. Men, there sure are a whole lot of nasty men around. However, I have learned something of immense value to me. All men are not bastards, though I thought they were for most of my entire life. If you look about you, there are some very worthy men, like Andre here. We are going to get married one day." Her rising anger gave way to love, and they both smiled at each other.

The Lady in Blue had regained some of her composure and managed to squeak, "I had no idea."

Her husband asked the next question, "So how is it that fifty of you could manage to eliminate a force ten times your size?" Lenkova flushed; she had sworn to me not to reveal our role for several years.

"We had some help is all that I am allowed to say at this time," she stayed true to her pledge.

"Accepted, Lenkova. Although that must have been some enormous help at ten to one odds," he replied. "Dear may I ask a follow up question?" His wife smiled and permitted him to ask, "I could not help noticing that some indirectly refer to you, Bethany, as also a Guardian. I am to conclude that you are one too? Does that mean that there are these Guardians in other lands besides the Greenway? And what exactly are these Guardians? What do they guard?" Looking at his wife, he said, "Sorry dear, that seems to be more than one question." Both grinned.

"Yes, I am one too. At this time, there are no Guardians in any lands but the Greenway, ourselves, excepted, at least none that I know about. The people in the Greenway were originally farmers and gatherers. None knew anything about defensive fighting to protect themselves. They are a peaceful folk who pride themselves on raising great crops of grain and have no thought of conquest of other lands. However, long ago, the Guardians were formed. Our basic purpose is to watch over the common folks, heal their injuries, advise them on matters that they cannot resolve, and to protect them from the aggression of others. Long have we had to fight the roving bands of Galts of the Northern Steppes, who infiltrated the eastern portions of the Greenway. Now, we are in a desperate struggle against the Axemen from the far north, who have cut a path through the Greenway so that they can attack the Galts and seize the gold and jewels that the barbarians took from the lands that they conquered. So all, in all, a Guardian merely looks after the well-being of the people who live there. Nothing more."

Alton added, "Long ago when the Centurions invaded the Sea Princes, we became allies of the Sisterhood, helping them to survive that mess. Later on, we were able to find a peaceful solution with the Centurions. The Greenway was next on their hit list, but we defused it completely. So we do prefer to find peaceful ways to handle the problems of life and resort to fighting only when there is no possible other choice."

"I see, a very noble purpose you have indeed. I am pleased to meet four Guardians. In some ways, you are much like the messiahs of old Juda Arad, except that they were more into fighting than much else," Emil commented. "Well, it's your turn once more, my dear."

She thought for a moment; I detected that there was some inner turmoil going through her mind. Finally, she seemed to have reached a decision. "There is something that I have been wondering about for a very, very long time. As a young girl, I was told all sorts of stories about there being Evil Witches in the Greenway. You know, the kind of stories meant to frighten young children into behaving. It was said that these Evil Witches could bring down fires from the sky, great bolts of lightning from the storm clouds, and even conjure sheets of ice, if the fairy tales are believed. I have always wondered about this. Is there any truth to this? Are there Evil Witches in the Greenway?"

Oh brother! I was on the spot, along with the other Guardians! You could hear a pin drop, so quiet was the room. Sisters nervously fiddled with their teacups, not daring to look up. Even though I could refuse to answer this direct question, our hosts could see that they were very near the truth just from all of the nervous reactions around me. I had to say something. "One of our principles is that only the truth sets one free. We believe that there are Seven Aspects of Live in which we dwell. In each Aspect, a man struggles to flourish and prosper. Naturally, the first one is self; one must do well in life. Next, comes the family unit; we all wish our families to flourish. All men belong to one or more social groups and these ought to survive well also. All of mankind should flourish, though for quite some time now, wars are blasting this Aspect nearly into rubble. Plants and animals around one need to survive and thrive, for we all would die if the plants and animals suddenly vanished. Then, there is the physical world itself and finally the realm of our true selves, the immortal spiritual beings. I must admit that the Great Messiah, while he lived, did more for this Seventh Aspect than any person I have even known."

"Thus, a Guardian is highly attuned to all of life, Nature, one might call it. As such, a Guardian has *command* of it, especially that of the physical world itself. An action is deemed poor if it hinders or harms more of these Aspects of Life than it helps. Only then do we call upon the natural forces of Nature to come to our aid to make right the imbalance. Yes, a Guardian can bring down fire and lightning from the sky, even bring ice into being for a short time. However, it is only ever done to bring balance back to Nature. Let me give you one example from my own childhood."

"Back around 550, I was a young girl in a small village of about fifty people; Uru, was its name. Uru was a peaceful farming community. That day, the men were out tending the fields, and I was playing in the dirt with my bare feet. Suddenly, a band of raiding Galts came racing out of the nearby woods, killing one of the defenseless farmers. They rushed into the village long before any of our fathers could get there. All of us children and our mothers gathered in a group beside the central well. We were lucky to have a Guardian living in our village. Ellen, though old, stood alone to face these men, who were waving their swords and shouting obscenities. Yes, if they had their way, the women would have been raped or worse. Anyway, Ellen conjured a circle wall of fire around us to prevent them from reaching us. Outside of that, she placed a circular wall of ice. She told them to go away and leave us alone. Instead, they hacked their way through the ice. Several tried to walk through the fire but were turned back after getting severe burns. Their leader tried to shoot Ellen next. Only then did she attack the leader back, killing him. Then, the rest fled, never to return."

"So no, there are no Evil Witches in the Greenway. There are male and female Guardians, who will do anything they can to protect their villagers from harm. Until recently, there was at least one Guardian in every town and village throughout the Greenway. Normally, however, we spend the vast majority of our time healing broken bones, illnesses, and settling disputes in a peaceful manner. Hence, of necessity, we have learned a great deal about healing mortal bodies."

I thought of a great way to end this discussion. "That's why Jes, the Great Messiah, so often called upon me to heal others who were sick or wounded. He claimed it was better to use what we know than to always rely upon Jehosa to heal our every wound. Still, when I could not heal someone, Jes would lay his hands upon them and work his miracles via Jehosa."

With Emil, that did the trick; it put everything into a proper perspective. However, I was still unsure of the reactions of the Lady in Blue. At first, she seemed somehow vindicated in some way, but then her attitude began to lean, not just to acceptance, but also to empathy. I found her most difficult to read.

Emil commented, "Well, Bethany, you are so right about the truth. After all these many years, I now have come to understand some of the Great Messiah's actions that until just now seemed a mystery to me. Now it is so clear. Yes, one should not depend upon Jehosa to do those things that you can do for yourself. Jes was a very wise man indeed! Only now am I beginning to see why it was that he had more respect for his wife than he did for his disciples, and that is saying something. Thank you."

He went on, "I should tell you a little bit about our story, about the Grey Havens. After the era of the invasions and the coming of the extortion plots of the Old Man of the Mountain, my village was in dire peril. Daily life was a nightmare, little food and constant threat of being attacked yet again over a crumb of bread. Hence, as the village prophet, I prayed to Jehosa for guidance. In his infinite wisdom, Jehosa gave me a vision to follow. I was to take all those who would follow me, pack up all our meager possessions, and travel into the foothills, heading south. In the vision, I would meet a Lady in Blue, riding atop a giant of a stallion. She would provide for us, giving us sanctuary. I did as the vision directed. Some hundred of us slowly walked this way, up out of the desert lands into this high country. Those few animals we had pulled our rickety carts loaded with tools with which to rebuild our lives."

"For days we walked and walked, knowing not wither we were going. Then one day, we saw the Lady in Blue riding a huge stallion our way. That did make believers out of my flock, I might add. Indeed, she has given us sanctuary here. Together we have rebuilt this ancient town, added new stone buildings and are thriving. To this day, her words to me are burned into my mind; I can quote them; she said:

> I have reached my decision. I will grant your desire for a new place to stay for as long as you desire under certain precise conditions. First, it is my obligation to help all people of whatever nationality or color of their skin that need assistance and are willing to accept my help. Do not ever ask why I do this or why I live with such an obligation. Realize that I may grant sanctuary to a person from the

Southlands, from the Sea Princes, from the Arad, or, yes, even from the Northern Steppes. Never ask why I do this. Just know that the person will be in great need, and I am able to assist him or her. Second, never ask about my past. Third, I will be raising a large number of horses, so there will always be horses around in quantity. Fourth, through my horse herd, I will provide for all our needs for as long as you desire to stay at the Grey Haven. Fifth, it would help us all immensely if you could lend a hand with helping to rebuild the place and helping to make us all self-sufficient. When winter comes, I expect the snowfall will be heavy. We will be completely isolated from the rest of the world. By then, we must be able to survive on our own. These are my only conditions. Are they acceptable to you?

I noticed tears forming in the Lady in Blue's eyes. He went on, "She has always been true to her word. We've sheltered hundreds upon hundreds of people, even Centurions and a few Galts as well. Her herd of horses numbers over five hundred; she has an uncanny way with horses. The Grey Havens has been just that a haven for one and all these past thirty-two years. Naturally, in time we fell in love and were married. You've seen our three children, and now we even have ten grandchildren to keep our days fully occupied. Oh yes, currently five hundred thirty-three people now reside permanently at the Grey Havens."

Lenkova, now that he had told us about the havens, asked the single question that she had wanted to ask since arriving. "How frequently has the Grey Havens been attacked? I need to know so that I can be prepared in case of trouble while we are here. It would be dereliction of duty for me to lower my guard. I am responsible for the safety of this party."

Emil actually laughed, "Sister Lenkova, rest assured that you and your Sisters can relax and live in peace, free from worries about attacks while you are here."

"You mean no one has ever come here to attack you?" she asked in complete disbelief.

"Oh you misunderstand me. Yes, yes, several times now various ones have come here seeking to raid or steal from us. However, the Lady in Blue always handles the situation nicely, or rather her horses do. The last time a band of Galts charged up here demanding gold. It's beside the point that we do not have hardly any, just what we exchange with nearby villages for supplies we cannot make here. The Lady in Blue merely summoned her herd of horses here to the buildings. You would be amazed how fast a band of ruffians will flee from five hundred plus angry horses! Every time we are threatened, the horses always drive them off. No one gets hurt. So you can indeed lower your guard while you are under our roof."

He yawned, "My how time flies in good conversations. We ought to let you get some sleep, hadn't we my dear?"

She smiled, replying, "Yes, the hour has grown late. There are more days that we can talk. Thank you all." Both got up and so did we. As we were preparing to head off to our building and rooms, the Lady in Blue said, "Would you Guardians and Lenkova stay just a bit longer? I would like a brief personal word with you. Emil, you too, please stay."

The others filed out, even Elona, who thought better of sticking around, for she was still just an apprentice. When the room was empty and the door shut, she said, "If you will promise me that you will tell no one outside of this room, I will tell you my name. It is only fair that you know it. There is power in a name; mine must remain unknown while I yet live. When you know it, you will understand why it must remain secret. Do you so promise?"

Naturally, we all did. She said, "My name is Zdlenka Al Amir; but you would probably know me better as Zdlenka Strokova." Suddenly so much made perfect sense. Lenkova gasped in complete shock, covering her mouth to keep from shrieking. "I am your aunt which you so despise. As you so wisely said, Bethany, we have all done things of which we are not proud. I have devoted my entire adult life to helping others who are in great need. Only by doing this can I find sleep at night. Lenkova, I cannot undo the atrocities, which I did in my youth. God, how I wish I could do that! But it is in my power to now be a force to help and so I have for the last thirty-two years and will continue to do so until this body fails me. Yes, Lenkova, there are some good men in this world, if you only look. I have been so incredibly lucky to have found Emil."

"It was the Will of Jehosa, Zdlenka, that brought us together," Emil corrected her.

Quickly, Andre put his strong arms around the trembling and shaking Lenkova. He carefully helped her sit back down. Her wounds made walking more difficult than normal, and this sudden shock was more than she could handle. Crying and talking at the same time, Lenkova tried to deal with the wild emotions flooding through her. "I have spent my whole life cursing the ground that you walked on! Now I find out that you are doing great deeds of which any Sister would be proud! Instead of reviling you, I should have been praising you. I am so sorry, Aunt Zdlenka. I just didn't know."

"Of course, you didn't. I did not even know that you were alive until a while ago when I finally worked out who you must be. Honestly, I nearly cried when I heard that you too had changed and have even fallen in love. You don't know how much such a simple thing means to me, Lenkova." She too began crying.

Hesitatingly, Lenkova extended her hand toward Zdlenka. The older woman did not hesitate; she grasped it firmly in both her hands. At once, the two women hugged each other tightly, both crying, both not saying a word. Emotions ruled for quite some time.

Finally, Lenkova explained, "I would never have changed if it weren't for the help of the Guardians and Andre here in particular. I'd still be a man-hater. I'm so confused right now!"

I offered a bit of wisdom, "That is only natural, Lenkova. All your life you held on to the datum that Zdlenka was a bad person. Now you discover that while she used to be so, she has been completely opposite for thirty-two years. Your stable datum is no longer stable, for it is blowing in the wind. Just pick out a new datum and latch on to that."

Between sobs, she said, "You mean like my aunt did terrible things when she was young, but has been doing great and noble things ever since?"

"Sure, is that the way you would say it?"

She brightened up suddenly; the massive confusion in her mind evaporated nearly as suddenly as it had come upon her, "Oh, yes. Wow. Yes. Oh, oh. This is strange, but Aunt Zdlenka, I do suddenly feel affection toward you and Uncle Emil! That's magic!" They hugged even tighter.

"Better only call me Uncle Emil when we are in private. Most folks around here do not know her name. You understand, there are many, many people who would come here just to seek revenge against her. Revenge never solves anything and only cripples the one who attempts revenge. So we must keep her identity a secret so those that would harm her do not get the chance to harm themselves out of their own ignorance of the way life works."

Andre commented, "Emil, that is an astute observation, if ever I heard one."

"Well, I am a prophet," he said wryly, adding a touch of humor to this emotionally packed scene, lighting the mood slightly. He added, "I suppose that we men folk ought to let these women have some time for themselves."

"One minute," Zdlenka insisted. "There is one thing that I must tell you Guardians. I don't know how things are in the steppes at the present. However, thirty years ago, the Galts were terrified of the Evil Witches in the Greenway. So much so, that they put off attacking the Greenway until last. So I don't think that you will have to worry too much about Galts invading your land anymore, perhaps isolated raids on the very borders would be about it. I thought you ought to know. I'm sorry that I thought of you all as Evil Witches way back then, but my thinking was totally clouded and completely self-centered and wrong. What you are doing is just fabulous. Speaking for just people, we thank you."

To Lenkova she said, "Do you feel up to more talking tonight? If not, there is always tomorrow."

"I've so much to ask you, but can Andre stay with me? My leg and arm hurts and, though I would never admit it to the others, I do feel very weak," she acknowledged. What a change in her attitude, I thought; before now, she would never have admitted it.

We headed to our rooms, leaving Andre, Lenkova, and Zdlenka alone in the large dining room. Andre and Lenkova had an arm around each other, while she held on to the hand of her aunt across the table from her. Andre reported that they talked for several more hours that night.

On our way back, Waverly suggested, "You know, these people would make a great ally on the humanitarian aid side."

"I was thinking the same thing," I replied. "I suppose that I ought to get an okay to do so from Wid John Henry."

She chuckled, "It would be the prudent thing to do. I'll contact him later tonight and see what he has to say. We are pledged not to reveal her name, and I can certainly see why. I will abide by my pledge."

Chapter 28 The Healing of Alabaster

The next day, Andre filled me in on the rest of their conversation last night. "So you see, Zdlenka has been through a hell of a lot. She has had the spiritual strength to open her eyes and see truth. Honestly, Lenkova was utterly shocked at what her aunt had endured. I can tell you that she is so excited about having an aunt that she can love and respect that she can hardly sit still!"

I explained, "Just so you know, I am having Waverly get an okay from Wid John Henry so that we can officially extend our alliance to these people here. I think that they are well worth assisting in any way that we can. The more pockets of true aid and assistance for the people of Tarra, the better."

"I kind of suspected you might do that. See, even more reason for me to end up staying in Zargarb when this is all over," he teased.

"I'm going to begin work on Alabaster. Want to tag along?"

"No way, not unless you need me. I am a Protector. Insanity is way out of my line. I don't have a clue what to do for him or her, now. Confounded confusing, isn't it?" We parted ways, as I knocked and entered the women's room.

"Hi, here to check on my patient," I said cheerily.

"Thank you so much," said Yannah, "Lenka said that we can stay here forever, if we want. I know how to sew and she said that skill would really be useful here. Say, if you are going to be a while with her, can I go out for a walk and get more familiar with this place?"

"Sure thing. You don't need to be back until lunch time." She readily grabbed a shawl and left me alone with Alabaster, er Allyah. "Hi, it's me, Bethany. I've come to check up on how you are doing today. How do you feel? Are your feet feeling better?"

She was awake, but as usual, I got a stream of dis-related sentences. Buried in the mist of the nonsense, was the fact that she felt a little better, but that her feet and bottom still ached. I was getting nowhere fast. When chatting with someone, it is terribly difficult to see what is going on in the other person's mind. At last, I decided to take a peek, alright, pry. I made the Mind Link and then asked her a question and watched what went on in her mind. Flabbergasted, I did this several more times to be sure of what I was seeing. Now it all made complete sense to me. I broke the connection and began to think about how I could possibly undo the damage.

Just then, Waverly peeked in. She'd heard from Andre that I was going to work on Alabaster and had come to offer her assistance.

"I've just had a look at what is going on in his mind. It all fits. I guess I'd better fill you in completely. Every time I have observed someone get sucked into their pole machine, from the outside looking in on them, I see that the machine takes their memories and scrambles them, shuffles them into a random order, and then adds in new, fake memories as well. Once the person's memories are a complete mess, they are then given the command to go find a new baby body and to report back here when that body dies."

"Now when you ask Alabaster a question, his mind is doing this same thing. First a bit of one memory appears and he says that part. Then, another random memory pops up and he recites it. Somewhere in the middle of the confusion, he does manage to get the right answer out to you. The real question is now what the heck do we do about it to fix him up?"

"Now I understand your comment the other night! We know a good deal about the workings of the physical world about us, we know some about spiritual beings, ourselves, that is. Yet, we know almost nothing about our own minds!" Waverly observed. She teased me, "So why haven't you Wids got this all solved already?" We both laughed.

"You aren't paying us enough," I countered, still laughing. "My initial reasoning goes like this. The Grey Creatures and the mantises used a physical universe machine to scramble memories. It probably uses some kind of energy as we do with our lightning bolts. If this physical machine can affect our minds, then we ought to be able to find a way to remedy the damage done. Only the how remains elusive."

Days stretched into weeks, the solution continued to remain just as elusive as it was that first day. One morning when I was quite frustrated at making no progress whatsoever, I left the room and went for a stroll around the sprawling complex. At least going for a long walk should clear my mind. Quite by accident, I came across a mother trying to teach her daughter how to weave a basket with which to carry produce from the many nearby fields. The young girl was all thumbs, trying to force the wet wicker this way and that. "No, no, like this. The first weave goes like this right here." She took the loose end and positioned it where it was to go. "Now this one goes over and under it like this," she patiently explained, showing her how it went.

Like a blast, I suddenly had an idea of how to help Alabaster! His memories were scrambled. However, some of them I knew because I was a part of them or I had seen him while he was trying to help Jes. I could show him how to put some of the pieces of dis-related memories back together, rather like stringing beads! I ran back to his room, eager to try my plan.

After making mental contact, I explained what I was going to do. I knew that I would be of no use with this lifetime memories, but then those were not scrambled. I decided to start with the last ones I'd had of him, when he was pulled into the machine trying to extract Jes from it. It took me an hour to find that bit of memory, there at the last instant before I had lost mental contact with him. I worked with him for four more hours, and we had finally gotten six bits of memory connected back together once more! Okay, so it was a sequence that lasted perhaps five minutes, but it was a start!

The Adventures of Elizabeth Stanton Series Volume 3 Of Kings and Queens and Troubadours

After two more days working eight hours each day, I had a nearly complete sequence from the point where I had begged him to help Jes up to his becoming sucked in himself. However, now that the whole sequence was restored, a new problem arose. As he began recalling or remembering that time span, he would dope off, go foggy on me, almost as if he was asleep! At first, I let him sleep, but soon gave that idea up. She slept for an hour!

Frustrated once more, I took a walk around the complex. Happen chance, I ran into Emil, who was inspecting a field of maize. "How are you coming on her insanity?" he asked.

"Not so good. I have some of his memories put back into their proper sequence, but each time I try to have him recall them, he falls asleep on me, sort of dopes off."

"A sequence of memories, funny way to put it, but you know, you're right, our memories are in a sequence, rather like memory following memory. Where was he at in these memories you've put back into sequence?"

"He was going to help a friend of mine and he got zapped," I dared not elaborate further. It was the Great Messiah that Alabaster was trying to rescue, and he was supposed to have long ago died on the cross back in Jerilum!

"Ah, and where is she now?" he asked.

"Oh, up in her room. Her feet are healing nicely, and I think that she can now come outside for short walks," I replied.

"Yes, but does she know where she is really at? Sometimes when a child gets sick with a fever, they don't seem to know where their body is really located. Perhaps she is not really aware that she is here," Emil suggested.

"Hum, I hadn't quite thought of it that way. You might be right. Excuse me. I've got to check this out." I fairly ran back to her room.

"Okay, Allyah, it's time to go outside and see the world. Here, lean on me. I know your feet are still tender, but the fresh air will do you good."

"Ducks swim until the ice forms, you know."

"Yes, they do," I replied. Slowly we hobbled out of the room and the stone building, out into the bright sunlit day. I stopped a little ways out so that she could see the steep mountain rising behind the buildings, the buildings, and the neatly terraced farming plots out in front of the buildings. In fact, we could see way out over the green rolling foothills, for miles.

"Where are you now?" I asked.

"I'm in my home," she replied.

"Fine, take a look. Where are you now?"

"I'm fighting the pull."

"Okay. Take a look around you, where are you now?"

I persisted, primarily because I could see that she considered herself many, many places other than right here outside the stone buildings of the

487

Grey Havens. After an hour, she brightened up considerably and began truly looking around. Finally, she said excitedly, "I'm here beside this stone building. Such a beautiful place. What is it called?"

"The Grey Havens. We are at the very edge of the foothills of the Kathas Mountains. See, right there the mountain rises sharply to the sky." She gazed around, seeing it for the first time. However, after a couple minutes, I noticed that she was slipping back into that dopiness, fogging out on me again. Sorry, but there are just no words to describe these phenomena.

Inspiration struck again. I asked, "Where were you when you got zapped by the Grey Creatures? Point toward the place." I realized that if I had not had her point to the location here in the real world, she would point to the memories in her mind, but those were only memories, not the real place. Somehow, I felt that the real place was what was important to locate.

She fumbled around and finally pointed off in some direction, not even vaguely the right direction. I asked, "Okay. Now where are you now?"

She looked around and replied, "Right here."

"Okay, now where were you when you got zapped? Point to it."

Another hour passed by quickly. At first when she came close to pointing to the actual direction of the Grey Creature's trap, she would suddenly fog out, as if this was getting too close to it, somehow. I just kept at it and noticed as she pointed out her surroundings that she pulled out of all that dopiness. Finally, she began to tire, and I ended up having to carry her back to her bed. Yet, I did feel like we had made some progress.

For two more days, I kept up this vigil. Emil dropped by to watch, became convinced that I was indeed making progress, and encouraged me to continue. Now I noticed that she was doing a considerable amount of yawning, especially when she examined where she now was. I took a quick peek into her mind and saw a much more orderly arrangement! Thus encouraged, I continued the procedure.

On the third day, she stopped yawning and suddenly looked all around. "Oh, I'm here. You're here. Bethany, right? Of course, Bethany. Ah yes, ah yes indeed. I feel so much better. Why do my feet hurt? Why does my bottom, whatever it is called, ache? Ah, you have come for me as I asked. Thank you. I believe that I needed some assistance. My, what a splendid view! I've never been here before. Where did you say we were? So peaceful."

I had tears of joy running down my face. "Alabaster!"

"Yes," he looked at me. "Yes, I am very glad to see you too. Hum, do you have a male body this time?"

"Yes, yes, not adapting to it at all well. How about yours?"

"Oh dear me! What are these protrusions on my chest? Have I been badly wounded?" He felt them and his face turned beet red. "Oh my. Breasts. Looks like the tables have turned on both of us."

"Yes, it certainly has. Your body was raped a number of times, and your womb got a terrible infection. I think it is healing, but none of us know if you will be able to bear children."

"What? Bear children, that's women's task. Oops." He realized what she was saying. "I'm afraid this will take some getting used to, won't it?"

"Yes, most definitely. Your younger sister has spent her life keeping you alive all these years. Your name is now Allyah and hers is Yannah."

He repeated them several times, before he said, "Arad names?"

"Yes. We've been speaking in the Greenway tongue, but you had better get your Arad up to speed or no one around here will understand you, especially Yannah, who thinks dearly of you."

"Hum, I do seem to have a lot of memories here. I had better scan over them and see what all I have more or less missed," she said.

"Let's do it back in your room. Your body is still on the mend. I don't want you to overdo it on your first day of recovery." Supporting a lot of her weight on my shoulder, we slowly went back inside.

I had her scan back over the memories of this lifetime. Now they all made sense to her. Any number of times, she would yawn deeply. After we scanned over them for the fourth time, she brightened up. "Well, I certainly can say for sure that this body would have been dead several times over if it wasn't for Yannah. She is all that remains of our family, correct?" I nodded.

Later on, the dinner bell sounded, and Yannah came by to help her sister. Usually, she would ask her what she would like to eat and then bring whatever was closest to that back here to the room. "Yannah, I have a surprise for you. Allyah has recovered and wants to go down to the dining hall and eat with the rest of us."

"Dear sister," Allyah said, "how can I ever possibly thank you for having taken such good care of me all these years?"

Yannah nearly fainted. Tears flowing like fountains, she rushed over to her sister and held her tightly. "Thank you. Thank you," she blubbered between sobs. I gave them a few minutes to recover, and then with Yannah on one side of her and I on the other, we three proudly walked into the dining room.

Of course, everyone knew about the insanity case that had been given sanctuary here. When we three walked in, a hush fell over the whole room. Allyah broke the awkward silence, "Hello everyone. I look forward to meeting each of you in good time. Just at the moment, I do feel rather hungry." The room broke into a spontaneous round of cheering and clapping. Yes, they firmly believed that they had just witnessed a miracle, another testimony to Jehosa. Certainly, nothing I could say would ever convince them otherwise.

We sat down at my customary table, with the other Guardians, Adriana, Lenkova, Zdlenka, and Emil. Allyah apologized, "I am truly sorry that I have not yet had the pleasure of meeting all of you fine people. I only recognize Bethany here and my sister Yannah."

While the food was being served, Emil said, "This is the Lady in Blue, your host who has provided you with sanctuary here in the Grey Havens. I am her husband, Prophet Emil Al Amir. We call ourselves the Holy Order of the Blue Servants of Jehosa at the Grey Havens. We're rather fond of blue, you see. She provides sanctuary for all those who are in need, regardless of who they are or where they come from."

"What a magnificent Lady in Blue you are indeed. The world needs more like you. You radiate such beauty and peace. I must say, I am deeply fond of your Grey Haven. Magnificent location, nay spectacular. Remote and out of the way too. Are all of the women from the steppes as beautiful as you? I recognize your skin color. Never forget a skin color."

She flushed, but realized that he had deduced this fact and that we had not told her, "No more so than here in the Arad. Beauty is really found within," she added.

"Wisdom too. Ah, Emil, you have a treasure here! Ah, food. I seem to be awfully hungry." We all chuckled and began to eat.

Later on, I introduced the others, giving him time to absorb the names and identities. True to her word, Allyah chatted with as many people as she could after dinner. Many just wanted to feel the touch of her hand, to prove to themselves that she was real. Alabaster knew that too. Finally, because I insisted that we not overly tax her on her first time here in the dining room, we graciously were able to get her back to my room. Alton, Andre, Waverly, and I were now alone with our founder.

"Thanks for helping Bethany rescue me. It seems I really needed rescuing," Allyah began. This name thing is becoming just a tad confusing — Alabaster — Allyah. You were awfully clever with your name, Ket Bethany," he teased. "Should I follow suit, Allyah Alabaster or Alabaster Allyah. No, Alabaster is definitely not a woman's name. Of course, the juxtaposition of an Arad name with a Greenway name is a bit unusual."

"No worse than mine, Sir. Oops, ma'am. This sex thing causes more problems. When I visited the fortress at Mont Blanc, everyone there knew me as the woman Bethany, so I dressed the role. Yes, it did make everyone feel far more comfortable when speaking to me."

"Okay, I assume that you all are under pressure to bring me up to date? Are there crisis that are pressing?"

"Yes, and no. They will wait another day. I'd rather you take all the time you need to get accustomed to life once more. While things are grim in some ways, the Guardians are coping and adjusting to meet the situations," I answered truthfully.

"Okay then, I am tired, physically — not mentally anymore. Give me a few days to get used to this woman thing. Then, I really do need to know what has been going on all these years."

The next day, I received the okay to offer Guardian assistance to our new friends. Mid-morning, I met with Zdlenka and Emil. Before I could bring up our offer, Emil commented, "Very nicely done, your healing of Allyah, I mean. I can see now why Jes chose you for his wife. I don't know of another person on Tarra who could have done what you have, save Jes when he was here on Tarra."

"Thanks, but I couldn't have done it without your guidance. Actually, your idea worked the miracle, so it is you, Prophet Emil, that I should be thanking." He grinned with a wise look upon his face. "The reason I wanted to see you both today is that I am authorized to extend the bonds of friendship and alliance of the Guardians to you. If we can help you in any way or if you should ever need anything, you only have to ask, and we will do everything in our power to aid you. Just send a message to the Zargarb Sisterhood, and they can relay it across the Sea Princes to Fortress d'Grange who can then get it to us. Also, Andre will also likely be staying in Zargarb, so you could also contact him directly, once he and Lenkova are married and settled down somewhere. Already I can see one thing that you could use that we could provide: seed grain and a stockpile of grain for the long winters."

Zdlenka smiled, though I could see that she was trying hard not to cry, "Long have I done all this on my own. Assistance would be most reassuring. I suspect little escapes your observation, Bethany."

"Aye," Emil added, "our goals and purposes to aid those in need on Tarra do seem to be closely allied. I must admit that finding sufficient seed has become nearly impossible. The villagers are in such plight that in desperation they consume the grain, which should be used to plant the next year's crops."

"But what can we do in exchange for your aid?" Zdlenka asked. "We must give back something of value to you. It would not be honest of us if we did not."

"Zdlenka, you are also very wise. Yes, if a man only receives and is not allowed to contribute in some way, he loses his self-respect. You have two things here which we could readily use and need in the Greenway."

"What could they possibly be?" she replied. "The Greenway sounds like a paradise."

"Quality horses. We are not breeders of horses, except by the lowest of standards. I'm afraid that no one really possesses the knowledge to raise much beyond a plow horse. Most are farmers, after all. We can send you Sea Prince ship loads of grain, and you can send back a ship of horses. I'm not sure how many can be shipped on a boat, but one ship did carry six of ours when we came over from West Reach to the mainland."

"That is easily done. I have been raising and trading horses all these years to provide for everyone here. A few more is easily handled. But what is the second thing?" she asked, still a bit puzzled.

"The second you might not be willing to share, and if so, give it no further thought." Now I did have her curiosity perked. "Let me explain a bit further. While all Guardians receive the same basic training, in our later years of study, we specialize in one of seven areas. Andre, Alton, and Elona, are Protectors. That is, they specialize in all forms of combat, usually defensive, mind you. But their job is to provide protection for the others in their group, similar to Lenkova's task. Waverly is a Communicator; she specializes in communicating via minds; telepathy you may call it. When I said that I received the okay to extend our aid, she first contacted our leaders back in the Greenway, explained the situation to them, and got their backing, all via telepathy."

A shocked look suddenly appeared on Zdlenka's face. Then, she turned beet red. I knew that I had accidentally touched a raw nerve somehow. I gave her time to recover. "Forgive me, but that has reminded me of something that I had forgotten about. Mikhailovich and I used to be able to do this. I abused it to give us an unfair advantage in all combat situations; I was his eyes in back of his head, so to speak. I did not know that it could be done over such great distances, however. I can see now that had we actually invaded the Greenway, we would have fared even worse than we had ever imagined. However, since I had abused my gift back then, ever since I have tried to forget that I could do that."

"But you still do it, am I not correct?"

She gave me a very startled look. Emil looked at her as if he had never seen her before. No, she had never tried it with him, of that I was certain, though I had actually not considered that aspect. "How could you know?"

"Let me finish my descriptions and then explain. It will become very clear; it is obvious that you do." She agreed, listening carefully hoping to see where I was headed. "Others chose to become expert Healers. In hindsight, we ought to have brought a Healer along with us. While the rest of us can do elementary healing, the real Healers are much better at it than we are. Then, there those who specialize in helping others settle or resolve disputes, the Judgers, we call them. Planners make their mark by knowing quite a lot about how to build and construct things. They assist our people in the design of a new stable, for example, or even an inn. The Loremaster is wise about all things involving Nature, plants and animals and even trails. Finally, in every group there is one special person whom we call the Wid, who is their leader. The Wid is very special in that they have a strong desire to learn all about everything. It is joked that a Wid never stops learning new things. We just keep on asking more questions and then set about finding answers. If you haven't already guessed, I'm the Wid of our party."

"Now to answer your question. You have a skill and an ability that far exceeds anything that any Guardian knows. That skill and ability is sorely needed but totally lacking, for none in the Greenway has any real knowledge about it."

Zdlenka was no dummy. "Let me guess. It has to do with horses, right?"

Grinning from ear to ear, I replied, "You guessed it! From the very little I have observed thus far — horses meeting us, leading us, ordering us on to the right path, even your description about the horses protecting you from harm — all this tells me that you not only have a vast knowledge of their breeding, but that you also communicate with these noble steeds. If you would be willing to share even a tiny bit of that with us, such would be more valuable than ship loads of grain! Don't misunderstand me; we aren't interested in becoming super-riders, as are the Galts of the Northern Steppes. Rather, we need to know how to breed them so we can obtain quality horses, whose spirits are keen and not suppressed into an apathy behind some plow. I think that if we could somehow communicate with these noble beasts, we could provide far better for their needs instead of beating them into subservience."

Zdlenka looked most relieved. I knew that she would balk completely if I had asked for training combat horses and becoming superb cavalry, as were the Galts. "It is rare among outsiders, those not from the steppes, as well as those within the Northern Steppes to elevate the care and needs of these magnificent animals above the base needs of men. Those special few in the steppes we call bredas, breeders of horses. A tribe is very lucky if it has one such person. Nearly always a breda is a woman, because men just cannot ever seem to get their needs separated from those of the horse, and thus have always failed since the dawn of time."

"I can see what you mean. While I love horses and just love to ride them, I doubt that I would make a good breda. If asked, I would try my very best, mind you." She smiled; I knew that she knew that I definitely would not make a good breda, not only because I had a male body this time, but rather my temperament, as witnessed back in Zargarb with the Axemen.

"However, Zdlenka, what you have told me about your mental skills leads me down another avenue that I had not considered before. Telepathy is a very rare skill, even among the Guardians. It is a gift from Nature — Emil may claim that it is a gift from someone else — but it is a gift. You have it. Perhaps at one time you mis-used it, but I would bet anything that you were never ever trained in its proper usage. It is a gift that is meant to be used and not just with horses. To deny your gift is like denying a part of you exists and that is just awful. Every now and then, we come across a child in the Greenway who has this gift. We do everything in our power to help them learn how to use it wisely and not become socially ostracized as a freak of Nature or fall victim to abusing their special gift. Thus, what I am saying is, if you are willing, we would be honored if you would allow us to help you learn more fully about your gift and how to use it honestly and ethically, so that you don't have to pretend you don't have such a gift. You don't have to make up your mind right now, take all the time you want to think it over."

"I've been so embarrassed about it. You know I so abused it thirty some years ago. I've tried to pretend I don't, but I know I am lying to myself. I lay awake at night and see through Big Boy II's eyes. It would be nice to know about it. Yes, if you can teach an old woman, I will try to learn. I promise never to abuse it again."

"I know that you would never abuse it or I would not have made my offer," I replied validating her. "By the way, I think I have already figured out how to get the grain to you safely. We can ship it to this New Barq city. From there, a caravan can bring it overland by traveling along the Centurion controlled paved roads to the junction with the great north-south road. The only hazardous part would then be getting from that point to here. Since they would be traveling along the river boundary and since they would be right next to the Southlands and Centurion controlled lands, I think the shipment ought to arrive unmolested. What do you think?"

Emil answered, "I had not thought of that route. Yes, I see what you mean. Hardly anyone lives that close to the Infidels. It just might work out."

"Especially, if you hire Centurions to bring it to us," Zdlenka added. "Many of those people are desperate for work as well. All is not going so well with them either. However, any shipment must arrive between late April and early October. Outside of those times, we are pretty much snowed in up here."

We shook hands, and I left to make some arrangements. There might still be time to get a shipload of grain through. Plus, I needed to talk with Waverly.

"Well, I suspected as much," Waverly replied, after I told her that Zdlenka had rogue telepathic skills. "We need to train her, if she will accept it, even though she is awfully old. We normally begin their training before their teens."

"She's already said she would love to be trained. Now all we have to do is get a Communicator here to do it," I replied. After a short pause, I added, "She has also agreed to exchange her horse breeding skills for the loads of grain we can send. Plus, she will help train someone in how to communicate with the noble steeds!"

"What? You mean she'll share how it is that she can get her horses to act so human-like? I swore those horses were giving us orders when we were on our way here!"

"Yes indeed, they actually were doing just that! And she will trade that knowledge for grain."

"What an opportunity this has become! Very well done, Wid Bethany." She paused, I could see her mind racing. "Ah, we do have a Communicator already here," she said sheepishly, and I knew that I had her.

"You are hereby hired for the task!"

"Yes, but," she began to protest.

"No but's. I know that this is not your original mission. However, we have found Alabaster, and we have cured him. So realistically, you have completed your assigned task, at least more or less. I can't order you to stay, but I will back you all the way if you wish to tackle this new assignment."

"Yes! I'll do it! When do I start?"

"Anytime you want. However, I can see that I'm going to have to tell them both about the mantises and the Grey Creatures for their own safety. Heaven help us if we teach her how to use her skills and that brings the Grey Creatures down on the people here!"

"I had not thought about that! You are right, but I wonder how they will accept such a far-fetched thing?"

An hour later, Adriana, Jolina, Alton, Andre, Elona, Waverly, Lenkova, and I sat across the dining room table from Emil and Zdlenka. Zdlenka was vibrant and excited, for Waverly had already spoken to her about her training. I began, "I have us all together because there is something that you both must know. Your lives and those around you depend upon knowing this information. I warn you right here at the start, what I am about to tell you is nearly unbelievable, almost incomprehensible, and downright terrifying. That's why I have asked these others to join us, for they can add their own observations to what I am about to tell you. Feel free to ask any questions you have as they arise."

"Many years ago, Alabaster and I discovered something absolutely horrific that is going on in utter secret here on Tarra. Something so despicable, so awful, so unimaginable, that no one knows about it or dares talk about it. It is perhaps the very worst thing that can be done to us humans." Thus, I began to tell them about the Grey Creatures and the mantises of the Red Desert. I told them about how they trap spiritual beings as we leave the body when it dies, how they scramble our memories, and how they then implant orders for us to go get a new baby body and to report back to them when it dies later on.

"Jes, the Great Messiah, discovered the truth of what I am saying. He understood at last why so many of us no longer know that we are spiritual beings, why we are so convinced we are fleshly bodies." The shocked look on Emil's face told me that he was beginning to understand something of great magnitude. "That's one reason that Jes died on the cross back there in Jerilum, he felt that he had to depart and to try to stop these Grey Creatures. Alabaster, whose own body had recently died, came to his aid. They tried to attack the creatures, and both failed utterly." I kept the precise details from them, however. It would destroy their religion suddenly to know that Jes had faked his death. Rather, I chose to let Emil believe that Jes, as a free being, had attacked these creatures. Certainly, Alabaster had.

"Back in West Reach, I embarked upon another plan. Using my Guardian skills, when someone's body died, I quickly use my telepathy skills to join them with their loved ones, allowing all of them to share parting thoughts and ideas, to form a closure on their lives. As a byproduct, by doing this, I overrode the implanted commands to return and be re-zapped, for want of a better word, by these Grey Creatures. Yes, as you can imagine, my ceremony became extremely effective. Eventually, the Grey Creatures found out about it, and they came after me. Their true forms are giants. One simply hit me in the face with his fist and completely crushed in my skull! My body, last lifetime, died instantly."

"To my horror, I discovered this lifetime that these creatures are now taking a more active role in controlling human affairs." First, I explained my theories about the Grey Creatures implanting ideas into others minds to nudge or force them to take actions that the creatures desired. When I finished explaining my theories on this, I noticed that Zdlenka began crying and stopped.

"I never knew!" she wailed. For several minutes, we sat stunned by her outpouring of grief. About all we could get out of her was, "I never knew." I could see that Adriana and Lenkova were becoming very ill at ease, not knowing how to deal with such an emotional outflowing. Even Elona began fidgeting nervously. I knew that Zdlenka was running out something terribly important to her and exceedingly personal. I kept everyone silent. Finally, she recovered a little.

"Mikhailovich and I kept getting strange ideas in our heads. Like 'Leave the Greenway for last,' 'Attack Juda Arad first,' 'Go after Zargarb this year.' Lots of them. We were used! I feel so utterly violated! We didn't know!" She began crying once more. "I am so humiliated. I am so ashamed. All the destruction that we did has come in upon my mind again!"

"Truth, Zdlenka, sets one free," I said quietly.

"I was used! All that because they wanted it!" Now she was coming up into anger. I knew I had to keep her at it. Now was definitely not the time to stop her.

"Damn, all these years, all this time I thought the blame lay solely on us! Curse them!" Now she moved on up to antagonism, and we were nearly there. I let her continue.

Just as suddenly as she had started crying, she began laughing. "They said just what I wanted to hear! Ha. Ha. Ha. I just used what they said as further proof to do what I had intended to do anyway. I feel so much lighter I could fly! It is like some immense burden has been lifted from me!"

"Well done, Zdlenka. Truth has set you free," I said softly.

"Good god!" exclaimed Lenkova. "The whole barbarian invasion was directly caused by these Grey Creatures!"

"Not entirely, niece, he and I carried out their orders. I am so ashamed to have to admit that. However, yes, things might have gone somewhat differently, if they had not so heavily encouraged us to go the route that we did."

"Damn, you are a victim too," Lenkova replied, now viewing her aunt in an entirely different light.

"Heck, I cut off my husband's balls," Adriana suddenly spoke up, startling us all. "I was a victim, but I am totally ashamed of my actions way back then. I had no right to retaliate on him like that. Zdlenka, we all carry the burdens of our past misdeeds with us. What matters is what we do now in the present. That is what I believe and follow."

Such wisdom from the Captain of Fighter Group One, I thought. Emil added, "All praise to Jehosa. Have we not seen yet another miracle right here before our very eyes?"

After some light comments, I continued with my tale, "It has gotten far worse in recent years." I went on to discuss how they were now posing as humans. I told them about the plot that we had uncovered in Vito, where the creature had gotten himself into the High Council. I related the imposter's impact on Solamina and Pieta, nearly bringing about a civil war. Finally, I told them about our discovery of a Grey Creature posing as a Deacon in the Church of Jehosa, living beside poor Bandar Dero. Next, I had Adriana and Jolina describe what they had seen with their own eyes and senses, which made the entire matter seem more real to the pair. If a blind woman could sense these creatures, they must be real! Further, Adriana's description of the reactions of the imposter, when it was found out, impressed upon them just how physically powerful these creatures were.

"The main reason I'm sharing this information with you is that soon Zdlenka you are going to be a practicing telepath." I told her about what could happen if she contacted one of them — that they would very likely seek her out and kill her, as they had done to me and hundreds of Guardians. "Waverly will be teaching you everything that we know about them and how to avoid gaining their attention, so that you can safely use your precious gift to benefit mankind."

"I don't know how we can ever thank you," exclaimed Emil, looking lovingly, although worriedly, at his wife.

Then, he started expounding, "This explains so much that has happened. Do you suppose that these are the ones who are really behind all of the wars we have seen over these many years? It would certainly appear to be so! Could these be the devils, those that Jehosa cast out from his realm? Could Jehosa be testing our purity? If so, we have failed utterly. They certainly are Evil Beings intent upon destroying not only humanity, but also our spiritual selves. Are they not actually making slaves out of us spiritual beings? Force us to lose our own identities, make us believe utterly that we are fleshly bodies, which we are not. Do you suppose that once they have got us completely convinced that we are bodies, then they will begin carting us off to some other place to be their slaves, much as we often do with our sheep and horses? Have people begun disappearing from towns and villages anywhere? You say that they are so utterly powerful physically and with magical powers. How can we ever hope to defeat them? Are we humans totally defeated then? Will Jehosa stand for this? Why hasn't Jehosa come to help us? Perhaps we need to pray to Jehosa for a miracle deliverance from these incredible enemies. Nothing in our scriptures has ever mentioned such a threat. Could that be because they have pretty much remained a secret organization? Perhaps there are even other aliens here on Tarra, as yet unseen and undetected. You say that you have only seen these two very tiny isolated groups. Could there not be far more of them who have gone as yet undetected? Who else on Tarra knows about these monstrosities anyway? Should we not spread the word everywhere across all lands? Refuse to do their bidding?" At last, he ran out of breath!

Alton spoke up, "That's a lot of questions, Emil. First, very few know about them. After all, who would believe us? Only a very few like yourselves. All the Guardians know and now we have the Sisterhoods in the Sea Princes alert for them as well. You two now know. I doubt that anyone else knows. You cannot just go about spreading the word. You will only be marked as a crazy man. It is too wild, too far beyond the reality of the normal man. The only people we have been able discuss this with are those who have had some direct contact with these creatures, such as the Sisterhood. However, you are a religious teacher and the first who has accepted the situation as it is. So that's something anyway. I'm not a religious prophet and would rather not speculate on the motives of these creatures. We could speculate all day and arrive nowhere."

I added, "I've traveled across much of the inhabited parts of Tarra. I've only come across these two alien groups. That doesn't preclude the possibility that there are other, as yet undetected groups, out there. However, based on my observations, I would be inclined to think not. I am currently going on the theory that these two groups are working against each other. Perhaps they are sworn enemies of each other. That's as far as I am willing to speculate, however. Now that we have rescued Alabaster, perhaps he will have some ideas."

"Good grief! I forgot all about Allyah!" exclaimed Emil. "So that is what caused her insanity! She, I mean he, was zapped by these creatures, had all his memories scrambled! I will be alert for others in this predicament. That is certainly a telltale symptom. But come to think of it, I haven't come across any who acted quite like Allyah did."

Zdlenka added, "We want to help. If there is ever anything that you think we can do to help defeat these vile creatures, please let us know. From what you have told us, they will not be defeated by swords; that much is clear. In a way, that is good, for we do not possess swords here. When the time comes for action against them, you can count on us if there is anything we could do. What they did to me I would not wish off onto my worst enemy. Until that time, we will maintain a place others can seek sanctuary."

"Excellent, Zdlenka. Right at this moment, sanctuary is what we most needed, so we have time to recover and plan our next move," I replied.

"Well, I am going to reread every holy scripture I have and see if these creatures actually are mentioned only we were too blind to see it," Emil promised. We adjourned our meeting. I was more than pleased that the two had taken this news so well.

Later that day, Waverly got news from Mont Blanc. Though the fall harvest was only just beginning, there was still a shipload of grains from last year available. John Henry had arranged to have it shipped to New Barq. It was to arrive there around October 1. He sent along shipping orders to have it transported to the crossroads where the north-south paved road in the Arad met the side spur running up to New Barq. One or more of us would have to meet the wagons and lead them to the Grey Havens. He also arranged to have another ship meet us in New Barq to bring the wagons, the horses, and us home safely.

When I told Adriana and Lenkova about this, both were very relieved that we would not have to fight our way back across the wild lands of the Arad. Their companions cheered when they heard that news.

Waverly met with Zdlenka and Emil to relay information about the grain shipment. When it finally did arrive just as the snows began falling in earnest, twelve heavily loaded wagons arrived. They received two loads of corn, two loads of barley, four loads of wheat, two loads of oats, and two of various other grains. For the first time in the history of the Grey Havens, there was plenty of grain for the long winter and an abundance for seed in the spring. The next year, their output more than doubled, and it continued on doubling for a number of years. Thus, in a small way, we had helped guarantee the long-term survival of this sanctuary.

A few days later, we met at length with Alabaster. Yes, it took us several long days to bring him fully up to date with all that had been going on during his long absence. He was most distressed about the massive loss of Guardians at the hands of these Grey Creatures. In fact, this bothered him more than the breakup of the Greenway into small kingdoms and the invasion of the Axemen.

Even the news Waverly received, that the Axemen had begun a significant invasion of the Velona sector, did not trouble him greatly. Elona, however, was upset over this dismal news. Fergus concluded that the Axemen had raided the forests of West Reach in order to obtain enough wood to build their fleet of ships with which they invaded Velona. For days, we all had things to discuss, and no one was bored, save the Sisters who were anxious to return home.

It so happened that Alabaster, Allyah rather, and I stayed up late one night discussing possible ways of dealing with the Creature Crisis, as she decided to name it. "In short, Allyah, there is just no way that we can bring enough force against even one of these groups to defeat them. If we exhaust all our resources fighting one, then the remaining one, likely the mantises, have nothing to keep them from taking over Tarra," I commented, or speculated on fairly sound footing. "It would seem that these two groups are always working against each other. Is there some way that we can use that against them? You know, make the bully defeat himself."

"You know, I think you're on to something with that line of reasoning.

Use their strengths against themselves. Ah, even better, use their strengths against each other," she hit upon a solid idea.

"I see, yes, get the Greys to attack the mantises that attack the Greys. But wait a minute. If we get the Greys to attack the mantises, what happens if they destroy the mantises and then they have full control of Tarra? Or the reverse, get the mantises to attack the Greys for us, but then that would leave the mantises, which might be even harder to defeat, though we have so little data on those creatures," I speculated further.

I continued my thinking, "I wish we could just get them to march out in fighting lines like the Centurions and the city defenders did back when Pieta was under attack. Let them face each other and do battle. Maybe they'd kill each other off."

Allyah's face became animated, "Bethany, that is it! We get them to fight each other. We get them to fight each other at their own home bases! Wipe out their bases of operation and we may gain much time, if nothing else. I wonder how we can do that?"

"Well, if they were kings, we could just send them each a message saying the other was planning a raid on their fortress on such and such a day and time. Make sure each thought the other was going to attack on the same day and time."

Allyah added, "A king might react in one of two ways. First, he could muster his forces, establish a strong defense, and await the attacker, intent upon crushing them as they arrived at his base of operations. That runs the risk of having his own base of operations sustaining collateral damage. Second, he could launch a counterattack somewhat before the other was planning to attack him and catch the other off guard, striking a killing blow on his opponent who is at their home base, not his."

Catching on, I added, "I'll wager the second. Look, these bases are full of this machinery and gadgets, whatever they are. I'd not want to risk my prized base of operations getting damaged while I was defending it, I'd strike first at the other's home base."

"Now how do we get the same message delivered to both sides?" Allyah thought out loud.

Midmorning the next day, Allyah and I both slept in. Once up, we got the Guardians together for a very private meeting. A smiling Allyah proclaimed, "We are pleased to announce the ABC Plan for Evil Creature removal. That's the Alabaster-Bethany-Crunch Plan." We could not resist a wee bit of humor in this deadly serious game."

I explained, "We know that the Grey Creatures are going about the Sea Princes disguised as locals. We accidentally let them overhear us talking about this really strange thing that we overheard during our travels. Mantises are planning a sneak attack on their base in the Appian Way on a certain day at a certain time. Simultaneously, a mantis overhears one of us talking about hearing that the Grey Creatures were planning a sneak attack

500

on the mantises and their pyramids on the very same day and time. We sit back and watch the fireworks."

Silence. After a minute, Alton commented, "You know, it might just work, especially if these two harbor animosity toward each other."

"It could go down quite differently," Waverly pointed out. "One side could launch a counter strike a day earlier. They could send out scouts to spy on the other and verify the attack was coming. Literally, all sorts of things could go astray." She was not happy with our plan, that's for sure. Waverly demanded an orderly, predictable universe. The ABC Plan did not fit even remotely within a predictable universe. "Worse still, have you considered what they might do to the messenger, whether the attack ever comes? We can't risk losing both of you Wids. There is so much at stake."

Alton countered, "At least right now we know where to find a Grey Creature to overhear the conversation as well as the mantises. Six months from now, we might not have that luxury. Besides, Waverly, they are killing us off one by one. How much longer can we cope with the massive losses we've been sustaining? We've had to hold back our help to the people of the Greenway just to avoid losing more of us to the creatures. I think if Alabaster and Bethany believe their crazy plan might work, we should back them up. I know I certainly don't have a single idea how to eliminate them."

Allyah surprised us by saying, "May I have a private word with Waverly? It will only take a minute or two. It may change her mind." I looked at her and wondered what she could possibly say that to get her to change her opinion about our wild plan. Worse, I was not to hear the words either. Reluctantly, the rest of us stepped outside my room, speculating like mad what he was about to tell her.

Indeed, about three minutes later, Allyah opened the door and beckoned us to re-enter. "Waverly has indeed changed her mind and is now ready to support my decision." We gaped at Waverly. What could he have said that so changed her mind? Her face was white; her eyes were watering. In addition, I caught a whiff of a noxious odor but could not place it.

She said, "Under the circumstances, we should give the ABC Plan a try." It was all she could manage to keep her emotions under control.

Allyah resumed control of the meeting, "This is how it will go down. I will journey to the pyramids out in the Red Desert alone. Bethany alone will get into position near the imposter priest in Zargarb. When I am in position, she, rather he, and I will make a Mind Link and coordinate the delivery of the messages, attempting to be as simultaneous as possible. Waverly has an assignment here in the Grey Havens, which will occupy her for many months to come. The rest of you are to escort the caravan and the Sisters back home. Try not to get into any more battles, please," she teased them.

"Now wait just a darn minute!" Alton protested, beating Andre to the punch. "We can't allow you two to go it alone; it's far, far too dangerous. I, we won't hear of that!"

"Bethany will be just fine with the Sisterhood to back him up in Zargarb. You trust them, right?" Of course we did. "As far as myself, I will take a tip from Bethany and Caitlyn and travel as a man. I don't expect to be coming back with this body." He dropped a bombshell on us all! Only Waverly did not react wildly to his simple statement.

She said softly, tears welling up in her eyes, "He won't be coming back because her body is actually dying from the diseases given to it from all the rapes. We haven't cured her, just delayed the inevitable. Already the infection is returning. That's what she told me while you were out, and I verified it."

Alabaster let the dismal news sink into our consciousness, thankfully, before he continued with, "Please have a body lined up for me in Mont Blanc. I plan on returning to the Greenway just as soon as the message is delivered."

I just had to ask, "You don't think that one of our Healers can help us deal with the body's infection?" I think that this was on all our minds right now. Surely, we hadn't yet exhausted all possible means of healing her body.

"Quite sure. I can tell what is slowly happening to the body and even its nervous system. I am sure I'll have enough time to carry out the plan, but not much more, I'm afraid. This time, the infection is much faster acting than it was with Isabel, Bethany."

Adjusting to the rapidly changing situation, Alton declared, "We can all travel together as far as New Barq before we split up, correct?"

"Yes, that would be wise. We should leave in two days. Now, if you will excuse me, I have to explain this to my sister, who, I'm afraid, is going to take this rather hard."

The next two days were a buzz of activities, loading the wagons with sufficient supplies for the journey, both food and water. Zdlenka presented her niece and Andre with a wedding gift. She knew she wouldn't be able to attend their wedding back in Zargarb; it was entirely too risky and would only stir up old memories best left in the past. Hence, her early present. She gave them a pair of extremely high quality horses, a matched pair, mare and stallion. In the back of her mind was the idea that the pair would produce great foals, even without breda knowledge.

Yannah took the news hard, but Alabaster had a way with easing her mind and concerns. Zdlenka gave her word that Yannah would be well cared for as long as she desired to stay at the Grey Havens. Allyah told her, "Sister, once I am gone, you are finally free to begin a new life of your own. Our past tragedies are finally behind us. Here you will be safe. There are wonderful, caring people here and plenty of men worthy of you. I wish I could live long here with you, but we both know that is no longer a possibility. In a month, this body will have succumbed to the rotting disease. I am so glad that you did not get it, Yannah, so very glad. To you our family burden falls, to carry our family heritage on into the future. May you have all the sons and daughters you desire." The two sisters hugged each other for a very long time.

Chapter 29 The ABC Plan

By the middle of October, our caravan reached the crossroads at the southern edge of Juda Arad, where the spur road from New Barq met the great north-south road, which runs the length of the Arad. Here, we made camp, awaiting the shipment of grain. Waverly had come along with us and would ride back to the Grey Havens with the wagons. Three men from the havens also tagged along so she wouldn't be alone with the drivers. The trip down from the foothills and across the bottom edge of the Arad went without any problems whatsoever. Largely, this region was uninhabited, except for the occasional Centurion outpost. Long ago, the Arads had vacated this extreme southern portion, giving the Centurions total control here.

We had to wait only four days before the dozen wagons slowly came our way down the spur road. After saying our farewells and thanks to Waverly, we headed on up the road to the single Centurion port city on the Med Sea, here at the extreme eastern edge of the sea. A week later, we entered the bustling port of New Bark.

It was built over the ruins of the original Arad city of Al Barq, which had been destroyed by the Galts when they took the town from the Centurions so long ago. I was surprised to see the construction details. Evidently, Megalos craftsmen had played a major role in its reconstruction. Everywhere stone buildings with great columned porticos were the norm. Occasionally, one saw an adobe building, but these were often on the edge of the city, housing blacksmith shops and stables. We rolled on down to the docks.

Alton checked with the Harbor Master and discovered that passage had already been booked for our group. All we had to do was wait on the next Sea Prince ship to dock and unload. Meanwhile, Alton and Andre purchased the supplies that Alabaster needed. When I last had been in the Red Desert, a thin dusting of a poisonous substance coated the land. The mere touch of it caused a rotting sickness and death. Hanging out at the local taverns, Andre picked up a bit of encouraging news. Several traders reported that they had seen people living out in the desert along with some scraggly palm trees. Nature had begun to heal itself, we all hoped. In any event, Alabaster planned to take two donkeys with him. One he would ride until it succumbed to the rotting sickness and the other would carry water and some food for the one-way journey.

While the men were obtaining the donkeys, supplies, and news, Alabaster and I Mind Linked, and I shared all the information I had on the location of the pyramids. Admittedly, it was scant data on which to find them. However, Alabaster felt confident that he could find them and that they were closer to New Barq than to the other end of the desert. Perhaps he had visited the pyramids when he was a free being and spying on the creatures, after his very aged body had died while my Lightning Circle was returning from our huge expedition into the Southlands some fifty years ago. However, he did not say so.

Two days later, we said our farewells to her and watched as the able dockhands loaded our wagons and horses onto the very large Sea Prince ship. True, we were quite overloaded, and the quarters were exceedingly cramped. However, most were going to be let off at Zargarb, which was only a few days sailing away. The ship, I noticed, hugged the coastline all the way, probably because they were so overloaded with all the horses, wagons, and people. I know for sure that the ship could not have weathered even the slightest squall! In hindsight, we ought to have taken two ships.

We landed without incident and here we parted company. Adriana and the twenty Fortress d'Grange Sisters continued on to their city, accompanied by Alton, Elona, Jolina, and Edgar. Try as I might, I couldn't convince Caitlyn to go with them, nor Fianna. Hence, Fergus refused to be parted as well. We, along with Andre and Lenkova, stood on the docks and waved farewell. If all went as planned, we would be joining them within a couple weeks.

Naturally, the Sisterhood put us up for free once more. I learned that they had kept a continual watch on the imposter priest, night and day. Thus, within a few minutes, I was fully briefed on his daily whereabouts. I did learn that on Friday nights, he visited a low-life tavern down by the docks. I guessed that he was probably picking up news there. I scouted the tavern and decided that it would be a perfect place to implement my side of the plan.

Since we had to wait until Alabaster found the pyramids before I we could implement the plan, we had a lot of spare time on our hands. Andre and Lenkova took care of this, however. They announced that they were going to get married on Sunday, five days from now, just enough time for Rosita and Antonio to make the journey to Zargarb. Andre refused to leave the city until I had finished my mission. Lenkova would not leave him here alone either. So we spent the ensuing days helping them get ready for their big day. They had already decided that they would have two homes, one in the city and one up at North Point, spending time in whichever location they were at. Lenkova, as Fighter Group Leader, spent a lot of time traveling; I suspected Andre would as well.

Their wedding was a simple one, and we remaining musicians played music for the ceremony, as well as for the party afterwards. In all, we truly enjoyed sharing their very special day. Naturally, both Caitlyn and Fianna insisted that we too begin making our wedding plans. Both women decided that we should be married as soon as we returned home, although neither could say just where "home" was going to be. The week passed slowly and we took to doing some shopping as well.

At last, Alabaster was in position, and we planned to implement our plan Friday night. We linked our minds so that we could coordinate our stories at precisely the same time. At dusk, I donned ragged clothing, complete with cloak that hid all my head, except my face. Caityln and Fianna had dusted my hair with lampblack so that it didn't look red. I thought it looked very dirty, but I had to be convincing in my part. I was pretending to be a trader just arriving from the Southlands. Earlier I received notice from the Sisters that our imposter priest had just headed for the tavern. After accepting all the "good luck's" from everyone, I left, walking down to the docks. Andre and Lenkova cleverly tailed me from a good distance back.

There was no escaping them, but we all knew that if this Grey Creature wanted me dead, there was nothing any of us could do about it. The tavern was dimly lit, but I knew who I was looking for, rather I could feel the alien coldness radiating from his form. I ordered an ale at the bar. I noticed that he was sitting in one corner, listening to the conversations going on around him. The place was crowded, perfect. I wandered more or less aimlessly over to the chair near him. "'Xcuse me. Need duh chair. Just got in from the Red Desert. Folks live there now. Pay good price fer t'ings. Heard a funny t'ing though. Crazy most likely. Said watch the skies tomorrow night o'er the Appains. Said there was going to be a big light show and some really big booms. Something about the mantises were 'goin to eliminate the giants, w'er that means. I reckon the desert dun got to 'em, you know. Din't make no sense ter me. But I's back in time. So's figure I'll poke me head out and look 'morrow night. Cain't hurt. Guy said t'wd be round midnight. I think the desert's done got to 'em. 'E's imagining strange creatures un'all. Don't ya think?"

I looked up and the man was gone. I had felt slight touch on my mind, and knew he saw my images of Alabaster standing close to the pyramids. I turned my head and saw his form racing out of the door, nearly knocking over two men who were entering. I sat there a while longer. My adrenaline rush was going full throttle! I had two more beers before I decided it was safe enough to leave. Outside, Andre and Lenkova quickly floated in out of the shadows, encircling me.

I pretended not to notice them; I could be being watched, so I pretended to be slightly drunk as I walked along. I muttered to them, "Easiest darn thing I ever did! He bought it."

Andre whispered, "We know. He flew out of the tavern and raced off through the city." We said nothing more until we were safely back inside the inn.

Simultaneously, Alabaster did his part. All along, he had kept me informed. Yes, the rumors were true, here and there where artesian water surfaced, date and palm trees now grew along with a bit of grass. Nomadic people camped by these watering holes, though she had given them a wide berth. She'd sent me the images of these encampments and those I had focused on while I was delivering my speech to the imposter. I knew that he had looked at them. Once at the pyramids, Alabaster had expanded his awareness to locate the mantises. He found them underground. Hence, when the time came, he crawled up on the side of a pyramid, which sounded some kind of alarm far below. As he sensed the mantises approaching, she began to act insane like she had been all her life, muttering about wanting to see for herself all the fire from the sky and loud booms from the pyramids. She rambled on about overhearing two giant Grey Creatures talking about making the sky light up and booms that would be heard all the way to the Sea Princes come tomorrow night at midnight. Insanely, she kept saying that she was right here, ready to see the show. Only a crazy person would sit on the pyramid which was about to be blown up. Soon, she noticed that the mantises that were stealthily creeping towards her had vanished back underground and knew that they had taken the bait. She then sat on the pyramid singing odd tunes, still playing the part of a crazy person waiting the show of the year. She was also very weak; the infection was running rampant. In fact, she was burning up with a fever. I could tell because of the Mind Link. My last communication to Alabaster was, *For heaven's sake, get out of there before they bomb it!* He chose not to reply, and I knew now what he intended.

"Did it take the bait?" Caitlyn asked the instant I returned. In fact, all my friends were gathered in my room waiting impatiently for my return. She had kept her fingers crossed the whole time I was gone, Fianna later told me. Even Lenkova looked very worried.

I related my brief experience. "Yes, it took the bait. Alabaster said that his likewise took our bait. So now, we wait and see. Tomorrow night we'll know the results, good or ill." After I was roundly congratulated and cleaned up, we all went out for an ale.

The next day seemed to last a week! Every so often, one of us would duck outside to see how much the sun had moved; we never wanted a day to pass so rapidly! After eating supper, we put on warm clothing and rode out of the city to the barren hill overlooking the city. Here, we would have a clear view in all directions.

"We probably won't be able to see anything," I cautioned everyone. "We are a long way from Barcella Sector. The Grey Creature's peak is in the Appian Way behind that sector. Actually, spatially, we are probably closer to the pyramids, though even that is a long way to the southeast."

"We'll watch anyway. I'm watching the mountains, and Fianna is watching the desert," Caitlyn explained. The two had worked this out during the day. If something happened, neither wanted to miss it. "As soon as anyone sees anything, holler." I was tempted to say that I see Lenkova and Andre kissing, but thought better of it.

Slowly the sky darkened and the stars came out. It was early evening in late October, and the air took on a definite chill. Winter would soon be coming, I mused. I hoped that I would be safe and warm in Caitlyn's arms somewhere at Mont Blanc when the snows came. I felt a distinct bulge growing in my pants and quickly ceased such musings and stared at the dark peaks outlined dimly against the night sky. Hours passed and we had to stomp around just to keep warm. It was definitely getting colder.

"I see something," called out Caitlyn. We all strained to see where she was pointing. Yes, a dim yellow light appeared in the distant mountains. It was very faint.

"Look here too," Fianna shouted, "there that way." All heads pivoted to the south. Again, a faint light appeared. "Is that all we are going to see?" she asked very disappointed at the poor light show.

"Hey, look up there in the sky over the Med!" called out Lenkova. Indeed, several bright flaming streaks were arcing their way towards the earth. "Falling stars?" she asked.

"Strange," I commented. "One is arcing from the north southward and down, while the other is coming from the south northward and down. Two different origin points. I doubt that they are shooting stars. Maybe it is a pair of their flying machines. We can hope so anyway."

"Hey gang, it's gone red now," Caitlyn called out. Far off the faint yellow glow was replaced by a reddish glow. "What does that mean?" None of us had any answer. A fire would not be visible even remotely from this extreme distance. It was several hundred miles away, though high in the mountains. We waited for another hour, but saw nothing more. Yet that very faint red glow remained. Finally, we called it a night.

Out in the Red Desert, in the numerous subterranean chambers the eternal lights of the Moon People suddenly went out, turning these dwelling rooms into a tomb-like darkness. Ventilation abruptly stopped. There was no one there to mark their passing.

The next day, Alana Ware, or Willow as I used to know her, the Communicator for the d'Grange Circle contacted us. *Your plan may have worked. We had scouts out some distance in the Landoc region observing. All reported a brilliant yellow flash followed by a very loud explosion of some kind. Shortly afterwards, a reddish glow appeared. Today, we have confirmed that a volcano has erupted where the Grey Creatures used to be. Ash has been blown high into the sky. Some of those who are the closest to the mountains report a light grey ash is falling on them at this very moment. When you sail past that area, you may be able to see it. Any word from Alabaster?* I told her that we had not as yet, but if there was an explosion at the pyramids, he might be out of commission for a time. I relayed the information to the others who cheered.

"Do we know that all the Grey Creatures are dead?" asked Lenkova. She did not miss a thing. This was the jackpot question, the all-important one.

"Part of our plan was to have me see if I can detect them, but not until we are safely at sea. Alabaster thought that I might be harder to locate if I was a moving target. Well, gang, we should get packed. Our ship sails tonight." The rest of the day, we spent packing and repacking, making sure that we had all that we might need for the long voyage home. However, I found saying farewell to everyone was the hardest part. I had become very close to Andre, Lenkova, and the Sisters who traveled with us. Yes, there were many hugs that afternoon before we rode down to the docks.

The Shining Star intended to sail at high tide, which was just after dark this day. An hour before sailing, we had all our many packs and sacks safely stowed and were standing on deck at the railings. Andre and Lenkova stood on the docks waving farewell, as the captain issued the order to cast off the four securing lines. We drifted free and slowly moved out to sea. Lanterns provided enough light for the crew of seven to carry out their activities, such as raising the large lateen sail. However, we went below deck because there was nothing to see but the nighttime stars.

Later, as the others drifted into sleep, I began expanding my awareness outward. My plan was to do a normal surveillance sensing, in which I just became aware of all the multitudes of minds and beings in the area being observed. I reached out over the Zargarb Sector and then expanded it further eastward. If all went well, I would eventually reach Alana in Fortress d'Grange. Secretly, I kept my fingers crossed. Could we have actually succeeded?

An hour later, I reached Alana. *All clear. Amazing, no Grey Creatures anywhere in the Sea Princes. I'm now going to move over the Appian Way into the Greenway.*

Careful, she sent. I broke contact, just in case I did encounter one. I was not about to risk her.

A few minutes later, I re-established contact with her. *No sign of any of them. Perhaps we have been successful after all. I'm now heading towards the mantises. I'll check back with you later on.*

I dropped my awareness of the northern lands and began moving out over the waters toward the southern shores and the Red Desert. This time I was overly cautious, remembering the frightful encounters that I had so long ago with these mantises. An hour passed before I was sure that I was over the pyramids. I spotted Alabaster. *Alabaster! Glad I found you. I cannot detect any Grey Creatures in any of their usual places. How are you doing?*

Dazed a bit. That was one big explosion here last night. I couldn't tell much of anything last night. But today, the pyramids are now about seventy feet lower. They've sunk. There is an amazing blast pattern here. Concentric circles of sand have formed into waves stretching for miles out into the desert sands. Look at this image. He sent me his view from earlier today. It looked like someone dropped a ball into a large pail of water, only the water was sand! *I believe that their underground chambers have collapsed. Conclusion: their chambers were directly under the pyramids. I've detected no sign of the mantises anywhere around the desert.*

Wow! The ABC Plan actually worked! I exclaimed.

Caution, my boy, caution. I've decided to cancel my plans to immediately return and pick up a new baby body. There are some things down here that I wish to examine first. I'll remain out of contact for some time. Nothing to worry about. No danger. If by chance I do find any of these aliens, I will let you know at once. Please pass this on to the others at Mount Blanc. It's been a long time since I was able to move around like this, free of a body. I do believe that I shall have a bit of fun and exploration before I take a new body. I leave the Guardians in the best of hands. In his usual way, he was saying that he had discovered something of interest, which might have an impact upon us all.

I made the connection to Alana and relayed his message. She said that in the morning, everyone would be celebrating the demise of the aliens that had been controlling our lives for such a long time. I cautioned her to keep up their guard. Some might have escaped the destruction. Honestly, I just couldn't accept the fact that we might have actually pulled this off: the total elimination of both alien groups! Then, I had another worrisome thought: what if more of them came from wherever they come from? What if both groups, not hearing from the others here, send others to find out what happened? Would we not be right back where we started, only this time we would not know where their base of operations were located? Honestly, I had so many what ifs that I dared not let myself become too confident, too relieved.

The others at last adopted my viewpoint of wait and see. For now, we, all the peoples of Tarra, we were now on our own. No alien minds whispering inside our heads, nudging us toward certain decisions. No overt manipulation of our plans. Sink or swim, we had destiny in our own hands to make of it what we chose. I hoped and prayed that we would make far better decisions than in the past when under their influence. Without these creatures coaxing one country after another to go to war with its neighbors, perhaps Tarra would see peace. Or had the pattern for our destruction already been laid? Far too many had learned the arts of war or suffered from such. For now at least, Nature seemed back in balance once more. For the first time in years, I slept soundly at night.

Ten days later, we passed by Barcella. Far off in the distance a giant smoke stack reached toward the sky from a peak high in the snow covered Appian Way. When spring came, I intended to send a scouting party to check on what remained of the Grey Creature's fortress. Yet, by the look of it now, they would find nothing at all. The destruction appeared to be complete.

Three days later, we sailed past Velona. Our captain gave the city a wide berth. Even from this distance of several miles out, we could make out the numerous long boats of the Axemen. We saw far too many smoke clouds, some thick. Velona was once more being sacked and pillaged by an invading force. I wondered how Elona took the sight when she and Alton passed by here some days before us. Velona was her city, her people.

Another four days later, we arrived safely at Fortress d'Grange. All the others were there waiting our arrival, warmly welcoming us back. However, from the grim looks on the faces of both Elona and Alton, I knew they were not at all happy with what was happening in Velona. Further, Laurence d'Grange, accompanied by his wife, Alana, was also in the welcoming crowd. Worry lined his face, though Alana was very glad to see me back alive and in one piece with the Grey Creatures eliminated. She, of course, could not tell her husband much about the ABC Plan, only enough to suggest that the threat of more imposters might have been eliminated.

After shaking hands, protocol dictated that I meet with their leader, Laurence. So I excused myself from Caitlyn and the welcoming throngs, and moved to meet these two, who were standing high on the steps of the Sisterhood tower. As I moved toward them, Alton and Elona moved to join up with me. Just then, it began to snow rather heavily, but none of us had any winter clothing with us.

Laurence spoke first, "Let me add my welcome to that of the many others. I trust you have had a safe voyage." I nodded, shivering slightly. He continued, "I am told that you are informed about our current crisis here — the Axemen are in Velona. Alton and Elona Po have asked me to council with you immediately upon your arrival. If you will follow me, let's get inside quickly. I see you don't have your furs with you. You'll catch your death of cold out here. Alana, will you kindly let Ket's friends know where I have taken him and see to it that they are properly housed and clothed? I fear the heavy snows have begun once more." She bowed and set off to carry out her husband's request, while the three of us headed into the Sisterhood tower.

Interesting, we were meeting in the Sisterhood's tower, Fortress Botini, and not his, I mused. We entered a side room on the first floor. Promptly, Adriana handed me a fur coat. The table held several steaming teapots with cups arranged for nine of us. Alana would join us soon. Besides Laurence, Elona, and Alton, several others were already present, including Adriana, Leroy and Maggie d'Grange, and Lucretia Botinni, the daughter of Rosita, the Fighter Group Leader here. I could not help but notice a large map of d'Grange and Velona sectors spread out on the table as well. I took the seat indicated by Laurence. This had every feeling of a serious meeting.

Alton began, "I'm sorry Ket to drag you into a meeting the second you arrived, but it is necessary. It's the Axeman invasion. Early June, a flotilla of some thirty longboats was spotted sailing down from Volksholm. They passed by here, but did not land — the assumption was that they would have immediately to attack these twin fortresses, not an easy task to say the least.

A week later, the flotilla just landed at the docks of Velona and began attacking everyone in sight who offered the slightest resistance. From the few reports that have reached Laurence, these invaders don't speak the Sea Prince dialect. As a result, many were killed just because of the language barrier; they were trying to find out what these invaders actually wanted."

Laurence added, "I have yet to receive any word from Velona requesting aid or supplies. However, the real problem is that now the invaders have pretty well looted Velona and are moving north towards us. When we suspected that they intended to invade Velona, I asked Lucretia to send out a fair number of scouts to keep an eye on things discretely, mind you. As we speak, the leading edge of their assault force is within fifty miles of the d'Grange Sector and showing no signs of stopping. I am forced to make the conclusion that they intend to attack us next from the south. It makes sense for them to have a source of strength from which to launch a siege. If they tried to invade down by the docks, we could push them back into the sea. We have long thought that the only possible way to assault d'Grange would be from the south."

He moved over to the map, pointing out a line of X's. "Here is where I have setup our initial line of defense. We have moved a stone barrier wall in place, blocking all reasonable foot or horse passage beyond this point. We've deployed five hundred of my men and an equal number of Sisterhood fighters to defend this line. Most are equipped with bows. The idea is to cut down their numbers before facing them in melee."

"Now this is where Elona and I come in," Alton picked up the discussion. "We heard about the invasion on our way home. Elona insisted that we stop for a day in Vito, one of the few sectors who still worship Tur. She has arranged for five hundred fighters to join her in taking back control of Velona, re-establishing Tur as their God and removing the despicable priests who have perverted the teachings of the Church of Jehosanity. Our plan is to sail later today for Velona, to rendezvous with the dozen ships from Vito out in the Med Sea and then land at the docks. From there, we will fight our way into the city, retaking it from the few Axemen who are being the rear guards. This way, we will get the Axemen in a vice grip. They will be unable to press on north and then will be unable to retreat to the south. With luck upon seeing the hopelessness of their position, they will surrender, especially now that the snows have begun. Do you see any flaws in our strategy or have any suggestions?"

He knew what my first comment would be, "What assistance has the Greenway offered?" I kept it simple, though the Guardians here all knew what I meant and implied.

"John Henry is sending fourteen Guardians to help defend the front lines and the twin towers here. They are due to arrive in a couple days, bringing along a good supply of arrows, as well as healing supplies and rations. Additionally, two fighters have already arrived and are to accompany us when we leave tonight. Mentally, he sent, *No, I could not get permission for you to come along, so don't ask. John Henry would pop his cork if you did.*

"Laurence, this is indeed a high honor you are receiving, fourteen Guardians! While in Zargarb, Adriana here witnessed what one Guardian could do when pressed. Fourteen will make a huge difference in the outcome of any battle. However, you asked about flaws. Yes, there is one major flaw. From all that I have seen of them, the Axemen are highly unlikely to surrender. Instead, if you get them in this pincher movement where they cannot go north or retreat south and the Med prevents them from going west, they will go east on through the outlying villages of Velona, right on into Barcella. From there they will likely attempt to reach the sea, perhaps commandeering a ship to use for evacuation. Either that or else fight to the last man in a brutal melee."

While they were digesting my statement and its ramifications, I continued, "Has anyone gotten any idea of what these men are really after? Surely not gold, how much can there be any more in Velona after all the recent sackings?"

Maggie spoke up, "That, Ket, remains an unanswered question. We have been brainstorming until late at night trying to make some sense of it all. Why they are attacking just makes no sense to any of us, unless their objective is really to take Fortress d'Grange, which is the only Sea Prince sector that has never been invaded and looted. One theory is that they might be trying to get to Calgary via Fortress d'Grange, but there are so many far better places they could have landed their flotilla in relative safety north of Calgary, that it makes little sense to go this roundabout way. No one has any real idea of what the Axeman objective might be. However, I will point out one salient detail from your homeland. Remember that Axeman village that you four discovered just before you came here? Well, it seems that the armies of West Reach were unable to drive them back into the sea. The Axemen are still in control of that village, although they have taken huge casualties in the process. We suspect that they need that bridgehead in order to build the large number of longboats needed for further invasions."

"It would seem that the inhabitants of West Reach need some help in pushing these Axemen from their shores," I concluded and Maggie nodded.

Both Adriana and Lucretia grasped the significance of my suggested flaw. Lucretia spoke up for the first time; her voice sounded very serious, "That means that by invading, we are endangering the Sisterhood in Barcella. Do we have that right to jeopardize our fellow Sisters?" She did not need to add, "I think not." We all took that as a certainty.

"Lucretia, do we know just where within the Velona sector their forces are currently located?" I asked. I knew that I would have to invent a safer plan that would not endanger Barcella's inhabitants.

"Not really, Ket. Velona has not been friendly to our Sisters in the recent years. Since the invasion, I have dared to send in some scouts, but not nearly enough to get an accurate picture. Our best guess, and this is only a guess mind you, is that they are concentrated along the western edge of the sector, moving northwards towards us."

"An educated guess is better than nothing at all, thanks, Lucretia," I replied, still thinking like mad. "You know Elona, if you actually destroy all their ships, then you have committed to having to slay every last one of them. Winter is coming and that may prove challenging. I wonder what they were planning to do for food supplies during the winter? Hundreds of men require a rather large amount of provisions."

While we were pondering where this might lead us, a loud gong sounded from the top of this tower. Instantly, Laurence and Lucretia jumped up. He called out, "Emergency! We are being threatened. Come on," and he dashed outside to see what the alarm was about. We all followed rapidly. Indeed everyone who was outside was staring out to sea, pointing and talking. I spied another flotilla of longboats about a mile off shore slowly moving towards the south.

Instantly, I had my answer! Each longboat had only six crew and a small square sail. Most of the ship's central area was filled with cargo. Here was their expected winter supplies. While I was deciding the best course of action to take, a familiar voice sounded behind our group. "Looketh, there be ships still a sail'en still. I ask again, cannot you spare a ship to take us to yonder island?" It was the gypsy leader, Bardia Zoreh!

Laurence barked angrily, "No, can you not see that we are at war? I have no time to send a ship over to West Reach. I thought you people left already."

I turned around and cheerily said, "Bardia Zoreh! We meet again!" His wife, Reza, was standing beside him. I said to her, "I did not go south." She smiled and nodded, very happy that I had taken her advice.

Laurence said, "You know these gypsies? Don't encourage them. I simply cannot seem to get rid of them." He was not at all pleased to see they were still in d'Grange.

"What we need is to find someone who can speak the language of these men from the north, the Axemen," I commented. I knew that none of we druwids knew it. Certainly, I had no hope that the folks in d'Grange would somehow know that tongue.

Laurence's reply said all, "Of course not. There's no reason to know it."

"Well, it would certainly make things a whole lot easier if we had someone who could translate for us," I explained.

Bardia Zoreh spoke up, "Reza speaks it. We makes deal. Reza does speaking for you. You take us gypsies to big island over there."

"I may need Reza to translate more than one time. If she will help us out today and later on when we need it again in a few days, I will personally see that you get your passage over to West Reach, wagons and all," I declared. We shook hands, sealing the deal. Laurence grimaced, but wisely said nothing.

"Okay, Elona, Alton, Reza, come with me. We need to get down to the docks at once." Quickly, we ran down the steps to the wharfs. Caitlyn, Fergus, and Fianna watched us go, and decided to come and see what was going on. Further, the two Sisterhood leaders and Laurence came down, Alana and Maggie on each arm.

"Adriana, commandeer us a small dingy and fix up a white flag on a pole. Alton, Elona, we need to make your wall of fire appear out there in front of them, forcing them to stop. Move the wall around as needed to keep them from leaving before Reza and I get there. I aim to have a word with these Axemen, not kill them." Elona and Alton began chanting their spell; I muttered mine quietly, for these spells were nearly second nature to me. Adriana and Lucretia brought a dingy with two sets of oars. Hastily, they fastened a pole with a white flag on top. My spell detonated and I let Alton take over the control of its positioning, I only needed to keep a tiny awareness of it in order to keep the fires burning.

Reza and I climbed into the dingy, but Lucretia and Adriana hopped in too. Adriana teased me, "Security is our job." I knew that she did not want to miss this encounter for the world; neither did Lucretia!

Reza exclaimed excitedly, "Look! Fires from the sky! No, it be a giant wall of fire from the Gods! Zea ships will burn up if zea goes thruz it!"

"Our fires, Reza. That's precisely the point! See, they are stopping. Ah, good they see us and our flag," I commented.

Adriana scowled, "I hope that these men honor the white flag!"

"Me too!" Reza added, realizing the situation in which I was putting her so she could translate for me.

It took us quite a while to paddle our way out to meet the flotilla of some twenty-five ships. Long before we reached them, they had come to a halt, some distance from the crackling walls of fire. Finally, we were within talking distance. "Reza ask them who is their leader that we may talk directly with him."

She obeyed, calling out the words slowly. I suspected she had a terrible accent, but the nearest man seemed to understand. He yelled to another longboat, which in turn relayed the message on back. Soon I spied another longboat moving out of the line toward me. Shortly, it pulled alongside our dingy; the longboat literally dwarfed our boat! A burly man with bushy beard and long hair who must weigh at least two hundred fifty pounds, spoke and Reza translated for me.

"He zaiz he'z Raul. Wantz to know meaning of firez?"

I'm with you, Bethany. Maggie placed her comforting though in my mind. *Can I help?*

Can you make these men see a distant illusion of an enormous wall of water, which would sink their ships? If so, ready it and wait for my signal to execute the illusion. They may need some convincing.

"Reza, tell him this. These supplies are for your army in Velona." I had to go slow, one sentence at a time.

"We cannot allow these supplies to reach them."

"In a few days they will not need them because they will have been defeated."

"Take them back to your village on the northeast coast of West Reach."

"Wait there until you receive word from your army in Velona."

"If you try to sneak around us at night or on the other side of West Reach, then we will cause a great wave to sink your ships. Just like this." *Now, Maggie, see what you can do to convince him further.*

Far off in the distance, Raul saw an enormous wave moving towards his ship. He began to panic, as did all of the other crew members. Suddenly the wave vanished.

"You see we mean this. We mean you no harm."

"But if you insist on taking these boats to Velona, we will sink all of them. Do you understand, Raul?"

Reza replied that he said that he did. She also added a curious translation. "Zea one over there in zea other boatz. He sayz he see dez flames once before near Bregia, West Reach. He sayz zea flames, zea burned hez boats." I had a flash back to the fight Jes and I had when we first got to West Reach only to find the Axemen had invaded our port town. I had brought down fire to stop them and save the town from being sacked.

One by one, the longboats began a wide turn, heading back northward. We let the walls of fire drop harmlessly into the ocean; a small cloud of steam erupted, further convincing these Axemen that we were serious. "Excellent, everyone. Well done, Reza," I complimented everyone. "No one got hurt and mission accomplished."

"Reza no understand Ket man-woman. Youz make dez fires?"

"Yes, we made the fires. It was a real fire too."

"Now I have something to tell my grandchildren about," declared Lucretia. "Adriana has been having all of the exciting adventures, while I sit in yonder tower all my life! Doesn't seem fair." Adriana laughed, and we began to oar back to shore. Can you really create such a mighty wave and sink their ships?"

"No, not really. It was just a threat," I replied honestly. "However, if they do try to sneak past us or go a very long way around all of West Reach, I think that Alton and I may just summon up a really nasty storm and let Nature sink the ships."

"Ah, then you are Holy Servants of Tur after all?" Lucretia asked rather perplexed. "Tur is the God of the Sea."

"No, we are just lovers of Nature and her balance," I answered her truthfully. It seemed to satisfy her for now. When we reached shore, I was very grateful that Alton had already fully briefed Laurence on what we had just done. Thus, I found a hearty handshake awaiting me, along with profuse thanks.

"Let's get back to our discussion, Laurence, for there goes their winter supplies. Now their situation has changed for the worst." I told Bardia Zoreh and Reza that I would come to their wagon tonight and explain further. Within minutes, we all headed back indoors and resumed our seats, while outside Sisters kept watch on the retreating longboats.

"Now we are making progress," I began. "By the time that Alton and Elona arrive in Velona, the Axemen will realize that their supply ships are not coming. That should make them more amenable to discussions. I will now make a critical assumption and that is that their leader is with the advancing forces heading this way and not sitting cozily back in Velona. Given the nature of these men, I think that is a safe assumption to make. Alton and Elona, when you attack Velona, don't try to slay every one of them. Rather, try to push them back northward. It is vital that at least one man brings the news to their leader of the fall of Velona to your army. Once that news reaches him, then we go into action on this end. I will ride forth with as many riders as we can muster and attempt to parley with their leader and arrange some settlement that does not cost more lives. Should he refuse, then we have mobility on our side. That will restrain the Axemen from trying to make a break eastward into Barcella Sector. We can tail them all the way back to Velona if need be."

Laurence slammed one fist into his other hand, declaring, "Ket, I do like your style! If they do not surrender, they will be caught like a rat in a maze and crushed between our forces. Thus, Lucretia, you need not worry about the fighting spilling over into Barcella. Such strategy from a fifteen year old boy who barely has reddish peach fuzz on his chin!" He meant it as a compliment, so I took no offense, though I hated to be having to think about this whole beard thing!

Maggie sent mentally, *That sure is a clever way around John Henry's direct orders that you are not to sail with Alton to Velona!* I smiled her way and she winked.

Alana then acted as a gracious hostess, "Then, that about wraps this meeting up, doesn't it? Why don't we let Ket get settled in. He probably would like a warm bath, a change of clothes, and a hot meal."

Alton's face reddened slightly, "Ah, Ket, if you please, there is one other tiny detail." We all looked at him. "Ah, Elona and I wish to be married before we sail. You know, just in case something happens. We want to be man and wife." Elona just grinned and beamed, her face flush with happiness. "And we want you to officiate, Ket, as Wid, if you don't mind, unless you have other plans or don't want to do it, that is. You don't have to reply right away." He was offering me many ways out of this one!

"Congratulations to the both of you! Maybe we can combine all our weddings. Caitlyn has been hounding me about it, and I know Fianna and Fergus want to marry soon. Let's talk about this after dinner." He agreed and Alana walked me to the inn where we would be staying. Already, the Sisters had brought all our gear from the docks to the inn. I found we again had the same rooms that we had the last time we were here months ago. Caitlyn, Fergus, and Fianna were sitting impatiently in our room, waiting for me to return.

When I walked in, Caitlyn commented, "Ket, will this happen every time that we travel anywhere? I mean crisis at every turn in the road? Don't you ever travel *anywhere* without finding troubles?" She was teasing and jesting, but I could see a grain of truth in her pronouncement.

I announced the news that Alton and Elona were going to be married very soon. Also, I explained what all had been going on, so that they didn't feel left out of the events surrounding us and Fortress d'Grange. Finally, I asked, "Caitlyn, I know that we have not talked about our marriage details yet, you know, the when and the where and all that. Same with you two, Fianna, Fergus. But if we want, we could make it a three couples ceremony." I added hastily, "Unless you would prefer some other arrangements. We could, for example, wait until we can get back to Cymry and have your extended families in attendance."

Caitlyn looked at Fianna, I knew the two were up to something. She said demurely, "Fianna and I wish to wait a while longer. Besides, if all of us got married together, it would take away some of the moment from Alton and Elona. Those two deserve to have a very special day. We aren't in a rush. Is that alright with you?"

"You bet, as long as we get married sometime fairly soon," I grinned. That settled, we headed for the pubic bath.

After dinner, Alton and I talked about their wedding. Since we were putting ours off a little longer, he and Elona decided to move theirs up to tomorrow. They had already made all the arrangements, save the precise day. Elona had suggested that they hold out to see if we wanted to join them. Since we weren't, they wanted to get married and to get sailing just as soon as possible. However, Elona mentioned that she would prefer a traditional Tur wedding. After all, Fortress d'Grange, while not a deeply religious city, was still firmly worshiping Tur, although many would convert to Jehosanity, if and when it ever arrived here. Hence, I was off the hook, so to speak; I would not have to officiate.

The hour was set for ten in the morning; the captain wished to sail with the tide at noon. So midmorning, a large crowd gathered on the docks, close to the water. Elona wore a traditional white linen dress, symbolizing purity of mind, body, and spirit. Likewise, Alton wore white linen pants and shirt. However, because it was still snowing, everyone wore heavy fur coats over their clothes. The local Priest of Tur, an elderly man who wore the traditional purple robes befitting his office, officiated.

Much of what the priest said we could not hear clearly, for the winds were blowing out to sea. I did catch a part of it. "Alton, do you freely and without malice accept Elona Po to be your lawful wife, to cherish and support her so long as you both shall live?"

"I certainly do," he replied boldly.

"Elona, do you accept freely and without malice or force accept Alton Woodgrove to be your lawful husband, to cherish and support for as long as you both shall live?"

"Yes, I do," she said quietly.

"To symbolize your union and bless it, please toss your bouquets into the waters of Tur together." Both tossed them; shortly, I could see them bobbing in the chilly waters. "Tur, accept this offering from these two. Know them as now married, bonded together as one. Bless them always." He turned to face the crowd, now we could hear clearly. "I present to you the couple now blessed by Tur himself. I give you Alton and Elona Woodgrove Po." The crowd cheered and clapped as the couple blushed and kissed loving before us.

Caitlyn whispered, "He took her last name, didn't he?"

"It sounds like it," I whispered back.

Ever the astute observer, Caitlyn commented, "Clever. Now when they retake control of Velona, once more a Po will be back in power. Her heritage does not die with her. Clever woman." I realized what she was saying. I ought to have already figured that out. Can I claim I was preoccupied?

I gave her a hug and said, "I bet you are right, my love. I wonder what we can get them for a wedding present? They didn't give us enough time to get them anything."

"Oh, let's wait and see what happens, and get them something appropriate later on," she replied. Next, came a long round of hand shaking with all their guests.

Finally, Alton yelled, "There is a party tonight in the Sisterhood Dance Hall. While we must leave shortly, please come and have fun on us. We will be preoccupied while we are sailing," he winked, and everyone noticed their intention. I thought it was great that they would have at least a week to themselves before they had to go into action again. Maybe there would be a little Alton or Elona next summer.

We helped them get their gear stowed onboard the ship, as well as giving them our private hugs and well wishes. "Remember, Alton, keep me informed at all times," I ordered. I knew that he would mostly do so, when it was convenient for him. Alton always was rather difficult to hold to a schedule. I couldn't help wonder if Elona would be able to do that better than I had with him. Just at the last minute, the two promised Protectors arrived. They waved hello to me and rushed to get their gear onboard in time. With only minutes to spare, they succeeded.

We watched as their ship cast off the bow lines and then the stern lines, drifting away from the dock along with the outgoing tide rush. Watching the ship slowly move away from the dock, I realized why these large ships preferred to leave as the high tide retreated. The natural action of the ocean would tend to pull the huge ship out towards the open sea where it could begin to maneuver more readily. Clever, these ship captains. We four stood in the falling snow watching them sail off into the distance and were the last to return from the docks.

Chapter 30 The New Velona

Later that afternoon, I asked Maggie who the Protectors were. I didn't know them, or at least I didn't think that I did. She said they were Thomas Algrove and Benjamin Thrush, two Protectors whose Circles had been decimated by the Grey Creatures. Both men were looking for a good fight, she explained, to relieve much of their frustrations. That's why John Henry sent these particular two. Yes, he was doing a good job running the Guardians.

Fortress d'Grange was a flurry of action during the next few days. Squads regularly formed up and took combat practice in the ever-increasing snow. Wagons of supplies were made ready. Everywhere the average person was concerned about the coming battle and its impact upon their lives. I hated this part of war. Yet, if we didn't do our part, they could well be fighting for their very existence against these heavyset Axemen. Finally, the promised two Circles arrived, along with the remaining members of the d'Grange Circle. One was the Hedgehog Circle, formerly the West Reach Circle. The other I didn't know, the Firefly Circle, whose members were all in their early twenties. This group was one of the more recently formed Circles made from joining together the surviving members of Grey Creature damaged Circles.

At long last and just about the time that Alton and Elona arrived off the port city of Velona, Lucretia ordered her forces to move out heading southwards. Twenty supply wagons rolled behind us, bringing sufficient supplies for a couple of weeks. The accumulated snowfall here at d'Grange was already six inches. However, the further south we traveled, the depth decreased significantly, until it was barely an inch when we entered the Velona sector proper.

On the ship, Alton introduced the rushed newcomers to Elona, "Thomas Algrove and Benjamin Thrush. These are two Protectors. Seldom are four Protectors found at the same place. I take it you two are itching for a fight?"

They grinned, with Thomas speaking for both of them, "You bet!"

"Welcome indeed," Elona replied. "I feel more confident by the minute! Let's get your gear stowed. This is supposed to be our month of honey; we just got married."

"We heard," Ben acknowledged, "congratulations are in order. We'll leave you two alone until we get there. That way you can have a short one at least." He grinned, thinking that Alton had latched onto a very pretty woman; certainly, he, Ben, wouldn't mind taking a relaxing week with her.

When the two newlyweds were finally alone, she hugged her husband and said, "Thanks my love. You are incredible. You know how much it means to me that our children carry the Po last name. I'm so glad you went along with me on this. Are you sure that you are going to be comfortable with it? You know, having to answer to Mister Po?" She'd asked this of him several times already, but she still couldn't believe her luck — that a man would be willing to use her surname instead of his.

"Honey, you have the heritage. The Po's settled Velona in the first place. Woodgrove's have been farmers mostly. Not much heritage there," he replied. "Besides, Alton Po sounds so much better than Alton Woodgrove. Now enough of this, let's take advantage of the time we have alone." They did just that for the next several days.

A week later, the ship arrived just off the coast of Velona, about two miles due south. Already twenty other ships had arrived here with the volunteers she'd acquired from Vito. Each ship carried twenty-five fighting men along with two cooks and supplies to last a couple of weeks. In the distance, a keen-sighted eye could make out the numerous longboats of the Axemen pulled up on the docks.

This was Elona's operation. Hence, she ordered the first conference, requesting a representative from each ship to come over to hers. An hour later, the twenty representatives and Elona's group met, crowed around the cargo bay, sitting on boxes. She looked at the faces of these men. While a few were veterans of some long ago combats, most were young men, some in their late teens. Uniformly, all displayed some nervousness; after all, they knew that they were about to go up against a formidable foe, far stronger than they were and certainly better fighters.

"Gentlemen, thank you for answering my summons to help me free Velona from both the Axemen and from the vile so-called priests of Jehosanity," she began. A round of cheers, curses, and applause greeted her ears. She knew how much the removal of these priests meant to these followers of Tur. "One of my goals is to re-establish Tur as the god of Velona, ousting these nasty priests. I'll not withhold from you that we face a very formidable opponent. Hence, one of my secondary goals is not to get either you or your men killed either. I will be honest with you, as High Priestess of Tur, I say unto you, wars and battles have never solved any problem, only created new ones. In a war, both sides lose. Tur doesn't want to see the shores of Velona run red in either our blood or that of the Axemen." She paused, letting her words sink into their minds.

"But are we not to fight them?" asked one veteran, others nodded in agreement with his question.

"Yes, we fight if there is no other alternative. However, I do firmly believe that there is another way to achieve all that we desire. Here is the basic plan." She described in some detail the plan that she and Alton had worked out several days before. "Will you follow my orders to the letter?" she added when she finished.

Smiles and cheers accompanied their many aye-aye's and "yes, High

Priestess." "Then, go back to your ships and tell the others what we are going to do. We begin an hour before sunrise tomorrow. Remember as we approach the docks, remain quiet. We need to surprise them, if at all possible."

Later that evening after eating a light supper, Elona lay beside Alton. "I can't sleep," she sighed.

"I know. An awful lot rests upon your shoulders tomorrow. You can do it, I know you can." He began rubbing her tense shoulder muscles, gradually moving over the rest of her body. She relaxed, and the next thing she realized was Alton nudging her awake. It was pitch black outside. "Time to get ready, my love," he whispered.

"Have I been asleep?" she asked, though she already realized that she had slept through the night. He gave her a morning kiss, and the two ate a light breakfast. Then, the four went up on deck, armed with their weapons, ready for the battle. She gave the captain his signal and slowly the ship sailed silently toward the docks of Velona. Far in the east, twilight began faintly at first, slowly increasing as the ships drew closer to the deserted docks. All four were as far forward as they could safely get on deck, without interfering with the crew's activities. For the tenth time, she looked to either side, counting the ships following this one. All twenty slid as silently through the Med Sea as hers.

When they were about a hundred yards from the docks, in the growing dawn, they could see some fifty longboats of the Axemen lining the wharf. They had been pulled ashore and stored off to either side. Unfortunately, these invaders were not stupid. Two guards were on duty watching over their precious longboats, their only means to return home to Volksholm in the far north. Suddenly, these guards spotted the incoming armada. One began blowing a loud horn that broke the stillness. After a short period of frantic noise, both men rushed away from the docks, heading to warn their leaders. "So far, so good," Elona commented to Alton.

"I agree," he replied, as he watched their ship slowly nudge up close to the dock. Quickly, the crew threw mooring lines onto the wooden platform; half hopped off and began securing the ship. On either side, several other ships were following suit. At once, the four climbed off the ship onto the dock proper, moving out in front to take up their positions at the very front of the attacking force. "Wait until they react," Alton whispered to her. Now, more horns began sounding from all parts of the city around them. "It won't be long now."

For Elona, time seemed to stand still. Here she was finally standing on the docks of Velona, ready to assume her birthright heritage, leader of Velona. It seemed so surreal in the early morning twilight. No people were up yet; here and there a dog barked along with roosters announcing the coming of a new winter's day. She heard the footsteps of men forming up ranks behind her, but did not turn to look. She strained her eyes to see the inevitable charge of the Axemen. Heavy thumping of boots echoed in the stillness, along with a lot of yelling in a foreign tongue, sent warning signals to her nervous system. Barely, she could see men rushing towards their line from the depths of the city in front of them. "Now!" called out Alton. She acted, raising her voice into her full chant.

Simultaneously, her five hundred men behind her saw a blazing wall of fire appear out in front of their High Priestess. A wall crackling and blazing some ten feet tall, but not touching the wooden docks, stretched out in a line across their entire front between them and the charging Axemen. In the growing light, they saw not a warrior priestess, but a reverend High Priestess of Tur, her flowing purple robes standing in stark contrast to the leather clothes of the three standing close to her. Alton was on her right, Ben on her left, Tom just behind her. Further, floating above the nicely arrayed longboats was yet another sheet of flames. This one was horizontal, and if left to the forces of gravity, it would descend upon most of these longboats. But it did not fall, not just yet. Elona took a deep breath and waited. She had played her card; now it was the Axemen's turn. What card would they play?

The wall of flames, though bright, didn't obscure vision completely. She watched the Axemen arrive and begin to form up battle lines. However, she saw the startled and shocked looks on the men closest to her as they gazed first on the barrier separating them from these newly arrived opponents and then gazed upon the floating wall of flames over their longboats.

The three Protectors were not idle. Their task was to identify the leader or leaders and let Elona know who was the most likely man in charge. While Alton had seen the Axemen in combat back in Zargarb, he hadn't had an opportunity to study their organization and leadership system. Neither Tom nor Ben had actually fought against Axemen. Hence, they had a challenge in rapid identification. They compared observations in whispers behind her, while she kept a sharp eye on those nearest her. At last they agreed, Alton relaying to her, "That one there with the huge horned helmet, the horn, and the raised battleaxe. We think he is their leader. Only a guess, mind you. Are you sure you want to proceed with the plan?"

She didn't answer but began walking forward into the flames. Behind her, she heard the gasps of her men as they saw their High Priestess walk up to the wall of crackling flames. In awe, they watched as the flames parted, allowing her to pass through unscathed. She stopped three feet beyond the wall of flames, facing several hundred hastily dressed Axemen. She called out in a steady voice, though looking straight at the presumed leader, "Do any of you speak our language?" This was the part she had fretted the most about — things would be so much easier if at least one of them could carry on a conversation with her. Yet, she was prepared to have Alton help her out if none could. However, she hoped and prayed that she could do this all on her own and not have to rely upon her husband. "Can any of you speak Sea

Prince?"

She saw several men speaking to others and hoped that one at least understood her. Out of the corner of her eye, she noticed one man on the far left flank notching an arrow. *On your left. Arrow.* Alton sent her, but she didn't need this warning. She watched his actions, and sure enough, the man shot an arrow at her, intent upon slaying this pretentious woman standing before them. Without moving her body in the slightest and without turning her head, she acted with a well-practiced rapidity. Her hand appeared at precisely the correct location at precisely the correct time. Her fingers closed upon the shaft, halting its flight mid-flight only inches from her head. Using her fingers, she snapped the shaft and let the halves drop onto the ground. She repeated her request, "Do any of you speak our language?"

She saw the presumed leader say something to another man at his side, who took a short step forward. "Yes, a little. Who are you and what do you want?" His accent was horrific, but she understood what he was asking.

"I am Elona Po, High Priestess of Tur. I have returned to retake the city my ancestors founded hundreds of years ago. I am now the sole ruler of Velona. I wish to speak with the leader of you men from the north here in my sector of Velona. I know that he is far away to the north. Go to him and tell him I wish to speak to him." She paused to give the man time to try to translate all this to the leader at his side. She had to repeat it several times before the Axeman got it straight. Meanwhile, she spied a hand signal from the presumed leader and saw once again from the corner of her right eye a man move out of the line.

This time, the man moved cautiously up to the wall of flames. She knew what he was about to do and let him. He gingerly stuck his hand into the flames. Shrieking in burning, searing pain, he violently retracted his arm, his furs aflame! Two others came to his assistance, patting the flames out. He retreated behind the lines. Yes, these flames were real, not an illusion or imaginary. She allowed herself a slight grin.

The presumed leader now replied, and then the translator explained crudely in Sea Prince, "Eric the Bold is many days to the north." That was all he said. *Okay, more force,* she thought to herself.

"Tell your leader that he and all you Axemen are to immediately leave Velona and march north until you find this Eric the Bold. Tell him I want to speak to him. If you do not leave at once or if you attempt to attack us, I will drop yonder wall of fire down upon your longboats. As dry as they are, they will catch fire at once. Long before you get through us, your only means to get home will be destroyed."

Hastily, the man began his fumbling translation. She had to repeat the message twice more before he got it straight. She added, "Do not look for your supply longboats to arrive. We have already sent them back from where they came. No longboats with supplies will be arriving this winter. Are they not already long overdue?" She added that last to help drive the point home. She knew that those supply longboats should have arrived nearly a week ago.

Still, the question remained: would this leader be reasonable? Would he take his men, pack up, and march north to find Eric the Bold? Or would they choose to attack and the heck with their losses? She knew if they chose to charge and attack that, while the flames would cause some damage, still these men were powerful enough to wipe out much of her small force of mostly untrained, but brave men. With four Guardians, very likely they would win the battle, but the cost in lives on her side would be staggering. This would then jeopardize her further plans. She had to make them retreat without a major melee.

She spied the leader glancing at the flames hovering above their longboats. Tom did too, and he cleverly lowered his flames a foot closer to the boats, an unmistakable sign, he hoped. At that instant, Elona saw the tiniest signs of doubt form upon the leader's countenance. She knew she had him now. Slowly, she moved the wall of flames closer to her, moving the line toward the Axemen, while she took a pair of steps toward their leader. Yes, it was a threatening nudge intended to pressure the man into making a decision to leave now. Involuntarily, the line of Axemen backed up a step, yet another good sign her plan was working.

"Go now. Take all your men with you. We will follow behind you. We know that he is up by d'Grange, so only go north or we will destroy your boats at once," she added taking yet another bold step forward while the flames followed her.

Alton sent to her, *He needs a tad bit more convincing. Allow me.* In the next instant, the leader saw in his mind the sequence of images Alton placed there. The man saw his supply ships returning to West Reach, retreating from a similar wall of flames. He saw his own men begin to fight, but becoming balls of flames in their winter furs; he saw his precious longboats aflame. Then, he acted. Yelling to his men, they waved their axes menacingly, but began an orderly retreat, moving on up the wide street that lead north and eventually out of the city.

Behind her, she heard the combined yelling and cheering of her five hundred men and knew she had just accomplished a minor miracle, sparing her men from the butchering axes of these wild men from the north. However, now there was an awful lot to do and fast.

Although the flames remained, she stepped back behind the wall, and Tom moved to cover her rear as she faced her cheering soldiers. Accepting graciously their yells of praise, she raised her arms for quiet. "Half of you will come with us to follow the Axemen, making sure that they are indeed going north to find the rest of their men and leaders. The remainder, you are to find the four noble houses and deliver my message to them. It is simply this: High Priestess Elona Po has now returned and has taken over complete control over Velona. Any that do not like this are free to leave today. Tell them that once I have handled the Axemen, I will meet with them to outline my rule here. Once you have let them know this, visit every last one of these despicable Churches of Jehosanity and tell them that they have until dark to leave Velona forever. After dark, you have my permission to hunt every one of them down and slay them as the rabid dogs they are. Half of you follow us."

She turned to face the flames once more. Slowly the four Protectors began walking north through this thirty-foot wide main street, moving the wall of flames before them. Thomas cancelled his flame spell over the longboats and fell into his place behind Elona, protecting her from all sides, keeping a sharp lookout. His task was to observe all that went on around them, to be the eyes and ears of this small group. The three others needed to concentrate on moving their walls of flames along the street, careful not to touch nearby buildings and local inhabitants.

Indeed, many of the nearby inhabitants of Velona had opened their doors to see what the commotion was about. Many had heard the words of Elona; many here in the docks region knew her and cheered her as she passed. Tur was worshiped here at the docks. The true test would be the reactions of those beyond the docks; they had been forcibly converted to Jehosanity and forsaking Tur. Elona hoped and prayed that the spectacle just witnessed here by the docks would convince many that indeed Tur hadn't forsaken Velona, perhaps renewing their ancient faiths. Time would tell, however.

As the group moved along the street, many citizens of Velona came out to watch this miracle as it happened. They had seen their invaders and oppressors retreating north out of the city without even a battle! They saw the Holy Flames of Tur moving like an impenetrable wall down their very streets! They saw a High Priestess of Tur in her traditional purple robes of office leading the small army right behind Tur's Wall of Flames. Some yelled "A miracle! Come and see the miracle of Tur!" Others cheered her; others just yelled as loudly as they could. Others stared in awe. A few stared in utter dismay, as their plans for the future evaporated in a puff of smoke. By the end of this day, the march of Elona Po up the main street had made a mighty impression on every person in the city; some for good, some for ill. No one went untouched by this day.

Elona forced herself to take one step and then another. The strain of the entire affair was taking its toll on her. When they reached the edge of the city and could see the line of Axemen in the distance ahead of them, she stopped and leaned on Alton. "I don't think I have the strength to take another step!" Strong arms encircled her body, steadying her.

Supporting much of her weight, Alton walked for her, "Very well done, my love. Relax a bit. Let's drop our spells for the time being." With great relief, she cancelled her wall; Alton and Ben followed suit. With her husband still supporting her, they began to follow the distant enemy heading northward. Tom verified that several wagons with their supplies were now following in their wake, just behind some two hundred-fifty proudly marching soldiers. "So far, perfect," Alton commented to her. She managed a weak smile.

"I never dreamed it could be so utterly draining, keeping the wall of flames going and then moving it while doing everything else!" she said. "Now I have a tiny appreciation of what Bethany must have gone through on that hilltop with the Axemen. How he could handle it is beyond my comprehension."

"You are still an apprentice, my love. You've a couple more years' worth of training to endure. Then you may not find it so taxing. Still, I must confess, I too am feeling the strain; so are Ben and Tom, but they wouldn't admit it unless forced to do so." She found his words encouraging. So different, men and women — here she was readily willing to say she was exhausted by the strain, but a man wouldn't so say.

"Manly pride, eh?" she managed to tease him. He chuckled.

"Ah, here come some horses," Alton relayed to her. Some kind souls in the city had brought them a dozen horses to use. She picked out eight others to accompany the four of them. These would be her messenger riders, should the Axemen try some trickery. The eight sat tall in their saddles, proud to be the "chosen ones" of their High Priestess.

Around four in the afternoon, the late afternoon sun cast long cold shadows on the snow-covered landscape around them. Ahead, the Axemen had stopped near a grove of trees and were preparing to gather firewood for the long cold night ahead of them. Alton quickly chose a similar spot, perhaps a quarter mile from their enemy's camp. While the supply wagons rolled up, the foot soldiers went about the task of making a camp here, likewise gathering firewood. However, all the wood was snow covered and thus became very hard to ignite. Alton, Tom, Ben, and Elona moved from campfire to campfire, bringing down a small wall of fire onto the wet wood, holding it in place until the wood dried out and ignited.

When their dozens of fires were going, the men warming themselves, and preparing the evening meal, Elona happened to notice the camp of the Axemen. Forced out of town as they had been, they were lacking many of the bare essentials. Not a single fire had started for these cold and hungry men. "Come on you guys; the Axemen are people just like us. Let's show a little kindness," Elona ordered. She and the three Protectors mounted up and walked their horses over to the Axeman encampment. Immediately, these men felt threatened with some new witchcraft, grabbed their weapons, and formed into battle lines. Elona called out, "Light fires." She and the Protectors then conjured small walls of flames above four campfires, lowered them onto the wet wood, holding them in position until the fires caught well. With four now blazing away, Elona looked at the presumed leader, met his eyes, and bowed her head slightly. The four returned to their camp.

The next day, they arrived at a small town that was now under the control of the Axemen. Elona ordered her group to pause a while, allowing these retreating troops to notify their comrades who were garrisoning the town and to pack up some vital supplies. She didn't want these men to arrive at Eric the Bold's location starving or frostbitten. After the Axemen left some two hours later, Elona ordered a dozen of her troops to meet with the townsfolk and their priest of Jehosanity, delivering unto them her commands. These twelve would ensure that the priests did indeed vacate the town within twenty-four hours.

Over the next ten days, four more towns and villages were similarly encountered and freed. She left a dozen or so in each after her small army passed through on the heels of the retreating Axemen, whose numbers had now grown to closer to six hundred men. Finally, the terrain became very rocky underfoot; they were getting close to the northern portion just south of the d'Grange Sector. They were very close to land's end; the ocean waves could be heard crashing far below them. Here the cliffs were nearly a thousand feet down to the sea. One slip and doom awaited on the jagged rocks below. Still, there was a trail built and maintained primarily by the Sisterhood and workers from d'Grange.

Huge bonfires told Elona that they had reached the main body of the invaders. She gave the retreating men time to reach this Eric the Bold and inform him of the vastly altered circumstances. Alton also pointed out that far above them, perhaps six miles further on up the trail, Bethany was camped with a large force of cavalry from d'Grange, awaiting orders and news from her. "Thanks, Alton. Here we wait a little longer. Have our men make camp and get fires going. I'm going to stand watch here. Give them time to understand their situation fully. Gosh, I hope they desire to communicate and not fight."

"Probably they are running low on supplies," Ben suggested, "which is why they are not pushing on up the trail to d'Grange."

She had patience; it was a requirement for her temperament and outlook on life. Charging headlong into a hasty battle was the very last thing she wanted, even though she took some comfort that the d'Grange cavalry and the large number of Guardians accompanying them could reach here within perhaps an hour, once summoned. Still, the killing of men went against what she believed. She therefore waited patiently astride her horse, watching for some hopeful sign.

Later on, Alton brought her a hot cup of tea heavily laced with honey. "Still no sign?" he asked.

Holding her fingers around the cup to warm them and sipping the warm fluid, she replied, "Not yet. Have faith. Thanks for the tea." By the time she had finished it, she spied some movement in the distance. "Heads up, everyone. Something is happening." Quickly, her forces grabbed their weapons and formed up a rag-tag set of skirmish lines. Ben and Tom took it upon themselves to arrange the men in a better formation.

Six men were walking their way; one waved a white flag back and forth. "Positive sign," she muttered. She and Alton dismounted and walked a bit towards the oncoming men, stopping when they were about twenty-five feet beyond their closest line of troops. Here they waited on the six.

She marveled at the heavy furs that seemed to make their already large bodies look more like small bears. At least they were warm and probably more than accustomed to the cold weather. One man whom she had not seen before spoke, "Eric the Bold wishes to talk with you. He wishes you to come to his camp and speak."

"I'd advise against that," Alton told Elona. "Going into the enemy's camp could be a very easy way to get oneself killed. Remember what happened to Bethany when she tried to parley with King Randolf."

"True, but thus far I haven't seen any sign that these men are insane or mad. Rather the contrary, they have acted from reason under the circumstance they faced." Facing the spokesman, she said, "I will come with you to speak to Eric the Bold." Turning to Alton, Ben, and Tom, she said, "You three don't have to come with me if you feel it is a trap."

"Where you go my love, so go I. I'll not have our children knowing their mother has more balls than their father!" he half-teased, but was also half-truthful.

She faced their spokesman and said, "Although you brought five with you, I'll only bring three with me. Lead the way, please." Ben and Tom fell in behind Alton and Elona, who followed behind the six. She was going into the enemy's camp and was aware of the possibility that she might not return alive. Yet, Elona knew that battles and wars have never solved man's problems, but discussion and compromise could. She steeled herself, knowing she would die trying to create a peaceful settlement without more loss of life on either side. She whispered to Alton, "One must have faith in what you believe or you are a traitor to yourself." He understood.

A few minutes later, the small group rounded a rocky bend and saw the main encampment. A huge bonfire crackled surrounded by crude huts housing the men. Large boulders had been moved around the fire, and two men now sat there warming themselves. Both rose when the group became visible. Elona made the correct assumption that one of these would be Eric the Bold. It was also rather obvious that the hundreds of other Axemen had been ordered to retire into their huts, which were now very overcrowded with all the newcomers from the south.

A tall, large man with flowing yellow locks neatly tied in several places down their length spoke first, hands extended in a welcoming gesture. He wore a huge helmet with protruding horns that looked fierce. However, no weapons could be seen in the area, which Elona took as an encouraging sign. He spoke crude but understandable Sea Prince dialect, "Velcome to the Fires of Eric the Bold. I be'st Eric. Comest and warmth thyselves beside the Fire of Life." The four took seats beside this man. Elona sat next to him, turning sideways on the rock to face him; he did likewise. Alton sat immediately behind her, while Ben and Tom moved around Eric and sat at his back. If he tired anything, they would react at once.

"I am Elona Po, my husband Alton and our friends. I am the High Priestess of Tur and heredity ruler of Velona. I have now returned and have taken control of this sector once more."

"Ah, the Queen?" Eric asked.

"Benevolent monarch, yes." She had not thought of herself being a Queen, but monarch certainly would fit her plans for sole rulership of Velona. "You have heard that I have arrived in Velona with a large force. You have heard that I command the Holy Fires from the Sky. You have heard that I have thus far spared your longboats from the Holy Flames. You have heard that we have turned back your supply longboats, which were en route from West Reach."

Eric roared with a hearty laughter, which Elona could not read properly. "Aye, Elona Po. This we have heard. Thus, it was spoken to me a dozen times. Never has a maiden so placed fear of the Gods into my men! Gudott had to show me his burns when he tested your Holy Flames in Velona. Verily, I canst not disprove that the mighty hand of Thog hast not broughst up a mighty winter storm, delaying our much needed supplies. Yet, Roag is very late in arriving. I give thee that you coulst have burned our fleet and slain five hundred defending Velona. A hundred tell the same tale, and I have Gudott's arm as proof, hadst I needed it. Verily, I didn't know that War Maidens dwelled here in this mariner's land. Thog the Mighty, it is said, has an army of War Maidens at his beck and call. Mighty are the blades of these Holy Maidens. Instead, I am told thee wisheth to speaketh with me. Speaketh then, mighty War Maiden Po, High Priestess of Tur."

Elona's mind raced to absorb the fragmentary details that Eric had dropped. *Evidently, he has deep respect for these War Maidens. He sees me as one. Perhaps I can make use of that.* "Eric the Bold, I will speak both truthfully with you and quite frankly. I hope that you will do me the same. When I learned that you had invaded our sector here, I was rather dumbstruck. What could you possibly want from Velona? Our sector has been decimated by two wars and the Black Plague, which killed over half of our people. The Galts of the Northern Steppes have recently completely sacked the entire land, carting way anything of monetary value. No doubt that you have noticed many villages are either ghost towns or only half occupied — the rest in rotting disuse. So I asked myself before returning here to Velona, what could this Axeman possibly desire from his invasion of Velona? Eric, I could not then and cannot now answer this question. You cannot be after gold or gems — all have long ago been looted. You cannot be after timber to make more boats, for the mariners have long ago used up the best forest stands. Indeed, there is a vast plain outside Velona where once great forests stood. Now others of your kind have been attacking the Galts, stealing their gold and gems, which they had stolen from the Sea Prince cities. This made sense to me, but invading Velona — this I simply cannot understand. Why?"

Eric let out a belly rolling roar of laughter, "Verily, thy words be'st not what I hast expected, War Maiden Po! Thee seeketh not terms for my surrender! Thee seeketh why! I liketh thee far better. Thee be'st akin to me. I seeketh not war or plunder of gold and gems as doth many of my fellow countrymen. I wilst tell thee, though I fear my command of thy language be'st not too good." All four Protectors were suddenly all ears; Bethany was listening in via Alton, though Elona was not aware of that at this point. If she had given it any thought, she could have predicted that Ket Bethany would be using a Mind Link to gain the information firsthand.

(For you benefit, as much as mine, I will clean up the language difficulties all experienced during this discussion.) Eric began, "We come from Volksholm, far to the north. Our country is a land of snow and ice for much of the year. Our growing season is but a few months long, barely enough time to grow crops. Hunting reindeer and other animals provides for our meat. Timber we have aplenty, though much of that which is closest to the fiords and coastal bays has been consumed, just as it has been here in Velona. We find it much more practical to land on the desolate coast of West Reach where great trees grow near the shores; there we may build more ships with ease, avoiding cumbersome transporting overland difficulties."

"But none of these is the real reason I have brought my men here. True, one of our ancient customs welcoming our youth into manhood requires that the youth raid outlying villages, thereby proving their manhood rights. But that custom is dying out and is also not the reason. I am here for two reasons. First, we Volksholm peoples are explorers by nature. We've sailed the seas far and wide. Exploring new lands is a passion with us. Some who have gone after the Galts have told me that they wish to explore beyond that land, once they line their pockets with all that gold. So you may see me as an explorer of Tarra. Still, why Velona? There is a second reason, which with me, is far more important. Indeed, with all my men, this is equally a burning reason."

"We have become too numerous for Volksholm to support. All of the good coves, bays, and fiords have become inundated with log settlements. When a man wishes to start his life, there is no reasonable land left on which he may settle and raise his new family. Many young men band together and raid other settlements. If victorious, they then capture that hamlet and dwell there. The alternative is to settle inland, cut off from the sea and people. Alas, most find this unacceptable. Some have chosen to follow me. My idea is to find other places where we can dwell outside of Volksholm. Some have tried to settle on West Reach, but many were slain in constant battles with those who already live on that large island. While one from Volksholm would never back down from a good fight, still there are some among us, myself included, that desires not constant combat and strife, but rather a time of building, of creation. I don't know your words to describe this. I chose Velona primarily because I thought that there was no real force here to hinder us. Until the War Maiden Elona Po appeared, I thought right. However, there appears to be quite a stronghold just a little further north of here. Stone castles we saw there when we passed by there earlier this summer. I thought to explore them and see if they would be a threat to us. If not and all proved safe, we were going to bring our wives and children here next spring. No Volksholm man would ever endanger his wife and children needlessly."

"Not even glorious battle victories could atone for allowing harm to befall one's wife and family. There would be no possibility of entrance into the Holy Realm of Thog, the Mighty, where we hope to go when our bodies fail here on Tarra. Until the unexpected War Maiden Elona Po arrived, we thought Velona was a good place to settle and bring our families hither, come spring. Alas, now Eric the Bold has brought ruin to his followers; it seems we are cut off from our longboats, trapped out here with winter's arrival."

Hearing his frank assessment of his goals and current situation, Elona was both inwardly excited and relieved. She knew she wouldn't have to fight these men. On the contrary, she imagined several future tracks that her sector might follow based upon some assumptions she was making in a hurry. One of these impressed her, and she spoke her mind. "Thank you Eric for being so frank with me. I have not destroyed your longboats as yet; we both realize the full ramifications of that happening. Unless you force me to, I will not set them ablaze. If you and your men wish to head back to Velona and leave in your longboats, I will support you all the way as I am able. You would not be harmed as you leave." He definitely showed a facial expression that indicated his relief; he would not be facing a major battle just to leave or to become stranded here with no hope of leaving.

Elona was not finished, she added, "However, we both know that if you leave now, you cannot get back home to Volksholm; the ice barrier has already begun forming in the northern lands. I believe that even Calgary, Greenway will shortly be frozen over until the spring thaw comes. You might be able to wait out the winter elsewhere, perhaps in West Reach, maybe." Elona was trying to be as logical about Eric's options as she could.

"I have another proposal to make, Eric. Fifty years ago, Velona itself boasted some eighty thousand people, with at least that number scattered in all of the outlying towns and villages. However, today our numbers are drastically smaller. More than half perished in the Great Plague of 560 or have abandoned Velona forever. Then came the Galt invasion and many more were lost during those years. Today, the Velona Sector is vastly under populated. We have more than enough room to accommodate new arrivals from the far north. As the new ruler of Velona, you have my permission for you and your families to settle here, making a new life for yourselves. Of course, there are a few conditions to all this. Would you be interested in making the Velona sector your new home?"

Eric cocked his head in surprise; his eyebrows rose slightly. "Well, yes we would. Until your arrival, we had all pretty much agreed that Velona would make an ideal location for us to settle. We had not quite decided just where, though. To dwell in the city would be taxing, because we have had to use force to keep the population under our control. I know we haven't made any real friends there, on the contrary."

"Excellent," Elona replied, the future she had just examined may well work out as she envisioned. "Though I have not yet worked out all of the details of my new government here in Velona, I know how I am going to run things. My role as supreme leader is going to be that of simply bringing in order, just order. I want to make the environment here very conducive toward allowing every person to be just as productive as they desire. Rulers should not be enforcing their will on everyone — no heavy-handed laws to be obeyed. I will, when needed, make judicial rulings to settle disputes and such. Every citizen of this sector should be free to make their own choices in life. I will step in only when those choices harm others here more broadly than they help. It is my duty and obligation as ruler to bring in as much order as I possibly can."

Alton interrupted her for the first time, "I notice that you did not say 'Law and Order.'"

She grinned, "You heard right. If we have to police our people heavily, forcing them under duress and threat of immediate punishment to do my bidding, then they have already lost their power of choice, have they not? I don't want a slave society here; no need for rebellious populations. Besides, heavy-handed policing actions are highly detrimental to a person's production. It's by having every person in Velona actually producing what they can to their fullest extent that will turn this mess around, making Velona a thriving place to live once more. I want to end up with a Velona in which a naive virgin with a large money pouch can walk the entire breadth of our land without encountering the slightest problem!"

"We do not even have that luxury at home," chuckled Eric.

"I have to admit that we do not have that safety in the Greenway either," Alton confessed.

"Well, I aim to have that here!" Elona declared. "It will be hard, I know. Expect many confusions to foment and boil off as I put in order here. For a while, it will seem like more chaos is resulting than order, but that always happens when one puts in order."

She continued, "Anyway, the few conditions for settling here are to support the local government, which is me, with a small fee. I am thinking about perhaps asking for one percent of everyone's production. Said fees will go toward projects that help everyone in the sector out in some way. For example, perhaps the wall should be built to protect the city, perhaps not. Perhaps a reserve of food and supplies should be established in case of emergencies, things like this. Wagons travel much faster on the Centurion paved roads, so perhaps we ought to extend the paved roads out to other towns. Perhaps more ships are needed to expand our merchant trading."

"Another condition is that we agree on the location where you wish to settle. The next condition is that you support the sector's ruler, me, or if you prefer to call it the local government, you may. Citizens of Velona should be supporting their government whose job it is to bring the order they need so that they can put their undivided attention onto producing their products, whatever they may be. Finally, I ask that in times of crisis when Velona is being attacked from some outside invader, that you lend your full support to the defense of Velona. Do you find these terms acceptable, Eric?"

"War Maiden Elona Po, are you sure that you are not a Goddess from the Holy Realm of Thog, the Mighty?" Eric commented sincerely. "Thy terms are more than acceptable!"

"Great! Then, the first order of business is to find you a good place to live, especially now that winter is upon us. I suspect that you will find our winters positively mild compared to what you are used to way up north. Have you already found a place that you were considering?" Elona asked, eager to get on with bringing order.

"We would like to have a sheltered bay area with access to these rugged valleys. There are good minerals here, coal and iron ore. We can make good metals from these. We do not like your mud houses, though. Great timbered long houses are common place in Volksholm, but such trees are scarce here, we have seen. I meant to ask, what happened to the town back there. We found it totally deserted; the buildings still stand, but not in good shape. Yet, no signs of people."

"Fifty years ago, the Great Plague struck. There are quite a few outlying villages, which now lie abandoned. You are welcome to adopt any of these villages as yours, if you find them close to where you wish to establish your mining and fabrication operations. I can see that it would be advantageous to you to live close to where your raw materials are found. Still, you will need some base of operations in Velona, right?"

"Ah, this would be ideal. The hills around here are teeming with everything we need, but we do need to have a bay town. Your docks in Velona are way too high for our longboats, you see."

"How about just south of Velona? Deadman's Bay has not been used in ages. We can extend the road a few hundred feet to the bay. Of course, about the only building materials we have down on the coast are adobe and stone. If you cut the timber, which is further down the coast from there, you would raise the ire of our ship builders. That is about the last tall stands of forest that remain, though I am told that new growth can be expected to be ready in a few more years. If you need timber, perhaps we can trade for some from the folks in West Reach," she suggested.

Elona continued, "You see, we are a trading people, sailing the high seas nearly everywhere on Tarra. We make our living by trading to others what they need in return for something we need or that we can trade to someone else. It becomes all interconnected at times. What kinds of metal things can you make?"

"Battleaxes and swords are in demand in our land, but perhaps only swords outside of Volksholm. But I expect that we could sell more pots, pans, shovels, pick axes, adzes, axes, and woodworking knives and such, right?" he actually smiled at Elona, knowing that she would totally agree.

"You bet, those we can trade nearly anywhere. Though I suppose that there will always be a market for swords and knives," she replied, knowing that she alone could not stop the spread of weapons. Indeed, she figured that she might well have to purchase some for those that she would be hiring to help defend the sector from invaders. "A more pressing problem is do you have enough supplies to last you for a few weeks until we can get those longboats with your supplies docked in or around Velona? If not, we can send you something to tide you over until your supplies do get here."

"If we are allowed to hunt, why, we ought to be able to do fine until the longboats arrive. How will you let them know that it is now safe for them to come?" asked Eric rather pointedly.

Coyly, Elona explained, "I happen to know of at least one ship that will be sailing up into that area very soon now. Probably the wisest course would be for you to send one of your trusted men who knows where the supply longboats may have put in to shore. He can then deliver the message. As long as that man can speak well enough to tell the ship's captain where to go, it should be fine. I don't need to know, just the ship's captain. I'll have the harbor master prepare the ledgers for you. On it, we can keep an accurate record of our trades. Incidentally, if you do turn out good metal tools, why, I think that in a few years' time, you'll find yourselves fabulously wealthy, though perhaps not in gold or gems, unless that is what you desire in payments."

"You do not want to know the location of our base in West Reach?" he asked, rather surprised.

"Not really. I am bringing order to Velona, not West Reach. Shall we get the show on the road now?"

"You never cease to amaze me, War Maiden Elona Po! Ah, there is one small thing that I would like to ask you."

"Yes?" she replied, her curiosity roused.

"Before you go, can you show me this Holy Wall of Flames that my men have reported seeing in Velona? It's not that I doubt what they say," his voice trailed off. He couldn't bring himself to admit that he, too, wanted to see this gift from the Gods.

Men! She thought. *If this is what it takes to bring order, I will do it.* She chanted briefly and formed a small circular wall of flames around the campsite, ten feet in diameter yet twenty tall. She watched as Eric the Bold stared at it in amazement. He picked up a fire log and inserted it into the flames. Shortly it burst into flames. He had a sheepish look on his face as he tossed the log onto the large bonfire. "Verily, thou be'st a Holy War Maiden, Elona Po!" He bowed to her.

A half hour later, she and Alton rejoined their small regiment, explaining to welcome ears that no battles would be needed. Indeed, these Axemen were now officially immigrants to Velona and had been given some land on which to live. "Now don't despair; you may yet have some small fights. We now have to take control of all the villages and towns, driving the evil priests of Jehosanity out of here once and for all. I suspect even the nobles may offer some resistance." Her volunteers from Vito actually enjoyed hearing the news; they could return home both alive and victorious, even with some money in their pouches, compliments of the High Priestess herself.

Later that evening, the four Guardians held a private conference. Alton began, "Are you sure that you should have trained to be a Protector, my love? Surely, a Wid or a Judger would have been proud of your accomplishments today!" All four laughed.

"Nope, I definitely don't want to know all about everything! I can barely keep up on what I need to know. Yes, it was a tossup between Protector and Judger. Since I can't be both, I chose Protector because I must stay alive and be able to enforce or backup the order I intend to put in on this whole sector. Anytime you put in some order, there is always a pile of confusion that bubbles off."

"Ah, now I see what you mean," put in Ben. "My, you have a clever mind!" It was both a tease and a sincere compliment.

"What I don't grasp is why you left out the Law part. Usually, we say bring Law and Order to an area," Alton asked. This detail had been festering in the back of his mind ever since he pointed this fact out to her when she explained it to Eric the Bold. "Surely, we are going to have to stem the lawlessness of the outlying areas, are we not?"

"I am and will always be a Priestess of Tur. Until I heard Ket explain something, I never could quite put my inner feelings into words that made any sense except to another priest. He said something that said it all. I'm paraphrasing him now. The key is a person's power of choice over matters. If you take away a person's power of choice, they will fight back or succumb to an apathy doing nothing. If I go around issuing Laws that everyone must obey or else I have them forcibly arrested, confined to a dungeon, beatenm or whatever, then at once they lose their power of choice. People in apathy produce little and of poor quality. Rebellious people turn out products with defects, getting even, so to speak. I want people here to act because they believe what they're doing is the best for everyone, including themselves, their families, and the sector. I think if I can bring in enough order, the vast majority of people here will slowly come around, since it is, after all, in their best interests to do so. Still, I'm not a dreamer. There will be a few that will not, no matter how much order I bring to the sector. It is those few that I expect will cause us the most trouble. I'll need everyone's ideas and input on how to deal with those few."

She went on, "So the first bit of order is to remove all these nutty Jehosanity priests. By now, I expect they have all been visited by those that we left behind when we left Velona over a week ago. When we get back to the city, I expect that all will have fled. Next, I need to bring order into the noble houses and their High Council. From there, I expand outward to the tradesmen and ultimately on out to the remoter towns and villages. We've got our work cut out for us."

"I've been wondering when you would get around to the city leaders, the nobles, and those on the council," Tom broke in, adding, "I sure would like to see their reactions to all this. I don't think I could do it without using force, making them do it my way. But as you say, that would violate their power of choice."

"Yes, but are you not violating their power of choice by unilaterally taking over total control of the sector?" Ben interjected. Tom nodded in agreement with him.

"They've already proved to everyone that they aren't up to the task. They allowed the city to be sacked by these Axemen and allowed the sector to be overrun with these nutty priests of Jehosanity preaching their crazy fire and brimstone balderdash. They had their chance and blew it."

"You've had your chance and you blew it!" Elona declared a week later in Velona. She had gotten all the noble houses and the other members of the High Council together for their first meeting. A dozen key tradesmen were also present, joining the two dozen wealthiest members of Velona. Actually, only four of the noble houses remained, all others had long ago abandoned the city. "I repeat, I'm now the sole ruler of Velona. Besides being my birthright, I'm the sole living Po, and I have earned the right to rule. I have ended the Axemen invasion amicably by bringing them into our folds. In time, you will see a highly productive group and reap large profits from their trade goods. All these years and you still have not begun to use our mineral resources to make metal goods, now have you? I suspect within a year or so these immigrants will be producing vast quantities of infinitely tradable goods. What wife of yours wouldn't love to have new metal cooking pans? Shipwrights, new quality woodworking tools. Even quality swords to trade. Gentlemen, I'm giving you the opportunity to put Velona back on the map, expanding into a thriving economy that vastly exceeds all the other sectors! Need I add that you will have more wealth than you can possibly spend?"

"Yes, yes," broke in Alonza Moreno in a sarcastic, condescending tone; he was the head of the wealthiest house that remained in the city. "But how will you do this? Are you going to issue orders we must follow? Besides, the other sectors are doing quite nicely with the High Councils, are they not? Why should we revert to a single ruler once more? Didn't that just get us where we are today? The Prince nearly wiped Velona off the face of Tarra. We know he was responsible for the Great Plague."

"Aye, High Priestess," added Thomasio, who was the head of the shipwright's guild, though he felt slightly ill at ease confronting directly a High Priestess of Tur. His relations many years ago with the earlier Po's had been less than satisfactory. He'd seen a lot in his sixty years in Velona. "The High Council did function well," he quickly added, "for ordinary matters, that is."

"Oh, I agree, gentlemen. I agree completely. All that I am doing and am ever going to do is put in more and more order. This is precisely why I have called you all here today. No, it was not to tell you that I am now the sole ruler and you must follow my laws or face death. That has not ever worked nor will it ever work. I am truly ashamed that so many of my deceased family chose to go that route. No gentlemen, I am only going to establish lots of order in Velona. I already have begun that by ousting those nutty so-called priests of Jehosanity. From my vast travels, I can say honestly and truthfully, there is much good in that religion, the worship of Jehosa. However, those priests who came to Velona have perverted that religion almost beyond recognition. I assure you that the Priests of Zargarb would be flabbergasted to hear the perversions done here in Velona in the guise of their religion. They might even arrest those priests if they could find them. I will allow proper Priest of Jehosanity to enter Velona and re-establish their church, but only proper ones. No more of these nutty ones."

"With the Axeman crisis resolved to our *great* benefit and the suppressive priests ousted, the next area that I must address is you folks. All of you gathered here today are the most important figures in our sector. You, all of you, are among the highest opinion leaders here. What you say to others carries a huge weight, a great significance. Look, haven't all of you taken an enormous backlash from your friends and acquaintances over allowing the Axemen to overrun Velona?" She knew she struck a sore wound with this one. Several could not conceal their immediate grimacing reactions as her words struck home.

Uniformly, they muttered and grumbled under their breaths. Yes, nearly everyday someone had bitterly complained to them about the mess, the destruction, the loss of life. Daily, they had been hounded to do something about the Axemen, but had been utterly powerless to do much of anything. It was indeed a very sore spot with these men.

"Well, I handled it and did it to everyone's great benefit. Time will show just how great that benefit will actually be. Further, I did it without harming any person on either side, no battles, no destruction. Okay, one man foolishly stuck his arm into the flames and got burned. I brought in order. Now I am going to do this with you all here," Elona continued.

"First, I want the High Council expanded to thirteen members at least. The four noble houses are already on it. I will appoint a Priest of Tur to be on it, that's five. We no longer have the Sisterhood present in our sector; otherwise, I would place one of them on it as well. I reserve the right to do so, if they ever make their presence felt here in our sector again. A seat goes to the Shipwright's Guild and one goes to the Mariner's Guild. Where will we be without those two? Nowhere. They must have a vital say in the running of Velona. That makes seven. What of the other six? I want these filled with a representative of six other guilds that you here deem the most vital to the recovery and expansion of Velona. So your first action is to decide what other six guilds will be represented on the High Council. I expect to have your decision within twenty-four hours."

"Now what exactly is the High Council to do under my rule? Help bring more order into our sector. Look, isn't there some part of your lives that you think you could bring a little better order into? Alonzo, how about you? Isn't there something in your own life which could do with a little more order?"

The old man hemmed and hawed, "Well, I don't know."

"Surely there is something in your life you aren't totally satisfied with and which could stand a little more order being brought into it," she pushed her point home.

"Well, I guess you could say that my sons need some ordering. The four of them are constantly bickering with each other, trying to get one up over the others, instead of putting their attention on how to make better and more trades," he finally admitted. Several others who knew him had to restrain themselves from laughing. His four sons were notorious around Velona, often involved in out-right fighting over who would gain control over the Moreno House when Alonzo departed.

"Good, Alonza. Can you think of some ways that you could bring more order into that situation?" Elona proceeded to drive her argument home.

After grumbling and protesting and with Elona's constant prodding, Alonzo finally said, "Well, I could cut off their allowances entirely. In place of that, I could pay them based upon their production. That might make them get back on the proper track."

"Well said, Alonzo. Let me know how it works out," Elona said quietly and confidently. She saw that while she had been concentrating on Alonzo, their unspoken leader of the High Council, everyone else here had been thinking about their own lives. Nearly everyone had at least one area, sometimes many, which they thought could use better order. One by one, they began to grasp what their High Priestess was asking.

"Gentlemen, what I want the High Council to do is just this: work out what areas of life here in our sector need more order brought into them. If possible, prioritize them. You know best what needs order brought to it the most. Write the findings down on an official document and bring it to me. If I concur with your analysis, together we will find ways and means of bringing more order to those. Let's begin with the areas that need it the most. Over time, all of us working together bringing more and more order to life here will make Velona prosper beyond our wildest imaginations."

"Additionally, I will provide the security. It will be my responsibility to prevent Velona from being attacked and sacked again. If I fail and let some army despoil our land, you have every right to dethrone me, because I'll deserve it, and I'll not stop you from removing me from my position. In fact, I will probably beat you to it," she jested.

"Aye, sounds fair enough," put in Alonzo, "but what is all this protection going to cost us?" More than a few catcalled in agreement.

"Before I answer you, how much were you all paying for protection services before the Axemen came? Mind you, I already have a fair idea of those expenses," she stated bluntly.

Making sure that he was not to blame, Alonzo said, "The High Council ruled that everyone donate ten percent of their profits to the guard forces. Some were patrolling the city streets; some were working on the barrier walls; some were trying to keep the bandits at bay."

"That's a pretty steep price to have paid, isn't it?" she asked rhetorically. "And were the results of all that money increased security? No more crime in the city? No more bandit problems?" Of course, she already knew that it had not really accomplished any of those, but she wanted them to admit it to her.

"Well, we could walk the streets more safely," one noble commented.

"With armed men at every corner? You felt safe? Or did you feel even more worried because there must be a lot of people who would rob you if these guards were not present?"

"Well, yes. But without them, we would have been robbed!" he protested, though he knew precisely what she meant.

"Isn't ten percent an enormous amount to pay out? Doesn't that cut deeply into your profits?" she asked, knowing that it literally crippled their abilities to make good deals.

"Of course!" Alonzo replied rather testily, if not outright angrily.

"I can answer your question now. I am going to ask that one percent of your trades be given to the government of Velona — me in this case. From those funds, I will see that order is brought, that the city is protected from further invasions, and that those members of the High Council are paid for their services. After all, gentlemen, I am asking you to donate a good deal of your time to working on council matters. It is only fair that you be reimbursed at least a little for your efforts." This scored a direct hit with the tradesmen present. The nobles had vast sums of money, rumors said, but the tradesmen lived by their own sweat and blood. Donating a lot of time to the council would deprive them of time spent on their own trades.

"Surely you jest," one called out. "One percent?"

"I admit I will be on a very tight budget here at the onset, but gentlemen, I fully expect that shortly the overall production of goods here in Velona will be escalating to undreamed of highs. That one percent will mushroom into a small fortune. In fact, I reserve the right to lower the percentage when I deem it is producing far too much revenue for our needs."

"In summary, gentlemen, I give you twenty-four hours to get me a written list of who is to be on the High Council. I will reciprocate and let you know the accountant of mine who will handle the record keeping so that an accurate assessment of the percent can be made fairly. Within a week, I expect to receive a document listing the ten most critical areas of life here in Velona that need order brought to them so that we may put our heads together to bring said order."

She sensed general agreement on this and continued, "Finally, you ought to know how I will be evaluating your documents. I will be looking for two key data. One: the actions we take must be for the greater good for all individuals directly involved, for our families, and for the good of all of us in the sector. Secondly and lastly, I am partial to always giving a person some power of choice over how matters are handled or resolved. Know then, that if a request meets both of these as I see it, then I will back you completely with all my resources. If a request fails to meet both of these as I see it, I will unilaterally reject it in writing and state precisely why I reject it. Said rejection will specifically be because it would do more harm than good or eliminate people's power of choice. We have a lot of work to do, but we are all up to the challenge. A few years from now, we can all look back on this day and mark it as the turning point in the history of Velona. I fully expect Velona to be the most prosperous city in the Sea Princes and the safest in which to live and raise a family."

As she rose to leave with Alton, who had not said a single word the entire meeting, one lone tradesman began clapping. Soon, the whole group joined in giving her a round of applause. She graciously accepted it. Arm in arm, she and Alton left the men to work out their details.

"God you are good!" he whispered in her ear when they were finally out on the street. She blushed.

"I'm rather drained. It was touchy there for a while, I will admit. I sure am glad that I singled out Alonzo. Getting him to see what I'm after was the turning point."

"I still say you would make an incredibly fine Judger, my love," he added.

"Now we have the challenge to stay alive. Expect tons of confusion to rain down upon us from all quarters. People will be demanding this and that, right and left. Solve this. Solve that. It cannot be done. How can we possible do this? We are going to be bombarded with confusions. I fully expect that some will try to kill me outright. I think you're going to have your hands full keeping me alive, dear. Please do. I think we are going to have a new addition to our family next fall." She surprised him with the news.

He stopped in his tracks. "You're — we're — a baby?" She nodded. He hugged her tightly and then relaxed his grip, fearing to overdo it — in her condition. She nudged his hug back to tightly once more. *Men*, she thought.

"Better ask where are we going to live?" she said, finally pushing him away. "Winter's here and there's no time to build anything. I believe we shall just have to confiscate one of the Jehosanity churches as our place for now. You guys go check on all of them, see which one is the most defensible. Our fighters have removed all the nasty priests from Velona, so you should have no troubles. Gentlemen, we have at most a week to get ourselves settled in before we get inundated in confusions from the High Council."

"Aye, aye, boss," Alton teased. He spun on his heels as he left their temporary quarters at an inn near the docks. Then, he called out, "I just remembered. Bethany said to tell you that you did a fabulous job. He's totally behind you. If we need anything, give a holler. I think that you really impressed him with your handling of the Axemen. He seemed really awestruck with your actions, and I've not seen Ket get very awestruck often." He gave her a bye kiss and left with Ben and Tom to check out the ten churches.

Chapter 31 A New Circle

By the time that our forces and I finally returned without incident to Fortress d'Grange, four ships from Velona had just arrived. A fifth was continuing onward with the Axeman representative, who was directing that ship to where the supply longboats had likely retreated. "Zo, zea didn't need me after all," Reza commented as we stood on the steps of the fortress looking down at the unloading ships. She had accompanied us when we headed south intending on intercepting the Axemen. However, the brilliant actions of Elona made that unnecessary. Still, several of us Guardians spent the two weeks having Reza teach us something of the Axemen's language. None of us was quite sure of our words; however, Reza had an awful accent even when she was not speaking that language.

"Yes, I sure do thank you for risking your life to lend us a hand. As promised, there are your ships. Once they are unloaded, they will begin ferrying your group over to West Reach. Of course, as I understand it, one ship can carry at most just four of your wagons at a time. Another ship will join in the transporting in a couple days. Still, it will take them something like eight trips to get you all over there."

"Wez all thanks zea, truly wez do. Without dez ships, we no cross," she replied. "How long it takes for one trip?"

"I think that between the loading and unloading, it will take a day. It is just a short haul from here. Yet, this is the stormy season and that could cause delays, and the winter ice buildup has already begun. We Guardians are going to try to keep the storms at bay for the next week so we can get you all safely across. How long do you plan to stay on the island?"

"Who knowz? Never fear, Reza will seez you and blonde woman when you get there. I better see to dez packing. Zoreh never packz dings well. No want my pots broke. Bye," she gaily wandered down toward the docks where the hundred or so gaily-painted wagons were parked in anticipation of their short crossing of the channel between Fortress d'Grange and West Reach. I wondered what she meant about seeing Caitlyn and myself again and back on the island. Right now, I had no such plans.

If the truth were known, I had no plans whatsoever. Edgar and Jolina had announced that they were going to get married soon. We saw very little of them once our fighting group returned from the north of the Velona sector. It was just the four of us once more, alone in our two rooms in the Sisterhood inn.

"Well, laddie, now what?" Fergus asked as we sat in our room sipping the fresh tea Caitlyn had made and munching on the biscuits Fianna had found in the Sisterhood kitchen. She was good at ferreting out delicious treats. "Fianna and I want to get married soon as well, if you hadn't

544

noticed." My eyes caught my sister's and she blushed. I knew that she had really fallen in love with Fergus.

"Yes, and what about us?" Caitlyn demurely inquired, hoping that I would want to set our date soon as well. However, she also knew that I was intimately tied to the Guardians and probably would be offered the leadership of the druwids. Knowing how important this was to me, she had not been pressuring me about getting married, let alone where we would settle down to live. In fact, she was not sure that I would actually "settle down." Ever since she had met me, I had been continually on the move, though the purpose of that constant travel now seemed to have all been settled.

"It is easier for you two," I answered Fergus. "You see, as her closest relative, I have already given you her hand and my blessings for your marriage. Yet, with Caitlyn, I owe her the honor of asking for her hand. Her parents are gone now, so I guess I ought to ask her Uncle King Emil Amir for her hand in marriage." Caitlyn blushed, but looked very pleased with my reply, though I know she would marry me even if I did not formally ask for her hand.

"Aye, laddie, that would be most proper for Caitlyn — her being the daughter of a King and all, even if he was, well not such a good man," Fergus acknowledged. "But what about the Guardians? You see, we three, well, we've had an awful lot of time to talk about this amongst ourselves. The way we have it figured is that they'll be want'n you to come back to Mont Blanc and lead them or Wid them or whatever you call it."

I sighed. My dear friends were further into my own future than I was. "Gang, I will admit that I've been entirely wrapped up in this lengthy mission and everything. I have not even thought this far ahead. Honestly, you are way ahead of me, but you are right. I really cannot make any plans until I figure out what I am going to do with them. I promise you that will be the very next thing I work on, so how would you all like to take a sleigh ride over the snows to Mont Blanc for a few days with me so I can meet with John Henry and the others?"

"What exactly is a sleigh ride?" asked Caitlyn. The others added their queries as well.

The next day, I made the arrangements. By ten, a two-horse sleigh stood outside the Sisterhood inn. These three had never seen such a large sleigh nor traveled any distance on one. We spent another hour loading cold weather gear and plenty of supplies in the back. Then, dressed in very warm furs, our breaths blowing white clouds in front of our excited faces, we climbed aboard. A number of Sisters had stepped outside braving the cold to wave us goodbye. Then, we were off, accompanied by a constant jingling of bells attached to the horse harnesses. Besides adding merriment to the trip, the bells also warned others we were near, should visibility drop.

Four days later, we arrived at the snow-covered fortress at Mont

Blanc, cold, yes, but with heightened spirits. It was not often that one could afford the luxury of a four-day sleigh ride across pristine snows. "Gang, I will admit to you that I have never had as much fun as I have had these last few days with you," I sincerely told them as we finally started up the grade toward the entrance gates. However, they replied that this was the most fun that they had ever had in the cold winter times.

Once inside the fortress, everyone we met gave us a cheer and hollered "Thanks Bethany!" There was no escaping their heartfelt praise for having gotten rid of the evil Grey Creatures. We were led into two adjoining rooms, given hot ale, and plied with numerous questions for at least an hour, before John Henry joined the throng, which had gathered outside our two rooms. His face, unlike the others, was serious, and I knew that he had come to fetch me for a critical meeting. "Excuse me gang; got to go to a meeting. Will you all answer all their questions about our adventures?" Fergus needed no further encouragement; neither did Fianna for that matter. For hours, the three were the center of attention.

I followed John Henry up the circular steps. He said nothing, so I followed suit. If I had thought ahead, I probably could have predicted what would be said when we met. However, I had relaxed and enjoyed the sleigh ride along with the company of my friends instead. It felt great not to have that awful pressure upon my shoulders any longer. To me, the world seemed to have come alive with renewed life.

In the familiar meeting room, only the Moon Circle was present. I nodded to Misty Simone, Robert Roy, Ellen Sarah, Henry, Lilly Elizabeth, and Ellie Ann. All looked very somber. As I took a seat facing them, I realized that I had not worn a dress, but looked like a young man. I hoped that this did not cause them too much confusion. John Henry began formally, "I call this meeting begun. We have not yet heard from Alabaster, however, he did say he would be away for a time and not to worry." It was his way of letting me know that the topic of discussion was the leadership of the druwid movement. Subtle, but effective.

"The first order of business is to formally congratulate Bethany and Alabaster for their incredible handling of the worst opponents of all mankind. Few beyond our circles even knew the evil existed and fewer know just what these two have done for all of us. On behalf of every druwid everywhere, let me formally thank you in person. Very well done, Ket Bethany. Just incredible!" As if well-rehearsed, the Moon Circle began applauding. I wondered why John Henry had just not let them be spontaneous in their gratitude. They certainly would have. Yet, he was being formal, ah well.

"The next order of business is the handing of the reins of control of the Guardians over to Wid Ket Bethany. Normally, our Circle would yield to his Circle, however, Ket does not at this time have a Circle. Two solutions thus present themselves: Ket, we can put together a new Circle for you or the

Moon Circle is willing to have you replace me as their Wid, and I'll put together a new Circle. Which would you prefer?" Having said his rehearsed words, I could tell that he finally did relax; tension seeped out of his muscles, as he sat down at his usual place, thinking probably for the last time.

Damn, I should have expected something like this. "I'm honored that you, the effectively All Greenway Circle, would desire to have me become the highest ranking Wid, even allowing me to be your Wid. I'm pleased, actually. However, I will not break up any Circle willingly. Circles bond for life. If you recall your history, when I last took up the reins of leadership of the Guardians, it was because I had the most experience dealing with the Centurions who were planning to invade the Greenway. Yet, I kept Alabaster's All Greenway Circle in place doing exactly what they had been doing, running the entire druwid network on a day to day basis"

"You, like them, are totally confident and have much experience in running us, through some incredibly trying times, I might add, and have done a remarkable job. I am proud of what all you have accomplished as well. I can see no reason to break up a completely well running organization such as yours. I am not power hungry or desirous of a high-ranking position. It is my decision that you, the Moon Circle, should continue to run the Guardians, until such time as age becomes a dominate factor or Alabaster decides otherwise."

"Notice also, that at this point in time, we are no longer facing nasty enemies. None of us really knows anything about the Axemen, for that matter, though through the actions of Protector Elona Po and Alton, in time we should know a whole lot more about them. So unless there is some other critical problem facing us, I do not see any need for me to have to step up to the ultimate leadership position. This time, Alabaster said nothing about my taking over the reins when I returned. He did so the last time. Of course, I am always willing to help in any way I can on anything that arises. It's just that at this time, I don't see any real need suddenly to change leadership. You all are doing a fine job."

"I probably ought to go back over to West Reach and help get things squared away on that island. Petty wars have cost them dearly, and they are not strong enough to drive the Axemen off the island. We should try to bring some order to that large island neighbor of ours. I would prefer not to have to go it alone there, so I would not be opposed to your helping me form up a Circle for West Reach, though they must all be willing to relocate to the island."

My speech worked; all their stoic attempt at formality evaporated. Misty Simone volunteered, "Bethany, we all thought for sure that you would want to jump back into the top position when you returned, especially after all that you have done for us. We just assumed," her voice trailed off.

"I told you we shouldn't assume anything when it comes to mother, I

547

mean Bethany," Robert Roy got in his self-righteousness. I gathered he had argued against this formal affair John Henry had insisted upon.

Lilly Elizabeth declared, "Now we can get down to more practical matters, like planning?" She teased the others. I suspected that she was also of the same opinion as Robert Roy.

In an effort to regain his control, John Henry waved his hand and said, "Okay, okay. I sit here chastised. Bethany, you can have your pick of all those that would be qualified to form a new Circle. I assume that you would desire most the younger druwids?" I nodded that I would. "Okay, then today, I will make a list of the most likely candidates, and we can interview them."

"Terrific, John Henry," I said sincerely. What a treat to be a part of a full Circle once more!

He declared, "Now then, Lilly is right. We need to get to more practical matters. Here I would very much like your input. What do we do about the Sea Princes? I mean Alton is going to stay in Velona. Andre, in Zargarb."

I replied, "John Henry, Zargarb is a powder keg of potential troubles. Velona is going to undergo massive re-organizational confusions, but nothing serious I hope. However, Zargarb is right at the crossroads for future trouble. If possible, I know we are spread unbelievably thin at this point, but if possible, we should have a full Circle in Zargarb. It would probably be advantageous to Alton and Elona if they had the backup of a full Circle there as well, but since they are both Protectors, it would be an unusual Circle. So perhaps we send supporting Guardians and not try for a complete Circle there."

"I am inclined to agree with your opinion of the situation, Bethany. Will you help us pick out the best candidates for these two groups?" he asked and I agreed, naturally. He continued, "There is also the matter of the Old Man of the Mountain assassin cult. Do we need to intervene directly there? Alton has talked of his ideas of sending a group of Protectors to destroy their base of operations."

"Do we have the personnel to spare at the moment?" I asked. "Are we in a position to expand our services that far from the Greenway? Have we become the Guardians for many other countries?"

Lilly answered curtly, "Definitely no to all three, Bethany. As you know, our numbers have been so radically reduced by the Grey Creatures that we have lost effective control of the Greenway. How can we possibly take on the responsibility of so many more lands? We need to maintain what we have and make an attempt to regain the Greenway, if that is even possible. Perhaps the design of some new fortresses based upon the d'Grange Towers might help convince some of these Kings to allow us back in control."

"Precisely, Lilly," I replied. "We need to take this breather time and re-organize ourselves, recruit, and train. Build up our numbers and see if others can do as Percival and Sarah have done, become the elected Kings of their territories. If the Circle at Zargarb later on deems it vital that we take action against the assassins, then we can send a group of Protectors for that single mission. Honestly, I think that the real concern may lie in quite another corner. As you know, there are two opposing Churches of Jehosanity now in operation. From what I can tell, they have become bitter enemies. I would expect that once again, the Arad would become a powder keg of religious troubles. Meanwhile, we have our hands full dealing with these Axemen."

For a moment, I became very quiet, in that instant, I found myself looking at possible future time tracks of our civilizations. The Moon Circle saw that something had my complete attention and wisely didn't interrupt my speculations. Suddenly, I duplicated the utter silence and rather embarrassedly said, "Excuse me. I was thinking about something Lilly said. Building fortresses. You know, that might not be a bad idea. I was kind of looking at possible futures there for a moment. I think it prudent that in all the territories that we firmly control, we should construct d'Grange type fortresses. While other kings around us may fall, ours may withstand the sieges. Old Count d'Grange may have been way ahead of our times with his vision of an impregnable fortress defense. These wooden palisades offer some protection but can be breeched. Stone is much harder. Lilly, I think that it would be prudent to begin drawing up designs for stone fortresses on a large scale. What do you all think?" I wisely threw it back at them.

Of course, Lilly was all for my plan and so said before anyone else could comment. For once, everyone agreed in principle, including John Henry. His only concern was what would happen if one of these fortresses should fall into the wrong hands and thus be used against us. He insisted, "They should only be built in territories in which we are in control." Considering that building such constructions would take scores of years, I thought this was quite agreeable.

Next came the picking of my new Circle and those for Alton and for Andre. Okay, so I picked my old original Lightning Circle members, except for Roy who was much older than the rest of us, married, and already part of another Circle. Admittedly, some were barely of age and a couple were not quite finished with their training. I chose them anyway.

Three were the youngest children of Roger Alan and Sue Ellen Wilkins. Benjamin (Thomas, Loremaster) was now fifteen and just finished with his training as a Loremaster. To study the fauna of West Reach was an excellent opportunity for this nature lover who jumped at the chance. The younger twins, I found inseparable. Paul Wilkins (Simon, Judger) was barely fourteen. This time he chose the ways of a Protector. His twin sister, Paulette (Sandy, Communicator) was very dear to me. She, as expected, was a Communicator.

Allan Albert Donegal (Raphael, Planner), eldest son of Willow Jane and Tom Albert, was seventeen and already had great plans for more great constructions. Yes, he continued down the path of Planner. Our Healer was Beth Ann Penton (Sarah Jane, Healer) and her nearly identical twin Lilly Ann was a Judger. Both were sixteen and the twin daughters of Percival and Sarah Penton Amir.

Paulette's (er, Sandy's) comment spoke for all of them, "Golly, this is just great! We are all back together again! Well, except for Roy." None of us let his absence put a damper on our newfound enthusiasm. The name of our new Circle? The Cymry Circle, what else?

Yes, Percival and Sarah just had to come and see their twins off. Sarah, extremely proud, said, "Okay mom. You promise to take good care of my twins here." We all had a good laugh over that one. I replied that we would be making frequent trips back and forth between the island and Greenway. I promised that we would stay in good communication with everyone this time.

Also, it was not too difficult to find enough older Guardians to form a Circle for Andre in Zargarb. The ravages of the Grey Creatures had left us with numerous broken Circles. Andre's Circle was complete and named the Zargarb Circle, what else? Additionally, since Ben and Tom really enjoyed working with Alton in Velona, they agreed to stay on indefinitely. That made four Protectors in Velona, guaranteeing, I hoped, the safety of Elona. I sent along a Planner, a Communicator, and a Healer. Since Elona was the ruler, I left the Judger role for her to fill, since she had already proven she could handle many of those actions a Judger was called upon to perform.

Caitlyn was ecstatic that we were actually going to go back to West Reach and live there, though neither of us could say where we might live. I gave my new Cymry Circle members ten days to get everything of theirs together and get to Fortress d'Grange. Meanwhile, we four returned in the sleigh, and I arranged for us to be transported after the ships finished with the gypsies.

My new Circle, eager to get started, arrived two days ahead of schedule! What a two-day conversation we all had! I had so much to ask them all and they, me, that we chatted from dawn til dusk daily. Cleverly, Sandy, I mean Paulette, made Caitlyn feel an integral part of the long conversations. Easily she could have felt very left out or worse. Yet, Paulette kept on bringing her in to everything, making her feel close to our Circle as well. I admit that I was so excited about my friends that I forgot the potential devastating emotional impact it could have on Caitlyn. Here I could have my pick of three charming druwids to marry and not her. Privately, once I realized this, I thanked Paulette heartily.

The day before we were to leave, Fergus brought us all back to reality. "Laddie, have you given any thought to where we are to land and where we are to go first?" Obviously, I had not. We were taking horses for everyone including four spares carrying our gear, instruments, and supplies. "By now, the northern bays are iced up, laddie. Bregia is probably the best choice, don't you think? I know that there was a war going on down there when we left, but perhaps we can just ride on up the road and get to Caitlyn's uncle's town first. It is not that far, perhaps seventy-five miles on a good road." I went with his suggestion, knowing that he was allowing me the first opportunity to ask for Caitlyn's hand in marriage.

After saying our farewells to our many friends in d'Grange, we boarded the last ship that would travel to West Reach before the spring thaw came. Once settled on board for the day trip, I suddenly realized that my Circle needed a crash course in the local language! We four spent the rest of the day and the ensuing days of overland travel working with the six Guardians. By the time we reached Caitlyn's uncle's town, the six could speak at least the very basics of our language. Fianna and I did tease them with some thick Tewdwr dialect, which Paulette said sounded awful, like our mouths were full of food. We'd not heard it described quite that way, and we roared with laughter.

Chapter 32 Queen Caitlyn

The ship crunched through the thin ice sheet that surrounded the docks in Bregia, West Reach. Several townsfolk came out to watch this unexpected docking. Indeed, no one expected to see another Sea Prince ship until the spring thaw. The temperature was probably twenty degrees at best, and the crew unloaded the horses as fast as they could. Even so, a thin coating of ice slowly began hardening on the decks, making footing extremely treacherous. An hour later, the horses were saddled, and the ship was backing out of the bay, crunching and tearing its way through the ice that had reformed during the hour the boat was in port.

We mounted up and followed Fergus, who knew the way from here on the extreme southern coast of Layamon up to the towns of our destination. Of course, I knew the roads as well, but I let Fergus lead us. Caitlyn also knew the way, for that matter. The late King Ahmad Amir, my eldest son last lifetime ruled over Nuadilan and Amathon, while King Emil, my youngest son, ruled over Bedwyn and Brea. All four towns lay in the north-central portion of Layamon, just south of the highlands of Ruadan. Caitlyn was the sole living member of Ahmad's family.

Fergus, on the other hand, came from the highlands, the son of Queen Ros and the King of Aine. Ros was the daughter of Jes's brother, Josh, making he and Caitlyn cousins. Josh's elder son, King Hadid dwelled more to the east of Bedwyn and Brea; his lands extended in a narrow strip down to the eastern seacoast.

Caitlyn had been living with her Uncle Emil and Aunt Carmine during that period when her father had come under the control of the Grey Creature. Her Uncle had helped her flee for her life when her father had ordered her to marry a rogue king in the south of Layamon. When Caitlyn had left them, King Emil lived in his home within the fortified town of Bedwyn. Hence, Bedwyn was our immediate destination. There, I intended to ask King Emil for Caitlyn's hand in marriage. Beyond this point, we had no plans, except that Fergus suggested that we go visit his parents in the highlands.

I knew that it was going to be a bit awkward asking Emil, who was my son, for permission to marry his daughter, my granddaughter. I guess, the real question is this. Do these familial relations still exist for one after their body dies and they are reborn? This physical body came from Tewdwr and had no connection to the Amir lines. Still, I could not help but think of Emil as my son.

Compounding matters was the inescapable fact that in these four towns the people held the Blessed Holy Mother, me or rather Bethany Madelyn Amir, in high reverence, actually worshiping her, I was told. If I revealed who I was, what then? Here was the actual spiritual being whom they were worshiping, returned in another incarnation or with another body. Awkward would be an understatement indeed. Only now that we were riding through the six inches of snow on the road north did the magnitude of what I was becoming involved in sink home in my mind and thoughts.

I remembered the great reverence that Caitlyn had held for me when she discovered that I was the very person whom she worshiped. Yet, in time, she had come to accept me as I am, not as the priests had portrayed me. Had she not, I would not be here asking for her hand in marriage.

The going was slow in the snow; Fergus estimated that it would take three days to reach Bedwyn. Hence, the prime concern was finding warm inns for the two nights that we were spending on the open road in the wintertime. He and Caitlyn conferred daily upon just how far we ought to travel each day. Our worst fear would be having darkness fall when we were miles from the nearest town or village. In the Sea Princes, the winters were relatively mild, due to the presence of the warm Med Sea. However, here in West Reach or Cymry the cold northwesterly winds made for bitterly cold winters and a lot of snow, which as a child made a fun time to play out of doors. Mommy was always there with a warm cocoa when we got cold and wet.

One night while we were snuggling to stay warm before we fell asleep, Caitlyn asked, "Are you going to tell Uncle Emil who you really are? It will be quite a shock for him, I expect. At least it was for me."

"Dear, I've been thinking about that ever since we set foot on the docks back there. I've decided that I won't until I've asked for your hand. After that, I really have no choice but to tell him. If I withhold it from him, we will drift apart. Besides, he is going to be my father-in-law, I hope." That satisfied her. I realized that he was now forty-one years old! He was barely twenty when I last saw him. I wondered how the years had treated him and fell asleep.

The sun was casting its last rays of twilight on January 1, 623, as we ten and our four packhorses rode up to the sprawling town of Bedwyn. For a minute, we paused and looked at this town, or more of a city now. When I was last here, I had designed it to house about five thousand. During these years, it had swelled to nearly double that. Bedwyn sat, like the other three towns, high on a large hill. The King's dwellings stood at the very top of the hill. Originally, seven log palisade walls encircled the hill, each one greater in diameter than the other was. I had purposely positioned the four gates into each circular wall at different compass angles so an invader could not breech the outer gates and come charging straight up the hill to take the King. I saw that King Emil had simply extended my basic design. Now nine walls of timber lay between us and his buildings at the top, along with ten thousand people and hundreds and hundreds of wooden buildings, all with rising and curling smoke clouds coming from the chimneys. It was picturesque, no doubt about that.

As we entered the outermost gate, the gatekeeper commented, "Yea be just in time. Another couple of minutes and I would have locked the gates for the night." We thanked him; I noticed that no fee was charged for entering the city. In fact, we were not even challenged. Evidently, things were now peaceful around Bedwyn, which I found encouraging. "Celebrations begin in a few minutes; find yourselves an inn and party along with us," the gatekeeper continued. "New Year's celebration." Again, we thanked him and headed on towards the next gate.

None of the other gates was closed, just the outermost ones. Only when we finally reached the last gate before the hilltop were we challenged in any way. As we approached this last gate, we could hear music coming from a large building just inside. However, three armed men moved to block our entrance. "Halt in the name of King Emil. Who goes there? What is your business here?"

I had not counted on being challenged. However, Caitlyn had the perfect reply. "It is I, Caitlyn Amir. I have returned and want to see my Uncle Emil, please."

"Caitlyn? Is that you?" the guard said very surprised. He squinted and held his lantern close to her face. "By golly! It is you! We thought you were dead! Come on in! King Emil will be most happy to see you again! He's out in the common hall officiating at the New Year's Ceremonies. You come at a happy time of the near, no discounting that. Come, come."

She thanked him and we rode the short distance to the large common hall. We tied our horses up beside three others and then followed Caitlyn to the main door. Again, two guards were on duty at the door. Once more, Caitlyn repeated her announcement with similar exclamations of wonderment and excitement. One guard, dressed in his finest ceremonial clothing, asked us to follow him. We entered and blinked from the bright lights of so many lanterns hanging from the ceiling. Over fifty people were inside, celebrating the coming of the new year. A small band of musicians, seated on a raised minstrel's gallery, was playing a dance song.

Two trumpeters stood just inside the door. As we entered, they stood at attention, raised their horns, and blew a short fanfare. The guard, who had led us in, spoke clearly and loudly filling the instant silence that the trumpet fanfare had created. "King Amil, Queen Carmine, I present Caitlyn Amir and her party!" Gasps filled the room; everyone turned to stare at us, particularly at Caitlyn who was standing out in front of our group.

The King and Queen were plainly obvious, sitting upon their oversized and raised thrones at the far end of the room. Both got up immediately and came rushing towards Caitlyn. Carmine held her hand over her mouth, as if she might shriek or cry. Caitlyn handed me her heavy fur coat and rushed towards them as the crowd parted to let them meet. Everyone was speaking in hushed whispers; I could not tell if it was shock or surprise or worse. I didn't have any intuition that anything ought to be amiss, however. As they met mid-room, King Emil welcomed her warmly, "Caitlyn, my dear! We thought you were dead, but we hoped against all odds that you would return."

They hugged and Carmine joined in a moment later, tears of joy coming from her eyes. Cathleen, their daughter and co-conspirator who had helped Caitlyn escape, dressed in a fancy gown rushed to join them. "It's you! How glad I am to see you! It worked then," she referred to the disguising of Caitlyn as a young man.

"I'm so glad to see you all!" Caitlyn exclaimed, wiping a tear from her eye. "Yes, it saved my life several times, Cathleen."

"I am sorry to have to inform you of the sad news about your father," Uncle Emil pulled himself up straight, stiff, and serious, knowing that he needed to let his niece know about her father's death nearly a year ago now.

"I know, uncle, he died. We heard about it on the mainland. Not the details, just that he was killed waging war in the south," she deftly replied, putting her uncle more at ease.

"Ah, then you know. Yes, killed by the upstart king way down south. Lost the battle too. However, I stepped in and took over control over Nuadilan and Amathon on your behalf," he replied. "However, where have you been? We were worried sick about you. No news at all, like you just disappeared off the face of Tarra."

"Oh uncle, have I got stories to tell all of you! I met Ket Bethany, and we formed the Cymry Minstrels, along with my cousin, Fergus. We toured Cymry for a time and then went over to the mainland. We've played the Greenway, all across the eight Sea Prince sectors, and even across Juda Arad and then back again!"

Cathleen let out a squeal of surprise, while the Queen gasped and held her hand over her mouth. Uncle Emil's eyebrows rose higher than I imagined they could. Caitlyn realized that she needed to introduce me and the rest of our group, and she motioned for me, Fianna, and Fergus to join her. We handed our heavy furs to my Circle's members and walked across the room to join them. All eyes marked our every step, gaping and staring at us, especially our flaming red hair.

"Uncle Emil, Aunt Carmine, Cathleen, this is our leader, Ket Bethany of Cuch Glyn and his sister Fianna. Fergus, you already know," Caitlyn explained. "This is my uncle, King Emil Amir, his wife Queen Carmine, and their daughter Cathleen."

I stepped forward and shook his hand, "Very pleased to meet you at long last, King Emil. Caitlyn has told me quite a lot about you and your family. It is good to finally meet all of you." I lowered my voice so that only these three could hear me. "I have returned your virgin niece back to you unspoiled and unharmed in any way. During our long travels, I have protected her with my life, sire." These were the proper words one should say to royalty, and I hoped they would break the ice between us. Emil was just as I had remembered him when he was twenty. Yes, the years had greyed his hair slightly, and he had definitely put on some weight. Yet, he was still my son Emil.

His reply came in the Arad language, "Thou do'est honor me with thy deeds. Standing in for her father, I accept all that you have done on her behalf and will make it right with you as per the codes." He bowed to me.

Without thinking, I replied in Arad, "Thank you sire. There is nothing to be made right. She is a good musician and has always earned her own way. In fact, we have gotten quite a large amount of funds from our concerts."

His eyes opened wide in surprise. Now speaking in Layamon, he said, "Amazing Ket Bethany. Tewdwr by your hair, yet no sign of that thick, nearly incomprehensible accent. Yet, you speak fluent Arad and the local Layamon." He looked long into my eyes; I, his. Finally, he said, "I feel that I know you somehow, but the red hair tells me no. My mother used to have such long hair, only hers was brown. Like you, she could speak many tongues. Tis strange that you bear her first name as your sir name." He continued to stare at me.

Before he actually did recognize me, I wanted to gain the hand of Caitlyn on my own. "Sire, I have come here today with two other purposes in mind beyond returning Caitlyn to you, now that it is safe to do so. It is safe for your sister, Queen Sarah, to come here to visit all of you. She will bring her children when she comes in the spring. She is married to King Percival Penton and has achieved her birthright."

"What? You know of my sister? Sarah? We've heard nothing all these years; it was not safe for her to send any word of her whereabouts to us, you see. Married? Children? Queen? How is all this possible?"

"Indeed, Sire, we do come bringing much news, joyous, happy news. However, there is one additional purpose." I got down on one knee and asked, "King Emil, as Caitlyn's closest benefactor, I humbly beseech thee to grant me thy grace to wed Caitlyn. She has already consented; however, I have insisted that we gain first thy blessing."

Cathleen giggled and squealed; Carmine, her hand still over her mouth — I think she had forgotten it was there — made an indecipherable noise, which I assume was surprise. King Emil looked once more at me, eye to eye. "I swear that I somehow know thee, Ket Bethany of Cuch Glyn. However, knowing thee not, I defer to Caitlyn. Caitlyn, dear, doest thou desire to wed Ket of thy own free will?"

"Oh yes, Uncle!" she bubbled and exclaimed simultaneously; her cheeks were flushed.

"Then, Ket Bethany, I do hereby grant my blessing upon this union. Arise and taketh the hand of Caitlyn as I present it to you." He placed her hand into mine. Speaking loudly so that everyone present could hear, "I have just given my blessing to the union of Caitlyn Amir and Ket Bethany." A loud round of applause and cheering greeted our ears. While this was going on, King Emil, still holding our hands, looking at Caitlyn and then me, said once more, "Caitlyn, should I know this man? I feel that I do, yet Tewdwr? Ought I know him, niece?" Caitlyn could hardly keep from gushing out everything.

She forced herself to say, "Uncle, look deep, deep beyond the fleshly body." She dared not say more, but did give him a clue. I held my breath; it would be far, far better if my son actually recognized me, the spiritual being he called mother, than if I just said so.

He whispered in Arad, "When I was five, I always played with Rosa."

In Arad, I replied, "Ah, testing me. Ha, it was Ros not Rosa that you played with."

"Mother? Is this really you?"

"What do you think?"

"It feels right somehow. Admittedly, I am not an expert on spiritual beings as was the Blessed Holy Mother, Bethany Adid."

"Bethany Madelyn Amir," I corrected him. "I was married, after all. I trust that Sarah explained my sudden disappearance to you? That was the biggest regret I had, fleeing like that without being able to say goodbye to you."

"But you have a male body? Tewdwr, no less," he replied. "Ah, the hair is a dead give-away. I know that folks in Tewdwr only have first names. You ought to have been introduced as Ket of Cuch Glyn, which by the way ceased to exist as a village around the time Caitlyn was forced to flee here."

"Talk about confusing! That has been an understatement, son. Hence, I find others still know me as Bethany, besides I love that name as much as I love long hair. So I have a couple of petty desires. Now you can grasp the full meaning of my previous words. The creatures that killed my body last lifetime and very nearly also killed Sarah have been permanently dealt with, and it is now safe to travel once more. That threat is completely over. I will tell you more about it all in private. You know that I was a Guardian from the Greenway before I was married to Jes. I used my influence to ensure that your sister Sarah also achieved her birthright. Even better news for Cymry, I have brought back with me an entire Circle of Guardians once more. They are pledged to do all that they can for this island and her peoples."

I introduced my new Circle members to the King. To say that King Emil was surprised and incredibly pleased would be an understatement. He kept shaking their hands repeatedly, saying, "Thank you for coming" over and over.

Finally, Queen Carmine got things back to normal, "Dear, why don't you let these young folks relax now, and let's all get back to the New Year's Celebration. You can always talk to them tomorrow. Everyone's still waiting for our party to resume." A bit embarrassed, he realized that the room of people was watching us out in the center of the floor.

"Let the music begin!" he called out. "Cathleen, why don't you show them to the guest rooms so they can unload their things. Then, let them return and join our merrymaking." His daughter jumped at this opportunity. All the while we were unloading our horses and carrying our many bags into the guest rooms in a nearby building, Cathleen chatted endlessly with Caitlyn, who answered nearly as fast as Cathleen talked. These were two very close cousins.

When we finally returned to the dance, King Emil said to me, "Please, all of you, come join me for breakfast in the Great Hall. Caitlyn knows the way. Now go have some fun. I, too, was once young." We needed no further encouragement.

While Caitlyn and I danced, she whispered in my ear, "See, it went super well, don't you think? He recognized you. I knew he would. How can you forget your own mother? Anyway, now you have no excuse for not marrying me," she teased me.

"You are right, dear. Let's do it soon!" She blushed and we danced. Cathleen broke in, desiring to have a dance with her cousin's fiancé. I must say that we did more chatting than dancing; she wanted to know everything that had happened to Caitlyn, and know it all at once. For these few hours, I just relaxed and thoroughly enjoyed life's pleasures, something I had not been able to do for so long.

The next morning, over a very lengthy breakfast, with several fresh pots of tea, I related all that had happened during the past year plus. At least I told him what was proper for him to hear — I could not betray confidences or secrets, naturally. Slowly, the magnitude of what had been accomplished was grasped.

When we finished, King Emil stretched and said, "Okay. Ket, have you given any thought to where you and Caitlyn will be living once you are married? She is the rightful ruler over Nuadilan and Amathon; I've held her throne for her."

"I agree. I think she should assume the throne vacated by her father, if only to help ensure that the damage he wreaked upon the towns is fully repaired," I replied.

"I like the sound of Queen Caitlyn," she said. "But that means you'll have to be king, Ket."

"Yes, but I don't want to be a king," I answered truthfully. "I'm a musician and a Guardian and perhaps even could be a spiritual leader, just not a king."

"That's what I was thinking about last night before I fell asleep," Emil commented. "You realized that, in spite of everything I have said and done, the common people in this whole area now worship the Blessed Holy Mother? You," he added for emphasis. "So how are you going to deal with all this?"

"I would like to take on a role of spiritual leader, musician, and ambassador to neighboring kingdoms, bringing as much order as I can to the island. Caitlyn can run the actual internal affairs of the kingdom as Queen. Hopefully, the people will respect her, since I am an outsider, in their eyes a Tewdwr man. I don't want them to think they have a foreign king."

"Aye that does sound like a good beginning," Emil acknowledged. "I believe she is up to the task. How soon are you planning to wed?"

"Well, we owe it to Fergus to go and meet his parents, the King and Queen of Aine. Ros is Josh's daughter. I should also meet King Hadid as well. I am not going to tell them who I was last lifetime unless they, like you, recognize me. I suspect that they will not, because we were just not as close, but we shall see. I haven't really answered your question, have I? I think that we will have a double ceremony just as soon as we all get back from meeting Fergus's parents. What do you think, dear? Two weeks long enough notice?"

"You bet! Cathleen and Carmine can help Fianna and me work out all the details," she eagerly replied, greatly relieved that we had at long last set a date.

"Would you do me the honor of allowing me to provide the location for the wedding? We can use our Church of Jehosanity of the Blessed Holy Mother right nearby here on the hilltop. I'm sure that the King of Aine and Ros would not mind returning here for the ceremony. Perhaps you all can return at the same time."

He went on, "I will send messengers to the two towns notifying them of Queen Caitlyn's return. Also, I will get the house servants to get the place cleaned up ready for your arrival. Leave those details to me." I was very thankful for his generosity; one less mess with which to deal.

Later that afternoon, we all packed up once more and hit the road, heading for Aine, Ruadan, the home of Fergus. Normally, in the summer, Fergus explained that we'd only need a good long day to get there. However, with the heavy snow, cold, and shortened days, he was allowing two. He was correct.

The town of Aine comprised several hundred buildings, most made from stones. Here at the edge of the Highlands of Ruadan trees were in short supply. Peat from the moors provided warmth and cooking fuel. Even with all the snow, the stubby stone boundary lines between fields and pastures were quaint, like a patchwork quilt of irregular sized blocks. Naturally, the King and Queen lived in the largest building in Aine, the Manor House was its name.

We received a warm welcome indeed. The King was a thin, wiry man of forty-two, with a medium length black beard and moustache. In his youth, he cut a dashing figure, so I could see why Ros had fallen for him. While we sat at his great table and munched on hot cider and scones, Fergus related much of his many adventures. I could tell that his parents had been somewhat concerned about his welfare. His father was grooming him to take his place as King. Thus, he had allowed Fergus to wander around Tarra. In his view, Fergus had gained an invaluable education which would make him a powerful ruler one day.

Queen Ros, who was the same age as her husband, definitely looked very relieved with her son's arrival home. I suspected that she worried far more about Fergus than the King of Aine. However, when Fergus announced that he was soon to wed Fianna, she looked positively radiant. She knew that Fergus would at last settle down somewhere close; her days of fretting over his safety were at an end.

"Aye, laddie, marrying so soon, are yea? And to a Tewdwr lassie no less! Well, she is not who I would have chosen, but then I am not marrying her, now am I, laddie?" He grinned, "Congratulations son! You've become a man while you have been gone. Well done." Turning to Fianna, he said, "Lassie with the brilliant red hair, you realize that when you marry my son here, why, you will become a Princess? See, he is really Prince Fergus of Aine. One day when I am old, he will become the next King of Aine and you will become her Queen. Are yea ready for all that lassie?"

For the first time in a long while, Fianna looked worried and downright frightened. Meekly, she replied, "Sire, I am just a simple fisherman's daughter. I don't know anything about being a princess, let alone a queen. Perhaps, Fergus, we should not do this." She was definitely afraid that her lack of knowledge would seriously hurt Fergus and wanted to give him a gracious way out of their pledge to wed.

"Well, lassie, you have already taken a good first step. You've lost your heavy Tewdwr accent. I was expecting you to have one thick accent. But, Fianna, you do surprise me all the more," the King said.

"Now don't you fret about that business, lassie," Queen Ros interrupted her husband. "When I married him, I knew almost nothing about being a queen. If I can learn on the job, so to speak, I'm sure you can too. Besides, I can teach you everything you need to know."

"Will you mom? That would be terrific!" Fergus acknowledged, greatly relieved. He had not given this aspect of his marriage any thought; he should have, however. "See, Fianna dear, it has all worked out for the best. Besides, you won't have to worry about being a queen for the longest time. Dad is still young, so there is no rush." He tried to put her at ease.

The King turned to Caitlyn and changed the topic, "Caitlyn, my dear. It is so good to see you adorning my hall once more. And you are to wed her brother. My, it seems we now have great long red locks in our families." Everyone chuckled at his attempt to lighten up the conversation. "When are you getting married?"

"In a couple of weeks when we get back," she replied.

"It'll be a double wedding," Fergus added. "Them and us."

"Two weeks! Gracious, are you going to have time to make all the preparations for the special day?" asked Queen Ros, genuinely concerned that sufficient plans could not be made in so short a time.

"Uncle Emil and Aunt Carmine are working on the plans even now," Caitlyn replied. "I do hope you two can come."

"Of course," said Ros dryly, "we certainly would not miss our own son's wedding day, now would we?" Caitlyn suddenly felt rather silly. Just then, Fergus's siblings came barging into the room.

"How come you didn't tell us Fergus was back?" protested Rhett, who was seventeen. Rhoslyn was nineteen and already married and expecting her first child in a few months. She happened to be visiting her mother when she got the news that her brother had returned. Rhiannon was only thirteen with long golden pigtails dangling behind her. Rather than talk, she just rushed up to her older brother and gave him a big hug. Fergus was the eldest at twenty-one.

"Missed you, big brother," Rhiannon exclaimed. The family reunion was now complete. The day passed swiftly with everyone wanting to hear all the exciting things that Fergus had done while he was gone.

I note here that at no time did Ros recognize who I was; she merely accepted me as Ket from Cuch Glyn. I found that promising indeed. We spent two days here before returning to Bedwyn. Because a new snowstorm had just dumped a large amount of snow to the east of the Highlands, travel to King Hadid's town would have to wait. The King of Aine did try to send a messenger to King Hadid, but he returned, stating the roads were impassible to the east. Indeed our own return went even slower because the roads now had several more inches of new snow on them.

On January 15, 623, Caitlyn and I were married and moved into our new home, the home in which she grew up, the home of her late father. While it was filled with sorrowful memories, we quickly changed that somber mood into one of light and gaiety. Simultaneously, Fianna and Fergus were wedded, and they moved into a house in Aine, only a day's ride from us in good weather.

As we two coupled kissed at the climax of the ceremonies, I realized that now I was embarking on a new phase of my life. Somehow, I had now become a king, whether or not I desired it or liked it. Caitlyn, of course, was our queen. As I kissed her, I knew that now I would be facing an entirely new set of problems to have to solve. Yet, perhaps now I could finally live a normal life, raise a loving family, and have the enjoyment of my dear friends of the Cymry Circle.

However, that was merely wishful thinking on my wedding day.
The End.

Other Books by Vic Broquard

<u>Without Warning (fantasy)</u>

The Trident Series: (fantasy)
<u>Volume 1 The Trident and the Book</u>
<u>Volume 2 The Trident and the Scepter</u>
<u>Volume 3 The Trident and the Resurrection</u>

The Adventures of Elizabeth Stanton Series: (science fiction)
<u>Volume 1 The Evolution of the Path</u>
<u>Volume 2 The Great Messiah</u>
<u>Volume 3 Of Kings and Queens and Troubadours</u>
<u>Volume 4 Chaos in the Aftermath</u>
<u>Volume 5 Power Plays</u>
<u>Volume 6 Age of Exploration</u>
<u>Volume 7 Abducted</u>
<u>Volume 8 The Emperor and Empress</u>
<u>Volume 9 A Job Worth Doing</u>
<u>Volume 10 Degradation</u>
<u>Volume 11 The Second Crusade</u>
<u>Volume 12 When Worlds Collide</u>
<u>Volume 13 Dark Ages</u>

The Lindsey Barron Series: (fantasy)
<u>Volume 1 The Rod of the Apocalypse</u>
<u>Volume 2 The Board of Governors</u>
<u>Volume 3 The Crown of Moses</u>
<u>Volume 4 Dominus for President</u>
<u>Volume 5 The National Health Care Program</u>
<u>Volume 6 States Justice</u>
<u>Volume 7 Cross and Double-cross</u>

Zoran Chronicles Series: (fantasy)
<u>Volume 1 A Dragon in Our Town</u>
<u>Volume 2 Dragons, Power, Courts, and War</u>

Planet of the Orange-red Sun Series: (science fiction)
<u>Volume 1 When Kingdoms Fall</u>
<u>Volume 2 Dark Ages</u>
<u>Volume 3 Age of the Towers</u>
<u>Volume 4 Difficillis Exitus</u>
<u>Volume 5 Age of the Lords</u>
<u>Volume 6 The Renegade Tower</u>

The Return of the Wizards: Twelve Companions – The Making of Wizards (fantasy)

www.ingramcontent.com/pod-product-compliance
Lightning Source LLC
Chambersburg PA
CBHW081127020726
47505CB00010B/2266